C000163576

VIXEN

MARY E. BRADDON

VIXEN

ALAN SUTTON

First published in 1879

First published in this edition in the United Kingdom in 1993
Alan Sutton Publishing Ltd · Phoenix Mill · Far Thrupp · Stroud · Gloucestershire

First published in this edition in the United States of America in 1993
Alan Sutton Publishing Inc · 83 Washington Street · Dover · NH 03820

British Library Cataloguing in Publication Data

Braddon, M.E.
  Vixen. – New ed. – (Pocket Classics)
  I. Title II. Series
  823.8 (F)

ISBN 0-7509-0445-3

Library of Congress Cataloging in Publication Data applied for

Cover picture: detail from Love's Shadow *by Anthony Frederick Augustus Sandys
(1829–1904). (Forbes Magazine Collection, New York/photograph The Bridgeman Art
Library, London)*

Typeset in 10/11 pt Bembo.
Typesetting and origination by
Alan Sutton Publishing Limited.
Printed in Great Britain by
The Guernsey Press Company Limited,
Guernsey, Channel Islands.

CONTENTS

INTRODUCTION

M.E. BRADDON by the time of her death in 1915 had achieved notoriety, literary fame and wealth. She was known as the queen of the circulating libraries; she counted among her admirers Dickens, Hardy, Henry James, Charles Reade and Bulmer Lytton; she had survived and prospered despite a scandalous marriage and a disreputable past. Indeed her own life echoes elements of the Sensational novels for which she was renowned and which established her reputation.

Born in London in 1837, M.E. Braddon was the third child of educated middle-class parents. Her father, Henry, was a solicitor whose successes within the law were squandered by philandering and good living. Her mother, Fanny, was a resourceful Irish woman whose patience with her husband's excesses ran out when her youngest daughter was four. The couple separated permanently, divorce at this time being virtually impossible.

Fanny assumed custody and financial responsibility for her children and moved them to Sussex. They returned to London in 1843 and settled in Kensington where M.E. Braddon received a sound education at a respectable private school. Like hundreds of other similarly well-brought up, well-educated young ladies, she looked set to follow an established path of marriage, children and a life of prosperous suburban domesticity. However, something happened that irretrievably altered such plans. Fanny Braddon's money had run out and she was faced with the harsh reality of having to survive financially in a society in which middle-class women were neither expected nor trained to earn a living. It was her daughter who stepped into the breach.

M.E. Braddon left home in 1857 to work as an actress under the name of Miss Seyton – her mother's maiden name. This she continued for three years, appearing in a variety of popular plays across the country. No doubt her theatrical training contributed to the pronounced sense of the dramatic that features in her novels, for she had already begun writing. As a teenager she had written for 'amusement' but with the advent of her mother's financial difficulties writing for profit became more important. She could not expect to work on the stage indefinitely, particulary if she wished to be socially respectable. Acting was associated with commonness and lewdness; nice girls did not make public exhibitions of themselves. It was this episode in M.E. Braddon's life that was to earn her a reputation for having a disreputable past and it comes as little surprise to note that it remained largely unconfirmed until after her death.

As is the nature of rumour, speculation surrounds her amorous experiences as an actress and the reason why she abruptly gave up the theatre in 1860 to concentrate on her writing. According to Charles Reade, with whom M.E. Braddon regulary communicated, the young actress received the patronage of 'a simple, noble-minded Yorkshire Squire' called Gilby who was a 'father, lover, and friend' to the aspiring author. Whatever their relationship it did not last, but he performed her an invaluable service: he enabled her to publish her first serialized fiction, *The Trail of the Serpent*. An unremarkable piece of work, it nevertheless established her writing career and also reveals her penchant for the lurid, ghastly and macabre. Less than two years later she published *Lady Audley's Secret* and became a leading popular novelist.

Lady Audley's Secret was initially published in serial form in 1862 by a publisher called John Maxwell. Thus began a lifelong personal and business partnership between M.E. Braddon and 'Max' which ended only with his death in 1895. However, it was not an easy relationship. When they met, Max was already married; his wife having been pronounced insane had been committed to a lunatic asylum in Dublin leaving him to rear their five children. Quietly and unobtrusively Max and M.E. Braddon began living together as man and wife, she bearing not only his children but also the financial burden of supporting the entire household when Max was struggling in business. They eventually married in 1874 after the death of his wife.

Rumour and gossip surrounded their early relationship, particularly when it became public knowledge that they were living together unmarried. It is no coincidence that the first of their five children was born amid the creation of what M.E. Braddon called her pair of 'bigamy novels' – *Lady Audley's Secret* and *Aurora Floyd*. Like so many of her heroines, M.E. Braddon understood what it was like to struggle for money and reputation in a deeply censorious society. Like Dickens she wrote compulsively and prolifically, conscious always of consolidating her financial security.

Her literary output was phenomenal. She completed at least seventy-four novels between 1862 and 1915; she edited a popular magazine, *the Belgravia*, which featured articles and serialized fiction, while also frequently submitting anonymous stories for the extremely popular 'penny dreadfuls' of the time. These tales she described as 'piratical stuff', full of 'crime, tradegy, murder, slow poisoning and general infamy'. They were written solely for profit and had no pretension to literary merit. While some of her novels can be similarly dismissed, and her writing was generally condemned and criticized by many contemporary reviewers for being immoral, outrageous and of harmful influence, it is not sufficient to limit her to such an assessment. She was a writer of extraordinary appeal and popularity as well as ability. Henry James, for example, described her writing as 'brilliant, lively, ingenious and destitute of a ray of sentiment'.

M.E. Braddon can in many ways be regarded as the founder of the Sensation novel as written by women for women. The principle subscribers to the circulating libraries that distributed her novels were middle-class women, confined by upbringing, society and expectation to limited lives of domesticity and dependence upon others. They were required to be passive, submissive, undemanding and selfless. Fulfilment was to be found through others: husbands, children and families. M.E. Braddon's novels feature much more resourceful active women who exert themselves in order to achieve social respectability and financial security. Unlike the unattractive, masculine women of similiar qualities as depicted by a male Sensation novelist such as Wilkie Collins, M.E. Braddon is the 'inventor of the fair-haired demon of modern fiction' (Margaret Oliphant, 1867). Her women are respectable, 'the daintiest, prettiest of blonde creatures'; they are intelligent and retaliate against injustice, poverty, unfavourable circumstances as well as men, to whom they are often openly hostile. It could be argued that they articulate the suppressed grievances and frustrations of the ordinary women who read about them, hence part of their extraordinary popularity. They provided escapism, fantasy and release from the mundane, the oppressive and the unescapable.

After its publication in volume form *Lady Audley's Secret* was never out of print during M.E. Braddon's lifetime. Unfortunately she was to some extent a victim of her own early success. Having achieved such popularity with her first novel she found herself compelled to write to a similar popular formula. What is interesting is how she manipulates this to produce changes and developments in the established Sensation novel form.

Vixen, written in 1879, is one such example. While it features lurid and ghastly events typical of the Sensation novel it is more subtle and psychological. It is also an examination of Victorian marriage. Violet Tempest is Vixen, the heroine. She is single, beautiful, wealthy and eminently marriageable. Ironically, this renders her vulnerable because, although she has the economic stability that so many women lacked, she is open to the machinations of ambitions and unscrupulous men such as Captain Winstanley. Privileged but poor he needs money; the easiest way to obtain it is to marry it. Refused by Vixen whose heart belongs to her childhood sweetheart Rorie, the dashing Captain applies himself more successfully to Vixen's recently widowed mother. Mrs Tempest represents ideal dependent, passive, submissive womanhood. It is these very qualities which are seen to make her susceptible, undiscerning and pathetic. The determination, outspoken integrity and 'wild' rebellion of her daughter who is renowned for being a 'minx' and for having an unpredictable temper prove to be her salvation.

A further aspect of the relationship between money and

marriage is considered when Rorie is forced by family loyalty and honour to engage himself to a cousin for whom he feels nothing. Only the resourcefulness and stubbornness of Vixen prevent him from contracting a loveless union. Both he and his unenthusiastic fiancée are seen to be saved from a life of emotional ennui and unhappiness. M.E. Braddon clearly condemns marriages calculated and contracted on mercenary grounds.

Vixen is an interesting herione. She is not small, blonde and apparently helpless but of much more solid build. Her hair is red, her mouth large; she is always engaged in active outdoor pursuits. Yet this does not make her in any way masculine. She is obviously feminine, respectable, attractive and striking; she exudes a sexuality that derives from her very vitality. While contradicting most of the contemporary qualities of ideal womanhood she is represented as equally virtuous and desirable, and she is seen to be rewarded by a romantic high-class, prosperous, love match. In her portrayal of Vixen — a most unlikely name for an herione with its connotations of cunning and shrewishness — M.E. Braddon is surreptitiously undermining the established Victorian perception of women. She replaces it with a much more robust emotional woman who is prepared to manipulate and mould her life without compromising integrity, dignity or femininity.

Vixen is a sensational novel in more than plot and event. It is more than simply a compelling read; it is a quiet act of rebellion.

FIONN O'TOOLE

CHAPTER 1

A PRETTY HORSEBREAKER

The moon had newly risen, a late October moon, a pale almost imperceptible crescent, above the dark pine spires in the thicket through which Roderick Vawdrey came, gun in hand, after a long day's rabbit-shooting. It was not his nearest way home, but he liked the broad clearing in the pine wood, which had a ghostly look at dusk, and was so still and lonely that the dart of a squirrel through the fallen leaves seemed a startling event. Here and there a sturdy old oak that had been stripped of its bark lay among the fern, like the naked corpse of a giant. Here and there a fir-tree lay across the track. The ground was soft and spongy, slippery with damp dead leaves, and inclined in a general way to bogginess; but it was ground that Roderick Vawdrey had known all his life, and it seemed more natural to him than any other spot upon mother earth.

On the edge of this thicket there was a broad ditch, with more mud and dead fern in it than water, a ditch strongly suspected of snakes, and beyond the ditch the fence that enclosed Squire Tempest's domain – an old manor house in the heart of the New Forest. It had been an abbey before the Reformation, and was still best known as the Abbey House.

'I wonder whether I'm too late to catch her,' speculated Roderick, shifting his bag from one shoulder to the other; 'she's no end of fun.'

In front of the clearing there was a broad five-barred gate, and beside the gate a keeper's cottage. The flame of a newly-lighted candle flashed out suddenly upon the autumn dusk, while Roderick stood looking at the gate.

1

'I'll ask at the lodge,' he said, 'I should like to say good-bye to the little thing before I go back to Oxford.'

He walked quickly on to the gate. The keeper's noisy children were playing at nothing particular just inside it.

'Has Miss Tempest gone for her ride this afternoon?' he asked.

'Ya-ase,' drawled the eldest shock-headed youngster.

'And not come back yet?'

'Noa. If she doant take care her'll be bogged.'

Roderick hitched his bag on to the top of the gate, and stood at ease waiting. It was late for the little lady of Tempest Manor to be out on her pony; but then it was an understood thing within a radius of ten miles or so that she was a self-willed young person, and even at fifteen years of age had a knack of following her own inclination with that noble disregard of consequences which characterises the heaven-born ruler.

Mr Vawdrey had not waited more than ten minutes when there came the thud of hoofs upon the soft track, a flash of gray in the distance, something flying over those forky branches sprawling across the way, then a half-sweet, half-shrill call, like a bird's, at which the keeper's children scattered themselves like a brood of scared chickens, and now a rush, and a gray pony shooting suddenly into the air and coming down on the other side of the gate, as if he were a new kind of skyrocket.

'What do you think of that, Rorie?' cried the shrill sweet voice of the gray pony's rider. 'Titmouse took the gate in pretty good style, didn't he?'

'I'm ashamed of you, Vixen,' said Roderick, 'you'll come to a bad end some of these days.'

'I don't care if I do, as long as I get my fling first,' replied Vixen, tossing her tawny mane.

She was a slim young thing, in a short Lincoln-green habit. She had a small pale face, brown eyes that sparkled with life and mischief, and a rippling mass of reddish-auburn hair falling down her back under a coquettish little felt hat.

'Hasn't your mamma forbidden jumping, Vixen?' remonstrated Roderick, opening the gate and coming in.

'Yes, that she has, sir,' said the old groom, riding up at a jog-trot on his thickset brown cob. 'It's quite against Mrs Tempest's orders, and it's a great responsibility to go out with Miss Violet. She will do it.'

'You mean the pony will do it, Bates,' cried Vixen. 'I don't jump. How can I help it if papa has given me a jumping pony? If I didn't let Titmouse take a gate when he was in the humour he'd kick like old boots, and pitch me a cropper. It's an instinct of self-preservation that makes me let him jump. And as for poor dear, pretty little mamma,' continued Vixen, addressing herself to Roderick, and changing her tone to one of patronising tenderness, 'if she had her way, I should be brought up in a little box wrapped in jeweller's wool, to keep me safe. But you see I take after papa, Rorie; and it comes as natural to me to fly over gates as it does to you to get ploughed for smalls. There, Bates' – jumping off the pony – 'you may take Titmouse home, and I'll come presently and give him some apples, for he has been a dear, darling, precious treasure of a ponykins.'

She emphasised this commendation with a kiss on Titmouse's gray nose, and handed the bridle to Bates.

'I'm going to walk home with Mr Vawdrey,' she said.

'But, Vixen, I can't really,' said Roderick; 'I'm due at home at this moment, only I couldn't leave without saying good-bye to little Vix.'

'And you're over due at Oxford, too, aren't you?' cried Vixen, laughing; 'you're always due somewhere – never in the right place. But whether you are due or not, you're coming up to the stables with me to give Titmouse his apples, and then you're coming to dine with us on your last night at home. I insist upon it; papa insists; mamma insists – we all insist.'

'My mother will be as angry as——'

'Old boots!' interjected Vixen. 'That's the best comparison I know.'

'Awfully vulgar for a young lady.'

'You taught it me. How can I help being vulgar when I associate with you? You should hear Miss McCroke preach at me – sermons so long' – here Vixen extended her arms to the uttermost – 'and I'm afraid they'd make as much impression on Titmouse as they do upon me. But she's a dear old thing, and I love her immensely.'

This was Vixen's usual way, making up for all shortcomings with the abundance of her love. The heart was always atoning for the errors of the head.

'I wouldn't be Miss McCroke for anything. She must have a bad time of it with you.'

'She has,' assented Vixen, with a remorseful sigh; 'I fear I'm bringing her sandy hairs with sorrow to the grave. That hair of hers never could be gray, you know, it's too self-opinionated in its sandiness. Now come along, Rorie, do. Titmouse will be stamping about his box like a maniac if he doesn't get those apples.'

She gave a little tug with both her small doeskin-covered hands at Roderick's arm. He was still standing by the gate irresolute, inclination drawing him to the Abbey House, duty calling him home to Briarwood, seven miles off, where his widowed mother was expecting his return.

'My last night at home, Vix,' he said remonstrantly; 'I really ought to dine with my mother.'

'Of course you ought; and that's the very reason why you'll dine with us. So "Kim over now," as Bates says to the horses; I don't know what there is for dinner,' she added confidentially, 'but I feel sure it's something nice. Dinner is papa's particular vanity, you know. He's very weak about dinner.'

'Not so weak as he is about you, Vixen.'

'Do you really think papa is as fond of me as he is of his dinner?'

'I'm sure of it!'

'Then he must be very fond of me,' exclaimed Vixen, with conviction. 'Now, are you coming?'

Who could resist those little soft hands in doeskin? Certainly not Rorie. He resigned himself to the endurance of his mother's anger in the future as a price to be paid for the indulgence of his inclination in the present, gave Vixen his arm, and turned his face towards the Abbey House.

They walked through shrubberies that would have seemed a pathless wilderness to a stranger, but every turn in which was familiar to these two. The ground was undulating, and vast thickets of rhododendron and azalea rose high above them, or

sank in green valleys below their path. Here and there a group
of tall firs towered skyward above the dark entanglement of
shrubs, or a great beech spread its wide limbs over the hollows;
here and there a pool of water reflected the pale moonshine.

The house lay low, sheltered and shut in by those
rhododendron thickets, a long rambling pile of building, which
had been added to, and altered, and taken away from, and
added to again, like that well-known puzzle in mental
arithmetic which used to amuse us in our childhood. It was all
gables and chimney-stacks and odd angles and ivy-mantled wall
and richly-mullioned windows, or quaint little diamond-paned
lattices, peeping like a watchful eye from under the shadow of a
jutting cornice. The stables had been added in Queen
Elizabeth's time, after the monks had been routed from their
snug quarters, and the Abbey had been bestowed upon one of
the Tudor favourites. These Elizabethan stables formed the four
sides of a quadrangle, stone-paved, with an old marble basin in
the centre – a basin which the Vicar pronounced to be an early
Saxon font, but which Squire Tempest refused to have removed
from the place it had occupied ever since the stables were built.
There were curious carvings upon the six sides, but so covered
with mosses and lichens that nobody could tell what they
meant; and the Squire forbade any scraping process by officious
antiquarians, which might lead to somebody's forcible
appropriation of the ancient basin.

The Squire was not so modern in his ideas as to set up his
own gasometer, so the stables were lighted by lanterns, with an
oil-lamp fixed here and there against the wall. Into this dim
uncertain light came Roderick and Vixen, through the deep
stone archway which opened from the shrubbery into the
stable-yard, and which was solid enough for the gate of a
fortified town.

Titmouse's stable was lighted better than the rest. The door
stood open, and there was Titmouse, with the neat little quilted
doeskin saddle still on his back, waiting to be fed and petted by
his young mistress. It was a pretty picture, the old low-ceiled
stable, with its wide stalls and roomy loose-boxes, and carpet of
plaited straw, golden against the deep brown of the woodwork.

Vixen ran into the box, and took off Titmouse's bridle, he holding down his head, like a child submitting to be undressed. Then, with many vigorous tugs at straps and buckles and a good deal of screwing up of her rosy lips in the course of the effort, Vixen took off her pony's saddle.

'I like to do everything I can for him,' she explained, as Rorie watched her with an amused smile; 'I'd wisp him down if they'd let me.'

She left the leather panel on Titmouse's back, hung up saddle and bridle, and skipped off to a córn-chest to hunt for apples. Of these she brought half a dozen or so in the skirt of her habit, and then swinging herself lightly into a comfortable corner of the manger, began to carry out her system of reward for good conduct, with much coquetry on her part and Titmouse's, Rorie watching it all from the empty stall adjoining, his folded arms resting on the top of the partition. He said not another word about his mother, or the duty that called him home to Briarwood, but stood and watched this pretty horsebreaker in a dreamy contentment.

What was Violet Tempest, otherwise Vixen, like, this October evening, just three months before her fifteenth birthday? She made a lovely picture in this dim light, as she sat in the corner of the old manger holding a rosy-cheeked apple at a tantalising distance from Titmouse's nose; yet she was perhaps not altogether lovely. She was brilliant rather than absolutely beautiful. The white skin was powdered with freckles. The rippling hair was too warm an auburn to escape an occasional unfriendly remark from captious critics; but it was not red hair for all that. The eyes were brownest of the brown, large, bright, and full of expression. The mouth was a thought too wide; but it was a lovely mouth notwithstanding. The lips were full and firmly moulded – lips that could mean anything, from melting tenderness to sternest resolve. Such lips, a little parted to show the whitest, evenest teeth in Hampshire, seemed to Rorie lovely enough to please the most critical connoisseur of feminine beauty. The nose was short and straight, but had a trick of tilting itself upward with a little impatient jerk that made it seem *retroussé*; the chin was round and full and dimpled;

the throat was full and round also, a white column supporting the tawny head, and indicated that Vixen was meant to be a powerful woman, and not one of those ethereal nymphs who lend themselves most readily to the decorative art of a court milliner.

'I'm afraid Violet will be a dreadfully large creature,' Mrs Tempest murmured plaintively, as the girl grew and flourished; that lady herself being ethereal, and considering her own appearance a strictly correct standard of beauty. How could it be otherwise, when she had been known before her marriage as 'the pretty Miss Calthorpe'?

'This is very nice, you know, Vixen,' said Roderick critically, as Titmouse made a greedy snap at an apple, and was repulsed with a gentle pat on his nose; 'but it can't go on for ever. What'll you do when you are grown up?'

'Have a horse instead of a pony,' answered Vixen unhesitatingly.

'And will that be all the difference?'

'I don't see what other difference there can be. I shall always love papa, I shall always love hunting, I shall always love mamma – as much as she'll let me. I shall always have a corner in my heart for dear old Crokey; and, perhaps,' looking at him mischievously, 'even an odd corner for you. What difference can a few more birthdays make in me? I shall be too big for Titmouse, that's the only misfortune; but I shall always keep him for my pet; and I'll have a basket-carriage and drive him when I go to see my poor people. Sitting behind a pony is an awful bore when one's natural place is on his back; but I'd sooner endure it than let Titmouse fancy himself superannuated.'

'But when you're grown up you'll have to come out, Vixen. You'll be obliged to go to London for a season and be presented, and go to no end of balls, and ride in the Row; and make a grand marriage, and have a page all to yourself in the *Court Journal.*'

'Catch me – going to London!' exclaimed Vixen, ignoring the latter part of the sentence. 'Papa hates London, and so do I. And as to riding in Rotten Row, *je voudrais bien me voir faisant cela*,' added Vixen, whose study of the French language chiefly resulted in the endeavour to translate English slang into that tongue. 'No, when I grow up I shall take papa the tour of Europe. We'll see all those places I'm worried about at lessons – Marathon, Egypt, Naples, the Peloponnesus, *tout le tremblement* – and I shall say to each of them, "O, this is you, is it? What a nuisance you've been to me on the map." We shall go up Mount Vesuvius, and the Pyramids, and do all sorts of wild things; and by the time I come home I shall have forgotten the whole of my education.'

'If Miss McCroke could hear you!'

'She does, often. You can't imagine the wild things I say to her. But I love her – fondly.'

A great bell clanged out with a vigorous peal, that seemed to shake the old stable.

'There's the first bell. I must run and dress. Come to the drawing-room and see mamma.'

'But, Vixen, how can I sit down to dinner in such a costume?' remonstrated Rorie, looking down at his brown shooting-suit, leather gaiters, and tremendous boots – boots, which, instead of being beautified with blacking, were suppled with tallow; 'I can't do it, really.'

'Nonsense,' cried Vixen, 'what does it matter? Papa seldom dresses for dinner. I believe he considers it a sacrifice to mamma's sense of propriety when he washes his hands after coming in from the home farm. And you are only a boy – I beg pardon – an undergraduate. So come along.'

'But upon my word, Vixen, I feel too much ashamed of myself.'

'I've asked you to dinner, and you've accepted,' cried Vixen, pulling him out of the stable by the lapel of his shooting-jacket.

He seemed to relish that mode of locomotion, for he allowed himself to be pulled all the way to the hall-door, and into the glow of the great beech-wood fire; a ruddy light which shone upon many a sporting trophy, and reflected itself on many a gleaming pike and cuirass, belonging to days of old, when gentlemanly sport for the most part meant man-hunting.

It was a fine old vaulted hall, a place to love and remember lovingly when far away. The walls were all of darkly bright oak panelling, save where here and there a square of tapestry hung before a door, or a painted window let in the moonlight. At one end there was a great arched fireplace, the arch surmounted with Squire Tempest's armorial bearings, roughly cut in freestone. A mailed figure of the usual stumpy build, in helm and hauberk, stood on each side of the hearth; a large three-cornered chair covered with stamped and gilded leather was drawn up to the fireside, the Squire's favourite seat on an autumn or winter afternoon. The chair was empty now, but, stretched at full length before the blazing logs, lay the Squire's chosen companion, Nip, a powerful liver-coloured pointer; and beside him, in equally luxurious rest, reclined Argus, Vixen's mastiff. There was a story about Vixen and the mastiff, involving the only incident in that young lady's life the recollection whereof could make her blush.

The dog, apparently coiled in deepest slumber, heard the light footsteps on the hall floor, pricked up his tawny ears, sprang to his feet, and bounded over to his young mistress, whom he nearly knocked down in the warmth of his welcome. Nip, the pointer, blinked at the intruders, yawned desperately, stretched himself a trifle longer, and relapsed into slumber.

'How fond that brute is of you,' said Rorie; 'but it's no wonder, when one considers what you did for him.'

'If you say another word I shall hate you,' cried Vixen savagely.

'Well, but you know when a fellow fights another fellow's battles, the other fellow's bound to be fond of him; and when a young lady pitches into a bird-boy with her riding-whip to save a mastiff-pup from ill-usage, that mastiff-pup is bound——'

'Mamma,' cried Vixen, flinging aside a tapestry *portière*, and bouncing into the drawing-room, 'here's Roderick, and he's come to dinner, and you must excuse his shooting-dress, please. I'm sure pa will.'

'Certainly, my dear Violet,' replied a gentle voice from the fire-lit dimness near the velvet-curtained hearth. 'Of course I am always glad to see Mr Vawdrey when your papa asks him. Where did you meet the Squire, Roderick?'

'Upon my word, Mrs Tempest,' faltered Rorie, coming slowly forward into the ruddy glow, 'I feel quite awfully ashamed of myself; I've been rabbit-shooting, and I'm a most horrid object. It wasn't the Squire asked me to stay. It was Vixen.'

Vixen made a ferocious grimace at him – he could just see her distorted countenance in the firelight – and further expressed her aggravation by a smart crack of her whip.

'Violet, my love, you have such startling ways,' exlaimed Mrs Tempest, with a long-suffering air. 'Really, Miss McCroke, you ought to try and correct her of those startling ways.'

On this Roderick became aware of a stout figure in a tartan dress, knitting industriously on the side of the hearth opposite Mrs Tempest's sofa. He could just see the flash of those active needles, and could just hear Miss McCroke murmur placidly that she had corrected Violet, and that it was no use.

Rorie remembered that plaid poplin dress when he was at Eton. It was a royal Stuart, too brilliant to be forgotten. He used to wonder whether it would ever wear out, or whether it was not made of some indestructible tissue, like asbestos – a fabric that neither time nor fire could destroy.

'It was Rorie's last night, you see, mamma,' apologised Vixen, 'and I knew you and papa would like him to come, and that you wouldn't mind his shooting-clothes a bit, though they do make him look like the under-keeper, except that the under-keeper's better looking than Rorie, and has finished growing his whiskers, instead of living in the expectation of them.'

And, with this Parthian shot, Vixen made a pirouette on her neat little morocco-shod toes, and whisked herself out of the room; leaving Roderick Vawdrey to make the best of his existence for the next twenty minutes with the two women he always found it most difficult to get on with, Mrs Tempest and Miss McCroke.

The logs broke into a crackling blaze just at this moment and lighted up that luxurious hearth and the two figures beside it.

It was the prettiest thing imaginable in the way of a drawing-room, that spacious low-ceiled chamber in the Abbey House.

The oak panelling was painted white, a barbarity on the part of those modern Goths the West End decorators, but a charming background for quaint Venetian mirrors, hanging shelves of curious old china, dainty little groups of richly-bound duodecimos, brackets, bronzes, freshest flowers in majolica jars; water-colour drawings by Hunt, Prout, Cattermole, and Edward Duncan; sage-green silk curtains; black and gold furniture, and all the latest prettinesses of the new Jacobean school. The mixture of real mediaevalism and modern quaintness was delightful. One hardly knew where the rococo began or the mediaeval left off. The good old square fireplace, with its projecting canopy, and columns in white and coloured marbles, was as old as the days of Inigo Jones; but the painted tiles were the newest thing from Minton's factory.

Even Rorie felt that the room was pretty, though he did above all things abhor to be trapped in it, as he found himself this October evening.

'There's a great lot of rubbish in it,' he used to say of Mrs Tempest's drawing-room, 'but it's rather nice altogether.'

Mrs Tempest, at five-and-thirty, still retained the good looks which had distinguished Miss Calthorpe at nineteen. She was small and slim, with a delicate complexion. She had large soft eyes of a limpid innocent azure, regular features, rosebud lips, hands after Velasquez, and an unexceptionable taste in dress, the selection of which formed one of the most onerous occupations of her life. To attire herself becomingly, and to give the Squire the dinners he best liked, in an order of succession so dexterously arranged as never to provoke satiety, were Mrs Tempest's cardinal duties. In the intervals of her life she read modern poetry, unobjectionable French novels, and reviews. She did a little high-art needle-work, played Mendelssohn's lieder, sang three French *chansons* which her husband liked, slept, and drank orange pekoe. In the consumption of this last article Mrs Tempest was as bad as a dram-drinker. She declared her inability to support life without that gentle stimulant, and required to be wound up at various hours of her languid day with a dose of her favourite beverage.

'I think I'll take a cup of tea,' was Mrs Tempest's inevitable remark at every crisis of her existence.

'And so you are going back to Oxford, Roderick?' the lady began, with a languid kindness.

Mrs Tempest had never been known to be unkind to anyone. She regarded all her fellow-creatures with a gentle tolerance; they were there, a necessary element of the universe, and she bore with them. But she had never attached herself particularly to anybody except the Squire. Him she adored. He took all the trouble of life off her hands, and gave her all good things. She had been poor, and he had made her rich; nobody, and he had elevated her into somebody. She loved him with a canine fidelity, and felt towards him as a dog feels towards his master – that in him this round world begins and ends.

'Yes,' assented Rorie, with a sigh; 'I'm going up to-morrow.'

'Why up?' inquired Miss McCroke, without lifting her eyes from her needles. 'It isn't up on the map.'

'I hope you are going to get a grand degree,' continued Mrs Tempest, in that soft conciliatory voice of hers; 'Senior Wrangler, or something.'

'That's the other shop,' exclaimed Rorie; 'they grow that sort of timber at Cambridge. However, I hope to pull myself through somehow or other this time, for my mother's sake. She attached a good deal of importance to it, though for my own part I can't see what good it can do me. It won't make me farm my own land better, or ride straighter to hounds, or do my duty better to my tenants.'

'Education,' said Miss McCroke sententiously, 'is always a good, and we cannot too highly estimate its influence upon——'

'O yes, I know,' answered Rorie quickly, for he knew that when the floodgates of Miss McCroke's eloquence were once loosened the tide ran strong; 'when house and lands are gone and spent a man may turn usher in an academy, and earn fifty pounds a year and his laundress's bill by grinding Caesar's Commentaries into small boys. But I shouldn't lay in a stock of learning with that view. When my house and lands are gone I'll go after them – emigrate, and go into the lumber trade in Canada.'

'What a dreadful idea!' said Mrs Tempest; 'but you are not going to lose house and lands, Roderick – such a nice place as Briarwood.'

'To my mind it's rather a commonplace hole,' answered the young man carelessly, 'but the land is some of the best in the county.'

It must be nearly seven by this time, he thought. He was getting through this period of probation better than he had expected. Mrs Tempest gave a little stifled yawn behind her huge black fan, upon which Cupids and Graces, lightly sketched in French gray, were depicted dancing in the airiest attitudes, after Boucher. Roderick would have liked to yawn in concert, but at this juncture a sudden ray of light flashed upon him and showed him a way of escape.

'I think I'll go to the gentleman's room, and make myself decent before the second bell rings,' he said.

'Do,' assented Mrs Tempest, with another yawn; and the young man fled.

He had only time to scramble through a hurried toilet, and was still feeling very doubtful as to the parting of his short crisp hair, when the gong boomed out its friendly summons. The gentleman's room opened from the hall, and Rorie heard the Squire's loud and jovial voice uplifted as he raised the tapestry curtain.

Mr Tempest was standing in front of the log fire, pulling Vixen's auburn hair. The girl had put on a picturesque brown velvet frock; a scarlet sash was tied loosely round her willowy waist, and a scarlet ribbon held back the rippling masses of her bright hair.

'A study in red and brown,' thought Rorie, as the fire-glow lit up the picture of the Squire in his hunting-dress, and the girl in her warm velvet gown.

'Such a run, Rorie,' cried the Squire; 'we dawdled about among the furze from twelve till four doing nothing, and just as it was getting dark started a fox up on the high ground this side of Picket Post, and ran him nearly into Ringwood. Go in and fetch my wife, Rorie. O, here she is' – as the *portière* was lifted by a white hand, all a-glitter with diamonds – 'you must excuse me sitting down in pink to-day, Pamela; I only got in as the gong began to sound, and I'm as hungry as the proverbial hunter.'

'You know I always think you handsomest in your scarlet coat, Edward,' replied the submissive wife, 'but I hope you're not very muddy.'

'I won't answer for myself; but I haven't been actually up to my neck in a bog.'

Rorie offered his arm to Mrs Tempest, and they all went in to dinner, the Squire still playing with his daughter's hair, and Miss McCroke solemnly bringing up the rear.

The dining-room at the Abbey House was the ancient refectory, large enough for a mess-room; so, when there were no visitors, the Tempests dined in the library – a handsome square room, in which old family portraits looked down from the oak panelling above the dwarf bookcases, and where the literary element was not obtrusively conspicuous. You felt that it was a room quite as well adapted for conviviality as for study. There was a cottage piano in a snug corner by the fireplace. The Squire's capacious arm-chair stood on the other side of the hearth, Mrs Tempest's low chair and gipsy table facing it. The old oak buffet opposite the chimney-piece was a splendid specimen of Elizabethan carving, and made a rich background for the Squire's racing-cups, and a pair of Oliver Cromwell tankards, battered and dinted with much service, and unornamental as that illustrious Roundhead himself.

It was a delightful room on a chill October evening like this; the logs roaring up the wide chimney, a pair of bronze candelabra lighting buffet and table, Mrs Tempest smiling pleasantly at her unbidden guest, and the Squire stooping, red-faced and plethoric, over his mulligatawny; while Vixen, who was at an age when dinner is a secondary consideration, was amusing herself with the dogs, gentlemanly animals, too well bred to be importunate in their demands for an occasional tit-bit, and content to lie in superb attitudes, looking up at the eaters patiently, with supplication in their great pathetic brown eyes.

'Rorie is going up to-morrow – not in a balloon, but to Magdalen College, Oxford – so, as this was his last night, I made him come to dinner,' explained Vixen presently. 'I hope I didn't do wrong.'

'Rorie knows he's always welcome. Have some more of that mulligatawny, my lad, it's uncommonly good.'

Rorie declined the mulligatawny, being at this moment deeply engaged in watching Vixen and the dogs. Nip, the liver-coloured pointer, was performing his celebrated statue feat. With his forelegs stiffly extended, and his head proudly poised, he simulated a dog of marble; and if it had not been for the occasional bumping of his tail upon the Persian carpet, in an irresistible wag of self approbation, the simulation would have been perfect.

'Look, papa, isn't it beautiful? I went out of the room the other day, while Nip was doing the statue, after I'd told him not to move a paw and I stayed away quite five minutes, and then stole quietly back; and there he was, lying as still as if he'd been carved out of stone. Wasn't that fidelity?'

'Nonsense!' cried the Squire. 'How do you know that Nip didn't wind you as you opened the door, and get himself into position? What are these?' as the old silver *entrée* dishes came round. 'Stewed eels? You never forget my tastes, Pamela.'

'Stewed eels, sir; *sole maître d'hôtel*,' said the butler, in the usual suppressed and deferential tone.

Rorie helped himself automatically, and went on looking at Vixen.

Her praises of Nip had kindled jealous fires in the breast of Argus, her own particular favourite; and the blunt black muzzle had been thrust vehemently under her velvet sleeve.

'Argus is angry,' said Rorie.

'He's a dear old foolish thing to be jealous,' answered Vixen, 'when he knows I'd go through fire and water for him.'

'Or even fight a big boy,' cried the Squire, throwing himself back in his chair with the unctuous laughter of a man who is dining well, and knows it.

Vixen blushed rosiest red at the allusion.

'Papa, you oughtn't to say such things,' she cried; 'I was a little bit of a child then.'

'Yes, and flew at a great boy of fourteen and licked him,' exclaimed the Squire rapturously. 'You know the story, don't you, Rorie?'

Rorie had heard it twenty times, but looked the picture of ignorant expectancy.

'You know how Vixen came by Argus? What, you don't? Well, I'll tell you. This little yellow-haired lass of mine was barely nine years old, and she was riding through the village on her pony, with young Stubbs behind her on the sorrel mare – and, you know, to her dying day, that sorrel would never let anyone dismount her quietly. Now what does Vixen spy but a lubberly lad and a lot of small children ill-using a mastiff-pup. They'd tied a tin-kettle to the brute's tail, and were doing their best to drown him. There's a pond just beyond Mrs Farley's cottage, you know, and into that pond they'd pelted the puppy, and wouldn't let him get out of it. As fast as the poor little brute scrambled up the muddy bank they drove him back into the water.'

'Papa darling,' pleaded Vizen despairingly, 'Rorie has heard it all a thousand times before. Haven't you now, Rorie?'

'It's as new to me as to-morrow's *Times*,' said Roderick, with effrontery.

'Vixen was off the pony before you could say "Jack Robinson." She flew into the midst of the dirty little ragamuffins, seized the biggest ruffian by the collar, and trundled him backwards into the pond. Then she laid about her right and left with her whip till the little wretches scampered off, leaving Vixen and the puppy masters of the situation; and by this time the sorrel mare had allowed Stubbs to get off her, and Stubbs rushed to the rescue. The young ringleader had been too much surprised by his ducking to pull himself together again before this, but he came up to time now, and had it out with Stubbs, while the sorrel was doing as much damage as she conveniently could to Mrs Farley's palings. "Don't quite kill him, please, Stubbs," cried Vixen, "although he richly deserves it;" and then she took the muddy little beast up in her arms and ran home, leaving her pony to fate and Stubbs. Stubbs told me the whole story, with tears in his eyes. "Who'd ha' thought, Squire, the little lady would ha' been such a game 'un?" said Stubbs.'

'It's very horrid of you, papa, to tell such silly old stories,' remonstrated Vixen. 'That was nearly seven years ago, and Dr Dewsnap told us the other day that everybody undergoes a complete change of – what is it? – all the tissues – in seven years. I'm not the same Vixen that pushed the boy into the pond. There's not a bit of her left in me.'

And so the dinner went on and ended, with a good deal of distraction, caused by the dogs, and a mild little remark now and then from Mrs Tempest, or an occasional wise interjection from Miss McCroke, who in a manner represented the Goddess of Wisdom in this somewhat frivolous family, and came in with a corrective and severely rational observation when the talk was drifting towards idiocy.

The filberts, bloomy purple grapes, and ruddy pippins, and yellow William pears had gone their rounds – all home produce – and had been admired and praised, and the Squire's full voice was mellowing after his second glass of port, when the butler came in with a letter on a salver, and carried it, with muffled footfall and solemn visage, as of one entrusted with the delivery of a death-warrant, straight to Roderick Vawdrey.

The young man looked at it as if he had encountered an unexpected visitor of the adder tribe.

'My mother,' he faltered.

It was a large and handsome letter with a big red seal.

'May I?' asked Rorie, with a troubled visage, and having received his host and hostess's assent, broke the seal.

'DEAR RODERICK, – Is it quite kind of you to absent yourself on this your last night at home? I feel very sure that this will find you at the Abbey House, and I send the brougham at a venture. Be good enough to come home at once. The Dovedales arrived at Ashbourne quite unexpectedly this afternoon, and are dining with me on purpose to see you before you go back to Oxford. If your own good feeling did not urge you to spend this last evening with me, I wonder that Mr and Mrs Tempest were not kind enough to suggest to you which way your duty lay. Yours anxiously,
'JANE VAWDREY.'

Roderick crumpled the letter with an angry look. That fling at the Tempests hit him hard. Why was it that his mother was always so ready to find fault with these chosen friends of his?

'Anything wrong, Rorie?' asked the Squire.

'Nothing; except that the Dovedales are dining with my mother, and I'm to go home directly.'

'If you please, ma'am, Master Vawdrey's servant has come for him,' said Vixen, mimicking the style of announcement at a juvenile party. 'It's quite too bad, Rorie,' she went on, 'I had made up my mind to beat you at pyramids. However, I daresay you're very glad to have the chance of seeing your pretty cousin before you leave Hampshire.'

But Rorie shook his head dolefully, made his adieux, and departed.

CHAPTER 2

LADY JANE VAWDREY

'It is not dogs only that are jealous!' thought Roderick, as he went home in the brougham, with the windows down, and the cool night breeze blowing his cigar smoke away into the forest, to mix with the mist wreaths that were curling up from the soft ground. It was an offence of the highest grade to smoke in his mother's carriage; but Rorie was in an evil temper just now, and found a kind of bitter pleasure in disobedience.

The carriage bowled swiftly along the straight, well-made road, but Rorie hated riding in a brougham. The soft padded confinement galled him.

'Why couldn't she send me my dog-cart?' he asked himself indignantly.

Briarwood was a large white house in a small park. It stood on much higher ground than the Abbey House, and was altogether different from that good old relic of a bygone

civilisation. Briarwood was distinctly modern. Its decorations
savoured of the Regency; its furniture was old-fashioned,
without being antique. The classic stiffness and straightness of
the First French Empire distinguished the gilded chairs and
tables in the drawing-room. There were statues by Chantrey
and Canova in the spacious lofty hall; portraits by Lawrence and
Romney in the dining-room; a historical picture by Copley
over the elephantine mahogany sideboard; a Greek sarcophagus
for wines under it.

At its best, the Briarwood house was commonplace; but to
the mind of Lady Jane Vawdrey, the gardens and hothouses
made amends. She was a profound horticulturist, and spent half
her income on orchids and rare newly-imported flowers; and by
this means she had made Briarwood one of the show places of
the neighbourhood.

'A woman must be distinguished for something, or she is no
better than her scullery-maid,' said Lady Jane to her son,
excusing herself for these extravagances. 'I have no talent for
music, painting, or poetry, so I devote myself to orchids; and
perhaps my orchids turn out better than many people's music
and poetry.'

Lady Jane was not a pleasant-tempered woman, and enjoyed
the privilege of being more feared than liked; a privilege of
which she made the most, and which secured her immunity
from many annoyances to which good-natured people are
subject. She did good to her poor neighbours, in her own
formal way, but the poor people about Briarwood did not send
to her for wine and brandy as if she kept a public-house, and
was benefited by their liberal patronage; the curate at the little
Gothic church, down in the tiny village in a hollow of the
wooded hills, did not appeal to Lady Jane in his necessities for
church or parish. She subscribed handsomely to all orthodox
old-established charities, but was not prone to accidental
benevolence. Nobody ever disappointed her when she gave a
dinner, or omitted the duty-call afterwards; but she had no
unceremonious gatherings, no gossipy kettledrums, no hastily-
arranged picnics or garden-parties. When people in the
neighbourhood wanted to take their friends to see the orchids,

they wrote to Lady Jane first, and made it quite a state affair;
and on an appointed afternoon, the lady of Briarwood received
them, richly clad in a dark velvet gown and a point-lace cap, as
if she had just walked out of an old picture, and there were
three or four gardeners in attendance to open doors, and cut
specimen blossoms for the guests.

'She's a splendid woman, admirable in every way,' said
Roderick to an Oxford chum, with whom he had been
discussing Lady Jane's virtues; 'but if a fellow could have a voice
in the matter, she's not the mother I should have chosen for
myself.'

Ambition was the leading characteristic of Lady Jane's mind.
As a girl, she had been ambitious for herself, and that ambition
had been disappointed; as a woman, her ambition transferred
itself to her son. She was the eldest daughter of the Earl of
Lodway, a nobleman who had been considerably overweighted
in the handicap of life, having nine children, seats in three
counties, a huge old house in St James's Square, and a small
income – his three estates consisting of some of the barrenest
and most unprofitable land in Great Britain. Of Lord Lodway's
nine children, five were daughters, and of these Lady Jane was
the eldest and the handsomest. Even in her nursery she had a
very distinct notion that, for her, marriage meant promotion.
She used to play at being married in Westminster Abbey, and
would never consent to have the ceremony performed by less
than two bishops; even though the part of one hierarch had to
be represented by the nursery hearth-broom. In due course
Lady Jane Umleigh made her *début* in society, in all the bloom
and freshness of her stately Saxon beauty. She was admired and
talked about, and acknowledged as one of the belles of that
season; her portrait was engraved in the Book of Beauty, and
her ball programmes were always filled with the very best
names; but at the end of the season, Lady Lodway went back to
Yorkshire with a biting sense of failure and mortification. Her
handsome daughter had not sent her arrow home to the gold.
Lady Jane had not received a single offer worth talking about.

'Don't you think you could consent to be married by one
bishop and a dean, Jenny, if the Marquis comes to the scratch

soon after the twelfth?' asked Lady Jane's youngest brother derisively.

He had been made to do bishop in those play-weddings of Lady Jane's, very often when the function went against the grain.

The Marquis thus familiarly spoken about was Lord Strishfogel, the richest nobleman in Ireland, and a great sea-rover, famous for his steam yachts, and his importance generally. He had admired Lady Jane's statuesque beauty, and had been more particular in his attentions than the rest of her satellites, who for the most part merely worshipped her because it was the right thing to do. Lord Strishfogel had promised to come to Heron's Nest, Lord Lodway's place in the North Riding, for the grouse-shooting; but instead of keeping his promise, this erratic young peer went off to the Golden Horn, to race his yacht against the vessel of a great Turkish official. This was Lady Jane Umleigh's first disappointment. She had liked Lord Strishfogel just well enough to fancy herself deeply in love with him, and she was unconscious of the influence his rank and wealth had exercised upon her feelings. She had thought of herself so often as the Marchioness of Strishfogel, had so completely projected her mind into that brilliant future, that to descend from this giddy height to the insignificance of unwedded girlhood was as sharp a fall as if she had worn a crown and lost it.

Her second season began, and Lord Strishfogel was still a rover. He was in the South Seas by this time, writing a book, and enjoying halcyon days among the friendly natives, swimming like a dolphin in those summery seas, and indulging in harmless flirtations with dusky princesses, whose chief attire was made of shells and flowers, and whose untutored dancing was more vigorous than refined. At the end of that second season, Jane Umleigh had serious thoughts of turning philanthropist, and taking a shipload of destitute young women to Queensland. Anything would be better than this sense of a wasted life and ignominious failure.

She was in this frame of mind when Mr Vawdrey came to Heron's Nest for the shooting. He was a commoner, but his family was one of the oldest in Hampshire, and he had lately distinguished himself by some rather clever speeches in the House of Commons. His estate was worth fifteen thousand a year, and he was altogether a man of mark. Above all, he was handsome, manly, and a gentleman to the marrow of his bones, and he was the first man who ever fell over head and ears in love with Jane Umleigh.

The charms that had repelled more frivolous admirers attracted John Vawdrey. That haughty beauty of Lady Jane's seemed to his mind the perfection of womanly grace. Here was a wife for a man to adore upon his knees, a wife to be proud of, a wife to rule her vassals like a queen, and to lead him, John Vawdrey, on to greatness.

He was romantic, chivalrous, aspiring, and Lady Jane Umleigh was the first woman he had met who embodied the heroine of his youthful dreams. He proposed and was refused, and went away despairing. It would have been a good match, undoubtedly – a truth which Lord and Lady Lodway urged with some iteration upon their daughter – but it would have been a terrible descent from the ideal marriage which Lady Jane had set up in her own mind, as the proper prize for so fair a runner in life's race. She had imagined herself a marchioness, with a vast territory of mountain, vale, and lake, and an influence in the sister island second only to that of royalty. She could not descend all at once to behold herself the wife of a plain country gentleman, whose proudest privilege was to write M.P. after his name.

The Earl and Countess were urgent, for they had another daughter ready for the matrimonial market, and were inclined to regard Lady Jane as an 'old shopkeeper,' but they knew their eldest daughter's temper, and did not press the matter too warmly.

Another season, Lady Jane's fourth, and Lady Sophia's first, began and ended. Lady Sophia was piquant and witty, with a snub nose and a playful disposition. She was a first-rate horse-woman, an exquisite waltzer, good at croquet, archery, billiards, and all games requiring accuracy of eye and aim, and Lady Sophia brought down her bird in a single season. She went home to Heron's Nest a duchess in embryo. The Duke of Dovedale, a bulky, middle-aged nobleman, with a passion for field sports and high farming, had seen Lady Sophia riding a dangerous horse in Rotten Row, and had been so charmed by her management of the brute, as to become from that hour her slave. A pretty girl, with such a seat in her saddle, and such a light hand for a horse's mouth, was the next best thing to a goddess. Before the season was over the Duke had proposed, and had been graciously accepted by the young lady, who felt an inward glow of pride at having done so much better than the family beauty.

'Can I ever forget how that girl Jane has snubbed me?' said Lady Sophia to her favourite brother. 'And to think that I shall be sitting in ermine robes in the House of Lords, while she is peeping through the nasty iron fretwork in the Ladies' Gallery to catch a glimpse of the top of her husband's head in the House of Commons.'

This splendid engagement of Lady Sophia's turned the tide for the faithful John Vawdrey. Lady Jane met her rejected lover at Trouville, and was so gracious to him that he ventured to renew his suit, and, to his delighted surprise, was accepted. Anything was better than standing out in the cold while the ducal engagement was absorbing everybody's thoughts and conversation. Lady Sophia had boasted, in that playful way of hers, of having her beauty-sister for chief bridesmaid; and the beauty-sister had made up her mind that this thing should not be. Perhaps she would have married a worse man than John Vawdrey to escape such infamy.

And John Vawdrey was by no means disagreeable to her; nay, it had been pride, and not any disinclination for the man himself that had bidden her reject him. He was clever, distinguished, and he loved her with a romantic devotion which flattered and pleased her. Yes, she would marry John Vawdrey.

Everybody was delighted at this concession, the lady's parents and belongings most especially so. Here were two daughters disposed of; and if the beauty had made the inferior match, it was only one of those capricious turns of fortune that are more to be expected than the common order of things.

So there was a double marriage the following spring at St George's, and Lady Jane's childish desire was gratified. There were two bishops at the ceremony. True that one was only colonial, and hardly ranked higher than the nursery hearth-brush.

Fate was not altogether unkind to Lady Jane. Her humble marriage was much happier than her sister's loftier union. The Duke, who had been so good-natured as a lover, proved stupid and somewhat tiresome as a husband. He gave his mind to hunting and farming, and cared for nothing else. His chief conversation was about cattle and manure, guano and composts, the famous white Chillingham oxen, or the last thing in strawberry roans. He spent a small fortune — a fortune that would have been large for a small man — in the attempt to acclimatise strange animals in his park in the Midlands. Sophia, Duchess of Dovedale, had seven country seats, and no home. Her children were puny and feeble. They sickened in the feudal Scotch castle, they languished in the Buckinghamshire Eden — an Athenian palace set among the woods that overhang the valley of the Thames. No breezes that blow could waft strength or vitality to those feeble lungs. At thirty the Duchess of Dovedale had lost all her babies, save one frail sapling, a girl of two years old, who promised to have a somewhat better constitution than her perished brothers and sisters. On this small paragon the Duchess concentrated her cares and hopes. She gave up hunting — much to the disgust of that Nimrod, her husband — in order to superintend her nursery. From the most pleasure-loving of matrons, she became the most domestic. Lady Mabel Ashbourne was to grow up the perfection of health, wisdom, and beauty, under the mother's loving care. She would have a great fortune for there was a considerable portion of the Duke's property which he was free to bequeath to his daughter. He had coal-pits in the North, and a tin-mine in the West. He had a house at Kensington which he had built for himself, a model Queen Anne mansion, with every article of furniture made on the strictest aesthetic principles, and not an anachronism from the garrets to the cellars. The Scottish castle and the Buckinghamshire Paradise would go with the title; but the Duke, delighted with the easy-going sport of the New Forest, had bought six hundred acres between Stony Cross and Romsey, and had made for himself an archetypal home-farm, and had built himself a hunting-box; and this estate, together with the Queen Anne house, and the pits and the mine, was his very own to dispose of as he pleased.

Lady Jane's married life was cloudless, but too brief. Her husband, always egged on by her ambitious promptings, made himself an important figure in the senate, and was on the eve of entering the Cabinet as Colonial Secretary, when death cut short his career. A hard winter and a sharp attack of bronchitis nipped the aspiring senator in the bud.

Lady Jane was as nearly broken-hearted as so cold a woman could be. She had loved her husband better than anything in this life, except herself. He left her with one son and a handsome jointure, with the full possession of Briarwood until her son's majority. Upon that only child Lady Jane lavished all her care, but did not squander the wealth of her affection. Perhaps her capacity for loving had died with her husband. She had been proud and fond of him, but she was not proud of the little boy in velvet knickerbockers, whose good looks were his only merit, and who was continually being guilty of some new piece of mischief; laming ponies, smashing orchids, glass, china, and generally disturbing the perfect order which was Briarwood's first law.

When the boy was old enough to go to Eton, he seemed still more remote from his mother's love and sympathy. He was passionately fond of field sports, and those Lady Jane Vawdrey detested. He was backward in all his studies, despite the careful coaching he had received from the mild Anglican curate of Briarwood village. He was intensely pugilistic, and rarely came home for the holidays without bringing a black eye or a swollen nose as the result of his latest fight. He spent a good deal of money, and in a manner that to his mother's logical mind appeared simply idiotic. His hands were always grubby, his nails wore almost perpetual mourning, his boots were an outrage upon good taste, and he generally left a track of muddy footmarks behind him along the crimson-carpeted corridors.

What could any mother do for such a boy, except tolerate him?
Love was out of the question. How could a delicate, high-bred
woman, soft-handed, velvet-robed, care to have such a lad
about her? a boy who smelt of stables and wore hob-nailed
boots, whose pockets were always sticky with toffee, and his
handkerchiefs a disgrace to humanity, who gave his profoundest
thoughts to pigeon-fancying, and his warmest affections to
ratting terriers, nay, who was capable of having a live rat in his
pocket at any moment of his life.

But while all these habits made the lad abominable in the eyes
of his mother, the Duke and Duchess of Dovedale admired the
young Hercules with a fond and envious admiration. The Duke
would have given coal-pits and tin-mine, all the disposable
property he held, and deemed it but a small price for such a
son. The Duchess thought of her feeble boy-babies who had
been whooping-coughed or scarlet-fevered out of the world,
and sighed, and loved her nephew better than ever his mother
had loved him since his babyhood. When the Dovedales were
at their place in the Forest, Roderick almost lived with them;
or, at any rate, divided his time between Ashbourne Park and
the Abbey House, and spent as little of his life at home as he
could. He patronised Lady Mabel, who was his junior by five
years, rode her thoroughbred pony for her, under the pretence
of improving its manners, until he took a header with it into a
bog, out of which pony and boy rolled and struggled
indiscriminately, boy none the worse, pony lamed for life. He
played billiards with the Duke, and told the Duchess all his
school adventures, practical jokes, fights, apple-pie beds, booby-
traps, surreptitious fried sausages, and other misdemeanours.

Out of this friendship arose a brilliant vision which reconciled
Lady Jane Vawdrey to her son's preference for his aunt's house
and his aunt's society. Why should he not marry Mabel by-and-
by, and unite the two estates of Ashbourne and Briarwood, and
become owner of the pits and the mine, and distinguish himself
in the senate, and be created a peer? As the husband of Lady
Mabel Ashbourne, he would be rich enough to command a
peerage, almost as a right; but his mother would have had him
deserve it. With this idea Lady Jane urged on her son's

education. All his Hampshire friends called him clever, but he
won no laurels at school. Lady Jane sent for grinders and had
the boy ground; but all the grinding could not grind a love of
classics or metaphysics into this free son of the forest. He went
to Oxford, and got himself ploughed for his Little Go, with a
wonderful facility. For politics he cared not a jot, but he could
drive tandem better than any other undergraduate of his year.
He never spoke at the Union, but he pulled stroke in the
'Varsity boat. He was famous for his biceps, his good-nature,
and his good looks; but so far he had distinguished himself for
nothing else, and to this stage of non-performance had he come
when the reader first beheld him.

CHAPTER 3

'I WANT A LITTLE SERIOUS TALK WITH YOU'

It was only half-past nine when the brougham drove up to the
pillared porch at Briarwood. The lighted drawing-room
windows shone out upon the vaporous autumn darkness — a
row of five tall French casements — and the sound of a piano
caught Roderick's ear as he tossed the end of his cigar into the
shrubbery and mounted the wide stone door-steps.

'At it again,' muttered Rorie, with a shrug of disgust, as he
entered the hall, and heard, through the half-open drawing-
room door, an interlacement of pearly runs. At this stage of his
existence, Rorie had no appreciation of brilliant pianoforte
playing. The music he liked best was of the simplest, most
inartificial order.

'Are the Duke and Duchess here?' he asked the butler.

'Her Grace and Lady Mabel is here, sir; not the Dook.'

'I suppose I must dress before I face the quality,' muttered
Rorie sulkily, and he went leaping upstairs — three steps at a
time — to exchange his brown shooting-clothes and leather

gaiters for that dress-suit of his which was continually getting too small for him. Rorie detested himself in a dress-suit and a white tie.

'You beast,' he cried, addressing his reflection in the tall glass door of his *armoire*, 'you are the image of a waiter at The Clarendon.'

The Briarwood drawing-room looked a great deal too vast and too lofty for the three women who were occupying it this evening. It was a finely-proportioned room, and its amber satin hangings made a pleasing background for the white and gold furniture. White, gold, and amber made up the prevailing tone of colour. Clusters of wax lights against the walls, and a crystal chandelier with many candles, filled the room with a soft radiance. It was a room without shadow. There were no recesses, no deepset windows or doors. All was coldly bright, faultlessly elegant. Rorie detested his mother's drawing-room almost as much as he detested himself in a dress-coat that was too short in the sleeves.

The matrons were seated on each side of the shining gold and steel fireplace, before which there stretched an island of silky white fur. Lady Jane Vawdrey's younger sister was a stout, comfortable-looking woman in gray silk, who hardly realised one's preconceived notion of a duchess. Lady Jane herself had dignity enough for the highest rank in the 'Almanach de Gotha.' She wore dark green velvet and old rose-point, and looked like a portrait of an Austrian princess by Velasquez. Years had not impaired the purity of her blonde complexion. Her aquiline nose, thin lips, small firm chin, were the features of one born to rule. Her light brown hair showed no streak of gray. An admirable woman, no doubt, for anybody else's mother, as Rorie so often said to himself.

The young lady was still sitting at the piano, remote from the two elders, her slim white fingers running in and out and to and fro in those wondrous intricacies and involutions which distinguish modern classical music. Rorie hated all that running about the piano to no purpose, and could not perceive his cousin's merit in having devoted three or four hours of her daily life for the last seven years to the accomplishment of this melodious meandering. She left off playing, and held out her small white hand to him as he came to the piano, after shaking hands with his aunt.

What was she like, this paragon formed by a mother's worshipping love and ceaseless care, this one last pearl in the crown of domestic life, this child of so many prayers, and hopes, and fears, and deep pathetic rejoicings?

She was very fair to look upon – complete and beautiful as a pearl – with that outward purity, that perfect delicacy of tint and harmony of detail which is in itself a charm. Study her as captiously as you would, you could find no flaw in this jewel. The small features were so delicately chiselled, the fair fine skin was so transparent, the fragile figure so exquisitely moulded, the ivory hand and arm were so perfect – no, you could discover no bad drawing or crude colouring in this human picture. She lifted her clear blue eyes to Rorie's face, and smiled at him in gentle welcome; and though he felt intensely savage at having been summoned home like a schoolboy, he could not refuse her a responsive smile, or a gentle pressure of the taper fingers.

'And so you have been dining with those horrid people!' she exclaimed with an air of playful reproach, 'and on your last night in Hampshire – quite too unkind to Aunt Jane.'

'I don't know whom you mean by horrid people, Mabel,' answered Rorie, chilled back into sulkiness all at once; 'the people I was with are all that is good and pleasant.'

'Then you've not been at the Tempests' after all?'

'I have been at the Tempests'. What have you to say against the Tempests?'

'O, I have nothing to say against them,' said Lady Mabel, shrugging her pretty shoulders in her fawn-coloured silk gown. 'There are some things that do not require to be said.

'Mr Tempest is the best and kindest of men; his wife is – well, a nonentity, perhaps, but not a disagreeable one; and his daughter——'

Here Rorie came to a sudden stop, which Lady Mabel accentuated with a silvery little laugh.

'His daughter is charming,' she cried, when she had done laughing: 'red hair, and a green habit with brass buttons, a

yellow waistcoat like her papa's, and a rose in her button-hole.
How I should like to see her in Rotten Row!'

'I'll warrant there wouldn't be a better horsewoman or a
prettier girl there,' cried Rorie, scarlet with indignation.

His mother looked daggers. His cousin gave another silvery
laugh, clear as those pearly treble runs upon the Erard; but that
pretty artificial laugh had a ring which betrayed her
mortification.

'Rorie is thorough,' she said; 'when he likes people he thinks
them perfection. You do think that little red-haired girl quite
perfection, now don't you, Rorie?' pursued Lady Mabel, sitting
down before the piano again, and touching the notes silently as
she seemed to admire the slender diamond hoops upon her
white fingers — old-fashioned rings that had belonged to a
patrician great-grandmother. 'You think her quite a model
young lady, though they say she can hardly read, and makes her
mark — like William the Conqueror — instead of signing her
name, and spends her life in the stables, and occasionally, when
the fox gets to earth — swears.'

'I don't know who they may be,' cried Roderick, savagely,
'but they say a pack of lies. Violet Tempest is as well educated
as — any girl need be. All girls can't be paragons; or, if they
could, this earth would be intolerable for the rest of humanity.
Lord deliver us from a world overrun with paragons. Violet
Tempest is little more than a child, a spoiled child, if you like,
but she has a heart of gold, and a firmer seat in her saddle than
any other woman in Hampshire.'

Roderick had turned from scarlet to pale by the time he
finished this speech. His mother had paled at the first mention
of poor Vixen. That young lady's name acted upon Lady Jane's
feelings very much as a red rag acts on a bull.

'I think after keeping you away from your mother on the last
night of your vacation, Mr Tempest might at least have had the
good taste to let you come home sober,' said Lady Jane with
suppressed rage.

'I drank a couple of glasses of hock at dinner, and not a drop
of anything else from the time I entered the Abbey House till I
left it; and I don't think, considering how I've seasoned myself

with Bass at Oxford, that two glasses of Rudesheimer would floor me,' explained Rorie, with recovered calmness.

'O, but you were drinking deep of a more intoxicating nectar,' cried Lady Mabel, with that provokingly distinct utterance of hers. She had been taught to speak as carefully as girls of inferior rank are taught to play Beethoven – every syllable studied, every tone trained and ripened to the right quality. 'You were with Violet Tempest.'

'How you children quarrel!' exclaimed the Duchess; 'you could hardly be worse if you were lovers. Come here, Rorie, and tell me all that has happened to you since we saw you at Lord's in July. Never mind these Tempest people. They are of the smallest possible importance. Of course, Rorie must have somebody to amuse himself with while we are away.'

'And now we are come back, he is off to Oxford,' said Mabel with an aggrieved air.

'You shouldn't have stayed so long in Switzerland then,' retorted Rorie.

'O, but it was my first visit, and everything is so lovely. After all the Swiss landscapes I have done in chalk, and pencil, and water-colours, I was astonished to find what a stranger I was to the scenery. I blushed when I remembered those dreadful landscapes of mine. I was ashamed to look at Mont Blanc. I felt as if the Matterhorn would fall and crush me.'

'I think I shall do Switzerland next long,' said Rorie patronisingly, as if it would be a good thing for Switzerland.

'You might have come this year while we were there,' said Lady Mabel.

'No, I mightn't. I've been grinding. If you knew what a dose of Aristotle I've had, you'd pity me. That's where you girls have the best of it. You learn to read a story-book in two or three modern languages, to meander up and down the piano, and spoil Bristol board, or Whatman's hot-pressed imperial, and then you call yourselves educated; while we have to go back to the beginning of civilisation, and find out what a lot of Greek blokes were driving at when they sat in the sunshine and prosed like old boots.'

Lady Mabel looked at him with a serene smile.

'Would you be surprised to hear that I know a little Greek,' she said, 'just enough to struggle through the Socratic dialogues with the aid of my master?'

Roderick started as if he had been stung.

'What a shame,' he cried. 'Aunt Sophia, what do you mean by making a Lady Jane Grey or an Elizabeth Barrett Browning of her?'

'A woman who has to occupy a leading position can hardly know too much,' answered the Duchess sententiously.

'Ah, to be sure, Mabel will marry some diplomatic swell, and be entertaining ambassadors by-and-by. And when some modern Greek envoy comes simpering up to her with a remark about the weather, it will be an advantage for her to know Plato. I understand. Wheels within wheels.'

Here the butler entered, and approaching the Duchess with bent head and confidential air, insinuated that her carriage was at the door.

Mabel rose at once from the piano, and came to say good-night to her aunt.

'My dear child, it's quite early,' said Lady Jane; 'Roderick's last night, too. And your mother is in no hurry.'

Mabel looked at Roderick, but that young gentleman was airing himself on the hearth-rug, and gazing absently at the ceiling. It evidently signified very little to him whether his aunt and cousin went or stayed.

'You know you told papa you would be home soon after ten,' said Lady Mabel, and the Duchess rose immediately.

She had a way of yielding to her only daughter which her strong-minded sister highly disapproved. The first duty of a mother, in Lady Jane's opinion, was to rule her child, the second to love it. The idea was no doubt correct in the abstract; but the practice was not succeeding too well with Roderick.

'Good-night and good-bye,' said Lady Mabel, when the maid had brought her wraps, and Rorie had put them on.

'Not good-bye,' said the good-natured Duchess; 'Rorie must come to breakfast to-morrow, and see the Duke. He has just bought some wonderful shorthorns, and I am sure he would like to show them to you, Rorie, because you can appreciate them. He was too tired to come out to-night, but I know he wants to see you.'

'Thanks. I'll be there,' answered Rorie, and he escorted the ladies to their carriage; but not another word did Mabel speak till the brougham had driven away from Briarwood.

'What a horrid young man Roderick has grown, mamma,' she remarked decisively, when they were outside the park-gates.

'My love, I never saw him look handsomer.'

'I don't mean his looks. Good looks in a man are a superfluity. But his manners — I never saw anything so underbred. Those Tempest people are spoiling him.'

'Roderick,' said Lady Jane, just as Rorie was contemplating an escape to the billiard-room and his cigar, 'I want a little serious talk with you.'

Rorie shivered in his shoes. He knew too well what his mother's serious talk meant. He shrugged his shoulders with a movement that indicated a dormant resistance, and went quietly into the drawing-room.

CHAPTER 4

RORIE COMES OF AGE

'Bless my soul!' cried the Squire; 'it's a vixen, after all.'

This is how Squire Tempest greeted the family doctor's announcement of his first baby's sex. He had been particularly anxious for a son to inherit the Abbey House estate, succeed to his father's dignities as master of the fox-hounds, and in a general way sustain the pride and glory of the family name; and behold! Providence had given him a daughter.

'The deuce is in it,' ejaculated the Squire, 'to think that it should be vixen!'

This is how Violet Tempest came by her curious pet name. Before she was short-coated, she had contrived to exhibit a very spirited, and even vixenish temper, and the family doctor, who loved a small joke, used to ask after Miss Vixen when he paid his professional visits. As she grew older, her tawny hair was not unlike a red fox's brush in its bright golden-brown hue, and her temper grew decidedly vixenish.

'I wish you wouldn't call Violet by that dreadful nickname, dear,' Mrs Tempest remonstrated mildly.

'My darling, it suits her to a nicety,' replied the Squire, and he took his own way in this as in most things.

The earth rolled round, and the revolving years brought no second baby to the Abbey House. Every year made the Squire fonder of his little golden-haired girl. He put her on a soft white ball of a pony as soon as she could sit up straight, and took her about the forest with a leading-rein. No one else was allowed to teach Vixen to ride. Young as she was, she soon learnt to do without the leading-rein, and the gentle white pony was discarded as too quiet for little Miss Tempest. Before her eleventh birthday she rode to hounds, rose before the sun to hunt the young fox-cubs in early autumn, and saw the stag at bay on the wild heathery downs above the wooded valleys that sink and fall below Boldrewood. She was a creature full of life, and courage, and generous impulses, and spontaneous leanings to all good thoughts; but she was a spoilt child, liked her own way, and had no idea of being guided by anybody else's will – unless it had been her father's, and he never thwarted her.

Him she adored with the fondest love that child ever gave to parent: a blind worshipping love, that saw in him the perfection of manhood, the beginning and end of earthly good. If anyone had dared to say in Vixen's hearing that her father could, by any possible combination of circumstances, do wrong, act unjustly, or ungenerously, it would have been better for that man to have come to handy grips with a tiger-cat than with Violet Tempest. Her reverence for her father, and her belief in him were boundless.

There never, perhaps, was a happier childhood than Violet's. She was daughter and heiress to one of the most popular men in that part of the country, and everybody loved her. She was not much given to visiting in a methodical way among the poor, and it had never entered into her young mind that it was her mission to teach older people the way to heaven; but if there was trouble in the neighbourhood – a sick child, a husband in prison for rabbit snaring, a dead baby, a little boy's pinafore set on fire – Vixen and her pony was always to the fore; and it was an axiom in the village that, where Miss Tempest did 'take,' it was very good for those she took to. Violet never withdrew her hand when she had put it to the plough. If she made a promise, she always kept it. However long the sickness, however dire the poverty, Vixen's patience and benevolence lasted to the end.

The famous princess in the story, whose sleep was broken because there was a pea under her seven feather-beds, had scarcely a more untroubled life than Vixen. She had her own way in everything. She did exactly what she liked with her comfortable, middle-aged governess, Miss McCroke, learnt what she pleased, and left what she disliked unlearned. She had the prettiest ponies in Hampshire to ride, the prettiest dresses to wear. Her mother was not a woman to bestow mental culture upon her only child, but she racked her small brain to devise becoming costumes for Violet: the coloured stockings which harmonised best with each particular gown, the neat little buckled shoes, the fascinating Hessian boots. Nothing was too beautiful or too costly for Violet. She was the one thing her parents possessed in the world, and they lavished much love upon her; but it never occurred to Mr and Mrs Tempest, as it had occurred to the Duchess of Dovedale – to make their daughter a paragon.

In this perpetual sunshine Violet grew up, fair as most things are that grow in the sunshine. She loved her father with all her heart, and mind, and soul; she loved her mother with a lesser love; she had a tolerant affection for Miss McCroke; she loved her ponies, and the dog Argus; she loved the hounds in the kennels; she loved every honest familiar face of nurse, servant, and stable-man, gardener, keeper, and huntsman, that had looked upon her with friendly, admiring eyes, ever since she could remember.

Not to be loved and admired would have been the strangest thing to Violet. She would hardly have recognised herself in an unappreciative circle. If she could have heard Lady Mabel talking about her, it would have been like the sudden revelation of an unknown world – a world in which it was possible for people to dislike and misjudge her.

This is one of the disadvantages of being reared in a little heaven of domestic love. The outside world seems so hard, and bleak, and dreary afterwards, and the inhabitants thereof passing cruel.

Miss Tempest looked upon Roderick Vawdrey as her own particular property – a person whom she had the right to order about as she pleased. Rorie had been her playfellow and companion in his holiday-time for the last five years. All their tastes were in common. They had the same love for the brute creation, the same wild delight in rushing madly through the air on the backs of unreasoning animals; widely different in their tastes from Lady Mabel, who had once been run away with in a pony-carriage, and looked upon all horses as incipient murderers. They had the same love of nature, the same indifference to books, and the same careless scorn of all the state and ceremony of life.

Vixen was 'rising fifteen,' as her father called it, and Rorie was just five years her senior. The Squire saw them gay and happy together without one serious thought of what might come of their childish friendship in the growth of years. That his Vixen could ever care for anyone but her 'old dad,' was a notion which had not yet found its way into the Squire's brain. She seemed to him quite as much his own property, his own to do what he liked with, singly and simply attached to him, as his favourite horse or his favourite dog. So there were no shadowings forth in the paternal mind as to any growth and development which the mutual affection of these two young people might take in the future.

It was very different with Lady Jane Vawdrey, who never saw her son and his cousin Mabel together without telling herself how exactly they were suited to each other, and what a nice thing it would be for the Briarwood and Ashbourne estates to be united by their marriage.

Rorie went back to college, and contrived to struggle through his next examinations with an avoidance of actual discredit; but when Christmas came he did not return to the Forest though Violet had counted on his coming, and had thought that it would be good fun to have his help in the decorations for the little Gothic church in the valley – a pretty little new church, like a toy, which the Squire had built and paid for, and endowed with a perpetual seventy pounds a year out of his own pocket. It would have been fun to see poor Rorie prick his clumsy fingers with the holly. Vixen laughed at his awkwardness in advance, when she talked to Miss McCroke about him, and drew upon herself that lady's mild reproval.

But Christmas came and brought no Rorie. He had gone off to spend his Christmas at the Duke of Dovedale's Scotch castle. Easter came, but still no Rorie. He was at Putney, with the 'Varsity crew, or in London with the Dovedales, riding in the Row, and forgetting dear old Hampshire and the last of the hunting, for which he would have been just in time.

Even the long vacation came without Rorie. He had gone for that promised tour in Switzerland, at his mother's instigation, and was only to come home late in the year to keep his twenty-first birthday, which was to be honoured in a very subdued and unhilarious fashion at Briarwood.

'Mamma,' said Violet at breakfast-time one August morning, with her nose scornfully tilted, 'what is Mr Vawdrey like – dark or fair?'

'Why, Violet, you can't have forgotten him,' protested her mother, with languid astonishment.

'I think he has been away long enough for me to forget even the colour of his hair, mamma; and as he hasn't written to anybody, we may fairly suppose he has forgotten us.'

'Vixen misses her old playfellow,' said the Squire, busy with the demolition of a grouse. 'But Rorie is a young man now, you know, dear, and has work to do in the world – duties, my pet – duties.'

'And is a young man's first duty to forget his old friends?' inquired Vixen naïvely.

'My pet, you can't expect a lad of that kind to write letters. I
am a deuced bad hand at letter-writing myself, and always was.
I don't think a man's hand was ever made to pinch a pen.
Nature has given us a broad strong grasp, to grip a sword or a
gun. Your mother writes most of my letters, Vixen, you know,
and I shall expect you to help her in a year or two. Let me see;
Rorie will be one-and-twenty in October, and there are to be
high jinks at Briarwood, I believe, so there's something for you
to look forward to, my dear.'

'Edward!' exclaimed Mrs Tempest reproachfully; 'you forget
that Violet is not out. She will not be sixteen till next
February.'

'Bless her!' cried the Squire, with a tender look at his only
child, 'she has grown up like a green bay-tree. But if this were
to be quite a friendly affair at Briarwood, she might go, surely.'

'It will not be a friendly affair,' said Mrs Tempest; 'Lady Jane
never gives friendly parties. There is nothing friendly in her
nature, and I don't think she likes us – much. But I daresay we
shall be asked, and if we go I must have a new gown,' added
the gentle lady with a sigh of resignation. 'It will be a dinner,
no doubt; and the Duke and the Duchess will be there, of
course.'

The card of invitation came in due course, three weeks
before the birthday. It was to be a dinner, as Mrs Tempest had
opined. She wrote off to her milliner at once, and there was a
passage of letters and fashion-plates and patterns of silk to and
fro, and some of Mrs Tempest's finest lace came out of the
sandal-wood chest in which she kept her treasures, and was sent
off to Madame Theodore.

Poor Vixen beheld these preparations with an aching heart.
She did not care about dinner-parties in the least, but she would
have liked to be with Roderick on his birthday. She would
have liked it to have been a hunting-day, and to have had a
wild scamper across the hills with him – to have seen the rolling
downs of the Wight blue in the distance – to have felt the soft
south wind blowing on her face, and to have ridden by his side,
neck and neck, all day long; and then to have gone home to the
Abbey House to dinner, to the snug round table in the library,

and the dogs, and papa in his happiest mood, expanding over his port and walnuts. That would have been a happy birthday for all of them, in Violet's opinion.

The Squire and his daughter had plenty of hunting in this merry month of October, but there had been no sign of Rorie and his big raking chestnut in the field, nor had anyone in the Forest heard of or seen the young Oxonian.

'I daresay he is only coming home in time for the birthday,' Mrs Tempest remarked placidly, and went on with her preparations for that event.

She wanted to make a strong impression on the Duchess, who had not behaved too well to her, only sending her invitations for indiscriminate afternoon assemblies, which Mrs Tempest had graciously declined, pleading her feeble health as a reason for not going to garden-parties.

Vixen was in a peculiar temper during those three weeks, and poor Miss McCroke had hard work with her.

'*Der, die, das,*' cried Vixen, throwing down her German grammar in a rage one morning, when she had been making a muddle of the definite article in her exercise, and the patient governess had declared that they really must go back to the very beginning of things. 'What stupid people the Germans are! Why can't they have one little word for everything, as we have? T, h, e, the. Any child can learn that. What do they mean by chopping up their language into little bits, like the pieces in a puzzle? Why, even the French are more reasonable – though they're bad enough, goodness knows, with their hes and shes – feminine tables, and masculine beds. Why should I be bothered to learn all this rubbish? I'm not going to be a governess, and it will never be any use to me. Papa doesn't know a single sentence in French or German, and he's quite happy.'

'But if your father were travelling on the Continent, Violet, he would find his ignorance of the language a great deprivation.'

'No, he wouldn't. He'd have a courier.'

'Are you aware, my dear, that we have wasted five minutes already in this discursive conversation?' remarked Miss McCroke, looking at a fat useful watch, which she wore at her side in the good old fashion. 'We will leave the grammar for the present, and you can repeat the first part of Schiller's Song of the Bell.'

'I'd rather say the Fight with the Dragon,' said Vixen, 'there's more fire and life in it. I do like Schiller, Crokey dear. But isn't it a pity he didn't write in English?'

And Vixen put her hands behind her, and began to recite the wonderful story of the knight who slew the dragon, and very soon her eyes kindled and her cheeks were aflame, and the grand verses were rolled out rapidly, with a more or less faulty pronunciation, but plenty of life and vehemence. This exercise of mind and memory suited Vixen a great deal better than dull plodding at the first principles of grammar, and the perpetual *der*, *die*, *das*.

This day was the last of October, and Roderick Vawdrey's birthday. He had not been seen at the Abbey House yet. He had returned to Briarwood before this, no doubt, but had not taken the trouble to come and see his old friends.

'He's a man now, and has duties, and has done with us,' thought Vixen savagely.

She was very glad that it was such a wretched day – a hideous day for anyone's twenty-first birthday, ominous of all bad things, she thought. There was not a rift in the dull gray sky; the straight fine rain came down persistently, soaking into the sodden earth, and sending up an odour of dead leaves. The smooth shining laurels in the shrubbery were the only things in nature that seemed no worse for the perpetual downpour. The gravel drives were spongy and sloppy. There was no hunting, or Vixen would have been riding her pony through rain and foul weather, and would have been comparatively independent of the elements. But to be at home all day, watching the rain, and thinking what a horrid, ungrateful young man Rorie was! That was dreary.

Mrs Tempest went to her room to lie down directly after luncheon. She wanted to keep herself fresh for the evening. She made quite a solemn business of this particular dinner-party. At five precisely, Pauline was to bring her a cup of tea. At half-past five she was to begin to dress. This would give her an hour and a half for her toilet, as Briarwood was an hour's drive from the Abbey House. So for the rest of that day – until she burst upon their astonished view in her new gown – Mrs Tempest would be invisible to her family.

'What a disgusting birthday,' cried Vixen, sitting in the deep embrasure of the hall window, with Argus at her side, dog and girl looking out at the glistening shrubbery.

Miss McCroke had gone to her room to write letters, or Vixen would have hardly been allowed to remain peacefully in such an inelegant position, her knees drawn up to her chin, her arms embracing her legs, her back against the stout oak shutter. Yet the girl and dog made rather a pretty picture, despite the inelegance of Vixen's attitude. The tawny hair, black velvet frock, and careless amber sash, amber stockings, and broad-toed Cromwell shoes; the tawny mastiff curled in the opposite corner of the deep recess; the old armorial bearings, sending pale shafts of parti-coloured light across Vixen's young head; – these things made a picture full of light and colour, framed in the dark brown oak.

'What an abominable birthday!' ejaculated Vixen; 'if it were such weather as this on my twenty-first birthday I should think Nature had taken a dislike to me. But I don't suppose Rorie cares. He is playing billiards with a lot of his friends, and smoking, and making a horror of himself, I daresay, and hardly knows whether it rains or shines.'

Drip, drip, drip, came the rain on the glistening leaves, berberis and laurel, bay and holly, American oaks of richest red and bronze, copper beeches, tall rhododendrons, cypress of every kind, and behind them a dense black screen of yew. The late roses looked miserable. Vixen would have liked to have brought them in and put them by the hall fire – the good old hearth with its pile of blazing logs, before which Nip the pointer was stretched at ease, his muscular toes stiffening themselves occasionally as if he were standing at a bird in his dreams.

Vixen went on watching the rain. It was rather a lazy way of spending the afternoon certainly, but Miss Tempest was out of humour with her little world, and did not feel equal to groping out the difficulties, the inexorable double sharps and odious double flats, in a waltz of Chopin's. She watched the straight thin rain, and thought about Rorie – chiefly to the effect that she hated him, and never could, by any possibility, like him again.

Gradually the trickle of the rain from an overflowing waterpipe took the sound of a tune. No *berceuse* by Gounod was ever more rest-compelling. The full white lids dropped over the big brown eyes, the little locked hands loosened, the soft round chin fell forward on the knees, Argus gave a snort of satisfaction, and laid his heavy head on the velvet gown. Girl and dog were asleep. There was no sound in the wide old hall except the soft falling of wood ashes, the gentle breathing of girl and dogs.

Too pretty a picture assuredly to be lost to the eye of mankind.

Whose footstep was this sounding on the wet gravel half an hour later? Too quick and light for the Squire's. Who was this coming in softly out of the rain, all dripping like a water god? Who was this whose falcon eye took in the picture at a glance, and who stole cat-like to the window, and bending down his dark wet head, gave Violet's sleeping lips the first lover's kiss that had ever saluted them?

Violet awoke with a faint shiver of surprise and joy. Instinct told her from whom that kiss came, though it was the first time Roderick had kissed her since he went to Eton. The lovely brown eyes opened and looked into the dark gray ones. The ruddy brown head rested on Rorie's shoulder. The girl – half child, half woman, and all loving trustfulness – looked up at him with a glad smile. His heart was stirred with a new feeling as those softly bright eyes looked into his. It was the early dawn of a passionate love. The head lying on his breast seemed to him the fairest thing on earth.

'Rorie, how disgracefully you have behaved, and how utterly I detest you!' exclaimed Vixen, giving him a vigorous push, and scrambling down from the window seat. 'To be all this time in Hampshire and never come near us.'

A moment ago, in that first instant of a newly awakened delight, she was almost betrayed into telling him that she loved him dearly, and had found life empty without him. But having had just time enough to recover herself, she drew herself up as straight as a dart, and looked at him as Kate may have looked at Petruchio during that remarkably unpleasant interview in which they made each other's acquaintance.

'All this time!' cried Rorie. 'Do you know how long I have been in Hampshire?'

'Haven't the least idea,' retorted Vixen haughtily.

'Just half an hour – or, at least it is exactly half an hour since I was deposited with all my goods and chattels at the Lyndhurst Road Station.'

'You are only just home from Switzerland?'

'Within this hour!'

'And you have not even been to Briarwood?'

'My honoured mother still awaits my duteous greetings.'

'And this is your twenty-first birthday, and you came here first of all.'

And, almost uninvited, the tawny head dropped on to his shoulder again, and the sweet childish lips allowed themselves to be kissed.

'Rorie, how brown you have grown.'

'Have I!'

The gray eyes were looking into the brown ones admiringly, and the conversation was getting a trifle desultory.

Swift as a flash Violet recollected herself. It dawned upon her that it was not quite the right thing for a young lady 'rising sixteen' to let herself be kissed so tamely. Besides, Rorie never used to do it. The thing was a new development, a curious outcome of his Swiss tour. Perhaps people did it in Switzerland, and Rorie had acquired the habit.

'How dare you do such a thing?' exclaimed Vixen, shaking herself free from the traveller's encircling arm.

'I didn't think you minded,' said Rorie innocently; 'and when a fellow comes home from a long journey he expects a warm welcome!'

'And I am glad to see you,' cried Vixen, giving him both her hands with a glorious frankness; 'but you don't know how I have been hating you lately.'

'Why, Vixen?'

'For being always away. I thought you had forgotten us all – that you did not care a jot for any of us.'

'I had not forgotten any of you, and I did care – very much – for some of you.'

This, though vague, was consoling.

The brown became Roderick. Dark of visage always, he was now tanned to a bronze, as of one born under southern skies. Those deep gray eyes of his looked black under their black lashes. His dark hair was cut close to his well-shaped head. An incipient moustache shaded his upper lip, and gave manhood to the strong, firm mouth. A manly face altogether, Roderick's, and handsome withal. Vixen's short life had shown her none handsomer.

He was tall and strongly built, with a frame that had been developed by many an athletic exercise – from throwing the hammer to pugilism. Vixen thought him the image of Richard Coeur de Lion. She had been reading 'The Talisman' lately, and the Plantagenet was her ideal of manly excellence.

'Many happy returns of the day, Rorie,' she said softly. 'To think that you are of age to-day. Your own master.'

'Yes, my infancy ceased and determined at the last stroke of midnight yesterday. I wonder whether my anxious mother will recognise that fact?'

'Of course you know what is going to happen at Briarwood. There is to be a grand dinner-party.'

'And you are coming? How jolly!'

'O, no, Rorie. I'm not out yet, you know. I sha'n't be for two years. Papa means to give me a season in town. He calls it having me broken to harness. He'll take a furnished house, and we shall have the horses up, and I shall ride in the Row. You'll be with us part of the time, won't you, Rorie?'

'*Ca se peut*. If papa will invite me.'

'O, he will, if I wish it. It's to be my first season, you know, and I'm to have everything my own way.'

'Will that be a novelty?' demanded Roderick, with intention.

'I don't know. I haven't had my own way in anything lately.'

'How is that?'

'You have been away.'

At this naïve flattery, Roderick almost blushed.

'How you've grown, Vixen,' he remarked presently.

'Have I really? Yes, I suppose I do grow. My frocks are always getting too short.'

'Like the sleeves of my dress-coats a year or two ago.'

'But now you are of age, and can't grow any more. What are you going to be, Rorie? What are you going to do with your liberty? Are you going into Parliament?'

Mr Vawdrey indulged in a suppressed yawn.

'My mother would like it,' he said, 'but upon my word I don't care about it. I don't take enough interest in my fellow-creatures.'

'If they were foxes you'd be anxious to legislate for them,' suggested Vixen.

'I would certainly try to protect them from indiscriminate slaughter. And in fact, when one considers the looseness of existing game laws, I think every country gentleman ought to be in Parliament.'

'And there is the Forest for you to take care of.'

'Yes, forestry is a subject on which I should like to have my say. I suppose I shall be obliged to turn senator. But I mean to take life easily – you may be sure of that, Vixen; and I intend to have the best stud of hunters in Hampshire. And now I think I must be off.'

'No, you mustn't,' cried Violet. 'The dinner is not till eight. If you leave here at six you will have no end of time for getting home to dress. How did you come?'

'On these two legs.'

'You shall have four to take you to Briarwood. West shall drive you home in papa's dog-cart, with the new mare. You don't know her, do you? Papa only bought her last spring. She is such a beauty, and goes – goes – O, like a skyrocket. She bolts occasionally; and there are a good many things she doesn't like; but you don't mind that, do you?'

'Not in the least. It would be rather romantic to be smashed on one's twenty-first birthday. Will you tell them to order West to get ready at once?'

'O, but you are to stop to tea with Miss McCroke and me – that's part of our bargain. No kettledrum, no Starlight Bess! And you'd scarcely care about walking to Briarwood under such rain as that!'

'So be it, then; kettledrum and Starlight Bess, at any hazard of maternal wrath. But really now, I'm doing a most ungentlemanly thing, Vixen, to oblige you!'

'Always be ungentlemanly then for my sake – if it's ungentlemanly to come and see me,' said Vixen coaxingly.

They were standing side by side in the big window looking out at the straight thin rain. The two pairs of lips were not very far away from each other, and Rorie might have been tempted to commit a third offence against the proprieties, if Miss McCroke had not fortunately entered at this very moment. She was wonderfully surprised at seeing Mr Vawdrey, congratulated him ceremoniously upon his majority, and infused an element of stiffness into the small assembly.

'Rorie is going to stay to tea,' said Vixen. 'We'll have it here by the fire, please, Crokey dear. One can't have too much of a good fire this weather. Or shall we go to my den? Which would you like best, Rorie?'

'I think we had better have tea here, Violet,' interjected Miss McCroke, ringing the bell.

Her pupil's *sanctum sanctorum* – that pretty upstairs room, half schoolroom, half boudoir, and wholly untidy – was not, in Miss McCroke's opinion, an apartment to be violated by the presence of a young man.

'And as Rorie hasn't had any luncheon, and has come ever so far out of his way to see me, please order something substantial for him,' said Vixen.

Her governess obeyed. The gipsy table was wheeled up to the broad hearth, and presently the old silver teapot and kettle, and the yellow cups and saucers, were shining in the cheery firelight. The old butler put a sirloin and a game-pie on the sideboard, and then left the little party to shift for themselves in pleasant picnic fashion.

Vixen sat down before the hissing tea-kettle with a pretty important air, like a child making tea out of toy tea-things.

Rorie brought a low square stool to a corner close to her, and seated himself with his chin a little above the tea-table.

'You can't eat roast beef in that position,' said Vixen.

'O yes I can – I can do anything that's mad or merry this evening. But I'm not at all sure that I want beef, though it is nearly three months since I've seen an honest bit of ox beef. I think thin bread and butter – or roses and dew even – quite substantial enough for me this evening.'

'You're afraid of spoiling your appetite for the grand dinner,' said Vixen.

'No, I'm not. I hate grand dinners. Fancy making a fine art of eating, and studying one's *menu* beforehand to see what combination of dishes will harmonise best with one's internal economy. And then the names of the things are always better than the things themselves. It's like a show at a fair, all the best outside. Give me a slice of English beef or mutton, and a bird that my gun has shot, and I let all the fine-art dinners go hang.'

'Cut him a slice of beef, dear Miss McCroke,' said Vixen.

'Not now, thanks; I can't eat now. I'm going to drink orange pekoe.'

Argus had taken up his position between Violet and her visitor. He sat bolt upright, like a sentinel keeping guard over his mistress.

'Are you very glad to come of age, Rorie?' asked Vixen, turning her bright brown eyes upon him, full of curiosity.

'Well, it will be rather nice to have as much money as I want without asking my mother for it. She was my only guardian, you know. My father had such confidence in her rectitude and capacity that he left everything in her hands.'

'Do you find Briarwood much improved?' inquired Miss McCroke.

Lady Jane had been doing a good deal to her orchid-houses lately.

'I haven't found Briarwood at all yet,' answered Rorie, 'and Vixen seems determined I sha'n't find it.'

'What, have you only just returned?'

'Only just.'

'And you have not seen Lady Jane yet?' exclaimed Miss
McCroke with a horrified look.

'It sounds rather undutiful, doesn't it? I was awfully tired, after
travelling all night; and I made this a kind of halfway house.'

'Two sides of a triangle are invariably longer than anyone
side,' remarked Vixen gravely. 'At least that's what Miss
McCroke has taught me.'

'It was rather out of my way, of course. But I wanted to see
whether Vixen had grown. And I wanted to see the Squire.'

'Papa has gone to Ringwood, to look at a horse; but you'll
see him at the grand dinner. He'll be coming home to dress
presently.'

'I hope you had an agreeable tour, Mr Vawdrey,' said Miss
McCroke.

'O, uncommonly jolly.'

'And you like Switzerland?'

'Yes; it's nice and hilly.'

And then Roderick favoured them with a sketch of his
travels, while they sipped their tea, and while Vixen made the
dogs balance pieces of cake on their big blunt noses.

It was all very nice – the Tête Noire, and Mont Blanc, and
the Matterhorn. Rorie jumbled them all together, without the
least regard to geography. He had done a good deal of climbing,
had worn out and lost dozens of alpenstocks, and had brought
home a case of Swiss carved work for his friends.

'There's a clock for your den, Vixen – I shall bring it to-
morrow – with a little cock-robin that comes out of his nest
and sings – no end of jolly.'

'How lovely!' cried Violet.

The tall eight-day clock in a corner of the hall chimed the
half-hour.

'Half-past five, and Starlight Bess not ordered,' exclaimed
Roderick.

'Let's go out to the stables and see about her,' suggested
Vixen. 'And then I can show you my pony. You remember
Titmouse, the one that *would* jump?'

'Violet!' ejaculated the aggrieved governess. 'Do you suppose
I would permit you to go out of doors in such weather?'

'Do you think it's still raining?' asked Vixen innocently. 'It may have cleared up. Well, we'd better order the cart,' she added meekly, as she rang the bell. 'I'm not of age yet, you see, Rorie. Please, Peters, tell West to get papa's dog-cart ready for Mr Vawdrey, and to drive Starlight Bess.'

Rorie looked at the bright face admiringly. The shadows had deepened; there was no light in the great oak-panelled room except the ruddy fire-glow, and in this light Violet Tempest looked her loveliest. The figures in the tapestry seemed to move in the flickering light – appeared and vanished, vanished and appeared, like the phantoms of a dream. The carved bosses of the ceiling were reflected grotesquely on the oaken wall above the tapestry. The stags' heads had a goblin look. It was like a scene of enchantment, and Violet, in her black frock and amber sash, looked like the enchantress – Circe, Vivien, Melusine, or somebody of equally dubious antecedents.

It was Miss McCroke's sleepiest hour. Strong tea, which has an awakening influence upon most people, acted as an opiate upon her. She sat blinking owlishly at the two young figures.

Rorie roused himself with a great effort.

'Unless Starlight Bess spins me along the road pretty quickly, I shall hardly get to Briarwood by dinner-time,' he said; 'and upon my honour, I don't feel the least inclination to go.'

'O, what fun if you were absent at your coming-of-age dinner!' cried Vixen, with her brown eyes dancing mischievously. 'They would have to put an empty chair for you, like Banquo's.'

'It would be a lark,' acquiesced Rorie, 'but it wouldn't do; I should hear too much about it afterwards. A fellow's mother has some kind of claim upon him, you know. Now for Starlight Bess.'

They went into the vestibule, and Rorie opened the door, letting in a gust of wind and rain, and the scent of autumn's last ill-used flowers.

'O, I so nearly forgot,' said Violet, as they stood on the threshold, side by side, waiting for the dog-cart to appear. 'I've got a little present for you – quite a humble one for a grand young landowner like you – but I never could save much of my

pocket-money; there are so many poor children always having
scarlet-fever, or tumbling into the fire, or drinking out of
boiling tea-kettles. But here it is, Rorie. I hope you won't hate
it very much.'

She put a little square packet into his hand, which he
proceeded instantly to open.

'I shall love it, whatever it is.'

'It's a portrait.'

'You darling! The very thing I should have asked for.'

'The portrait of someone you're fond of.'

'Someone I adore,' said Rorie.

He had extracted the locket from its box by this time. It was
a thick oblong locket of dead gold, plain and massive; the
handsomest of its kind that a Southampton jeweller could
supply.

Rorie opened it eagerly, to look at the portrait.

There was just light enough from the newly-kindled vestibule
lamp to show it to him.

'Why it's a dog,' cried Rorie, with deep-toned disgust. 'It's
old Argus.'

'Who did you think it was?'

'You, of course.'

'What an idea! As if I should give anyone my portrait. I knew
you were fond of Argus. Doesn't his head come out beautifully?
The photographer said he was the best sitter he had had for ever
so long. I hope you don't quite detest the locket, Rorie.'

'I admire it intensely, and I'm deeply grateful. But I feel
inexpressibly sold, all the same. And I am to go about the world
with Argus dangling at my breast. Well, for your sake, Vixen,
I'll submit even to that degradation.'

Here came the cart, with two flaming lamps, like angry eyes
flashing through the shrubberies. It pulled up at the steps. Rorie
and Vixen clasped hands and bade good-night, and then the
young man swung himself lightly into the seat beside the driver,
and away went Starlight Bess, making just that sort of dashing
and spirited start which inspires the timorous beholder with the
idea that the next proceeding will be the bringing home of the
driver and his companion upon a brace of shutters.

CHAPTER 5

RORIE MAKES A SPEECH

Somewhat to his surprise, and much to his delight, Roderick Vawdrey escaped the maternal lecture which he was wont undutifully to describe as a 'wigging.' When he entered the drawing-room in full dress just about ten minutes before the first of the guests was announced, Lady Jane received him with a calm affectionateness, and asked him no questions about his disposal of the afternoon. Perhaps this unusual clemency was in honour of his twenty-first birthday, Rorie thought. A man could not come of age more than once in his life. He was entitled to some favour.

The dinner-party was as other dinners at Briarwood: all the arrangements perfect; the *menu* commendable, if not new; the general result a little dull.

The Ashbourne party were among the first to arrive; the Duke portly and affable; the Duchess delighted to welcome her favourite nephew; Lady Mabel looking very fragile, flower-like, and graceful in her pale blue gauze dinner-dress. Lady Mabel affected the palest tints, half-colours which were more like the shadows in a sunset sky than any earthly hues.

She took possession of Rorie at once, treating him with a calm superiority, as if he had been a younger brother.

'Tell me all about Switzerland,' she said, as they sat side by side on one of the amber ottomans. 'What was it that you liked best?'

'The climbing, of course,' he answered.

'But which of all the landscapes? What struck you most? What impressed you most vividly? Your first view of Mont Blanc, or that marvellous gorge below the Tête Noire – or——?'

'It was all uncommonly jolly. But there's a family resemblance in Swiss mountains, don't you know? They're all white – and they're all peaky. There's a likeness in Swiss lakes, too, if you come to think of it. They're all blue, and they're all wet. And Swiss villages, now – don't you think they are rather disappointing? – such a cruel plagiarism of those plaster châlets

the image-men carry about the London streets, and no candle-
ends burning inside to make 'em look pretty. But I liked
Lucerne uncommonly, there was such a capital billiard-table at
the hotel.'

'Roderick!' cried Lady Mabel, with a disgusted look. 'I don't
think you have a vestige of poetry in your nature.'

'I hope I haven't,' replied Rorie devoutly.

'You could see those sublime scenes, and never once feel
your heart thrilled or your mind exalted – you can come home
from your first Swiss tour and talk about billiard-tables!'

'The scenery was very nice,' said Rorie thoughtfully. 'Yes;
there were times, perhaps, when I was a trifle stunned by all
that grand calm beauty, the silence, the solitude, the awfulness
of it all: but I had hardly time to feel the thrill when I came
bump up against a party of tourists, English or American, all
talking the same twaddle, and all patronising the scenery. That
took the charm out of the landscape somehow, and I coiled up,
as the Yankees say. And now you want me to go into secondhand raptures, and repeat my emotions, as if I were writing a
tourist's article for a magazine. I can't do it, Mabel.'

'Well, I won't bore you any more about it,' said Lady Mabel,
'but I confess my disappointment. I thought we should have
such nice long talks about Switzerland.'

'What's the use of talking of a place? If it's so lovely that one
can't live without it, one had better go back there.'

This was a practical way of putting things which was too
much for Lady Mabel. She fanned herself gently with a great fan
of blue cloudy looking feathers, such as Titania might have used
that midsummer night near Athens. She relapsed into a placid
silence, looking at Rorie thoughtfully with her calm blue eyes.

His travels had improved him. That bronze hue suited him
wonderfully well. He looked more manly. He was no longer a
beardless boy, to be patronised with that gracious elder-sister air
of Lady Mabel's. She felt that he was farther off from her than
he had been last season in London.

'How late you arrived this evening,' she said after a pause. 'I
came to five-o'clock tea with my aunt, and found her quite
anxious about you. If it hadn't been for your telegram from

Southampton, she would have fancied there was something wrong.'

'She needn't have fidgeted herself after three o'clock,' answered Rorie coolly; 'my luggage must have come home by that time.'

'I see. You sent the luggage on before, and came by a later train?'

'No, I didn't. I stopped halfway between here and Lyndhurst to see some old friends.'

'Flattering for my aunt,' said Mabel. 'I should have thought she was your oldest friend.'

'Of course she has the prior claim. But as I was going to hand myself over to her bodily at seven o'clock, to be speechified about and rendered generally ridiculous, after the manner of young men who come of age, I felt I was entitled to do what I liked in the interval.'

'And therefore you went to the Tempests',' said Mabel, with her blue eyes sparkling. 'I see. That is what you do when you do what you like.'

'Precisely. I am very fond of Squire Tempest. When I first rode to hounds it was under his wing. There's my mother beckoning me; I am to go and do the civil to people.'

And Roderick walked away from the ottoman to the spot where his mother stood, with the Duke of Dovedale at her side, receiving her guests.

It was a very grand party, in the way of blue blood, landed estate, diamonds, lace, satin, and velvet, and self-importance. All the magnates of the soil, within accessible distance of Briarwood, had assembled to do honour to Rorie's coming of age. The dining-tables had been arranged in a horse-shoe, so as to accommodate fifty people in a room which, in its every-day condition, would not have been too large for thirty. The orchids and ferns upon his horse-shoe table made the finest floricultural show that had been seen for a long time. There were rare specimens from New Granada and the Philippine Islands; wondrous flowers lately discovered in the Sierra Madre; blossoms of every shape and colour from the Cordilleras; richest varieties of hue – golden yellow, glowing crimson, creamy white; rare eccentricities of form and colour beside which any other flower would have looked vulgar; butterfly flowers and pitcher-shaped flowers that had cost as much money as prize pigeons, and seemed as worthless, save to the connoisseur in the article. The Vawdrey racing-plate, won by Roderick's great-grandfather, was nowhere by comparison with those marvellous tropical blossoms, that fairy forest of fern. Everybody talked about the orchids, confessed his or her comparative ignorance of the subject, and complimented Lady Jane.

'The orchids made the hit of the evening,' Rorie said afterwards. 'It was their coming of age, not mine.'

There was a moderate and endurable amount of speechifying by-and-by, when the monster double-crowned pines had been cut, and the purple grapes, almost as big as pigeons' eggs, had gone round.

The Duke of Dovedale assured his friends that this was one of the proudest moments of his life, and that if Providence had permitted a son of his own to attain his majority, he, the Duke, could have hardly felt a deeper interest in the occasion than he felt to-day. He had – arra – arra – known this young man from childhood, and – had – er – um – never found him guilty of a mean action – or – arra – discovered in him a thought unworthy of an English gentleman.

This last was felt to be a strong point, as it implied that an English gentleman must needs be much better than any other gentleman.

A continental gentleman might, of course, be guilty of an unworthy thought and yet pass current, according to the loose morality of his nation. But the English article must be flawless.

And thus the Duke meandered on for five minutes or so and there was a subdued gush of approval, and then an uncomfortable little pause, and then Rorie rose in his place, next the Duchess, and returned thanks.

He told them all how fond he was of them and the soil that bred them. How he meant to be a Hampshire Squire, pure and simple, if he could. How he had no higher ambition than to be useful and to do good in this little spot of England which Providence had given him for his inheritance. How, if he should go into Parliament by-and-by, as he had some thoughts of attempting to do, it would be in their interests that he would join that noble body of legislators; that it would be they and their benefit he would have always nearest his heart.

'There is not a tree in the Forest that I do not love,' cried Rorie, fired with his theme, and forgetting to stammer; 'and I believe there is not a tree, from the Twelve Apostles to the Knightwood Oak, or a patch of gorse from Picket Post to Stony Cross, that I do not know as well as I know the friends round me to-night. I was born in the Forest, and may I live and die and be buried here. I have just come back from seeing some of the finest scenery in Europe; yet, without blushing for my want of poetry, I will confess that the awful grandeur of those snow-clad mountains did not touch my heart so deeply as our beechen glades and primrose-carpeted bottoms close at home.'

There was a burst of applause after Rorie's speech that made all the orchids shiver, and nearly annihilated a thirty-guinea *Odontoglossum Vexillarium*. His talk about the Forest, irrelevant as it might be, went home to the hearts of the neighbouring landowners. But, by-and-by, in the drawing-room, when he rejoined his cousin, he found that fastidious young lady by no means complimentary.

'Your speech would have been capital half a century ago, Rorie,' she said, 'and you don't arra – arra – as poor papa does, which is something to be thankful for; but all that talk about the Forest seemed to me an anachronism. People are not rooted in their native soil nowadays, as they used to be in the old stage-coach times, when it was a long day's journey to London. One might as well be a vegetable at once if one is to be pinned down to one particular spot of earth. Why, the Twelve Apostles,' exclaimed Mabel, innocent of irreverence, for she meant certain ancient and fast-decaying oaks so named, 'see as much of life as your fine old English gentleman. Men have wider ideas nowadays. The world is hardly big enough for their ambition.'

'I would rather live in a field, and strike my roots deep down like one of those trees, than be a homeless nomad with a world-wide ambition,' answered Rorie. 'I have a passion for home.'

'Then I wonder you spend so little time in it.'

'O, I don't mean a home inside four walls. The Forest is my home, and Briarwood is no dearer to me than any other spot in it.'

'Not so dear as the Abbey House, perhaps?'

'Well no. I confess that fine old Tudor mansion pleases me better than his abode of straight lines and French windows, plate-glass and gilt mouldings.'

They sat side by side upon the amber ottoman, Rorie with Mabel's blue feather fan in his hand, twirling and twisting it as he talked, and doing more damage to that elegant article in a quarter of an hour than a twelvemonth's legitimate usage would have done. People, looking at the pretty pair, smiled significantly, and concluded that it would be a match, and went home and told less privileged people about the evident attachment between the Duke's daughter and the young commoner. But Rorie was not strongly drawn towards his cousin this evening. It seemed to him that she was growing more and more of a paragon; and he hated paragons.

She played presently, and afterwards sang some French *chansons*. Both playing and singing were perfect of their kind. Rorie did not understand Chopin, and thought there was a good deal of unnecessary hopping about the piano in that sort of thing – nothing concrete, or that came to a focus; a succession of airy meanderings, a fairy dance in the treble, a goblin hunt in the bass. But the French *chansons*, the dainty little melodies with words of infantine innocence, all about leaves and buds, and birds' nests and butterflies, pleased him infinitely. He hung over the piano with an enraptured air; and again his friends made note of his subjugation, and registered the fact for future discussion.

CHAPTER 6

HOW SHE TOOK THE NEWS

It was past midnight when the Tempest carriage drove through the dark rhododendron shrubberies up to the old Tudor porch. There was a great pile of logs burning in the hall, giving the home-comers cheery welcome. There was an antique silver spirit stand with its accompaniments on one little table for the Squire, and there was another little table on the opposite side of the hearth for Mrs Tempest, with a dainty tea-service sparkling and shining in the red glow.

A glance at these arrangements would have told you that there were old servants at the Abbey House, servants who knew their master's and mistress's ways, and for whom service was more or less a labour of love.

'How nice,' said the lady, with a contented sigh. 'Pauline has thought of my cup of tea.'

'And Forbes has not forgotten my soda-water,' remarked the Squire.

He said nothing about the brandy, which he was pouring into the tall glass with a liberal hand.

Pauline came to take off her mistress's cloak, and was praised for her thoughtfulness about the tea, and then dismissed for the night.

The Squire liked to stretch his legs before his own fireside after dining out; and with the Squire, as with Mr Squeers, the leg-stretching process involved the leisurely consumption of a good deal of brandy and water.

Mr and Mrs Tempest talked over the Briarwood dinner-party, and arrived – with perfect good nature – at the conclusion that it had been a failure.

'The dinner was excellent,' said the Squire, 'but the wine went round too slow; my glasses were empty half the time. That's always the way where you've a woman at the helm. She never fills her cellars properly, or trusts her butler thoroughly.'

'The dresses were lovely,' said Mrs Tempest, 'but everyone looked bored. How did you like my dress, Edward? I think it's

rather good style. Theodore will charge me horribly for it, I
daresay.'

'I don't know much about your dress, Pam, but you were the
prettiest woman in the room.'

'O Edward, at my age!' exclaimed Mrs Tempest, with a
pleased look, 'when there was that lovely Lady Mabel
Ashbourne.'

'Do you call her lovely? – I don't. Lips too thin; waist too
slim; too much blood, and too little flesh.'

'O, but surely, Edward, she is grace itself; quite an ethereal
creature. If Violet had more of that refined air——'

'Heaven forbid. Vixen is worth twenty such fine-drawn
misses. Lady Mabel has been spoiled by over-training.'

'Roderick is evidently in love with her,' suggested Mrs
Tempest, pouring out another cup of tea.

The clocks had just struck two, the household was at rest, the
logs blazed and cracked merrily, the red light shining on those
mail-clad effigies in the corners, lighting up helm and hauberk,
glancing on greaves and gauntlets. It was an hour of repose and
gossip which the Squire dearly loved.

Hush! what is this creeping softly down the old oak staircase?
A slender white figure with cloudy hair; a small pale face, and
two dark eyes shining with excitement; little feet in black velvet
slippers tripping lightly upon the polished oak.

Is it a ghost? No; ghosts are noiseless, and those little slippers
descend from stair to stair with a gentle pit-a-pit.

'Bless my soul and body!' cried the Squire; 'what's this?'

A gush of girlish laughter was his only answer.

'Vixen!'

'Did you take me for a ghost, papa?' cried Violet, descending
the last five stairs with a flying leap, and then, bounding across
the hall to perch, light as a bird, upon her father's knee. 'Did I
really frighten you? Did you think the good old Abbey House
was going to set up a family ghost; a white lady, with a dismal
history of a broken heart? You darling papa! I hope you took
me for a ghost!'

'Well, upon my word, you know, Vixen, I was just the least
bit staggered. Your little white figure looked like something

uncanny against the black oak balustrades, half in light, half in shadow.'

'How nice,' exclaimed Violet.

'But, my dear Violet, what can have induced you to come downstairs at such an hour?' ejaculated Mrs Tempest in an aggrieved voice.

'I want to hear all about the party, mamma,' answered Vixen coaxingly. 'Do you think I could sleep a wink on the night of Rorie's coming of age? I heard the joy-bells ringing in my ears all night.'

'That was very ridiculous,' said Mrs Tempest, 'for there were no joy-bells after eleven o'clock yesterday.'

'But they rang all the same, mamma. It was no use burying my head in the pillows; those bells only rang the louder. Ding-dong, ding-dong, dell, Rorie's come of age; ding-dong, dell, Rorie's twenty-one. Then I thought of the speeches that would be made, and I fancied I could hear Rorie speaking. Did he make a good speech, papa?'

'Capital, Vix; the only one that was worth hearing!'

'I am so glad! And did he look handsome while he was speaking? I think the Swiss sunshine has rather over-cooked him, you know; but he is not unbecomingly brown.'

'He looked as handsome a young fellow as you need wish to set eyes on.'

'My dear Edward,' remonstrated Mrs Tempest, languidly, too thoroughly contented with herself to be seriously vexed about anything, 'do you think it is quite wise of you to encourage Violet in that kind of talk?'

'Why should she not talk of him? She never had a brother, and he stands in the place of one to her. Isn't Rorie the same to you as an elder brother, Vix?'

The girl's head was on her father's shoulder, one slim arm round his neck, her face hidden against the Squire's coat-collar. He could not see the deep warm blush that dyed his daughter's cheek at this home question.

'I don't quite know what an elder brother would be like, papa. But I'm very fond of Rorie – when he's nice, and comes to see us before anyone else, as he did to-day.'

'And when he stays away?'

'O, then I hate him awfully,' exclaimed Vixen, with such
energy that the slender figure trembled faintly as she spoke. 'But
tell me all about the party, mamma. Your dress was quite the
prettiest, I am sure?'

'I'm not certain of that, Violet,' answered Mrs Tempest with
grave deliberation, as if the question were far too serious to be
answered lightly. 'There was a cream-coloured silk, with silver
buillion fringe, that was very striking. As a rule, I detest gold or
silver trimmings; but this was really elegant. It had an effect like
moonlight.'

'Was that Lady Mabel Ashbourne's dress?' asked Vixen eagerly.

'No; Lady Mabel wore blue gauze – the very palest blue, all
puffings and ruchings – like a cloud.'

'O mamma! the clouds have no puffings and ruchings.'

'My dear, I mean the general effect – a sort of shadowiness
which suits Lady Mabel's ethereal style.'

'Ethereal!' repeated Violet thoughtfully; 'you seem to admire
her very much, mamma.'

'Everybody admires her, my dear.'

'Because she is a duke's only daughter.'

'No; because she is very lovely, and extremely elegant, and
most accomplished. She played and sang beautifully to-night.'

'What did she play, mamma?'

'Chopin!'

'Did she!' cried Vixen. 'Then I pity her. Yes, even if she
were my worst enemy I should still pity her.'

'People who are fond of music don't mind difficulties,' said
Mrs Tempest.

'Don't they? Then I suppose I'm not fond of it, because I
shirk my practice. But I should be very fond of music if I could
grind it on a barrel organ.'

'O Violet, when will you be like Lady Mabel Ashbourne?'

'Never, I devoutly hope,' said the Squire.

Here the Squire gave his daughter a hug which might mean
anything.

'Never, mamma,' answered Violet with conviction. 'First and
foremost, I never can be lovely, because I have red hair and a

wide mouth. Secondly, I can never be elegant – much less ethereal because it isn't in me. Thirdly, I shall never be accomplished, for poor Miss McCroke is always giving me up as the baddest lot in the shape of pupils that ever came in her way.'

'If you persist in talking in that horrible manner, Violet——'

'Let her talk as she likes, Pam,' said the fond father. 'I won't have her bitted too heavily.'

Mrs Tempest breathed a gentle sigh of resignation. The Squire was all that is dear and good as husband and father, but refinement was out of his line.

'Do go on about the party, mamma. Did Rorie seem to enjoy himself very much?'

'I think so. He was very devoted to his cousin all the evening. I believe they are engaged to be married.'

'Mamma!' exclaimed Vixen, starting up from her reclining attitude upon her father's shoulder, and looking intently at the speaker; 'Rorie engaged to Lady Mabel Ashbourne!'

'So I am told,' replied Mrs Tempest. 'It will be a splendid match for him.'

The pretty chestnut head dropped back into its old place upon the Squire's shoulder, and Violet answered never a word.

'Past two o'clock,' cried her mother. 'This is really too dreadful. Come Violet, and you and I must go upstairs at any rate.'

'We'll all go,' said the Squire, finishing his second brandy and soda.

So they all three went upstairs together. Vixen had grown suddenly silent and sleepy. She yawned dolefully, and kissed her mother and father at the end of the gallery, without a word; and then scudded off, swift as a scared rabbit, to her own room.

'God bless her!' exclaimed the Squire; 'she grows prettier and more winning every day.'

'If her mouth were only a little smaller,' sighed Mrs Tempest.

'It's the prettiest mouth I ever saw upon woman – bar one,' said the Squire.

What was Vixen doing while the fond father was praising her?

She had locked her door, and thrown herself face downwards on the carpet, and was sobbing as if her heart would break.

Rorie was going to be married. Her little kingdom had been overturned by a revolution: her little world had crumbled all to pieces. Till to-night she had been a queen in her own mind; and her kingdom had been Rorie, her subjects had begun and ended in Rorie. All was over. He belonged to someone else. She could never tyrannize over him again — never scold him and abuse him and patronize him and ridicule him any more. He was her Rorie no longer.

Had she ever thought that a time might come when he would be something more to her than playfellow and friend? No, never. The young bright mind was too childishly simple for any such foresight or calculation. She had only thought that he was in somewise her property, and would be so till the end of both their lives. He was hers, and he was very fond of her; and she thought him a rather absurd young fellow, and looked down upon him with airs of ineffable superiority from the altitude of her childish womanliness.

And now he was gone. The earth had opened all at once and swallowed him, like that prophetic gentleman in the Greek play, whose name Vixen could never remember — chariot and horses and all. He belonged henceforth to Lady Mabel Ashbourne. She could never be rude to him any more. She could not take such a liberty with another young lady's lover.

'And to think that he should never have told me he was going to be engaged to her,' she said. 'He must have been fond of her from the very beginning; and he never said a word; and he let me think he rather liked me — or at least tolerated me. And how could he like two people who are the very antipodes of each other? If he is fond of her, he must detest me. If he respects her, he must despise me.'

The thought of such treachery rankled deep in the young warm heart. Vixen started up to her feet, and stood in the midst of the fire-lit room, with clenched fists, like a young fury. The light chestnut tresses should have been Medusa's snakes to have harmonised with that set white face. God had given Violet

Tempest a heart to feel deeply, too deeply for perfect peace, or that angelic softness which seems to us most worthy in woman – the power to suffer and be patient.

CHAPTER 7

RORIE HAS PLANS OF HIS OWN

Roderick Vawdrey's ideas of what was due to a young man who attains his majority were in no wise satisfied by his birthday dinner-party. It had been pleasant enough in its way, but far too much after the pattern of all other dinner-parties to please a young man who hated all common and hackneyed things, and all the beaten tracks of life – or who, at any rate, fancied he did, which comes to nearly the same thing.

'Mother,' he began at breakfast next morning, in his loud cheery voice, 'we must have something for the small tenants, and shopkeepers, and cottagers.'

'What do you mean, Roderick?'

'Some kind of entertainment to celebrate my majority. The people will expect it. Last night polished off the swells very nicely. The whole thing did you credit, mother.'

'Thank you,' said Lady Jane, with a slight contraction of her thin lips.

This November morning, so pleasant for Rorie, was rather a bitter day for his mother. She had been reigning sovereign at Briarwood hitherto; henceforth she could only live there on sufferance. The house was Rorie's. Even the orchid-houses were his. He might take her to task if he pleased for having spent so much money on glass.

'But I must have my humble friends round me,' continued Rorie. 'The young people, too – the boys and girls. I'll tell you what, mother. We must have a lawn meet. The hounds have never met here since my grandfather's time – fifty years ago.

The Duke's stud-groom was telling me about it last year. He's a Hampshire man, you know, born and bred in the Forest. We'll have a lawn meet and a hunting breakfast; and it shall be open house for everyone – high and low, rich and poor, gentle and simple. Don't be frightened, mother,' interjected Rorie, seeing Lady Jane's look of horror; 'we won't do any mischief. Your gardens shall be respected.'

'They are your gardens now, Roderick. You are sole master here, and can do what you please.'

'My dear mother, how can you talk like that? Do you suppose I shall ever forget who made the place what it is? The gardens have been your particular hobby, and they shall be your gardens to the end of time.'

'That is very generous of you, my dear Roderick; but you are promising too much. When you marry, your wife will be mistress of Briarwood, and it will be necessary for me to find a new home.'

'I am in no hurry to get married. It will be half-a-dozen years before I shall even think of anything so desperate.'

'I hope not, Roderick. With your position and your responsibilities you ought to marry young. Marriage – a suitable marriage, that is to say – would give you an incentive to earnestness and ambition. I want to see you follow in your father's footsteps; I want you to make a name by-and-by.'

'I'm afraid it will be a distant by-and-by,' said Rorie, with a yawn. 'I don't feel at all drawn towards the senate. I love the country, my dogs, my horses, the free fresh air, the stir and movement of life too well to pen myself up in a study and pore over blue-books, or to waste the summer evenings listening to the member for Little Peddlington laying down the law about combination drainage, or the proposed loop-line that is intended to connect his borough with the world in general. I'm afraid it isn't in me, mother, and that you'll be sorely disappointed if you set your heart upon my making a figure as a senator.'

'I should like to see you worthy of your father's name,' Lady Jane said, with a regretful sigh.

'Providence hasn't made me after the same pattern,' answered Rorie. 'Look at my grandfather's portrait over the mantelpiece in pink and mahogany tops. What a glorious fellow he must have been. You should hear how the old people talk of him. I think I inherit his tastes, instead of my father's. Hereditary genius crops up in curious ways, you know. Perhaps, if I have a son, he will be a heaven-born statesman, and you may have your ambition gratified by a grandson. And now about the hunting breakfast. Would this day week suit you?'

'This is your house, Roderick. It is for you to give your orders.'

'Bosh!' exclaimed the son impatiently. 'Don't I tell you that you are mistress here, and will be mistress——'

'My dear Roderick, let us look things straight in the face.' said Lady Jane. 'If I were sole mistress here there would be no hunting breakfast. It is just the very last kind of entertainment I should ever dream of giving. I am not complaining, mind. It is natural enough for you to like that kind of thing; and, as master of this house, it is your right to invite whomsoever you please. I am quite happy that it should be so, but let there be no more talk about my being mistress of this house. That is too absurd.'

Rorie felt all his most generous impulses turned to a sense of constraint and bitterness. He could say no more.

'Will you give me a list of the people you would like to be asked?' said his mother, after rather an uncomfortable silence.

'I'll go and talk it over with the Duke,' answered Rorie. 'He'll enter into the spirit of the thing.'

Rorie found the Duke going the round of his loose-boxes, and uncle and nephew spent an hour together pleasantly, overhauling the fine stud and hunters which the Duke kept at Ashbourne, and going round the paddocks to look at the brood-mares and their foals; these latter being eccentric little animals, all head and legs, which nestled close to the mother's side for a minute, and then took fright at the whisking of their own tails, and shot off across the field, like a skyrocket travelling horizontally, or suddenly stood up on end, and executed a wild waltz in mid air.

The Duke and Roderick decided which among these leggy little beasts possessed the elements of future excellence; and after an hour's perambulation of the paddocks they went to the house, where they found the Duchess and Lady Mabel in the morning-room; the Duchess busy making scarlet cloth cloaks for her school-children, Lady Mabel reading a German critic on Shakespeare.

Here the hunt breakfast was fully discussed. Everybody was to be asked. The Duchess put in a plea for her school-children. It would be such a treat for the little things to see the meet, and their red cloaks and hoods would look so pretty on the lawn.

'Let them come, by all means,' said Roderick; 'your school – half-a-dozen schools. I'll have three or four tents rigged up for refreshments. There shall be plenty to eat and drink for everybody. And now I'm off to the Tempests' to arrange about the hounds. The Squire will be pleased, I know.'

'Of course,' said Lady Mabel, 'and the Squire's daughter.'

'Dear little thing,' exclaimed Rorie, with an elder brother's tenderness; 'she'll be as pleased as Punch. You'll hunt, of course, Mabel?'

'I don't know. I don't shine in the field, as Miss Tempest does.'

'O, but you must come, Mab. The Duke will find you a safe mount.'

'She has a hunter I bred on purpose for her,' said the Duke; 'but she'll never be such a horsewoman as her mother.'

'She looks lovely on Mazeppa,' said Rorie; 'and she must come to my hunting breakfast.'

'Of course, Rorie, if you really wish it I shall come.'

Rorie stayed to luncheon, and then went back to Briarwood to mount his horse and ride to the Abbey House.

The afternoon was drawing in when Rorie rode up to the old Tudor porch – a soft, sunless, gray afternoon. The door stood open, and he saw the glow of the logs on the wide hearth, and the Squire's stalwart figure sitting in the great arm-chair, leaning forward with a newspaper across his knee, and Vixen on a stool at his feet, the dogs grouped about them.

'Shall I send my horse round to the stables, Squire?' asked Rorie.

'Do, my lad,' answered Mr Tempest, ringing the bell, at which summons a man appeared and took charge of Roderick's big chestnut.

'Been hunting to-day, Squire?' asked Rorie, when he had shaken hands with Mr Tempest and his daughter, and seated himself on the opposite side of the hearth.

'No,' answered the Squire, in a voice that had a duller sound than usual. 'We had the hounds out this morning at Hilberry Green, and there was a good muster, Jack Purdy says; but I felt out of sorts, and neither Vixen nor I went. It was a loss for Vixen, poor little girl.'

'It was a grief to see you ill, papa,' said Violet, nestling closer to him.

She had hardly taken any notice of Roderick to-day, shaking hands with him in an absent-minded way, evidently full of anxiety about her father. She was very pale, and looked older and more womanly than when he saw her yesterday, Roderick, thought.

'I'm not ill, my dear,' said the Squire, 'only a little muddled and queer in my head; been riding too hard lately, perhaps. I don't get lighter, you know, Rorie, and a quick run shakes me more than it used. Old Martin, our family doctor, has been against my hunting for a long time; but I should like to know what kind of life men of my age would lead if they listened to the doctors. They wouldn't let us have a decent dinner.'

'I'm so sorry,' said Rorie; 'I came to ask you a favour, and now I feel as if I hardly ought to say anything about it.'

And then Roderick proceeded to tell the Squire his views about a lawn meet at Briarwood, and a hunting breakfast for rich and poor.

'It shall be done, my boy,' answered the Squire heartily. 'It's just the sort of thing you ought to do to make yourself popular. Lady Jane is a charming woman, you know, thoroughbred to the finger-nails; but she has kept herself a little too much to herself. There are people old enough to remember what Briarwood was in your grandfather's time. This day week you say? I'll arrange everything. We'll have such a gathering as hasn't been seen for the last twenty years.'

'Vixen must come with you,' said Rorie.

'Of course.'

'If papa is well and strong enough to hunt.'

'My love, there is nothing amiss with me – nothing that need trouble me this day week. A man may have a headache, mayn't he, child, without people making any fuss about it?'

'I should like you to see Dr Martin, papa. Don't you think he ought to see the doctor, Rorie? It's not natural for him to be ill.'

'I'm not going to be put upon half-rations, Vixen. Martin would starve me. That's his only idea of medical treatment. Yes, Vixen shall come, Rorie.'

CHAPTER 8

GLAS IST DER ERDE STOLZ UND GLUCK

The morning of the Briarwood Meet dawned fairly. Roderick watched the first lifting of the darkness from his bed-room window, and rejoiced in the promise of fine weather. The heavens, which had been so unpropitious upon his birthday, seemed to promise better things to-day. He did not desire the traditional hunting morning – a southerly wind and a cloudy sky. He cared very little about the scent lying well, or the actual result of the day's sport. He wanted rather to see the kind familiar faces round him, the autumn sunshine lighting up all the glow and colour of the picture, the scarlet coats, the rich bay and brown of the horses, the verdant background of lawn and shrubberies. Two huge marquees had been erected for the commonalty – one for the school-children, the other for the villagers. There were long tables in the billiard-room for the farming class; and for the quality there was the horse-shoe table in the dining-room, as at Roderick's birthday dinner. But on this occasion the table was decorated only with hardy ferns and flowers. The orchids were not allowed to appear.

Roderick noticed the omission.

'Why, where are the thing-um-tites, mother?' he asked, with some surprise; 'the pitcher-plants, and tropical what's-its-names?'

'I did not think there was any occasion to have them brought out of the houses, Roderick,' Lady Jane answered quietly; 'there is always a risk of their being killed, or some of your sporting friends might be picking my prize blossoms to put in their button-holes. Men who give their minds to horses would hardly appreciate orchids.'

'All right, mother. As long as there is plenty to eat, I don't suppose it much matters,' answered Rorie.

He had certainly no cause for complaint upon this score. Briarwood had been amply provisioned for an unlimited hospitality. The red coats and black coats, and blue coats and brown coats, came in and out, slashed away at boar's head and truffled turkey, sent champagne corks flying, and added more dead men to the formidable corps of tall hock bottles, which the astonished butler ranged rank and file in a lobby outside the dining-room. He had never seen this kind of thing at Briarwood since he had kept the keys of the cellars; and he looked upon this promiscuous hospitality with a disapproving eye.

The Duke supported his nephew admirably, and was hail-fellow-well-met with everybody. He had always been popular at Ashbourne. It was his own place, his particular selection, bought with his own money, improved under his own eye, and he liked it better than any of his hereditary seats.

'If I had only had a son like you, Rorie,' he said, as he stood beside the young man, on the gravel sweep before the hall door, welcoming the new-comers, 'I should have been a happy man. Well, I suppose I must be satisfied with a grandson; but it's a hard thing that the title and estates are to go to that scamp of a cousin of mine.'

Roderick, on this particular morning, was a nephew whom any uncle might be proud to own. His red coat and buckskins became him; so did his position as host and master at Briarwood. His tall erect figure showed to advantage amidst the crowd. His smile lit up the dark sunburnt face like sunshine. He had a kind word, a friendly hand-clasp for everybody – even for gaffers and goodies who had hobbled from their village shanties to see the sport, and to get their share of cold sirloin and old

October. He took the feeble old creatures into the tent, and saw that they found a place at the board.

Squire Tempest and his daughter were among the later arrivals. The meet was to be at one, and they only rode into the grounds at half-past twelve, when everyone else had breakfasted. Mrs Tempest had not come. The entertainment was much too early for a lady who never left her rooms till after noon.

Vixen looked lovely in her smart little habit. It was not the Lincoln green with brass buttons, which Lady Mabel had laughed at a year ago. To-day Miss Tempest wore a dark brown habit, moulded to the full erect figure, with a narrow rim of white at the throat, a little felt hat of the same dark brown with a brown feather, long white gauntlets, and a hunting-crop with a strong bone hook for opening gates.

The golden bay's shining coat matched Violet's shining hair. It was the prettiest picture in the world, the rider in dark brown on the bright bay horse, the daintily quilted saddle, the gauntleted hands playing so lightly with the horse's velvet mouth – horse and rider devotedly attached to each other.

'How do you like him?' asked Vixen, directly she and Rorie had shaken hands. 'Isn't he absolutely lovely?'

'Absolutely lovely,' said Rorie, patting the horse's shoulder and looking at the rider.

'Papa gave him to me on my last birthday. I was to have ridden Titmouse another year; but I got the brush one day after a hard run when almost everybody else was left behind, and papa said I should have a horse. Poor Titmouse is put into a basket-chaise. Isn't it sad for him?'

'Awfully humiliating.'

Lady Mabel was close by on her chestnut thoroughbred, severely costumed in darkest blue and chimney-pot hat.

'I don't think you've ever met my cousin?' said Rorie. 'Mabel, this is Miss Tempest, whom you've heard me talk about. Miss Tempest, Lady Mabel Ashbourne.'

Violet Tempest gave a startled look, and blushed crimson. Then the two girls bowed and smiled: a constrained smile on Vixen's part, a prim and chilly smile from Lady Mabel.

'I want you two to be awful good friends,' said Rorie; 'and when you come out, Vixen, Lady Mabel will take you under her wing. She knows everybody, and the right thing to be done on every occasion.'

Vixen turned from red to pale, and said nothing. Lady Mabel looked at the distant blue line of the Wight, and murmured that she would be happy to be of use to Miss Tempest if ever they met in London. Rorie felt, somehow, that it was not encouraging. Vixen stole a glance at her rival. Yes, she was very pretty – a delicate patrician beauty which Vixen had never seen before. No wonder Rorie was in love with her. Where else could he have seen anything so exquisite? It was the most natural thing in the world that these cousins should be fond of each other, and engaged to be married. Vixen wondered that the thing had never occurred to her as inevitable – that it should have come upon her as a blow at the last.

'I think Rorie ought to have told me,' she said to herself. 'He is like my brother; and a brother would not hide his love affairs from his sister. It was rather mean of Rorie.'

The business of the day began presently. Neither Vixen nor the Squire dismounted. They had breakfasted at home; and Vixen, who did not care much for Lady Jane Vawdrey, was glad to escape with no further communication than a smile and a bow. At a quarter-past one they were all moving quietly away towards the old woods.

Vixen and her father were riding side by side.

'You are so pale, papa. Is your head bad again to-day?'

'Yes, my dear. I'm afraid I've started a chronic headache. But the fresh air will blow it away presently, I daresay. You're not looking over-well yourself, Vixen. What have you done with your roses?'

'I – I – don't care much about hunting to-day, papa,' said Violet, sudden tears rushing into her eyes. 'Shall we go home together?' You're not well, and I'm not enjoying myself. Nobody wants us either; so why should we stay?'

Rorie was a little way behind them, taking care of Lady Mabel, whose slim-legged chestnut went through as many

manoeuvres as if he had been doing the *manège* business in a
circus, and got over the ground very slowly.

'Nonsense, child! Go back! I should think not! Jack Purdy
may do all the work, but people like to see me to the fore. We
shall find down in Dingley Bottom, I daresay, and get a capital
run across the hills to Beaulieu.'

They found just as the Squire had anticipated, and after that
there was a hard run for the next hour and a quarter. Roderick
was at the heel of the hunt all the time, opening gates, and
keeping his cousin out of bogs and dangers of all kinds. They
killed at last on a wild bit of common near Beaulieu, and there
were only a few in at the death, amongst them Vixen on her
fast young bay, flushed with excitement and triumph by this
time, and forgetting all her troubles in the delight of winning
one of the pads. Mrs Millington, the famous huntress from the
shires, was there to claim the brush.

'How tired you look, papa,' said Vixen, as they rode slowly
homewards.

'A little done up, my dear; but a good dinner will set me all
right again. It was a capital run, and your horse behaved
beautifully. I don't think I made a bad choice for you. Rorie
and his cousin were miles behind, I daresay. Pretty girl, and sits
her horse like a picture – but she can't ride. No hands. We shall
meet them going home, perhaps.'

A mile or two farther on they met Roderick alone. His
cousin had gone home with her father.

'It was rather a bore losing the run,' he said, as he turned his
horse's head and rode by Vixen; 'but I was obliged to take care
of my cousin.'

One of the Squire's tenants, a seventeen-stone farmer, on a
stout gray cob, overtook them presently, and Mr Tempest rode
on by his side, talking agricultural talk about over-fed beasts and
cattle shows – the last popular form of cruelty to animals.

Roderick and Violet were alone, riding slowly side by side in
the darkening gray, between woods where solitary robins
carolled sweetly, or the rare gurgle of the thrush sounded now
and then from thickets of beech and holly.

A faint colour came back to Vixen's cheek. She was very angry with her playfellow for his want of confidence, for his unfriendly reserve. Yet this was the one happy hour of her day. There had been a flavour of desolateness and abandonment in all the rest.

'I hope you enjoyed the run,' said Rorie.

'I don't think you can care much whether we did or didn't,' retorted Vixen, shrouding her personality in a vague plural. 'If you had cared you would have been with us. Sultan,' meaning the chestnut, 'must have felt cruelly humiliated by being kept so far behind.'

'If a man could be in two places at once, half of me, the better half of me, would have been with you, Vixen; but I was bound to take care of my cousin. I had insisted upon her coming.'

'Of course,' answered Vixen, with a little toss of her head; 'it would have been quite wrong if she had been absent.'

They rode on in silence for a little while after this. Vixen was longing to say: 'Rorie, you have treated me very badly. You ought to have told me you were going to be married.' But something restrained her. She patted her horse's neck, listened to the lonely robins, and said not a word. The Squire and his tenant were a hundred yards ahead, talking loudly.

Presently they came to a point at which their roads parted; but Rorie still rode on by Vixen.

'Isn't that your nearest way?' asked Vixen, pointing down the cross-road with the ivory handle of her whip.

'I am not going the nearest way. I am going to the Abbey House with you.'

'I wouldn't be so rude as to say don't; but I think poor Sultan must be tired.'

'Sultan shall have a by-day to-morrow.'

They went into an oak plantation, where a broad open alley led from one side of the enclosure to the other. The wood had a mysterious look in the late afternoon, when the shadows were thickening under the tall thin trees. There was an all-pervading ghostly grayness as in a shadowy underworld. They rode silently over the thick wet carpet of fallen leaves, the horses starting a little now and then at the aspect of a newly-barked trunk lying white across the track. They were silent, having, in sooth, very little to say to each other just at this time. Vixen was nursing her wrathful feelings; Rorie felt that his future was confused and obscure. He ought to do something with his life, perhaps, as his mother had so warmly urged. But his soul was stirred by no ambitious promptings.

They were within two hundred yards of the gate at the end of the enclosure, when Vixen gave a sudden cry:

'Did papa's horse stumble?' she asked; 'look how he sways in his saddle.'

Another instant, and the Squire reeled forward, and fell head foremost across his horse's shoulder. The fall was so sudden and so heavy that the horse fell with him, and then scrambled up on to his feet again affrighted, swung himself round, and rushed past Roderick and Vixen along the plashy track.

Vixen was off her horse in a moment, and had flown to her father's side. He lay like a log, face downwards upon the sodden leaves just inside the gate. The farmer had dismounted, and was stooping over him, bridle in hand, with a frightened face.

'O, what is it?' cried Violet frantically. 'Did the horse throw him? – Bullfinch, his favourite horse. Is he much hurt? O, help me to lift him up – help me – help me!'

Rorie was by her side by this time, kneeling down with her beside the prostrate Squire, trying to raise the heavy figure which lay like lead across his arm.

'It wasn't the horse, miss,' said the farmer. 'I'm afraid it's a seizure.'

'A fit!' cried Vixen. 'O papa, papa – darling – darling——'

She was sobbing, clinging to him, trembling like a leaf, and turning a white stricken face up towards Roderick.

'Do something to help him – for God's sake – do something,' she cried; 'you won't let him lie there and die for want of help. Some brandy – something,' she gasped, stretching out her trembling hand.

The farmer had anticipated her thought. He had taken his flask from the saddle-pocket, and was kneeling down by the Squire. Roderick had lifted the heavy head, and turned the ghastly face to the waning light. He tried to force a little brandy between the livid lips – but vainly.

'For God's sake, get her away,' he whispered to John Wimble, the farmer. 'It's all over with him.'

'Come away with me, my dear Miss Tempest,' said Wimble, trying to raise Violet from her knees beside the Squire. She was gazing into that awful face distractedly – half divining its solemn meaning – yet watching for the kind eyes to open and look at her again. 'Come away with me, and we'll get a doctor. Mr Vawdrey will take care of your father.'

'You go for the doctor,' she answered firmly; 'I'll stay with papa. Take my horse, he's faster than yours. O, he'll carry you well enough. You don't know how strong he is. Go – quick, quick – Dr Martin, at Lyndhurst; it's a long way, but you must get him. Papa will recover and be able to ride home perhaps before you can get back to us; but go, go.'

'You go for the doctor, miss; your horse will carry you fast enough. He'd never carry such a heavy weight as me, and my cob is dead beat. You go, and Mr Vawdrey will go with you. I'll take care of the Squire.'

Violet looked from one to the other helplessly.

'I'd rather stay with papa,' she said. 'You go, Rorie – yes – go, go; I'll stay with papa.'

She crouched down beside the prostrate figure on the damp marshy ground, took the heavy head on her lap, and looked up at the two men with a pale set face, which indicated a resolve that neither of them was strong enough to overrule. They tried their utmost to persuade her, but in vain. She was fixed as a new Niobe – a stony image of young despair. So Roderick mounted his horse and rode off towards Lyndhurst, and honest Jack Wimble tied the other two horses to the gate, and took his stand beside them, a few paces from those two motionless figures on the ground, patiently waiting for the issue of this bitter hour.

It was one of the longest, weariest, saddest hours that ever youth and hope lived through. There was an awful heart-sickening fear in Violet's mind, but she gave it no definite shape. She would not say to herself, 'My father is dead.' The position in which he was lying hampered her arms, so that she could not reach out her hand to lay it upon his heart. She bent her face down to his lips.

O God! not a flutter stirred upon her soft cheek as she laid it against those pallid lips. The lower jaw had fallen in an awful-looking way; but Violet had seen her father look like that sometimes as he slept, with open mouth, before the hall fire. It might be only a long swoon, a suspension of consciousness. Dr Martin would come presently – O, how long, how long the time seemed – and make all things right.

The crescent moon shone silver pale above that dim gray wood. The barked trunks gleamed white and spectral in the gathering dark. Owls began to hoot in the distance, frogs were awaking near at hand, belated rabbits flitted ghost-like across the track. All nature seemed of one gray shadowy hue, silvery where the moonbeams fell.

The November air was chill and penetrating. There was a dull aching in Violet's limbs from the weight of her burden, but she was hardly conscious of physical pain. It seemed to her that she had been sitting there for hours, waiting for the doctor's help. She thought the night must have nearly worn itself out.

'Dr Martin could not have been at home,' she said, speaking for the first time since Roderick rode away. 'Mr Vawdrey would fetch someone else surely.'

'My dear young lady, he hasn't had time to ride to Lyndhurst yet.'

'Not yet,' cried Vixen despairingly, 'not yet! and it has been so long. Papa is getting so cold; the chill will be so bad for him.'

'Worse for you, miss; I do wish you'd let me take you home.'

'And leave papa here – alone – unconscious! How can you be so cruel as to think of such a thing?'

'Dear Miss Tempest, we're not doing him any good, and you may be getting a chill that will be nigh your death. If you would only go home to your mamma now – it's hard upon her not to know – she'll be fretting about you, I daresay.'

'Don't waste your breath talking to me,' cried Vixen indignantly: 'I shall not leave this spot till papa goes with me.'

They waited for another quarter of an hour in dismal silence.
The horses gnawed the lower branches of the trees, and gave
occasional evidence of their impatience. Bullfinch had gone
home to his stable no doubt; they were only about a mile and a
half from the Abbey House.

Hark! what was that? The splish-splash of horses' hoofs on
the soft turf. Another minute and Rorie rode up to the gate
with a stranger.

'I was lucky enough to meet this gentleman,' he said, 'a
doctor from Southampton, who was out with us to-day. Violet
dear, will you let me take you home now, and leave the doctor
and Mr Wimble with your father?'

'No,' answered Vixen decisively.

The strange doctor knelt down and looked at his patient. He
was a middle-aged man, grave-looking, with iron-gray hair – a
man who impressed Vixen with a sense of power and authority.
She looked at him silently, with a despairing appealing look that
thrilled him, familiar as he was with such looks. He made his
examination quietly, saying not a word, and keeping his face
hidden. Then he turned to the two men who were standing
close by, watching him anxiously.

'You must get some kind of litter to carry him home,' he
whispered.

And then, with gentle firmness, with strong irresistible hands,
he separated the living from the dead, lifted Violet from the
ground and led her towards her horse.

'You must let Mr Vawdrey take you home, my dear young
lady,' he said. 'You can do nothing here.'

'But you – you can do something,' sobbed Violet; 'you will
bring him back to life – you——'

'I will do all that can be done,' answered the doctor gently.'

His tone told her more than his words. She gave one wild
shriek, and threw herself down beside her dead father. A cloud
came over the distracted brain, and she lay there senseless. The
doctor and Rorie lifted her up and carried her to the gate,
where her horse was waiting. The doctor forced a little brandy
through her locked lips, and between them, Rorie and he,
placed her in the saddle. She had just consciousness enough by

this time to hold the bridle mechanically, and to sit upright on
her horse; and thus, led by Roderick, she rode slowly back to
the home that was never any more to be the same home that she
had known and lived in through the joyous sixteen years of her
life. All things were to be different to her henceforward. The joy
of life was broken short off, like a flower snapped from its stem.

CHAPTER 9

A HOUSE OF MOURNING

There was sorrow at the Abbey House deeper and wilder than
had entered within those doors for many a year. To Mrs
Tempest the shock of her husband's death was overwhelming.
Her easy, luxurious, monotonous life had been very sweet to
her, but her husband had been the dearest part of life. She had
taken little trouble to express her love for him, quite willing
that he should take it for granted. She had been self indulgent
and vain; seeking her own ease, spending money and care on
her own adornment; but she had not forgotten to make the
Squire's life pleasant to him also. Newly-wedded lovers in the
fair honeymoon-stage of existence could not have been fonder
of each other than the middle-aged Squire and his somewhat
faded wife. His loving eyes had never seen Time's changes in
Pamela Tempest's pretty face, the lessening brightness of the
eyes, the duller tints of the complexion, the loss of youth's glow
and glory. To him she had always appeared the most beautiful
woman in the world.

And now the fondly-indulged wife could do nothing but lie
on her sofa and shed a rain of incessant tears, and drink strong
tea, which had lost its power to comfort or exhilarate. She
would see no one. She could not even be roused to interest
herself in her mourning, though, with a handsome widow,
Pauline thought that ought to be all important.

'There are so many styles of widows' caps now, ma'am. You really ought to see them, and choose for yourself,' urged Pauline, an honest young Englishwoman, who had begun life as Polly, but whom Mrs Tempest had elevated into Pauline.

'What does it matter, Pauline? Take anything you like. *He* will not be there to see.'

Here the ready tears flowed afresh. That was the bitterest of all. That she should look nice in her mourning, and Edward not be there to praise her. In her feebleness she could not imagine life without him. She would hear his step at her door surely, his manly voice in the corridor. She would awake from this awful dream, in which he was not, and find him, and fall into his arms, and sob out her grief upon his breast, and tell him all she had suffered.

That was the dominant feeling in this weak soul. He could not be gone for ever.

Yet the truth came back upon her in hideous distinctness every now and then – came back suddenly and awfully, like the swift revelation of a desolate plague-stricken scene under a lightning flash. He was gone. He was lying in his coffin, in the dear old Tudor hall where they had sat so cosily. Those dismal reiterated strokes of the funeral-bell meant that his burial was at hand. They were moving the coffin already, perhaps. His place knew him no more.

She tottered to the darkened window, lifted the edge of the blind, and looked out. The funeral train was moving slowly along the carriage sweep, through the winding shrubberied road. How long, and black, and solemnly splendid the procession looked. Everybody had loved and respected him. It was a grand funeral. The thought of this general homage gave a faint thrill of comfort to the widow's heart.

'My noble husband,' she ejaculated. 'Who could help loving you?'

It seemed to her only a little while ago that she had driven up to the Tudor porch for the first time after her happy honeymoon, when she was in the bloom of youth and beauty, and life was like a schoolgirl's happy dream.

'How short life is,' she sobbed; 'how cruelly short for those who are happy!'

With Violet grief was no less passionate; but it did not find its
sole vent in tears. The stronger soul was in rebellion against
Providence. She kept aloof from her mother in the time of
sorrow. What could they say to each other? They could only
cry together. Violet shut herself in her room, and refused to see
anyone, except patient Miss McCroke, who was always
bringing her cups of tea, or basins of arrowroot, trying to coax
her to take some kind of nourishment, dabbing her hot
forehead with eau-de-cologne — doing all those fussy little
kindnesses which are so acutely aggravating in a great sorrow.

'Let me lie on the ground alone, and think of him, and wail
for him.'

That is what Violet Tempest would have said, if she could
have expressed her desire clearly.

Roderick Vawdrey went back to the Abbey House after the
funeral, and contrived to see Miss McCroke, who was full of
sympathy for everybody.

'Do let me see Violet, that's a dear creature,' he said. 'I can't
tell you how unhappy I am about her. I can't get her face out of
my thoughts, as I saw it that dreadful night when I led her horse
home — the wild sad eyes, the white lips.'

'She is not fit to see anyone,' said Miss McCroke: 'but
perhaps it might rouse her a little to see you.'

Miss McCroke had an idea that all mourners ought to be
roused; that much indulgence in grief for the dead was
reprehensible.

'Yes,' answered Rorie eagerly, 'she would see me, I know.
We are like brother and sister.'

'Come into the schoolroom,' said the governess, 'and I'll see
what I can do.'

The schoolroom was Vixen's own particular den, and was
not a bit like the popular idea of a schoolroom.

It was a pretty little room, with a high wooden dado, painted
olive green, and a high-art paper of amazing ugliness, whereon
brown and red storks disported themselves on a dull green
ground. The high-art paper was enlivened with sporting
sketches by Leech, and a menagerie of pottery animals on
various brackets.

A pot or a pan had been stuck into every corner that would
hold one. There were desks, and boxes, and wickerwork
baskets of every shape and kind, a dwarf oak bookcase on either
side of the fireplace, with the books all at sixes and sevens,
leaning against each other as if they were intoxicated. The
broad mantelpiece presented a confusion of photographs, cups
and saucers, violet jars, and Dresden shepherdesses. Over the
old Venetian glass dangled Vixen's first trophy, the fox's brush,
tied with a scarlet ribbon. There were no birds, or squirrels, or
dormice, for Vixen was too fond of the animal creation to shut
her favourites up in cages; but there was a black bearskin spread
in a corner for Argus to lie upon. In the wide low windows
there were two banks of bright autumn flowers, pompons and
dwarf roses, mignonette and veronica.

Miss McCroke drew up the blind, and stirred the fire.

'I'll go and ask her to come,' she said.

'Do, like a dear,' said Rorie.

He paced the room while she was gone, full of sadness. He
had been very fond of the Squire, and that awfully sudden
death, an apoplectic seizure, instantaneous as a thunderbolt, had
impressed him very painfully. It was his first experience of the
kind, and it was infinitely terrible to him. It seemed to him a
long time before Vixen appeared, and then the door opened,
and a slim black figure came in, a white fixed face looked at
him piteously, with tearless eyes made big by a great grief. She
came leaning on Miss McCroke, as if she could hardly walk
unaided. The face was stranger to him than an altogether
unknown face. It was Violet Tempest with all the vivid joyous
life gone out of her, like a lamp that is extinguished.

He took her cold trembling hands and drew her gently to a
chair, and sat down beside her.

'I wanted so much to see you, dear,' he said, 'to tell you how
sorry we all are for you – my mother, my aunt, and cousin' –
Violet gave a faint shiver – 'all of us. The Duke liked your dear
father so much. It was quite a shock to him.'

'You are very good,' Violet said mechanically.

She sat by him, pale and still as marble, looking at the
ground. His voice and presence impressed her but faintly, like

something a long way off. She was thinking of her dead father. She saw nothing but that one awful figure. They had laid him in his grave by this time. The cold cruel earth had fallen upon him and hidden him for ever from the light; he was shut away for ever from the fair glad world; he who had been so bright and cheerful, whose presence had carried gladness everywhere.

'Is the funeral quite over?' she asked presently, without lifting her heavy eyelids.

'Yes, dear. It was a noble funeral. Everybody was there – rich and poor. Everybody loved him.'

'The poor most of all,' she said. 'I know how good he was to them.'

Somebody knocked at the door and asked something of Miss McCroke, which obliged the governess to leave her pupil. Roderick was glad at her departure. That substantial figure in its new black dress had been a hindrance to freedom of conversation.

Miss McCroke's absence did not loosen Violet's tongue. She sat looking at the ground, and was dumb. That silent grief was very awful to Roderick.

'Violet, why don't you talk to me about your sorrow?' he said. 'Surely you can trust me – your friend – your brother!'

That last word stung her into speech. The hazel eyes shot a swift angry glance at him.

'You have no right to call yourself that,' she said, 'you have not treated me like a sister.'

'How not, dear?'

'You should have told me about your engagement – that you were going to marry Lady Mabel Ashbourne.'

'Should I?' exclaimed Rorie, amazed. 'If I had I should have told you an arrant falsehood. I am not engaged to my cousin Mabel. I am not going to marry her.'

'O, it doesn't matter in the least whether you are or not,' returned Vixen, with a weary air. 'Papa is dead, and trifles like that can't affect me now. But I felt it unkind of you at the time I heard it.'

'And where and how did you hear this wonderful news, Vixen?' asked Rorie, very pleased to get her thoughts away from her grief, were it only for a minute.

'Mamma told me that everybody said you were engaged, and that the fact was quite obvious.'

'What everybody says, and what is quite obvious, is very seldom true, Violet. You may take that for a first principle in social science. I am not engaged to anyone. I have no thought of getting married – for the next three years.'

Vixen received this information with chilling silence. She would have been very glad to hear it, perhaps, a week ago – at which time she had found it a sore thing to think of her old playfellow as Lady Mabel's affianced husband – but it mattered nothing now. The larger grief had swallowed up all smaller grievances. Roderick Vawdrey had receded into remote distance. He was no one, nothing, in a world that was suddenly emptied of all delight.

'What are you going to do, dear?' asked Roderick presently. 'If you shut yourself up in your room and abandon yourself to grief, you will make yourself very ill. You ought to go away somewhere for a little while.'

'For ever!' exclaimed Vixen passionately. 'Do you think I can ever endure this dear home without papa? There is not a thing I look at that doesn't speak to me of him. The dogs, the horses. I almost hate them for reminding me so cruelly. Yes, we are going away at once, I believe. Mamma said so when I saw her this morning.'

'Your poor mamma! How does she bear her grief?'

'O, she cries, and cries, and cries,' said Vixen, rather contemptuously. 'I think it comforts her to cry. I can't cry. I am like the dogs. If I did not restrain myself with all my might I should howl. I should like to lie on the ground outside his door – just as his dog does – and to refuse to eat or drink till I died.'

'But, dear Violet, you are not alone in the world. You have your poor mamma to think of.'

'Mamma – yes. I am sorry for her, of course. But she is only like a lay-figure in my life. Papa was everything.'

'Do you know where your mamma is going to take you?'

'No; I neither know nor care. It will be to a house with four walls and a roof, I suppose. It will be all the same to me wherever it is.'

What could Roderick say? It was too soon to talk about hope
or comfort. His heart was rent by this dull silent grief; but he
could do nothing except sit there silently by Vixen's side with
her cold unresponsive hands held in his.

Miss McCroke came back presently, followed by a maid
carrying a pretty Japanese tea-tray.

'I have just been giving your poor mamma a cup of tea,
Violet,' said the governess. 'Mr Clements has been telling
her about the will, and it has been quite too much for her.
She was almost hysterical. But she's better now, poor dear.
And now we'll all have some tea. Bring the table to the fire,
Mr Vawdrey, please, and let us make ourselves comfortable,'
concluded Miss McCroke with an assumption of mild
cheerfulness.

Perhaps there is not in all nature so cheerful a thing as a good
sea-coal fire, with a log of beech-wood on the top of the coals.
It will be cheerful in the face of affliction. It sends out its gushes
of warmth and brightness, its gay little arrowy flames that appear
and disappear like pixies dancing their midnight waltzes on a
barren moor. It seems to say: 'Look at me and be comforted!
Look at me and hope! So from the dull blackness of sorrow rise
the many-coloured lights of new-born joy.'

Vixen suffered her chair to be brought near that cheery fire,
and just then Argus crept into the room and nestled at her knee.
Roderick seated himself at the other side of the hearth – a
bright little fireplace bordered with high-art tiles, illustrative of
the story of 'Mary, Mary, quite contrary.' Miss McCroke
poured out the tea, and valiantly sustained that assumption of
cheerfulness. She would not have permitted herself to smile
yesterday; but now the funeral was over, the blinds were drawn
up, and a mild cheerfulness was allowable.

'If you would condescend to tell me where you are going,
Vixen, I might contrive to come there too, by-and-by. We
could have some rides together. You'll take Arion, of course.'

'I don't know that I shall ever ride again,' answered Violet
with a shudder.

Could she ever forget that awful ride? Roderick hated himself
for his foolish speech.

'Violet will have to devote herself to her studies very assiduously for the next two years,' said Miss McCroke. 'She is much more backward than I like a pupil of mine to be at sixteen.'

'Yes, I am going to grind at three or four foreign grammars, and to give my mind to latitude and longitude, and fractions, and decimals,' said Vixen, with a bitter laugh. 'Isn't that cheering?'

'Whatever you do, Vixen,' cried Roderick earnestly, 'don't be a paradigm.'

'What's that?'

'An example, a model, a paragon, a perfect woman, nobly planned, &c. Be anything but that, Vixen, if you love me.'

'I don't think there is much fear of any of us being perfect,' said Miss McCroke severely. 'Imperfection is more in the line of humanity.'

'Do you think so?' interrogated Rorie. 'I find there is a great deal too much perfection in this world, too many faultless people – I hate them.'

'Isn't that a confession of faultiness on your side?' suggested Miss McCroke.

'It may be. But it's the truth.'

Vixen sat with dry hollow eyes staring at the fire. She had heard their talk as if it had been the idle voices of strangers sounding in the distance, ever so far away. Argus nestled closer and closer at her knee, and she patted his big blunt head absently, with a dim sense of comfort in this brute love, which she had not derived from human sympathy.

Miss McCroke went on talking and arguing with Rorie, with a view to sustaining that fictitious cheerfulness which might beguile Vixen into brief oblivion of her griefs. But Vixen was not so to be beguiled. She was with them, but not of them. Her haggard eyes stared at the fire, and her thoughts were with the dear dead father, over whose newly-filled grave the evening shadows were closing.

CHAPTER 10

CAPTAIN WINSTANLEY

Two years later, and Vixen was sitting with the same faithful
Argus nestling beside her, by the fireside of a spacious Brighton
drawing-room, a large, lofty, commonplace room, with tall
windows facing seawards. Miss McCroke was there, too,
standing at one of the windows taking up a dropped stitch in
her knitting, while Mrs Tempest walked slowly up and down
the expanse of Brussels carpet, stopping now and then at a
window to look idly out at the red sunset beyond the low-
lying roofs and spars of Shoreham. Those two years had
changed Violet Tempest from a slender girl to a nobly-formed
woman; a woman whom a sculptor would have worshipped as
his dream of perfection, whom a painter would have
reverenced for her glow and splendour of colouring; but about
whose beauty the common run of mankind, and more
especially womankind, had not quite made up their minds.
The pretty little women with eighteen-inch waists opined that
Miss Tempest was too big.

'She's very handsome, you know, and all that,' they said
deprecatingly, 'and her figure is quite splendid; but she's on
such a very large scale. She ought to be painted in fresco, you
know, on a high cornice. As Autumn, or Plenty, or Ceres, or
something of that kind, carrying a cornucopia. But in a
drawing-room she looks so very massive.'

The amber-haired women − palpably indebted to auricomous
fluids for the colour of their tresses − objected to the dark
burnished gold of Violet Tempest's hair. There was too much
red in the gold, they said, and a colour so obviously natural was
very unfashionable. That cream-white skin of hers, too, found
objectors, on the score of a slight powdering of freckles; spots
which the kindly sun leaves on the fruit he best loves. In fact,
there were many reservations made by Miss Tempest's
pretended admirers when they summed up her good looks; but
when she rode her pretty bay horse along the King's Road,
strangers turned to look at her admiringly; when she entered a

crowded room she threw all paler beauties in the shade. The cabbage-rose is a vulgar flower, pehaps, but she is queen of the garden notwithstanding.

Lest it should be supposed, after this, that Vixen was a giantess, it may be as well to state that her height was five feet six, her waist twenty-two inches at most, her shoulders broad but finely sloping, her arms full and somewhat muscular, her hands not small, but exquisitely tapering, her foot long and narrow, her instep arched like an Arab's, and all her movements instinct with an untutored grace and dignity. She held her head higher than is common to women, and on that score was found guilty of pride.

'I think we ought to go back before Christmas, Violet,' said Mrs Tempest, continuing a discussion that had been dragging itself slowly along for the last half-hour.

'I am ready, mamma,' answered Vixen submissively. 'It will break our hearts afresh when we go home, but I suppose we must go home some day.'

'But you would like to see the dear old house again, surely, Violet?'

'Like to see the frame without the picture? No, no, no, mamma. The frame was very dear while the picture was in it – but – yes,' cried Vixen passionately, 'I should like to go back. I should like to see papa's grave, and carry fresh flowers there every day. It has been much neglected.'

'Neglected, Violet! How can you say such a thing? When Manotti's bill for the monument was over six hundred pounds.'

'O mamma, there is more love in a bunch of primroses that my own hand gathers and carries to the grave than in all the marble or granite in Westminster Abbey.'

'My dear, for poor people wild flowers are very nice, and show good feeling – but the rich must have monuments. There could be nothing too splendid for your dear papa,' added the widow tearfully.

She was always tearful when she spoke of her dear Edward, even now; though she was beginning to find that life had some savour without him.

'No,' said Vixen, 'but I think papa will like the flowers best.'

'Then, if all is well, Miss McCroke,' pursued Mrs Tempest, 'we will go back at the end of November. It would be a pity to lose the season here.'

Vixen yawned despondently.

'What do we care about the season, mamma?' she exclaimed. 'Can it matter to us whether there are two or three thousand extra people in the place? It only makes the King's Road a little more uncomfortable.'

'My dear Violet, at your age gaiety is good for you,' said Mrs Tempest.

'Yes, and, like most other things that are good, it's very disagreeable,' retorted Vixen.

'And now, about this ball,' pursued Mrs Tempest, taking up a dropped stitch in the previous argument; 'I really think we ought to go, if it were only on Violet's account. Don't you, Maria?'

Mrs Tempest always called her governess Maria when she was anxious to conciliate her.

'Violet is old enough to enter society, certainly,' said Miss McCroke, with some deliberation; 'but whether a public ball——'

'If it's on my account, mamma, pray don't think of going,' protested Vixen earnestly; 'I hate the idea of a ball – I hate——'

'Captain Winstanley,' announced Forbes, in the dusky end of the drawing-room by the door.

'He has saved me the trouble of finishing my sentence,' muttered Vixen.

The visitor came smiling through the dusk into the friendly glow of the fire. He shook hands with Mrs Tempest with the air of an old friend, went over to the window to shake hands with Miss McCroke, and then came back to Vixen, who gave him a limp cold hand, with an indifference that was almost insolent, while Argus lifted his head an inch or so from the carpet and saluted him with a suppressed growl. Whether this arose from a wise instinct in the animal, or from a knowledge that his mistress disliked the gentleman, would be too nice a point to decide.

'I was that moment thinking of you, Captain Winstanley,' said the widow.

'An honour and a happiness for me,' murmured the Captain.

Mrs Tempest seated herself in her own particular chair, beside which was her own particular table with one of those pretty tea-services which were her chief delight.

'You'll take a cup of tea?' she said insinuatingly.

'I shall be delighted. I feel as if I ought to go home and write verses or smart paragraphs for the society papers after drinking your tea, it is inspiring. Addison ought to have drunk just such tea before writing one of his *Spectators*, but unfortunately his muse required old port.'

'If the *Spectator* came out nowadays I'm afraid we should think it stupid,' suggested Mrs Tempest.

'Simply because the slipshod writers of the present day have spoiled our taste for fine English,' interjected Miss McCroke severely.

'Well, I fear we should find Addison a little thin,' said Captain Winstanley; 'I can't imagine London society existing for a week on such literary pabulum as "The Vision of Mirza." We want something stronger than that. A little scandal about our neighbours, a racy article on field sports, some sharpish hits at the City, a libel or two upon men we know, a social article sailing very near the wind, and one of Addison's papers on cherry-coloured hoods, or breast-knots, patches or powder, thrown in by way of padding. Our dear Joseph is too purely literary for the present age.'

'What monsters newspapers have grown,' remarked Mrs Tempest. 'It's almost impossible to get through them.'

'Not if you read anything else,' answered the Captain. 'The majority do not.'

'We were talking about the ball just as you came in,' said Mrs Tempest. 'I really think Violet ought to go.'

'I am sure she ought,' said the Captain.

Vixen sat looking at the fire and patting Argus. She did not favour the Captain with so much as a glance; and yet he was a man upon whom the eyes of women were apt to dwell favourably. He was not essentially handsome. The most attractive men rarely are. He was tall and thin, with a waist as small as a woman's, small hands, small feet – a general delicacy

of mould that was accounted thoroughbred. He had a long
nose, a darkly-pale complexion, keen gray eyes under dark
brows, dark hair, cropped close to his small head; thin lips,
white teeth, a neat black moustache, and a strictly military
appearance, though he had sold out of a line regiment three
years ago, and was now a gentleman at large, doing nothing,
and living in a gentlemanlike manner on a very small income.
He was not in debt, and was altogether respectable. Nothing
could be said against him, unless it was some dark hint of a
gambling transaction at a fast and furious club, the kind of
rumour which is apt to pursue a man who, like Bulwer's
Dudley Smooth, does not cheat but always wins.

Despite these vague slanders, which are generally baseless –
the mere expression of society's floating malice, the scum of ill-
nature on the ocean of talk – Captain Winstanley was a universal
favourite. He went everywhere, and was liked wherever he
went. He was gifted with that adaptability and handiness which
is, of all cleverness, most valuable in polite society. Of him, as of
Goldsmith, it might be said that he touched nothing he did not
adorn. True, that the things he touched were for the most part
small things; but they were things that kept him before the eye
of society, and found favour in that eye.

He was a good horseman, a good oarsman, a good swimmer,
a good cricketer. He played and sang; he was a first-rate
amateur actor; he was great at billiards and all games of skill; he
could talk any language society wanted him to talk – society not
requiring a man to excel in Coptic or Chinese, or calling upon
him suddenly for Japanese or Persian; he dressed with perfect
taste, and without the slightest pretence of dandyism; he could
write a first-rate letter, and caricature his dearest friends of last
year in pen and ink for the entertainment of his dearest friends
of this year; he was known to have contributed occasionally to
fashionable periodicals, and was supposed to have a reserve of
wit and satire which would quite have annihilated the hack
writers of the day had he cared to devote himself to literature.

Mrs Tempest and her daughter had met the Captain early in
the previous spring among Swiss mountains. He knew some of
Mrs Tempest's Hampshire friends, and with no other credentials

had contrived to win her friendship. Vixen took it into her obstinate young head to detest him. But then, Vixen at seventeen and a half, was full of ridiculous dislikes and irrational caprices. Mrs Tempest, in her lonely and somewhat depressed condition, considered the Captain a particularly useful acquaintance. Miss McCroke was dubious, but finding any expression of her doubts ungraciously received, took the safer line of silence.

The ball in question was a charity ball at the Pavilion, a perfectly unobjectionable ball. The list of patronesses bristled with noble names. There was nothing to be said against Vixen's appearance there, except Miss McCroke's objection, that Squire Tempest's daughter and heiress ought not to make her *début* in society at any public ball whatever; ought, in a manner, hardly to be seen by the human eye as a grown-up young lady, until she had been presented to her gracious sovereign. But Mrs Tempest had set her heart upon Vixen's going to the ball; or, in other words, she had set her heart upon going herself. On her way through Paris, in September, she had gone to Worth's – out of curiosity, just to see what the great man's salons were like – and there she had been tempted into the purchase of an artistic arrangement in black silk and jet, velvet and passementerie. She did not require the costume, but the thing in itself was so beautiful that she could not help buying it. And having spent a hundred guineas upon this masterpiece, there arose in her mind a natural craving to exhibit it; to feel that she was being pointed out as one of the best-dressed women in the crowded room; to know that women were whispering to each other significantly, 'Worth,' as the nocturne in velvet and silk and glimmering jet swept by them.

There was a good deal more discussion, and it was ultimately settled that Vixen should go to the ball. She had no positive objection. She would have liked the idea of the ball well enough perhaps, if it had not been for Captain Winstanley. It was his advocacy that made the subject odious.

'How very rudely you behaved to Captain Winstanley, Violet,' said Mrs Tempest, when her visitor had departed.

'Did I, mamma?' inquired Vixen listlessly. 'I thought I was extraordinarily civil. If you knew how I should have liked to behave to him, you would think so too.'

'I cannot imagine why you are so prejudiced against him,'
pursued Mrs Tempest fretfully.

'It is not prejudice, mamma, but instinct, like Argus's. That
man is destined to do us some great wrong, if we do not escape
out of his clutches.'

'It is shameful of you to say such things,' cried the widow,
pale with anger. 'What have you to say against him? What fault
can you find with him? You cannot deny that he is most
gentlemanlike.'

'No, mamma; he is a little too gentlemanlike. He makes a
trade of his gentlemanliness. He is too highly polished for me.'

'You prefer a rough young fellow, like Roderick Vawdrey,
who talks slang, and smells of the stables.'

'I prefer anyone who is good and true,' retorted Vixen.
'Roderick is a man, and not to be named in the same breath
with your fine gentleman.'

'I admit that the comparison would be vastly to his
disadvantage,' said the widow. 'But it's time to dress for dinner.'

'And we are to dine with the Mortimers,' yawned Vixen.
'What a bore!'

This young lady had not that natural bent for society which is
symptomatic of her age. The wound that pierced her young
heart two years ago had not healed so completely that she could
find pleasure in inane conversation across a primeval forest of
sixpenny ferns, and all the factitious liveliness of a fashionable
dinner-table.

CHAPTER 11

'IT SHALL BE MEASURE FOR MEASURE'

The night of the ball came, and, in spite of her aversion for
Captain Winstanley and general dislike of the whole thing,
Violet Tempest began the evening by enjoying herself. She was

young and energetic, and had an immense reserve of animal
spirits after her two years of sadness and mourning. She danced
with the partners her friends brought her – some of the most
eligible men in the room – and was full of life and gaiety; yet
the festival seemed to her in somewise horrible all the time.

'If papa could know that we are dancing and smiling at each
other, as if all life was made up of gladness, when he is lying in
his cold grave!' thought Vixen, after joining hands with her
mother in the ladies' chain.

The widow looked as if she had never known a care. She was
conscious that Worth's *chef-d'oeuvre* was not thrown away. She
saw herself in the great mirrors which once reflected George
and his lovely Fitzherbert in their days of gladness – which
reflected the same George later, old, and sick, and weary.

'That French *grande dame* was right,' thought Mrs Tempest,
'who said, "*Le noir est si flatteur pour les blondes*," '

Black was flattering for Vixen's auburn hair also. Though her
indifferent eye rarely glanced at the mirrored walls, she had
never looked lovelier. A tall graceful figure, in billowy black
tulle, wreathed with white chrysanthemums; a queen-like head,
with a red-gold coronal; a throat like an ivory pillar, spanned
with a broad black ribbon, fastened with a diamond clasp;
diamond stars in her ears, and a narrow belt of diamonds round
each white arm.

'How many waltzes have you kept for me?' Captain
Winstanley asked presently, coming up to Vixen.

'I have not kept waltzes for anyone,' she answered
indifferently.

'But surely you were under a promise to keep some for me? I
asked you a week ago.'

'Did you? I am sure I never promised anything of the kind.'

'Here is only one little shabby waltz left,' said the Captain,
looking at her programme. 'May I put my name down for that?'

'If you like,' answered Vixen indifferently; and then, with the
faintest suspicion of malice, she added, 'as mamma does not
dance round dances.'

She was standing up for the Lancers presently, and her partner
had just led her to her place, when she saw that she had her

mother and Captain Winstanley again for her *vis-à-vis*. She grew
suddenly pale, and turned away.

'Will you let me sit this out?' she said. 'I feel awfully ill.'

Her partner was full of concern, and carried her off at once to
a cooler room.

'It is too bad!' she muttered to herself. 'The Lancers! To go
romping round with a lot of wild young men and women. It is
as bad as the Queen in *Hamlet*.'

This was the last dance before supper. Vixen went into the
supper-room presently with her attentive partner, who had kept
by her side devotedly while the lively scramble to the good old
English tunes was going on in the dancing-room.

'Are you better?' he asked tenderly, fanning her with her big
black fan, painted with violets and white chrysanthemums. 'The
room is abominably hot.'

'Thanks. I'm quite well now. It was only a momentary
faintness. But I rather hate the Lancers, don't you?'

'Well, I don't know. I think, sometimes, you know, with a
nice partner, they're good fun. Only one can't help treading on
the ladies' trains, and they wind themselves round one's legs like
snakes. I've seen fellows come awful croppers, and the lady who
has done it look so sweetly unconcerned.'

Vixen's supper was the merest pretence. Her mother sat
opposite her, with Captain Winstanley still in attendance. Vixen
gave them one scathing look, and then sat like an image of
scorn. Her partner could not get a word from her, and when he
offered her the fringed end of a cracker bonbon, she positively
refused to have anything to do with it.

'Please don't,' she said. 'It's too inane. I couldn't pretend to
be interested in the motto.'

When she went back to the ball-room Captain Winstanley
followed her and claimed his waltz. The band was just striking
up the latest love-sick German melody, '*Weit von dir*!' a strain of
drawling tenderness.

'You had better go and secure your supper,' said Vixen
coldly.

'I despise all ball-suppers. This one most particularly, if it
were to deprive me of my waltz.'

Vixen shrugged her shoulders, and submitted to take those few preliminary steps which are like the strong swimmer's shiverings on the bank ere he plunges in the stream. And then she was whirling round to the legato strains, '*Weit von dir! Weit von dir! Wo ist mein Leben's Lust – Weit von dir – weit von dir!*'

Captain Winstanley's waltzing was simple perfection. It was not the Liverpool Lurch, or the Scarborough Scramble, the Bermondsey Bounce, or the Whitechapel Wiggle; it was waltzing pure and simple, unaffected, graceful; the waltzing of a man with a musical ear, and an athlete's mastery of the art of motion. Vixen hated the Captain, but she enjoyed the waltz. They danced till the last bar died away in a tender diminuendo.

'You look pale,' said the Captain, 'let us go into the garden.' He brought her cloak and wrapped it round her, and she took his offered arm without a word. It was one of those rare nights in late October, when the wind is not cold. There was hardly the flutter of a leaf in the Pavilion garden. The neighbouring sea made the gentlest music – a melancholy ebb and flow of sound, like the murmuring of some great imprisoned spirit.

In the searching light of day, when its adjacent cab-stands and commonnesses are visible, and its gravelled walks are peopled with nursemaids and small children, the Pavilion garden can hardly be called romantic. But by this tender moonlight, in this cool stillness of a placid autumn midnight, even the Pavilion garden had its air of romance and mystery. And, after all, this part of Brighton has a peculiar charm which all the rest of Brighton lacks. It speaks of the past, it tells its story of the dead. They were not great or heroic, perhaps, those departed figures, whose ghosts haunt us in the red and yellow rooms, and in the stiff town garden; but they had their histories. They lived, and loved, and suffered; and, being dead so long, come back to us in the softened light of vanished days, and take hold of our fancy with their quaint garments and antique head-gear, their powder, and court-swords, and diamond shoe-buckles, and little loves and little sorrows.

Vixen walked slowly along the shining gravel-path, with her black and gold mantle folded round her, looking altogether statuesque and unapproachable. They took one turn in absolute silence, and then Captain Winstanley, who was not inclined to beat about the bush when he had something particular to say, and a good opportunity for saying it, broke the spell.

This was perhaps the first time, in an acquaintance of more than six months, that he had ever found himself alone with Violet Tempest, without hazard of immediate interruption. 'Miss Tempest,' he began, with a firmness of tone that startled her, 'I want to know why you are so unkind to me?'

'I hardly know what you mean by unkindness. I hope I have never said anything uncivil?'

'No; but you have let me see very plainly that you dislike me.'

'I am sorry nature has given me an unpleasantly candid disposition.'

Those keen gray eyes of the Captain's were watching her intently. An angry look shot at her from under the straight dark brows – swift as an arrow.

'You admit then that you do not like me?' he said.

Vixen paused before replying. The position was embarrassing.

'I suppose if I were ladylike and proper, I should protest that I like you immensely; that there is no one in the world, my mother excepted, whom I like better. But I never was particularly proper or polite, Captain Winstanley, and I must confess there are very few people I do like, and——'

'And I am not one of them,' said the Captain.

'You have finished my sentence for me.'

'That is hard upon me – no, Violet, you can never know how hard. Why should you dislike me? You are the first woman who ever told me so' (flushing with an indignant recollection of all his victories). 'I have done nothing to offend you. I have not been obtrusive. I have worshipped at a distance – but the Persian's homage of the sun is not more reverent——'

'O, pray don't talk about Persians and the sun,' cried Violet. 'I am not worthy that you should be so concerned about my likes and dislikes. Please think of me as an untaught inexperienced girl. Two years ago I was a spoiled child. You don't know how my dearest father spoiled me. It is no wonder I am rude. Remember this, and forgive me if I am too truthful.'

'You are all that is lovely,' he exclaimed passionately, stung by her scorn and fired by her beauty, almost beside himself as they stood there in the magical moonlight – for once in his life forgetting to calculate every move on life's chessboard. 'You are too lovely for me. From the very first, in Switzerland, when I was so happy – no, I will not tell you. I will not lay down my heart to be trampled under your feet.'

'Don't,' cried Vixen, transfixing him with the angry fire of her eyes, 'for I'm afraid I should trample on it. I am not one of those gentle creatures who go out of their way to avoid treading on worms – or other reptiles.'

'You are as cruel as you are lovely,' he said, 'and your cruelty is sweeter than another woman's kindness. Violet, I laugh at your dislike. Yes, such aversion as that is often the beginning of closest liking. I will not be disheartened. I will not be put off by your scornful candour. What if I were to tell you that you are the only woman I ever loved?'

'Pray do not. It would transform passive dislike into active hatred. I should be sorry for that, because,' looking at him deliberately, with a slow scorn, 'I think my mother likes you.'

'She has honoured me with her confidence, and I hope I shall not prove unworthy of the trust. I rarely fail to repay any benefit that is bestowed upon me.'

'October nights are treacherous,' said Vixen, drawing her cloak closer round her. 'I think we had better go back to the ball-room.'

She was shivering a little with agitated feeling, in spite of that mantle of scorn in which she had wrapped herself. This was the first man who had ever called her lovely, who had ever talked to her of love with manhood's strong passion.

The Captain gave her his arm, and they went back to the glare and heat of the yellow dragons and scarlet griffins. Another Lancer scramble was in full progress, to the old-fashioned jigging tunes, but Mrs Tempest was sitting among the matrons in a corner by an open window.

'Are we ever going home any more, mamma?' inquired Vixen.

'My dear Violet, I have been waiting for you ever so long.'

'Why should you leave so early?' exclaimed Captain Winstanley. 'There are half-a-dozen more dances, and you are engaged for them all, I believe, Miss Tempest.'

'Then I will show mercy to my partners by going away,' said Violet. 'Are all balls as long as this? We seem to have been here ages; I expect to find my hair gray to-morrow morning.'

'I really think we had better go,' said Mrs Tempest, in her undecided way.

She was a person who never quite made up her mind about anything, but balanced every question gently, letting somebody else turn the scale for her – her maid, her governess, her daughter; she was always trying to have her own way, but never quite knew what her own way was, and just managed things skilfully enough to prevent other people having theirs.

'If you are determined, I will see you to your carriage, and then the ball is over for me,' said the Captain gallantly.

He offered Mrs Tempest his arm, and they went out into the vestibule, where the Captain left them for a few minutes, while he went into the porch to hasten the arrival of the carriage.

'Where were you and Captain Winstanley all that time, Violet?' asked Mrs Tempest.

'In the garden.'

'How imprudent!'

'Indeed, dear mamma, it wasn't cold.'

'But you were out there so long. What could you find to talk about all that time?'

'We were not talking all the time, only enjoying the cool air and the moonlight.'

'Mrs Tempest's carriage!' roared one of the door-keepers, as if it had been his doing that the carriage had appeared so quickly.

Captain Winstanley was ready to hand them to their brougham.

'Come and take a cup of tea to-morrow afternoon, and let us talk over the ball,' said the widow.

'With infinite pleasure.'

'Shall we drop you at your house?'

'A thousand thanks – no – my rooms are so close, I'll walk home.'

He went back for his overcoat, and then walked slowly away, without another glance at the crowded ball-room, or the corridors where the ladies who were waiting for their carriages were contriving to improve the time by a good deal of quiet, or even noisy, flirtation. His lodgings were on the Old Steine, close by. But he did not go home immediately. There are times in a man's life when four walls are too small to hold the bigness of his thoughts. Captain Winstanley paced the Marine Parade for half an hour or so before he went home.

'*Va pour la mère*,' he said to himself, at the close of that half hour's meditations; 'she is really very nice, and the position altogether advantageous, perhaps as much as one has the right to expect in the general decadence of things. But, good heavens, how lovely that girl is! She is the first woman who ever looked me in the face and told me she disliked me; the first woman who ever gave me contemptuous looks and scornful words. And yet — for that very reason perhaps — I——'

The dark brows contracted over the keen eyes, which seemed closer than usual to the hawk nose.

'Look to yourself, my queen, in the time to come,' he said, as he turned his back on the silvery sea and moonlight sky. 'You have been hard to me and I will be hard to you. It shall be measure for measure.'

CHAPTER 12

'I HAVE NO WRONG, WHERE I CAN CLAIM NO RIGHT'

Going home again. That was hard to bear. It reopened all the old wounds. Violet Tempest felt as if her heart must really break, as if this new grief were sharper than the old one, when the carriage drove in through the familiar gates, in the December dusk, and along the winding shrubberied drive, and up to the Tudor porch, where the lion of the Tempest stood, *passant regardant*, with lifted paw and backward gaze, above the stone shield. The ruddy firelight was shining across the wide doorway. The old hearth looked as cheerful as of old. And there stood the empty chair beside it. That had been Vixen's particular wish.

'Let nothing be disturbed, dear mamma,' she had said ever so many times, when her mother was writing her orders to the housekeeper. 'Beg them to keep everything just as it was in papa's time.'

'My dear, it will only make you grieve more.'

'Yes; but I had rather grieve for him than forget him. I am more afraid of forgetting him than of grieving too much for him,' said Vixen.

And now, as she stood on the hearth after her journey, wrapped in black furs, a little black fur *toque* crowning her ruddy gold hair, fancy filled the empty chair as she gazed at it. Yes, she could see her father sitting there in his hunting-clothes, his whip across his knee.

The old pointer, the Squire's favourite, came whining to her feet. How old he looked! Old, and broken, and infirm, as if from much sorrow.

'Poor Nip! poor Nip!' she said, patting him. 'The joy of your life went with papa, didn't it?'

'It's all very sad,' murmured Mrs Tempest, loosening her wraps. 'A sad, sad home-coming. And it seems only yesterday that I came here as a bride. Did I ever tell you about my travelling-dress, Violet? It was a shot-silk – they were fashionable then, you know – bronze and blue – the loveliest combination of colour!'

'I can't imagine a shot-silk being anything but detestable,' said Vixen curtly. 'Poor Nip! How faithful dogs are! The dear thing is actually crying!'

Tears were indeed running from the poor old eyes, as the pointer's head lay in Vixen's lap; as if memory, kindled by her image, brought back the past too keenly for that honest canine heart.

'It is very mournful,' said Mrs Tempest. 'Pauline, let us have a cup of tea.'

She sank into an arm-chair opposite the fire. Not the Squire's old carved oak chair, with its tawny leather cushions. That must needs be sacred evermore — a memento of the dead, standing beside the hearth, revered as the image of an honoured ancestor in a Roman citizen's home.

'I wonder if anyone is alive that we knew here?' said Vixen, lying back in her low chair, and idly caressing the dogs.

'My dear Violet, why should people be dead? We have only been away two years.'

'No; but it seems so long. I hardly expect to see any of the old faces. He is not here,' with a sudden choking sob. 'Why should all be left — except him?'

'The workings of Providence are full of mystery,' sighed the widow. 'Dear Edward! How handsome he looked that day he brought me home. And he was a noble-looking man to the last. Not more than one spoonful of pekoe, Pauline. You ought to know how I like it by this time.'

This is to the handmaiden, who was making tea at the gipsy table in front of the fire — the table at which Vixen and Rorie had drunk tea so merrily on that young man's birthday.

After tea mother and daughter went the round of the house. How familiar, how dear, how strange, how sad all things looked! The faithful servants had done their duty. Everything was in its place. The last room they entered was the Squire's study. Here were all his favourite books. The *Sporting Magazine* from its commencement, in crimson morocco. *Nimrod* and the *Druid*, Assheton Smith's *Memoirs*, and many others of the same class. Books on farming and farriery, on dogs and guns. Here were the Squire's guns and whips, a motley collection, all neatly aranged by his own hands. The servants had done nothing but keep them free from dust. There, by the low and cosy fireplace, with its tiled hearth, stood the capacious crimson morocco chair, in which the master of the Abbey House had been wont to sit, when he held audience with his kennel-huntsman, or gamekeeper, his farm-bailiff, or stud-groom.

'Mamma, I should like you to lock the door of this room and keep the key, so that no one may ever come here,' said Vixen.

'My dear, that is just the way to prolong your grief; but I will
do it if you like.'

'Do, dear mamma. Or, if you will let me keep the key, I will
come in and dust the room every day. It would be a pleasure
for me, a mournful one, perhaps, but still a pleasure.'

Mrs Tempest made no objection, and, when they left the
room, Vixen locked the door and put the key in her pocket.

Christmas was close at hand. The saddest time for such a
home-coming, Vixen thought. The gardeners brought in their
barrows of holly and fir and laurel; but Vixen would take no
part in the decoration of hall and corridors, staircase and gallery
– she who, in former years, had been so active in the labour.
The humble inhabitants of the village rejoiced in the return of
the family at the great house, and Vixen was pleased to see the
kind faces again, the old men and women, the rosy-cheeked
children, and care-worn mothers, withered and wrinkled
before their time with manifold anxieties. She had a friendly
word for every one, and gifts for all. Home was sweet to her
after her two years' absence, despite the cloud of sadness that
overhung all things. She went out to the stables and made
friends with the old horses, which had been out at grass all
through the summer, and had enjoyed a paradise of rest for the
last two years. Slug and Crawler, Mrs Tempest's carriage-
horses, sleek even-minded bays, had been at Brighton, and so
had Vixen's beautiful thoroughbred, and a handsome brown
for the groom; but all the rest had stayed in Hampshire. Not
one had been sold, though the stud was a wasteful and useless
one for a widow and her daughter. There was Bullfinch, the
hunter Squire Tempest had ridden in his last hour of life.
Violet went into his box, and caressed him, and fed him, and
cried over him with bitterest tears. This home-coming brought
back the old sorrow with overwhelming force. She ran out of
the stables to hide her tears, and ran up to her own room, and
abandoned herself to her grief, almost as utterly as she had
done on those dark days when her father's corpse was lying in
the house.

There was no friendly Miss McCroke now to be fussy and
anxious, and to interpose herself between Violet Tempest and

her grief. Violet was supposed to be 'finished,' or, in other words, to know everything under the sun which a young lady of good birth and ample fortune can be required to know. Everything, in this case, consisted of a smattering of French, Italian, and German, a dubious recollection of the main facts in modern history, a few vague notions about astronomy, some foggy ideas upon the constitution of plants and flowers, seaweeds and shells, rocks and hills, – and a general indifference for all literature except poetry and novels.

Miss McCroke, having done her duty conscientiously, after her lights, had now gone to finish three other young ladies, the motherless daughters of an Anglo-Indian colonel, over whom she was to exercise maternal authority and guidance, in a tall narrow house in Maida Vale. She had left Mrs Tempest with all honours, and Violet had lavished gifts upon her at parting, feeling fonder of her governess in the last week of their association than at any other period of her tutelage. To-day, in her sorrow, it was a relief to Violet to find herself free from the futile consolations of friendship. She flung herself into the arm-chair by the fire, and sobbed out her grief.

'O, kindest, dearest, best of fathers,' she cried, 'what is home without you!'

And then she remembered that awful day of the funeral, when Roderick Vawdrey had sat with her beside this hearth, trying to comfort her, and remembered how she had heard his voice as a sound far away, a sound that had no meaning. That was the last time she had seen him.

'I don't suppose I thanked him for his pity or his kindness,' she thought. 'He must have gone away thinking me cold and ungrateful; but I was like a creature at the bottom of some dark dismal pit. How could I feel thankful to someone happy looking down at me and talking to me from the free happy world at the top?'

Her sobs ceased gradually, she dried her tears, and that unconscious pleasure in life, which is a part of innocent youth, came slowly back. She looked round the room in which so much of her childhood had been spent – a room full of her own fancies and caprices, a room whose prettiness had been bought with her own money, and was for the most part the work of her own hands.

In spite of home's sorrowful association she was glad to find herself at home. Mountains and lakes, and sunny bays, and dark pathless forests, may be ever so good to see, but there is some pleasure in being shut snugly within four familiar walls, surrounded by one's own belongings.

The wood-fire burnt merrily. Outside the deep mullioned windows the winter blast was howling, with occasional spurts of flying snow. Argus crept in presently, and stretched himself at full length upon the fleecy rug. Vixen lay back in her low chair, musing idly in the glow of the fire, and by-and-by the lips which had been convulsed with grief parted in a smile, the lovely brown eyes shone with happy memories.

She was thinking of her old playfellow and friend, Rorie.

'I wonder if he will come to-day?' she mused. 'I think he will. He is sure to be at home for the hunting. Yes, he will come to-day. What will he be like, I wonder? Handsomer than he was two years ago? No, that could hardly be. He is quite a man now – three-and-twenty! I must not laugh at him any more.'

The thought of his coming thrilled her with a new joy. She seemed to have been living an artificial life in the two years of her absence – to have been changed in her very self by change of surroundings. It was almost as if the old Vixen had been sent into an enchanted sleep, while some other young lady, a model of propriety and good manners, went about the world in Vixen's shape. Her life had been made up, more or less, of trifles and foolishness, with a background of grand scenery. Tepid little friendships with agreeable fellow-travellers at Nice; tepid little friendships of the same order in Switzerland; well-dressed young people smiling at each other, and delighting in each other's company; and parting, probably for ever, without a pang.

But now she had come back to the friends, the horses, the dogs, the rooms, the gardens, the fields, the forests of youth, and was going to be the real Vixen again – the wild, thoughtless, high-spirited girl, whom Squire Tempest and all the peasantry round about had loved.

'I have been ridiculously well-behaved,' she said to herself, 'quite a second edition of mamma; but now I am back in the Forest, my good manners may go hang. My foot's on my native heath, and my name is McGregor.'

Somehow in all her thoughts of home – after that burst of grief for her dead father – Roderick Vawdrey was the central figure. He filled the gap cruel death had made.

Would Rorie come soon to see her? Would he be very glad to have her at home again? What would he think of her? Would he fancy her changed? For the worse? For the better?

'I wonder whether he would like my good manners, or the original Vixen, best?' she speculated.

The morning wore on, and still Violet Tempest sat idly by the fire. She had made up her mind that Roderick would come to see her at once. She was sufficiently aware of her own importance to feel sure that the fact of her return had been duly chronicled in the local papers. He would come to-day – before luncheon, perhaps, and they three, mamma, Rorie, and herself, would sit at the round table in the library, the snug warm room where they had so often sat with papa. This thought brought back the bitterness of her loss.

'I can bear it better if Rorie is with us,' she thought, 'and he is almost sure to come. He would not be so unkind as to delay bidding welcome to such poor lonely creatures as mamma and I.'

She looked at her watch. It was one o'clock already, and luncheon would be at half-past.

'Only half an hour for Rorie,' she thought.

The minute-hand crept slowly to the half-hour, the luncheon-gong sounded below, and there had been no annoucement of Mr Vawdrey.

'He may be downstairs with mamma all this time,' thought Vixen. 'Forbes would not tell me, unless he were sent.'

She went downstairs and met Forbes in the hall.

'O, if you please, ma'am, Mrs Tempest does not feel equal to coming down to luncheon. She will take a wing of chicken in her own room.'

'And I don't feel equal to sitting in the library alone, Forbes,' said Violet; 'so you may tell Phoebe to bring me a cup of tea and a biscuit. Has nobody called this morning?'

'No, ma'am.'

Vixen went back to her room, out of spirits and out of temper. It was unkind of Rorie, cold, neglectful, heartless.

'If he had come home after an absence of two years – absence under such sad circumstances – how anxious I would be to see him,' she thought. 'But I don't suppose there is frost enough to stop the hunting, and I daresay he is tearing across the heather on some big raw-boned horse, and not giving me a thought. Or perhaps he is dancing attendance upon Lady Mabel. But no, I don't think he cares much for that kind of thing.'

She moved about the room a little, rearranging things that were already arranged exactly as she had left them two years ago. She opened a book and flung it aside; tried the piano, which sounded muffled and woolly.

'My poor little Broadwood is no better for being out at grass,' she said.

She went to one of the windows, and stood there looking out, expecting every instant to see a dog-cart with a rakish horse, a wasp-like body, and high red wheels, spin round the curve of the shrubbery. She stood thus for a long time, as she had done on that wet October afternoon of Rorie's home-coming; but no rakish horse came swinging round the curve of the carriage-drive. The flying snow drifted past the window, the winter sky looked blue and clear between the brief showers, the tall feathery fir-trees stood up against the afternoon light, and Vixen gazed at them with angry eyes, full of resentment against Roderick Vawdrey.

'The ground is too hard for the scent to lie well, that's one comfort,' she reflected savagely.

And then she thought of the dear old kennels given over to a new master; the hounds whose names and idiosyncrasies she had known as well as if they had been human acquaintance. She had lost all interest in them now. Ponto and Gellert, Lightfoot, Juno, Ringlet, Lord Dundreary – they had forgotten her, no doubt.

Here was someone at last, but not the one for whom she was watching. A figure clothed in a long loose black coat and slouched felt hat, and carrying a weedy umbrella, trudged sturdily round the curve, and came briskly towards the porch. It was Mr Scobel, the incumbent of the pretty little Gothic church in the village – a church like a toy.

He was a good man and benevolent, this Mr Scobel; a hard-worker, and a blessing in the neighbourhood. But just at this moment Violet Tempest did not feel grateful to him for coming.

'What does he want?' she thought. 'Blankets and coals and things, I suppose.'

She turned sullenly from the window, and went back to her seat beside the fire, and threw on a log, and gave herself up to disappointment. The blue winter sky had changed to gray; the light was fading behind the feathery fir-tops.

'Perhaps he will come to afternoon tea,' she thought; and then, with a discontented shrug of her shoulders, 'No, he is not coming at all. If he cared about us he would have been the first to bid us welcome; knowing, as he must, how miserable it was for me to come home at all – without papa!'

She sat looking at the fire.

'How idle I am!' she mused; 'and poor Crokey did so implore me to go on with my education, and read good useful books and enlarge my mind. I don't think my poor little mind would bear any more stretching, or that I should be much happier if I knew all about old red sandstone, and tertiary, and the rest of them. What does it matter to me what the earth is made of, if I can but be happy upon it? No, I shall never try to be a highly cultivated young woman. I shall read Byron, and Tennyson, and Wordsworth, and Keats, and Bulwer, and Dickens, and Thackeray, and remain an ignoramus all the days of my life. I think that would be quite enough for Rorie, if he and I were to be much together; for I don't believe he ever opens a book.'

Phoebe, Miss Tempest's fresh-faced Hampshire maid, appeared at this moment.

'O, if you please, miss, your ma says would you go to the drawing-room? Mr Scobel is with her, and would like to see you.'

Violet rose with a sigh.

'Is my hair awfully untidy, Phoebe?'

'I think I had better arrange the plaits, miss.'

'That means that I'm an object. It's four o'clock; I may as well change my dress for dinner. I suppose I must go down to dinner?'

'Lor' yes, miss; it will never do to shut yourself up in your own room and fret. You're as pale as them there Christmas roses already.'

Ten minutes later Vixen went down to the drawing-room, looking very stately in her black Irish poplin, whose heavy folds became the tall full figure, and whose dense blackness set off the ivory skin and warm auburn hair. She had given just one passing glance at herself in the cheval-glass, and Vanity had whispered,

'Perhaps Rorie would have thought me improved; but he has not taken the trouble to come and see. I might be honeycombed by the small-pox or bald from the effects of typhus for aught he cares.'

The drawing-room was all aglow with blazing logs, and the sky outside the windows looked pale and gray, when Violet went in. Mrs Tempest was in her favourite arm-chair by the fire, Tennyson's latest poem on the velvet-covered gipsy table at her side, in company with a large black fan and a smelling-bottle. Mr Scobel was sitting in a low chair on the other side of the hearth, with his knees almost up to his chin and his trousers wrinkled up ever so far above his stout Oxford shoes, leaving a considerable interval of gray stocking. He was a man of about thirty, pale, and unpretending of aspect, who fortified his native modesty with a pair of large binoculars, which interposed a kind of barrier between himself and the outer world.

He rose as Violet came towards him, and turned the binoculars upon her, glittering in the glow of the fire.

'How tall you have grown,' he cried, when they had shaken hands. 'And how——' here he stopped, with a little nervous laugh; 'I really don't think I should have known you if we had met elsewhere.'

'Perhaps Rorie would hardly know me,' thought Vixen.

'How are all the poor people?' she asked, when Mr Scobel
had resumed his seat, and was placidly caressing his knees, and
blinking, or seeming to blink, at the fire with his binoculars.

'O poor souls!' he sighed. 'There has been a great deal of
sickness and distress, and want of work. Yes, a very great
deal. The winter began early; and we have had some severe
weather. James Parsons is in prison again for rabbit-snaring.
I'm really afraid James is incorrigible. Mrs Roper's eldest son
Tom — I daresay you remember Tom, an idle little ruffian,
who was always birdnesting — has managed to get himself
run over by a pair of Lord Ellangowan's wagon-horses, and
now Lady Ellangowan is keeping the whole family. An aunt
came from Salisbury to sit up with the boy, and was quite
angry because Lady Ellangowan did not pay her for nursing
him.'

'That's the worst of the poor,' said Mrs Tempest languidly,
the firelight playing upon her diamond rings, as she took her fan
from the velvet table and slowly unfolded it, to protect her
cheek from the glare, 'they are never satisfied.'

'Isn't it odd they are not,' cried Vixen, coming suddenly out
of a deep reverie, 'when they have everything that can make
life delightful?'

'I don't know about everything, Violet; but really, when they
have such nice cottages as your papa built for them, so well-
drained and ventilated, they ought to be more contented.'

'What a comfort good drainage and ventilation must be,
when there is no bread in the larder!' said Violet.

'My dear, it is ridiculous to talk in that way; just in the style
of horrid Radical newspapers. I am sure the poor have an
immense deal done for them. Look at Mr Scobel, is he not
always trying to help them?'

'I do what I can,' said the clergyman modestly; 'but I only
wish it were more. An income of sixteen shillings a week for a
family of seven requires a good deal of ekeing out. If it were
not for the assistance I get here, and in one or two other
directions, things would be very bad in Beechdale.'

Beechdale was the name of the village nearest the Abbey
House, the village to which belonged Mr Scobel's toy-church.

'Of course, we must have the usual distribution of blankets and wearing apparel on Christmas-eve,' said Mrs Tempest. 'It will seem very sad without my dear husband. But we came home before Christmas on purpose.'

'How good of you! It was very sad last year when the poor people came up to the Hall to receive your gifts, and there were no familiar faces except the servants'. There were a good many tears shed over last year's blankets, I assure you.'

'Poor dear things!' sighed Mrs Tempest, not making it too clear whether she meant the blankets or the recipients thereof.

Violet said nothing after her little ironical protest about the poor. She sat opposite the fire, between her mother and Mr Scobel, but at some distance from both. The ruddy light glowed on her ruddy hair, and lit up her pale cheeks, and shone in her brilliant eyes. The incumbent of Beechdale thought he had never seen anything so lovely. She was like a painted window; a Madonna, with the glowing colour of Rubens, the devine grace of Raffaelle. And those little speeches about the poor had warmed his heart. He was Violet's friend and champion from that moment.

Mrs Tempest fanned herself listlessly.

'I wish Forbes would bring the tea,' she said.

'Shall I ring, mamma?'

'No, dear. They have not finished tea in the housekeeper's room, perhaps. Forbes doesn't like to be disturbed. Is there any news, Mr Scobel? We only came home yesterday evening, and have seen no one.'

'News! Well, no, I think not much. Lady Ellangowan has got a new orchid.'

'And there has been a new baby, too, hasn't there?'

'O yes. But nobody talks about the baby, and everybody is in raptures with the orchid.'

'What is it like?'

'Rather a fine boy. I christened him last week.'

'I mean the orchid.'

'O, something really magnificent; a butterfly-shaped blossom that positively looks as if it were alive. They say Lord Ellangowan gave five hundred guineas for it. People come from the other side of the county to see it.'

'I think you are all orchid mad,' exclaimed Mrs Tempest. 'O, here comes the tea!' as Forbes entered with the cups and saucers. 'You'll take some, of course, Mr Scobel. I cannot understand this rage for orchids – old china, or silver, or lace, I can understand, but orchids – things that require no end of trouble to keep them alive, and which I daresay are as common as buttercups and daisies in the savage places where they grow. There is Lady Jane Vawdrey now, a perfect slave to her orchid-houses.'

Violet's pale face flamed crimson at this mention of Lady Jane. Not for worlds would she have asked a question about her old playfellow, though she was dying to hear about him. Happily no one saw that sudden blush, or it passed for a reflection of the fire-glow.

'Poor Lady Jane!' sighed the incumbent of Beechdale, looking very solemn, 'she has gone to a land in which there are fairer flowers than ever grew on the banks of the Amazon.'

'What do you mean?'

'Surely you have heard——'

'Nothing,' exclaimed Mrs Tempest. 'I have corresponded with nobody but my housekeeper while I have been away. I am a wretched correspondent at the best of times, and, after dear Edward's death, I was too weary, too depressed to write letters. What is the matter with Lady Jane Vawdrey?'

'She died at Florence early in November of bronchitis. She was very ill last winter, and had to be taken to Cannes; but she came back in May quite well and strong, as everyone supposed, and spent the summer at Briarwood. Her doctors told her, however, that she was not to risk another winter in England; so in September she went to Italy, taking Lady Mabel with her.'

'And Roderick?' inquired Vixen. 'He went with them of course.'

'Naturally,' replied Mr Scobel. 'Mr Vawdrey was with his mother till the last.'

'Very nice of him,' murmured Mrs Tempest approvingly; 'for, in a general way, I don't think they got on too well together. Lady Jane was rather dictatorial. And now, I suppose, Roderick will marry his cousin as soon as he is out of mourning.'

'Why should you suppose so, mamma?' exclaimed Violet. 'It was quite a mistake of yours about their being engaged. Roderick told me so himself. He was not engaged to Lady Mabel. He had not the least idea of marrying her.'

'He has altered his mind since then, I conclude,' said Mr Scobel cheerily – those binoculars of his could never have seen through a stone-wall, and were not much good at seeing things under his nose – 'for it is quite a settled thing that Mr Vawdrey and Lady Mabel are to be married. It will be a splendid match for him, and will make him the largest landowner in the Forest, for Ashbourne is settled on Lady Mabel. The Duke bought it himself, you know, and it is not in the entail,' added the incumbent, explaining a fact that was as familiar as the church catechism to Violet, who sat looking straight at the fire, holding her head as high as Queen Guinevere after she had thrown the diamonds out of the window.

'I always knew that it would be so,' said Mrs Tempest, with the air of a sage. 'Lady Jane had set her heart upon it. Worldly greatness was her idol, poor thing! It is sad to think of her being snatched away from everything. What has become of the orchids?'

'Lady Jane left them to her niece. They are building houses to receive them at Ashbourne.'

'Rather a waste of money, isn't it?' suggested Violet, in a cold hard voice. 'Why not let them stay at Briarwood till Lady Mabel is mistress there?'

Mr Scobel did not enter into this discussion. He sat serenely blinking at the fire, and sipping his tea, enjoying this hour of rest and warmth after a long day's fatigue and hard weather. He had an Advent service at seven o'clock that evening, and would but just have time to tramp home through the winter dark and take a hurried meal before he ran across to his neat little vestry and shuffled on his surplice, while Mrs Scobel played her plaintive voluntary on the twenty-guinea harmonium.

'And where is young Vawdrey now?' inquired Mrs Tempest blandly.

She could only think of the Squire of Briarwood as the lad from Eton – clump, shy, given to breaking teacups, and leaving the track of his footsteps in clay or mud upon the Aubusson carpets.

'He has not come home yet. The Duke and Duchess went to Florence just before Lady Jane's death, and I believe Mr Vawdrey is with them in Rome. Briarwood has been shut up since September.'

'Didn't I tell you, mamma, that somebody would be dead?' cried Violet. 'I felt when we came into this house yesterday evening that everything in our lives was changed.'

'I should hardly think mourning can be very becoming to Lady Mabel,' ruminated Mrs Tempest. 'Those small sylph-like figures rarely look well in black.'

Mr Scobel rose with an effort to make his adieux. The delicious warmth of the wood-fire, the perfume of arbutus logs, had made him sleepy.

'You'll come and see our new school, I hope,' he said to Violet, as they shook hands. 'You and your dear mamma have contributed so largely to its erection that you have a right to be critical; but I really think you will be pleased.'

'We'll come to-morrow afternoon, if it's fine,' said Mrs Tempest graciously. 'You must bring Mrs Scobel to dinner at seven, and then we can talk over all we have seen.'

'You are very kind. I've my young women's scripture-class at a quarter-past eight; but if you will let me run away for an hour——'

'Certainly.'

'I can come back for Mrs Scobel. Thanks. We shall be delighted.'

When he was gone, Violet walked towards the door without a word to her mother.

'Violet, are you going away again? Pray stop, child, and let us have a chat.'

'I have nothing to talk about, mamma.'

'Nonsense. You have quite deserted me since we came home. And do you suppose I don't feel dull and depressed as well as you? It is not dutiful conduct, Violet. I shall really have to engage a companion if you go on so. Miss McCroke was dreary, but she was not altogether uncompanionable. One could talk to her.'

'You had better have a companion, mamma. Someone who will be lively, and talk pleasantly about nothing particular all day long. No doubt a well-trained companion can do that. She has an inexhaustible well-spring of twaddle, in her own mind. I feel as if I could never be cheerful again.'

'We had better have stopped at Brighton——'

'I hate Brighton!'

'Where we knew so many nice people——'

'I detest nice people!'

'Violet, do you know that you have an abominable temper?'

'I know that I am made up of wickedness!' answered Vixen vehemently.

She left the room without another word, and went straight to her den upstairs, not to throw herself on the ground, and abandon herself to a childish unreasoning grief, as she had done on the night of Roderick's coming of age, but to face the situation boldly. She walked up and down the dim fire-lit room, thinking of what she had just heard.

'What does it matter to me?' Why should I be so angry?' she asked herself. 'We were never more than friends and playfellows. And I think that, on the whole, I rather disliked him. I know I was seldom civil to him. He was papa's favourite. I should hardly have tolerated him but for that.'

She felt relieved at having settled this point in her mind. Yet there was a dull blank sense of loss, a vague aching in her troubled heart, which she could not get rid of easily. She walked to and fro, to and fro, while the fire faded out and the pale windows darkened.

'I hate myself for being so vexed about this,' she said, clasping her hands above her head with a vehemence that showed the intensity of her vexation. 'Could I – I – Violet Tempest – ever be so despicable a creature as to care for a man who does not care for me; to be angry, sorry, broken-hearted, because a man does not want me for his wife? Such a thing is not possible; if it were, I think I would kill myself. I should be ashamed to live. I could not look human beings in the face. I should take poison, or turn Roman Catholic and go into a convent, where I should never see the face of a man again. No; I am not such an odious creature. I have no regard for Rorie, except as my old playfellow, and when he comes home I will walk straight up to him and give him my hand, and congratulate him heartily on his approaching marriage. Perhaps Lady Mabel will ask me to be one of her bridesmaids. She will have a round dozen, I daresay. Six in pink and six in blue, no doubt, like wax dolls at a charity fair. Why can't people be married without making idiots of themselves?'

The half-hour gong sounded at his moment, and Vixen ran down to the drawing-room, where the candles and lamps were lighted, and where there was plenty of light literature lying about to distract the troubled mind. Violet went to her mother's chair and knelt beside it.

'Dear mamma, forgive me for being cross just now,' she said gently; 'I was out of spirits. I will try to be better company in future; so that you may not be obliged to engage a companion.'

'My dear, I don't wonder at your feeling low-spirited,' replied Mrs Tempest graciously. 'This place is horribly dull. How we ever endured it, even in your dear papa's time, is more than I can understand. It is like living on the ground floor of one of the Egyptian pyramids. We must really get some nice people about us, or we shall both go melancholy mad.'

CHAPTER 13

'HE BELONGS TO THE TAME-CAT SPECIES'

Life went on smoothly enough at the Abbey House after that evening. Violet tried to make herself happy among the surroundings of her childhood, petted the horses, drove her basket-carriage with the favourite old pony, went among the villagers, rode her thoroughbred bay for long wild explorations of the Forest and neighbouring country, looked with longing eyes, sometimes, at the merry groups riding to the meet, and went her lonely way with a heavy heart. No more hunting for her. She could not hunt alone, and she had declined all friendly offers of escort. It would have seemed a treason against her beloved dead to ride across country by anyone else's side.

Everyone had called at the Abbey House and welcomed Mrs Tempest and her daughter back to Hampshire. They had been asked to five o'clock tea at Ellangowan Park, to see the marvellous orchid. They had been invited to half-a-dozen dinner-parties.

Violet tried her utmost to persuade her mother that it was much too soon after her father's death to think of visiting.

'My dear Violet,' cried the widow, 'after going to that ball at Brighton, we could not possibly decline invitations here. It would be an insult to our friends. If we had not gone to the ball——'

'We ought not to have gone,' exclaimed Vixen.

'My love, you should have said so at the time.'

'Mamma, you know I was strongly against it.'

Mrs Tempest shrugged her shoulders as who should say: 'This is too much!'

'I know your dress cost a fortune, and that you danced every waltz, Violet,' she answered, 'that is about all I do know.'

'Very well, mamma, let us accept all the invitations. Let us be merry as grigs. Perhaps it will make papa more comfortable in Paradise to know how happy we are without him. He won't be troubled by any uneasy thoughts about our grief, at all events,' added Vixen, with a stifled sob.

'How irreverently you talk. Mr Scobel would be dreadfully shocked to hear you,' said Mrs Tempest.

The invitations were all accepted, and Mrs Tempest for the rest of the winter was in a flutter about her dresses. She was very particular as to the exact shade of silver-gray or lavender which might be allowed to relieve the sombre mass of black; and would spend a whole morning in discussing the propriety of a knot of scarlet ribbon, or a border of gold passementerie.

They went to Ellangowan Park and did homage to the wonderful orchid, and discussed Roderick's engagement to the Duke's only daughter. Everybody said that it was Lady Jane's doing, and there were some who almost implied that she had died on purpose to bring about the happy conjuncture. Violet was able to talk quite pleasantly about the marriage, and to agree with everybody's praises of Lady Mabel's beauty, elegance, good style, and general perfection.

Christmas and the New Year went by, not altogether sadly. It is not easy for youth to be full of sorrow. The clouds come and go, there are always glimpses of sunshine. Violet was grateful for the kindness that greeted her everywhere among her old friends, and perhaps a little glad of the evident admiration accorded to her beauty in all circles. Life was just tolerable, after all. She thought of Roderick Vawdrey as of something belonging to the past; something which had no part, never would have any part, in her future life. He too was dead and passed away, like her father. Lady Mabel's husband, the master of Briarwood *in esse*, and of Ashbourne *in posse*, was quite a different being from the rough lad with whom she had played at battledore and shuttlecock, billiards, croquet, and rounders.

Early in February Mrs Tempest informed her daughter that she was going to give a dinner.

'It will seem very dreadful without dearest Edward,' she said; 'but of course having accepted hospitalities, we are bound to return them.'

'Do you really think we ought to burst out into dinner-parties so soon, mamma?'

'Yes, dear, as we accepted the dinners. If we had not gone it would have been different.'

'Ah,' sighed Vixen, 'I suppose it all began with that ball at Brighton, like "Man's first disobedience, and the fruit——"'

'I shall miss poor McCroke to fill in the invitation cards.'

'Let me do it, mamma. I can write a decent hand. That is one of the few ladylike accomplishments I have been able to master; and even that is open to objection as being too masculine.'

'If you would slope more, Violet, and make your up-strokes finer, and not cross your T's so undeviatingly,' Mrs Tempest murmured amiably. 'A lady's T ought to be less pronounced. There is something too assertive in your consonants.'

Violet wrote the cards. The dinner was to be quite a grand affair, three weeks' notice, and a French cook from The Dolphin in Southampton to take the conduct of affairs in the

kitchen; whereby the Abbey House cook declared afterwards
that there was nothing that Frenchman did which she could not
have done quite as well, and that his wastefulness was enough to
make a Christian woman's hair stand on end.

Three days before the dinner, Vixen, riding Arion home
through the shrubbery, after a long morning in the Forest, was
startled by the vision of a dog-cart a few yards in front of her, a cart
which, at the first glance, she concluded must belong to Roderick
Vawdrey. The wheels were red, the horse had a rakish air, the light
vehicle swung from side to side as it spun round the curve.

No; that slim figure, that neat waist, that military air did not
belong to Roderick Vawdrey.

'He here!' ejaculated Vixen inwardly, with infinite disgust. 'I
thought we had seen the last of him.'

She had been out for two hours and a half, and felt that Arion
had done quite enough, or she would have turned her horse's
head and gone back to the Forest, in order to avoid the
unwelcome visitor.

'I only hope mamma won't encourage him to come here,'
she thought; 'but I'm afraid that smooth tongue of his has too
much influence over her. And I haven't even poor Crokey to
stand by me. I shall feel like a bird transfixed by the wicked
green eyes of a velvet-pawed murdering cat.'

'And I have not a friend in the world,' she thought. 'Plenty
of pleasant acquaintance, ready to simper at me and pay me
compliments, because I am Miss Tempest of the Abbey House,
but not one honest friend to stand by me, and turn that man
out of doors. How dare he come here? I thought I spoke
plainly enough that night at Brighton.'

She rode slowly up to the house, slipped lightly out of her
saddle, and led her horse round to the stables, just as she had led
the pony in her happy childish days. The bright thoroughbred
bay was as fond of her as if he had been a dog, and as tame. She
stood by his manger caressing him while he ate his corn, and
feeling very safe from Captain Winstanley's society in the warm
clover-scented stable.

She dawdled away half-an-hour in this manner, before she
went back to the house, and ran up to her dressing-room.

'If mamma sends for me now, I sha'n't be able to go down,' she thought. 'He can hardly stay more than an hour. O, horror! he is a tea-drinker; mamma will persuade him to stop till five o'clock.'

Violet dawdled over her change of dress as she had dawdled in the stable. She had never been more particular about her hair.

'I'll have it all taken down, Phoebe,' she told her Abigail; 'I'm in no hurry.'

'But really miss, it's beautiful——'

'Nonsense, after a windy ride; don't be lazy, Phoebe. You may give my hair a good brushing while I read.'

A tap at the door came at this moment, and Phoebe ran to open it.

'Mrs Tempest wishes Miss Tempest to come down to the drawing-room directly,' said a voice in the corridor.

'There now, miss,' cried Phoebe, 'how lucky I didn't take your hair down. It never was nicer.'

Violet put on her black dress, costly and simple as the attire Polonius recommended to his son. Mrs Tempest might relieve her costume with what bright or delicate hues she liked. Violet had worn nothing but black since her father's death. Her sole ornaments were a pair of black earrings, and a large black enamel locket, with one big diamond shining in the middle of it, like an eye. This locket held the Squire's portrait, and his daughter wore it constantly.

The Louis Quatorze clock on the staircase struck five as Violet went down.

'Of course he is staying for tea,' she thought, with an impatient shrug of her shoulders. 'He belongs to the tame-cat species, and has an inexhaustible flow of gossip, spiced with mild malevolence. The kind of frivolous ill-nature which says: "I would not do anyone harm for the world, but one may as well think the worst of everybody."'

Yes, kettledrum was in full swing. Mrs Scobel had come over from her tiny vicarage for half-an-hour's chat, and was sitting opposite her hostess's fire, while Captain Winstanley lounged with his back to the canopied chimney-piece, and looked benignantly down upon the two ladies. The Queen Anne kettle was hissing merrily over its spirit-lamp, the perfume of the pekoe was delicious, the logs blazed cheerily in the low fireplace, with its shining brass andirons. Not a repulsive picture, assuredly; yet Vixen came slowly towards this charmed circle, looking black as thunder.

Captain Winstanley hurried forward to receive her.

'How do you do?' she said, as stiffly as a child brought down to the drawing-room, bristling in newly-brushed hair and a best frock, and then turning to her mother, she asked curtly: 'What did you want with me, mamma?'

'It was Captain Winstanley who asked to see you, my dear. Won't you have some tea?'

'Thanks, no,' said Vixen, seating herself in a corner between Mrs Scobel and the mantelpiece, and beginning to talk about the schools.

Conrad Winstanley gave her a curious look from under his dark brows, and then went on talking to her mother. He seemed hardly disconcerted by her rudeness.

'Yes, I assure you, if it hadn't been for the harriers, Brighton would have been unbearable after you left,' he said. 'I ran across to Paris directly the frost set in. But I don't wonder you were anxious to come back to such a lovely old place as this.'

'I felt it a duty to come back,' said Mrs Tempest, with a pious air. 'But it was very sad at first. I never felt so unhappy in my life. I am getting more reconciled now. Time softens all griefs.'

'Yes,' said the Captain, in a louder tone than before, 'Time is a clever horse. There is nothing he won't beat if you know how to ride him.'

'You'll take some tea?' insinuated Mrs Tempest, her attention absorbed by the silver kettle, which was just now conducting itself as spit-fireishly as any blackened block-tin on a kitchen hob.

'I can never resist it. And perhaps after tea you will be so good as to give me the treat you talked about just now.'

'To show you the house,' said Mrs Tempest. 'Do you think we shall have light enough?'

'Abundance. An old house like this is seen at its best in the twilight. Don't you think so, Mrs Scobel?'

'O, yes,' exclaimed Mrs Scobel, with a lively recollection of her album. '"They who would see Melrose aright should see it" – I think, by-the-bye, Sir Walter Scott says, "by moonlight."'

'Yes, for an ancient Gothic abbey; but twilight is better for a Tudor manor house. Are you sure it will not fatigue you?' inquired the Captain, with an air of solicitude, as Mrs Tempest rose languidly.

'No; I shall be very pleased to show you the dear old place. It is full of sad associations, of course, but I do not allow my mind to dwell upon them more than I can help.'

'No,' cried Vixen bitterly. 'We go to dinner-parties, and kettledrums, and go into raptures about orchids and old china and try to cure our broken hearts that way.'

'Are you coming, Violet?' asked her mother sweetly.

'No, thanks, mamma. I am tired after my ride. Mrs Scobel will help you to play cicerone?'

Captain Winstanley left the room without so much as a look at Violet Tempest. Yet her rude reception had galled him more than any cross that fate had lately inflicted upon him. He had fancied that time would have softened her feelings towards him, that rural seclusion and the society of rustic nobodies would have made him appear at an advantage, that she would have welcomed the brightness and culture of metropolitan life in his person. He had hoped a great deal from the lapse of time since their last meeting. But this sullen reception, this silent expression of dislike, told him that Violet Tempest's aversion was a plant of deep root.

'The first woman who ever disliked me,' he thought. 'No wonder that she interests me more than other women. She is like that chestnut mare that threw me six times before I got the better of her. Yet she proved the best horse I ever had, and I rode her till she hadn't a leg to stand upon, and then sold her for twice the money she cost me. There are two conquests a man can make over a woman, one to make her love him, the other——'

'That suit of chain-armour was worn by Sir Gilbert Tempest at Acre,' said the widow. 'The plate-armour belonged to Sir Percy, who was killed at Barnet. Each of them was knighted before he was five-and-twenty years old, for prowess in the field. The portrait over the chimney-piece is the celebrated Judge Tempest, who was famous for – Well, he did something wonderful, I know. Perhaps Mrs Scobel remembers,' concluded Mrs Tempest feebly.

'It was at the trial of the seven bishops,' suggested the Vicar's wife.

'In the time of Queen Elizabeth,' assented Mrs Tempest. 'That one with the lace cravat and steel breastplate was an admiral in Charles the Second's reign, and was made a baronet for his valiant behaviour when the Dutch fleet were at Chatham. The baronetcy died with his son, who left only daughters. The eldest married a Mr Percival, who took the name of Tempest, and sat for the borough of – perhaps Mrs Scobel knows. I have such a bad memory for these things; though I have heard my dear husband talk about them often.'

Captain Winstanley looked round the great oak-panelled hall dreamily, and heard very little of Mrs Tempest's vague prattling about her husband's ancestors.

What a lovely old place, he was thinking. A house that would give a man importance in the land, supported, as it was, by an estate bringing in something between five and six thousand a year. How much military distinction, how many battles must a soldier win before he could make himself master of such a fortune?

'And it needed but for that girl to like me, and a little gold ring would have given me the freehold of it all,' thought Conrad Winstanley bitterly.

How many penniless girls, or girls with fortunes so far beneath the measure of a fine gentleman's needs as to be useless, had been over head and ears in love with the elegant Captain; how many pretty girls had tempted him by their beauty and winsomeness to be false to his grand principle that marriage meant promotion. And here was an obstinate minx who could have realised all his aims, and whom he felt himself able to love to distraction into the bargain; and, behold, some adverse devil had entered into her mind, and made Conrad Winstanley hateful to her.

'It's like witchcraft,' he said to himself. 'Why should this one woman be different from all other women? Perhaps it's the colour. That ruddy auburn hair, the loveliest I ever saw, means temper. But I conquered the chestnut, and I'll conquer Miss Tempest – or make her smart for it.'

'A handsome music-gallery, is it not?' said the widow. 'The carved balustrade is generally admired.'

Then they went into the dining-room, and looked cursorily at about a dozen large dingy pictures of the Italian school, which a man who knew anything about art would have condemned at a glance. Fine examples of brown varnish, all of them. Thence to the library, with its carved-oak dwarf bookcases, containing books which nobody had opened for a generation – Livy, Gibbon, Hume, Burke, Smollett, Plutarch, Thompson. These sages, clad in shiny brown leather and gilding, made as good a lining for the walls as anything else, and gave an air of snugness to the room in which the family dined when there was no company.

They came presently to the Squire's den, at the end of a corridor.

'That was my dear husband's study,' sighed Mrs Tempest. 'It looks south, into the rose garden, and is one of the prettiest rooms in the house. But we keep it locked, and I think Violet has the key.'

'Pray don't let Miss Tempest be disturbed,' said Captain Winstanley. 'I have seen quite enough to know what a delightful house you have – all the interest of days that are gone, all the luxuries of to-day. I think that blending of past and present is most fascinating. I should never be a severe restorer of antiquity, or refuse to sit in a chair that wasn't undeniably Gothic.'

'Ah,' sighed the Vicar's wife, who was an advanced disciple in the school of Eastlake, 'but don't you think that everything should be in harmony? If I were as rich as Mrs Tempest, I wouldn't have so much as a teapot that was not strictly Tudor.'

'Then I'm afraid you'd have to go without a teapot, and drink your tea out of a tankard,' retorted Captain Winstanley.

'At any rate, I would be as Tudor as I could be.'

'And not have a brass bedstead, a spring mattress, a moderator lamp, or a coal-scuttle in your house,' said the Captain. 'My dear madam, it is all very well to be mediaeval in matters ecclesiastic, but home comforts must not be sacrificed to the pursuit of the aesthetic, or a modern luxury discarded because it looks like an anachronism.'

Mrs Scobel was delighted with Captain Winstanley. He was just the kind of man to succeed in a rustic community. His quiet self-assurance set other people at their ease. He carried with him an air of life and movement, as if he were the patentee of a new pleasure.

'My husband would be so pleased to see you at the vicarage, if you are staying any time in the neighbourhood,' she said.

But after the little gush of friendliness, she reflected that there could not be much sympathy between the man of society and her Anglican parson; and that it was she, and not Ignatius Scobel, who would be glad to see Captain Winstanley at the vicarage.

'I shall be charmed,' he replied. 'I never was so delighted with any place as your Forest. It is a new world to me. I hate myself for having lived in England so long without knowing this beautiful corner of the land. I am staying with my old chief, Colonel Pryke, at Warham Court, and I am only here for a few days.'

'But you are coming to my dinner-party?' said Mrs Tempest.

'That is a pleasure I cannot deny myself.'

'And you will come and see our church and schools?' said Mrs Scobel.

'I shall be more than pleased. I passed your pretty little church, I think, on my way here. There was a tin tea-ket – a bell ringing——'

'For vespers,' exclaimed Mrs Scobel.

The exploration of the house took a long time, conducted in this somewhat desultory and dawdling manner; but the closing in of night and the sound of the dinner-gong gave the signal for Captain Winstanley's departure.

Mrs Tempest would have liked to ask him to dinner; but she had an idea that Violet might make herself objectionable, and refrained from this exercise of hospitality. He was coming to the great dinner. He would see her dress with the feather trimming, which was really prettier than Worth's masterpiece, or, at any rate, newer; though it only came from Madame Theodore, of Bruton Street. Sustained by this comforting reflection, she parted with him quite cheerfully.

CHAPTER 14

'HE WAS WORTHY TO BE LOVED A LIFETIME'

Conrad Winstanley had come to the New Forest with his mind resolved upon one of two things. He meant to marry Violet Tempest or her mother. If the case was quite hopeless with the daughter, he would content himself with winning the lesser prize; and though Vanity whispered that there was no woman living he might not win for himself if he chose to be sufficiently patient and persevering, instinct told him that Violet frankly detested him.

'After all,' argued Worldly Wisdom, 'the alternative is not to be despised. The widow is somewhat rococo; an old-fashioned jewel kept in cotton-wool, and brought out on occasions, to shine with a factitious brilliancy, like old Dutch garnets backed with tinfoil; but she is still pretty. She is ductile, amiable, and weak to a degree that promises a husband the sovereign dominion. Why break your heart for this fair devil of a daughter, who looks capable, if offended, of anything in the way of revenge, from a horsewhip to slow poison? Are a pair of brown eyes and coronal of red gold hair worth all this wasted passion?'

'But the daughter is the greater catch,' urged Ambition. 'The dowager's jointure is well enough, and she had the Abbey House and gardens for her life, but Violet will be sole mistress of the estate when she comes of age. As Violet's husband, your position would be infinitely better than it could be as her stepfather. Unhappily, the cantankerous minx has taken it into her head to dislike you.'

'Stay,' interjected the bland voice of Vanity, 'may not this dislike be only an assumption, a mask for some deeper feeling? There are girls who show their love in that way. Do not be in a hurry to commit yourself to the mother until you have made yourself quite sure about the daughter.'

Mrs Tempest's dinner-party was a success. It introduced Captain Winstanley to all that was best in the surrounding society; for although in Switzerland he had seemed very familiar with the best people in the Forest, in Hampshire he appeared almost a stranger to them. It was generally admitted, however, that the Captain was an acquisition, and a person to be cultivated. He sang a French comic song almost as well as Monsieur de Roseau, recited a short Yankee poem, which none of his audience had ever heard before, with telling force. He was at home upon every subject, from orchids to steam-ploughs, from ordnance to light literature. A man who sang so well, talked so well, looked so well, and behaved so well, could not be otherwise than welcome in county society. Before the evening was over, Captain Winstanley had been offered three hunters for the next day's run, and had been asked to write his name in four birthday-books.

Violet did not honour him with so much as a look, after her one cold recognition of his first appearance in the drawing-room. It was a party of more than twenty people, and she was able to keep out of his way without obvious avoidance of him. He was stung, but had no right to be offended.

He took Mrs Scobel in to dinner, and Mrs Scobel played the accompaniment of his song, being a clever little woman, able to turn her hand to anything. He would have preferred to be told off to some more important matron, but was not sorry to be taken under Mrs Scobel's wing. She could give him the *carte du pays*, and would be useful to him, no doubt, in the future; a social Iris, to fetch and carry for him between Beechdale and the Abbey House.

'Do you know that I am quite in love with your Forest?' he said to Mrs Tempest, standing in front of the ottoman where that lady sat with two of her particular friends; 'so much so, that I am actually in treaty for Captain Hawbuck's cottage, and mean to stay here till the end of the hunting.'

Everybody knew Captain Hawbuck's cottage, a verandahed box of a house, on the slope of the hill above Beechdale.

'I'm afraid you'll find the drawing-room chimney smokes,' said a matter-of-fact lady in sea-green; 'poor Mrs Hawbuck was a martyr to that chimney.'

'What does a bachelor want with a drawing-room? If there is one sitting-room in which I can burn a good fire, I shall be satisfied. The stable is in very fair order.'

'The Hawbucks kept a pony-carriage,' assented the sea-green lady.

'If Mrs Hawbuck accepts my offer, I shall send for my horses next week,' said the Captain.

Mrs Tempest blushed. Her life had flowed in so gentle and placid a current, that the freshness of her soul had not worn off, and at nine-and-thirty she was able to blush. There was something so significant in Captain Winstanley's desire to establish himself at Beechdale, that she could not help feeling flattered by the fact. It might be on Violet's account, of course, that he came; yet Violet and he had never got on very well together.

'Poor fellow!' she thought blandly, 'if he for a moment supposes that anything would tempt me to marry again, he is egregiously mistaken.'

And then she looked round the lovely old room, brightened by a crowd of well-dressed people, and thought that next to being Edward Tempest's wife, the best thing in life was to be Edward Tempest's widow.

'Dear Edward!' she mused, 'how strange that we should miss him so little to-night.'

It had been with everyone as if the Squire had never lived. Politeness exacted this ignoring of the past, no doubt; but the thing had been so easily done. The noble presence, the jovial laugh, the friendly smile were gone, and no one seemed conscious of the void – no one but Violet, who looked round the room once when conversation was liveliest, with a pale indignant face, resenting this forgetfulness.

'I wish papa's ghost would come in at that door and scare his hollow-hearted friends,' she said to herself; and she felt as if it would hardly have been a surprise to her to see the door open slowly and that familiar figure appear.

'Well, Violet,' Mrs Tempest said sweetly, when the guests were gone, 'how do you think it all went off?'

'It,' of course, meant the dinner-party.

'I suppose, according to the nature of such things, it was all right and proper,' Vixen answered coldly; 'but I should think it must have been intensely painful to you, mamma.'

Mrs Tempest sighed. She had always a large selection of sighs in stock, suitable to every occasion.

'I should have felt it much worse if I had sat in my old place at dinner,' she said; 'but sitting at the middle of the table instead of at the end made things less painful. And I really think it's better style. How did you like the new arrangement of the glasses?'

'I didn't notice anything new.'

'My dear Violet, you are frightfully unobservant.'

'No, I am not,' answered Vixen quickly. 'My eyes are keen enough, believe me.'

Mrs Tempest felt uncomfortable. She began to think that, after all, it might be a comfortable thing to have a companion – as a fender between herself and Violet. A perpetually present Miss Jones or Smith would ward off these unpleasantnesses.

There are occasions, however, on which a position must be faced boldly – in proverbial phrase, the bull must be taken by the horns. And here, Mrs Tempest felt, was a bull which must be so encountered. She knew that her poor little hands were too feeble for the office; but she told herself that she must make the heroic attempt.

'Violet, why have you such a rooted dislike to Captain Winstanley?'

'Why is my hair the colour it is, mamma, or why are my eyes brown instead of blue? If you could answer my question, I might be able to answer yours. Nature made me what I am, and nature has implanted a hatred of Captain Winstanley in my mind.'

'Do you not think it wrong to hate anyone — the very word hate was considered unladylike when I was a girl — without cause?'

'I have cause to hate him, good cause, sufficient cause. I hate all self-seekers and adventurers.'

'You have no right to call him one or the other.'

'Have I not? What brings him here, but the pursuit of his own interest? Why does he plant himself at our door as if he were come to besiege a town? Do you mean to say, mamma, that you can be so blind as not to see what he wants?'

'He has come for the hunting.'

'Yes, but not to hunt our foxes or our stags. He wants a rich wife, mamma. And he thinks that you or I will be foolish enough to marry him.'

'There would be nothing unnatural in his entertaining some idea of that kind about you,' replied Mrs Tempest, with a sudden assertion of matronly dignity. 'But for him to think of me in that light would be too absurd. I must be some years, perhaps four or five years, his senior, to begin with.'

'O, he would forgive you that: he would not mind that.'

'And he ought to know that I should never dream of marrying again.'

'He ought, if he had any idea of what is right and noble in a woman,' answered Vixen. 'But he has not. He has no ideas that do not begin and end in himself and his own advantage. He sees you here with a handsome house, a good income, and he thinks that he can persuade you to marry him.'

'Violet, you must know that I shall never marry.'

'I hope I do know it. But the world ought to know it too. People ought not to be allowed to whisper, and smile, and look significant; as I saw some of your friends do to-night when Captain Winstanley was hanging over your chair. You ought not to encourage him, mamma. It is a treason against my father to have that man here.'

Here was a bull that required prompt and severe handling, but Mrs Tempest felt her powers inadequate to the effort.

'I am surprised at you, Violet!' she exclaimed; 'as if I did not know, as well as you, what is due to my poor Edward; as if I should do anything to compromise my own dignity. Is it to encourage a man to ask him to a dinner-party, when he happens to be visiting in the neighbourhood? Can I forbid Captain Winstanley to take the Hawbucks' cottage?'

'No, you have gone too far already. You gave him too much encouragement in Switzerland, and at Brighton. He has attached himself to us like a limpet to a rock. You will not easily get rid of him; unless you let him see that you understand and despise him.'

'I see nothing despicable in him, and I am not going to insult him at your bidding,' answered the widow, tremulous with anger. 'I do not believe him to be a schemer or an adventurer. He is a gentleman by birth, education, profession. It is a supreme insolence on your part to speak of him as you do. What can you know of the world? How can you judge and measure a man like Captain Winstanley? A girl like you, hardly out of the nursery! It is too absurd. And understand at once and for ever, Violet, that I will not be hectored or lectured in this manner, that I will not be dictated to, or taught what is good taste, in my own house. This is to be my own house, you know, as long as I live.'

'Yes; unless you give it a new master,' said Violet gravely. 'Forgive me if I have been too vehement, mamma. It is my love that is bold. Whom have I in this world to love now, except you? And when I see you in danger – when I see the softness of your nature – Dear mother, there are some instincts that are stronger than reason. There are some antipathies which are implanted in us for warnings. Remember what a happy life you led with my dear father – his goodness, his overflowing generosity, his noble heart. There is no man worthy to succeed him, to live in his house. Dear mother, for pity's sake——'

She was kneeling at her mother's feet, clinging to her hands, her voice half-choked with sobs. Mrs Tempest began to cry too.

'My dearest Violet, how can you be so foolish? My love, don't cry. I tell you that I shall never marry again – never. Not if I were asked to become a countess. My heart is true to your dear father; it always will be. I am almost sorry that I consented to these scarlet bows on my dress, but the feather trimming looked so heavy without them, and Theodore's eye for colour is perfect. My dear child, be assured I shall carry his image with me to my grave.'

'Dear mother, that is all I ask. Be as happy as you can; but be true to him. He was worthy to be loved for a lifetime; not to be put off with half a life, half a heart.'

CHAPTER 15

LADY SOUTHMINSTER'S BALL

Captain Winstanley closed with Mrs Hawbuck for the pretty little verandah-surrounded cottage on the slope of the hill above Beechdale. Captain Hawbuck, a retired naval man, to whom the place had been very dear, was in his grave, and his wife was anxious to try if she and her hungry children could not live on less money in Belgium than they could in England. The good old post-captain had improved and beautified the place from a farm-labourer's cottage into a habitation which was the quintessence of picturesque inconvenience. Ceilings which you could touch with your hand; funny little fireplaces in angles of the rooms; a corkscrew staircase, which a stranger ascended or descended at peril of life or limb; no kitchen worth mentioning, and stuffy little bedrooms under the thatch. Seen from the outside the cottage was charming; and if the captain and his family could only have lived over the way, and looked at it, they would have had full value for the money invested in its improvement. Small as the rooms were, however, and despite that dark slander which hung over the chimneys, Captain Winstanley declared that the cottage would suit him admirably.

'I like the situation,' he said, discussing his bargain in the coffee-room at The Crown, Lyndhurst.

'I should rather think you did!' cried Mr Bell, the local surgeon. 'Suits you down to the ground, doesn't it?'

Whereby it will be seen that there was already a certain
opinion in the neighbourhood as to the Captain's motive for
planting himself at Beechdale — so acute is a quiet little
community of this kind in divining the intentions of a stranger.

Captain Winstanley took up his quarters at Beechdale
Cottage in less than a week after Mrs Tempest's dinner-party.
He sent for his horses, and began the business of hunting in real
earnest. His two hunters were unanimously pronounced screws;
but it is astonishing how well a good rider can get across
country on a horse which other people call a screw. Nobody
could deny Captain Winstanley's merits as a horseman. His
costume and appointments had all the finish of Melton
Mowbray, and he was always in the first flight.

Before he had occupied Captain Hawbuck's cottage a month
the new-comer had made friends for himself in all directions.
He was as much at home in the Forest as if he had been native
and to the manner born. His straight riding, his good looks, and
agreeable manners won him everybody's approval. There was
nothing dissipated or Bohemian about him. His clothes never
smelt of stale tobacco. He was as punctual at church every
Sunday morning as if he had been a family man, bound to set a
good example. He subscribed liberally to the hounds, and was
always ready with those stray florins and half-crowns by which a
man purchases a cheap popularity among the horse-holding and
ragged-follower class.

Having distinctly asserted her intention of remaining a widow
to Violet, Mrs Tempest allowed herself the privilege of being
civil to Captain Winstanley. He dropped in at afternoon tea at
least twice a week; he dined at the Abbey House whenever the
Scobels or any other intimate friends were there 'in a quiet
way.' He generally escorted Mrs Tempest and her daughter
from church on a Sunday morning, Violet persistently loitering
twenty yards or so behind them on the narrow woodland path
that led from Beechdale to the Abbey House.

After walking home from church with Mrs Tempest, it was
only natural that the Captain should stop to luncheon, and after
luncheon — the Sabbath afternoon being, in a manner, a
legitimate occasion for dawdling — it was equally natural for him

to linger, looking at the gardens and greenhouses, or talking beside the drawing-room fire, till the appearance of the spitfire Queen Anne tea-kettle and Mrs Tempest's infusion of orange pekoe.

Sometimes the Scobels were present at these Sunday luncheons, sometimes not. Violet was with her mother, of course, on these occasions; but, while bodily present, she contrived to maintain an attitude of aloofness which would have driven a less resolute man than Conrad Winstanley to absent himself. A man more sensitive to the opinions of others could hardly have existed in such an atmosphere of dislike; but Captain Winstanley meant to live down Miss Tempest's aversion, or to give her double cause for hating him.

'Why have you given up hunting, Miss Tempest?' he asked one Sunday afternoon, when they had gone the round of the stables, and Arion had been fondled and admired – a horse as gentle as an Italian greyhound in his stable, as fiery as a wildcat out of it.

'Because I have no one I care to hunt with, now papa is gone.'

'But here in the Forest, where everybody knows you, where you might have as many fathers as the Daughter of the Regiment——'

'Yes, I have many kind friends. But there is not one who could fill my father's place – for an hour.'

'It is a pity,' said the Captain sympathetically. 'You were so fond of hunting, were you not?'

'Passionately.'

'Then it is a shame you should forego the pleasure. And you must find it very dull, I should think, riding alone in the Forest.'

'Alone! I have my horse.'

'Surely he does not count as a companion.'

'Indeed he does. I wish for no better company than Arion, now papa is gone.'

'Violet is so eccentric!' Mrs Tempest murmured gently.

Captain Winstanley had taken Mrs Hawbuck's cottage till the first of May. The end of April would see the last of the hunting, so this arrangement seemed natural enough. He hunted in good earnest. There was no pretence about him. It was only the extra knowing ones, the little knot of choice spirits at The Crown, who saw some deeper motive than a mere love of sport for his residence at Beechdale. These advanced minds had contrived to find out all about Captain Winstanley by this time – the date of his selling out, his ostensible and hidden reasons for leaving the army, the amount of his income, and the general complexion of his character. There was not much to be advanced against him. No dark stories; only a leading notion that he was a man who wanted to improve his fortunes, and would not be over-scrupulous as to the means. But as your over-scrupulous man is one in a thousand, this was ranking Captain Winstanley with the majority.

The winter was over; there were primroses peeping out of the moss and brambles, and a shy little dog-violet shining like a blue eye here and there. The flaunting daffodils were yellow in every glade, and the gummy chestnut buds were beginning to swell. It was mid-March, and as yet there had been no announcement of home-coming from Roderick Vawdrey or the Dovedales. The Duke was said to have taken a fancy to the Roman style of fox-hunting; Lady Mabel was studying art; the Duchess was suspected of a leaning to Romanism; and Roderick was dancing attendance upon the family generally.

'Why should he not stay there with them?' said Mr Scobel, sipping his pekoe in a comfortable little circle of gossipers round Mrs Tempest's gipsy table. 'He has very little else to do with his life. He is a young man utterly without views or purpose. He is one of our many Gallios. You could not rouse him to an interest in those stirring questions that are agitating the Catholic Church to her very foundation. He has no mission. I have sounded him, and found him full of a shallow good-nature. He would build a church if people asked him, and hardly know, when it was finished, whether he meant it for Jews or Gentiles.'

Vixen sat in her corner and said nothing. It amused her rather – with a half-bitter sense of amusement – to hear them talk about Roderick. He had quite gone out of her life. It interested her to know what people thought of him in his new world.

'If the Duke doesn't bring them all home very soon the Duchess will go over to Rome,' said Mrs Scobel, with conviction. 'She had been drifting that way ever so long. Ignatius isn't high enough for her.'

The Reverend Ignatius sighed. He hardly saw his way to ascending any higher. He had already, acting always in perfect good faith and conscientious desire for the right, made his pretty little church obnoxious to many of the simple old Foresters, to whom a pair of brazen candlesticks on an altar were among the abominations of Baal, and a crucifix as hateful as the image of Ashtaroth; obstinate old people of limited vision, who wanted Mr Scobel to stick to what they called the old ways, and read the Liturgy as they had heard it when they were children. In the minds of these people, Mr Scobel's self-devotion and hard service were as nothing, while he cut off the ten commandments from the Sunday morning service, and lighted his altar candles at the early celebration.

It was in this month of March that an event impended which caused a considerable flutter among the dancing population of the Forest. Lord Southminster's eldest daughter, Lady Almira Ringwood, was to marry Sir Ponto Jones, the rich ironmaster – an alliance of ancient aristocracy and modern wealth which was considered one of the grandest achievements of the age, like the discovery of steam or the electric telegraph; and after the marriage, which was to be quietly performed in the presence of about a hundred and fifty blood relations, there was to be a ball, to which all the county families were bidden, with very little more distinction or favouritism than in the good old fairy-tale times, when the king's herald went through the streets of the city to invite everybody, and only some stray Cinderella, cleaning boots and knives in a back kitchen, found herself unintentionally excluded. Lady Southminster drew the line at county families, naturally, but her kindly feelings allowed a wide margin for parsons, doctors, and military men – and among these last Captain Winstanley received a card.

Mrs Scobel declared that this ball would be a grand thing for Violet. 'You have never properly come out, you know, dear,' she said; 'but at Southminster you will be seen by everybody;

and, as I daresay Lady Ellangowan will take you under her wing, you'll be seen to the best advantage.'

'Do you think Lady Ellangowan's wing will make any difference – in me?' inquired Vixen.

'It will make a great deal of difference in the Southminster set,' replied Mrs Scobel, who considered herself an authority upon all social matters.

She was a busy good-natured little woman, the chosen confidante of all her female friends. People were always appealing to her on small social questions, what they ought to do or to wear on such and such an occasion. She knew the wardrobes of her friends as well as she knew her own. 'I suppose you'll wear that lovely pink,' she would say when discussing an impending dinner-party. She gave judicious assistance in the composition of a *menu*. 'My love, everyone has pheasants at this time of year. Ask your poulterer to send you guinea-fowls, they are more *distingué*,' she would suggest. Or: 'If you have dessert ices, let me recommend you coffee-cream. We had it last week at Ellangowan Park.'

Vixen made no objection to the Southminster ball. She was young, and fond of waltzing. Whirling easily round to the swing of some German melody, in a great room garlanded with flowers, was a temporary cessation of all earthly care, the idea of which was in no wise unpleasant to her. She had enjoyed her waltzes even at that charity-ball at the Pavilion, to which she had gone so unwillingly.

The March night was fine, but blustery, when Mrs Tempest and her daughter started for Southminster. The stars were shining in a windy sky, the tall forest trees were tossing their heads, the brambles were shivering, and a shrill shriek came up out of the woodland every now and then like a human cry for help.

Mrs Tempest had offered to take Mrs Scobel and Captain Winstanley in her roomy carriage. Mr Scobel was not going to the ball. All such entertainments were an abhorrence to him; but this particular ball, being given in Lent, was more especially abhorrent.

'I shouldn't think of going for my own amusement,' Mrs Scobel told her husband, 'but I want to see Violet Tempest at her first local dance. I want to see the impression she makes. I believe she will be the belle of the ball.'

'That would mean the belle of South Hants,' said the parson. 'She has a beautiful face for a painted window – there is such a glow of colour.'

'She is absolutely lovely, when she likes,' replied his wife, 'but she has a curious temper; and there is something very repellent about her when she does not like people. Strange, is it not, that she should not like Captain Winstanley?'

'She would be a very noble girl under more spiritual influences,' sighed the Reverend Ignatius. 'Her present surroundings are appallingly earthly. Horses, dogs, a table loaded with meat in Lent and Advent, a total ignoring of vigils and saints' days. It is sad to see those we like treading the broad path so blindly. I feel sorry, my dear, that you should go to this ball.'

'It is only on Violet's account,' repeated Mrs Scobel. 'Mrs Tempest will be thinking of nothing but her dress; there will be nobody interested in that poor girl.'

Urged thus, upon purely benevolent grounds, Mr Scobel could not withhold his consent; more especially as he had acquired the habit of letting his wife do what she liked on most occasions – a marital custom not easily broken through. So Mrs Scobel, who was an economical little woman, 'did up' her silver-gray silk dinner-dress with ten shillings' worth of black tulle and pink rosebuds, and felt she had made a success that Madame Ellise might have approved. Her faith in the silver-gray and rosebuds was just a little shaken by her first view of Mrs Tempest and Violet: the widow in black velvet, rose-point, and scarlet – Spanish as a portrait by Velasquez; Violet in black and gold, with stephanotis in her hair.

The drive was a long one, well over ten miles, along one of those splendid straight roads which distinguish the New Forest. Mrs Tempest and Mrs Scobel were in high spirits, and prattled agreeably all the way, only giving Captain Winstanley time to get a word in edgeways now and then. Violet looked out of the window and held her peace. There was always a charm for her in that dark silent forest, those waving branches and flitting clouds, stars gleaming like lights on a stormy sea. She was not much elated at the idea of the ball, and 'that small, small, imperceptibly small talk' of her mother's and Mrs Scobel's was beyond measure wearisome to her.

'I hope we shall get there after the Ellangowans,' said Mrs Scobel, when they had driven through the little town of Ringwood, and were entering a land of level pastures and fertilising streams, which seemed wonderfully tame after the undulating forest; 'it would be so much nicer for Violet to be in the Ellangowan set from the first.'

'I beg to state that Miss Tempest has promised me the first waltz,' said Captain Winstanley. 'I am not going to be ousted by any offshoot of nobility in Lady Ellangowan's set.'

'O, of course, if Violet has promised—— What a lot of carriages! I'm afraid there'll be a block presently.'

There was every prospect of such a calamity. A confluence of vehicles had poured into a narrow lane bounded on one side by a treacherous water-meadow, on the other by a garden-wall. They all came to a standstill, as Mrs Scobel had prophesied. For a quarter of an hour there was no progress whatever, and a good deal of recrimination among coachmen, and then the rest of the journey had to be done at a walking pace.

The reward was worth the labour when, at the end of a long winding drive, the carriage drew up before the Italian front of Southminster House; a white marble portico, long rows of tall windows brilliantly lighted, a vista of flowers, and statues, and lamps, and pictures, and velvet hangings, seen through the open doorway.

'O, it is too lovely!' cried Violet, fresh as a schoolgirl in this new delight; 'first the dark forest and then a house like this – it is like Fairyland.'

'And you are to be the queen of it – my queen,' said Conrad Winstanley in a low voice. 'I am to have the first waltz, remember that. If the Prince of Wales were my rival I would not give way.'

He detained her hand in his as she alighted from the carriage. She snatched it from him angrily.

'I have a good mind not to dance at all,' she said.

'Why not?'

'It is paying too dearly for the pleasure to be obliged to dance with you.'

'In what school did you learn politeness, Miss Tempest?'

'If politeness means civility to people I despise, I have never learnt it,' answered Vixen.

There was no time for further skirmishing. He had taken her cloak from her, and handed it to the attendant nymph, and received a ticket; and now they were drifting into the tea-room, where a row of ministering footmen were looking at the guests across a barricade of urns and teapots, with countenances that seemed to say: 'If you want anything, you must ask for it. We are here under protest, and we very much wonder how our people could ever have invited such rabble!'

'I always feel small in a tea-room when there are only men in attendance,' whispered Mrs Scobel, 'they are so haughty. I would sooner ask Gladstone or Disraeli to pour me out a cup of tea than one of those supercilious creatures.'

Lady Southminster was stationed in the Teniers room, a small apartment at the beginning of the suite which ended in the picture-gallery or ball-room. She was what Joe Gargery called 'a fine figure of a woman,' in ruby velvet and diamonds, and received her guests with an indiscriminating cordiality, which went far to heal the gaping wounds of county politics.

The Ellangowans had arrived, and Lady Ellangowan, who was full of good-nature, was quite ready to take Violet under her wing when Mrs Scobel suggested that operation.

'I can find her any number of partners,' she said. 'O, there she goes – off already – with Captain Winstanley.'

The Captain had lost no time in exacting his waltz. It was the third on the programme, and the band were beginning to warm to their work. They were playing a waltz by Offenbach – 'Les Traineaux' – with an accompaniment of jingling sleigh-bells – music that had an almost maddening effect on spirits already exhilarated.

The long lofty picture-gallery made a magnificent ball-room – a polished floor of dark wood – a narrow line of light under the projecting cornice, the famous Paul Veronese, the world-

renowned Rubens, the adorable Titian, to which Dr Waagen
had devoted pages of criticism – ideal beauty looking down with
art's eternal tranquillity upon the whisk and whirl of actual life –
here a calm Madonna, contemplating, with deep unfathomable
eyes, these brief ephemera of a night – there Judith with a white
muscular arm holding the tyrant's head aloft above the dancers –
yonder Philip of Spain frowning on this Lenten festival.

Violet and Captain Winstanley waltzed in a stern silence. She
was vexed with herself for her loss of temper just now. In his
breast there was a deeper anger. 'When will my day come?' he
asked himself. 'When shall I be able to bow this proud head, to
bend this stubborn will?' It must be soon – he was tired of
playing his submissive part – tired of holding his cards hidden.

They held on to the end of the waltz – the last clash of the
sleigh-bells.

'Who's that girl in black and gold?' asked a Guardsman of
Lady Ellangowan; 'those two are the best dancers in the room –
it's a thousand to nothing on them.'

That final clash of the bells brought the Captain and his
partner to anchor at the end of the gallery, which opened
through an archway into a spacious palm-house with a lofty
dome. In the middle of this archway, looking at the dancers,
stood a figure, at sight of which Violet Tempest's heart gave a
great leap, and then stood still.

It was Roderick Vawdrey. He was standing alone, listlessly
contemplating the ball-room, with much less life and expression
in his face than there was in the pictured faces on the walls.

'That was a very nice waltz, thanks,' said Vixen, giving the
Captain a little curtsy.

'Shall I take you back to Mrs Tempest?'

Roderick had seen her by this time, and was coming towards
her with a singularly grave and distant countenance, she
thought; not at all like the Rorie of old times. But of course
that was over and done with. She must never call him Rorie
any more, not even in her own thoughts. A sharp sudden
memory thrilled her, as they stood face to face in that brilliant
gallery – the memory of their last meeting in the darkened
room on the day of her father's funeral.

'How do you do?' said Roderick, with a gush of originality. 'Your mamma is here, I suppose.'

'Haven't you seen her?'

'No; we've only just come.'

'We,' no doubt, meant the Dovedale party, of which Mr Vawdrey was henceforth a member.

'I did not know you were to be here,' said Vixen, 'or even that you were in England.'

'We only came home yesterday, or I should have called at the Abbey House. We have been coming home, or talking about it, for the last three weeks. A few days ago the Duchess took it into her head that she ought to be at Lady Almira's wedding – there's some kind of relationship, you know, between the Ashbournes and the Southminsters – so we put on a spurt, and here we are.'

'I am very glad,' said Vixen, not knowing very well what to say; and then seeing Captain Winstanley standing stiffly at her side, with an aggrieved expression of countenance, she faltered: 'I beg your pardon, I don't think you have ever met Mr Vawdrey. Captain Winstanley – Mr Vawdrey.'

Both gentlemen acknowledged the introduction with the stiffest and chilliest of bows; and then the Captain offered Violet his arm, and she, having no excuse for refusing it, submitted quietly to be taken away from her old friend. Roderick made no attempt to detain her.

The change in him could hardly have been more marked, Vixen thought. Yes, the old Rorie – playfellow, scapegoat, friend of the dear old childish days – was verily dead and gone.

'Shall we go and look at the presents?' asked Captain Winstanly.

'What presents?'

'Lady Almira's wedding presents. They are all laid out in the library. I hear they are very splendid. Everybody is crowding to see them.'

'I daresay mamma would like to go, and Mrs Scobel,' suggested Vixen.

'Then we will all go together.'

They found the two matrons side by side on a settee, under a lovely girlish head by Greuze. They were both delighted at the idea of seeing the presents. It was something to do. Mrs Tempest had made up her mind to abjure even square dances this evening. There was something incongruous in widowhood and the Lancers; especially in one's own neighbourhood.

CHAPTER 16

RORIE ASKS A QUESTION

The library was one of the finest rooms at Southminster. It was not like the library at Althorpe – a collection for a nation to be proud of. There was no priceless Decameron, no Caxton Bible, no inestimable 'Book of Hours,' or early Venetian Virgil; but as a library of reference, a library for all purposes of culture or enjoyment, it left nothing to be desired. It was a spacious and lofty room, lined from floor to ceiling with exquisitely bound books; for, if not a collector of rare editions, Lord Southminster was at least a connoisseur of bindings. Creamy vellum, flowered with gold, antique brown calf, and russia in every shade of crimson and brown, gave brightness to the shelves, while the sombre darkness of carved oak made a background for this variety of colour.

Not a mortal in the crowded library this evening thought of looking at the books. The room had been transformed into a bazaar. Two long tables were loaded with the wedding gifts which rejoicing friends and aspiring acquaintances had lavished upon Lady Almira. Each gift was labelled with the name of the giver; and the exhibition was full of an intensely personal interest. Everybody wanted to see what everybody else had given. Most of the people looking at the show had made their offerings, and were anxious to see if their own particular contributions appeared to advantage.

Here Mrs Scobel was in her element. She explained everything, expatiated upon the beauty and usefulness of everything. If she had assisted at the purchase of all these gifts, or had actually chosen them, she could not have been more familiar with their use and merits.

'You must look at the silver candelabra presented by Sir Ponto's workpeople, so much more sensible than a bracelet. I don't think Garrard — yes, it is Garrard — ever did anything better; so sweetly mythological — a goat and a dear little chubby boy, and ever so many savage-looking persons with cymbals.'

'The education of Jupiter, perhaps,' suggested Captain Winstanley.

'Of course. The savage persons must be teaching him music. And this lovely, lovely screen in crewels, by the Ladies Ringwood, after a picture by Alma Tadema,' continued Mrs Scobel. 'Was there ever anything so perfect? And to think that our poor mothers worked staring roses and gigantic lilies in Berlin wool and glass beads, and imagined themselves artistic!'

The ladies went the round of the tables, in a crush of other ladies, all rapturous. The Louis-Quatorze fans, the carved ivory, the Brussels point, the oxydised silver glove-boxes, and malachite blotting-books, the pearls, opals, ormolu; the antique tankards and candlesticks, Queen-Anne teapots; diamond stars, combs, tiaras; prayer-books, and *Christian Years*. The special presents which stood out from this chaos of commonplace were — a *rivière* of diamonds from the Earl of Southminster, a cashmere shawl from her Majesty, a basket of orchids, of fabulous value, from Lady Ellangowan, a pair of priceless crackle jars, a Sèvres dinner-service of the old *bleu-du-roi*, a set of knives of which the handles had all been taken from stags slaughtered by the Southminster hounds.

'This is all very well for the wallflowers,' said Captain Winstanley to Violet, 'but you and I are losing our dances.'

'I don't much care about dancing,' answered Vixen wearily.

She had been looking at this gorgeous display of bracelets and teacups, silver-gilt dressing-cases, and ivory hairbrushes, without seeing anything. She was thinking of Roderick Vawdrey, and how odd a thing it was that he should seem so utter a stranger to her.

'He has gone up into the ducal circle,' she said to herself. 'He is translated. It is almost as if he had wings; he is certainly as far away from me as if he were a bishop.'

They struggled back to the picture-gallery, and here Lady Ellangowan took possession of Violet, and got her distinguished partners for all the dances till supper-time. She found herself receiving a gracious little nod from Lady Mabel Ashbourne in the ladies' chain. Neither the lapse of two years nor the experiences of foreign travel had made any change in the hope of the Dovedales. She was still the same sylph-like being, dressed in palest green, the colour of a duck's egg, with a parure of pearls that would have done honour to a princess.

'Do you think Lady Mabel Ashbourne very beautiful?' Vixen asked Lady Ellangowan, curious to hear the opinion of experience and authority.

'No; she's too shadowy for my taste,' replied her ladyship, who was the reverse of sylph-like. 'Wasn't there someone in Greek mythology who fell in love with a cloud? Lady Mabel would just suit that sort of person. And then she is over-educated and conceited; sets up for a modern Lady Jane Grey, quotes Greek plays, I believe, and looks astounded if people don't understand her. She'll end by establishing a female college, like Tennyson's princess.'

'O, but she is engaged to be married to Mr Vawdrey.'

'Her cousin? Very foolish! That may go off by-and-by. First engagements seldom come to anything.'

Violet thought herself a hateful creature for being inwardly grateful to Lady Ellangowan for this speech.

She had seen Roderick spinning round with his cousin. He was a good waltzer, but not a graceful one. He steered his way well, and went with a strong swing that covered a great deal of ground; but there was a want of finish. Lady Mabel looked as if she were being carried away by a maelstrom. And now people began to move towards the supper-rooms, of which there were two, luxuriously arranged with numerous round tables in the way that was still a novelty when *Lothair* was written. This gave more room for the dancers. The people for whom a ball meant a surfeit of perigord pie, truffled turkey, salmon *mayonnaise*, and early strawberries, went for their first innings, meaning to return to that happy hunting-ground as often as proved practicable. Violet was carried off by a partner who was so anxious to take her to supper that she felt sure he was dying to get some for himself.

Her cavalier found her a corner at a snug little table with three gorgeous matrons. She ate a cutlet and a teaspoonful of peas, took three sips from a glass of champagne, and wound up with some strawberries, which tasted as if they had been taken by mistake out of the pickle-jar.

'I'm afraid you haven't had a very good supper,' said her partner, who had been comfortably wedged between two of the matrons, consuming *mayonnaise* and *pâté* to his heart's content.

'Excellent, thanks. I shall be glad to make room for someone else.' Whereat the unfortunate young man was obliged to stand up, leaving the choicest morsel of truffled goose-liver on his plate.

The crowd in the picture-gallery was thinner when Violet went back. In the doorway she met Roderick Vawdrey.

'Haven't you kept a single dance for me, Violet?' he asked.

'You didn't ask me to keep one.'

'Didn't I? Perhaps I was afraid of Captain Winstanley's displeasure. He would have objected, no doubt.'

'Why should he object, unless I broke an engagement to him?'

'Would he not? Are you actually free to be asked by anyone? If I had known that two hours ago! And now, I suppose, your programme is full. Yes, to the very last galop; for which, of course, you won't stop. But there's to be an extra waltz presently; you must give me that.'

She said neither yes nor no, and he put her hand through his arm and led her up the room.

'Have you seen my mother?'

'Yes; she thinks I am grown. She forgets that I was one-and-twenty when we last met. That does not leave much margin for growing, unless a man went on getting taller indefinitely, like Lord Southminster's palms. He had to take the roof off his palm-house last year, you know. What a dreadful thing if I were to become a Norfolk giant – giants are indigenous to Norfolk, aren't they? – and were obliged to take the roof off Briarwood. Have you seen the Duchess?'

'Only in the distance. I hardly know her at all, you know.'

'That's absurd. You ought to know her very well. You must be quite intimate with her by-and-by, when we are all settled down as steady-going married people.'

The little gloved hand on his arm quivered ever so slightly. This was a distinct allusion to his approaching marriage.

'Lovely room, isn't it? Just the right thing for a ball. How do you like the Rubens? Very grand – a magnificent display of carmines – beautiful, if you are an admirer of Rubens. What a draughtsman! The Italian school rarely achieved that freedom of pencil. Isn't that Greuze enchanting? There is an innocence, a freshness about his girlish faces that nobody has ever equalled. His women are not Madonnas, or Junos, or Helens – they are the incarnation of girlhood; girlhood without care or thought; girlhood in love with a kitten, or weeping over a wounded robin-redbreast.'

How abominably he rattled on. Was it the overflow of joyous spirits? No doubt. He was so pleased with life and fate, that he was obliged to give vent to his exuberance in this gush of commonplace.

'You remind me of Miss Bates, in Jane Austen's *Emma*,' said Vixen, laughing.

The band struck up 'Trauriges Herz,' a waltz like a wail, but with a fine swing in it.

'Now for the old three-time,' said Roderick; and in the next minute they were sailing smoothly over the polished floor, with all the fair pictured faces, the crimson draperies, the pensive Madonnas, Dutch boors, Italian temples, and hills, and skies, circling round them like the figures in a kaleidoscope.

'Do you remember our boy-and-girl waltzes in the hall at the Abbey House?' asked Rorie.

Happily for Vixen her face was so turned that he could not see the quiver of her lips, the sudden look of absolute pain that paled her cheeks.

'I am not likely to forget any part of my childhood,' she answered gravely. 'It was the one happy period of my life.'

'You don't expect me to believe that the last two years have been altogether unhappy.'

'You may believe what you like. You, who knew my father, ought to know——'

'The dear Squire! Do you think I am likely to undervalue him, or to forget your loss? No, Violet, no. But there are compensations. I heard of you at Brighton. You were very happy there, were you not?'

'I liked Brighton pretty well. And I had Arion there all the while. There are some capital rides on the Downs.'

'Yes, and you had agreeable friends there.'

'Yes, we knew a good many pleasant people, and went to a great many concerts. I heard all the good singers, and Madame Goddard ever so many times.'

They went on till the end of the waltz, and then walked slowly round the room, glancing at the pictures as they went by. The Duchess was not in sight.

'Shall we go and look at the palms?' asked Roderick, when they came to the archway at the end of the gallery.

'If you like.'

'This was the roof that had to be taken off, you know. It is a magnificent dome, but I daresay the palms will outgrow it within Lord Southminster's time.'

It was like entering a jungle in the tropics, if one could fancy a jungle paved with encaustic tiles, and furnished with velvet-covered ottomans for the repose of weary sportsmen.

There was only a subdued light from lamps thinly sprinkled among the ferns and flowers. There were four large groups of statuary, placed judiciously, and under the central dome there was a fountain, where, half hidden by a veil of glittering spray, Neptune was wooing Tyro, in the aspect of a river-god, amongst bulrushes, lilies, and water-plants.

Violet and her companion looked at the tropical plants, and admired, with a delightful ignorance of the merits of these specimens. The tall shafts and the thick tufts of huge leaves were not Vixen's idea of beauty.

'I like our beeches and oaks in the Forest ever so much better,' she exclaimed.

'Everything in the Forest is dear,' said Rorie.

Vixen felt, with a curious choking sensation, that this was a good opening for her to say something polite. She had always intended to congratulate him, in a straightforward sisterly way, upon his engagement to Lady Mabel.

'I am so glad to hear you say that,' she began. 'And how happy you must be to think that your fate is fixed here irrevocably; doubly fixed now; for you can have no interest to draw you away from us, as you might if you were to marry a stranger. Briarwood and Ashbourne united will make you the greatest man among us.'

'I don't highly value that kind of greatness, Violet – a mere question of acreage; but I am glad to think myself anchored for life on my native soil.'

'And you will go into Parliament and legislate for us, and take care that we are not disforested. They have taken away too much already, with their horrid enclosures.'

'The enclosures will make splendid pine woods by-and-by.'

'Yes, when we are all dead and gone.'

'I don't know about Parliament. So long as my poor mother was living I had an incentive to turn senator, she was so eager for it. But now that she is gone, I don't feel strongly drawn that way. I suppose I shall settle down into the approved pattern of country squire: breed fat cattle – the aristocratic form of cruelty to animals – spend the best part of my income upon agricultural machinery, talk about guano, like the Duke, and lecture delinquents at quarter-sessions.'

'But Lady Mabel will not allow that. She will be ambitious for you.'

'I hope not. I can fancy no affliction greater than an ambitious wife. No. My poor mother left Mabel her orchids. Mabel will confine her ambition to orchids and literature. I believe she writes poetry, and some day she will be tempted to publish a small volume, I daresay. *Aeolian Echoes*, or *Harp Strings*, or *Broken Chords*, or *Consecutive Fifths*, or something of that kind.'

'You believe!' exclaimed Vixen. 'Surely you have read some of Lady Mabel's poetry, or heard it read. She must have read some of her verses to you.'

'Never. She is too reserved, and I am too candid. It would be a dangerous experiment. I should inevitably say something rude. Mabel adores Shelley and Browning; she reads Greek, too. Her poetry is sure to be unintelligible, and I should expose my obtuseness of intellect. I couldn't even look as if I understood it.'

'If I were Lady Mabel, I think under such circumstances I should leave off writing poetry.'

'That would be quite absurd. Mabel has a hundred tastes which I do not share with her. She is devoted to her garden and hothouses. I hardly know one flower from another, except the forest wildlings. She detests horses and dogs. I am never happier than when among them. She reads Aeschylus as glibly as I can read a French newspaper. But she will make an admirable mistress for Briarwood. She has just that tranquil superiority which becomes the ruler of a large estate. You will see what cottages and schools we shall build. There will not be a weed in our allotment gardens, and our farm-labourers will get all the prizes at cottage flower-shows.'

'You will hunt, of course?'

'Naturally; don't you know that I am to have the hounds next year? It was all arranged a few days ago. Poor Mabel was strongly opposed to the plan. She thought it was the first stage on the road to ruin; but I think I convinced her that it was the natural thing for the owner of Briarwood; and the Duke was warmly in favour of it.'

'The dear old kennels!' said Vixen. 'I have never seen them since − since I came home. I ride by the gate very often, but I have never had courage to go inside. The hounds woudn't know me now.'

'You must renew your friendship with them. You will hunt, of course, next year?'

'No, I shall never hunt again!'

'O, nonsense; I hear that Captain Winstanley is a mighty Nimrod − quite a Leicestershire man. He will wish you to hunt.'

'What can Captain Winstanley have to do with it?' asked Vixen, turning sharply upon him.

'A great deal, I should imagine, by next season.'

'I haven't the least idea what you mean.'

It was Roderick Vawdrey's turn to look astonished. He looked both surprised and angry.

'How fond young ladies are of making mysteries about these things,' he exclaimed impatiently; 'I suppose they think it enhances their importance. Have I made a mistake? Have my informants misled me? Is your engagement to Captain Winstanley not to be talked about yet — only an understood thing among your own particular friends? Let me at least be allowed the privilege of intimate friendship. Let me be among the first to congratulate you.'

'What folly have you been listening to?' cried Vixen; 'you, Roderick Vawdrey, my old playfellow — almost an adopted brother — to know me so little.'

'What could I know of you to prevent my believing what I was told? Was there anything strange in the idea that you should be engaged to Captain Winstanley? I heard that he was a universal favourite.'

'And did you think that I should like a universal favourite?'

'Why should you not? It seemed credible enough, and my informant was positive; he saw you together at a picnic in Switzerland. It was looked upon as a settled thing by all your friends.'

'By Captain Winstanley's friends, you mean. They may have looked upon it as a settled thing that he should marry someone with plenty of money, and they may have thought that my money would be as useful as anyone else's.'

'Violet, are you mystifying me? are you trying to drive me crazy? or is this the simple truth?'

'It is the simple truth.'

'You are not engaged to this man? — you never have been: you don't care for him, never have cared for him?'

'Never, never, never, never!' said Violet, with unmistakable emphasis.

'Then I have been the most consummate——'

He did not finish his sentence, and Violet did not ask him to finish it. The ejaculation seemed involuntary. He sat staring at the palms, and said nothing for the next minute and a half, while Vixen unfurled her great black and gold fan, and looked at it admiringly, as if she had never seen it before.

'Do you really think those palms will break through the roof again, in the present Lord Southminster's time?' Roderick inquired presently, with intense interest.

Vixen did not feel herself called upon to reply to a question so purely speculative.

'I think I had better go and look for mamma and Mrs Scobel,' she said; 'they must have come back from the supper-room by this time.'

Roderick rose and offered her his arm. She was surprised to see how pale he looked when they came out of the dusk into the brilliant light of the gallery. But in a heated room, and between two and three o'clock in the morning, a man may naturally be a little paler than usual.

Roderick took Violet straight to the end of the room, where his quick eye had espied Mrs Tempest in her striking black and scarlet costume. He said nothing more about the Duchess or Lady Mabel; and, indeed, took Violet past the elder lady, who was sitting in one of the deep-set windows with Lady Southminster, without attempting to bring about any interchange of civilities.

'Captain Winstanley has been kind enough to go and look for the carriage, Violet,' said Mrs Tempest. 'I told him we would join him in the vestibule directly I could find you. Where have you been all this time? You were not in the Lancers. Such a pretty set. O, here is Mrs Scobel!' as the Vicar's wife approached them on her partner's arm, in a piteous state of dilapidation – not a bit of tulle puffing left, and all her rosebuds crushed as flat as dandelions.

'Such a delightful set!' she exclaimed gaspingly.

'I'm afraid your dress has suffered,' said her partner.

'Not in the least,' protested Mrs Scobel.

'Your carriage will be the third,' the Captain told Mrs Tempest, while Roderick was putting Violet's cloak round her in the vestibule; 'there are a good many people leaving already.'

Roderick went with them to the carriage door, and stayed in the porch till they were gone. The last object Vixen saw under the Southminster lamps was the pale grave face of her old playfellow.

He went straight from the porch to the supper-room, not to find himself a place at one of the snug little tables, but to go to the buffet and pour out a glass of brandy, which he drank at a draught. Yet, in a general way, there was no man more abstemious than Roderick Vawdrey.

A quarter of an hour afterwards he was waltzing with Lady Mabel – positively the last dance before their departure.

'Roderick,' she said in an awe-stricken undertone, 'I am going to say something very dreadful. Please forgive me in advance.'

'Certainly,' he said, with a somewhat apprehensive look.

'Just now, when you were talking to me, I fancied you had been drinking brandy.'

'I had.'

'Absolute undiluted brandy!'

'Neat brandy, sometimes denominated "short."'

'Good heavens! were you ill?'

'I had had what people call "a turn."'

CHAPTER 17

WHERE THE RED KING WAS SLAIN

May had come. The red glow of the beech branches had changed to a tender green; the oaks were amber; the winding forest-paths, the deep inaccessible glades where the cattle led such a happy life, were blue with dog-violets and golden with primroses. Whitsuntide was close at hand, and good Mr Scobel had given up his mind to church decoration, and the entertainment of his school-children with tea and buns in that delightful valley, where an iron monument, a little less artistic than a pillar post-office, marks the spot where the Red King fell.

Vixen, though not particularly fond of school-feasts, had promised to assist at this one. It was not to be a stiff or ceremonious affair. There was to be no bevy of young ladies, oppressively attentive to their small charges, causing the children to drink scalding tea in a paroxysm of shyness. The whole thing was to be done in an easy and friendly manner, with no aid but that of the schoolmistress and master. The magnates of the land were to have no part in the festival.

'The children enjoy themselves so much more when there are no finely-dressed people making believe to wait upon them,' said Mrs Scobel; 'but I know they'll be delighted to have you, Violet. They positively adore you!'

'I'm sure I can't imagine why they should,' answered Violet truthfully.

'O, but they do. They like to look at you. When you come into the schoolroom they're all in a flutter; and they point at you awfully, don't they, Miss Pierson?' said Mrs Scobel, appealing to the schoolmistress.

'Yes, ma'am. I can't cure them of pointing, do what I will.'

'O, they are dear little children,' exclaimed Violet, 'and I don't care how much they point at me if they really like me. They make me such nice little bob-curtsies when I meet them in the Forest, and they all seem fond of Argus. I'm sure you have made them extremely polite, Miss Pierson. I shall be very pleased to come to your school-feast, Mrs Scobel; and I'll tell our good old Trimmer to make no end of cakes.'

'My dear Violet, pray don't think of putting Mrs Trimmer to any trouble. Your dear mamma might be angry.'

'Angry at my asking for some cakes for the school-children, after being papa's wife for seventeen years! That couldn't be.'

The school-feast was fixed, three weeks in advance, for the Wednesday in Whitsun week, and during the interval there were many small meteorologists in Beechdale school intent upon the changes of the moon, and all those varied phenomena from which the rustic mind draws its auguries of coming weather. The very crowing of early village cocks was regarded suspiciously by the school-children at this period; and even the harmless domestic pussy, sitting with his back to the fire, was deemed a cat of evil omen.

It happened that the appointed Wednesday was a day on which Mrs Tempest had chosen to invite a few friends in a quiet way to her seven o'clock dinner; among the few Captain Winstanley, who had taken Mrs Hawbuck's cottage for an extended period of three months. Mrs Tempest had known all about the school-feast a fortnight before she gave her invitations, but had forgotten the date at the moment when she arranged her little dinner. Yet she felt offended that Violet should insist upon keeping her engagement to the Scobels.

'But, dear mamma, I am of no use to you at our parties.' pleaded Vixen; 'if I were at all necessary to your comfort I would give up the school-feast.'

'My dear Violet, it is not my comfort I am considering; but I cannot help feeling annoyed that you should prefer to spend your evening with a herd of vulgar children – playing Oranges and Lemons, or Kiss in the Ring, or some other ridiculous game, and getting yourself into a most unbecoming perspiration – to a quiet home evening with a few friends.'

'You see, mamma, I know our quiet home evenings with a few friends so well. I could tell you beforehand exactly what will happen, almost the very words people will say – how your *jardinières* will be admired, and how the conversation will glance off from your ferns and pelargoniums to Lady Ellangowan's orchids, and then drift back to your old china; after which the ladies will begin to talk about dress, and the wickedness of giving seven guineas for a summer bonnet, as Mrs Jones, or Green, or Robinson has just done; from which their talk will glide insensibly to the iniquities of modern servants; and when those have been discussed exhaustively, one of the younger ladies will tell you the plot of the last novel she has had from Mudie's, with an infinite number of you knows and you sees, and then perhaps Captain Winstanley – he is coming, I suppose – will sing a French song, of which the company will understand about four words in every verse, and then you will show Mrs Carteret your last piece of art needlework——'

'What nonsense you talk, Violet. However, if you prefer the children at Stony Cross to the society of your mother and your mother's friends, you must take your own way.'

'And you will forgive me in advance, dear mamma?'

'My love, I have nothing to forgive. I only deplore a bent of mind which I can but think unladylike.'

Vixen was glad to be let off with so brief a lecture. In her heart of hearts she was not at all sorry that her mother's friendly dinner should fall on a day which she had promised to spend elsewhere. It was a treat to escape the sameness of that polite entertainment. Yes, Captain Winstanley was to be there, of course, and prolonged acquaintance had not lessened her dislike to that gentleman. She had seen him frequently during his residence at the Hawbuck cottage, not at her mother's house only, but at all the best houses in the neighbourhood. He had done nothing to offend her. He had been studiously polite; and that was all. Not by one word had he reminded Violet of that moonlight walk in the Pavilion garden; not by so much as a glance or a sigh had he hinted at a hidden passion. So far she could make no complaint against him. But the attrition of frequent intercourse did not wear off the sharp edge of her dislike.

Wednesday afternoon came, and any evil auguries that had been drawn from the noontide crowing of restless village cocks were set at naught, for the weather was peerless; a midsummer sky and golden sunlight shone upon all things; upon white-walled cottages and orchards, and gardens where the pure lilies were beginning to blow, upon the yellow-green oak leaves and deepening bloom of the beech, and the long straight roads cleaving the heart of the Forest.

Violet had arranged to drive Mr and Mrs Scobel in her pony-carriage. She was at the door of their snug little vicarage at three o'clock; the vivacious Titmouse tossing his head and jingling his bit in a burst of pettishness at the aggravating behaviour of the flies.

Mrs Scobel came fluttering out, with the Vicar behind her. Both carried baskets, and after them came an old servant, who had been Mrs Scobel's nurse, a woman with a figure like a hogs-head of wine, and a funny little head at the top, carrying a third basket.

'The buns and bread have gone straight from the village,' said the Vicar's wife. 'How well you are looking, Violet. I hope dear Mrs Tempest was not very angry at your coming with us.'

'Dear Mrs Tempest didn't care a straw,' Vixen answered, laughing. 'But she thinks me wanting in dignity for liking to have a romp with the school-children.'

All the baskets were in by this time, and Titmouse was in a paroxysm of impatience; so Mr and Mrs Scobel seated themselves quickly, and Vixen gave her reins a little shake that meant Go, and off went the pony at a pace which was rather like running away.

The Vicar looked slightly uneasy.

'Does he always go as fast as this?' he inquired.

'Sometimes a good deal faster. He's an old fencer, you know, and hasn't forgotten his jumping days. But of course I don't let him jump with the carriage.'

'I should think not,' ejaculated the Vicar; 'unless you wanted to commit murder and suicide. Don't you think you could make him go a little steadier? He's going rather like a dog with a tin kettle at his tail, and if the kettle were to tip over——'

'O, he'll settle down presently,' said Vixen coolly. 'I don't want to interfere with him; it makes him ill-tempered. And if he were to take to kicking——'

'If you'll pull him up I think I'll get out and walk,' said Mr Scobel, the back of whose head was on a level with the circle which the pony's hoofs would have been likely to describe in the event of kicking.

'O, please don't!' cried Vixen. 'If you do that I shall think you've no confidence in my driving.'

She pulled Titmouse together, and coaxed him into an unobjectionable trot; a trot which travelled over the ground very fast, without giving the occupants of the carriage the uncomfortable sensation of sitting behind a pony intent on getting to the sharp edge of the horizon and throwing himself over.

They were going up a long hill. Halfway up they came to the gate of the kennels. Violet looked at it with a curious half-reluctant glance that expressed the keenest pain.

'Poor papa,' she sighed. 'He never seemed happier than when he used to take me to see the hounds.'

'Mr Vawdrey is to have them next year,' said Mrs Scobel. 'That seems right and proper. He will be the biggest man in this part of the country when the Ashbourne and Briarwood estates are united. And the Duke cannot live very long – a man who gives his mind to eating and drinking, and is laid up with the gout twice a year.'

'Do you know when they are to be married?' asked Vixen, with an unconcerned air.

'At the end of this year, I am told. Lady Jane died last November. They would hardly have the wedding before a twelvemonth was over. Have you seen much of Mr Vawdrey since he came back?'

'I believe I have seen him three times: once at Lady Southminster's ball; once when he came to call upon mamma; once at a kettledrum at Ellangowan, where he was in attendance upon Lady Mabel. He looked rather like a little dog at the end of a string; he had just that meekly-obedient look, combined with an expression of not wanting to be there, which you see in a dog. If I were engaged, I should not take my *fiancé* to kettledrums.'

'Ah, Violet, when are you going to be engaged?' cried Mrs Scobel, in a burst of playfulness. 'Where is the man worthy of you?'

'Nowhere; unless Heaven would make me such a man as my father.'

'You and Mr Vawdrey were such friends when you were girl and boy. I used sometimes to fancy that childish friendship of yours would lead to a lasting attachment.'

'Did you? That was a great mistake. I am not half good enough for Mr Vawdrey. I was well enough for a playfellow, but he wants something much nearer perfection in a wife.'

'But your tastes are so similar.'

'The very reason we should not care for each other.'

'"In joining contrasts lieth love's delight." That's what a poet
has said, yet I can't quite believe it, Violet.'

'But you see the event proves the poet's axiom true. Here is
my old playfellow, who cares for nothing but horses and
hounds and a country life, devotedly attached to Lady Mabel
Ashbourne, who reads Greek plays with as much enjoyment as
other young ladies derive from a stirring novel, and who hasn't
an idea or an attitude that is not strictly aesthetic.'

'Do you know, Violet, I am very much afraid that this
marriage is rather the result of calculation than of genuine
affection?' said Mrs Scobel solemnly.

'O, no doubt it will be a grand thing to unite Ashbourne and
Briarwood, but Roderick Vawdrey is too honourable to marry
a girl he could not love. I would never believe him capable of
such baseness,' answered Violet, standing up for her old friend.

Here they turned out of the Forest and drove through a
peaceful colony consisting of half-a-dozen cottages, a rustic inn
where reigned a supreme silence and sleepiness, and two or
three houses in old-world gardens.

Vixen changed the conversation to buns and school-children,
which agreeable theme occupied them till Titmouse had
walked up a tremendously steep hill, the Vicar trudging through
the dust beside him; and then the deep green vale in which
Rufus was slain by smiling in the sunshine below their feet.

Perhaps the panorama to be seen from the top of that hill is
absolutely the finest in the Forest – a vast champaign, stretching
far away to the white walls, tiled roofs, and ancient abbey-
church of Romsey; here a glimpse of winding water, there a
humble village – nameless save to its inhabitants – nestling
among the trees, or basking in the broad sunshine of a
common.

At the top of the hill, Bates, the gray-headed groom, who
had attended Violet ever since her first pony-ride, took
possession of Titmouse and the chaise, while the baskets were
handed over to a lad, who had been on the watch for their
arrival. Then they all went down the steep path into the valley,
at the bottom of which the children were swarming in a cluster,
as thick as bees, while a pale flame and a cloud of white smoke

went up from the midst of them like the fire beneath a sacrifice. This indicated the boiling of the kettle, in true gipsy fashion.

For the next hour and a half tea-drinking was the all-absorbing business with everybody. The boiling of the kettle was a grand feature in the entertainment. Cups and saucers were provided by a little colony of civilised gipsies, who seem indigenous to the spot, and whose summer life is devoted to assisting at picnics and tea-drinkings, telling fortunes, and selling photographs. White cloths were spread upon the short sweet turf, and piles of bread-and-butter, cake and buns, invited the attention of the flies.

Presently arose the thrilling melody of a choral grace, with the sweet embellishment of a strong Hampshire accent. And then, with a swoop as of eagles on their quarry, the school-children came down upon the mountains of bread-and-butter, and ate their way manfully to the buns and cake.

Violet had never been happier since her return to Hampshire than she felt this sunny afternoon, as she moved quickly about, ministering to these juvenile devourers. The sight of their somewhat bovine contentment took her thoughts away from her own cares and losses; and presently, when the banquet was concluded – a conclusion only arrived at by the total consumption of everything provided, whereby the hungry-eyed gipsy attendants sunk into despondency – Vixen constituted herself Lord of Misrule, and led off a noisy procession in the time-honoured game of Oranges and Lemons, which entertainment continued till the school-children were in a high fever. After this they had Kiss in the Ring; Vixen only stipulating, before she began, that nobody should presume to drop the handkerchief before her. Then came Touchwood – a game charmingly adapted to that wooded valley, where the trees looked as if they had been planted at convenient distances on purpose for this juvenile sport.

'O, I am so tired,' cried Violet at last, when church clocks – all out of earshot in this deep valley – were striking eight, and the low sun was golden on the silvery beech-boles, and arrowy gleams of light touched the quiet half-hidden water-pools under the trees yonder; 'I really don't think I can have anything to do with the next game.'

'O, if you please, miss,' cried twenty shrill young voices, 'O, if you please, miss, we couldn't play without you – you're the best on us!'

This soothing flattery had its effect.

'O, but I really don't think I can do more than start you,' sighed Vixen, flushed and breathless, 'what is it to be?'

'Blindman's Buff,' roared the boys.

'Hunt the Slipper,' screamed the girls.

'O, Blindman's Buff is best,' said Vixen. 'This little wood is a splendid place for Blindman's Buff. But mind, I shall only start you. Now then, who's to be Blindman?'

Mr Scobel volunteered. He had been a tranquil spectator of the sports hitherto; but this was the last game, and he felt that he ought to do something more than look on. Vixen blindfolded him, asked him the usual question about his father's stable, and then sent him spinning amongst the moss-grown beeches, groping his way fearfully, with outstretched arms, amidst shrillest laughter and noisiest delight.

He was not long blindfold, and had not had many bumps against the trees before he impounded the person of a fat and scant-of-breath scholar, a girl whose hard breathing would have betrayed her neighbourhood to the dullest ear.

'That's Polly Sims, I know,' said the Vicar.

It was Polly Sims, who was incontinently made as blind as Fortune or Justice, or any other of the deities who dispense benefits to man. Polly floundered about among the trees for a long time, making frantic efforts to catch the empty air, panting like a human steam-engine, and nearly knocking out what small amount of brains she might possess against the gray branches, outstretched like the lean arms of Macbeth's weird women across her path. Finally Polly Sims succeeded in catching Bobby Jones, whom she clutched with the tenacity of an octopus; and then came the reign of Bobby Jones, who was an expert at the game, and who kept the whole party on the *qui vive* by his serpentine windings and twistings among the stout old trunks.

Presently there was a shrill yell of triumph. Bobby had caught Miss Tempest.

'I know'd her by her musling gownd, and the sweet-smelling stuff upon her pocket-handkercher,' he roared.

Violet submitted with a good grace.

'I'm dreadfully tired,' she said, 'and I'm sure I sha'n't catch anyone.'

The sun had been getting lower and lower. There were splashes of ruddy light on the smooth gray beech-boles, and that was all. Soon these would fade, and all would be gloom. The grove had an awful look already. One would expect to meet some ghostly Druid, or some witch of eld, among the shadowy tracks left by the forest wildlings. Vixen went about her work languidly. She was really tired, and was glad to think her day's labours were over. She went slowly in and out among the trees, feeling her way with outstretched arms, her feet sinking sometimes into deep drifts of last year's leaves, or gliding noiselessly over the moss. The air was soft and cool and dewy, with a perfume of nameless wild flowers – a faint aromatic odour of herbs, which the wise women had gathered for medicinal uses in days of old, when your village sorceress was your safest doctor. Everywhere there was the hush and coolness of fast-coming nights. The children's voices were stilled. This last stage of the game was a thing of breathless interest.

Vixen's footsteps drifted lower down into the wooded hollow; insensibly she was coming towards the edge of the treacherously green bog which has brought many a bold rider to grief in these districts, and still she had caught no one. She began to think that she had roamed ever so far away, and was in danger of losing herself altogether, or at least losing everybody else, and being left by herself in the forest darkness. The grassy hollow in which she was wandering had an atmosphere of solitude.

She was on the point of taking off the handkerchief that Mr Scobel had bound so effectually across her eyes, when her outstretched arms clasped something – a substantial figure, distinctly human, clad in rough cloth.

Before she had time to think who it was she had captured, a pair of strong arms clasped her; she was drawn to a broad chest;

she felt a heart beating strong and fast against her shoulder, while lips that seemed too familiar to offend kissed hers with all the passion of a lover's kiss.

'Don't be angry,' said a well-known voice. 'I believe it's the rule of the game. If it isn't I'm sure it ought to be.'

A hand, at once strong and gentle, took off the handkerchief, and in the soft woodland twilight she looked up at Roderick Vawdrey's face, looking down upon her with an expression which she presumed must mean a brotherly friendliness – the delight of an old friend at seeing her after a long interval.

She was not the less angry at that outrageous unwarrantable kiss.

'It is not the rule of the game amongst civilised people; though it possibly may be among ploughboys and servant-maids!' she exclaimed indignantly. 'You are really a most ungentlemanlike person! I wonder Lady Mabel Ashbourne has not taught you better manners.'

'Is that to be my only reward for saving you from plunging – at least ankle-deep – in the marshy ground yonder? But for me you would have been performing a boggy version of Ophelia by this time.'

'How did you come here?'

'I have been to Langley Brook for a day's fly-fishing, and was tramping home across country in a savage humour at my poor sport, when I heard the chatter of small voices, and presently came upon the Scobels and the school-children. The juveniles were in a state of alarm at having lost you. They had been playing the game in severe silence, and at a turn in the grove had missed you altogether. O, here comes Scobel, with his trencher on the back of his head.'

The Vicar came forward, rejoicing at sight of Violet's white gown.

'My dear, what a turn you have given us!' he cried; 'those silly children, to let you out of their sight! I don't think a wood is a good place for Blindman's Buff.'

'No more do I,' answered Vixen, very pale.

'You look as if you had been frightened too,' said the Vicar.

'It did feel awfully lonely; not a sound, except the frogs croaking their vespers, and one dismal owl screaming in the distance. And how cold it has turned now the sun has gone down; and how ghostly the beeches look in their green mantles; there is something awful in a wood at sunset.'

She ran on in an excited tone, masking her agitation under an unnatural vivacity. Roderick watched her keenly. Mr and Mrs Scobel went back to their business of getting the children together, and the pots, pans, and baskets packed for the return journey. The children were inclined to be noisy and insubordinate. They would have liked to make a night of it in the woody hollow, or on the gorse-clothed heights up yonder by Stony Cross. To go home after such a festival, and be herded in small stuffy cottages, was doubtless trying to free-born humanity, always more or less envious of the gipsies.

'Shall we walk up the hill together,' Roderick asked Violet humbly, 'while the Scobels follow with their flock?'

'I am going to drive Mr and Mrs Scobel,' replied Vixen curtly.

'But where is your carriage?'

'I don't know. I rather think it was to meet us at the top of the hill.'

'Then let us go up together and find it – unless you dislike me too much to endure my company for a quarter of an hour – or are too angry with me for my impertinence just now.'

'It is not worth being serious about,' answered Vixen quietly, after a little pause. 'I was very angry at the moment, but after all – between you and me – who were like brother and sister a few years ago, it can't matter very much. I daresay you may have kissed me in those days, though I have forgotten all about it.'

'I think I did – once or twice,' admitted Rorie with laudable gravity.

'Then let your impertinence just now go down to the old account, which we will close, if you please, to-night. But,' seeing him drawing nearer her with a sudden eagerness, 'mind it is never to be repeated. I could not forgive that.'

'I would do much to escape your anger,' said Rorie softly.

'The whole situation just now was too ridiculous,' pursued Vixen, with a spurious hilarity. 'A young woman wandering blindfold in a wood all alone – it must have seemed very absurd.'

'It seemed very far from absurd – to me,' said Rorie.

They were going slowly up the grassy hill, the short scanty herbage looking gray in the dimness. Glow-worms were beginning to shine here and there at the foot of the furze-bushes. A pale moon was rising above the broad expanse of wood and valley, which sank with gentle undulations to the distant plains, where the young corn was growing and the cattle were grazing in a sober agricultural district. Here all was wild and beautiful – rich, yet barren.

'I'm afraid when we met last – at Lady Southminster's ball – that I forgot to congratulate you upon your engagement to your cousin,' said Vixen by-and-by, when they had walked a little way in perfect silence.

She was trying to carry out an old determination. She had always meant to go up to him frankly, with outstretched hand, and wish him joy. And she fancied that at the ball she had said too little. She had not let him understand that she was really glad. 'Believe me, I am very glad that you should marry someone close at home – that you should widen your influence among us.'

'You are very kind,' answered Rorie, with exceeding coldness. 'I suppose all such engagements are subjects for congratulation, from a conventional point of view. My future wife is both amiable and accomplished, as you know. I have reason to be very proud that she has done me so great an honour as to prefer me to many worthier suitors; but I am bound to tell you – as we once before spoke of this subject, at the time of your dear father's death, and I then expressed myself somewhat strongly – I am bound to tell you that my engagement to Mabel was made to please my poor mother. It was when we were all in Italy together. My mother was dying. Mabel's goodness and devotion to her had been beyond all praise; and my heart was drawn to her by affection, by gratitude; and I knew that it would make my poor mother happy to see us irrevocably bound to each other; and so the thing came about somehow, almost unawares, and I have every reason to be proud and happy that fate should have favoured me so far above my deserts.'

'I am very glad that you are happy,' said Violet gently.

After this there was a silence which lasted longer than the previous interval in their talk. They were at the top of the hill before either of them spoke.

Then Vixen laid her hand lightly upon her old playfellow's arm, and said, with extreme earnestness.

'You will go into Parliament by-and-by, no doubt, and have great influence. Do not let them spoil the Forest. Do not let horrid grinding-down economists, for the sake of saving a few pounds or gaining a few pounds, alter and destroy scenes that are so beautiful and a delight to so many. England is a rich country, is she not? Surely she can afford to keep something for her painters and her poets, and even for the humble holiday-folks who come to drink tea at Rufus's stone. Don't let our Forest be altered, Rorie. Let all things be as they were when we were children.'

'All that my voice and influence can do to keep them so shall be done, Violet,' he answered in tones as earnest. 'I am glad that you have asked me something to-night. I am glad, with all my heart, that you have given me something to do for you. It shall be like a badge in my helmet, by-and-by, when I enter the lists. I think I shall say, "For God and for Violet," when I run a tilt against the economic devastators who want to clear our woods and enclose our commons.'

He bent down and kissed her hand, as in token of knightly allegiance. He had just time to do it comfortably before Mr and Mrs Scobel, with the children and their master and mistress, came marching up the hill, singing, with shrill glad voices one of the harvest-home processional hymns.

> 'All good gifts around us
> Are sent from Heaven above,
> Then thank the Lord, O thank the Lord,
> For all His love.'

'What a delicious night!' cried Mr Scobel. 'I think we ought all to walk home. It would be much nicer than being driven.'

This he said with a lively recollection of Titmouse's performances on the journey out, and a lurking dread that he might behave a little worse on the journey home. A lively animal of that kind, going home to his stable, through the uncertain lights and shadows of woodland roads, and driven by such a charioteer as Violet Tempest, was not to be thought of without a shudder.

'I think I had better walk, in any case,' said Mr Scobel thoughtfully. 'I shall be wanted to keep the children together.'

'Let us all walk home.' suggested Roderick. 'We can go through the plantations. It will be very jolly in the moonlight. Bates can drive your pony back, Violet.'

Violet hesitated.

'It's not more than four miles through the plantations,' said Roderick.

'Do you think I am afraid of a long walk?'

'Of course not. You were a modern Atalanta three years ago. I don't suppose a winter in Paris and a season at Brighton have quite spoiled you.'

'It shall be as you like, Mrs Scobel,' said Vixen, appealing to the Vicar's wife.

'O, let us walk by all means,' replied Mrs Scobel, divining her husband's feelings with respect to Titmouse.

'Then you may drive the pony home, Bates,' said Violet; 'and be sure you give him a good supper.'

Titmouse went rattling down the hill at a pace that almost justified the Vicar's objection to him. He gave a desperate shy in the hollow at sight of a shaggy donkey, with a swollen appearance about the head, suggestive, to the equine mind, of hobgoblins. Convulsed at this appalling spectre, Titmouse stood on end for a second or two, and then tore violently off, swinging his carriage behind him, so that the groom's figure swayed to and fro in the moonlight.

'Thank God we're not sitting behind that brute!' ejaculated the Vicar devoutly.

The pedestrians went off in the other direction, along the brow of the hill, by a long white road that crossed a wide sweep of heathy country, brown ridges and dark hollows, distant groups of firs standing black against the moonlit sky, here and there a solitary yew that looked as if it were haunted – just such a landscape as that Scottish heath upon which Macbeth met the three weird women at set of sun, when the battle was lost and won. Vixen and Rorie led the way; the procession of school-children followed, singing hymns as they went with a vocal power that gave no token of diminution.

'Their singing is very melodious when the sharp edge is taken off by distance,' said Roderick; and he and Violet walked at a pace which soon left the children a good way behind them.

Mellowed by a quarter of a mile or so of intervening space, the music lent a charm to the tranquil, perfumed night.

By-and-by they came to the gate of an enclosure which covered a large extent of ground, and through which there was a near way to Beechdale and the Abbey House. They walked along a grassy track through a plantation of young pines – a track which led them down into a green and mossy bottom, where the trees were old and beautiful, and the shadows fell darker. The tall beech-trunks shone like silver, or like wonderful frozen trees in some region of eternal ice and snow. It was a wilderness in which a stranger would incontinently lose himself; but every foot of the way was familiar to Vixen and Rorie. They had followed the hounds by these green ways, and ridden and rambled here in all seasons.

For some time they had walked almost in silence, enjoying the beauty of the night, the stillness only broken by the distant chorus of children singing their pious strains – old hymn-tunes that Violet had known and loved all her life.

'Doesn't it almost seem as if our old childish days had come back?' said Roderick by-and-by. 'Don't you feel as if you were a little girl again, Vixen, going for a ramble with me – fern-hunting or primrose-gathering?'

'No,' answered Vixen firmly. 'Nothing can ever bring the past back for me. I shall never forget that I had a father – the best and dearest – and that I have lost him.'

'Dear Violet,' Roderick began, very gently, 'life cannot be made up of mourning for the dead. We may keep their images enshrined in our hearts for ever, but we must not shut our youth from the sunshine. Think how few years of youth God gives us; and if we waste those upon vain sorrow——'

'No one can say that I have wasted my youth, or shut myself from the sunshine. I go to kettledrums and dancing-parties. My mother and I have taken pains to let the world see how happy we can be without papa.'

'The dear old Squire,' said Rorie tenderly; 'I think he loved me.'

'I am sure he did,' answered Vixen.

'Well, you and I seem to have entered upon a new life since last we rode through these woods together. I daresay you are right, and that it is not possible to fancy oneself back in the past, even for a moment. Consciousness of the present hangs so heavily upon us.'

'Yes,' assented Vixen.

They had come to the end of the enclosure, and stood leaning against a gate, waiting for the arrival of the children.

'And after all, perhaps, it is better to live in the present, and look back at the past, as at an old picture which we shall sooner or later turn with its face to the wall.'

'I like best to think of my old self as if it were someone else,' said Violet. 'I know there was a little girl whom her father called Vixen, who used to ride after the hounds, and roam about the Forest on her pony; and who was herself almost as wild as the Forest ponies. But I can't associate her with this present me,' concluded Violet, pointing to herself with a half-scornful gesture.

'And which is the better, do you think,' asked Rorie, 'the wild Violet of the past, or the elegant exotic of the present?'

'I know which was the happier.'

'Ah,' sighed Rorie, 'happiness is a habit we outgrow when we get out of our teens. But you, at nineteen, ought to have a year or so to the good.'

The children came in sight, tramping along the rutty green walk, singing lustily, Mr Scobel walking at their head, and swinging his stick in time with the tuneful choir.

> 'He only is the Maker
> Of all things near and far;
> He paints the wayside flower,
> He lights the evening star.'

CHAPTER 18

'SHALL I TELL YOU THE SECRET?'

For the rest of the way Violet walked with Mrs Scobel, and at the garden-gate of the vicarage Roderick Vawdrey wished them both good-night, and tramped off, with his basket on his back and his rod on his shoulder, for the long walk to Briarwood.

Here the children separated, and ran off to their scattered homes, dropping bob-curtsies to the last − 'louting' as they called it in their Forest dialect.

'You must come in and have some tea, Violet,' said Mrs Scobel. 'You must be very tired.'

'I am rather tired; but I think it's too late for tea. I had better get home at once.'

'Ignatius shall see you home, my dear,' cried Mrs Scobel. At which the indefatigable Vicar, who had shouted himself hoarse in leading his choir, protested himself delighted to escort Miss Tempest.

The church clock struck ten as they went along the narrow forest-path between Beechdale and the Abbey House.

'O,' cried Vixen, 'I do hope mamma's people will have gone home.'

A carriage rolled past them as they came out into the road.

'That's Mrs Carteret's landau,' said Vixen. 'I breathe more freely. And there goes Mrs Horwood's brougham; so I suppose everything is over. How nice it is when one's friends are so unanimous in their leave-taking.'

'I shall try to remember that the next time I dine at the Abbey House,' said Mr Scobel, laughing.

'O, please don't!' cried Violet. 'You and Mrs Scobel are different. I don't mind you; but those dreadful stiff old ladies mamma cultivates, who think of nothing but their dress and their own importance − a little of them goes a very long way.'

'But, my dear Miss Tempest, the Carterets and the Horwoods are some of the best people in the neighbourhood.'

'Of course they are,' answered Vixen. 'If they were not they would hardly venture to be so stupid. They take the full license of their acres and their quarterings. People with a coat-of-arms found yesterday, and no land to speak of, are obliged to make themselves agreeable.'

'Like Captain Winstanley,' suggested Mr Scobel. 'I don't suppose he had land enough to sod a lark. But he is excellent company.'

'Very,' suggested Vixen, 'for the people who like him.'

They were at the gate by this time.

'You sha'n't come any farther unless you are coming in to see mamma,' protested Vixen.

'Thanks, no; it's too late to think of that.'

'Then go home immediately, and have some supper,' said Vixen imperatively. 'You've had nothing but a cup of weak tea since two o'clock this afternoon. You must be worn out.'

'On such an occasion as to-day a man must not think of himself,' said the Vicar.

'I wonder when you ever do think of yourself,' said Vixen.

And indeed Mr Scobel, like many another Anglican pastor of modern times, led a life which, save for its liberty to go where he listed, and to talk as much as he liked, was but little less severe in its exactions upon the flesh and the spirit than that of the monks of La Trappe.

The Abbey House looked very quiet when Vixen went into the hall, whose doors stood open to the soft spring night. The servants were all at supper, treating themselves to some extra comforts on the strength of a dinner-party, and talking over the evening's entertainment and its bearings on their mistress's life. There was a feeling in the servants' hall that these little dinners, however seemingly harmless, had a certain bent and tendency inimical to the household, and household peace.

'He was more particular in his manner to-night than hever,' said the butler, as he dismembered a duck which had been 'hotted up' after removal from the dining-room. 'He feels hisself master of the whole lot of us already. I could see it in his hi. "Is that the cabinet 'ock, Forbes?" he says to me, when I was a-filling round after the bait. "No," says I, "it is not. We ain't got so much of our cabinet 'ock that we can afford to trifle with 'em.' Of course I said it in a hundertone, confidential like; but I wanted him to know who was master of the cellar.'

'There'll be nobody master but him when once he gets his foot inside these doors,' said Mrs Trimmer, the housekeeper, with a mournful shake of the head. 'No, Porline, I'll have a noo pertater. Them canister peas ain't got no flaviour with them.'

While they were enjoying themselves, with a certain chastening touch of prophetic melancholy, in the servants' hall, Violet was going slowly upstairs and along the corridor which led past her mother's rooms.

'I must go in and wish mamma good-night,' she thought; 'though I am pretty sure of a lecture for my pains.'

Just at this moment a door opened, and a soft voice called 'Violet,' pleadingly.

'Dear mamma, I was just coming in to say good-night,'

'Were you, darling? I heard your footstep, and I was afraid you were going by. And I want very particularly to see you to-night, Violet.'

'Do you mamma? I hope not to scold me for going with the school-children. They had such a happy afternoon; and ate! it was like a miracle. Not so little serving for so many, but so few devouring so much.'

Pamela Tempest put her arm round her daughter, and kissed her, with more warmth of affection than she had shown since the sad days after the Squire's death. Violet looked at her mother wonderingly. She could hardly see the widow's fair delicate face in the dimly-lighted room. It was one of the prettiest rooms in the house – half boudoir half dressing-room, crowded with elegant luxuries and modern inventions, gipsy tables, book-stands, toy-cabinets of egg-shell china, a toilet table à la Pompadour, a writing-desk à la Sevigné. Such small things had made the small joys of Mrs Tempest's life. When she mourned her kind husband she lamented him as the someone who had bought her everything she wanted.

She had taken off her dinner-dress, and looked particularly fair and youthful in her soft muslin dressing-gown, trimmed with Mechlin lace which had cost as much as a small holding on the outskirts of the Forest. Even in that subdued light Violet could see that her mother's cheeks were pinker than usual, that her eyes were clouded with tears, and her manner anxiously agitated.

'Mamma,' cried the girl, 'there is something wrong, I know. Something has happened.'

'There is nothing wrong, love. But something has happened. Something which I hope will not make you unhappy – for it has made me very happy.'

'You are talking in enigmas, mamma, and I am too tired to be good at guessing riddles, just now,' said Violet, becoming suddenly cold as ice.

A few minutes ago she had been all gentleness and love, responding to the unwonted affection of her mother's caresses. Now she drew herself away and stood aloof, with her heart beating fast and furiously. She divined what was coming. She had guessed the riddle already.

'Come and sit by the fire, Violet, and I will tell you – everything,' said Mrs Tempest coaxingly, seating herself in the low semi-circular chair which was her especial delight.

'I can hear what you have to tell just as well where I am,' answered Violet curtly, walking to the latticed window, which was open to the night. The moon was shining over the rise and fall of the woods; the scent of the flowers came stealing up from the garden. Without, all was calm and sweetness, within, fever and smothered wrath. 'I can't think how you can endure a fire on such a night. The room is positively stifling.'

'Ah, Violet, you have not my sad susceptibility to cold.'

'No, mamma. I don't keep myself shut up like an unset diamond in a jeweller's strong-box.'

'I don't think I can tell you – the little secret I have to tell, Violet, unless you come over to me and sit by my side, and give me your hand, and let me feel as if you were really fond of me,' pleaded Mrs Tempest, with a little gush of piteousness. 'You seem like an enemy, standing over there with your back to me, looking out at the sky.'

'Perhaps there is no need for you to tell me anything, mamma,' answered Violet, in a tone which, to that tremulous listener in the low seat by the fire, sounded as severe as the voice of a judge pronouncing sentence. 'Shall I tell you the secret?'

There was no answer.

'Shall I, mamma?'

'I don't think you can, my love.'

'Yes; I am afraid I can. The secret – which is no secret to me or to anyone else in the world, any more than the place where the ostrich has put his head is a secret when his body is sticking up out of the sand – the secret is that, after being for seventeen happy honourable years the wife of the best and truest of men – the kindest, most devoted, and most generous of husbands – you are going to take another husband, who comes to you with no better credentials than a smooth tongue and a carefully-drilled figure, and who will punish your want of faith and constancy to my dead father by making the rest of your life miserable – as you will deserve that it shall be. Yes, mother, I, your only child, say so. You will deserve to be wretched if you marry Captain Winstanley.'

The widow gave a faint scream, half indignation, half terror. For the moment she felt as if some prophetic curse had been hurled at her. The tall straight figure in the white gown, standing in the full flood of the moonlight, looked awful as Cassandra, prophesying death and doom in the wicked house at Argos.

'It is too bad,' sobbed Mrs Tempest; 'it is cruel, undutiful, disrespectful, positively wicked for a daughter to talk to a mother as you have talked to me to-night. How can Miss McCroke have brought you up, I wonder, that you are capable of using such language? Have you forgotten the Fifth Commandment?'

'No. It tells me to honour my father and my mother. I honour my dead father, I honour you, when I try to save you from the perdition of a second marriage.'

'Perdition!' echoed Mrs Tempest faintly, 'what language!'

'I knew when that adventurer came here, that he intended to make himself master of this house – to steal my dead father's place,' cried Vixen passionately.

'You have no right to call him an adventurer. He is an officer and a gentleman. You offer him a cruel, an unprovoked insult.

You insult me still more deeply by your abuse of him. Am I so old or ugly, or so altogether horrid, that a man cannot love me for my own sake?'

'Not such a man as Captain Winstanley. He does not know what love means. He would have made me marry him if he could, because I am to have the estate by-and-by. Failing that, he has made you accept him for your husband. Yes, he has conquered you, as a cat conquers a bird, fascinating the poor wretch with its baleful green eyes. You are quite young enough and pretty enough to win a good man's regard, if you were a penniless unprotected widow, needing a husband to shelter you and provide for you. But you are the natural victim of such a man as Captain Winstanley.'

'You are altogether unjust and unreasonable,' exclaimed Mrs Tempest, weeping very copiously. 'Your poor dear father spoiled you. No one but a spoiled child would talk as you are talking. Who made you a judge of Captain Winstanley? It is not true that he ever wanted to marry you. I don't believe it for an instant.'

'Very well, mother. If you are wilfully blind——'

'I am not blind. I have lived twice as long as you have. I am a better judge of human nature than you can be.'

'Not of your admirer's, your flatterer's nature,' cried Vixen. 'He has slavered you with pretty speeches and soft words, as the cobra slavers his victim, and he will devour you, as the cobra does. He will swallow up your peace of mind, your self-respect, your independence, your money – all good things you possess. He will make you contemptible in the eyes of all who know you. He will make you base in your own eyes.'

'It is not true. You are blinded by prejudice.'

'I want to save you from yourself, if I can.'

'You are too late to save me, as you call it. Captain Winstanley has touched my heart by his patient devotion. I have not been so easily won as you seem to imagine. I have refused him three times. He knows that I had made up my mind never to marry again. Nothing was farther from my thought than a second marriage. I liked him as a companion and friend. That he knew. But I never intended that he should be more to me than a friend. He knew that. His patience has conquered me. Such devotion as he has given me has not often been offered to a woman. I do not think any woman living could resist it. He is all that is good and noble, and I am assured, Violet, that as a second father——'

Vixen interrupted her with a cry of horror.

'For God's sake, mamma, do not utter the word "father" in conjunction with his name. He may become your husband – I have no power to prevent that evil – but he shall never call himself my father.'

'What happiness can there be for any of us, Violet, when you start with such prejudices?' whimpered Mrs Tempest.

'I do not expect there will be much,' said Vixen. 'Good-night, mamma.'

'You are very unkind. You won't even stop to hear how it came about – how Conrad persuaded me to forego my determination.'

'No, mamma. I don't want to hear the details. The fact is enough for me. If it would be any use for me to go down upon my knees and entreat you to give up this man, I would gladly do it; but I fear it would be no use.'

'It would not, Violet,' answered the widow, with modest resoluteness. 'I have given Conrad my word. I cannot withdraw it.'

'Then I have nothing more to say,' replied Vixen, with her hand upon the door, 'except good-night.'

'You will not even kiss me?'

'Excuse me, mamma; I am not in a kissing humour.'

And so Vixen left her.

Mrs Tempest sat by the fading fire, and cried herself into a gentle slumber. It was very hard. She had longed to pour the story of this second courtship – its thrilling, unexpected joys, its wondrous surprises – into a sympathetic ear. And Violet, the natural recipient of these gentle confidences, had treated her so cruelly.

She felt herself secretly ill-used; and then came soothing thoughts about her *trousseau*, her wedding-dress, the dress in which she would start for her wedding-tour. All things would of course be chastened and subdued. No woman can be a bride twice in her life; but Mrs Tempest meant that the *trousseau* should, in its way, be perfect. There should be no rush or excitement in the preparation; nothing should be scamped or hurried. Calmness, deliberation, and a faultless taste should pervade all things.

'I will have no trimming but Valenciennes for my underlinen,' she decided; 'it is the only lace that never offends. And I will have old English monograms in satin-stitch upon everything. My *peignoirs* will require a good deal of study; they admit of so much variety. I will have only a few gowns, but those shall be from Paris. Theodore must go over and get them from Worth. She knows what suits me better than I do myself. I am not going to be extravagant; but Conrad so appreciates elegance and taste; and of course he will wish me to be well dressed.'

And so, comforted by these reflections, Mrs Tempest sank into a gentle slumber, from which she was awakened by Pauline, who had discussed her mistress's foolishness over a heavy supper, and now came to perform the duties of the evening toilet.

'O Pauline!' cried the widow, with a shiver, 'I am glad you awoke me. I've just had such an awful dream.'

'Lor', ma'am! What about?'

'O, an awful dream. I thought Madame Theodore sent me home a *trousseau* and that there was not a single thing that would fit. I looked an object in every one of the dresses.'

CHAPTER 19

WEDDING GARMENTS

After that night Vixen held her peace. There were no more bitter words between Mrs Tempest and her daughter, but the mother knew that there was a well-spring of bitterness — a

Marah whose waters were inexhaustible – in her daughter's heart; and that domestic happiness, under one roof, was henceforth impossible for these two.

There were very few words of any kind between Violet and Mrs Tempest at this time. The girl kept herself as much as possible apart from her mother. The widow lived her languid drawing-room life, dawdling away long slow days that left no more impression behind them than the drift of rose-leaves across the velvet lawn before her windows. A little point-lace, deftly worked by slim white fingers flashing with gems; a little Tennyson; a little Owen Meredith; a little Browning – only half understood at best; a little scandal; a great deal of orange pekoe, sipped out of old Worcester teacups of royal blue or flowered Swansea; an hour's letter-writing on the last fashionable note-paper; elegantly-worded insanity, delicately penned in a flowing Italian hand, with long loops to the Y's and G's and a serpentine curve at the end of every word.

No life could well have been more useless or vapid. Even Mrs Tempest's charities – those doles of wine and soup, bread and clothing, which are looked for naturally from the mistress of a fine old mansion – were vicarious. Trimmer, the housekeeper, did everything. Indeed, in the eyes of the surrounding poor, Mrs Trimmer was mistress of the Abbey House. It was to her they looked for relief; it was her reproof they feared; and to her they louted lowest. The faded beauty, reclining in her barouche, wrapped in white raiment of softest China crape, and whirling past them in a cloud of dust, was as remote as a goddess. They could hardly have realised the fact that she was fashioned out of the same clay that made themselves.

Upon so smooth and eventless an existence Captain Winstanley's presence came like a gust of north wind across the sultry languor of an August noontide. His energy, his prompt resolute manner of thinking and acting upon all occasions, impressed Mrs Tempest with an extraordinary sense of his strength of mind and manliness. It seemed to her that she must always be safe where he was. No danger, no difficulty could assail her while his strong arm was there to ward it off. She felt very much as Mary Stuart may have done about Bothwell; when, moved to scornful aversion by the silken boy-profligate Darnley, her heart acknowledged its master in the dark freebooter who had slain him. There had been no Darnley in Pamela Tempest's life; but this resolute clear-brained soldier was her Bothwell. She had the Mary Stuart temperament, the love of compliments and fine dresses, dainty needlework and luxurious living, without the Stuart craft. In Conrad Winstanley she had found her master, and she was content to be so mastered; willing to lay down her little sum of power at his feet, and live henceforward like a tame falcon at the end of a string. Her position, as a widow, was an excellent one. The Squire's will had been dictated in fullest confidence in his wife's goodness and discretion; and doubtless also with the soothing idea common to most hale and healthy men, that it must be a long time before their testamentary arrangements can come into effect. It was a holograph will, and the Squire's own composition throughout. 'He would have no lawyer's finger in that pie,' he had said. The disposal of his estate had cost him many hours of painful thought before he rang the bell for his bailiff and his butler, and executed his will in their presence.

Mrs Tempest was mistress of the Abbey House for her life; and at her death it was to become Violet's property. Violet was not to come of age until she was twenty-five, and in the mean time her mother was to be her sole guardian, and absolute mistress of everything. There was no question of an allowance for the maintenance of the heiress, no question as to the accumulation of income. Everything was to belong to Mrs Tempest till Violet came of age. She had only to educate and maintain her daughter in whatever manner she might think fit. At Violet's majority the estate was to pass into her possession, charged with an income of fifteen hundred a year, to be paid to the widow for her lifetime. Until her twenty-fifth birthday, therefore, Violet was in the position of a child, entirely dependent on her mother's liberality, and bound to obey her mother as her natural and only guardian. There was no court of appeal nearer than the Court of Chancery. There was no one to whom the two women could make their complaints or refer their differences.

Naturally, Captain Winstanley had long before this made himself acquainted with the particulars of the Squire's will. For six years he saw himself sole master of a very fine estate, and at the end of six years reduced to an income which seemed, comparatively, a pittance, and altogether inadequate for the maintenance of such a place as the Abbey House. Still, fifteen hundred a year and the Abbey House were a long way on the right side of nothing; and Captain Winstanley felt that he had fallen on his feet.

That was a dreary June for Vixen. She hugged her sorrow, and lived in a mental solitude which was almost awful in so young a soul. She made a confidante of no one, not even of kind-hearted Mrs Scobel, who was quite ready to pity her and condole with her, and who was secretly indignant at the widow's folly.

The fact of Mrs Tempest's intended marriage had become known to all her friends and neighbours, with the usual effect of such intelligence. Society said sweet things to her; and praised Captain Winstanley; and hoped the wedding would be soon; and opined that it would be quite a nice thing for Miss Tempest to have such an agreeable stepfather, with whom she could ride to hounds, as she had done with the dear Squire. And the same society, driving away from the Abbey House in its landaus and pony-carriages, after half-an-hour's pleasant gossip and a cup of delicately-flavoured tea, called Mrs Tempest a fool, and her intended husband an adventurer.

Vixen kept aloof from all the gossip and tea-drinking. She did not even go near her old friends the Scobels, in these days of smothered wrath and slow consuming indignation. She deserted the schools, her old pensioners, even the little village children, to whom she had loved to carry baskets of good things, and pocketfuls of halfpence, and whose queer country dialect had seemed as sweet to her as the carolling of finches and blackbirds in the woods. Everything in the way of charity was left to Mrs Trimmer now. Vixen took her long solitary rides in the Forest, roaming wherever there was a footway for her horse under the darkening beeches, dangerously near the swampy ground where the wet grass shone in the sunlight, the green reedy patches that

meant peril; into the calm unfathomable depths of Mark Ash, or
Queen's Bower; up to the wild heathy crest of Boldrewood;
wherever there was loneliness and beauty.

Roderick had gone to London for the season, and was riding
with Lady Mabel in the Row, or dancing attendance at garden-
parties, exhibitions, and flower-shows.

'I wonder how he likes the dusty days, and the crowded
rooms, the classical music, and high-art exhibitions?' thought
Vixen savagely. 'I wonder how he likes being led about like a
Pomeranian terrier? I don't think I could endure it if I were a
man. But I suppose when one is in love———'

And then Vixen thought of their last talk together, and how
little of the lover's enthusiasm there had been in Roderick's
mention of his cousin.

'In the bottom of my heart I know that he is going to marry
her for the sake of her estate, or because his mother wished it
and urged it, and he was too weak-minded to go on saying No.
I would not say it for the world, or let anyone else say it in my
hearing, but, in my heart of hearts, I know he does not love
her.'

And then, after a thoughtful silence, she cried to the mute
unresponsive woods:

'O, it is wicked, abominable, mad, to marry without love!'

The woods spoke to her of Roderick Vawdrey. How often
she had ridden by his side beneath these spreading beech-
boughs, dipping her childish head, just as she dipped it to-day,
under the low branches, steering her pony carefully between
the prickly holly-bushes, plunging deep into the hollows where
the dry leaves crackled under his hoofs.

'I fancied Rorie and I were to spend our lives together –
somehow,' she said to herself. 'It seems very strange for us to be
quite parted.'

She saw Mr Vawdrey's name in the fashionable newspapers,
in the lists of guests at dinners and drums. London life suited
him very well, no doubt. She heard that he was a member of
the Four-in-hand Club, and turned out in splendid style at
Hyde Park Corner. There was no talk yet of his going into
Parliament. That was an affair of the future.

Since that evening on which Mrs Tempest announced her intention of taking a second husband, Violet and Captain Winstanley had only met in the presence of other people. The Captain had tried to infuse a certain fatherly familiarity into his manner; but Vixen had met every attempt at friendliness with a sullen disdain, which kept even Conrad Winstanley at arm's length.

'We shall understand each other better by-and-by,' he said to himself, galled by this coldness. 'It would be a pity to disturb these halcyon days by anything in the way of a scene. I shall know how to manage Miss Tempest – afterwards.'

He spoke of her, and to her, always as Miss Tempest. He had never called her Violet since that night in the Pavilion garden.

These days before her wedding were indeed a halcyon season for Mrs Tempest. She existed in an atmosphere of millinery and pretty speeches. Her attention was called away from a ribbon by the sweet distraction of a compliment, and oscillated between tender whispers and honiton lace. Conrad Winstanley was a delightful lover. His enemies would have said that he had done the same kind of thing so often, that it would have been strange if he had not done it well. His was assuredly no 'prentice hand in the art. Poor Mrs Tempest lived in a state of mild intoxication, as dreamily delicious as the effects of opium. She was enchanged with her lover, and still better pleased with herself. At nine-and-thirty it was very sweet to find herself exercising so potent an influence over the Captain's strong nature. She could not help comparing herself to Cleopatra, and her lover to Antony. If he had not thrown away a world for her sake, he was at least ready to abandon the busy career which a man loves, and to devote his future existence to rural domesticity. He confessed that he had been hardened by much contact with the world, that he did not love now for the first time: but he told his betrothed that her influence had awakened feelings which had never before been called into life, that this love which he felt for her was to all intents and purposes a first love, the first pure and perfect affection that had subjugated and elevated his soul.

After that night in Mrs Tempest's boudoir, it was only by tacit avoidance of her mother that Vixen showed the intensity

of her disapproval. If she could have done any good by
reproof or entreaty, by pleading or exhortation, she would
assuredly have spoken; but she saw the Captain and her
mother together every day, and she knew that, opposed to his
influence, her words were like the idle wind which bloweth
where it listeth. So she held her peace, and looked on with an
aching angry heart, and hated the intruder who had come to
steal her dead father's place. To take her father's place; that in
Violet's mind was the unpardonable wrong. That any man
should enter that house as master, and sit in the Squire's seat,
and rule the Squire's servants, and ride the Squire's horses, was
an outrage beyond endurance. She might have looked more
leniently on her mother's folly, had the widow chosen a
second husband with a house and home of his own, who
would have carried off his wife to reign over his own
belongings, and left the Abbey House desolate – a temple
dedicated to the dead.

Mrs Tempest's manner towards her daughter during this
period was at once conciliatory and reproachful. She felt it a
hard thing that Violet should have taken up such an obnoxious
position. This complaint she repeated piteously, with many
variations, when she discussed Violet's unkindness with her
lover. She had no secrets from the Captain, and she told him all
the bitter things Violet had said about him.

He heard her with firmly-set lips and an angry sparkle in his
dark eyes, but his tone was full of paternal indulgence presently,
when Mrs Tempest had poured out all her woes.

'Is it not hard upon me, Conrad?' she asked in conclusion.

'My dear Pamela, I hope you are too strong-minded to
distress yourself seriously about a wilful girl's foolishness. Your
daughter has a noble nature, but she has been spoilt by too
much indulgence. Even a race-horse – the noblest thing in
creation – has to be broken in; not always without severe
punishment. Miss Tempest and I will come to understand each
other perfectly by-and-by.'

'I know you will be a second father to her,' said Mrs Tempest
tearfully.

'I will do my duty to her, dearest, be assured.'

Still Mrs Tempest went on harping upon the cruelty of her daughter's conduct. The consciousness of Violet's displeasure weighed heavily upon her.

'I dare not even show her my *trousseau*,' she complained, 'all confidence is at an end between us. I should like to have had her opinion about my dresses – though she is sadly deficient in taste, poor child! and has never even learnt to put on her gloves perfectly.'

'And your own taste is faultless, love,' replied the Captain soothingly. 'What can you want with advice from an inexperienced girl, whose mind is in the stable?'

'It is not her advice I want, Conrad, but her sympathy. Fanny Scobel is coming this afternoon. I can show her my things. I really feel quite nervous about talking to Violet of her own dress. She must have a new gown for the wedding, you know; though she cannot be a bridesmaid. I think that is really unfair. Don't you Conrad?'

'What is unfair, dearest?' asked the Captain, whose mind had scarcely followed the harmless meanderings of his lady's speech.

'That a widow is not allowed to have bridesmaids or orange-blossoms. It seems like taking the poetry out of a wedding, does it not?'

'Not to my mind, Pamela. The poetry of wedlock does not lie in these details – a sugared cake, and satin favours; a string of carriages, and a Brussels veil. The true poetry of marriage is in the devotion and fidelity of the two hearts it binds together.'

Mrs Tempest sighed gently, and was almost resigned to be married without bridesmaids or orange-blossoms.

It was now within a month of the wedding, which was to be solemnised on the last day of August – a convenient season for a honeymoon tour in Scotland. Mrs Tempest liked to travel when other people travelled. Mountain and flood would have had scarcely any charm for her 'out of the season.' The time had come when Violet's dress must be talked about, as Mrs Tempest told the Vicar's wife solemnly. She had confided the secret of her daughter's unkindness to Mrs Scobel, in the friendly hour of afternoon tea.

'It is very hard upon me,' she repeated — 'very hard that the only drawback to my happiness should come from my own child.'

'Violet was so fond of her father,' said Mrs Scobel excusingly.

'But is that any reason she should treat me unkindly? Who could have been fonder of dear Edward than I was? I studied his happiness in everything. There never was an unkind word between us. I do not think anyone could expect me to go down to my grave a widow, in order to prove my affection for my dearest Edward. That was proved by every act of my married life. I have nothing to regret, nothing to atone for. I feel myself free to reward Captain Winstanley's devotion. He has followed me from place to place for the last two years; and has remained constant, in spite of every rebuff. He proposed to me three times before I accepted him.'

Mrs Scobel had been favoured with the history of these three separate offers more than once.

'I know, dear Mrs Tempest,' she said somewhat hurriedly, lest her friend should recapitulate the details. 'He certainly seems very devoted. But, of course, from a worldly point of view, you are an excellent match for him.'

'Do you think I would marry him if I thought that consideration had any weight with him?' demanded Mrs Tempest indignantly. And Mrs Scobel could say no more.

There are cases of physical blindness past the skill of surgery, but there is no blindness more incurable than that of a woman on the verge of forty who fancies herself beloved.

'But Violet's dress for the wedding ,' said Mrs Scobel, anxious to get the conversation upon safer ground. 'Have you really said nothing to her about it?'

'No. She is so headstrong and self-willed. I have been absolutely afraid to speak. But it must be settled immediately. Theodore is always so busy. It will be quite a favour to get the dress made at so short a notice, I daresay.'

'Why not speak to Violet this afternoon?'

'While you are here? Yes, I might do that,' replied Mrs Tempest eagerly.

She felt that she could approach the subject more comfortably in Mrs Scobel's presence. There would be a kind of protection in a third person. She rang the bell.

'Has Miss Tempest come home from her ride?'

'Yes, ma'am. She has just come in.'

'Send her to me at once then. Ask her not to stop to change her dress.'

Mrs Tempest and Mrs Scobel were in the drawing-room, sitting at a gipsy table before an open window; the widow wrapped in a China-crape shawl, lest even the summer breeze should be too chill for her delicate frame, the Worcester cups and saucers, and antique silver teapot and caddy and kettle set out before her, like a child's toys.

Violet came running in, flushed after her ride, her habit muddy.

'Bogged again!' cried Mrs Tempest, with ineffable disgust. That horse will be the death of you some day.'

'I think not, mamma. How do you do, Mrs Scobel?'

'Violet,' said the Vicar's wife gravely, 'why do you never come to our week-day services now?'

'I – I – don't know. I have not felt in the humour for coming to church. It's no use to come and kneel in a holy place with rebellious thoughts in my head. I come on Sundays for decency's sake; but I think it's better to keep away from the week-day services till I am in a better temper.'

'I don't think that's quite the way to recover your temper, dear.'

Violet was silent, and there was a rather awkward pause.

'Will you have a cup of tea, dear?' asked Mrs Tempest.

'No, thanks, mamma. I think, unless you have something very particular to say to me, I had better take my muddy habit off your carpet. I feel rather warm and dusty. I shall be glad to change my dress.'

'But I have something very particular to say, Violet. I won't detain you long. You'd better have a cup of tea.'

'Just as you please, mamma.'

And forgetful of her clay-bespattered habit, Violet sank into one of the satin-covered chairs, and made a wreck of an antimacassar worked in crewels by Mrs Tempest's own hands.

'I am going to write to Madame Theodore by this evening's post, Violet,' said her mother, handing her a cup of tea, and making believe not to see the destruction of that exquisite antimacassar; 'and I should like to order your gown for – the – wedding. I have been thinking that cream-colour and pale blue would suit you to perfection. A cream-coloured hat – the Vandyke shape – with a long blue ostrich——'

'Please don't take any trouble about it, mamma,' said Vixen whose cheek had paled at the word 'wedding,' and who now sat very erect in her chair, holding her cup and saucer firmly. 'I am not going to be present at your wedding, so I shall not want a gown.'

'Violet!' cried Mrs Tempest, beginning to tremble. 'You cannot mean what you say. You have been very unkind, very undutiful. You have made me perfectly miserable for the last seven weeks; but I cannot believe that you would – grossly insult me – by refusing to be present at my wedding.'

'I do not wish to insult you, mamma. I am very sorry if I have pained you, but I cannot and will not be present at a marriage the very idea of which is hateful to me. If my presence could give any sanction to this madness of yours, that sanction shall not be given.'

'Violet, have you thought what you are doing? Have you considered what will be said – by the world?'

'I think the world – our world – must have made up its mind about your second marriage already, mamma.' Vixen answered quietly. 'My absence from your wedding can make very little difference.'

'It will make a very great difference, and you know it!' cried Mrs Tempest, roused to as much passion as she was capable of feeling. 'People will say that my daughter sets her face against my marriage – my daughter, who ought to sympathise with me, and rejoice that I have found a true friend and protector.'

'I cannot either sympathise or rejoice, mamma. It is much better that I should stop away from your wedding. I should look miserable, and make other people uncomfortable.'

'Your absence will humiliate and lower me in the sight of my friends. It will be a disgrace. And you take this course on purpose to wound and injure me. You are a wicked undutiful daughter.'

'O mamma!' cried Vixen, with grave voice and reproachful eyes — eyes, before whose steady gaze the tearful widow drooped and trembled, 'is duty so one-sided? Do I owe all to you, and you nothing to me? My father left us together, mother and daughter, to be all the world to each other. He left us mistresses of the dear old home we had shared with him. Do you think he meant a stranger to come and sit in his place — to be master over all he loved? Do you think it ever entered his mind that, in three little years, his place would be filled by the first-comer — his daughter asked to call another man father?'

'The first-comer!' whimpered Mrs Tempest. 'O, this is too cruel!'

'Violet!' exclaimed Mrs Scobel reprovingly, 'when you are calmer you will be sorry for having spoken so unkindly to your dear mamma.'

'I shall not be sorry for having spoken the truth,' said Violet. 'Mamma has heard the truth too seldom in her life. She will not hear it from Captain Winstanley — yet awhile.'

And after flinging this last poisoned dart, Vixen took up the muddy skirt of her habit and left the room.

'It was rather a pity that Arion and I did not go to the bottom of that bog and stay there,' she reflected. 'I don't think anybody wants us above ground.'

'Did you ever know anything so humiliating, so shameful, so undutiful?' demanded Mrs Tempest piteously, as the door closed on her rebellious daughter. 'What will people say if Violet is not at my wedding?'

'It would be awkward, certainly; unless there were some good reason for her absence.'

'People are so ill-natured. Nobody would believe in any excuse that was made. That cruel girl will disgrace me.'

'She seems strongly prejudiced against Captain Winstanley. It is a great pity; but I daresay she will relent in time. If I were you, dear Mrs Tempest, I should order the gown.'

'Would you really, Fanny?'

'Yes; I should order the gown, and trust in Providence for the result. You may be able to bring her round somehow between now and the wedding.'

'But I am not going to humiliate myself. I am not going to be trampled on by my daughter.'

'Of course not; but you must have her at your wedding.'

'If I were to tell Captain Winstanley what she has said this afternoon——'

'He would be very angry, no doubt; but I would not tell him if I were you.'

'No, I shall not say anything about it.'

Yet, before night, Captain Winstanley had heard every syllable that Vixen had said; with some trifling and unconscious exaggerations, hardly to be avoided by a woman of Mrs Tempest's character, in the narration of her own wrongs.

CHAPTER 20

'I SHALL LOOK LIKE THE WICKED FAIRY'

Nothing in Captain Winstanley's manner during the sultry summer days which went before his marriage betrayed his knowledge of Violet Tempest's rebellious spirit. He would not see that he was obnoxious to her. He spoke to her and looked at her as sweetly as if there had been the friendliest understanding between them. In all his conduct, in any act of his which approached the assumption of authority, he went to work with supreme gentleness. Yet he had his grip upon everything already, and was extending his arms in every direction, like an octopus. There were alterations being made in the gardens which Violet knew were his, although Mrs Tempest was supposed to have originated them. He had, in some measure, assumed dominion over the stables; his two hunters were already quartered there. Vixen saw them when she went her morning round with a basket of bread. They were long-bodied, hungry-looking animals, and the grooms reported them ravenous and insatiable in their feeding.

'When they've eat their corn they eats their 'ay, and when they've eat their 'ay they eats their bed, and then they takes and gnaws the wooden partitions. They'll eat up all the woodwork in the stable before they've done. I never see such brutes,' complained Bates, the head-groom.

Vixen fancied these animals were in some wise typical of their owner.

One morning when Vixen was leaning upon the half-door of Arion's loose-box, giving herself up to a quarter of an hour's petting of that much-loved animal, Captain Winstanley came into the stable.

'Good-morning, Miss Tempest. Petting that pretty little bay of yours?' I'm afraid you spoil him. You ought to hunt him next October.'

'I shall never hunt again.'

'Pshaw! At your age there's no such word as never. He's the neatest little hunter in the Forest. And on his by-days you might ride one of mine.'

'Thanks,' said Vixen, with a supercilious glance at the most leggy of the two hunters, 'I shouldn't care to be up there. I should feel myself out of everything.'

'O, by-the-way,' said Winstanley, opening the door of another loose-box, 'what are we to do with this fellow?'

'This fellow' was a grand-looking bay, with herculean quarters, short legs, and a head like a war-horse. He snorted indignantly as the Captain slapped his flank, and reared his splendid crest, and seemed as if he said 'Ha, ha!'

'I don't quite know of whom you are speaking when you say "we,"' said Vixen, with an unsmiling countenance.

'Naturally of your mother and myself. I should like to include you in all our family arrangements, present or future; but you seem to prefer being left outside.'

'Yes,' replied Vixen, 'I prefer to stand alone.'

'Very well then. I repeat my question – though, as you decline to have any voice in our arrangements, it's hardly worth while to trouble you about it — what are we to do with this fellow?'

'Do with him? My father's horse!' exclaimed Vixen; 'the horse he rode to his dying day! Why, keep him, of course!'

'Don't you think that is rather foolish? Nobody rides or drives him. It takes all one man's time to groom him and exercise him. You might just as well keep a white elephant in the stables.'

'He was my father's favourite horse,' said Vixen, with indignant tears clouding the bright hazel of her eyes; 'I cannot imagine mamma capable of parting with him. Yet I ought not to say that, after my experience of the last few months,' she added in an undertone.

'Well, my dear Miss Tempest, family affection is a very charming sentiment, and I can quite understand that you and your mamma would be anxious to secure your father's horse a good home and a kind master; but I cannot comprehend your mamma being so foolish as to keep a horse which is of no use to any member of her family. If the brute were of a little lighter build, I wouldn't mind riding him myself, and selling one of mine. But he's too much of a weight-carrier for me.'

Vixen gave Arion a final hug, drying her angry tears upon his soft neck, and left the stable without another word. She went straight to her mother's morning-room, where the widow was sitting at a table covered with handkerchief-cases and glove-boxes, deeply absorbed in the study of their contents, assisted by the faithful Pauline, otherwise Polly, who had been wearing smarter gowns and caps ever since her mistress's engagement, and who was getting up a *trousseau* on her own account, in order to enter upon her new phase of existence with due dignity.

'We shall keep more company, I make no doubt, with such a gay young master as the Captain,' she had observed in the confidences of Mrs Trimmer's comfortable parlour.

'I can never bring myself to think Swedish gloves pretty,' said Mrs Tempest, as Vixen burst into the room, 'but they are the fashion, and one must wear them.'

'Mamma,' cried Vixen, 'Captain Winstanley wants you to sell Bullfinch. If you let him be sold, you will be the meanest of women.'

And with this startling address Vixen left the room as suddenly as she had entered it, banging the door behind her.

Time, which brings all things, brought the eve of Mrs Tempest's wedding. The small but perfect *trousseau*, subject of such anxious thoughts, so much study, was completed. The travelling-dresses were packed in two large oilskin-covered baskets, ready for the Scottish tour. The new travelling-bag, with monograms in pink coral on silver-gilt, a wedding present from Captain Winstanley, occupied the place of honour in Mrs Tempest's dressing-room. The wedding-gown, of cream-coloured brocade and old point-lace, with a bonnet of lace and water-lilies, was spread upon the sofa. Everything in Mrs Tempest's apartment bore witness to the impending change in the lady's life. Most of all, the swollen eyelids and pale cheeks of the lady, who, on this vigil of her wedding-day, had given herself up to weeping.

'O mum, your eyes will be that red to-morrow,' remonstrated Pauline, coming into the room with another dainty little box, newly-arrived from the nearest railway-station, and surprising her mistress in tears. 'Do have some red lavender. Or let me make you a cup of tea.'

Mrs Tempest had been sustaining nature with cups of tea all through the agitating day. It was a kind of dram-drinking, and she was as much a slave of the teapot as the forlorn drunken drab of St Giles's is a slave of the gin-bottle.

'Yes, you may get me another cup of tea, Pauline. I feel awfully low to-night.'

'You seem so, mum. I'm sure if I didn't want to marry him, I wouldn't, if I was you. It's never too late for a woman to change her mind, not even when she's inside the church. I've known it done. I wouldn't have him, mum, if you feel your mind turn against him at the last,' concluded the lady's-maid energetically.

'Not marry him, Pauline, when he is so good and noble, so devoted, so unselfish!'

Mrs Tempest might have extended this list of virtues indefinitely, if her old servant had not pulled her up rather sharply.

'Well, mum, if he's so good and you're so fond of him, why cry?'

'You don't understand, Pauline. At such a time there are many painful feelings. I have been thinking, naturally, of my dear Edward, the best and most generous of husbands. Twenty years last June since we were married. What a child I was, Pauline, knowing nothing of the world. I had a lovely *trousseau*; but I daresay if we could see the dresses now we should think them absolutely ridiculous. Dear Edward! He was one of the handsomest men I ever saw. How could Violet believe that I should sell his favourite horse?'

'Well, mum, hearing Captain Winstanley talk about it, she naturally——'

'Captain Winstanley would never wish me to do anything I did not like.'

The Captain had not said a word about Bullfinch since that morning in the stable. The noble brute still occupied his loose-box, and was fed and petted daily by Vixen, and was taken for gallops in the dry glades of the Forest, or on the grassy crest of Boldrewood.

Mrs Tempest had dined – or rather had not dined – in her own room on this last day of her widowhood. Captain Winstanley had business in London, and was coming back to Hampshire by the last train. There had been no settlements. The Captain had nothing to settle, and Mrs Tempest confided in her lover too completely to desire to fence herself round with legal protections and precautions. Having only a life interest in the estate, she had nothing to leave, except the multifarious ornaments, frivolities, and luxuries which the Squire had presented to her in the course of their wedded life.

It had been altogether a trying day, Mrs Tempest complained: in spite of the diversion to painful thought which was continually being offered by the arrival of some interesting item of the *trousseau*, elegant trifles, ordered ever so long ago, which kept dropping in at the last moment. Violet and her mother had not met during the day, and now night was hurrying on. The owls were hooting in the Forest. Their monotonous cry sounded every now and then through the evening silence like a prophecy of evil. In less than twelve hours the wedding was to take place; and as yet Vixen had shown no signs of relenting.

The dress had come from Madame Theodore's. Pauline had thrown it over a chair, with an artistic carelessness which displayed the tasteful combination of cream colour and pale azure.

Mrs Tempest contemplated it with a pathetic countenance.

'It is simply perfect!' she exclaimed. 'Theodore has a most delicate mind. There is not an atom too much blue. And how exquisitely the drapery falls! The Vandyke hat too! Violet would look lovely in it. I do not think if I were a wicked mother I should take so much pains to select an elegant costume for her. But I have always studied her dress. Even when she was in pinafores I took care that she should be picturesque. And she rewards my care by refusing to be present at my wedding. It is very cruel.'

The clock struck twelve. The obscure bird clamoured a little louder in his woodland haunt. The patient Pauline, who had packed everything and arranged everything, and borne with her mistress's dolefulness all day long, began to yawn piteously.

'If you'd let me brush your hair now, ma'am,' she suggested at last, 'I could get to bed. I should like to be fresh to-morrow morning.'

'Are you tired?' exclaimed Mrs Tempest wonderingly.

'Well, mum, stooping over them dress-baskets is rather tiring, and it's past twelve.'

'You can go. I'll brush my hair myself.'

'No, mum, I wouldn't allow that anyhow. It would make your arms ache. You ought to get to bed as soon as ever you can, or you'll look tired and 'aggard to-morrow.'

That word haggard alarmed Mrs Tempest. She would not have objected to look pale and interesting on her wedding-day, like one who had spent the previous night in tears; but haggardness suggested age; and she wanted to look her youngest when uniting herself to a husband who was her junior by some years.

So Pauline was allowed to hurry on the evening toilet. The soft hair, not so abundant as it used to be, was carefully brushed;

the night-lamp was lighted; and Pauline left her mistress sitting by her dressing-table in her flowing white raiment, pale, graceful, subdued in colouring, like a classic figure in a faded fresco.

She sat with fixed eyes, deep in thought, for some time after Pauline had left her, then looked uneasily at the little watch dangling on its ormolu stand. A quarter to one. Violet must have gone to bed hours ago; unless, indeed, Violet were like her mother, too unhappy to be able to sleep. Mrs Tempest was seized with a sudden desire to see her daughter.

'How unkind of her never to come near me to say good-night, on this night of all others!' she thought. 'What has she been doing all day, I wonder? Riding about the Forest, I suppose, like a wild girl, making friends of dogs and horses, and gipsies, and fox-cubs, and charcoal-burners, and all kinds of savage creatures.'

And then, after a pause, she asked herself truthfully:

'What will people say if my own daughter is not at my wedding?'

The idea of possible slander stung her sharply. She got up and walked up and down the room, inwardly complaining against Providence for using her so badly. To have such a rebellious daughter! It was sharper than a serpent's tooth.

The time had not been allowed to go by without some endeavour being made to bring Violet to a better state of feeling. That was the tone taken about her by Mrs Tempest and the Vicar's wife in their conferences. The headstrong, misguided girl was to be brought to a better state of mind. Mrs Scobel tackled her, bringing all her diplomacy to bear, but without avail. Vixen was rock. Then Mr Scobel undertook the duty, and, with all the authority of his holy office, called upon Violet to put aside her unchristian prejudices, and behave as a meek and dutiful daughter.

'Is it unchristian to hate the man who has usurped my father's place?' Violet asked curtly.

'It is unchristian to hate anyone. And you have no right to call Captain Winstanley a usurper. You have no reason to take your mother's marriage so much to heart. There is nothing sinful, or even radically objectionable in a second marriage; though I admit, that to my mind, a woman is worthier in remaining faithful to her first love; like Anna, the prophetess, who had been a widow fourscore-and-four years. Who shall say that her exceptional gift of prophecy may not have been a reward for the purity and fidelity of her life?'

Mr Scobel's arguments were of no more effect than his wife's persuasion. His heart was secretly on Violet's side. He had loved the Squire, and he thought this marriage of Mrs Tempest's a foolish, if not a shameful thing. There was no heartiness in the feeling with which he supervised the decoration of his pretty little church for the wedding.

'If she were only awake,' thought Mrs Tempest, 'I would make a last appeal to her feelings – late as it is. Her heart cannot be stone.'

She took her candle, and went through the dark silent house to Violet's room, and knocked gently.

'Come in,' said the girl's clear voice with a wakeful sound.

'Ah!' thought Mrs Tempest triumphantly, 'obstinate as she is, she knows she is doing wrong. Conscience won't let her sleep.'

Vixen was standing at her window, leaning with folded arms upon the broad wooden ledge, looking out at the dim garden, over which pale stars were shining. There was a moon, but it was hidden by drifting clouds.

'Not in bed, Violet,' said her mother sweetly.

'No, mamma.'

'What have you been doing all these hours?'

'I don't know – thinking.'

'And you never came to wish me good-night.'

'I did not think you would want me. I thought you would be busy packing – for your honeymoon.'

'That was not kind, Violet. You must have known that I should have many painful thoughts to-night.'

'I did not know it. And if it is so, I can only say it is a pity the painful thoughts did not come a little sooner.'

'Violet, you are as hard as iron, as cold as ice!' cried Mrs Tempest, with passionate fretfulness.

'No, I am not, mamma; I can love very warmly, where I love deeply. I have given this night to thoughts of my dead father, whose place is to be usurped in this house from to-morrow.'

'I never knew anyone so obstinately unkind. I could not have believed it possible in my own daughter. I thought you had a good heart, Violet; and yet you do not mind making me intensely wretched on my wedding-day.'

'Why should you be wretched, mamma, because I prefer not to be present at your wedding? If I were there, I should be like the bad fairy at the princess's christening. I should look at everything with a malevolent eye.'

Mrs Tempest flung herself into a chair and burst into tears.

The storm of grief which had been brooding over her troubled mind all day, broke suddenly in a tempest of weeping. She could have given no reason for her distress; but all at once, on the eve of that day which was to give a new colour to her life, panic seized her, and she trembled at the step she was about to take.

'You are very cruel to me, Violet,' she sobbed. 'I am a most miserable woman.'

Violet knelt beside her and gently took her hand, moved to pity by wretchedness so abject.

'Dear mother, why miserable?' she asked. 'This thing which you are doing is your own choice. Or, if it is not – if you have yielded weakly to persuasion – it is not too late to draw back. No, dear mother, even now it is not too late. Let us run away as soon as it is light, you and I, and go off to Spain, or Italy, anywhere, leaving a letter for Captain Winstanley, to say you have changed your mind. He could not do anything to us. You have a right to draw back, even at the last.'

'Don't talk nonsense, Violet,' cried Mrs Tempest peevishly. 'Who said I had changed my mind? I am as devoted to Conrad as he is to me. I should be a heartless wretch if I could throw him over at the last moment. But this has been a most agitating day. Your unkindness is breaking my heart.'

'Indeed, mamma, I have no wish to be unkind – not to you. But my presence at your wedding would be a lie. It would seem to give my approval to an act I hate. I cannot bring myself to do that.'

'And you will disgrace me by your absence? You do not care what people may say of me.'

'Nobody will care about my absence. You will be the queen of the day.'

'Everybody will care – everybody will talk. I know how malicious people are, even one's most intimate friends. They will say my own daughter turned her back upon me on my wedding-day.'

'They can hardly say that, when I shall be here in your house!'

Mrs Tempest went on weeping. She had reduced herself to a condition in which it was much easier to cry than to leave off crying. The fountain of her tears seemed inexhaustible.

'A pretty object I shall look to-morrow,' she murmured plaintively, and this was all she said for some time.

Violet walked up and down the room, sorely distressed, sorely perplexed. To see her mother's grief, and to be able to give comfort, and to refuse. That must be undutiful, undaughterly, rebellious. But had not her mother forfeited all right to her obedience? Were not their hearts and lives completely sundered by this marriage of to-morrow? To Violet's stronger nature it seemed as if she were the mother – offended, outraged by a child's folly and weakness. There sat the child, weeping piteously, yearning to be forgiven. It was a complete reversal of their positions.

Her heart was touched by the spectacle of her mother's weakness, by the mute appeal of those tears.

'What does it matter to me, after all, whether I am absent or present?' she argued at last. 'I cannot prevent this man coming to take possession of my father's house. I cannot hinder the outrage to my father's memory. My mother has been very kind to me – and I have no one else in the world to love.'

She took a few more turns, and then stopped by her mother's chair.

'Will it really make you happier, mamma, if I am at your wedding?'

'It will make me quite happy.'

'Very well, then; it shall be as you please. But, remember, I shall look like the wicked fairy. I can't help that.'

'You will look lovely. Theodore has sent you home the most exquisite gown. Come to my room and try it on,' said Mrs Tempest, drying her tears, and as quickly comforted as a child who has obtained its desire by means of copious weeping.

'No, dear mamma; not to-night, I'm too tired,' sighed Violet.

'Never mind, dear. Theodore always fits you to perfection. Go to bed at once, love. The gown will be a pleasant surprise for you in the morning. Good-night, pet. You have made me so happy.'

'I am glad of that, mamma.'

'I wish you were going to Scotland with us.' (Vixen shuddered.) 'I'm afraid you'll be dreadfully bored here.'

'No, mamma; I shall have the dogs and horses. I shall get on very well.'

'You are such a curious girl. Well, good-night, darling. You are my own Violet again.'

And with this they parted; Mrs Tempest going back to her room with restored peace of mind.

She looked at the reflection of her tear-blotted face anxiously as she paused before the glass.

'I'm afraid I shall look an object to-morrow,' she said. 'The morning sunshine is so searching.'

CHAPTER 21

THE VOW IS VOWED

Only a chosen few had been bidden to Mrs Tempest's wedding. She had told all her friends that she meant everything to be done very quietly.

'There is so much that is saddening in my position,' she said pensively. But she was resolved that those guests who were asked to lend their countenance to her espousals should be the very best people.

Lord and Lady Ellangowan had been asked and had accepted, and their presence alone would lend dignity to the occasion. Colonel and Mrs Carteret, from Copse Hall; the Chopnells, of Chopnell Park; and about half-a-dozen other representative landowners and commoners made up the list.

'There is such a satisfaction in knowing they are all the best people,' Mrs Tempest said to Captain Winstanley, when they went over the list together.

His own friends were but two, Major Pontorson, his best man, and a clerical cousin, with a portly figure and a portwiney nose, who was to assist Mr Scobel in the marriage service.

It was a very pretty wedding, the neighbourhood declared unanimously, despite the absence of that most attractive feature in more youthful bridals —a string of girlish bridesmaids. The little church at Beechdale was a bower of summer flowers. The Abbey House conservatories had been emptied – the Ellangowans had sent a waggon-load of ferns and exotics. The atmosphere was heavy with the scent of yellow roses and stephanotis.

Violet stood among the guests, no gleam of colour on her cheeks except the wavering hues reflected from the painted windows in the low Gothic chancel – the ruddy gold of her hair shining under the Vandyke hat with its sweeping azure feather. She was the loveliest thing in that crowded church, whither people had come from ten miles off to see Squire Tempest's widow married; but she had a spectral look in the faint light of the chancel, and seemed as strange an image at this wedding as the ghost of Don Ramiro at Donna Clara's bridal dance, in Heine's ghastly ballad.

Violet did not look like the malevolent fairy in the old story, but she had a look and air which told every one that this marriage was distasteful to her.

When all was over, and the register had been signed in the vestry, Captain Winstanley came up to her, with both hands extended, before all the company.

'My dear Violet, I am your father now,' he said. 'You shall not find me wanting in my duty.'

She drew back involuntarily; and then, seeing herself the focus of so many eyes, suffered him to touch the tips of her fingers.

'You are very kind,' she said. 'A daughter can have but one father, and mine is dead. I hope you will be a good husband to my mother. That is all I can desire of you.'

All the best people heard this speech, which was spoken deliberately, in a low clear voice; and they decided inwardly that whatever kind of wife Captain Winstanley might have won for himself, he had found his match in his stepdaughter.

Now came the drive to the Abbey House, which had put on a festive air, and where smartly-dressed servants were lending their smiles to a day which they all felt to be the end of a peaceful and comfortable era, and the beginning of an age of uncertainty. It was like that day at Versailles when the Third Estate adjourned to the Tennis Court, and the French Revolution began. People smiled, and were pleased at the new movement and expectancy in their lives, knowing not what was coming.

'We are bound to be livelier, anyhow, with a military master.' said Pauline.

'A little more company in the house wouldn't come amiss, certainly,' said Mrs Trimmer.

'I should like to see our champagne cellar better stocked,' remarked Forbes the butler. 'We're behind the times in our sparkling wines.'

Captain Winstanley entered the old oak-panelled hall with his wife on his arm, and felt himself master of such a house as a man might dream of all his life and never attain. Money could not have bought it. Taste could not have created it. The mellowing hand of time, the birth and death of many generations, had made it beautiful.

The wedding breakfast was as other wedding feasts. People ate and drank and made believe to be intensely glad, and drank more sparkling wine than was good for them at that early hour, and began to feel sleepy before the speeches, brief as they were, had come to an end. The August sun shone in upon the banquet, the creams and jellies languished and collapsed in the sultry air. The wedding-cake was felt to be a nuisance. The weather was too warm for enthusiasm. And Violet's pale set face was almost as disheartening as the skeleton of an Egyptian banquet. When Mrs Winstanley retired to put on her travelling-dress Violet went with her, a filial attention the mother had in no wise expected.

'Dear girl,' she said, squeezing her daughter's hand, 'to-day is not to make the slightest difference.'

'I hope not, mamma,' answered Violet gravely; 'but one can never tell what is in the future. God grant you may be happy!'

'I'm sure it will be my own fault if I am not happy with Conrad,' said the wife of an hour, 'and O, Violet! my constant prayer will be to see you more attached to him.'

Violet made no reply, and here happily Pauline brought the fawn-coloured travelling-dress, embroidered with poppies and cornflowers in their natural colours, after the style of South Kensington, a gown so distractingly lovely that it instantly put an end to serious conversation. The whole costume had been carefully thought out, a fawn-coloured parasol, edged with ostrich feathers; a fawn-coloured bonnet, fawn-coloured Hessian boots, fawn-coloured Swedish gloves, with ten buttons – all prepared for the edification of railway guards and porters, and Scotch innkeepers and their *valetaille*.

Violet stayed with her mother to the last, received the last embrace – a fond and tearful one – and watched the carriage drive away from the porch amidst a shower of rice. And then all was over. The best people were bidding her a kindly good-bye. Carriages drove up quickly, and in a quarter of an hour every one was gone except the Vicar and his wife. Vixen found herself standing between Mr and Mrs Scobel, looking blankly at the hearth, where an artistic group of ferns and scarlet geraniums replaced the friendly winter fire.

'Come and spend the evening with us, dear,' said Mrs Scobel kindly; 'it will be so lonely for you here.'

But Violet pleaded a headache, a plea which was confirmed by her pale cheeks and the dark rings round her eyes.

'I shall be better at home,' she said. 'I'll come and see you in a day or two, if I may.'

'Come whenever you like, dear; I wish you would come and stay with us altogether. Ignatius and I have been so pleased with your conduct to-day; and we have felt for you deeply, knowing what a conquest you have made over yourself.'

The Reverend Ignatius murmured his acquiescence.

'Poor mamma!' sighed Violet, 'I am afraid I have been very unkind.'

And then she looked absently round the old familiar hall, and her eye lighted on the Squire's favourite chair, which still stood in its place by the hearth. Her eyes filled with sudden tears. She fancied she could see a shadowy figure sitting there. The Squire in his red coat, his long hunting whip across his knee, his honest loving face smiling at her.

She squeezed Mrs Scobel's friendly hand, bade her and the Vicar a hurried good-bye, and ran out of the room, leaving them looking after her pityingly.

'Poor girl,' said the Vicar's wife, 'how keenly she feels it!'

'Ah!' sighed the Vicar, 'I have never been in favour of second marriages. I can but think with St Paul, that the widow is happier if she so abide.'

Vixen called Argus and went up to her room, followed by that faithful companion. When she had shut and locked her door, she flung herself on the ground, regardless of Madame Theodore's masterpiece, and clasped her arms round the dog's thick neck, and buried her face in his soft hide.

'O Argus, I have not a friend in the world but you!' she sobbed.

CHAPTER 22

WAR TO THE KNIFE

A strange stillness came upon the Abbey House after Mrs Tempest's wedding. Violet received a few invitations and

morning calls from friends who pitied her solitude; but the best
people were for the most part away from home in August and
September.

Violet did not want society. She made excuses for refusing all
invitations. The solitude of her life did not afflict her. If it could
have continued for ever, if Captain Winstanley and her mother
could have wandered about the earth, and left her in peaceful
possession of the Abbey House, with the old servants, old
horses, old dogs, all things undisturbed as in her father's times,
she would have been happy. It was the idea of change, a new
and upstart master in her father's place, which tortured her. Any
delay which kept off that evil hour was a blessed relief; but, alas!
the evil hour was close at hand, inevitable. That autumn proved
exceptionally fine. Scotland cast aside her mantle of mist and
cloud, and dressed herself in sunshine. The Trossachs blossomed
like the rose. Gloomy gray glens and mountains put on an
apparel of light. Mrs Winstanley wrote her daughter rapturous
letters about the tour.

'We move about very slowly,' she said, 'so as not to
fatigue me. Conrad's attention is more than words can
describe. I can see that even the waiters are touched by it.
He telegraphs beforehand to all the hotels, so that we have
always the best rooms. He thinks nothing too good for me.
It is quite saddening to see a herd of travellers sent away,
houseless, every evening. The fine weather is bringing
crowds to the Highlands. We could not have travelled at a
more favourable time. We have had only a few showers, but
in one, on Loch Katrine, my poor fawn-coloured dress
suffered. The scarlet of the poppies ran into the blue of the
cornflowers. Is it not a pity? I was quite unconscious of what
was going on at the time; and afterwards, when I discovered
it, I could have shed tears.

'I hope when you marry, darling, you will come to
Scotland for your honeymoon. The mountains seem to
appeal to one's highest feelings. There are ponies, too, for
the ascent; which is a great comfort if one is wearing pretty
boots. And you know, Violet, my idea that a woman should

be essentially feminine in every detail. I never could bring
myself to wear the horrid clump-soles which some women
delight in. They seem to me to indicate that strong-minded
and masculine character which I detest. Such women would
want the suffrage, and to have the learned professions thrown
open to them. I meet ladies or, at least, persons calling
themselves such – in horrid waterproof costumes and with
coarse cloth hats. Hideousness could go no farther. And
though I regret the wreck of my fawn-colour, I can but
remember with satisfaction what Theodore always says to me
when she shows me one of her *chef-d'oeuvres*: "Mrs Tempest,
it is a dress fit for a *lady*." There are ill-natured people who
declare that Theodore began life as a kitchen-maid in an Irish
inn, but I, for one, will never believe it. Such taste as hers
indicates a refined progeniture.'

With such letters as these did Mrs Winstanley comfort her
absent daughter. Vixen replied as best she might, with scraps of
news about the neighbours, rich and poor, the dogs, horses, and
gardens. It was hateful to her to have to direct her letters to Mrs
Winstanley.

The days went on. Vixen rode from early morning till noon,
and rambled in the Forest for the best part of the afternoon. She
used to take her books there, and sit for hours reading on a
mossy bank under one of the boughy beeches, with Argus at
her feet. The dog was company enough for her. She wanted no
one better. At home the old servants were more or less friends –
their faces always pleasant to see. Some of them had lived with
her grandfather; most of them had served her father from the
time he inherited his estate. The Squire had been the most
conservative and indulgent of masters; always liking to see the
old faces. The butler was old, and even on his underling's
bullet-head the gray hairs were beginning to show. Mrs
Trimmer was at least sixty, and had been getting annually
bulkier for the last twenty years. The kitchen-maid was a
comfortable-looking person of forty. There was an atmosphere
of domestic peace in the offices of the Abbey House which
made everybody fat. It was only by watchfulness and tight-

lacing that Pauline preserved to herself that grace of outline which she spoke of in a general way as 'figure.'

'And what a mite of a waist I had when I first went out to service,' she would say pathetically.

But Pauline was now in Scotland, harassed by unceasing cares about travelling-bags, bonnet-boxes, and extra wraps, and under-valuing Ben Nevis as not worth half the trouble that was taken to go and look at him.

The gardeners were gray-headed, and remembered potting the first fuchsia-slips that ever came to the Forest. They had no gusto for new-fangled ideas about cordon fruit-trees or root-pruning. They liked to go their own way, as their fathers and grandfathers had done before them; and, with unlimited supplies of manure, they were able to produce excellent cucumbers by the first of May, or a fair dish of asparagus by about the same time. If their produce was late it was because nature went against them. They could not command the winds, or tell the sun that he must shine. The gardens at the Abbey House were beautiful, but nature had done more for them than the Squire's old gardeners. The same rose-trees budded and bloomed year after year; the same rhododendrons and azaleas opened their big bunches of bloom. Eden could have hardly owed less to culture. The noble old cedars, the mediaeval yews, needed no gardener's hand. There was a good deal of weeding and mowing, and rolling done from week's end to week's end; and the borders were beautified by banks of geranium and golden calceolaria, and a few other old-fashioned flowers; but scientific horticulture there was none. Some alterations had been begun already under Captain Winstanley's directions; but the work languished in his absence.

It was the twentieth of September, and the travellers were expected to return within a few days – the exact date of their arrival not being announced. The weather was glorious, finer than it had been all through the summer; and Vixen spent the best part of her life out of doors. Sad thoughts haunted her less cruelly in the great wood. There was a brightness and life in the Forest which cheered her. It was pleasant to see Argus's enjoyment of the fair weather; his wild rushes in among the

underwood; his pursuit of invisible vermin under the thick
holly-bushes, brambles, and bracken; his rapturous rolling in the
dewy grass, where he flung himself at full length, and rolled
over and over, and leapt as if he had been revelling in a bath of
freshest water; pleasant to see him race up to a serious-minded
hog, and scrutinise that stolid animal closely, and then leave him
to his sordid researches after edible roots, with open contempt,
as who should say: 'Can the same scheme of creation include
me and that vulgar brute?'

All things had been set in order for the return of the newly-
married couple. Mrs Trimmer had her dinner arranged and ready
to be put in hand at a moment's notice. Violet felt that the end of
her peaceful life was very near. How would she bear the change?
How would she be able to behave herself decently? Well, she
would try her best, Heaven giving her strength. That was her last
resolve. She would not make the poor frivolous mother unhappy.

'Forgive me, beloved father, if I am civil to the usurper,' she
said. 'It will be for my mother's sake. You were always tender
and indulgent to her; you would not like to see her unhappy.'

These were Vixen's thoughts this bright September morning,
as she sat at her lonely little breakfast-table in the sunny window
of her den, with Argus by her side, intently watchful of every
morsel of bread-and-butter she ate, though he had already been
accommodated with half the loaf.

She was more amiably disposed than usual this morning. She
had made up her mind to make the best of a painful position.

'I shall always hate him,' she told herself, meaning Captain
Winstanley; 'but I will begin a career of Christianlike hypocrisy,
and try to make other people believe that I like him. No,
Argus,' as the big paw tugged her arm pleadingly, 'no; now
really this is sheer greediness. You can't be hungry.'

A piteous whine, as of a dog on the brink of starvation,
seemed to gainsay her. Just then the door opened, and the
middle-aged footman entered.

'O, if you please, miss, Bates says would you like to see
Bullfinch?'

'To see Bullfinch,' echoed Vixen. 'What's the matter? Is he
ill? Is he hurt?'

'No, miss; but Bates thought as how maybe you'd like to see 'un before he goes away. He's sold.'

Vixen turned very pale. She started up, and stood for a few moments silent, with her strong young hands clenched, just as she gripped them on the bridle sometimes when Arion was running away with her and there were bogs in front.

'I'll come,' she said in a half-suffocated voice.

'He has sold my father's horse, after all,' she said to herself, as she went towards the stables. 'Then I shall hate him openly all my life. Yes, everybody shall know that I hate him.'

She found the stables in some commotion. There were two strangers, groomy-looking men, standing in front of Bullfinch's loose-box, and all the stablemen had come out of their various holes, and were standing about.

Bates looked grave and indignant.

'There isn't a finer horse in the county,' he muttered; 'it's a shame to send him out of it.'

Vixen walked straight up to the strange men, who touched their caps, and looked at her admiringly; her dark blue cloth dress fitted her like a riding-habit, her long white throat was bare, her linen collar tied loosely with a black ribbon, her chestnut hair wound into a crown of plaits at the top of her head. The severe simplicity of her dress set off her fresh young beauty.

'She's the prettiest chestnut filly I've seen for a long time,' one of the grooms said of her afterwards. 'Thoroughbred to the tips of her ears.'

'Who has bought this horse?' she asked authoritatively.

'My master, Lord Mallow, miss,' answered the superior of the men. 'You needn't be anxious about him; he'll have a rare good home.'

'Will you let me see the order for taking him away?'

'Your groom has got it, miss.'

Bates showed her a sheet of paper on which Captain Winstanley had written:

'Trossachs Hotel, September 12.
'The bay horse, Bullfinch, is to be delivered, with clothing, &c., to Lord Mallow's groom.   C. WINSTANLEY.'

Vixen perused this paper with a countenance full of suppressed rage.

'Does your master give much money for this horse?' she asked, turning to the strange groom.

'I haven't heard how much, miss.' Of course the man knew the sum to a penny. 'But I believe it's a tidyish lot.'

'I don't suppose I have as much money in the world,' said Vixen, 'or I'd buy my father's horse of Captain Winstanley, since he is so badly in want of money, and keep him at a farm.'

'I beg your pardon, miss,' said the groom, 'but the hoss is sold. My master has paid his money. He's a friend of Captain Winstanley's. They met somewhere in Scotland the other day, and my lord bought the hoss on hearsay; and I must say I don't think he'll be disappointed in him.'

'Where are you going to take him?'

'Well, it's rather an awkward journey across country. We're going to Melton. My lord is going to hunt the hoss in October, if he turns out to my lord's satisfaction.'

'You are going to take him by rail?'

'Yes, miss.'

'He has never been by rail in his life. It will kill him!' cried Vixen, alarmed.

'O no, it won't, miss. Don't be frightened about him. We shall have a padded box and everything tip-top. He'll be as snug and as tight as a sardine in its case. We'll get him to Leicestershire as fresh as paint.'

Vixen went into the loose-box, where Bullfinch, all regardless of his doom, was idly munching a mouthful of upland meadow hay. She pulled down his noble head, and laid her cheek against his broad forehead, and let her tears rain on him unheeded. There was no one to see her in that dusky loose-box. The grooms were clustered at the stable-door, talking together. She was free to linger over her parting with the horse that her father had loved. She wound her arms about his arched neck, and kissed his velvet nose.

'O Bullfinch, have you a memory? Will you be sorry to find yourself in a strange stable?' she asked, looking into the animal's full soft eyes with a pathetic earnestness in her own.

She dried her tears presently; she was not going to make herself a spectacle for the scornful pity of stablemen. She came out of the loose-box with a serene countenance, and went up to Lord Mallow's groom. 'Please be kind to him,' she said, dropping a sovereign into the man's ready hand.

'No fear of that, miss,' he said; 'there are very few Christians that have as good a time of it as our hosses.'

That sovereign, taken in conjunction with the donor's beauty, quite vanquished Lord Mallow's stud-groom, and very nearly bought Violet Tempest a coronet.

Bullfinch was led out presently, looking like a king; but Violet did not stop to see him go away. She could hardly have borne that. She ran back to the house, put on her hat and jacket, called Argus, and set out for a long ramble, to walk down, if possible, the angry devil within her.

No; this she would never forgive – this sale of her father's favourite horse. It was as if some creature of her own flesh and blood had been sold into slavery. Her mother was rich, would squander hundreds on fine dresses, and would allow her dead husband's horse to be sold.

'Is Captain Winstanley such a tyrant that mamma cannot prevent this shameful thing?' she asked herself. 'She talks about his attention, his devotion, as if he were at her feet; and yet she suffers him to disgrace her by this unparalleled meanness!'

CHAPTER 23

AT THE KENNELS

It was a fresh sunny morning, a soft west wind blowing up all the sweetness of the woods and leas. The cattle were grouped in lazy stillness on the dewy grass; the year's pigs, grown to the hobbledehoy stage of existence, were grubbing about contentedly among the furze-bushes; by the roadside, a matronly sow lay stretched flat upon her side in the sunshine, just where carriage-wheels must pass over her were carriages frequent in those parts.

Even the brightness of the morning had no charm for Vixen. There was no delight for her in the green solemnity of the forest glades, where the beechen pillars led the eye away into innumerable vistas, each grandly mysterious as a cathedral aisle. The sun shot golden arrows through dark boughs, patching the moss with translucent lights, vivid and clear as the lustre of emeralds. The gentle plash of the forest stream, rippling over its pebbly bed, made a tender music that was wont to seem passing sweet to Violet Tempest's ear. To-day she heard nothing, saw nothing. Her brain was clouded with angry thoughts.

She left the Forest by-and-by, following one of the familiar cart-tracks, and came out into the peaceful little colony of Beechdale, where it was a chance if the noonday traveller saw anything alive except a youthful family of pigs enjoying an oasis of mud in a dry land, or an obtrusive dog rushing out of a cottage to salute the wayfarer with an inquiring bark. The children were still in school; the hum of their voices was wafted from the open windows. The church door stood open. The village graves the sunward-fronting slope were bright with common flowers; the dead lying with their feet to the west, ready to stand up and see their Lord at the resurrection morning.

Vixen hurried through the little village, not wanting to see Mrs Scobel, or anyone she knew, this morning. There was a long rustic lane opposite the church, that led straight to the kennels.

'I will go and see the foxhounds,' said Vixen; 'they are true and faithful. But perhaps all those I love best have been sold, or are dead by this time.'

It seemed to her ages since she had been to the kennels with her father. It had been his favourite walk, out of the hunting season, and he had rarely suffered a week to pass without making his visit of inspection. Since her return Violet had carefully avoided the well-known spot; but to-day, out of the very bitterness of her heart, came a desire to renew past associations. Bullfinch was gone for ever, but the hounds at least remained; and her father had loved them almost as well as he had loved Bullfinch.

Nothing was changed at the kennels. The same feeder in corduroy and fustian came out of the cooking-house when Vixen opened the five-barred gate. The same groom was lounging in front of the stables, where the horses were kept for the huntsman and his underlings. The whole place had the same slumberous out-of-season look she remembered so well of old in the days when hunting was over.

The men touched their caps to Miss Tempest as she passed them. She went straight to the kennels. There were the three wooden doors, opening into three square stone-paved yards, each door provided with a round eye-hole, through which the authorities might scrutinise the assembly within. A loud yelping arose as Vixen's footstep drew near. Then there were frantic snufflings under the doors, and a general agitation. She looked through the little eye-hole into the middle yard. Yes; there they were, fourteen or fifteen couple, tumultuously excited, as if they knew she was there: white and black and tan, pointed noses, beautiful intelligent eyes, bright tan spots upon marked brows, some with a streak of white running down the long sharp noses, some heavy in the jowl, some with muzzles sharp as a greyhound's, thirty tails erect and agitated.

The feeder remembered Miss Tempest perfectly, though it was more than three years since her last visit.

'Would you like to go in and see 'em, miss?' he said.

'Yes, if you please, Dawson. You have Gauntlet still, I see. That is Gauntlet, isn't it? And Dart, and Juno, and Ringlet, and Artful?'

'Yes, miss. There ain't many gone since you was here. But there's a lot o' poppies. You'd like to see the poppies, wouldn't you, miss? They be in the next kennel, if you'll just wait five minutes.'

Cleanliness was the order of the day at the kennels; but to do the late master's daughter more honour, Dawson the feeder called a bright-looking lad, his subordinate, and divers pails of water were fetched, and the three little yards were washed out vigorously before Miss Tempest was invited to enter. When she did go in, the yard was empty and clean as a new pin. The hounds had been sent into their house, where they were all grouped picturesquely on a bench littered with straw, looking as grave as a human parliament, and much wiser. Nothing could be more beautiful than their attitudes, or more intelligent than their countenances.

Vixen looked in at them through the barred window.

'Dear things,' she exclaimed; 'they are as lovely as ever. How fond papa was of them.'

And then the kennel-huntsman, who had appeared on the scene by this time, opened the door and smacked his whip; and the fifteen couple came leaping helter-skelter out into the little yard, and made a rush at Vixen, and surrounded her, and fawned upon her, and caressed her as if their recognition of her after long years was perfect, and as if they had been breaking their hearts for her in the interval. Perhaps they would have been just as affectionate to the next comer, having a large surplus stock of love always on hand ready to be lavished on the human race; but Vixen took these demonstrations as expressive of a peculiar attachment, and was moved to tears by the warmth of this canine greeting.

'Thank God! there are some living things that love me,' she exclaimed.

'Something that loves you!' cried a voice from the door of the yard. 'Does not everything noble or worthy love you, as it loves all that is beautiful?'

Turning quickly, with a scared look, Violet saw Roderick Vawdrey standing in the doorway.

He stood quietly watching her, his dark eyes softened with a look of tender admiration. There could hardly have been a prettier picture than the tall girlish figure and bright chestnut head, the fair face bending over the upturned noses of the hounds as they clustered round her, some standing up with their strong white paws upon her shoulder, some nestling at her knees. Her hat had fallen off, and was being trampled under a multitude of restless feet.

Rorie came into the little yard. The huntsman cracked his whip, and the hounds went tumbling one over the other into their house, where they leaped upon their straw bed, and grouped themselves as if they had been sitting for their portraits to Sir Edwin Landseer. Two inquisitive fellows stood up with their paws upon the ledge of the barred window, and looked out at Violet and the new master.

'I did not know you were at Briarwood,' she said, as they shook hands.

'I only came home last night. My first visit was naturally here. I wanted to see if everything was in good order.'

'When do you begin to hunt?'

'On the first of October. You are going to be amongst us this year, of course.'

'No. I have never followed the hounds since papa's death. I don't suppose I ever shall again.'

'What, not with your stepfather?'

'Certainly not with Captain Winstanley.'

'Then you must marry a hunting-man,' said Rorie gaily. 'We can't afford to lose the straightest rider in the Forest.'

'I am not particularly in love with hunting – for a woman. There seems something bloodthirsty in it. And Bates says that if ladies only knew how their horses' backs get wrung in the hunting season, they would hardly have the heart to hunt. It was very nice to ride by papa's side when I was a little girl. I would have gone anywhere with him – through an Indian jungle after tigers – but I don't care about it now.'

'Well, perhaps you are right; though I should hardly have expected such mature wisdom from my old playfellow, whose flowing locks used once to be the cynosure of the hunting-field. And now, Violet – I may call you Violet, may I not, as I did in the old days? – at least, when I did not call you Vixen.'

'That was papa's name,' she said quickly. 'Nobody ever calls me that now.'

'I understand; I am to call you Violet. And we are to be good friends always, are we not, with a true and loyal friendship?'

'I have not so many friends that I can afford to give up one who is staunch and true,' answered Violet sadly.

'And I mean to be staunch and true, believe me; and I hope, by-and-by, when you come to know Mabel, you and she will be fast friends. You may not cotton to her very easily at first, because, you see, she reads Greek, and goes in for natural science, and has a good many queer ways. But she is all that is pure-minded and noble. She has been brought up in an atmosphere of adulation, and that has made her a little self-opinionated. It is the only fault she has.'

'I shall be very glad if she will let me like her,' Violet said meekly.

They had strolled away from the kennels into the surrounding forest, where the free horses of the soil were roaming from pasture to pasture, and a few vagabond pigs were stealing a march on their brethren, for whom the joys of pannage-time had not yet begun. They walked along idly, following a cart-track that led into woody deeps where the earliest autumn leaves were dropping gently in the soft west wind. By-and-by they came to a fallen oak, lying by the side of the track, ready for carting, and it seemed the most natural thing in the world to sit down side by side on this rustic seat, and talk of days gone by, lazily watching the flickering shadows and darting sunrays in the opposite thicket, or along the slanting stretch of open turf – that smooth emerald grass, so inviting to the eye, so perilous to the foot of man or beast.

'And now, Violet, tell me all about yourself, and about this second marriage of your mother's,' Roderick began earnestly; 'I hope you have quite reconciled yourself to the idea of it by this time.'

'I have not reconciled myself; I never shall,' answered Violet with restrained anger. 'I know that mamma has heaped up sorrow for herself in the days to come, and I pity her too much to be angry with her. Yes; I, who ought to look up to and respect my mother, can only look down upon her and pity her. That is a hard thing, is it not, Rorie? She has married a bad man – mean, and false, and tyrannical. Shall I tell you what he has done within these last few days?'

'Do. I hope it is not anything very bad.'

Violet told how Bullfinch had been sold.

'It looks mean, certainly,' said Mr Vawdrey; 'but I daresay to Captain Winstanley, as a man of the world, it might seem a foolish thing to keep a horse nobody rode; especially such a valuable horse as Bullfinch. Your father gave two hundred and fifty for him at Andover, I remember. And you really have too many horses at Abbey House.'

'Arion will be the next to be sold, I daresay.'

'O, no, no. He could not be such an insolent scoundrel as to sell your horse. That would be too much. Besides, you will be of age in a year or two, and your own mistress.'

'I shall not be of age for the next seven years. I am not to come of age till I am five-and-twenty.'

'Phew!' whistled Rorie. 'That's a long shot off. How is that?'

'Papa left it so in his will. It was his care of me, no doubt. He never could have believed that mamma would marry again.'

'And for the next seven years you are to be in a state of tutelage, dependent on your mother for everything?'

'For everything. And that will really mean dependent upon Captain Winstanley; because I am very sure that as long as he lets mamma wear pretty dresses, and drink orange pekoe out of old china, she will be quite contented to let him be master of everything else.'

'But if you were to marry———?'

'I suppose that would entangle or disentangle matters somehow. But I am not likely to marry.'

'I don't see that,' said Rorie. 'I should think nothing was more likely.'

'Allow me to be the best judge of my own business,' exclaimed Vixen, looking desperately angry. 'I will go so far as to say that I never shall marry!'

'O, very well, if you insist upon it, let it be understood so. And now Vix — Violet, don't you think if you could bring yourself to conciliate Captain Winstanley — to resign yourself, in fact, to the inevitable, and take things pleasantly, it would make your life happier for the next seven years? I really would try to do it if I were you.'

'I had made up my mind to an existence of hypocrisy before he sold Bullfinch,' replied Vixen, 'but now I shall hate him frankly.'

'But, Violet, don't you see that unless you can bring yourself to live pleasantly with that man your life will be made miserable? Fate condemns you to live under the same roof with him.'

'I am not sure about that. I could go out as a governess. I am not at all clever, but I think I could teach as much as would be good value for twenty pounds a year; or at the worst I might give my services in exchange for a comfortable home, as the advertisements say. How I wish I could read Greek and play Chopin, like Lady Mabel Ashbourne. I'll write to dear old McCroke, and ask her to get me a place.'

'My dear Violet, how can you talk so absurdly? You, the future mistress of the Abbey House – you, with your youth and beauty and high spirit – to go meandering about the world teaching buttermen's or tea-dealers' children to spell B a, ba, and A b, ab?'

'It might be better than sitting at meat with a man I detest,' said Vixen. 'Am I to value the flesh-pots of Egypt more than my liberty and independence of mind?'

'You have your mother to think of,' urged Roderick. 'You owe duty and obedience to her, even if she has offended you by this foolish marriage. If you have so bad an opinion of Captain Winstanley, you are all the more bound to stand by your mother.'

'That is an argument worth listening to,' said Vixen. 'It might be cruel to leave poor mamma quite at his mercy. I don't suppose that he would actually ill-treat her. He knows his own interest too well for that. He will not lock her up in a cellar, or beat, or starve her. He will be content with making himself her master. She will have no more will of her own than if she were a prettily dressed doll placed at the head of the table for show. She will be lulled into a state of childish bliss, and go smiling through life, believing she has not a wish ungratified. Everybody will think her the happiest of women, and Captain Winstanley the best of husbands.'

Vixen said all this with prophetic earnestness, looking straight forward into the green glade before her, where the beech-nuts and acorns were dropping in a gentle rain of plenty.

'I hope things won't be quite so bad as you anticipate. I hope you will be able to make yourself happy, in spite of Captain Winstanley. And we shall see each other pretty often, I hope, Violet, as we used in old times. The Dovedales are at Wiesbaden: the Duke only holds existence on the condition of deluging himself with German waters once a year; but they are to be back early in November. I shall make the Duchess call on Mrs Winstanley directly she returns.'

'Thanks; mamma will be very pleased. I wonder you are not with them.'

'O, I had to begin my duties as M.F.H. I wouldn't have been away for the world.'

Violet looked at her watch. It was a good deal later than she had supposed. Time goes quickly when one is talking over a new grievance with an old friend. She was a long way from the Abbey House.

'I must go home,' she said; 'mamma and Captain Winstanley may arrive at any moment. There is no time named in mamma's last telegram; she said only that they are moving gently homeward.'

'Let us go, then,' said Rorie, rising from his rugged seat.

'But I am not going to take you out of your way. Every step of my journey home takes you farther from Briarwood.'

'Never mind if it does. I mean to walk to the Abbey House with you. I daresay, if I were very tired, Bates would lend me a mount home.'

'You can have Arion, if you like.'

'No thanks. Arion shall not have my thirteen stone; I want a little more timber under me.'

'You ought to have had Bullfinch,' said Vixen regretfully.

'I would have had him, if I had known he was in the market. The writing a figure or so more or less on a cheque should not have hindered me.'

CHAPTER 24

A BAD BEGINNING

That walk through the Forest was very pleasant to Violet. It was a day on which mere existence was a privilege; and now that her spirits had been soothed by her confidential talk with Rorie,

Vixen could enjoy those sights and sounds and sweet wild
scents of the woodland that had ever been a rapture to her.

This Forest-born girl loved her native woods as Wordsworth
loved his lakes and mountains, as Byron loved the bleak bare
landscape round the city of Aberdeen. Their poetry and beauty
filled her heart with a deep contentment. To walk or ride alone
through pathless forest glades, or in the scented darkness of fir
plantations, was enough for happiness. But it was comforting
to-day – on this day when her heart had been so cruelly
wounded – to have Roderick Vawdrey by her side. It was like a
leaf out of the closed volume of the past.

They talked freely and happily during that long homeward
walk, and their conversation was chiefly of bygone days.
Almost every speech began with 'Do you remember?' Vixen
was gayer than she had been for a long time, save once or
twice, when a pang shot through her heart at the idea that
Bullfinch was being shaken about in a railway-box, oscillating
helplessly with every vibration of the train, and panic-stricken
in every tunnel.

The sun had declined from his meridian; he had put on his
sober afternoon glory, and was sending shafts of mellower gold
along the green forest aisles, when Miss Tempest and her
companion drew near the Abbey House. They went in at the
gate by the keeper's cottage, the gate which Titmouse had
jumped so often in the days when he carried his childish
mistress. They went through the wood of rhododendrons, and
past the old archway leading to the stables, and round by the
shrubbery to the porch. The door stood open as usual, and the
Squire's old pointer was lying on the threshold; but within all
was commotion. Dress-baskets, hat-cases, bonnet-boxes, gun-
cases, travelling-bags, carriage-rugs, were lying about in every
direction. Mrs Winstanley was leaning back in the large chair by
the fireplace, fanning herself with her big black fan; Pauline was
standing by in attendance; and the silver tray, with the Swansea
tea-set, was being brought in by Forbes the butler, whose
honest old face wore a troubled aspect.

Captain Winstanley was standing with his back to the hearth,
his countenance and whole figure wearing the unmistakable air

of the master of a house who has returned to his domicile in an execrable temper.

Violet ran to Mrs Winstanley, every other thought forgotten in the pleasure of seeing her mother again. These three weeks were the longest parting mother and daughter had ever known; and, after all, blood is thicker than water; and there is a natural leaning in a child's mind even to the weakest of parents.

Mr Vawdrey stood in the background, waiting till those affectionate greetings natural to such an occasion should be over.

But to his surprise there were no such greetings. Mrs Winstanley went on fanning herself vehemently, with a vexed expression of countenance, while Violet bent over and kissed her. Captain Winstanley swayed himself slowly backwards and forwards upon the heels of his boots, and whistled to himself *sotto voce*, with his eyes fixed upon some lofty region of empty air. He vouchsafed not the faintest notice of his stepdaughter or Mr Vawdrey.

'It's really too bad of you, Violet,' the mother exclaimed at last.

'Dear mamma,' cried Vixen, in blank amazement, 'what have I done?'

'To go roaming about the country,' pursued Mrs Winstanley plaintively, 'for hours at a stretch, nobody knowing where to find you or what had become of you. And my telegram lying there unattended to.'

'Did you telegraph, mamma?'

'Did I telegraph? Should I come home without telegraphing? Should I be so mad as to expose myself knowingly to the outrage which has been offered to me to-day?'

'Dearest mamma, you alarm me. What has happened?'

'One of the deepest humiliations I ever had to endure. But you were roaming about the Forest. You were following the instincts of your wild nature. What do you care for my mortification? If I had telegraphed to my housekeeper, it would not have happened. But I trusted in my daughter.'

'Dear mamma,' pleaded Vixen, looking anxious and bewildered, 'if you would only explain. You make me miserable. What has happened?'

'Violet, your stepfather and I had to drive home from the station in a fly!'

'O, mamma!' cried Vixen, with a gasp. 'Is that all?'

'Is that all? Do you think that is not enough? Do you understand, child? – a fly – a common innkeeper's fly – that anybody may have for half-a-guinea; a fly with a mouldy lining, smelling of – other people! And on such an occasion, when every eye was upon us! No; I was never so degraded. And we had to wait – yes, a quarter of an hour, at least, and it seemed ages, while Pycroft's fly was got ready for us; yes, while a rough forest pony was dragged out of his wretched stable, and a man, whose face had not been washed for a week, shuffled himself into an old coachman's coat. And there were all the porters staring at me, and laughing inwardly, I know. And, as a last drop in the cup, Colonel Carteret drove up in his phaeton to catch the up-train just as we were getting into that disgraceful looking vehicle, and would stop to shake hands with us both, and insisted upon handing me into the horrid thing.'

'Dear mamma, I am more sorry than I can say,' said Vixen gently; 'but I was afraid it was something much worse.'

'Nothing could be worse, Violet.'

'Then the telegram was to order the carriage to meet you, I suppose?'

'Of course. We telegraphed from The Grosvenor at nine o'clock this morning. Who would imagine that you would be out of doors at such an hour?'

'I am not often out so early. But something happened this morning to put me out of temper, and I went for a ramble.'

'A ramble lasting from ten in the morning till half-past four in the afternoon,' remarked Captain Winstanley, with his gaze still fixed upon empty space. 'Rather a long walk for a solitary young lady.'

Vixen appeared unconscious that anyone had spoken. Roderick Vawdrey felt a burning desire to kick the new master of the Abbey House.

'Shall I pour out your tea, mamma?' asked Vixen meekly.

'If you like. I am utterly prostrate. To have no carriage to meet me on such an occasion! I daresay everybody in the Forest knows all about it by this time. When I came home from my honeymoon with your poor papa, the joy-bells rang all the afternoon, and the road was lined with people wanting to get a glimpse of us, and there were floral arches——'

'Ah, mamma, those things cannot happen twice in a lifetime,' said Vixen, with irrepressible bitterness. 'One happy marriage is as much as any woman can expect.'

'A woman has a right to expect her own carriage,' said Captain Winstanley.

'I am afraid I have paid my visit at rather an unfortunate moment,' said Roderick, coming forward and addressing himself solely to Mrs Winstanley; 'but I could not go without saying How do you do? I hope you had a pleasant journey from Scotland – bar the fly.'

'How do you do, Roderick? Yes, it was all pleasant except that last *contretemps*. Imagine the Duchess of Dovedale's feelings if she arrived at the station adjoining her own estate, and found no carriage to meet her!'

'My aunt would tuck up her petticoats and trudge home,' answered Roderick, smiling. 'She's a plucky little woman.'

'Yes, perhaps on an ordinary occasion. But to-day it was so different. Everybody will talk about our return.'

'Most people are still away,' suggested Rorie, with a view to comfort.

'O, but their servants will hear it, and they will tell their masters and mistresses. All gossip begins that way. Besides, Colonel Carteret saw us, and what he knows everybody knows.'

After this, Roderick felt that all attempts at consolation were hopeless. He would have liked to put Mrs Winstanley into a better temper, for Violet's sake. It was not a pleasant home atmosphere in which he was obliged to leave his old playfellow on this the first day of her new life. Captain Winstanley maintained a forbidding silence; Mrs Winstanley did not even ask anyone to have a cup of tea; Violet sat on the opposite side of the hearth, pale and quiet, with Argus at her knee, and one arm wound caressingly round his honest head.

'I've been inspecting the kennels this morning,' said Roderick, looking at the new master of the Abbey House with

a cheerful assumption that everything was going on pleasantly.
'We shall begin business on the first. You'll hunt, of course?'

'Well, yes; I suppose I shall give myself a day occasionally.'

'I shall not have a happy moment while you are out,' said Mrs
Winstanley. 'I used to be miserable about poor dear Edward.'

Vixen winced. These careless references to the dead hurt her
more than the silence of complete oblivion. To remember, and
to be able to speak so lightly. That seemed horrible.

'I doubt if I shall hunt much this season,' pursued Captain
Winstanley, as much as to say that he was not going to be
grateful to the new master of the fox-hounds as a public
benefactor, however many hundreds that gentleman might
disburse in order to make up the shortcomings of a scanty
subscription. 'I shall have a great deal to occupy me. This place
has been much neglected – naturally – within the last few years.
There is no end of work to be done.'

'Are you going to pull down the Abbey House and build an
Italian villa on its site?' asked Vixen, her upper lip curling
angrily. 'That would be rather a pity. Some people think it a
fine old place, and it has been in my father's family since the
reign of Henry the Eighth.'

To the Captain's ear this speech had a covert insolence. The
Abbey House was to belong to Violet in the future. Neither he
nor his wife had a right to touch a stone of it. Indeed, it was by
no means clear to him that there might not be ground for a
Chancery suit in his cutting down a tree.

'I hope I shall do nothing injudicious,' he said politely.

'My aunt will be back in a week or two, Mrs Winstanley,'
said Roderick. 'I shall bring her over to see you directly she
settles down at Ashbourne. And now I think I'd better be off;
I've a long walk home, and you must be too tired to care about
talking or being talked to.'

'I am very tired,' answered Mrs Winstanley languidly; 'but I
should have liked to hear all your news.'

'I'm afraid that's not much. I only came home last night; I
have been shooting grouse in Renfrew.'

'Plenty of birds this year?' inquired the Captain, with a
languid interest.

'Pretty fair. The rainy spring killed a good many of the young birds.'

'Do you remember any year in which that complaint was not made?' retorted Captain Winstanley.

Rorie took his departure after this, and contrived to give Violet's hand an encouraging squeeze at parting, accompanied with a straight steady look, which said as plainly as words: 'You have one friend who will be staunch and true, come what may.'

Vixen understood him, and sudden tears welled up to her eyes – the first that had clouded them since her parting with Bullfinch. She brushed them away hurriedly, but not so quickly as to escape Captain Winstanley's observation.

'If you'll excuse me, mamma. I'll run and dress for dinner,' she said, 'unless there is anything I can do for you. Your rooms are quite ready.'

'I'm glad of that,' replied Mrs Winstanley fretfully: 'for really after our reception at the railway-station, I expected to find everything at sixes and sevens.'

'Dear mamma, you must know that it was quite an accident.'

'An accident very likely to occur when a young lady indulges in *tête-à-tête* forest rambles with an old friend, instead of waiting at home for her mother's letters and telegrams,' remarked Captain Winstanley, caressing his neat whisker with his irreproachable hand.

'What do you mean?' said Vixen, turning sharply upon him. 'I went out alone this morning. Mr Vawdrey and I met at the kennels by accident.'

'A chapter of accidents,' sneered the Captain. 'I have no objection to make, Miss Tempest, if your mamma has none. But I am rather sorry for the young lady Mr Vawdrey is going to marry.'

'Mr Vawdrey was my father's friend, and will never cease to be mine,' said Vixen, with flashing eyes. 'There can be nothing offensive to Lady Mabel Ashbourne in our friendship.'

She was gone before her stepfather could reply, or her mother reprove her want of respect for that new relative.

'I suppose I had better go and dress too,' said Mrs Winstanley, 'and in the evening we can talk about our first dinner-party. I daresay we shall have a great many people calling to-morrow afternoon. It will be rather trying. There is such a painful feeling in being a bride and not a bride, as it were. People's congratulations hardly sound hearty.'

'I daresay they have rather a vapid flavour, like a warmed-up dinner,' said the Captain. 'That is the result of living in a neighbourhood where your first husband was known and popular. If we went among strangers, their congratulations would be a great deal heartier. But I hope you don't begin to repent already, my dear Pamela.'

'Conrad!' How can you imagine such a thing? – after your delicate attentions, your devoted care of me during our tour. What dress shall I wear this evening? Do you like me best in blue or amber?'

'To my eye all colours suit you. But I think a woman' – he was going to say 'of your age,' but checked himself and substituted – 'in the maturity of her beauty looks best in velvet, or some rich and heavy material that falls in massive folds, like the drapery in a portrait by Velasquez. A border of fur, too, is an artistic introduction in a woman's dress – you see it often in Velasquez. Heavy old laces are, of course, always admirable. And for colour, I like the warmer hues best – wine-dark purples or deep glowing reds; rich ruddy browns, with a knot of amber now and then for relief.'

'How beautifully you talk,' cried Mrs Winstanley, delighted. 'I only wish Theodore could hear you. It would give her new ideas; for, after all, the best dressmakers are *bornées*. It is too early in the year for velvet. I shall put on my dark green brocade with the old Flanders lace. I am so glad you like lace. It is my chief weakness. Even dear Edward, who was so generous, thought me a little extravagant in the matter of lace. But when one once begins to collect, the study is so interesting. One is led on.'

'Good heavens! is my wife a collector?' thought Captain Winstanley, horrified. 'That must be put a stop to, or she will ruin me.'

And then he went off to his dressing-room rather wearily, to put on full-dress for a home dinner; a sacrifice to his new state of existence which he found very irksome. He would have liked to dine in a shooting-jacket, and smoke all the evening. But his smoking now, instead of pervading the whole house, as it had done in his snug bachelor quarters, was an indulgence to be taken out of doors, or in a room appointed for the purpose. He was not even to smoke in the fine old hall, for it was one of the family sitting-rooms, and Mrs Winstanley could not endure smoke.

'I am not at all fanciful or capricious,' she told her husband early in the honeymoon, 'but smoking is one of my horrors. I hope, dear Conrad, it is not too much to ask you never to smoke in any room I use.'

Captain Winstanley pledged himself to respect this and every other wish of his wife's. It was his policy to be subservient in small matters, in order to be master in essentials. But that daily dressing for dinner was something of a bore; and the dinners themselves – *tête-à-tête* dinners, in which he had to take as much trouble to be amusing as at a dinner-party – had been apt to hang heavily upon him. He had even proposed dining at the *table-d'hôte*, while they were on their Scotch travels, but this idea Mrs Winstanley rejected with horror.

'I have never dined at a *table-d'hôte* in my life, Conrad,' she exclaimed, 'and I certainly should not begin during my wedding-tour.'

CHAPTER 25

ON HALF RATIONS

Captain Winstanley entered upon his new position with a fixed determination to make the best of it, and with a very clear view of its advantages and disadvantages. For seven years he was to be master of everything – or his wife was to be mistress, which, in his mind, was exactly the same. No one could question his use of the entire income arising from Squire Tempest's estates during that period. When Violet came of age – on her twenty-

fifth birthday – the estates were to be passed over to her *in toto*;
but there was not a word in the Squire's will as to the income
arising during her minority. Nor had the Squire made any
provision in the event of his daughter's marriage. If Violet were
to marry to-morrow, she would go to her husband penniless.
He would not touch a sixpence of her fortune till she was
twenty-five. If she were to die during her minority the estate
would revert to her mother.

It was a very nice estate, taken as a sample of a country
squire's possessions. Besides the New Forest property, there
were farms in Wiltshire and Dorsetshire; the whole yielding an
income of between five and six thousand a year. With such a
revenue, and the Abbey House and all its belongings rent free,
Captain Winstanley felt himself in a land of Canaan. But then
there was the edict that seven years hence he was to go forth
from this land of milk and honey; or, at any rate, was to find
himself living at the Abbey House on a sorely restricted income.
Fifteen hundred a year in such a house would mean genteel
beggary, he told himself despondently. And even this genteel
beggary would be contingent on his wife's life. Her death
would rob him of everything.

He had a mind given to calculations, and he entered upon the
closest calculations as to his future. He meant to enjoy life, of
course. He had always done that to the best of his ability. But he
saw that the chief duty he owed to himself was to save money; to
lay by against the evil inevitable day when Violet Tempest would
despoil him of power and wealth. The only way to do this was
by the cutting down of present expenses, and an immediate
narrowing of the lines on which the Abbey House was being
conducted; for the Captain had discovered that his wife, who was
the most careless and incompetent of women as regards money
matters, had been spending the whole of her income since her
husband's death. If she had not spent her money on society, she
had spent it on travelling, on lace, on old china, on dress, on
hothouse flowers, on a stable which was three times larger than
she could possibly require, on a household in which there were a
good many more cats than there were wanted to catch mice, on
bounties and charities that were given upon no principle, not

even from inclination, but only because Squire Tempest's widow had never been able to say No.

Captain Winstanley's first retrenchment had been the sale of Bullfinch, for which noble animal Lord Mallow, a young Irish viscount, had given a cheque for three hundred guineas. This money the Captain put on deposit at his banker's, by way of a nest-egg. He meant his deposit account to grow into something worth investing before those seven fat years were half gone.

He told his wife his views on the financial question one morning when they were breakfasting *tête-à-tête* in the library, where the Squire and his family had always dined when there was no company. Captain and Mrs Winstanley generally had the privilege of breakfasting alone, as Violet was up and away before her mother appeared. The Captain also was an early riser, and had done half his day's work before he had sat down to the luxurious nine-o'clock breakfast with his wife.

'I have been thinking of your ponies, pet,' he said, in a pleasant voice, half careless, half caressing, as he helped himself to a salmon cutlet. 'Don't you think it would be a very wise thing to get rid of them?'

'O, Conrad!' cried his wife, letting the water from the urn overflow the teapot in her astonishment; 'you can't mean that! Part with my ponies?'

'My dear love, how often do you drive them in a twelve-month?'

'Not very often, perhaps. I have felt rather nervous driving lately – carts and great waggon-loads of hay come out upon one so suddenly from cross-roads. I don't think the waggoners would care a bit if one were killed. But I am very fond of my gray ponies. They are so pretty. They have quite Arabian heads. Colonel Carteret says so, and he has been in Arabia.'

'But, my dear Pamela, do you think it worth while keeping a pair of ponies because they are pretty, and because Colonel Carteret, who knows about as much of a horse as I do of a megalosaurus, says they have Arabian heads? Have you ever calculated what those ponies cost you?'

'No, Conrad; I should hate myself if I were always calculating the cost of things.'

'Yes; that's all very well in the abstract. But if you are inclined to waste money, it's just as well to know how much you are wasting. Those ponies are costing you at the least a hundred and fifty pounds a year, for you could manage with a man less in the stables if you hadn't got them.'

'That's a good deal of money certainly,' said Mrs Winstanley, who hated driving, and had only driven her ponies because other people in her position drove ponies, and she felt it was a right thing to do.

Still the idea of parting with anything that appertained to her state wounded her deeply.

'I can't see why we should worry ourselves about the cost of the stables,' she said; 'they have gone on in the same way ever since I was married. Why should things be different now?'

'Don't you see that you have the future to consider, Pamela? This handsome income which you are spending so lavishly——'

'Edward never accused me of extravagance,' interjected Mrs Winstanley tearfully, 'except in lace. He did hint that I was a little extravagant in lace.'

'This fine income is to be reduced seven years hence to fifteen hundred a year, an income upon which – with mine added to it – you could not expect to be able to carry on life decently in such a house as this. So you see, Pamela, unless we contrive between us to put by a considerable sum of money before your daughter's majority, we shall be obliged to leave the Abbey House, and live in a much smaller way than we are living now.'

'Leave the Abbey House!' cried Mrs Winstanley with a horrified look. 'Conrad, I have lived in this house ever since I was married.'

'Am I not aware of that, my dear love? But, all the same, you would have to let this place, and live in a much smaller house, if you had only fifteen hundred a year to live upon.'

'It would be too humiliating! At the end of one's life. I should never survive such a degradation.'

'It may be prevented if we exercise reasonable economy during the next seven years.'

'Sell my ponies then, Conrad; sell them immediately. Why should we allow them to eat us out of house and home? Frisky shies abominably if she is the least bit fresh, and Peter has gone so far as to lie down in the road when he has had one of his lazy fits.'

'But if they are really a source of pleasure to you, my dear Pamela, I should hate myself for selling them,' said the Captain, seeing he had gained his point.

'They are not a source of pleasure. They have given me some awful frights.'

'Then we'll send them up to Tattersall's immediately, with the carriage.'

'Violet uses the carriage with Titmouse,' objected Mrs Winstanley. 'We could hardly spare the carriage.'

'My love, if I part with your ponies from motives of economy, do you suppose I would keep a pony for your daughter?' said the Captain with a grand air. 'No; Titmouse must go, of course. That will dispose of a man and a boy in the stables. Violet spends so much of her life on horseback, that she cannot possibly want a pony to drive.'

'She is very fond of Titmouse,' pleaded the mother.

'She has a tendency to lavish her affections on quadrupeds – a weakness which hardly needs fostering. I shall write to Tattersall about the three ponies this morning; and I shall send up that great raking brown horse Bates rides at the same time. Bates can ride one of my hunters. That will bring down the stable to five horses – my two hunters, Arion, and your pair of carriage-horses.'

'Five horses,' sighed Mrs Winstanley pensively; 'I shall hardly know those great stables with only five horses in them. The dear old place used to look so pretty and so full of life when I was first married, and when the Squire used to coax me to go with him on his morning rounds. The horses used to move on one side, and turn their heads so prettily at the sound of his voice – such lovely, sleek, shining creatures, with big intelligent eyes.'

'You would be a richer woman, if it had not been for those lovely, sleek, shining creatures,' said Captain Winstanley. 'And now, love, let us go round the gardens, and you will see the difference that young able-bodied gardeners are making in the appearance of the place.'

Mrs Winstanley gave a plaintive little sigh as she rose and rang
the bell for Pauline. The good old gray-haired gardeners – the
men who had seemed to her as much a part of the gardens as
the trees that grew in them – these hoary and faithful servants
had been cashiered, to make room for two brawny young
Scotchmen, whose dialect was as Greek to the mistress of the
Abbey House. It wounded her not a little to see these strangers
at work in her grounds. It gave an aspect of strangeness to her
very life out of doors. She hardly cared to go into her
conservatories, or to loiter on her lawn, with those hard
unfamiliar eyes looking at her. And it wrung her heart to think
of the Squire's old servants thrust out in their feeble age,
unpensioned, uncared for. Yet this was a change that had come
about with her knowledge, and, seemingly, with her consent.
That is to say, the Captain had argued her into a corner, where
she stood, like the last forlorn king in a game of draughts,
fenced round and hemmed in by opponent kings. She had not
the strength of mind to assert herself boldly, and say: 'I will not
have it so. This injustice shall not be.'

A change had come over the spirit of the Abbey House
kitchen, which was sorely felt in Beechdale and those half-
dozen clusters of cottages within a two-mile radius, which
called themselves villages, and all of which had turned to the
Abbey House for light and comfort, as the sunflower turns to
the sun. Captain Winstanley had set his face against what he
called miscellaneous charity. Such things should be done and no
other. His wife should subscribe liberally to all properly
organised institutions – schools, Dorcas societies, maternity
societies, soup-kitchens, regulated dole of bread or coals, every
form of relief that was given systematically and by line and rule;
but the Good Samaritan business – the picking up stray
travellers, and paying for their maintenance at inns – was not in
the Captain's view of charity. Henceforward Mrs Winstanley's
name was to appear with due honour upon all printed
subscription-lists, just as it had done when she was Mrs
Tempest; but the glory of the Abbey House kitchen had
departed. The beggar and the cadger were no longer sure of a
meal. The villagers were no longer to come boldly asking for

what they wanted in time of trouble – broth, wine, jelly, for the sick, allowances of new milk, a daily loaf when father was out of work, broken victuals at all times. It was all over. The kitchen-doors were to be closed against all intruders.

'My love, I do not wonder that you have spent every sixpence of your income,' said Captain Winstanley. 'You have been keeping an Irish household. I can fancy an O'Donoghue or a Knight of Glyn living in this kind of way; but I should hardly have expected such utter riot and recklessness in an English gentleman's house.'

'I am afraid Trimmer has been rather extravagant,' assented Mrs Winstanley. 'I have trusted everything to her entirely, knowing that she is quite devoted to us, poor dear soul.'

'She is so devoted, that I should think in another year or so, at the rate she was going, she would have landed you in the bankruptcy court. Her books for the last ten years – I have gone through them carefully – show an expenditure that is absolutely ruinous. However, I think I have let her see that her housekeeping must be done upon very different lines in future.'

'You made her cry very bitterly, poor thing,' said his wife. 'Her eyes were quite red when she came out of your study.'

'Made her cry!' echoed the Captain contemptuously. 'She is so fat that the slightest emotion liquefies her. It isn't water, but oil that she sheds when she makes believe to weep.'

'She has been a faithful servant to me for the last twenty years,' moaned Mrs Winstanley.

'And she will be a much more faithful servant to you for the next twenty years, if she lives so long. I am not going to send her away. She is an admirable cook, and now she knows that she is not to let your substance run out at the back door, I daresay she will be a fairly good manager. I shall look after her rather sharply, I assure you. I was caterer for our mess three years, and I know pretty well what a household ought to cost per head.'

'O, Conrad!' cried his wife piteously; 'you talk of us as if we were an institution, or a workhouse, or something horrid.'

'My love, a man of sense ought to be able to regulate a private establishment at least as well as a board of thick-headed guardians can manage a workhouse.'

Poor Mrs Trimmer had left her new master's presence sorely
bowed down in spirit. She was so abased that she could only
retire to her own snug sitting-room, a panelled parlour, with an
ivy-wreathed casement looking into the stable-yard, and
indulge herself with what she called 'a good cry.' It was not
until later that she felt equal to communicating her grief to
Forbes and Pauline, over the one-o'clock dinner.

She had had a passage of arms, which she denominated 'a
stand further,' with the Captain; but it appeared that her own
stand had been feeble. He had been going over the
housekeeping accounts for the last ten years – accounts which
neither the Squire nor his wife had ever taken the trouble to
examine – accounts honestly, but somewhat carelessly and
unskilfully made out. There had been an expenditure that was
positively scandalous, Captain Winstanley told Mrs Trimmer.

'If you're dissatisifed, sir, perhaps I'd better go,' the old
woman said, tremulous with indignation. 'If you think there's
anything dishonest in my accounts, I wouldn't sleep under this
roof another night, though it's been my home near upon forty
year – I was kitchen-maid in old Squire Tempest's time – no, I
wouldn't stay another hour – not to be doubted.'

'I have not questioned your honesty, Trimmer. The accounts
are honest enough, I have no doubt, but they show a most
unjustifiable waste of money.'

'If there's dissatisfaction in your mind, sir, we'd better part.
It's always best for both parties. I'm ready to go at an hour's
notice, or to stay my month, if it's more convenient to my
mistress.'

'You are a silly old woman,' said the Captain. 'I don't want
you to go. I am not dissatisfied with you, but with the whole
system of housekeeping. There has been a great deal too much
given away.'

'Not a loaf of bread without my mistress's knowledge,' cried
Trimmer. 'I always told Mrs Tempest every morning who'd
been for soup, or wine, or bread – yes, even to broken victuals –
the day before. I had her leave and license for all I did. "I'm not
strong enough to see to the poor things myself, Trimmer," she
used to say, "but I want them cared for. I leave it all to you."'

'Very well, Trimmer. That kind of thing must cease from this hour. Your mistress will contribute to all the local charities. She will give the Vicar an allowance of wine to be distributed by him in urgent cases; but this house will no longer be the village larder – no one is to come to this kitchen for anything.'

'What, sir? – not in the case of sickness?'

'No. Poor people are always sick. It is their normal state, when there is anything to be got by sickness. There are hospitals and infirmaries for such cases. My house is not to be an infirmary. Do you understand?'

'Yes, sir; I understand that everything is to be different from what it was in my late master's time.'

'Precisely. Expenses are to be kept within a certain limit. They are not to fluctuate, as they do in these books of yours. You must get rid of two or three women-servants. There are at least three too many. I am always seeing strange faces about upstairs. One might as well live in an hotel. Think it over, Trimmer, and make up your mind as to which you can best spare, and give them a month's wages, and pack them off. I don't care to have servants about me who are under notice to quit. They always look sulky.'

'Is that all, sir?' inquired the housekeeper, drying her angry tears upon her linen apron.

'Well, yes, that is all at present. Stay. What wages has my wife given you?'

'Sixty pounds a year,' replied Trimmer, quite prepared to be told that her stipend was to be reduced.

'Then I shall give you seventy.'

At this unexpected grace Trimmer began to tremble with an excess of indignation. She saw in this bounty a bribe to meanness.

'Thank you, sir; but I have never asked to have my wages raised, and I am quite contented to remain as I am,' she answered with dignity. 'Perhaps, if the ways of the house are to be so much altered, I may not feel myself comfortable enough to stay.'

'O, very well, my good soul please yourself,' replied the Captain carelessly; 'but remember what I have told you about cadgers and interlopers; and get rid of two or three of those idle young women. I shall examine your housekeeping accounts weekly, and pay all the tradespeople weekly.'

'They have not been used to it, sir.'

'Then they must get used to it. I shall pay every account weekly – corn-merchant, and all of them. Bring me up your book on Saturday morning at ten, and let me have all other accounts at the same time.'

Here was a revolution. Trimmer and Forbes and Pauline sat long over their dinner, talking about the shipwreck of a fine old house.

'I knew that things would be different,' said Pauline, 'but I didn't think it would be so bad as this. I thought it would be all the other way, and that there'd be grand doings and lots of company. What awful meanness! Not a drop of soup to be given to a poor family; and I suppose, if I asked my aunt and uncle to stop to tea and supper, anywhen that they call to ask how I am, it will be against the rules.'

'From what I gather, there's not a bit nor a sup to be given to mortal,' said Mrs Trimmer solemnly.

'Well, thank Providence, I can afford to buy a bit of tea and sugar and a quart loaf when a friend drops in,' said Pauline, 'but the meanness isn't any less disgusting. He'll want her to sell her cast-off dresses to the secondhand dealers, I shouldn't wonder.'

'And he'll be asking for the keys of the cellars, perhaps,' said Forbes 'after I've kept them for five-and-twenty years.'

CHAPTER 26

THE OWNER OF BULLFINCH

Captain Winstanley had been master of the Abbey House three months, and there had been no open quarrel between him and Violet Tempest. Vixen had been cold as marble, but she had been civil. For her mother's sake she had held her peace. She remembered what Roderick Vawdrey had said about her duty, and had tried to do it, difficult as that duty was to the girl's undisciplined nature. She had even taken the loss of Titmouse very quietly – her father's first gift, the pony that had carried her when she was a seven-year-old huntress with tawny hair flowing loose under her little velvet *toque*. She gave no expression to her indignation at the sale of this old favourite, as she had done in the case of Bullfinch. If she wept for him, her tears were shed in secret. She took the sale of her pet almost as a matter of course.

'The Captain thinks we have too many horses and ponies, dear, and you know dear papa was a little extravagant about his stables,' said her mother apologetically, when she announced the fate of Titmouse; 'but of course Arion will always be kept for you.'

'I am glad of that, mamma,' Vixen answered gravely. 'I should be sorry to part with the last horse papa gave me as well as with the first.'

To the Captain himself Vixen said no word about her pony, and he made no apology for or explanation of his conduct. He acted as if Heaven had made him lord of the Abbey House and all its belongings in his cradle, and as if his wife and her daughter were accidental and subordinate figures in the scene of his life.

Despite the era of retrenchment which the new master had inaugurated, things at the Abbey House had never been done with so much dignity and good style. There had been a slipshod ease, an old-fashioned liberality in the housekeeping during the Squire's reign, which had in some measure approximated to the popular idea of an Irish household. Now all was done by line and rule, and according to the latest standard of perfection. There was no new fashion in Belgravia – from a brand of champagne to the shape of a menu-holder – which Captain Winstanley had not at his fingers' ends. The old-style expensive heavy dinners at the Abbey House: the monster salmon under whose weight the serving-man staggered; the sprawling gigantic turbot, arabesqued with sliced lemon and barberries; the prize

turkey, too big for anything but a poultry show; these leviathans
and megatheria of the market were seen no more. In their stead
came the subdued grace of the *dîner à la Russe*, a well-chosen
menu, before composing which Captain Winstanley studied
Gouffé's artistic cookery-book as carefully as a pious Israelite
studies the Talmud. The new style was as much more
economical than the old as it was more elegant. The table, with
the Squire's old silver, and fine dark blue and gold Worcester
china, and the Captain's picturesque grouping of hothouse
flowers and ferns, was a study worthy of a painter of still life.
People exclaimed at the beauty of the picture. The grave old
dining-room was transformed from its heavy splendour to a
modern grace that delighted everybody. Mrs Winstanley's
bosom thrilled with a gentle pride as she sat opposite her
husband – he and she facing each other across the centre of the
oval table – at their first dinner-party.

'My love, I am delighted that you are pleased,' he said
afterwards, when she praised his arrangements. 'I think I shall be
able to show you that economy does not always mean
shabbiness. Our dinners shall not be too frequent, but they shall
be perfect after their kind.'

The Captain made another innovation in his wife's mode of
existence. Instead of a daily dropping-in of her acquaintance for
tea and gossip, she was to have her afternoon, like Lady
Ellangowan. A neat copper-plate inscription on her visiting-
card told her friends that she was at home on Tuesdays from
three to six, and implied that she was not at home on any other
day. Mrs Winstanley felt her dignity enhanced by this
arrangement, and the Captain hoped thereby to put a stop to a
good deal of twaddling talk, and to lessen the weekly
consumption of five-shilling tea, pound-cake, and cream.

The Duke and Duchess returned to Ashbourne with Lady
Mabel a short time before Christmas, and the Duchess and her
daughter came to one of Mrs Winstanley's Tuesday afternoons,
attended by Roderick Vawdrey. They came with an evident
intention of being friendly, and the Duchess was charmed with
the old oak hall, the wide hearth and Christmas fire of beech-
logs, the light flashing upon the men in armour, and reflected

here and there on the beeswaxed panels as on dark water. In this wintry dusk the hall looked its best, dim gleams of colour from the old painted glass mixing with the changeful glow of the fire.

'It reminds me a little of our place in Scotland,' said the Duchess, 'only this is prettier. It has a warmer homelier air. All things in Scotland have an all-pervading stoniness. It is a country overgrown with granite.'

Mrs Winstanley was delighted to be told that her house resembled one of the ducal abodes.

'I daresay your Scotch castle is much older than this,' she said deprecatingly. 'We only date from Henry the Eighth. There was an abbey, built in the time of Henry the First; but I am afraid there is nothing left of that but the archway leading into the stables.'

'O, we are dreadfully ancient at Dundromond; almost as old as the mountains, I should think,' answered the Duchess. 'Our walls are ten feet thick, and we have an avenue of yew trees said to be a thousand years old. But all that does not prevent the Duke getting bronchitis every time he goes there.'

Vixen was in attendance upon her mother, dressed in dark green cloth. Very much the same kind of gown she had on that day at the kennels, Rorie thought, remembering how she looked as she stood with quickened breath and tumbled hair, encircled by those boisterous hounds.

'If Landseer could have lived to paint her, I would have given a small fortune for the picture,' he thought regretfully.

Lady Mabel was particularly gracious to Violet. She talked about dogs and horses even, in her desire to let herself down to Miss Tempest's lower level; praised the Forest; made a tentative remark about point-lace; and asked Violet if she was fond of Chopin.

'I'm afraid I'm not enlightened enough to care so much for him as I ought,' Vixen answered frankly.

'Really! Who is your favourite composer?'

Violet felt as if she were seated before one of those awful books which some young ladies keep instead of albums, in which the sorely-tormented contributor is catechised as to his or her particular tastes, distastes, and failings.

'I think I like Mozart best.'

'Do you really?' inquired Lady Mabel, looking as if Violet had sunk fathoms lower in her estimation by this avowal. 'Don't you think that he is dreadfully tuney?'

'I like tunes,' retorted Vixen, determined not to be put down. 'I'd rather have written "*Voi chè sapete*," and "*Batti, batti*," than all Chopin's nocturnes and mazurkas.'

'I think you would hardly say that if you knew Chopin better,' said Lady Mabel gravely, as if she had been gently reproving someone for the utterance of infidel opinions. 'When are you coming to see our orchids?' she asked graciously. 'Mamma is at home on Thursdays. I hope you and Mrs Winstanley will drive over and look at my new orchid-house. Papa had it built for me with all the latest improvements. I'm sure you must be fond of orchids, even if you don't appreciate Chopin.'

Violet blushed. Rorie was looking on with a malicious grin. He was sitting a little way off in a low Glastonbury chair, with his knees up to his chin, making himself an image of awkwardness.

'I don't believe Violet cares twopence for the best orchid you could show her,' he said. 'I don't believe your *Dendrobium Formosum* would have any more effect upon her than it has upon me.'

'O, but I do admire them; or, at least, I should admire them immensely,' remonstrated Vixen, 'if I could see them in their native country. But I don't know that I have ever thoroughly appreciated them in a hothouse, hanging from the roof, and tumbling on to one's nose, or shooting off their long sprays at a tangent into awkward corners. I'm afraid I like the bluebells and foxgloves in our enclosures ever so much better. I have seen the banks in New Park one sheet of vivid blue with hyacinths, one blaze of crimson with foxgloves; and then there are the long green swamps, where millions of marsh marigolds shine like pools of liquid gold. If I could see orchids blooming like that I should be charmed with them.'

'You paint of course,' said Lady Mabel. 'Wild flowers make delightful studies, do they not?'

Vixen blushed violently.

'I can't paint a little bit,' she said. 'I am a dreadfully unaccomplished person.'

'That's not true,' remonstrated Rorie. 'She sketches capitally in pen and ink – dogs, horses, trees, you and me, everything, dashed off with no end of spirit.'

Here the Duchess, who had been describing the most conspicuous costumes at the German baths, to the delight of Mrs Winstanley, rose to go, and Lady Mabel, with her graceful, well-drilled air, rose immediately.

'We shall be so glad to see you at Ashbourne,' she murmured sweetly, giving Violet her slim little hand in its pearl-gray glove.

She was dressed from head to foot in artistically blended shades of gray – a most unpretending toilet. But to Violet's mind the very modesty of her attire seemed to say: 'I am a duke's only daughter, but I don't want to crush you.'

Vixen acknowledged her graciousness politely, but without any warmth; and it would hardly have done for Lady Mabel to have known what Miss Tempest said to herself when the Dovedale barouche had driven round the curve of the shrubbery, with Roderick smiling at her from his place as it vanished.

'I am afraid I have a wicked tendency to detest people,' said Vixen inwardly. 'I feel almost as bad about Lady Mabel as I do about Captain Winstanley.'

'Are they not nice?' asked Mrs Winstanley gushingly, when she and Violet were alone.

'Trimmer's drop-cakes?' said Vixen, who was standing by the tea-table munching a dainty little biscuit. 'Yes, they are always capital.'

'Nonsense, Violet; I mean the Duchess and her daughter.'

Vixen yawned audibly.

'I'm glad you do not find the Duchess insupportably dreary,' she said. 'Lady Mabel weighted me down like a nightmare.'

'O Violet! when she behaved so sweetly – quite caressingly, I thought. You really ought to cultivate her friendship. It would be so nice for you to visit at Ashbourne. You would have such opportunities——'

'Of doing what, mamma? Hearing polonaises and mazurkas in seven double flats; or seeing orchids with names as long as a German compound adjective.'

'Opportunities of being seen and admired by young men of position, Violet. Sooner or later the time must come for you to think of marrying.'

'That time will never come, mamma. I shall stay at home with you till you are tired of me; and when you turn me out I will have a cottage in the heart of the Forest – upon some wild ridge topped with a hat of firs – and good old McCroke to take care of me; and I will spend my days botanising and fern-hunting, riding and walking, and perhaps learn to paint my favourite trees, and live as happily and as remote from mankind as the herons in their nests at the top of the tall beeches on Vinny Ridge.'

'I am very glad there is no one present to hear you talk like that, Violet,' Mrs Winstanley said gravely.

'Why, mamma?'

'Because anybody hearing you might suppose you were not quite right in your mind.'

The Duchess's visit put Mrs Winstanley in good-humour with all the world, but especially with Roderick Vawdrey. She sent him an invitation to her next dinner; and when her husband seemed inclined to strike his name out of her list, she defended her right of selection with a courage that was almost heroic.

'I can't understand your motive for asking this fellow,' the Captain said, with a blacker look than his wife had ever before seen on his countenance.

'Why should I not ask him, Conrad? I have known him ever since he was at Eton; and the dear Squire was very fond of him.'

'If you are going to choose your acquaintance in accordance with the taste of your first husband, it will be rather a bad look out for your second,' said the Captain.

'What objection can you have to Roderick?'

'I can have, and I have, a very strong objection to him. But I am not going to talk about it yet awhile.'

'But, Conrad, if there is anything I ought to know——' began Mrs Winstanley, alarmed.

'When I think you ought to know it you will be told it, my dear Pamela. In the meantime, allow me to have my own opinion about Mr Vawdrey.'

'But, Conrad, in dear Edward's time he used to come to this house whenever he liked, as if he had been a near relation. And he is the Duchess's nephew, remember; and when he marries Lady Mabel, and the Duke dies, he will be one of the largest landowners in South Hampshire.'

'Very well, let him come to your dinner. It can make very little difference.'

'Now you are offended, Conrad,' said Mrs Winstanley, with a deprecating air.

'No, I am not offended; but I have my own opinion as to your wisdom in giving any encouragement to Mr Vawdrey.'

This sounded mysterious, and made Mrs Winstanley uncomfortable. But she was determined not to offend the Duchess, who had been so particularly gracious, and who had sent Captain and Mrs Winstanley a card for a dinner to be given on the last day of the year.

So Roderick got his invitation, and accepted it with friendly promptitude. He was master of the hounds now, and a good many of his days were given up to the pleasures of the hunting-field. He was an important person in his way, full of business; but he generally found time to drop in for an hour on Mrs Winstanley's Tuesday afternoons, to lounge with his back against the massive oaken chimney-breast and talk to Violet, or pat Argus, while the lady-visitors gossiped and tittered over their teacups.

This last dinner of Mrs Winstanley's was to take place a few days before Christmas, and was to be given in honour of a guest who was coming to spend the holidays at the Abbey House. The guest was Captain Winstanley's Irish friend, Lord Mallow, the owner of Bullfinch.

Vixen's heart gave an indignant bound when she heard that he was coming.

'Another person for me to hate,' she said to herself, almost despairingly. 'I am becoming a mass of envy, hatred, and malice, and all uncharitableness.'

Lord Mallow had spent the early morning of life in the army, it appeared, with no particular expectations. He and Captain Winstanley had been brother-officers. But the fell sergeant Death had promoted Patrick Hay to his elder brother's heritage, and he had surrendered a subaltern's place in a line regiment to become Viscount Mallow, and the owner of a fine stretch of fertile hill and valley in County Cork. He had set up at once as the model landlord, eager for his tenantry's welfare, full of advanced ideas, a violent politician, liberal to the verge of radicalism. If the Irish Church had not been disestablished before Lord Mallow went into Parliament, he would have gripped his destructive axe and had a chop or two at the root of that fine old tree. Protestant, and loyal to the Church of England in his own person – so far as such loyalty may be testified by regular attendance at divine service every Sunday morning, and a gentlemanlike reverence for bishops – it seemed to him not the less an injustice that his native land should be taxed with the maintenance of an alien clergy.

The late Lord Mallow had been a violent Tory, Orange to the marrow of his bones. The new Lord Mallow was violently progressive, enthusiastic in his belief in Hibernian virtues, and his indignation at Hibernian wrongs. He wanted to disestablish everything. He saw his country as she appears in the eyes of her poets and song-writers – a fair dishevelled female, oppressed by the cruel Sassenach, a lovely sufferer for whose rescue all true men and leal would fight to the death. He quoted the outrages of Elizabeth's reign, the cruelties of Cromwell's soldiery, the savagery of Ginkell, as if those wrongs had been inflicted yesterday, and the House of Commons of to-day were answerable for them. He made fiery speeches which were reported at length in the Irish newspapers. He was a fine speaker, after a florid pattern, and had a great command of voice, and a certain rugged eloquence that carried his hearers along with him, even when he was harping upon so hackneyed a string as the wrongs of 'Ould Ireland.'

Lord Mallow was not thirty, and he looked younger than his years. He was tall and broad-shouldered, robust, and a trifle clumsy in figure, and rode fourteen stone. He had a good-looking Irish face, smiling blue eyes, black hair, white teeth, bushy whiskers, and a complexion inclining to rosiness.

'He is the perfection of a commonplace young man,' Vixen said, when she talked him over with her mother on the day of his arrival at the Abbey House.

'Come Violet, you must admit that he is very handsome,' remonstrated Mrs Winstanley, who was sitting before her dressing-room fire, with her feet on a fender-stool of her own crewel-work, waiting for Pauline to commence the important ceremony of dressing for dinner. 'I think I never saw a finer set of teeth, and of course at his age they must all be real.'

'Unless he has had a few of the original ones knocked out in the hunting-field, mamma. They go over a good many stone walls in Ireland, you know, and he may have come to grief.'

'If you would only leave off talking in that horrid way, Violet. He is a very agreeable young man. How he enjoyed a cup of tea after his journey, instead of wanting soda-water and brandy. Conrad tells me he has a lovely place near Mallow – on the slope of a hill, sheltered on the north with pine woods; and I believe it is one of the prettiest parts of Ireland – so green, and fertile, and sweet, and such a happy peasantry.'

'I think I'd better leave you to dress for dinner, mamma. You like a clear hour, and it's nearly half-past six.'

'True, love; you may ring for Pauline. I have been wavering between my black and maize and my amethyst velvet, but I think I shall decide upon the velvet. What are you going to wear?'

'I? O, anything. The dress I wore last night.'

'My love, it is positively dowdy. Pray wear something better in honour of Lord Mallow. There is the gown you had for my wedding,' suggested Mrs Winstanley, blushing. 'You look lovely in that.'

'Mamma, do you think I am going to make a secondhand bridesmaid of myself to oblige Lord Mallow? No; that dress too painfully bears the stamp of what it was made for. I'm afraid it will have to rot in the wardrobe where it hangs. If it were woollen, the moths would inevitably have it; but, I suppose, as it is silk it will survive the changes of time; and some day it will be made into chair-covers, and future generations of Tempests will point to it as a relic of my great-aunt Violet.'

'I never heard anything so absurd,' cried Mrs Winstanley fretfully. 'It was Theodore's *chef-d'oeuvre*, and no doubt I shall have to pay an awful price for it.'

'Ah, mamma, we are continually doing things for which we have to pay an awful price,' said Vixen, with one of her involuntary bursts of bitter sadness.

CHAPTER 27

SOMETHING LIKE A RIDE

It was impossible to go on hating Lord Mallow for ever. He was a man whose overflowing good-nature would have conciliated the direct foe, could that enemy have been exposed long enough to its softening influence. He came upon the dull daily life of the Abbey House like a burst of sudden sunshine on a gloomy plain. The long winter evenings, when there was no company, had been sorely oppressive to Vixen. Out of respect to her mother she had kept her place in the drawing-room, reading, or working at some uninteresting strip of point-lace, which she had no hope of ever finishing, though it had been promised to Mr Scobel for his church. Captain Winstanley read the newspapers or the quarterlies, and paced the room thoughtfully at intervals. He talked to his wife just enough to escape the charge of neglect, but rarely spoke to or noticed Violet. Sometimes Mrs Winstanley asked for a little music; whereupon Violet went to the piano and played her scanty recollections of Mozart and Beethoven – all 'tuney' bits, remembered out of the sonatas or symphonies Miss McCroke had taught her; or, if asked to sing, the girl sang a ballad or two, to order, in her full round mezzo-soprano, which had a thrilling expression at times, when feeling got the better of her proud reserve, and all the pent-up sorrow of her heart broke loose into her song. But Captain Winstanley took no notice of these efforts, and even her mother's praises were not enthusiastic.

'Very sweet, very nice,' was the most Vixen ever heard from those maternal lips as she closed the piano.

But here was Lord Mallow, passionately fond of music and singing, and the beauties of nature, and all things that appeal to the sensitive Hibernian character. It seemed a new thing to Violet to have someone standing by the piano, turning over the leaves, applauding rapturously, and entreating for another and yet another Irish melody. When she sang 'The Minstrel Boy,' he joined in with a rich baritone that harmonised finely with her full ripe notes. The old room vibrated with the strong gush of melody, and even Captain Winstanley was impelled to praise.

'How well your voices harmonise,' he said. 'You ought to try some duets. I remember that fine baritone of yours in days of old, Mallow.'

Thereupon Lord Mallow asked Miss Tempest if she had any duets, and Vixen produced her small stock of vocal music. They tried one or two of Mendelssohn's, 'I would that my love,' and 'Greeting,' and discovered that they got on wonderfully well together. Vixen fell asleep that night wondering at her own amiability.

'To think that I should sing sentimental duets with him,' she said to herself. 'The man who has Bullfinch!'

Lord Mallow's presence at the Abbey House had a marked effect upon Captain Winstanley's treatment of his stepdaughter. Hitherto there had been a veiled bitterness in all his speeches, a constrained civility in his manners. Now he was all kindness, all expansion. Even his wife, who admired him always, and thought him the soul of wisdom in all he did, could not be blind to the change, and a new sense of peacefulness stole into her feeble mind. It was so pleasant to see dear Conrad so sweetly kind to Violet.

'What are we going to do with Lord Mallow this morning, Violet?' asked the Captain at breakfast, the day after the Irishman's arrival. 'We must try to amuse him somehow.'

'I don't think I have much to do with it,' Vixen answered
coldly. 'You will find plenty of amusement, I daresay, in the
billiard-room, in the stables, or in showing Lord Mallow your
improvements.'

'That would do very well for a wet morning, but it would be
a profligate waste of fine weather. No; I propose that you
should show Mallow some of the prettiest bits in the Forest. I
am not half so accomplished a guide as you; but we'll all go. I'll
order the horses at once if you like my plan, Mallow,' said
Captain Winstanley, turning to his friend, and taking Violet's
consent for granted.

'I shall be quite too delighted, if Miss Tempest will honour us
with her company,' replied the Irishman, with a pleasant look at
Vixen's fresh morning face, rosy-red with vexation.

It was the first time her stepfather had ever asked her to ride
with him, and she hated doing it. It was the first time she had
ever been asked to ride with anyone but her father or Roderick
Vawdrey. Yet to refuse would have been impossible, without
absolute discourtesy to her mother's husband and her mother's
guest. So she sat in her place and said nothing; and Lord
Mallow mistook that angry carnation for the warm red of happy
girlhood, which blushes it knows not wherefore.

Captain Winstanley ordered the horses to be at the door in
half-an-hour; and then he took Lord Mallow off to look at the
stables, while Violet went upstairs to put on her habit. Why was
the Captain so unusually amiable? she speculated. Was his little
soul so mean that he put on better manners to do honour to an
Irish peer?

She came tripping down the wide old staircase at the end of
the half-hour, in habit and hat of Lincoln green; with a cock's
feather in the neat little hat, and a formidable hooked hunting-
crop for opening gates, little feet daintily shod in patent leather,
but no spur. She loved her horse too well to run a needle into
his sleek side at the slightest provocation.

There were three horses, held by Bates and Lord Mallow's
groom. Bullfinch, looking as if he had just taken a prize at
Islington and was inclined to be bumptious about it. Arion,
tossing his delicately-modelled Greek head, and peering

furtively after bogies in the adjacent shrubbery. Captain Winstanley's well-seasoned hunter, Mosstrooper, nodding his long bony head, and swaying his fine-drawn neck up and down in a half-savage half-scornful manner, as if he were at war with society in general, like the Miller of Dee.

Vixen, who had looked the picture of vexation at the breakfast-table, was now all gaiety. Her hazel eyes sparkled with mischief. Lord Mallow stood in the porch, watching her as she came down the shining oak staircase, glorious in the winter sunlight. He thought her the perfection of a woman – nay, more than a woman, a goddess. Diana, the divine huntress, must have looked so, he fancied. He ran forward to mount her on the fidgety Arion; but honest old Bates was too quick for him; and she was looking down at Lord Mallow graciously from her perch on the well-worn doeskin saddle before he had time to offer his services.

She leant over to pat Bullfinch's massive crest.

'Dear old horse,' she murmured tenderly, remembering those winter mornings of old when he had stood before the porch as he stood to-day, waiting for the noble rider who was never more to mount him.

'Yet life goes on somehow without our beloved dead,' thought Violet.

Her changeful face saddened at the idea, and she rode along the shrubberied drive in silence.

'Where are you going to take us?' asked the Captain, when they had emerged from the Abbey House grounds, crossed the coach-road, and made their plunge into the first cart-track that offered itself.

'Everywhere,' answered Vixen, with a mischievous laugh. 'You have chosen me for your guide, and all you have to do is to follow.'

And she gave Arion a light touch with her hunting-crop, and cantered gaily down the gently sloping track to a green lawn, which looked, to Captain Winstanley's experienced eye, very much like a quaggy bog.

'Steer towards your left!' he cried anxiously to Lord Mallow.

If there was danger near, Vixen managed to avoid it; she made a sweeping curve, skirted the treacherous-looking lawn,

and disappeared in another cart-track, between silvery trunks of
veteran beeches, self-sown in the dark ages, with here and there
a gnarled old oak, rugged and lichen-mantled, with feathery tufts
of fern nestling in the hollow places between his gaunt limbs.

That was a ride! Lord Mallow could remember nothing like
it, and he was destined to carry this in his memory for a
lifetime. The ghostly trees; the silver-shining bark of the
beeches, varying with a hundred indescribable shades of green,
and purple, and warmest umber; the rugged gray of the grand
old oaks; the lichens and mosses, the mysterious wintry growths
of toadstool and weed and berry; that awful air of unearthliness
which pervaded the thicker portions of the wood, as of some
mystic underworld – half shadow and half dream. No, Lord
Mallow could never forget it; nor yet the way that flying figure
in Lincoln green led them by bog and swamp, over clay and
gravel – through as many varieties of soil as if she had been
trying to give them a practical lesson in geology; across snaky
ditches and pebbly fords; through furze-bushes and thickets of
holly; through everything likely to prove aggravating to the
temper of a well-bred horse; and finally, before giving them
breathing-time, she led them up the clayey side of a hill, as
steep as a house, on the top of which she drew rein, and
commanded them to admire the view.

'This is Acres Down, and there are the Needles,' she said,
pointing her whip at the dim blue horizon. 'If it were a clear
day, and your sight were long enough, I daresay you would see
Jersey, Guernsey, Alderney, and Sark. But, I think, to-day you
must be content with the Needles. Can you see them?' she
asked Lord Mallow.

'See them!' exclaimed the Irishman. 'I can see well enough to
thread one of them if I wanted.'

'Now, you've seen the Isle of Wight,' said Vixen. 'That's a
point accomplished. The ardent desire of everyone in the Forest
is to see the Isle of Wight. They are continually mounting hills,
and gazing into space, in order to get a glimpse at that chalky
little island. It seems the main object of everybody's existence.'

'They might as well go and live there at once, if they're so
fond of it,' suggested Lord Mallow.

'Yes; and then they would be straining their eyes in the endeavour to see the Great Horse – that's a group of firs on the top of a hill, and one of our Forest seamarks. That frantic desire to behold distant objects has always seemed to me to be one of the feeblest tendencies of the human mind. Now you have seen the Needles, we have accomplished a solemn duty, and I may show you our woods.'

Vixen shook her rein and trotted recklessly down a slippery track, jumped a broad black ditch, and plunged into the recesses of the wood, Bullfinch and Mosstrooper following meekly.

They went a wonderful round, winding in and out of Bratley Wood, piercing deep into the wintry mysteries of Mark Ash; through mud and moss and soft pitfalls, where the horses sank up to their hocks in withered leaves; avoiding bogs by a margin of a yard or so; up and down, under spreading branches, where the cattle-line but just cleared the heads of the riders; across the blackened bracken; by shining hollies, whose silvery trunks stood up like obelisks out of a thicket of dwarf bushes; through groves, where the tall beech-trunks had a solemn look like the columns of some gigantic temple; then into wondrous plantations of Scotch firs, where the air was balmy as in summer, and no breath of the December wind penetrated the dense wall of foliage. Then to higher ground, where the wintry air blew keen again, and where there was a soft green lawn, studded with graceful conifers – cypress, deodora, Douglas fir – tall with a growth of thirty years; the elegant importations of an advanced civilisation. Anon by the gray lichened walls of a deserted garden, which had a strangely-romantic look, and was as suggestive of a dreamy idyllic world as a poem by Tennyson; and so down into the green-and-gray depths of Mark Ash again, but never returning over the same ground; and then up the hill to Vinny Ridge and the Heronry, where Captain Winstanley cracked his whip to scare the herons, and had the satisfaction of scaring his own and the other two horses, while the herons laughed him to scorn from their cradles in the tree-tops, and would not stir a feather for his gratification. Then by a long plantation to a wide stretch of common, where Vixen told her companions that they were safe for a good mile, and set them

an example by starting Arion across the short smooth turf at a
hand-gallop. They pulled up just in time to escape a small gulf
of moss and general sponginess, waded a stream or two,
splashed through a good deal of spewy ground, and came to
Queen's Bower; thence into the oak plantations of New Park;
then across Gretnam Wood; and then at a smart trot along the
road towards home.

'I hope I haven't kept you out too long?' said Vixen politely.

'We've only been five hours,' answered the Captain with
grim civility; 'but if Mallow is not tired, I shall not complain.'

'I never enjoyed anything so much in my life, never,'
protested Lord Mallow.

'Well, to-morrow we can shoot the pheasants. It will be a rest
for us after this.'

'It will be dull work after the enchantments of to-day,' said
the Irishman.

Captain Winstanley rode homeward a few paces in the rear of
the other two, smiling to himself grimly, and humming a little
song of Heine's:

> 'Est ist ein alte Geschichte,
>   Doch bleibt es immer neue.'

CHAPTER 28

RORIE OBJECTS TO DUETS

Mrs Winstanley's little dinner went off smoothly and pleasantly,
as all such entertainments had done under the new *régime*. The
Captain knew how to select his guests, as well as he knew how
to compose a *menu*. People felt pleased with themselves and
their neighbours at his table. There were nothing heavy in the
dinner or in the conversation; there were no long sittings over
old port or particular claret. The wines were of the first quality;

but there was no fuss made about them. Colonel Carteret remembered how he and the Squire had sat prosing over their port or Château Lafitte, and felt as if he were living in a new world – a world in which full-blooded friendship and boisterous hospitality were out of fashion. People whose talk had hitherto been intensely local – confined, for the most part, to petty sessions, commoners' rights, hunting, and the parish church and schools – found themselves discussing the widest range of topics, from the prospect of a European war – that European war which has been impending more or less distinctly for the last twenty years – to the latest social scandal in the upper currents of London society. Captain and Mrs Winstanley's country friends, inspired by one or two clever young men just imported from the London clubs, were surprised to discover how well they were able to criticise the latest productions in literature, art, and the drama; the newest results of scientific investigation; or the last record of African or Central Asian exploration. It was quite delightful to quiet country people, who went to London on an average once in three years, to find themselves talking so easily about the last famous picture, the latest action for libel in artistic circles, or the promised adaptation of Sardou's last comedy at a West End theatre, just as glibly as if they knew all about art, and had read every play of Sardou's.

Roderick Vawdrey enjoyed himself wonderfully at this particular dinner-party, so long as the dinner lasted; for Captain Winstanley, by an oversight which made him inwardly savage all dinner-time, had placed Mr Vawdrey and Miss Tempest side by side. There had been some confusion in his mind as he finished his plan of the table; his attention had been called away at the last moment, or this thing could not have happened – for nothing was farther from Captain Winstanley's intention than that Violet and her old playfellow should be happy in each other's society. And there they sat, smiling and sparkling at each other in the exuberance of youth and high spirits, interchanging little confidential remarks that were doubtless to the disparagement of some person or persons in the assembly. If dark electric glances shot from the covert of bent brows could

have slain those two happy triflers, assuredly neither of them
would have lived to the end of that dinner.

'How do you like him?' asked Rorie, stooping to sniff at the
big Maréchal Niel bud, in the specimen glass by his plate.

'Whom?'

'The man who has Bullfinch.'

Lord Mallow was in the place of honour next his hostess.
Involuntarily Violet glanced in that direction, and was startled
to find the Irishman's good-humoured gaze meeting hers, just
as if he had been watching her for the last half-hour.

'How do I like him? Well, he seems very good-natured.'

'Seems good-natured. You ought to be able to give me a more
definite answer by this time. You have lived in the same house
with him – let me see, is it three or four days since he came?'

'He has been here nearly a week.'

'A week! Why then you must know him as well as if he were
your brother. There is no man living who could keep himself
dark for a week. No; I don't believe the most inscrutable of
men, born and bred in diplomatic circles, could keep the secret
of a solitary failing from the eyes of those who live under the
same roof with him for seven days. It would leak out somehow
– if not at breakfast, at dinner. Man is a communicative animal,
and so loves talking of himself that if he has committed murder
he must tell somebody about it sooner or later. And as to that
man,' continued Rorie, with a contemptuous glance at the
single-minded Lord Mallow, 'he is a creature whom the merest
beginner in the study of humanity would know by heart in
half-an-hour.'

'What do you know about him?' asked Vixen laughing. 'You
have had more than half-an-hour for the study of his character.'

'I know ever so much more than I want to know.'

'Answered like a Greek oracle.'

'What, have you taken to reading Greek?'

'No; but I know the oracles were a provoking set of creatures
who answered every inquiry with an enigma. But I won't have
you abuse Lord Mallow. He has been very kind to Bullfinch,
and has promised me that he will never part with him. The dear
old horse is to have a comfortable stable and kindly treatment to

his dying day – not to be sent out to grass in his old age, to shiver in a dreary solitude, or to be scorched by the sun and tormented by the flies.'

'He has promised all that, has he? He would promise a good deal more, I daresay,' muttered Rorie, stooping over his rosebud. 'Do you think him handsome? Do women admire a fresh complexion and black whiskers, and that unmistakable air of a hairdresser's wax model endowed with animation?'

'I see you consider him an idiot,' said Vixen laughing. 'But I assure you he is rather clever. He talks wonderfully about Ireland, and the reforms he is going to bring about for her.'

'Of course. Burke, and Curran, and Castlereagh, and O'Connell, and fifty more have failed to steer that lumbering old vessel off the mudbank on which she stranded at some time in the dark ages; in fact, nobody except Oliver Cromwell ever did understand how to make Ireland prosperous and respectable, and he began by depopulating her. And here is a fresh-coloured young man, with whiskers *à la côtelette de mouton*, who thinks he was born to be her pilot, and to navigate her into a peaceful haven. He is the sort of man who will begin by being the idol of a happy tenantry, and end by being shot from behind one of his own hedges.'

'I hope not,' said Vixen, 'for I am sure he means well. And I should like him to outlive Bullfinch.'

Roderick had been very happy all dinner-time. From the soups to the ice-puddings the moments had flown for him. It seemed the briefest dinner he had ever been at; and yet when the ladies rose to depart the silvery chime of the clock struck the half-hour after nine. But Lord Mallow's hour came later, in the drawing-room, where he contrived to hover over Violet, and fence her round from all other admirers for the rest of the evening. They sang their favourite duets together, to the delight of every one except Rorie, who felt curiously savage at 'I would that my love,' and icily disapproving at 'Greeting;' but vindictive to the verge of homicidal mania at 'O, wert thou in the cauld blast!'

'His "plaidie," indeed,' he ejaculated inwardly. 'The creature never possessed anything so comfortable or civilised. How

preposterous it is to hear an Irishman sing Scotch songs. If an
Irishman had a plaidie, he would pawn it for a drop o' the
cratur.'

Later Violet and Lord Mallow sang a little duet by Masini,
'O, *que la mer est belle!*' the daintiest, most bewitching music –
such a melody as the Lorelei might have sung when the Rhine
flowed peacefully onward below mountain-peaks shining in the
evening light, and the sweet unearthly voice floated on the
summer air, bringing foolish fishermen to their doom.
Everybody was delighted. It was just the kind of music to please
the unlearned in the art. Mrs Carteret came to the piano to
compliment Violet.

'I had no idea you could sing so sweetly,' she said. 'Why have
you never sung to us before?'

'Nobody ever asked me,' Vixen answered frankly. 'But
indeed I am no singer.'

'You have one of the freshest, brightest voices I ever had the
happiness of hearing,' Lord Mallow exclaimed enthusiastically.

He would have liked to go on singing duets for an indefinite
period. He felt lifted into some strange and delightful region – a
sphere of love and harmony – while he was mingling his voice
with Violet's. It made the popular idea of heaven, as a place
where there is nothing but singing – an eternal, untiring choir –
clearer and more possible to him than it had ever seemed before.
Paradise would be quite endurable if he and Violet might stand
side by side in the serried ranks of choristers. There was quite a
little crowd round the piano, shutting in Violet and Lord
Mallow, and Roderick Vawdrey was not in it. He felt himself
excluded, and held himself gloomily apart, talking hunting-talk
with a man for whom he did not care twopence. Directly his
carriage was announced – *sotto voce* by the considerate Forbes, so
as not to wound anybody's feelings by the suggestion that the
festivity was on its last legs – Mr Vawdrey went up to Mrs
Winstanley and took leave. He would not wait to say good-
night to Violet. He only cast one glance in the direction of the
piano, where the noble breadth of Mrs Carteret's brocaded
amber back obscured every remoter object, and then went away
moodily, denouncing duet-singing as an abomination.

When Lady Mabel asked him next day what kind of an evening he had had at the Abbey House, in a tone which implied that any entertainment there must be on a distinctly lower level as compared with the hospitalities of Ashbourne, he told her that it had been uncommonly slow.

'How was that? You had some stupid person to take in to dinner, perhaps?'

'No; I went in with Violet.'

'And you and she are such old friends. You ought to get on very well together.'

Rorie reddened furiously. Happily he was standing with his back to the light in one of the orchid-houses, enjoying the drowsy warmth of the atmosphere, and Mabel was engrossed with the contemplation of a fine zygopetalum, which was just making up its mind to bloom.

'O yes, that was well enough; but the evening was disgustingly slow. There was too much music.'

'Classical?'

'Lord knows. It was mostly French and German. I consider it an insult to people to ask them to your house, and then stick them down in their chairs and say h——sh——h! every time they open their mouths. If people want to give amateur concerts, let them say so when they send out their invitations, and then one would know what one has to expect.'

'I am afraid the music must have been very bad to make you so cross,' said Lady Mabel, rather pleased that the evening at the Abbey House should have been a failure. 'Who were the performers?'

'Violet, and an Irish friend of Captain Winstanley's – a man with a rosy complexion and black whiskers – Lord Mallow.'

'Lord Mallow! I think I danced with him once or twice last season. He is rather distinguished as a politician, I believe, among the young Ireland party. Dreadfully radical.'

'He looks it,' answered Rorie. 'He has a loud voice and a loud laugh, and they seem to be making a great deal of him at the Abbey House.'

' "Tommy loves a lord," ' said Lady Mabel brightly. Rorie hadn't the faintest idea whence the quotation came. 'I daresay

the Winstanleys are rather glad to have Lord Mallow staying
with them.'

'The Squire would have kicked him out of doors,' muttered
Rorie savagely.

'But why? Is he so very objectionable? He waltzes beautifully,
if I remember right; and I though him rather a well-meaning
young man.'

'O, there's nothing serious against him that I know of; only I
don't think Squire Tempest would have liked a singing man
any more than he would have liked a singing mouse.'

'I didn't know Miss Tempest sang,' said Lady Mabel. 'I
thought she could do nothing but ride.'

'O, she has a very pretty voice, but one may have too much
of a good thing, you know. One doesn't go out to dinner to
hear people sing duets.'

'I'm afraid they must have given you a very bad dinner, or
you would hardly be so cross. I know that is the way with papa.
If the dinner is bad he abuses everything, and declares the ladies
were all ugly.'

'O, the dinner was excellent, I believe. I'm not a connoisseur,
like my uncle. People might give me the most wonderful
dinner in the world, and I should hardly be the wiser; or they
might give me a wretched one, and I should not feel
particularly angry with them.'

The next day was Tuesday, and, as the Duchess and her
daughter happened to be driving within a mile or so of the
Abbey House, Lady Mabel suggested that they should call upon
Mrs Winstanley.

'I am rather anxious to see the wild Irishman they have
captured lately – Lord Mallow. We met him at Lady Dumdrum's,
if you remember, mamma. I danced with him twice.'

'My dear Mabel, do you think I can remember all your
partners?'

'But Lord Mallow is rather celebrated. He makes very good
speeches. Papa read one of them to us the other day when there
was a great debate going on upon the Irish land question.'

The Duchess remembered being read to one evening after
dinner, but the debates, as delivered by the Duke, had generally

a somnolent effect upon his wife. She had a faint idea of the beginning, and struggled heroically to discover what the speakers were talking about; then came a soft confusion of sound, like the falling of waters; and the middle and end of the lecture was dreamland. Lady Mabel was of a more energetic temper, and was interested in everything that could enlarge her sphere of knowledge, from a parliamentary debate to a Greek play.

The Duchess had never in her life refused compliance with any wish of her daughter's, so the horses' heads were turned towards the Abbey House, along a smooth hard road through a pine wood, then through a lodge-gate into a forest of rhododendrons.

'This is really a nicer place than Ashbourne, mamma,' remarked Lady Mabel disapprovingly.

It appeared to her quite a mistake in the arrangement of the universe that Violet Tempest should be heiress to a more picturesque estate than that which she, the Duke of Dovedale's only daughter, was to inherit.

'My dear, Ashbourne is perfect. Everyone says so. The stables, the offices, the way the house is lighted and heated, the ventilation.'

'Yes, mamma; but those are details which nobody thinks about except an architect or a house-agent. Ashbourne is so revoltingly modern. It smells of stucco. It will take a century to tone it down. Now this fine old place is like a dream of the past; it is a poem in wood and stone. Ashbourne would be very well for a hunting-box for anyone who had three or four other places, as my father has; but when my time comes, and I have only Ashbourne, I'm afraid I shall hate it.'

'But you will have a choice of places by-and-by,' said the Duchess consolingly. 'You will have Briarwood.'

'Briarwood is a degree uglier than Ashbourne,' sighed Mabel, leaning back in the carriage, wrapped to the chin in Russian sable, the image of discontent.

There are moments in every life, as in Solomon's, when all seems vanity. Lady Mabel Ashbourne's life had been cloudless – a continual summer, an unchangeable Italian sky; and yet there

were times when she was weary of it, when some voice within
her murmured 'This is not enough.' She was pretty, she was
graceful, accomplished, gifted with a self-confidence that
generally passed for wit; all the blood in her veins was the bluest
of the blue, everybody bowed down to her, more or less, and
paid her homage; the man she liked best in the world, and had
so preferred from her childhood, was to be her husband;
nobody had ever contradicted her, or hinted that she was less
than perfect; and yet that mysterious and rebellious voice
sometimes repeated, 'It is not enough.'

The rebellious voice expostulated loudly this winter
afternoon, as Lady Mabel's languid eyes scanned the dark
shining rhododendron bushes, rising bank above bank, a
veritable jungle, backed by tall beeches and towerlike Douglas
firs. A blackbird was whistling joyously amongst the greenery,
and a robin was singing on the other side of the drive. The
sunlit sky was soft and pearly. It was one of those mild winters
in which Christmas steals unawares upon the footprints of a
lovely autumn. The legendary oak was doubtless in full bud at
Cadenham, like its miraculous brother, the Glastonbury thorn.

'I don't think any of my father's places can compare with
this,' Lady Mabel said irritably.

She would not have minded the beauty of the grounds so
much had they been the heritage of any other heiress than
Violet Tempest.

The old hall was full of people and voices when the Duchess
and her daughter were announced. There was a momentary
hush at their entrance, as at the advent of someone of
importance, and Mrs Winstanley came smiling out of the
firelight to welcome them, in Theodore's last invention, which
was a kind of skirt that necessitated a peculiar gliding motion in
the wearer, and was built upon the lines of a mermaid's tail.

'How good of you!' exclaimed Mrs Winstanley.

'We were driving through Lyndhurst, and could not resist the
temptation of coming in to see you,' said the Duchess
graciously. 'How do you do, Miss Tempest? Were you out
with the hounds this morning? We met some people riding
home.'

'I have never hunted since my father's death,' Violet answered gravely; and the Duchess was charmed with the answer and the seriously tender look that accompanied it.

Lord Mallow was standing before the hearth, looking remarkably handsome in full hunting costume. The well-worn scarlet coat and high black boots became him. He had enjoyed his first day with the fox-hounds, had escaped the bogs, and had avoided making an Absalom of himself among the spreading beechen boughs. Bullfinch had behaved superbly over his old ground.

Mr and Mrs Scobel were among those dusky figures grouped around the wide fire-lit hearth, where the piled-up logs testified to the Tempest common of estovers. Mr Scobel was talking about the last advance movement of the Ritualists, and expatiating learnedly upon the Ornaments Rubric of 1559, and its bearing upon the Advertisements of 1566, with a great deal more about King Edward's first Prayer-book, and the Act of Uniformity, to Colonel Carteret, who, from an antique conservative standpoint, regarded Ritualists, Spirit-rappers, and Shakers in about the same category; while Mrs Scobel twittered cheerily about the parish and the schools to the Colonel's bulky wife, who was a liberal patroness of all philanthropic institutions in her neighbourhood.

Lord Mallow came eagerly forward to recall himself to the memories of Lady Mabel and her mother.

'I hope your grace has not forgotten me,' he said; and the Duchess, who had not the faintest recollection of his face or figure, knew that this must be Lord Mallow. 'I had the honour of being introduced to you at Lady Dumdrum's delightful ball.'

The Duchess said something gracious, and left Lord Mallow free to talk to Lady Mabel. He reminded her of that never to be, by him, forgotten waltz, and talked, in his low-pitched Irish voice, as if he had lived upon nothing but the recollection of it ever since.

It was idiosyncratic of Lord Mallow that he could not talk to any young woman without seeming to adore her. At this very moment he thought Violet Tempest the one lovable and soul-entrancing woman the world held for him; yet at sight of Lady

Mabel he behaved as if she and no other was his one particular star.

'It was a nice dance, wasn't it? but there were too many people for the rooms,' said Lady Mabel easily; 'and I don't think the flowers were so prettily arranged as the year before. Do you?'

'I was not there the year before.'

'No? I must confess to having been at three balls at Lady Dumdrum's. That makes me seem very old, does it not? Some young ladies in London make believe to be always in their first season. They put on a hoydenish freshness, and pretend to be delighted with everything, as if they were just out of the nursery.'

'That's a very good idea up to thirty,' said Lord Mallow. 'I should think it would hardly answer after.'

'O, after thirty they begin to be fond of horses and take to betting. I believe young ladies after thirty are the most desperate – what is that dreadful slang word? – plungers in society. How do you like our hunting?'

'I like galloping about the Forest amazingly; but I should hardly call it hunting, after Leicestershire.'

'Was my cousin, Mr Vawdrey, out to-day?'

'The M.F.H.? In the first flight. May I get you some tea?'

'If you please. Mrs Winstanley's tea is always so good.'

Mrs Winstanley was supremely happy in officiating at her gipsy table, where the silver tea-kettle of Queen Anne's time was going through its usual spluttering performances. To sit in a fashionable gown – however difficult the gown might be to sit in – and dispense tea to a local duchess, was Mrs Winstanley's loftiest idea of earthly happiness. Of course there might be a superior kind of happiness beyond earth; but to appreciate that the weak human soul would have to go through a troublesome ordeal in the way of preparation, as the gray cloth at Hoyle's printing-works is dashed about in gigantic vats, and whirled round upon mighty wheels, before it is ready for the reception of particular patterns and dyes.

Lady Mabel and Lord Mallow had a longish chat in the deepset window where Vixen watched for Rorie on his twenty-first birthday. The conversation came round to Irish politics somehow, and Lord Mallow was enraptured at discovering that Lady Mabel had read his speeches, or had heard them read. He had met many young ladies who professed to be interested in his Irish politics; but never before had he encountered one who seemed to know what she was talking about. Lord Mallow was enchanted. He had found his host's lively stepdaughter stonily indifferent to the Hibernian cause. She had said 'Poor things' once or twice, when he dilated on the wrongs of an oppressed people; but her ideas upon all Hibernian subjects were narrow. She seemed to imagine Ireland a vast expanse of bog, chiefly inhabited by pigs.

'There are mountains, are there not?' she remarked once; 'and tourists go there? But people don't live there, do they?'

'My dear Miss Tempest, there are charming country seats; if you were to see the outskirts of Waterford, or the hills above Cork, you would find almost as many fine mansions as in England.'

'Really?' exclaimed Vixen, with most bewitching incredulity; 'but people don't live in them? Now I'm sure you cannot tell me honestly that anyone lives in Ireland. You, for instance, you talk most enthusiastically about your beautiful country, but you don't live in it.'

'I go there every year for the fishing.'

'Yes; but gentlemen will go to the most uncomfortable places for fishing — Norway, for example. You go to Ireland just as you go to Norway.'

'I admit that the fishing in Connemara is rather remote from civilisation——'

'Of course. It is at the other end of everything. And then you go into the House of Commons, and rave about Ireland, just as if you loved her as I love the Forest, where I hope to live and die. I think all this wild enthusiasm about Ireland is the silliest thing in the world when it comes from the lips of landowners who won't pay their beloved country the compliment of six months' residence out of twelve.'

After this Lord Mallow gave up all hope of sympathy from Miss Tempest. What could be expected from a young lady who

could not understand patriotism in the abstract, but wanted to
pin a man down for life to the spot of ground for which his soul
burned with the ardour of an orator and a poet?

It was a relief, therefore, to Lord Mallow's active mind to
find himself in conversation with a young lady who really cared
for his subject and understood him. He could have talked to
Lady Mabel for ever. The limits of five-o'clock tea were far too
narrow. He was delighted when the Duchess paused as she was
going away, and said:

'I hope you will come and see us at Ashbourne, Lord
Mallow; the Duke will be very pleased to know you.'

Lord Mallow murmured something expressive of a mild
ecstasy, and the Duchess swept onward, Lady Mabel gliding in
her wake.

Lord Mallow was glad when the next day's post brought him
a card of invitation to the ducal dinner on December the 31st.
He fancied that he was indebted to Lady Mabel for this civility.

'You are going, of course,' he said to Violet, twisting the card
between his fingers meditatively.

'I believe I am asked.'

'She is,' answered Mrs Winstanley, from her seat behind the
urn; 'and I consider, under the circumstances, it is extremely
kind of the Duchess to invite her.'

'Why?' asked Lord Mallow, intensely mystified.

'Why, the truth is, my dear Lord Mallow, that Violet is in an
anomalous position. She has been to Lady Southminster's ball,
and a great many parties about here. She is out and yet not out,
if you understand.'

Lord Mallow looked as if he were very far from
understanding.

'She has never been presented,' explained Mrs Winstanley. 'It
is too dreadful to think of. People would call me the most
neglectful of mothers. But the season before last seemed too
soon after dear Edward's death; and last season, well' – blushing
and hesitating a little – 'my mind was so much occupied, and
Violet herself was so indifferent about it, that somehow or other
the time slipped by and the thing was not done. I feel myself
awfully to blame – almost as much so as if I had neglected her

confirmation. But early next season — at the very first drawing-room, if possible — she must be presented, and then I shall feel a great deal more comfortable in my mind.'

'I don't think it matters one little bit,' said Lord Mallow, with appalling recklessness.

'It would matter immensely if we were travelling. Violet could not be presented at any foreign court, or invited to any court ball. She would be an outcast. I shall have to be presented myself, on my marriage with Captain Winstanley. We shall go to London early in the spring. Conrad will take a small house in Mayfair.'

'If I can get one,' said the Captain doubtfully. 'Small houses in Mayfair are as hard to get nowadays as black pearls — and as dear.'

'I am charmed to think you will be in town,' exclaimed Lord Mallow; 'and, perhaps, some night when there is an Irish question on, you and Miss Tempest might be induced to come to the Ladies' Gallery. Some ladies rather enjoy a spirited debate.'

'I should like it amazingly,' cried Violet. 'You are awfully rude to one another, are you not? And you imitate cocks and hens; and do all manner of dreadful things. It must be capital fun.'

This was not at all the kind of appreciation Lord Mallow desired.

'O, yes; we are excruciatingly funny sometimes, I daresay, without knowing it,' he said, with a mortified air.

He was getting on the friendliest terms with Violet. He was almost as much at home with her as Rorie was, except that she never called him by his Christian-name, nor flashed at him those lovely, mirth-provoking glances which he surprised sometimes on their way to Mr Vawdrey. Those two had a hundred small jokes and secrets that dated back to Vixen's childhood. How could a new-comer hope to be on such delightful terms with her? Lord Mallow felt this, and hated Roderick Vawdrey as intensely as it was possible for a nature radically good and generous to hate even a favoured rival. That Roderick was his rival, and was favoured, were two ideas of which Lord Mallow could not dispossess himself, notwithstanding the established fact of Mr Vawdrey's engagement to his cousin.

'A good many men begin life by being engaged to their cousins,' reflected Lord Mallow. 'A man's relations take it into their heads to keep an estate in the family, and he is forthwith set at his cousin like an unwilling terrier at a rat. I don't at all feel as if this young man were permanently disposed of, in spite of all their talk; and I'm very sure Miss Tempest likes him better than I should approve of were I the cousin.'

While he loitered over his second cup of coffee, with the ducal card of invitation in his hand, it seemed to him a good opportunity for talking about Lady Mabel.

'A very elegant girl, Lady Mabel,' he said; 'and remarkably clever. I never talked to a young woman, or an old one either, who knew so much about Ireland. She's engaged to that gawky cousin, isn't she?'

Vixen shot an indignant look at him, and pouted her rosy underlip.

'You mean young Vawdrey. Yes; it is quite an old engagement. They were affianced to each other in their cradles. I believe,' answered Captain Winstanley.

'Just what I should have imagined,' said Lord Mallow.

'Why?'

'Because they seem to care so little for each other now.'

'O but, dear Lord Mallow, remember, Lady Mabel Ashbourne is too well-bred to go about the world advertising her affection for her future husband,' remonstrated Mrs Winstanley. 'I'm sure, if you had seen us before our marriage, you would never have guessed from our manner to each other that Conrad and I were engaged. You would not have a lady behave like a housemaid with her "young man." I believe in that class of life they always sit with their arms round each other's waists at evening parties.'

'I would have a lady show that she has a heart, and is not ashamed to acknowledge its master,' said Lord Mallow, with his eyes on Vixen, who sat stolidly silent, pale with anger. 'However, we will put down Lady Mabel's seeming coldness to

good-breeding. But as to Mr Vawdrey, all I can say about him
is, that he may be in love with his cousin's estate, but he is
certainly not in love with his cousin.'

This was more than Vixen could brook.

'Mr Vawdrey is a gentleman, with a fine estate of his own!'
she cried. 'How dare you impute such meanness to him!'

'It may be mean, but it is the commonest thing in life.'

'Yes, among adventurers who have no other road to fortune
than by marrying for money; but do you suppose it can matter
to Roderick whether he has a thousand acres less or more, or
two houses instead of one? He is going to marry Lady Mabel
because it was the dearest wish of his mother's heart, and
because she is perfect, and proper, and accomplished, and
wonderfully clever – you said as much yourself – and exactly the
kind of wife that a young man would be proud of. There are
reasons enough, I should hope,' concluded Vixen indignantly.

She had spoken breathlessly, in gasps of a few words at a
time, and her eyes flashed their angriest light upon the
astounded Irishman.

'Not half a reason if he does not love her,' he answered
boldly. 'But I believe young Englishmen of the present day
marry for reason and not for love. Cupid has been cashiered in
favour of Minerva. Foolish marriages are out of fashion.
Nobody ever thinks of love in a cottage. First, there are no
more cottages; and secondly, there is no more love.'

Christmas was close at hand: a trying time for Vixen, who
remembered the jolly old Christmas of days gone by, when the
poor from all the surrounding villages came to receive the
Squire's lavish bounty, and not even the tramp or the cadger
was sent empty-handed away. Under the new master all was
done by line and rule. The distribution of coals and blankets
took place down in Beechdale under Mr and Mrs Scobel's
management. Vixen went about from cottage to cottage, in the
wintry dusk, giving her small offerings out of her scanty
allowance of pocket-money, which Captain Winstanley had put
at the lowest figure he decently could.

'What can Violet want with pocket-money?' he asked, when
he discussed the subject with his wife. 'Your dressmaker

supplies all her gowns, and bonnets, and hats. You give her gloves – everything. Nobody calls upon her for anything.'

'Her papa always gave her a good deal of money,' pleaded Mrs Winstanley. 'I think she gave it almost all away to the poor.'

'Naturally. She went about pauperising honest people because she had more money than she knew what to do with. Let her have ten pounds a quarter to buy gloves and eau-de-cologne, writing-paper, and postage-stamps, and trifles of that kind. She can't do much harm with that, and it is quite as much as you can afford, since we have both made up our minds to live within our incomes.'

Mrs Winstanley sighed and assented, as she was wont to do. It seemed hard that there should be this need of economy, but it was in a manner Violet's fault that they were all thus restricted, since she was to take so much, and to reduce her mother almost to penury by-and-by.

'I don't know what would become of me without Conrad's care,' thought the dutiful wife.

Going among the poor this Christmas, with almost empty hands, Violet Tempest discovered what it was to be really loved. Honest eyes brightened none the less at her coming, the little children flocked as fondly to her knee. The changes at the Abbey House were very well understood. They were all put down to Captain Winstanley's account; and many a simple heart burned with indignation at the idea that the Squire's golden-haired daughter was being 'put upon.'

One bright afternoon in the Christmas holidays Vixen consented, half reluctantly, to let Lord Mallow accompany her in her visits among the familiar faces. That was a rare day for the Squire's old pensioners. The Irishman's pockets were full of half-crowns and florins and sixpences for the rosy-faced, bare-footed, dirty, happy children.

'It puts me in mind of the old country,' he said, when he had made acquaintance with the interior of half-a-dozen cottages. 'The people seem just as kind and friendly, and improvident, and idle, and happy-go-lucky as my friends at home. That old Forester, now, that we saw sitting in the winter sun, drinking his noonday pint, on a bench outside a rustic beer-shop, looking the very image of lazy enjoyment – what Irishman could take life more lightly or seem better pleased with himself? a freeborn child of the sun and wind, ready to earn his living anyhow, except by the work of his hands. Yes, Miss Tempest, I feel a national affinity to your children of the Forest. I wish I were Mr Vawdrey, and bound to spend my life here.'

'Why, what would life be to you if you had not Ould Ireland to fight for?' cried Vixen, smiling at him.

'Life would be simply perfect for me if I had——'

'What?' asked Vixen, as he came to a sudden stop.

'The dearest wish of my heart. But I dare not tell you what that is yet awhile.'

Vixen felt very sorry she had asked the question. She looked wildly round for another cottage. They had just done the last habitation in a straggling village in the heart of the woods. There was nothing human in sight by which the conversation might be diverted from the uncomfortable turn it had just taken. Yes; yonder under the beechen boughs Vixen descried a small child with red legs, like a Jersey partridge, dragging a small child by the arm, ankle-deep in the sodden leaves. To see them, and to dart across the wet grass towards them, were almost simultaneous.

'Tommy,' cried Vixen, seizing the red-legged child, 'why do you never come to the Abbey House?'

'Because Mrs Trimmer says theres nothing for me,' lisped the infant. 'The new master sells the milk up in Lunnun.'

'Laudable economy,' exclaimed Vixen to Lord Mallow, who had followed her into the damp woodland and heard the boy's answer. 'The poor old Abbey House can hardly know itself under such admirable management.'

'There is a big house where you might do what you liked; yes, and give away the cows as well as the milk, if you pleased, and none should say you nay,' said Lord Mallow in a low voice, full of unaffected tenderness.

'O, please don't!' cried Vixen; 'don't speak too kindly. I feel sometimes as if one little kind word too much would make me cry like a child. It's the last straw, you know, that crushes the camel; and I hate myself for being so weak and foolish.'

After this Vixen walked home as if she had been winning a match, and Lord Mallow, for his life, dared not say another tender word.

This was their last *tête-à-tête* for some time. Christmas came with its festivities, all of a placid and eminently well-bred character, and then came the last day of the year and the dinner at Ashbourne.

CHAPTER 29

'FADING IN MUSIC'

'Mrs Winstanley, on her marriage, by the Duchess of Dovedale.'

That was the sentence which went on repeating itself like a cabalistic formula in Pamela Winstanley's mind, as her carriage drove through the dark silent woods to Ashbourne on the last night of the year.

A small idea had taken possession of her small mind. The Duchess was the fittest person to present her to her gracious mistress, or her gracious mistress's representative, at the first drawing-room of the coming season. Mrs Winstanley had old friends, friends who had known her in her girlhood, who would have been happy to undertake the office. Captain Winstanley had an ancient female relative, living in a fossil state at Hampton Court, and vaguely spoken of as 'a connection,' who would willingly emerge from her aristocratic hermitage to present her kinsman's bride to her sovereign, and whom the Captain deemed the proper sponsor for his wife on that solemn occasion. But what social value had a fossilized Lady Susan Winstanley, of whom an outside world knew nothing, when weighed in the balance with the Duchess of Dovedale? No; Mrs Winstanley felt that to be presented by the Duchess was the one thing useful to her happiness.

It was a dinner of thirty people; quite a state dinner. The finest and newest orchids had been brought out of their houses, and the dinner-table looked like a tropical forest in little. Vixen went in to dinner with a strange young man from London. Roderick Vawdrey was ever so far away, between his betrothed and an enormous dowager in sky-blue velvet and diamonds.

After dinner there was music. Lady Mabel played a dreary minor melody, chiefly remarkable for its delicate modulation from sharps to flats and back again. A large gentleman sang an Italian buffo song, at which the company smiled tepidly; a small young lady sighed and languished through '*Non e ver*', and then Miss Tempest and Lord Mallow sang a duet.

This was the success of the evening. They were asked to sing again and again. They were allowed to monopolise the piano; and before the evening was over everyone had decided that Lord Mallow and Miss Tempest were engaged. Only the voices of plighted lovers could be expected to harmonise as well as that.

'They must have sung very often together,' said the Duchess to Mrs Winstanley.

'Only within the last fortnight. Lord Mallow never stayed with us before, you know. He is my husband's friend. They were brother-officers, and have known each other a long time. Lord Mallow insists upon Violet singing every evening. He is passionately fond of music.'

'Very pleasant,' murmured the Duchess approvingly: and then she glided on to shed the sunshine of her presence upon another group of guests.

Carriages began to be announced at eleven – that is to say, about half-an-hour after the gentlemen had left the dining-room – but the Duke insisted that people should stop till twelve.

'We must see the old year out,' he said. 'It is a lovely night. We can go out on the terrace and hear the Ringwood bells.'

This is how Violet and Lord Mallow happened to sing so many duets. There was plenty of time for music during the hour before midnight. After the singing, a rash young gentleman, pining to distinguish himself somehow – a young

man with a pimply complexion, who had said with Don Carlos,
'Three-and-twenty years of age, and nothing done for
immortality' – recited Tennyson's 'Farewell to this Old Year,'
in a voice which was like anything but a trumpet, and with
gesticulation painfully suggestive of Saint Vitus.

The long suite of rooms terminated in an orangery, a
substantial stone building with tessellated pavement, and wide
windows opening on the terrace. The night was wondrously
mild. The full moon shed her tender light upon the dark Forest,
the shining water-pools, the distant blackness of a group of
ancient yew-trees on the crest of a hill. Ashbourne stood high,
and the view from the terrace was at all times magnificent, but
perhaps finest of all in the moonlight.

The younger guests wandered softly in and out of the rooms,
and looked at the golden oranges glimmering against their dark
leaves, and put themselves into positions that suggested the
possibility of flirtation. Young ladies whose study of German
literature had never gone beyond Ollendorff gazed pensively at
the oranges, and murmured the song of Mignon. Couples of
maturer growth whispered the details of unsavoury scandals
behind perfumed fans.

Vixen and Rorie were among these roving couples. Violet
had left the piano, and Roderick was off duty. Lady Mabel and
Lord Mallow were deep in the wrongs of Ireland. Captain
Winstanley was talking agriculture with the Duke, whose mind
was sorely exercised about guano.

'My dear sir, in a few years we shall have used up all the
guano, and then what can become of us?' demanded the Duke.
'Talk about our exhausting our coal! What is that compared
with the exhaustion of guano? We may learn to exist without
fires. Our winters are becoming milder; our young men are
going in for athletics; they can keep themselves warm upon
bicycles. And then we have the gigantic coal-fields of America,
the vast basin of the Mississippi to fall back upon, with ever-
increasing facilities in the mode of transport. But civilisation
must come to a deadlock when we have no more guano. Our
grass, our turnips, our mangel, must deteriorate. We shall have
no more prize cattle. It is too awful to contemplate.'

'But do you really consider such a calamity at all probable, Duke?' asked the Captain.

'Probable, sir? It is inevitable. In 1868 the Chincha Islands were estimated to contain about six million tons of guano. The rate of exportation had at that time risen to four hundred thousand tons per annum. At this rate the three islands will be completely exhausted by the year 1888, and England will have to exist without guano. The glory of the English people, as breeders of prize oxen, will have departed.'

'Chemistry will have discovered new fertilisers by that time,' suggested the Captain, in a comforting tone.

'Sir,' replied the Duke severely, 'the discoveries of modern science tend to the chimerical rather than the practical. Your modern scientists can liquefy oxygen, they can light a city with electricity, but they cannot give me anything to increase the size and succulence of my turnips. Virgil knew as much about agriculture as your modern chemist.'

While the Duke was holding forth about guano, Vixen and Rorie were on the terrace, in the stillness and moonlight. There was hardly a breath of wind. It might have been a summer evening. Vixen was shrouded from head to foot in a white cloak which Rorie had fetched from the room where the ladies had left their wraps. She looked all white and solemn in the moonlight, like a sheeted ghost.

Although Mr Vawdrey had been civil enough to go in quest of Violet's cloak, and had seemed especially desirous of bringing her to the terrace, he was by no means delightful now he had got her there. They took a turn or two in silence, broken only by a brief remark about the beauty of the night, and the extent of the prospect.

'I think it is the finest view in the Forest,' said Vixen, dwelling on the subject for lack of anything else to say. 'You must be very fond of Ashbourne.'

'I don't exactly recognise the necessity. The view is superb, no doubt; but the house is frightfully commonplace. It is a little better than Briarwood. That is about all which an enthusiastic admirer could advance in its favour. How much longer does Lord Mallow mean to take up his abode with you?'

Vixen shrugged her cloaked shoulders with an action that seemed to express contemptuous carelessness.

'I haven't the least idea. That is no business of mine, you know.'

'I don't know anything of the kind,' retorted Rorie captiously. 'I should have thought it was very much your business.'

'Should you really?' said Vixen mockingly.

If the gentleman's temper was execrable, the lady's mood was not too amiable.

'Yes. Are not you the load-star? It is your presence that makes the Abbey House pleasant to him. Who can wonder that he protracts his stay?'

'He has been with us a little more than a fortnight.'

'He has been with you an age. Mortals who are taken up to Paradise seldom stay so long. Sweet dreams are not so long. A fortnight in the same house with you, meeting with you at breakfast, parting with you at midnight, seeing you at noontide and afternoon, walking with you, riding with you, singing with you, kneeling down to family prayer at your side, mixing his "Amen" with yours; why he might as well be your husband at once. He has as much delight in your society.'

'You forget the hours in which he is shooting pheasants and playing billiards.'

'Glimpses of purgatory, which make his heaven all the more divine,' said Rorie. 'Well, it is none of my business, as you said just now. There are people born to be happy, I suppose; creatures that come into the world under a lucky star.'

'Undoubtedly, and among them notably Mr Vawdrey, who has everything that the heart of a reasonable man can desire.'

'So had Solomon, and yet he made his moan.'

'O, there is always a crumpled rose-leaf in everybody's bed. And if the rose-leaves were all smooth, a man would crumple one on purpose, in order to have something to grumble about. Hark, Rorie!' cried Vixen, with a sudden change of tone, as the first silvery chime of Ringwood bells came floating over the wooded valleys – the low moonlit hills; 'don't be cross. The old year is dying. Remember the dear days that are gone, when you and I used to think a new year a thing to be glad about. And now, what can the new years bring us half so good as that which the old ones have taken away?'

She had slipped her little gloved hand through his arm, and drawn very near to him, moved by tender thoughts of the past. He looked down at her with eyes from which all anger had vanished. There was only love in them – deep love; love such as a very affectionate brother might perchance give his only sister – but it must be owned that brothers capable of such love are rare.

'No, child,' he murmured sadly. 'Years to come can bring us nothing so good or so dear as the past. Every new year will drift us farther.'

They were standing at the end of the terrace farthest from the orangery windows, out of which the Duchess and her visitors came trooping to hear the Ringwood chimes. Rorie and Vixen kept quite apart from the rest. They stood silent, arm-in-arm, looking across the landscape towards the winding Avon and the quiet market-town, hidden from them by intervening hills. Yonder, nestling among those grassy hills, lies Moyles Court, the good old English manor house where noble Alice Lisle sheltered the fugitives from Sedgemoor; paying for that one act of womanly hospitality with her life. Farther away, on the banks of the Avon, is the quiet churchyard where that gentle martyr of Jeffreys' lust for blood takes her long rest. The creeping spleenwort thrives amidst the gray stones of her tomb. To Vixen these things were so familiar, that it was as if she could see them with her bodily eyes, as she looked across the distance, with its mysterious shadows, its patches of silver light.

The bells chimed on with their tender cadence, half joyous, half sorrowful. The shallower spirits among the guests chattered about the beauty of the night, and the sweetness of the bells. Deeper souls were silent, full of saddest thoughts. Who is there who has not lost something in the years gone by, which earth's longest future cannot restore?

Violet's lips trembled and were dumb. Roderick saw the tears rolling down her pale cheeks, and offered no word of consolation. He knew that she was thinking of her father.

'Dear old Squire,' he murmured gently, after an interval of silence. 'How good he was to me, and how fondly I loved him.'

That speech was the sweetest comfort he could have offered. Vixen gave his arm a grateful hug.

'Thank God there is someone who remembers him, besides his dogs and me!' she exclaimed; and then she hardly dried her tears, and made herself ready to meet Lord Mallow and Lady Mabel Ashbourne, who were coming along the terrace towards them, talking gaily. Lord Mallow had a much wider range of subjects than Mr Vawdrey. He had read more, and could keep pace with Lady Mabel in her highest flights; science, literature, politics, were all as one to him. He had crammed his vigorous young mind with everything which it behoved a man panting for parliamentary distinction to know.

'Where have you two people been hiding yourselves for the last half-hour?' asked Lady Mabel. 'You were wanted badly just now for "Blow, Gentle Gales." I know you can manage the bass, Rorie, when you like.'

'"Lo, behold a pennant waving!"' sang Rorie in deep full tones. 'Yes, I can manage that much, at a push. You seem music mad to-night, Mabel. The old year is making a swanlike end – fading in music.'

Rorie and Vixen were still standing arm-in-arm; rather too much as if they belonged to each other, Lady Mabel thought. The attitude was hardly in good taste, according to Lady Mabel's law of taste, which was a code as strict as Draco's.

The bells rang on.

'The new year has come!' cried the Duke. 'Let us all shake hands, in the friendly German fashion.'

On this there was a general shaking of hands, which appeared to last a long time. It seemed rather as if the young people of opposite sexes shook hands with each other more than once. Lord Mallow would hardly let Violet's hand go, once having got it in his hearty grasp.

'Hail to the first new year we greet together,' he said softly. 'May it not be the last. I feel that it must not, cannot be the last.'

'You are wiser than I, then,' Vixen answered coldly; 'for my feelings tell me nothing about the future – except' – and here her faced beamed at him with a lovely smile – 'except that you will be kind to Bullfinch.'

'If I were an emperor I would make him a consul,' answered the Irishman.

He had contrived to separate Roderick and Vixen. The young man had returned to his allegiance, and was escorting Lady Mabel back to the house. Everybody began to feel chilly, now that the bells were silent, and there was a general hurrying off to the carriages, which were standing in an oval ring round a group of deodoras in front of the porch on the other side of the house.

Rorie and Vixen met no more that night. Lord Mallow took her to her carriage, and sat opposite her and talked to her during the homeward drive. Captain Winstanley was smoking a cigar on the box. His wife slumbered peacefully.

'I think I may be satisfied with Theodore,' she said, as she composed herself for sleep; 'my dress was not quite the worst in the room, was it, Violet?'

'It was lovely, mamma. You can make yourself quite happy,' answered Vixen truthfully; whereupon the matron breathed a gentle sigh of content, and lapsed into slumber.

They had the Boldrewood Road before them, a long hilly road cleaving the very heart of the Forest; a road full of ghosts at the best of times, but offering a Walpurgis revel of phantoms on such a night as this to the eye of the belated wanderer. How ghostly the deer were, as they skimmed across the road and flitted away into dim distances, mixing with and melting into the shadows of the trees. The little gray rabbits, sitting up on end, were like circles of hobgoblins that dispersed and vanished at the approach of mortals. The leafless old hawthorns, rugged and crooked, silvered by the moonlight, were most ghostlike of all. They took every form, from the most unearthly to the most grotesquely human.

Violet sat wrapped in her furred white mantle, watching the road as intently as if she had never seen it before. She never could grow tired of these things. She loved them with a love which was part of her nature.

'What a delightful evening, was it not?' asked Lord Mallow.

'I suppose it was very nice,' answered Violet coolly; 'but I have no standard of comparison. It was my first dinner at Ashbourne.'

'What a remarkably clever girl Lady Mabel is. Mr Vawdrey ought to consider himself extremely fortunate.'

'I have never heard him say that he does not so consider himself.'

'Naturally. But I think he might be a little more enthusiastic. He is the coolest lover I ever saw.'

'Perhaps you judge him by comparison with Irish lovers. Your nation is more demonstrative than ours.'

'O, an Irish girl would cashier such a fellow as Mr Vawdrey. But I may possibly misjudge him. You ought to know more about him than I. You have known him——'

'All my life,' said Violet simply. 'I know that he is good and staunch and true, that he honoured his mother, and that he will make Lady Mabel Ashbourne a very good husband. Perhaps if she were a little less clever and a little more human, he might be happier with her; but no doubt that will all come right in time.'

'Any way it will be all the same in a century or so,' assented Lord Mallow. 'We are going to have lovely weather as long as this moon lasts, I believe. Will you go for a long ride to-morrow – like that first ride of ours?'

'When I took you all over the world for sport?' said Vixen laughing. 'I wonder you are inclined to trust me after that. If Captain Winstanley likes I don't mind being your guide again to-morrow.'

'Captain Winstanley shall like. I'll answer for that. I would make his life unendurable if he were to refuse.'

CHAPTER 30

CRYING FOR THE MOON

Despite the glorious moonlight night which ushered in the new-born year, the first day of that year was abominable; a day of hopeless, incessant rain, falling from a leaden sky in which there was never a break, not a stray gleam of sunshine from morn till eve.

'The new year is like Shakespeare's Richard,' said Lord Mallow, when he stood in the porch after breakfast, surveying the horizon. '"Tetchy and wayward in his infancy." I never experienced anything so provoking. I was dreaming all night of our ride.'

'Were you not afraid of being like that dreadful man in "Locksley Hall"? –

        "Like a dog, he hunts in dreams,"'

asked Vixen mockingly.

She was standing on the threshold, playing with Argus, looking the picture of healthful beauty, in her dark green cloth dress and plain linen collar. All Vixen's morning costumes were of the simplest and neatest; a compact style of dress which interfered with none of her rural amusements. She could romp with her dog, make her round of the stables, work in the garden, ramble in the Forest, without fear of dilapidated flounces or dishevelled laces and ribbons.

'Violet's morning-dresses are so dreadfully strong-minded,' complained Mrs Winstanley. 'To look at her, one would almost think that she was the kind of girl to go round the country lecturing upon woman's rights.'

'No ride this morning,' said Captain Winstanley, coming into the hall, with a bundle of letters in his hand. 'I shall go to my den, and do a morning's letter-writing and accountancy – unless you want me for a shy at the pheasants, Mallow?'

'Let the pheasants be at rest for the first day of the year,' answered Lord Mallow. 'I am sure you would rather be fetching up your arrears of correspondence than shooting at dejected birds in a damp plantation; and I am luxurious enough to prefer staying indoors, if the ladies will have me. I can help Miss Tempest to wind her wools.'

'Thanks, but I never do any wool-work. Mamma is the artist in that line.'

'Then I place myself unreservedly at Mrs Winstanley's feet.'

'You are too good,' sighed the fair matron, from her arm-chair by the hearth; 'but I shall not touch my crewels to-day. I have one of my nervous headaches. It is a penalty I too often have to pay for the pleasures of society. I'm afraid I shall have to lie down for an hour or two.'

And with a languid sigh Mrs Winstanley wrapped her China crape shawl round her, and went slowly upstairs, leaving Violet and Lord Mallow in sole possession of the great oak-panelled hall; the lady looking at the rain from her favourite perch in the deep window-seat, the gentleman contemplating the same prospect from the open door. It was one of those mild winter mornings when a huge wood fire is a cheerful feature in the scene, but hardly essential to comfort.

Vixen thought of that long rainy day, years ago, the day on which Roderick Vawdrey came of age. How well she remembered sitting in that very window, watching the ceaseless rain, with a chilly sense of having been forgotten and neglected by her old companion. And then, in the gloaming, just when she had lost all hope of seeing him, he had come leaping in out of the wet night, like a lion from his lair, and had taken her in his arms and kissed her before she knew what he was doing.

Her cheeks crimsoned even to-day at the memory of that kiss. It had seemed a small thing then. Now it seemed awful – a burning spot of shame upon the whiteness of her youth.

'He must have thought I was very fond of him, or he would not have dared to treat me so,' she told herself, 'But then we had been playfellows so long. I had teased him, and he had plagued me; and we had been really like brother and sister. Poor Rorie! If we could have always been young we should have been better friends.'

'How thoughtful you seem this morning, Miss Tempest,' said a voice behind Vixen's shoulder.

'Do I?' she asked, turning quickly round. 'New Year's Day is a time to make one thoughtful. It is like beginning a new chapter in the volume of life, and one cannot help speculating as to what the chapter is to be about.'

'For you it ought to be a story full of happiness.'

'Ah, but you don't know my history. I had such a happy childhood. I drained my cup of bliss before I was a woman; and there is nothing left for me but the dregs, and they – they are dust and ashes.'

There was an intensity of bitterness in her tone that moved him beyond his power of self-control. That she – so fair, so lovely, so deeply dear to him already; she for whom life should be one summer-day of unclouded gladness; – that she should give expression to a rooted sorrow was more than his patience could bear.

'Violet, you must not speak thus; you wound me to the heart. O, my love, my love, you were born to be the giver of gladness, the centre of joy and delight. Grief should never touch you; sorrow and pain should never come near you. You are a creature of happiness and light.'

'Don't!' cried Vixen vehemently. 'O, pray don't. It is all vain – useless. My life is marked out for me. No one can alter it. Pray do not lower yourself by one word more. You will be sorry – angry with yourself and me – afterwards.'

'Violet, I must speak.'

'To what end? My fate is as fixed as the stars. No one can change it.'

'No mortal perhaps, Violet. But Love can. Love is a god. O, my darling, I have learnt to love you dearly and fondly in this little while, and I mean to win you. It shall go hard with me if I do not succeed. Dear love, if truth and constancy can conquer fate, I ought to be able to win you. There is no one else, is there, Violet?' he asked falteringly, with his eyes upon her downcast face.

A burning spot glowed and faded on her cheek before she answered him.

'Can you not see how empty my life is?' she asked with a bitter laugh. 'No; there is no one else. I stand quite alone. Death took my father from me; your friend has robbed me of my mother. My old playfellow, Roderick Vawdrey, belongs to his cousin. I belong to nobody.'

'Let me have you then, Violet. Ah, if you knew how I would cherish you! You should be loved so well that you would fancy yourself the centre of the universe, and that all the planets revolved in the skies only to please you. Love, let me have you – priceless treasure that others know not how to value. Let me keep and guard you.'

'I would not wrong you so much as to marry you without loving you, and I shall never love any more,' said Vixen, with a sad steadfastness that was more dispiriting than the most vehement protestation.

'Why not?'

'Because I spent all my store of love while I was a child. I loved my father – ah, I cannot tell you how fondly. I do not think there are many fathers who are loved as he was. I poured out all my treasures of affection at his feet. I have no love left for a husband.'

'What, Violet, not if your old friend Roderick Vawdrey were pleading?' asked Lord Mallow.

It was an unlucky speech. If Lord Mallow had had a chance, which he had not, that speech would have spoiled it. Violet started to her feet, her cheeks crimson, her eyes flashing.

'It is shameful, abominable of you to say such a thing!' she cried, her voice tremulous with indignation. 'I will never forgive you for that dastardly speech. Come, Argus.'

She had mounted the broad oak stairs with light swift foot before Lord Mallow could apologise. He was terribly crestfallen.

'I was a brute,' he muttered to himself. 'But I hit the bull's-eye. It is that fellow she loves. Hard upon me, when I ask for nothing but to be her slave and adore her all the days of my life. And I know that Winstanley would have been pleased. How lovely she looked when she was angry – her tawny hair gleaming in the firelight, her great brown eyes flashing. Yes, it's the Hampshire squire she cares for, and I'm out of it. I'll go and shoot the pheasants,' concluded Lord Mallow savagely; 'those beggars shall not have it all their own way to-day.'

He went off to get his gun, in the worst humour he had ever been in since he was a child and cried for the moon.

He spent the whole day in a young oak plantation, ankle-deep in oozy mud, moss, and dead fern, making havoc among the innocent birds. He was in so bloodthirsty a temper, that he felt as if he could have shot a covey of young children, had they come in his way, with all the ferocity of a modern Herod.

'I think I've spoiled Winstanley's coverts for this year, at any rate,' he said to himself, as he tramped homewards in the early darkness, with no small hazard of losing himself in one of those ghostly plantations, which were all exactly alike, and in which a man might walk all day long without meeting anything nearer humanity than a trespassing forest pony that had leapt a fence in quest of more sufficing food than the scanty herbage of the open woods.

Lord Mallow got on better than might have been expected. He went east when he ought to have gone west, and found himself in Queen's Bower when he fancied himself in Gretnam Wood; but he did not walk more than half-a-dozen miles out of his way, and he got home somehow at last, which was much for a stranger to the ground.

The stable clock was chiming the third quarter after five when he went into the hall, where Vixen had left him in anger that morning. The great wood fire was burning gaily, and Captain Winstanley was sitting in a Glastonbury chair in front of it. 'Went for the birds after all, old fellow,' he said, without looking round, recognising the tread of Lord Mallow's shooting-boots. 'You found it too dismal in the house, I suppose? Consistently abominable weather, isn't it? You must be soaked to the skin.'

'I suppose I am,' answered the other carelessly. 'But I've been soaked a good many times before, and it hasn't done me much harm. Thanks to the modern inventions of the waterproof-makers, the soaking begins inside instead of out. I should call myself parboiled.'

'Take off your oilskins and come and talk. You'll have a nip, won't you?' added Captain Winstanley, ringing the bell. 'Kirschenwasser, curaçoa, Glenlivat – which shall it be?'

'Glenlivat,' answered Lord Mallow, 'and plenty of it. I'm in the humour in which a man must either drink inordinately or cut his throat.'

'Were the birds unapproachable?' asked Captain Winstanley, laughing; 'or were the dogs troublesome?'

'Birds and dogs were perfect; but—— Well, I suppose I'd better make a clean breast of it. I've had a capital time here—— O, here comes the whisky. Hold your hand, old fellow!' cried Lord Mallow, as his host poured the Glenlivat somewhat recklessly into a soda-water tumbler. 'You mustn't take me literally. Just moisten the bottom of the glass with whisky before you put in the soda. That's as much as I care about.'

'All right. You were saying——'

'That my visit here has been simply delightful, and that I must go to London by an early train to-morrow.'

'Paradoxical!' said the Captain. 'That sounds like your well-bred servant, who tells you that he has nothing to say against the situation, but he wishes to leave you at the end of his month. What's the matter, dear boy? Do you find our Forest hermitage too dull?'

'I should ask nothing kinder from Fate than to be allowed to spend my days in your Forest. Yes, I would say good-bye to the green hills and vales of County Cork, and become that detestable being, an absentee, if – if – Fortune smiled on me. But she doesn't, you see, and I must go. Perhaps you may have perceived, Winstanley – perhaps you may not have been altogether averse from the idea – in a word, I have fallen over head and ears in love with your bewitching stepdaughter.'

'My dear fellow, I'm delighted. It is the thing I would have wished, had I been bold enough to wish for anything so good. And of course Violet is charmed. You are the very man for her.'

'Am I? So I thought myself till this morning. Unfortunately the young lady is of a different opinion. She has refused me.'

'Refused you! Pshaw, they all begin that way. It's one of the small diplomacies of the sex. They think they enhance their value by an assumed reluctance. Nonsense, man, try again. She can't help liking you.'

'I would try again, every day for a twelvemonth, if there were a scintilla of hope. My life should be a series of offers. But the thing is decided. I know from her manner, from her face, that I have no chance. I have been in the habit of thinking myself rather a nice kind of fellow, and the women have encouraged the idea. But I don't answer here, Winstanley. Miss Tempest will have nothing to say to me.'

'She's a fool,' said Captain Winstanley, with his teeth set, and that dark look of his which meant harm to somebody. 'I'll talk to her.'

'My dear Winstanley, understand I'll have no coercion. If I win her, I must do it off my own bat. Dearly as I love her, if you were to bring her to me conquered and submissive, like Iphigenia at the altar, I would not have her. I love her much too well to ask any sacrifice of inclination from her. I love her too well to accept anything less than her free unfettered heart. She cannot give me that, and I must go. I had much rather you should say nothing about me, either to her or her mother.'

'But I shall say a great deal to both,' exclaimed the Captain, desperately angry. 'I am indignant. I am outraged by her conduct. What in Heaven's name does this wilful girl want in a husband? You have youth, good looks, good temper, talent, tastes that harmonise with her own. You can give her a finer position than she has any right to expect. And she refuses you. She is a spoiled child, who doesn't know her own mind or her own advantage. She has a diabolical temper, and is as wild as a hawk. Egad, I congratulate you on your escape, Mallow. She was not born to make any man happy.'

'Small thanks for your congratulations,' retorted the Irishman. 'She might have made me happy if she had chosen. I would have forgiven her tempers, and loved her for her wildness. She is the sweetest woman I ever knew; as fresh and fair as your furzy hill-tops. But she is not for me. Fate never meant me to be so blessed.'

'She will change her mind before she is many months older,' said Captain Winstanley. 'Her father and mother have spoilt her. She is a creature of whims and fancies, and must be ridden on the curb.'

'I would ride her with the lightest snaffle-bit that ever was made,' protested Lord Mallow. 'But there's no use in talking about it. You won't think me discourteous or ungrateful if I clear out of this to-morrow morning, will you, Winstanley?'

'Certainly not,' answered his host; 'but I shall think you a confounded ass. Why not wait and try your luck again?'

'Simply because I know it would be useless. Truth and candour shine in that girl's eyes. She has a soul above the petty trickeries of her sex. No from her lips means No, between this and eternity. O, thrice blessed will that man be to whom she answers Yes; for she will give him the tenderest, truest, most generous heart in creation.'

'You answer boldly for her on so short an acquaintance.'

'I answer as a man who loves her, and who has looked into her soul,' replied Lord Mallow. 'You and she don't hit it over well, I fancy.'

'No. We began by disliking each other, and we have been wonderfully constant to our first opinions.'

'I can't understand——'

'Can't you? You will, perhaps, some day: if you ever have a handsome stepdaughter who sets up her back against you from the beginning of things. Have you ever seen a sleek handsome tabby put herself on the defensive at the approach of a terrier, her back arched, her eyes flashing green lightnings, her tail lashing itself, her whiskers bristling? That's my stepdaughter's attitude towards me, and I daresay before long I shall feel her claws. There goes the gong, and we must go too. I'm sorry Miss Tempest has been such a fool, Mallow; but I must repeat my congratulations, even at the risk of offending you.'

There were no duets that evening. Vixen was as cold as ice, and as silent as a statue. She sat in the shadow of her mother's arm-chair after dinner, turning over the leaves of Doré's *Tennyson*, pausing to contemplate Elaine with a half-contemptuous pity – a curious feeling that hurt her like a physical pain.

'Poor wretch!' she mused. 'Are there women in our days so weak as to love where they can never be loved again, I wonder?

It is foolish enough in a man; but he cures himself as quickly as the mungoose that gets bitten by a snake, and runs away to find the herb which is an antidote to the venom, and comes back ready to fight the snake again.'

'Are we not going to have any music?' asked Mrs Winstanley languidly, more interested in the *picots* her clever needle was executing on a piece of Italian point than in the reply.

'Lord Mallow, cannot you persuade Violet to join you in one of those sweet duets of Mendelssohn's?'

'Indeed, mamma, I couldn't sing a note. I'm as husky as a raven.'

'I'm not surprised to hear it,' said the Captain, looking up from his study of *The Gardeners' Chronicle*. 'No doubt you managed to catch cold last night, while you were mooning upon the terrace with young Vawdrey.'

'How very incautious of you, Violet,' exclaimed Mrs Winstanley, in her complaining tone.

'I was not cold, mamma; I had my warm cloak.'

'But you confess you have caught cold. I detest colds; they always go through a house. I shall be the next victim, I daresay; and with me a cold is martyrdom. I'm afraid you must find us very dull, Lord Mallow, for New Year's Day, when people expect to be lively. We ought to have had a dinner-party.'

'My dear Mrs Winstanley, I don't care a straw about New Year's Day, and I am not in a lively vein. This quiet evening suits me much better than high jinks, I assure you.'

'It's very good of you to say so.'

'Come and play a game of billiards,' said Captain Winstanley, throwing down his paper.

'Upon my honour I'd rather sit by the fire and watch Mrs Winstanley at her point-lace. I'm in an abominably lazy mood after my tramp in those soppy plantations,' answered Lord Mallow, who felt a foolish pleasure – mingled with bitterest regrets – in being in the same room with the girl he loved.

She was hidden from him in her shadowy corner; shrouded on one side by the velvet drapery of the fireplace, on the other by her mother's chair. He could only catch a glimpse of her auburn plaits now and then as her head bent over her open book. He never heard her voice, or met her eyes. And yet it was sweet to him to sit in the same room with her.

'Come, Mallow, you can sing us something, at any rate,' said the Captain, suppressing a yawn. 'I know you can play your own accompaniment, when you please. You can't be too idle to give us one of Moore's melodies.'

'I'll sing, if you like, Mrs Winstanley,' assented Lord Mallow, 'but I'm afraid you must be tired of my songs. My *répertoire* is rather limited.'

'Your songs are charming,' said Mrs Winstanley.

The Irishman seated himself at the distant piano, struck a chord or two, and began the old melody, with its familiar refrain:

> 'O, there's nothing half so sweet in life
> As love's young dream.'

Before his song was finished Violet had kissed her mother and glided silently from the room. Lord Mallow saw her go, and there was a sudden break in his voice as the door closed upon her, a break that sounded almost like a suppressed sob.

When Vixen came down to breakfast next morning she found the table laid only for three.

'What has become of Lord Mallow?' she asked Forbes, when be brought in the urn.

'He left by an early train, ma'am. Captain Winstanley drove him to Lyndhurst.'

The old servants of the Abbey House had not yet brought themselves to speak of their new lord as 'master.' He was always 'Captain Winstanley.'

The Captain came in while Violet knelt by the fire playing with Argus, whom even the new rule had not banished wholly from the family sitting-rooms.

The servants filed in for morning prayers, which Captain Winstanley delivered in a cold hard voice. His manual of family worship was of concise and businesslike form, and the whole ceremony lasted about seven minutes. Then the household dispersed quickly, and Forbes brought in his tray of covered dishes.

'You can pour out the tea, Violet. Your mother is feeling a little tired and will breakfast in her room.'

'Then I think, if you'll excuse me, I'll have my breakfast with her,' said Vixen. 'She'll be glad of my company, I daresay.'

'She has a headache and will be better alone. Stop where you are, if you please, Violet. I have something serious to say to you.'

Vixen left off pouring out the tea, clasped her hands in her lap, and looked at Captain Winstanley with the most resolute expression he had ever seen in a woman's face.

'Are you going to talk to me about Lord Mallow?' she asked.

'Yes.'

'Then spare yourself the trouble. It would be useless.'

'I cannot conceive that you should be so besotted as to refuse a man who offers so much. A man who has wealth, rank, youth, good looks——'

'Spare me the catalogue of your friend's merits. I think him a most estimable person. I acknowledge his rank and wealth. But I have refused him.'

'You will change your mind.'

'I never change my mind.'

'You will live to repent your folly then, Miss Tempest: and all I hope is that your remorse may be keen. It is not one woman in a thousand who gets such a chance. What are you that you should throw it away?'

'I am a woman who would sooner cut my throat than marry a man I cannot honestly love,' answered Vixen, with unblenching firmness.

'I think I understand your motive,' said Captain Winstanley. 'Lord Mallow never had a chance with you. The ground was occupied before he came. You are a very foolish girl to reject so good an offer for the sake of another woman's sweetheart.'

'How dare you say that to me?' cried Vixen. 'You have usurped my father's place; you have robbed me of my mother's heart. Is not that cause enough for me to hate you? I have only one friend left in the world, Roderick Vawdrey. And you would slander me because I cling to that old friendship, the last remnant of my happy childhood.'

'You might have a dozen such friends, if friendship is all you want, and be Lady Mallow into the bargain,' retorted Captain Winstanley scornfully. 'You are a simpleton to send such a man away despairing. But I suppose it is idle to ask you to hear reason. I am not your father, and even if I were, I daresay you would take your own way in spite of me.'

'*My* father would not have asked me to marry a man I did not love,' answered Vixen proudly, her eyes clouding with tears even at the thought of her beloved dead; 'and he would have valued Lord Mallow's rank and fortune no more than I do. But you are so fond of a bargain,' she added, her eye kindling and her lip curving with bitterest scorn. 'You sold Bullfinch, and now you want to sell me.'

'By Heaven, madam, I pity the man who may be fool enough to buy you!' cried the Captain, starting up from his untasted breakfast, and leaving Vixen mistress of the field.

CHAPTER 31

'KURZ IST DER SCHMERZ UND EWIG IST DIE FREUDE'

Captain Winstanley said no more about Lord Mallow; but Violet had to listen to much plaintive bemoaning from her mother, who could not understand how any well-brought-up young woman could refuse an Irish peer with a fine estate, and the delights of a *trousseau* made by the renowned Theodore. Upon this latter detail Mrs Winstanley dwelt at more length than upon that minor circumstance in a marriage – the bridegroom.

'It would have been such a pleasure to me to plan your *trousseau*, darling,' she said; 'such an occupation for my mind in these wretched winter afternoons when there is no possibility of driving or making calls. I should have attended to everything myself. Theodore's general way is to make a list of what she thinks necessary, allowing her customer to correct it; but I should not have been satisfied with that, even from Theodore, though I admit that her taste is perfect. And then, you know, she is hand in glove with Worth, and that alone is a liberal education, as somebody says somewhere about something. No, dear, I would have done it all myself. I know the exact shades that suit your complexion, the dashes of colour that contrast with and light up your hair, the style that sets off your figure. Your *trousseau* should be talked about in society, and even described in the fashion magazines. And then Lord Mallow is really so very nice – and has such a charming baritone – what more can you want?'

'Only to love him, mother dearest, which I do not, and never shall. That frank loud voice of his does not stir a fibre of my heart. I like him extremely, and so I do Mr Scobel, and Bates the groom. Lord Mallow is no more to me than either of those. Indeed, Bates is much nearer and dearer, for he loved my father.'

'My dear Violet, you have the most radical ideas. Imagine anyone putting Bates on a level with Lord Mallow!'

'I don't, mamma. I only say he is more to me than Lord Mallow could ever be.'

'Your travelling-dress,' murmured Mrs Winstanley, her mind still dwelling on the *trousseau*; 'that affords more scope for taste than the wedding-gown. Velvet suits your style, but is too heavy for your age. A soft clinging cashmere, now, one of those delicious neutral tints that have been so fashionable lately, over an underskirt of a warmer shade in *poult de soie*, a picturesque costume that would faintly recall Lely's portraits at Hampton Court.'

'Dear mamma, what is the use of talking about dresses I am never going to require? Not for all the finery that Theodore ever made would I marry Lord Mallow, or anybody else. I am happy enough with you, and my horse, and my dog, and all the dear old things, animal and vegetable, that belong to this dear old place. I shall never leave you, or the Forest. Can you not be content to know this and let me alone?'

'You are a very wilful girl, Violet, and ridiculously blind to
your own interests,' remarked Mrs Winstanley, throwing herself back in her chair with a fretful look, 'and you put me in an
absurd position. The Duchess quite congratulated me about
your brilliant prospects, when we were chatting together on
New Year's Eve. Anybody could see how devoted Lord
Mallow was, she said, and what a splendid match it would be
for you.'

'Let the Duchess marry her own daughter, and leave me
alone,' cried Vixen scornfully.

This was the kind of thing she had to endure continually,
during the chill winter months that followed Lord Mallow's
departure. Even her old friends the Scobels worried her about
the Irish peer, and lamented her inability to perceive his merits.
It was known throughout her particular circle that she had been
idiotic enough to refuse Lord Mallow. Mrs Winstanley had
whispered the fact to all her friends, under the seal of strictest
secrecy. Of all Vixen's acquaintance, Roderick Vawdrey was
the only one who said no word to her about Lord Mallow; but
he was much kinder to her after the Irishman's departure than
he had shown himself during his visit.

Spring put on her green mantle; and when the woods were
starred with primroses, and the banks lovely with heaven-hued
dog-violets, everyone of any pretension to importance in the
social scale began to flee from the Forest as from a loathsome
place. Lord Ellangowan's train of vans and waggons set out for
the railway-station with their load of chests and baskets. The
departure of the Israelites from Egypt was hardly a mightier
business than this emigration of the Ellangowan household. The
Duke and Duchess, and Lady Mabel Ashbourne, left for the
Queen Anne house at Kensington, whereat the fashionable
London papers broke out in paragraphs of rejoicing, and the
local journals bewailed the extinction of their sun.

The London season had begun, and only the nobodies stayed
in the Forest to watch the rosy sunsets glow and fade behind the
yellow oaks; to see the purple of the beech-boughs change
mysteriously to brightest green; and the bluebells burst into
blossom in the untrodden glades and bottoms. Captain

Winstanley found a small house in Mayfair, which he hired for six weeks, at a rent which he pronounced exorbitant. He sacrificed his own ideas of prudence to the gratification of his wife, who had made up her mind that she had scarcely the right to exist until she had been presented to her sovereign in her new name. But when Mrs Winstanley ventured to suggest the Duchess of Dovedale as her sponsor on this solemn occasion, her husband sternly tabooed the notion.

'My aunt, Lady Susan Winstanley, is the proper person to present you,' he said authoritatively.

'But is she really your aunt, Conrad? You never mentioned her before we were married.'

'She is my father's third cousin by marriage; but we have always called her Aunt. She is the widow of Major-General Winstanley, who distinguished himself in the last war with Tippoo Saïb, and had a place at Court in the reign of William the Fourth.'

'She must be dreadfully old and dowdy,' sighed Mrs Winstanley, whose only historical idea of the Sailor King's reign was as a period of short waists and beaver bonnets.

'She is not a chicken, and she does not spend eight hundred a year on her dressmaker,' retorted the Captain. 'But she is a very worthy woman, and highly respected by her friends. Why should you ask a favour of the Duchess of Dovedale?'

'Her name would look so well in the papers,' pleaded Mrs Winstanley.

'The name of your husband's kinswoman will look much more respectable,' answered the Captain; and in this, as in most matters, he had his own way.

Lady Susan Winstanley was brought from her palatial retirement to spend a fortnight in Mayfair. She was bony, wiggy, and snuffy; wore false teeth and seedy apparel; but she was well-bred and well-informed, and Vixen got on with her much better than with the accomplished Captain. Lady Susan took to Vixen; and these two went out for early walks together in the adjacent Green Park, and perambulated the picture-galleries, before Mrs Winstanley had braced herself up for the fatigues of a fashionable afternoon.

Sometimes they came across Mr Vawdrey at a picture-gallery or in the Park; and at the first of these chance meetings, struck by the obvious delight with which the two young people greeted each other, Lady Susan jumped to a conclusion.

'That's your young man, I suppose, my dear,' she said bluntly, when Rorie had left them.

'O, Lady Susan!'

'It's a vulgar expression, I know, my dear, but it comes natural to me; I hear it so often from my maid. I fancied that you and that handsome young fellow must be engaged.'

'O no; we are only old friends. He is engaged to Lady Mabel Ashbourne – a very grand match.'

'That's a pity,' said Lady Susan.

'Why?'

'Well, my dear,' answered the old lady hesitatingly; 'because when one hears of a grand match, it generally means that a young man is marrying for the sake of money, and that young old friend of yours looks too good to throw himself away like that.'

'O but indeed, Lady Susan, it is not so in Rorie's case. He has plenty of money of his own!'

The important day came; and Lady Susan, Mrs Winstanley, and Violet packed themselves and their finery into a capacious carriage, and set off for St James's. The fair Pamela's costume was an elaborate example of Theodore's highest art; colours, design, all of the newest – a delicate harmony of half tints, an indescribable interblending of feathers, lace, and flowers. Violet was simply and elegantly dressed by the same great artist. Lady Susan wore a petticoat and train that must have been made in the time of Queen Adelaide. Yes, the faded and unknown hue of the substantial brocade, the skimpiness of the satin, the quaint devices in piping-cord and feather-stitch – must assuredly have been coeval with that good woman's famous hat and spencer.

Poor Mrs Winstanley was horrified when she saw her husband's kinswoman attired for the ceremony, not a whit less wiggy and snuffy than usual, and with three lean ostrich feathers starting erect from her back hair, like the ladies in the proscenium boxes of Skelt's Theatre, whose gaily painted effigies were so dear to our childhood.

Poor Pamela felt inclined to shed tears. Even her confidence in the perfection of her own toilet could hardly sustain her against the horror of being presented by such a scarecrow.

The ceremony went off satisfactorily, in spite of Lady Susan's antiquated garments. Nobody laughed. Perhaps the *habitués* of St James's were accustomed to scarecrows. Violet's fresh young beauty attracted some little notice as she waited among the crowd of *débutantes*; but, on its being ascertained that she was nobody in particular, curiosity languished and died.

Mrs Winstanley wanted to exhibit her court-dress at the opera that evening, but her husband protested against this display as bad style. Vixen was only too glad to throw off her finery, the tulle puffings and festoonings, and floral wreaths and bouquets, which made movement difficult and sitting down almost impossible.

Those six weeks in town were chiefly devoted to gaiety. Mrs Winstanley's Hampshire friends called on her, and followed up their calls by invitations to dinner; and at the dinners she generally met people who were on the eve of giving a garden-party, or a concert, or a dance, and who begged to be allowed to send her a card for that entertainment, spoken of modestly as a thing of no account. And then there was a hurried interchange of calls, and Violet found herself meandering about an unknown croquet-lawn, amongst unknown nobodies, under a burning sun, looking at other girls, dressed like herself in gowns *à la* Theodore, with the last thing in sleeves, and the last cut in trains, all pretending to be amused by the vapid and languid observations of the cavalier told off to them, paired like companions of the chain at Toulon, and almost as joyless.

Violet Tempest attended no less than eight private concerts during those six weeks, and heard the same new ballad, and the same latest *gavotte* in C minor, at every one of them. She was taken to pianoforte recitals in fashionable squares and streets, and heard Bach and Beethoven till her heart ached with pity for the patient labour of the performers, knowing how poorly she and the majority of mankind appreciated their efforts. She went to a few dances that were rather amusing, and waltzed to her heart's content. She rode Arion in the Row, and horse and

rider were admired as perfect after their kind. Once she met Lord
Mallow, riding beside Lady Mabel Ashbourne and the Duke of
Dovedale. His florid cheek paled a little at the sight of her. They
passed each other with a friendly bow, and this was their only
meeting. Lord Mallow left cards at the house in Mayfair a week
before the Winstanley's went back to Hampshire. He had been
working hard at his senatorial duties, and had made some telling
speeches upon the Irish land question. People talked of him as a
rising politician; and, whenever his name appeared in the
morning papers, Mrs Winstanley uplifted her voice at the
breakfast-table, and made her wail about Violet's folly in refusing
such an excellent young man.

'It would have been so nice to be able to talk about my
daughter, Lady Mallow, and Castle Mallow,' said Pamela in
confidence to her husband.

'No doubt, my dear,' he answered coolly; 'but when you
bring up a young woman to have her own way in everything,
you must take the consequences.'

'It is very ungrateful of Violet,' sighed the afflicted mother,
'after the pains I have taken to dress her prettily, ever since she
was a baby. It is a very poor return for my care.'

CHAPTER 32

A MIDSUMMER NIGHT'S DREAM

They were all back at the Abbey House again early in June, and
Vixen breathed more freely in her sweet native air. How dear,
how doubly beautiful, everything seemed to her after even so
brief an exile. But it was a grief to have missed the applebloom
and the bluebells. The woods were putting on their ripe
summer beauty; the beeches had lost the first freshness of their
tender green, the amber glory of the young oak-leaves was
over, the last of the primroses was dead and buried under the

spreading bracken; masses of snowy hawthorn bloom gleamed white amidst the woodland shadows; blossoming beanfields filled the air with delicate odours; the summer winds swept across the long lush grass in the meadows, beautiful with ever-varying lights and shadows; families of sturdy black piglings were grubbing on the waste turf beside every road, and the forest-fly was getting strong upon the wing. The depths of Mark Ash were dark at noontide under their roof of foliage.

Vixen revelled in the summer weather. She was out from morning till evening, on foot or on horseback, sketching or reading a novel, in some solitary corner of the woods, with Argus for her companion and guardian. It was a purposeless existence for a young woman to lead, no doubt; but Violet Tempest knew of no better thing that life offered for her to do.

Neither her mother nor Captain Winstanley interfered with her liberty. The Captain had his own occupations and amusements, and his wife was given up to frivolities which left no room in her mind for anxiety about her only daughter. So long as Violet looked fresh and pretty at the breakfast-table, and was nicely dressed in the evening, Mrs Winstanley thought that all was well: or at least as well as ever could be with a girl who had been so besotted as to refuse a wealthy young nobleman. So Vixen went her own way, and nobody cared. She seemed to have a passion for solitude, and avoided even her old friends, the Scobels, who had made themselves odious by their championship of Lord Mallow.

The London season was at its height when the Winstanleys went back to Hampshire. The Dovedales were to be at Kensington till the beginning of July, with Mr Vawdrey in attendance upon them. He had rooms in Ebury Street, and had assumed an urban air which in Vixen's opinion made him execrable.

'I can't tell you how hateful you look in lavender gloves and a high hat,' she said to him one day in Clarges Street.

'I daresay I look more natural dressed like a gamekeeper,' he answered lightly; 'I was born so. As for the high hat, you can't hate it more than I do; and I have always considered gloves a foolishness on a level with pig-tails and hair-powder.'

Vixen had been wandering in her old haunts for something less than a fortnight, when, on one especially fine morning, she mounted Arion directly after breakfast and started on one of her rambles, with the faithful Bates in attendance, to open gates or to pull her out of bogs if needful. Upon this point Mrs Winstanley was strict. Violet might ride when and where she pleased – since these meanderings in the Forest were so great a pleasure to her – but she must never ride without a groom.

Old Bates liked the duty. He adored his mistress, and had spent the greater part of his life in the saddle. There was no more enjoyable kind of idleness possible for him than to jog along in the sunshine on one of the Captain's old hunters; called upon for no greater exertion than to flick an occasional fly off his horse's haunch, or to bend down and hook open the gate of a plantation with his stout hunting-crop. Bates had many a brief snatch of slumber in those warm enclosures, where the air was heavy with the scent of the pines, and the buzzing of summer flies made a perpetual lullaby. There was a delicious sense of repose in such a sleep, but it was not quite so pleasant to be jerked suddenly into the waking world by a savage plunge of the aggravated hunter's hind legs, goaded to madness by a lively specimen of the forest-fly.

On this particular morning Vixen was in a thoughtful mood, and Arion was lazy. She let him walk at a leisurely pace under the beeches of Gretnam Wood, and through the quiet paths of the New Park plantations. He came slowly out into Queen's Bower, tossing his delicate head and sniffing the summer air. The streamlets were rippling gaily in the noontide sun; far off on the yellow common a solitary angler was whipping the stream – quite an unusual figure in the lonely landscape. A delicious slumberous quiet reigned over all the scene. Vixen was lost in thought, Bates was dreaming, when a horse's hoofs came up stealthily beside Arion, and a manly voice startled the sultry stillness.

'I've got rid of the high hat for this year, and I'm my own man again,' said the voice; and then a strong brown hand was laid upon Vixen's glove, and swallowed up her slender fingers in its warm grasp.

'When did you come back?' she asked, as soon as their friendly greetings were over, and Arion had reconciled himself to the companionship of Mr Vawdrey's hack.

'Late last night.'

'And have the Duchess and her people come back to Ashbourne?'

'*Pas si bête*. The Duchess and her people – meaning Mabel – have engagements six deep for the next month – breakfasts, lawn-parties, music, art, science, horticulture, dancing, archery, every form of laborious amusement that the genius of man has invented. One of our modern sages has said that life would be tolerable but for its amusements. I am of that wise man's opinion. Fashionable festivities are my aversion. So I told Mabel frankly that I found my good spirits being crushed out of me by the weight of too much pleasure, and that I must come home to look after my farm. The dear old Duke recognised that duty immediately, and gave me all sorts of messages and admonitions for his bailiff.'

'And you are really free to do what you like for a month?' exclaimed Vixen naïvely. 'Poor Rorie! How glad you must be!'

'My liberty is of even greater extent. I am free till the middle of August, when I am to join the Dovedales in Scotland. Later, I suppose, the Duke will go to Baden, or to some newly-discovered fountain in the Black Forest. He could not exist for a twelvemonth without German waters.'

'And after that there will be a wedding, I suppose?' said Violet.

She felt as if called upon to say something of this kind. She wanted Rorie to know that she recognised his position as an engaged man. She hated talking about the business, but she felt somehow that this was incumbent upon her.

'I suppose so,' answered Rorie; 'a man must be married once in his life. The sooner he gets the ceremony over the better. My engagement has hung fire rather. There is always a kind of flatness about the thing between cousins, I daresay. Neither of us is in a hurry. Mabel has so many ideas and occupations, from orchids to Greek choruses.'

'She is very clever,' said Vixen.

'She is clever and good, and I am very proud of her,' answered Rorie loyally.

He felt as if he were walking on the brink of a precipice, and that it needed all his care to steer clear of the edge.

After this there was no more said about Lady Mabel. Vixen and Rorie rode on happily side by side, as wholly absorbed in each other as Launcelot and Guinevere – when the knight brought the lady home through the smiling land, in the glad boyhood of the year, by tinkling rivulet and shadowy covert, and twisted ivy and spreading chestnut fans – and with no more thought of Lady Mabel than those two had of King Arthur.

It was the first of many such rides in the fair June weather. Vixen and Rorie were always meeting in that sweet pathless entanglement of oak and beech and holly, where the cattle-line of the spreading branches was just high enough to clear Vixen's coquettish little hat, or in the long straight fir plantations, where the light was darkened even at noonday, and where the slumberous stillness was broken only by the hum of summer flies. It was hardly possible, it seemed to Violet, for two people to be always riding in the Forest without meeting each other very often. Various as the paths are they all cross somewhere: and what more natural than to see Roderick's brown horse trotting calmly along the grass by the wayside, at the first bend of the road? They made no appointments, or were not conscious of making any: but they always met. There was a fatality about it: yet neither Rorie nor Violet ever seemed surprised at this persistence of fate. They were always glad to see each other; they had always a world to tell each other. If the earth had been newly made every day, with a new set of beings to people it, those two could hardly have had more to say.

'Darned if I can tell what our young Miss and Muster Vawdrey can find to talk about,' said honest old Bates, over his dish of tea in the servants' hall; 'but their tongues ha' never done wagging.'

Sometimes Miss Tempest and Mr Vawdrey went to the kennels together, and idled away an hour with the hounds; while their horses stood at ease with their bridles looped round the five-barred gate, their heads hanging lazily over the topmost bar, and their big soft eyes dreamily contemplating the opposite pine wood, with that large capacity for perfect idleness common to their species. Bates was chewing a straw and swinging his hunting-crop somewhere in attendance. He went with his young mistress everywhere, and played the part of the 'dragon of prudery placed within call;' but he was a very amiable dragon, and nobody minded him. Had it come into the minds of Rorie and Vixen to elope, Bates would not have barred their way. Indeed he would have been very glad to elope with them himself. The restricted license of the Abbey House had no charm for him.

Whither were those two drifting in the happy summer weather, lulled by the whisper of forest leaves faintly stirred by the soft south wind, or by the low murmur of the forest river, stealing on its stealthy course under overarching boughs, mysterious as that wondrous river in Kubla Khan's dream, and anon breaking suddenly out into a clamour loud enough to startle Arion as the waters came leaping and brawling over the shining moss-green boulders? Where were these happy comrades going as they rode side by side under the glancing lights and wavering shadows? Everybody knows what became of Launcelot and Guinevere after that famous ride of theirs. What of these two, who rode together day after day in sun and shower, who loitered and lingered in every loveliest nook in the Forest, who had the same tastes, the same ideas, the same loves, the same dislikes? Neither dared ask that question. They took the happiness fate gave them, and sought not to lift the veil of the future. Each was utterly and unreasonably happy, and each knew very well that this deep and entire happiness was to last no longer than the long summer days and the dangling balls of blossom on the beechen boughs. Before the new tufts on the fir-branches had lost their early green, this midsummer dream would be over. It was to be brief as a schoolboy's holiday.

What was the good of being so happy, only to be so much the more miserable afterwards? A sensible young woman might have asked herself that question, but Violet Tempest did not. Her intentions were pure as the innocent light shining out of her hazel eyes – a gaze frank, direct, and fearless as a child's. She

had no idea of tempting Roderick to be false to his vows. Had
Lady Mabel, with her orchids and Greek plays, been alone in
question, Violet might have thought of the matter more lightly;
but filial duty was involved in Rorie's fidelity to his betrothed.
He had promised his mother on her death-bed. That was a
promise not to be broken.

One day – a day for ever to be remembered by Vixen and
Rorie – a day that stood out in the foreground of memory's
picture awfully distinct from the dreamy happiness that went
before it, these two old friends prolonged their ride even later
than usual. The weather was the loveliest that had ever blessed
their journeyings – the sky Italian, the west wind just fresh
enough to fan their cheeks and faintly stir the green feathers of
the ferns that grew breast-high on each side of the narrow
track. The earth gave forth her subtlest perfumes under the
fire of the midsummer sun. From Boldrewood the distant
heights and valleys had an Alpine look in the clear bright air,
the woods rising line above line in the far distance, in every
shade of colour, from deepest umber to emerald green, from
darkest purple to translucent azure, yonder, where the farthest
line of verdure met the sunlit sky. From Stony Cross the vast
stretch of wood and moor lay basking in the warm vivid light,
the yellow of the dwarf furze flashing in golden patches amidst
the first bloom of the crimson heather. This southern corner
of Hampshire was a glorious world to live in on such a day as
this. Violet and her cavalier thought so, as their horses
cantered up and down the smooth stretch of turf in front of
The Forester's Inn.

'I don't know what has come to Arion,' said Vixen, as she
checked her eager horse in his endeavour to break into a mad
gallop. 'I think he must be what Scotch people call "fey."'

'And pray what may that mean?' asked Rorie, who was like
the young lady made famous by Sydney Smith: what he did not
know would have made a big book.

'Why, I believe it means that in certain moments of life, just
before the coming of a great sorrow, people are wildly gay.
Sometimes a man who is doomed to die breaks out into
uproarious mirth, till his friends wonder at him. Haven't you

noticed that sometimes in the accounts of suicides, the suicide's friends declare that he was in excellent spirits the night before he blew out his brains?'

'Then I hope I'm not "fey,"' said Rorie, 'for I feel uncommonly jolly.'

'It's only the earth and sky that make us feel happy,' sighed Violet, with a sudden touch of seriousness. 'It is but an outside happiness after all.'

'Perhaps not; but it's very good of its kind.'

They went far afield that day; as far as the yews of Sloden; and the sun was low in the west when Vixen wished her knight good-bye, and walked her horse down the last long glade that led to the Abbey House. She was very serious now, and felt that she had transgressed a little by the length of her ride. Poor Bates had gone without his dinner, and that dismal yawn of his just now doubtless indicated a painful vacuity of the inner man. Rorie and she were able to live upon air and sunshine, the scent of the clover, and the freshness of the earth; but Bates was of the lower type of humanity, which requires to be sustained by beef and beer; and for Bates this day of sylvan bliss had been perhaps a period of deprivation and suffering.

Violet had been accustomed to be at home, and freshly dressed, in time for Mrs Winstanley's afternoon tea. She had to listen to the accumulated gossip of the day – complaints about the servants, praises of Conrad, speculations upon impending changes of fashion, which threatened to convulse the world over which Theodore presided; for the world of fashion seems ever on the verge of a crisis awful as that which periodically disrupts the French Chamber.

To have been absent from afternoon tea was a breach of filial duty which the mild Pamela would assuredly resent. Violet felt herself doomed to one of those gentle lectures, which were worrying as the perpetual dropping of rain. She was very late – dreadfully late – the dressing-bell rang as she rode into the stable-yard. Not caring to show herself at the porch, lest her mother and the Captain should be sitting in the hall, ready to pronounce judgement upon her misconduct, she ran quickly up to her dressing-room, plunged her face into cold water, shook

out her bright hair, brushed and plaited the long tresses with
deft swift fingers, put on her pretty dinner-dress of pale blue
muslin, fluttering all over with pale blue bows, and went
smiling down to the drawing-room like a new Hebe, dressed in
an azure cloud.

Mrs Winstanley was sitting by an open window, while the
Captain stood outside and talked to her in a low confidential
voice. His face had a dark look which Vixen knew and hated,
and his wife was listening with trouble in her air and
countenance. Vixen, who meant to have marched straight up to
her mother and made her apologies, drew back involuntarily at
the sight of those two faces.

Just at this moment the dinner-bell rang. The Captain gave
his wife his arm, and the two passed Vixen without a word. She
followed them to the dining-room, wondering what was
coming.

The dinner began in silence, and then Mrs Winstanley began
to falter forth small remarks, feeble as the twitterings of birds
before the coming storm. How very warm it had been all day,
almost oppressive: and yet it had been a remarkably fine day.
There was a fair at Emery Down – at least, not exactly a fair,
but a barrow of nuts and some horrid pistols, and a swing.
Violet answered, as in duty bound; but the Captain maintained
his ominous silence. Not a word was said about Violet's long
ride. It seemed hardly necessary to apologise for her absence,
since her mother made no complaint. Yet she felt that there was
a storm coming.

'Perhaps he is going to sell Arion,' she thought, 'and that's
why the dear thing was "fey."'

And then that rebellious spirit of hers arose within her, ready
for war.

'No, I would not endure that. I would not part with my
father's last gift. I shall be rich seven years hence, if I live so
long. I'll do what the young spendthrifts do. I'll go to the Jews.
I will not be Captain Winstanley's helot. One slave is enough
for him, I should think. He has enslaved poor mamma. Look at
her now, poor soul; she sits in bodily fear of him, crumbling her
bread with her pretty fingers, shining and sparkling with rings.

Poor mamma! it is a bad day for her when fine dresses and handsome jewels cannot make her happy.'

It was a miserable dinner. Those three were not wont to be gay when they sat at meat together; but the dinner of to-day was of a gloomier pattern than usual. The strawberries and cherries were carried round solemnly, the Captain filled his glass with claret, Mrs Winstanley dipped the ends of her fingers into the turquoise-coloured glass, and disseminated a faint odour of roses.

'I think I'll go and sit in the garden, Conrad,' she said, when she had dried those tapering fingers on her fringed doily. 'It's so warm in the house.'

'Do, dear. I'll come and smoke my cigar on the lawn presently,' answered the Captain.

'Can't you come at once, love?'

'I've a little bit of business to settle first. I won't be long!'

Mrs Winstanley kissed her hand to her husband, and left the room, followed by Vixen.

'Violet,' she said, when they were outside, 'how could you stay out so long? Conrad is dreadfully angry.'

'Your husband angry because I rode a few miles farther to-day than usual? Dear mother, that is too absurd. I was sorry not to be at home in time to give you your afternoon tea, and I apologize to you with all my heart; but what can it matter to Captain Winstanley?'

'My dearest Violet, when will you understand that Conrad stands in the place of your dear father?'

'Never, mamma, for that is not true. God gave me one father, and I loved and honoured him with all my heart. There is no sacrifice he could have asked of me that I would not have made; no command of his, however difficult, that I would not have obeyed. But I will obey no spurious father. I recognise no duty that I owe to Captain Winstanley.'

'You are a very cruel girl,' wailed Pamela, 'and your obstinacy is making my life miserable.'

'Dear mother, how do I interfere with your happiness? You live your life, and I mine. You and Captain Winstanley take your own way, I mine. Is it a crime to be out riding a little

longer than usual, that you should look so pale and the Captain
so black when I come home?'

'It is worse than a crime, Violet; it is an impropriety.'

Vixen blushed crimson, and turned upon her mother with an
expression that was half startled, half indignant.

'What do you mean, mamma?'

'Had you been riding about the Forest all those hours alone, it
would have been eccentric – unladylike – masculine even. You
know that your habit of passing half your existence on horseback
has always been a grief to me. But you were not alone.'

'No, mamma, I was not alone. I had my oldest friend with
me; one of the few people in this big world who cares for me.'

'You were riding about with Roderick Vawdrey, Lady Mabel
Ashbourne's future husband.'

'Why do you remind me of his engagement, mamma? Do
you think that Roderick and I have ever forgotten it? Can he
not be my friend as well as Lady Mabel's husband? Am I to
forget that he and I played together as children, that we have
always thought of each other and cared for each other as
brother and sister, only because he is engaged to Lady Mabel
Ashbourne?'

'Violet, you must know that all talk about brother and sister is
sheer nonsense. Suppose I had set up brother and sister with
Captain Winstanley! What would you – what would the world
have thought?'

'That would have been different,' said Vixen. 'You did not
know each other as babies. In fact you couldn't have done so,
for you had left off being a baby before he was born,' added
Vixen naïvely.

'You will have to put a stop to these rides with Roderick.
Everybody in the neighbourhood is talking about you.'

'Which everybody?'

'Colonel Carteret to begin with.'

'Colonel Carteret slanders everybody. It is his only
intellectual resource. Dearest mother, be your own sweet easy-
tempered self, not a speaking-tube for Captain Winstanley. Pray
leave me my liberty. I am not particularly happy. You might at
least let me be free.'

Violet left her mother with these words. They had reached the lawn before the drawing-room windows. Mrs Winstanley sank into a low basket-chair, like a hall-porter's, which a friend had sent her from the sands of Trouville; and Vixen ran off to the stables to see if Arion was in any way the worse for his long round.

The horses had been littered down for the night, and the stable-yard was empty. The faithful Bates, who was usually to be found at this hour smoking his evening pipe on a stone bench beside the stable pump, was nowhere in sight. Vixen went into Arion's loose-box, where that animal was nibbling clover lazily, standing knee-deep in freshly-spread straw, his fine legs carefully bandaged. He gave his mistress the usual grunt of friendly greeting, allowed her to feed him with the choicest bits of clover, and licked her hands in token of gratitude.

'I don't think you're any the worse for our canter over the grass, old pet,' she cried cheerily, as she caressed his sleek head, 'and Captain Winstanley's black looks can't hurt you.'

As she left the stable she saw Bates, who was walking slowly across the court-yard, wiping his honest old eyes with the cuff of his drab coat, and hanging his grizzled head dejectedly.

Vixen ran to him with her cheeks aflame, divining mischief. The Captain had been wreaking his spite upon this lowly head.

'What's the matter, Bates?'

'I've lived in this house, Miss Voylet, man and boy, forty year come Michaelmas, and I've never wronged my master by so much as the worth of a handful o' wuts or a carriage candle. I was stable-boy in your grandfather's time, miss, as is well-beknown to you; and I remember your feyther when he was the finest and handsomest young squire within fifty mile. I've loved you and yours better than I ever loved my own flesh and blood: and to go and pluck me up by the roots and chuck me out amongst strangers in my old age, is crueller than it would be to tear up the old cedar on the lawn, which I've heard Joe the gardener say be as old as the days when such-like trees was fust beknown in England. It's crueller, Miss Voylet, for the cedar ain't got not feelings – but I felt it down to the deepest fibres in me. The lawn 'ud look ugly and empty without the cedar, and mayhap nobody 'll miss me – but I've got the heart of a man, miss, and it bleeds.'

Poor Bates relieved his wounded feelings with this burst of eloquence. He was a man who, although silent in his normal condition, had a great deal to say when he felt aggrieved. In his present state of mind his only solace was in many words.

'I don't know what you mean, Bates,' cried Vixen, very pale now, divining the truth in part, if not wholly. 'Don't cry, dear old fellow, it's too dreadful to see you. You don't mean – you can't mean – that – my mother has sent you away?'

'Not your ma, miss, bless her heart. She wouldn't sack the servant that saddled her husband's horse, fair weather and foul, for twenty year. No, Miss Voylet, it's Captain Winstanley that's given me the sack. He's master here, now, you know, miss.'

'But for what reason? What have you done to offend him.'

'Ah, miss, there's the hardship of it! He's turned me off at a minute's notice, and without a character too. That's hard, ain't it, miss? Forty year in one service, and to leave without a character at last! That do cut a old feller to the quick.'

'Why don't you tell me the reason, Bates? Captain Winstanley must have given you his reason for such a cruel act.'

'He did, miss; but I ain't going to tell you.'

'Why not, in goodness' name?'

'Because it's an insult to you, Miss Voylet; and I'm not going to insult my old master's grand-daughter. If I didn't love you for your own sake – and I do dearly love you, miss, if you'll excuse the liberty – I'm bound to love you for the sake of your grandfeyther. He was my first master, and a kind one. He gave me my first pair o' tops. Lor, miss, I can call to mind the day as well as if it was yesterday. Didn't I fancy myself a buck in 'em!'

Bates grinned and sparkled at the thought of those first top-boots. His poor old eyes, dim with years of long service, twinkled with the memory of those departed vanities.

'Bates,' cried Vixen, looking at him resolutely, 'I insist upon knowing what reason Captain Winstanley alleged for sending you away.'

'He didn't allege nothing, miss: and I ain't agoing to tell you what he said.'

'But you must. I order you to tell me. You are still my servant, remember. You have always been a faithful servant, and I am sure you won't disobey me at the last. I insist upon knowing what Captain Winstanley said; however insulting his words may have been to me, they will not surprise me or wound me much. There is no love lost between him and me. I think everybody knows that. Don't be afraid of giving me pain, Bates. Nothing the Captain could say would do that. I despise him too much.'

'I'm right down glad o' that, miss. Go on a-despising of him. You can't give it him as thick as he deserves.'

'Now, Bates, what did he say?'

'He said I was a old fool, miss, or a old rogue, he weren't quite clear in his mind which. I'd been actin' as go-between with you and Mr Vawdrey, encouragin' of you to meet the young gentleman in your rides, and never givin' the Cap'en warnin', as your stepfather, of what was goin' on behind his back. He said it was shameful, and you was makin' yourself the talk of the county, and I was no better than I should be for aidin' and abettin' of you in disgracin' yourself. And then I blazed up a bit, miss, and maybe I cheeked him: and then he turned upon me sharp and short and told me to get out of the house this night, bag and baggage, and never to apply to him for a character; and then he counted out my wages on the table, miss, up to this evening, exact to a halfpenny, by way of showing me that he meant business, perhaps. But I came away and left his brass upon the table, staring him in the face. I ain't no pauper, praise be to God! I've had a good place and I've saved money: and I needn't lower myself by taking his dirty halfpence.'

'And you're going away, Bates, to-night?' exclaimed Vixen, hardly able to realise this calamity.

That Captain Winstanley should have spoken insultingly of her and of Rorie touched her but lightly. She had spoken truly just now when she said that she scorned him too much to be easily wounded by his insolence. But that he should dismiss her father's old servant as he had sold her father's old horse; that this good old man, who had grown from boyhood to age under her ancestral roof, who remembered her father in the bloom and glory of early youth; that this faithful servant should be thrust out at the bidding of an interloper – a paltry schemer, who, in Vixen's estimation, had been actuated by the basest and most mercenary motives when he married her mother; – that these things should be, moved Violet Tempest with an overwhelming anger.

She kept her passion under, so far as to speak very calmly to Bates. Her face was white with suppressed rage, her great brown eyes shone with angry fire, her lips quivered as she spoke, and the rings on one clenched hand were ground into the flesh of the slender fingers.

'Never mind, Bates,' she said very gently; 'I'll get you a good place before ten o'clock to-night. Pack up your clothes, and be ready to go where I tell you two hours hence. But first saddle Arion.'

'Bless yer heart, Miss Voylet, you're not going out riding this evening? Arion's done a long day's work.'

'I know that; but he's fresh enough to do as much more – I've just been looking at him. Saddle him at once, and keep him ready in his stable till I come for him. Don't argue, Bates. If I knew that I were going to ride him to death I should ride him to-night all the same. You are dismissed without a character, are you?' cried Vixen, laughing bitterly. 'Never mind, Bates, I'll give you a character; and I'll get you a place.'

She ran lightly off and was gone, while Bates stood stock still wondering at her. There never was such a young lady. What was there in life that he would not have done for her – were it to the shedding of blood? And to think that he was no more to serve and follow her; no longer to jog contentedly through the pine-scented Forest – watching the meteoric course of that graceful figure in front of him, the lively young horse curbed by the light and dexterous hand, the ruddy brown hair glittering in the sunlight, the flexible form moving in unison with every motion of the horse that carried it! There could be no deeper image of desolation in Bate's mind than the idea that this rider and this horse were to be henceforth severed from his existence. What had he in life save the familiar things and faces among which he had grown from youth to age? Separate him from these beloved surroundings, and he had no standpoint in the universe. The reason of his being would be gone. Bates was as strictly local in his ideas as the zoophyte which has clung all its life to one rock.

He went to the harness-room for Miss Tempest's well-worn saddle, and brought Arion out of his snug box, and wisped him and combed him, and blacked his shoes, and made him altogether lovely – a process to which the intelligent animal was inclined to take objection, the hour being unseemly and unusual. Poor Bates sighed over his task, and brushed away more than one silent tear with the back of the dandy-brush. It was kind of Miss Violet to think about getting him a place; but he had no heart for going into a new service. He would rather have taken a room in one of the Beechdale cottages, and have dragged out the remnant of his days within sight of the chimney-stacks beneath which he had slept for forty years. He had money in the bank that would last until his lees of life were spilt, and then he would be buried in the churchyard he had crossed every Sunday of his life on his way to morning service. His kindred were all dead or distant – the nearest, a married niece, settled at Romsey, which good old humdrum market-town was – except once a week or so by carrier's cart – almost as unapproachable as the Bermudas. He was not going to migrate to Romsey for the sake of a married niece; when he could stop at Beechdale, and see the gables and chimneys of the home from which stern fate had banished him.

He had scarcely finished Arion's toilet when Miss Tempest opened the stable-door and looked in, ready to mount. She had her hunting-crop, with the strong horn hook for opening gates, her short habit, and looked altogether ready for business.

'Hadn't I better come with you, miss?' Bates asked, as he lifted her into her saddle.

'No, Bates. You are dismissed, you know. It wouldn't do for you to take one of Captain Winstanley's horses. He might have you sent to prison for horse-stealing.'

'Lord, miss, so he might!' said Bates, grinning. 'I reckon he's capable of it. But I cheeked him pretty strong, Miss Voylet.

The thought o' that'll always be a comfort to me. You wouldn't ha' knowed me for your feyther's old sarvant if you'd heard me. I felt as if Satan had got hold o' my tongue, and was wagging it for me. The words came so pat. It seemed as if I'd got all the dictionary at the tip of my poor old tongue.'

'Open the gate,' said Vixen. 'I am going out by the wilderness.'

Bates opened the gate under the old brick archway, and Vixen rode slowly away, by unfrequented thickets of rhododendron and arbutus, holly and laurel, with a tall mountain-ash, or a stately deodora, rising up among them, here and there, dark against the opal evening sky.

It was a lovely evening. The crescent moon rode high above the tree-tops; the sunset was still red in the west. The secret depths of the wood gave forth their subtle perfume in the cool, calm air. The birds were singing in suppressed and secret tones among the low branches. Now and then a bat skimmed across the open glade, and melted into the woodland darkness, or a rabbit flitted past, gray and ghostlike. It was an hour when the woods assumed an awful beauty. Not to meet ghosts seemed stranger than to meet them. The shadows of the dead would have been in harmony with the mystic loveliness of this green solitude — a world remote from the track of men.

Even to-night, though her heart was swelling with indignant pain, Violet felt all the beauty of these familiar scenes. They were a part of her life, and so long as she lived she must love and rejoice in them. To-night as she rode quietly along, careful not to hurry Arion after his long day's work, she looked around her with eyes full of deep love and melancholy yearning. It seemed to her to-night that out of all that had been sweet and lovely in her life only these forest scenes remained. Humanity had not been kind to her. The dear father had been snatched away: just when she had grown to the height of his stout heart, and had fullest comprehension of his love, and greatest need of his protection. Her mother was a gentle, smiling puppet, to whom it were vain to appeal in her necessities. Her mother's husband was an implacable enemy. Rorie, the friend of her childhood — who might have been so much — had given himself to another. She was quite alone.

'The charcoal-burner in Mark Ash is not so solitary as I am,' thought Vixen bitterly. 'Charcoal-burning is only part of his life. He has his wife and children in his cottage at home.'

By-and-by she came out of the winding forest ways into the straight high-road that led to Briarwood, and now she put her horse at a smart trot, for it was growing dark already, and she calculated that it must be nearly eleven o'clock before she could accomplish what she had to do and get back to the Abbey House. And at eleven doors were locked for the night, and Captain Winstanley made a circuit of inspection, as severely as the keeper of a prison. What would be said if she should not get home till after the gates were locked, and the keys delivered over to that stern janitor?

At last Briarwood came in sight above the dark clumps of beech and oak, a white portico, shining lamplit windows. The lodge-gate stood hospitably open, and Violet rode in without question, and up to the pillared porch.

Roderick Vawdrey was standing in the porch smoking. He threw away his cigar as Vixen rode up, and ran down the steps to receive her.

'Why, Violet, what has happened?' he asked, with an alarmed look.

It seemed to him that only sudden death or dire calamity could bring her to him thus, in the late gloaming, pale, and deeply moved. Her lips trembled faintly as she looked at him, and for the moment she could find no words to tell her trouble.

'What is it, Violet?' he asked again, holding her gloved hand in his, and looking up at her, full of sympathy and concern.

'Not very much, perhaps, in your idea of things: but it seems a great deal to me. And it has put me into a tremendous passion. I have come to ask you to do me a favour.'

'A thousand favours if you like: and when they are all granted the obligation shall be still on my side. But come into the drawing-room and rest – and let me get you some tea – lemonade – wine – something to refresh you after your long ride.'

'Nothing, thanks. I am not going to get off my horse. I must not lose a moment. Why it must be long after nine already, and Captain Winstanley locks up the house at eleven.'

Rorie did not care to tell her that it was on the stroke of ten. He called in a stentorian voice for a servant, and told the man to get Blue Peter saddled that instant.

'Where's your groom, Violet?' he asked, wondering to see her unattended.

'I have no groom. That's just what I came to tell you. Captain Winstanley has dismissed Bates, at a minute's warning, without a character.'

'Dismissed old Bates, your father's faithful servant! But in Heaven's name what for?'

'I would rather not tell you that. The alleged reason is an insult to me. I can tell you that it is not for dishonesty, or lying, or drunkenness, or insolence, or any act that a good servant need be ashamed of. The poor old man is cast off for a fault of mine; or for an act of mine, which Captain Winstanley pleases to condemn. He is thrust out of doors, homeless, without a character, after forty years of faithful service. He was with my grandfather, you know. Now, Rorie, I want you to take Bates into your service. He is not so ornamental as a young man, perhaps; but he is ever so much more useful. He is faithful and industrious, honest and true. He is a capital nurse for sick horses; and I have heard my dear father say that he knows more than the common run of veterinary surgeon. I don't think you would find him an incumbrance. Now, dear Rorie,' she concluded coaxingly, with innocent childish entreaty, almost as if they had still been children and playfellows, 'I want you to do this for me – I want you to take Bates.'

'Why, you dear simple-minded baby, I would take a regiment of Bateses for your sake. Why this is not a favour——'

'"It is as if I should entreat you wear your gloves,"' cried Vixen, quoting Desdemona's speech to her general.

Rorie's ready promise had revived her spirits. She felt that, after all, there was such a thing as friendship in the world. Life was not altogether blank and dreary. She forgot that her old friend had given himself away to another woman. She had a knack of forgetting that little fact when she and Rorie were together. It was only in her hours of solitude that the circumstance presented itself distinctly to her mind.

'I am so grateful to you for this, Rorie,' she cried. 'I cannot tell you what a load you have taken off my mind. I felt sure you would do me this favour. And yet, if you had said No——! It would have been too dreadful to think of. Poor old Bates loafing about Beechdale, living upon his savings! I shall be able to pension him by-and-by, when I am of age; but now I have only a few pounds in the world, the remains of a quarter's pocket-money, according to the view and allowance of the forester.' added Vixen, quoting the Forest Law, with a little mocking laugh. 'And now good-night; I must go home as fast as I can.'

'So you must, but I am coming with you,' answered Rorie; and then he roared again in his stentorian voice in the direction of the stables, 'Where's that Blue Peter?'

'Indeed, there is no reason for you to come,' cried Vixen. 'I know every inch of the Forest.'

'Very likely; but I am coming with you, all the same.'

A groom led out Blue Peter, a strong useful-looking hack, which Mr Vawdrey kept to do his dirty work, hunting in bad weather, night-work, and extra journeys of all kinds. Rorie was in the saddle and by Vixen's side without a minute's lost time, and they were riding out of the grounds into the straight road.

They rode for a considerable time in silence. Violet had seldom seen her old friend so thoughtful. The night deepened, the stars shone out of the clear heaven, at first one by one: and then, suddenly, in a multitude that no tongue could number. The leaves whispered and rustled with faint mysterious noises, as Violet and her companion rode slowly down the long steep hill.

'What a beast that Winstanley is!' said Rorie, when they got to the bottom of the hill, as if he had been all this time arriving at an opinion about Violet's stepfather. 'I'm afraid he must make your life miserable.'

'He doesn't make it particularly happy,' answered Vixen quietly; 'but I never expected to be happy after mamma married. I did not think there was much happiness left for me after my father's death; but there was at least peace. Captain Winstanley has made an end of that.'

'He is a wretch, and I should like to shoot him,' said Rorie vindictively. 'Dear little Vixen – yes, I must call you by the old pet name – to think that you should be miserable, you whom I remember so bright and happy, you who were born for happiness! But you are not always wretched, dear,' he said, leaning over to speak to her in closer, more confidential tones, as if the sleepy birds and the whispering forest leaves could hear and betray him. 'You were happy – we were happy – this morning.'

He had laid his hand on hers. That useful Blue Peter needed no guidance. They were just leaving the road, and entering a long glade that led through a newly-opened fir plantation, a straight ride of a mile and a half or so. The young moon was gleaming cool and clear above the feathering points of the firs.

'Yes,' she answered recklessly, involuntarily, with a stifled sob, 'I am always happy with you. You are all that remains to me of my old life.'

'My dearest, my loveliest, then be happy for ever,' he cried, winding his arm round her slim waist, and leaning over her till his head almost rested on her shoulder. Their horses were close together, walking at a foot-pace, Blue Peter in nowise disconcerted by this extraordinary behaviour of his rider.

'My love, if you can be happy at so small a price, be happy always!' said Rorie, his lips close to the girl's pale cheek, his arm feeling every beat of the passionate heart. 'I will break the toils that bind me. I will be yours, and yours only. I have never truly loved anyone but you, and I have loved you all my life – I never knew and how dearly till of late. No, dearest love, never did I know how utterly I loved you till these last summer days which we have lived together, alone and supremely happy, in the forest that is our native land. My Violet, I will break with Mabel to-morrow. She and I were never made for one another. You and I were. Yes, love, yes: we have grown up together side by side, like the primroses and violets in the woods. It is my second nature to love you. Why should we be parted? Why should I go on acting a dismal farce, pretending love to Mabel, pretending friendship for you – alike false to both? There is no reason, Violet, none – except——'

'Except your promise to your dying mother,' said Violet, escaping from his arm, and looking at him steadily, bravely through the dim light. 'You shall not break that for my sake – you ought not, were I ten times a better woman than I am. No, Rorie, you are to do your duty, and keep your word. You are to marry Lady Mabel, and be happy ever after, like the prince in a fairy tale. Depend upon it, happiness always comes in the long run to the man who does his duty.'

'I don't believe it,' cried Roderick passionately; 'I have seen men who have done right all through life – men who have sacrificed feeling to honour, and been miserable. Why should I imitate them? I love you. I loved you always: but my mother worried and teased me, vaunting Mabel's perfections, trying to lessen you in my esteem. And then, when she was dying, and it seemed a hard thing to oppose her wishes, or to refuse her anything, were it even the happiness of my life, I was weak, and let myself be persuaded, and sold myself into bondage. But it is not too late, Violet. I will write Mabel an honest letter to-morrow, and tell her the truth for the first time in my life.'

'You will do nothing of the kind!' cried Violet resolutely. 'What, do you think I have no pride – no sense of honour? Do you think I would let it be said of me, that I, knowing you to be engaged to your cousin, set myself to lure you away from her; that we rode together, and were seen together, happy in each other's company, and as careless of slander as if we had been brother and sister; and that the end of all was that you broke your faith to your promised wife in order to marry me? No, Rorie, that shall never be said. If I could stoop so low I should be worthy of the worst word my mother's husband could say of me.'

'What does it matter what people say – your mother's husband above all? Malice can always find something evil to say of us, let us shape our lives how we may. What really matters is that we should be happy: and I can be happy with no one but you, Violet. I know that now. I will never marry Mabel Ashbourne.'

'And you will never marry me,' answered Vixen, giving Arion a light touch of her whip which sent him flying along the shadowy ride.

Blue Peter followed as swiftly. Rorie was by Violet's side again in a minute, with his hand grasping hers.

'You mean that you don't love me?' he exclaimed angrily. 'Why could you not have said so at the first; why have you let me live in a fool's paradise?'

'The paradise was of your own making,' she answered; 'I love you a little for the past, because my father loved you – because you are all that remains to me of my happy childhood. Yes, if it were not for you, I might look back and think those dear old days were only a dream. But I hear your voice, I look at you, and know that you are real, and that I once was very happy. Yes, Rorie, I do love you – love you – yes, with all my heart, dearer, better than I have ever loved anyone upon this earth, since my father was laid in the ground. Yes, dear.' Their horses were walking slowly now; and her hand was locked in his as they rode side by side. 'Yes, dear, I love you too well, and you and I must part. I had schooled myself to believe that I loved you only as I might have loved a brother; that you could be Lady Mabel's husband, and my true friend. But that was a delusion – that can never be. You and I must part, Rorie. This night-ride in the Forest must be our last. Never any more, by sun or moon, must you and I ride together. It is all over, Rorie, the old childish friendship. I mean to do my duty, and you must do yours.'

'I will never marry a woman I do not love.'

'You will keep your promise to your mother; you will act as a man of honour should. Think, Rorie, what a shameful thing it would be to do, to break off an engagement which has been so long publicly known, to wound and grieve your good aunt and uncle.'

'They have been very kind to me,' sighed Rorie. 'It would hurt me to give them pain.'

His conscience told him she was right, but he was angry with her for being so much wiser than himself.

Then, in a moment, love – that had slumbered long, idly happy in the company of the beloved, and had suddenly awakened to know that this summer-day idlesse meant a passion stronger than death – love got the better of conscience, and he cried vehemently:

'What need I care for the Duke and Duchess! They can have their choice of husbands for their daughter; an heiress like Mabel has only to smile, and a man is at her feet. Why should I sacrifice myself, love, truth, all that makes life worth having? Do you think I would do it for the sake of Ashbourne, and the honour of being a duke's son-in-law?'

'No, Rorie; but for the sake of your promise. And now look, there is Lyndhurst steeple above the woods. I am near home, and we must say good-night.'

'Not till you are at your own gate.'

'No one must see you. I want to ride in quietly by the stables. Don't think I am ashamed of my errand to-night. I am not; but I want to save my mother trouble, and if Captain Winstanley and I were to discuss the matter there would be a disturbance.'

Roderick Vawdrey seized Arion by the bridle.

'I shall not let you go so easily,' he said resolutely. 'Vixen, I have loved you ever since I can remember you. Will you be my wife?'

'No.'

'Why did you say that you love me?'

'Because I cannot tell a lie. Yes, I love you, Rorie; but I love your honour and my own better than the chance of a happiness that might fade and wither before we could grasp it. I know that your mother had a very poor opinion of me while she was alive; I should like her to know, if the dead know anything, that she was mistaken, and that I am not quite unworthy of her respect. You will marry Lady Mabel Ashbourne, Rorie; and ten years hence, when we are sober middle-aged people, we shall be firm friends once again, and you will thank and praise me for having counselled you to cleave to the right. Let go the bridle, Rorie, there's no time to lose. There's a glorious gallop from Queen's Bower to the Christchurch Road.'

It was a long grassy ride, safe only for those who knew the country well, for it was bordered on each side by treacherous bogs. Violet knew every inch of the way. Arion scented his stable afar off, and went like the wind; Blue Peter stretched his muscular limbs in pursuit. It was a wild ride along the grassy track beside watery marshes and reedy pools that gleamed in the dim light of a new moon. The distant woods showed black against the sky. There was no light to mark a human habitation within ken. There was nothing but night and loneliness and the solemn beauty of an unpeopled waste. A forest pony stood here and there – pastern-deep in the sedges – and gazed at those two wild riders, grave and gray, like a ghost. A silvery snake glided across the track; a water-rat plunged, with a heavy splash, into a black pool as the horses galloped by. It was a glorious ride. Miserable as both riders were, they could not but enjoy that wild rush through the sweet soft air, under the silent stars.

Vixen gave a long sigh, presently, when they pulled up their horses on the hard road.

'I think I am "fey" now,' she said. 'I wonder what is going to happen to me?'

'Whatever misfortunes come to you henceforth will be your own fault,' protested Rorie savagely. 'You won't be happy, or make me so.'

'Don't be angry with me, Rorie,' she answered quite meekly. 'I would rather be miserable in my own way than happy in yours.'

Arion, having galloped for his own pleasure, would now have liked to crawl. He was beginning to feel the effects of the unusual toil, and hung his head despondently; but Vixen urged him into a sharp trot, feeling that matters were growing desperate.

Ten minutes later they were at the lodge leading to the stables. The gate was locked, the cottage wrapped in darkness.

'I must go in by the carriage-drive,' said Vixen. 'It's rather a bore, as I am pretty sure to meet Captain Winstanley. But it can't be helped.'

'Let me go in with you.'

'No, Rorie; that would do no good. If he insulted me before you, his insolence would pain me.'

'And I believe I should pain him,' said Rorie. 'I should give him the sweetest horsewhipping he ever had in his life.'

'That is to say you would bring disgrace upon me, and make my mother miserable. That's a man's idea of kindness. No, Rorie, we part here. Good-night, and good-bye.'

'Fiddlesticks!' cried Rorie. 'I shall wait for you all to-morrow morning at the kennels.'

Vixen had ridden past the open gate. The lodge-keeper stood at his door waiting for her. Roderick respected her wishes and stayed outside.

'Good-night!' she cried again, looking back at him; 'Bates shall come to you to-morrow morning.'

The hall door was wide open, and Captain Winstanley stood on the threshold, waiting for his stepdaughter. One of the underlings from the stable was ready to take her horse. She dismounted unaided, flung the reins to the groom, and walked up to the Captain with her firmest step. When she was in the hall he shut the door, and bolted and locked it with a somewhat ostentatious care. She seemed to breathe less freely when that great door had shut out the cool night. She felt as if she were in a jail.

'I should like half-a-dozen words with you in the drawing-room before you go upstairs,' Captain Winstanley said stiffly.

'A hundred, if you choose,' answered Vixen, with supreme coolness.

She was utterly fearless. What risks or hazards had life that she need dread? She hoped nothing – feared nothing. She had just made the greatest sacrifice that fate could require of her: she had rejected the man she fondly loved. What were the slings and arrows of her stepfather's petty malice compared with such a wrench as that?

She followed Captain Winstanley to the drawing-room. Here there was more air; one long window was open, and the lace curtains were faintly stirred by the night winds. A large moderator lamp burned upon Mrs Winstanley's favourite table – her books and basket of crewels were there, but the lady of the house had retired.

'My mother has gone to bed, I suppose?' inquired Vixen.

'She has gone to her room, but I fear she is too much agitated to get any rest. I would not allow her to wait here any longer for you.'

'Is it so very late?' asked Vixen, with the most innocent air.

Her heart was beating violently, and her temper was not at its best. She stood looking at the Captain, with a mischievous sparkle in her eyes, and her whip tightly clenched.

She was thinking of that speech of Rorie's about the 'sweetest horsewhipping.' She wondered whether Captain Winstanley had ever been horsewhipped; whether that kind of chastisement was numbered in the sum of his experience. She opined not. The Captain was too astute a man to bring himself in the way of such punishment. He would do things that deserved horsewhipping, and get off scot free.

'It is a quarter-past eleven. I don't know whether you think that a respectable hour for a young lady's evening ride. May I ask the motive of this nocturnal expedition?'

'Certainly. You deprived Bates of a comfortable place – he has only been in the situation forty years – and I went to get him another. I am happy to say that I succeeded.'

'And pray who is the chivalrous employer willing to receive my dismissed servant without a character?'

'A very old friend of my father's – Mr Vawdrey.'

'I thought as much,' retorted the Captain. 'And it is to Mr Vawdrey you have been, late at night, unattended?'

'It is your fault that I went unattended. You have taken upon yourself to dismiss my groom – the man who broke my first pony, the man my father gave me for an attendant and protector, just as he gave me my horse. You will take upon yourself to see my horse next, I suppose?'

'I shall take a great deal more upon myself, before you and I have done with each other, Miss Tempest,' answered the Captain, pale with passion.

Never had Vixen seen him so strongly moved. The purple veins stood out darkly upon his pale forehead, his eyes had a haggard look; he was like a man consumed inwardly by some evil passion that was stronger than himself, like a man possessed by devils. Vixen looked at him with wonder. They stood facing each other, with the lamplit table between them, the light shining on both their faces.

'Why do you look at me with that provoking smile?' he asked. 'Do you want to exasperate me? You must know that I hate you.'

'I do,' answered Vixen; 'but God only knows why you should do so.'

'Do you know no reason?'

'No.'

'Can't you guess one?'

'No; unless it is because my father's fortune will belong to me by-and-by, if I live to be five-and-twenty, and your position here will be lessened.'

'That is not the reason; no, I am not so base as that. That is not why I hate you, Violet. If you had been some dumpy, homely, country lass, with thick features and a clumsy figure, you and I might have got on decently enough. I would have made you obey me; but I would have been kind to you. But you are something very different. You are the girl I would have perilled my soul to win – the girl who rejected me with careless scorn. Have you forgotten that night in Pavilion Garden at Brighton? I have not. I never look up at the stars without remembering it; and I can never forgive you while that memory lives in my mind. If you had been my wife, Violet, I would have been your slave. You forced me to make myself your stepfather; and I will be master instead of slave. I will make your life bitter to you if you thwart me. I will put a stop to your running after another woman's sweetheart. I will come between you and your lover, Roderick Vawdrey. Your secret meetings, your clandestine love-making, shall be stopped. Such conduct as you have been carrying on of late is a shame and disgrace to your sex.'

'How dare you say that?' cried Vixen, beside herself with anger.

She grasped the lamp with both her hands, as if she would have hurled it at her foe. It was a large moon-shaped globe upon a bronze pedestal – a fearful thing to fling at one's adversary. A great wave of blood surged up into the girl's brain. What she was going to do she knew not; but her whole being was convulsed by the passion of that moment. The room reeled before her eyes, the heavy pedestal swayed in her hands, and then she saw the big moonlike globe roll on to the carpet, and after it, and darting beyond it, a stream of liquid fire that ran, and ran, quicker than thought, towards the open window.

Before she could speak or move the flame had run up the lace curtain, like a living thing, swift as the flight of a bird or the gliding motion of a lizard. The wide casement was wreathed with light. They two – Vixen and her foe – seemed to be standing in an atmosphere of fire.

Captain Winstanley was confounded by the suddenness of the catastrophe. While he stood dumb, bewildered, Vixen sprang through the narrow space between the flaming curtains, as if she had plunged into a gulf of fire. He heard her strong clear voice calling to stablemen and gardeners. It rang like a clarion in the still summer night.

There was not a moment lost. The stablemen rushed with pails of water, and directly after them the Scotch gardener with his garden-engine, which held several gallons. His hose did some damage to the drawing-room carpet and upholstery, but the strong jet of water speedily quenched the flames. In ten minutes the window stood blank, and black, and bare, with Vixen standing on the lawn outside, contemplating the damage she had done.

Mrs Winstanley rushed in at the drawing-room door, ghost-like, in her white *peignoir*, pale and scared.

'O Conrad, what has happened?' she cried distractedly, just able to distinguish her husband's figure standing in the midst of the disordered room.

'Your beautiful daughter has been trying to set the house on fire,' he answered. 'That is all.'

CHAPTER 33

'THAT MUST END AT ONCE'

A quarter of an hour later, when all the confusion was over, Violet was kneeling by her mother's chair, trying to restore tranquillity to Mrs Winstanley's fluttered spirits. Mother and daughter were alone together in the elder lady's dressing-room, the disconsolate Pamela sitting like Niobe, amidst her scattered fineries, her pomade-pots and powder-boxes, fan-cases and jewel-caskets, and all the arsenal of waning beauty.

'Dear mother,' pleaded Violet, with unusual gentleness, 'pray don't give way to this unnecessary grief. You cannot surely believe that I tried to set this dear old house on fire — that I could be so foolish — granting even that I were wicked enough to do it — as to destroy a place I love — the house in which my father was born! You can't believe such a thing, mother.'

'I know that you are making my life miserable,' sobbed Mrs Winstanley, feebly dabbing her forehead with a flimsy Valenciennes bordered handkerchief, steeped in eau-de-cologne, 'and I am sure Conrad would not tell a falsehood.'

'Perhaps not,' said Vixen, with a gloomy look. 'We will take it for granted that he is perfection and could not do wrong. But in this case he is mistaken. I felt quite capable of killing him, but not of setting fire to this house.'

'O,' wailed Pamela distractedly, 'this is too dreadful! To think that I should have a daughter who confesses herself at heart a murderess.'

'Unhappily it is true, mother,' said Vixen, moodily contrite. 'For just that one moment of my life I felt a murderous impulse — and from the impulse to the execution is a very short step. I don't feel myself very superior to the people who are hanged at Newgate, I assure you.'

'What is to become of me?' inquired Mrs Winstanley in abject lamentation. 'It is too hard that my own daughter should be a source of misery in my married life, that she should harden her heart against the best of stepfathers, and try, yes, actually try, to bring discord between me and the husband I love. I don't know what I have done that I should be so miserable.'

'Dear mother, only be calm and listen to me,' urged Violet, who was very calm herself, with a coldly resolute air which presently obtained ascendency over her agitated parent. 'If I have been the source of misery, that misery cannot too soon come to an end. I have long felt that I have no place in this house — that I am one too many in our small family. I feel now

— yes, mamma, I feel and know that the same roof cannot cover me and Captain Winstanley. He and I can no longer sit at the same board, or live in the same house. That must end at once.'

'What complaint can you have to make against him, Violet?' cried her mother hysterically, and with a good deal more dabbing of the perfumed handkerchief upon her fevered brow. 'I am sure no father could be kinder than Conrad would be to you if you would only let him. But you have set yourself against him from the very first. It seems as if you grudged me my happiness.'

'It shall seem so no longer, mamma. I will cease to be a thorn in your garland of roses,' replied Vixen, with exceeding bitterness. 'I will leave the Abbey House directly any other home can be found for me. If dear old McCroke would take care of me I should like to go abroad, somewhere very far, to some strange place, where all things would be different and new to me,' continued Vixen, unconsciously betraying that aching desire for forgetfulness, natural to a wounded heart. 'Sweden, or Norway, for instance. I think I should like to spend a year in one of those cold strange lands, with good old McCroke for my companion. There would be nothing to remind me of the Forest,' she concluded with a stifled sob.

'My dear Violet, you have such wild ideas,' exclaimed her mother with an injured air. 'It is just as Conrad says. You have no notion of the proprieties. Sweden or Norway, indeed! Was there ever anything so outlandish? What would people say, I wonder?'

'Ah, what indeed, mamma? Perhaps they might for once say what is true: that I could not get on with Captain Winstanley, and so was forced to find another home.'

'And what a reproach that would be to me,' cried her mother. 'You are so selfish, Violet; you think of no one but yourself.'

'Perhaps that is because nobody else thinks of me, mother.'

'How can you say such abominable things, Violet? Am I not thinking of you this moment? I am sure I have thought of you this evening until my head aches. You force one to think about you, when you behave in such a disgraceful manner.'

'What have I done that is disgraceful, mamma? I have ridden out at an unusual hour to get a place for an old servant – a man who has served in this house faithfully for forty years. That is what I have done, and I should not be ashamed if it were known to everybody in Hampshire. Yes, even to Lady Mabel Ashbourne, that pattern of chilly propriety. The disgrace is Captain Winstanley's. It is he who ought to be ashamed of turning off my father and grandfather's old servant. What you have to be sorry for, mamma, is that you have married a man capable of such an action.'

'How dare you speak against him!' cried the offended wife. 'He has done everything for the best. It was your own foolish conduct that obliged him to dismiss Bates. To think that a daughter of mine should have so little self-respect as to go roaming about the Forest with an engaged man! It is too dreadful.'

'You need not make yourself unhappy about the engaged man, mamma,' said Vixen scornfully. 'He is out of danger. Rorie and I need never see each other again. I should be more than content that it should be so. Only arrange with Captain Winstanley for some allowance to be made me – just money enough to enable me to live abroad with dear old McCroke. I want no gaieties, I want no fine dresses. The simplest mode of life, in a strange country, will suit me best.'

'I can't bear the idea of your going away,' whimpered Mrs Winstanley. 'People will talk so. A stepfather's is such a delicate position. People are sure to say cruel things about Conrad. And it is all your fault, Violet. We might have lived so happily together if you had liked.'

'We might, perhaps, mamma; but I don't think any of us knew the way. Captain Winstanley could hardly expect that to sell my father's favourite horse was the shortest way to my liking; and that's how he began his reign in this house. Don't let us talk any more, my dear mother. Words are useless to heal such wounds as ours. Good-night. Sleep well, and forget all about me. To-morrow you and the Captain can give me my liberty.'

'I thought you were so fond of the Abbey House,' moaned her mother.

'So I was when it was home. It has ceased to be my home, and I shall be glad to leave it.'

'O, Violet, you have a hard heart.'

'Good-night, mamma.'

She was gone, leaving Mrs Winstanley feebly moaning, and vaguely dabbing her forehead, feeling that the Fates had not been kind to her. Life seemed to have gone all askew. It was as if Theodore had taken to sending home misfits. Nothing was smooth or pleasant in an existence whose halcyon calm had once been undisturbed by so much as a crumpled rose-leaf.

Vixen went straight to her room, accompanied by Argus, who had followed her from the hall to the door of her mother's dressing-room, and had waited patiently for her in the corridor, with his head leaning against the closed door, as if he scented trouble within.

When girl and dog were alone together, Violet flung herself on the ground, threw her arms round the mastiff's thick neck, and let her tears flow freely against that faithful head.

'O Argus,' she cried piteously, 'you are the only friend left me in this wide world!'

CHAPTER 34

GOING INTO EXILE

After a long sleepless night of tossing to and fro, Vixen rose with the first stir of life in the old house, and made herself ready to face the bleak hard world. Her meditations of the night had brought no new light to her mind. It was very clear to her that she must go away – as far as possible – from her old home. Her banishment was necessary for everybody's sake. For the sake of Rorie, who must behave like a man of honour, and keep his engagement with Lady Mabel, and shut his old playfellow out of his heart. For the sake of Mrs Winstanley, who could never be happy while there was discord in her home; and last of all, for Violet herself, who felt that joy and peace had fled from the Abbey House for ever, and that it would be better to be anywhere, in the coldest strangest region of this wide earth, verily friendless and alone among strange faces, than here among friends who were but friends in name, and among scenes that were haunted with the ghosts of dead joys.

She went round the gardens and shrubberies in the early morning, looking sadly at everything, as if she were bidding the trees and flowers a long farewell. The rhododendron thickets were shining with dew, the grassy tracks in that wilderness of verdure were wet and cold under Vixen's feet. She wandered in and out among the groups of wild growing shrubs, rising one above another to the height of forest trees, and then she went out by the old five-barred gate which Titmouse used to jump so merrily, and rambled in the plantation till the sun was high, and the pines began to breathe forth their incense as the day-god warmed them into life.

It was half-past eight. Nine was the hour for breakfast, a meal at which, during the Squire's time, the fragile Pamela had rarely appeared, but which, under the present *régime*, she generally graced with her presence. Captain Winstanley was an early riser, and was not sparing in his contempt for sluggish habits.

Vixen had made up her mind never again to sit at meat with her stepfather; so she went straight to her own den, and told Phoebe to bring her a cup of tea.

'I don't want anything else,' she said wearily when the girl suggested a more substantial breakfast; 'I should like to see mamma presently. Do you know if she has gone down?'

'No, miss. Mrs Winstanley is not very well this morning. Pauline has taken her a cup of tea.'

Vixen sat idly by the open window, sipping her tea, and caressing Argus's big head with a listless hand, waiting for the next stroke of fate. She was sorry for her mother, but had no wish to see her. What could they say to each other – they, whose thoughts and feelings were so wide apart? Presently Phoebe came in with a little three-cornered note, written in pencil.

'Pauline asked me to give you this from your ma, miss.'

The note was brief, written in short gasps, with dashes between them.

'I feel too crushed and ill to see you – I have told Conrad what you wish – he is all goodness – he will tell you what we have decided – try to be worthier of his kindness – poor misguided child – he will see you in his study, directly after breakfast – pray control your unhappy temper.'

'His study, indeed!' ejaculated Vixen, tearing up the little note and scattering its perfumed fragments on the breeze; 'my father's room, which he has usurped. I think I hate him just a little worse in that room than anywhere else – though that would seem hardly possible, when I hate him so cordially everywhere.'

She went to her looking-glass, and surveyed herself proudly as she smoothed her shining hair, resolved that he should see no indication of trouble or contrition in her face. She was very pale, but her tears of last night had left no traces. There was a steadiness in her look that befitted an encounter with an enemy. A message came from the Captain, while she was standing before her glass, tying a crimson ribbon under the collar of her white morning-dress.

Would she please to go to Captain Winstanley in the study? She went without an instant's delay; walked quietly into the room, and stood before him silently as he sat at his desk writing.

'Good-morning, Miss Tempest,' he said, looking up at her with his blandest air; 'sit down, if you please. I want to have a chat with you.'

Vixen seated herself in her father's large arm-chair. She was looking round the room absently, dreamily, quite disregarding the Captain. The dear old room was full of sadly sweet associations. For the moment she forgot the existence of her foe. His cold level tones recalled her thoughts from the lamented past to the bitter present.

'Your mother informs me that you wish to leave the Abbey House,' he began; 'and she has empowered me to arrange a suitable home for you elsewhere. I entirely concur in your opinion that your absence from Hampshire for the next year or so will be advantageous to yourself and others. You and Mr Vawdrey have contrived to get yourselves unpleasantly talked about in the neighbourhood. Any further scandal may possibly be prevented by your departure.'

'It is not on that account I wish to leave home,' said Vixen proudly. 'I am not afraid of scandal. If the people hereabouts are so wicked that they cannot see me riding by the side of an old friend for two or three days running without thinking evil of him and me, I am sorry for them, but I certainly should not regulate my life to please them. The reason I wish to leave the Abbey House is that I am miserable here, and have been ever since you entered it as its master. We may as well deal frankly with each other in this matter. You confessed last night that you hated me. I acknowledge to-day that I have hated you ever since I first saw you. It was an instinct.'

'We need not discuss that,' answered the Captain calmly. He had let passion master him last night, but he had himself well in hand to-day. She might be as provoking as she pleased, but she should not provoke him to betray himself as he had done last night. He detested himself for that weak outbreak of passion.

'Have you arranged with my mother for my leaving home?' inquired Vixen.

'Yes, it is all settled.'

'Then I'll write at once to Miss McCroke. I know she will leave the people she is with to travel with me.'

'Miss McCroke has nothing to do with the question. Your roaming about the world with a superannuated governess would be too preposterous. I am going to take you to Jersey by this evening's boat. I have an aunt living there who has a fine old manor house, and who will be happy to take charge of you. She is a maiden lady, a woman of superior cultivation, who devotes herself wholly to intellectual pursuits. Her refining influence will be valuable to you. The island is lovely, the climate delicious. You could not be better off than you will be at Les Tourelles.'

'I am not going to Jersey, and I am not going to your intellectual aunt,' said Vixen resolutely.

'I beg your pardon, you are going, and immediately. Your mother and I have settled the matter between us. You have expressed a wish to leave home, and you will be pleased to go where we think proper. You had better tell Phoebe to pack your trunks. We shall leave here at ten o'clock in the evening. The boat starts from Southampton at midnight.'

Vixen felt herself conquered. She had stated her wish, and it was granted; not in the mode and manner she had desired; but perhaps she ought to be grateful for release from a home that had become loathsome to her, and not take objection to details in the scheme of her exile. To go away, quite away, and immediately, was the grand point. To fly before she saw Rorie again.

'Heaven knows how weak I might be if he were to talk to me again as he talked last night!' she said to herself. 'I might not be able to bear it a second time. O Rorie, if you knew what it cost me to counsel you wisely, to bid you do your duty; when the vision of a happy life with you was smiling at me all the time, when the warm grasp of your dear hand made my heart thrill with joy, what a heroine you would think me! And yet nobody will ever give me credit for heroism; and I shall be remembered only as a self-willed young woman, who was troublesome to her relations, and had to be sent away from home.'

She was thinking this while she sat in her father's chair, deliberating upon the Captain's last speech. She decided presently to yield, and obey her mother and stepfather. After all, what did it matter where she went? That scheme of being happy in Sweden with Miss McCroke was but an idle fancy. In the depths of her inner consciousness Violet Tempest knew that she could be happy nowhere away from Rorie and the Forest. What did it matter, then, whether she went to Jersey or Kamtchatka, the sandy desert of Gobi or the Mountains of the Moon? In either case exile meant moral death, the complete renunciation of all that had been sweet and precious in her uneventful young life – the shadowy beech-groves; the wandering streams; the heathery upland plains; the deep ferny hollows, where the footsteps of humanity were almost unknown; the cluster of tall trees on the hill-top, where the herons came sailing home from their flight across Southampton Water; her childhood's companion; her horse; her old servants. Banishment meant a long farewell to all these.

'I suppose I may take my dog with me?' she asked, after a long pause, during which she had wavered between submission and revolt, 'and my maid?'

'I see no objection to your taking your dog; though I doubt whether my aunt will care to have a dog of that size prowling about her house. He can have a kennel somewhere, I daresay. You must learn to do without a maid. Feminine helplessness is going out of fashion; and one would expect an Amazon like you to be independent of lady's-maids, and milliners.'

'Why don't you state the case in plain English?' cried Vixen scornfully. 'If I took Phoebe with me she would cost money. There would be her wages and maintenance to be provided. If I leave her behind, you can dismiss her. You have a fancy for dismissing old servants.'

'Had not you better see to the packing of your trunks?' asked Captain Winstanley, ignoring this shaft.

'What is to become of my horse?'

'I think you must resign yourself to leave him to fate and me,' replied the Captain coolly; 'my aunt may submit to the infliction of your dog, but that she should tolerate a young lady's roaming about the island on a thoroughbred horse would be rather too much to expect from her old-fashioned notions of propriety.'

'Besides, even Arion would cost something to keep,' retorted Vixen, 'and strict economy is the rule of your life. If you sell him – and, of course, you will do so – please let Lord Mallow have the refusal of him. I think he would buy him, and treat him kindly, for my sake.'

'Wouldn't you rather Mr Vawdrey had him?'

'Yes, if I were free to give him away; but I suppose you would deny my right of property even in the horse my father gave me.'

'Well, as the horse was not specified in your father's will, and as all his horses and carriages were left to your mother, I think there cannot be any doubt that Arion is my wife's property.'

'Why not say your property? Why give unnatural prominence
to a cipher? Do you think I hold my poor mother to blame for
any wrong that is done to me, or to others, in this house? No,
Captain Winstanley, I have no resentment against my mother.
She is a blameless nullity, dressed in the latest fashion.'

'Go and pack your boxes!' cried the Captain angrily. 'Do you
want to raise the devil that was raised last night? Do you want
another conflagration? It might be a worse one this time I have
had a night of fever and unrest.'

'Am I to blame for that?'

'Yes – you beautiful fury. It was your image kept me awake.
I shall sleep sounder when you are out of this house.'

'I shall be ready to start at ten o'clock,' said Vixen, in a
business-like tone which curiously contrasted this sudden gust
of passion on the part of her foe, and humiliated him to the
dust. He loathed himself for having let her see her power to
hurt him.

She left him, and went straight upstairs to her room, and gave
Phoebe directions about the packing of her portmanteaux, with
no more outward semblance of emotion than she might have
shown had she been starting on a round of pleasant visits under
the happiest circumstances. The faithful Phoebe began to cry
when she heard that Miss Tempest was going away for a long
time, and that she was not to go with her; and poor Vixen had
to console her maid instead of brooding upon her own griefs.

'Never mind, Phoebe,' she said; 'it is as hard for me to lose
you as it is for you to lose me. I shall never forget what a
devoted little thing you have been, and all the muddy habits
you have brushed without a murmur. A few years hence I shall
be my own mistress, and have plenty of money, and then,
wherever I may be, you shall come to me. If you are married
you shall be my housekeeper, and your husband shall be my
butler, and your children shall run wild about the place, and be
made as much of as the litter of young foxes Bates reared in a
corner of the stable-yard, when Mr Vawdrey was at Eton.'

'O, miss, I don't want no husband nor no children, I only
want you for my missus. And when you come of age, will you
live here, miss?'

'No. Phoebe. The Abbey House will belong to mamma all her life. Poor mamma! may it be long before the dear old house comes to me. But when I am of age and my own mistress I shall find a place somewhere in the Forest, you may be sure of that, Phoebe.'

Phoebe dried her honest tears, and made haste with the packing, believing that Miss Tempest was leaving home for her own pleasure, and that she, Phoebe, was the only victim of adverse fate.

The day wore on quickly, though it was laden with sorrow. Vixen had a great deal to do in her den; papers to look over, old letters, pen-and-ink sketches, and scribblings of all kinds to destroy, books and photographs to pack. There were certain things she could not leave behind her. Then there was a melancholy hour to spend in the stables, feeding, caressing, and weeping over Arion, who snorted his tenderest snorts, and licked her hands with abject devotion – almost as if he knew they were going to part, Vixen thought.

Last of all came the parting with her mother. Vixen had postponed this with an aching dread of a scene, in which she might perchance lose her temper, and be betrayed into bitter utterances that she would afterwards repent with useless tears. She had spoken the truth to her stepfather when she told him that she held her mother blameless; yet the fact that she had but the smallest share in that mother's heart was cruelly patent to her.

It was nearly four o'clock in the afternoon when Pauline came to Violet's room with a message from Mrs Winstanley. She had been very ill all the morning, Pauline informed Miss Tempest, suffering severely from nervous headache, and obliged to lie in a darkened room. Even now she was barely equal to seeing anyone.

'Then she had better not see me,' said Vixen icily; 'I can write her a little note to say good-bye. Perhaps it would be just as well. Tell mamma that I will write, Pauline.'

Pauline departed with this message, and returned in five minutes with a distressed visage.

'O, miss!' she exclaimed, 'your message quite upset your poor mamma. She said, "How could she?" and began to get almost hysterical. And those hysterical fits end in such fearful headaches.'

'I will come at once,' said Vixen.

Mrs Winstanley was lying on a sofa near an open window, the Spanish blinds lowered to exclude the afternoon sunshine, the perfume of the gardens floating in upon the soft summer air. There were vases of flowers about the room, and an all-pervading perfume and coolness – a charm half sensuous, half aesthetic.

'Violet, how could you send me such a message?' remonstrated the invalid fretfully.

'Dear mother, I did not want to trouble you. I know how you shrink from all painful things; and you and I could hardly part without pain, as we are parting to-day. Would it not have been better to avoid any farewell?'

'If you had any natural affection, you would never have suggested such a thing.'

'Then perhaps I have never had any natural affection,' answered Vixen, with subdued bitterness; 'or only so small a stock that it ran out early in my life, and left me cold and hard and unloving. I am sorry we are parting like this, mamma. I am still more sorry that you could not spare me a little of the regard which you have bestowed so lavishly upon a stranger.'

'Violet, how can you?' sobbed her mother. 'To accuse me of withholding my affection from you, when I have taken such pains with you from your very cradle! I am sure your frocks, from the day you were short-coated, were my constant care; and when you grew a big, lanky girl, who would have looked odious in commonplace clothes, it was my delight to invent picturesque and becoming costumes for you. I have spent hours poring over books of prints, studying Vandyke and Sir Peter Lely, and I have let you wear some of my most valuable lace; and as for indulgence of your whims! Pray when have I ever thwarted you in anything?'

'Forgive me, mamma!' cried Vixen penitently. She divined dimly – even in the midst of that flood of bitter feeling in which her young soul was overwhelmed – that Mrs Winstanley had been a good mother, according to her lights. The tree had bourne such fruits as was natural to its kind. 'Pray forgive me! You have been good and kind and indulgent, and we should have gone on happily together to the end of the chapter, if fate had been kinder.'

'It's no use your talking of fate in that way, Violet,' retorted her mother captiously. 'I know you mean Conrad.'

'Perhaps I do, mamma; but don't let us talk of him any more. We should never agree about him. You and he can be quite happy when I am gone. Poor, dear, trusting, innocent-minded mamma!' cried Vixen, kneeling by her mother's chair and putting her ams round her ever so tenderly. 'May your path of life be smooth and strewn with flowers when I am gone. If Captain Winstanley does not always treat you kindly, he will be a greater scoundrel than I think him. But he has always been kind to you, has he not, mamma? You are not hiding any sorrow of yours from me?' asked Vixen, fixing her great brown eyes on her mother's face with earnest inquiry. She had assumed the maternal part. She seemed an anxious mother questioning her daughter.

'Kind to me,' echoed Mrs Winstanley. 'He has been all goodness. We have never had a difference of opinion since we were married.'

'No, mamma, because you always defer to his opinion.'

'Is not that my duty, when I know how clever and far-seeing he is?'

'Frankly, dear mother, are you as happy with this new husband of yours − so wise and far-seeing, and determined to have his own way in everything − as you were with my dear, indulgent, easy-tempered father?'

Pamela Winstanley burst into a passion of tears.

'How can you be so cruel?' she exclaimed. 'Who can give back the past, or the freshness and brightness of one's youth? Of course I was happier with your dear father than I can ever be again. It is not in nature that it should be otherwise. How could you be so heartless as to ask me such a question?'

She dried her tears slowly, and was not easily comforted. It seemed as if that speech of Violet's had touched a spring that opened a fountain of grief.

'This means that mamma is not happy with her second husband, in spite of her praises of him,' thought Vixen.

She remained kneeling by her mother's side comforting her as best she could, until Mrs Winstanley had recovered from the wound her daughter's heedless words had inflicted, and then Violet began to say good-bye.

'You will write to me sometimes, won't you, mamma, and tell me how the dear old place is going on, and about the old people who die – dear familiar white heads that I shall never see again – and the young people who get married, and the babies that are born? You will write often, won't you, mamma?'

'Yes, dear, as often as my strength will allow.'

'You might even get Pauline to write to me sometimes, to tell me how you are and what you are doing; that would be better than nothing.'

'Pauline shall write when I am not equal to holding a pen,' sighed Mrs Winstanley.

'And, dear mamma, if you can prevent it, don't let any more of the old servants be sent away. If they drop off one by one home will seem like a strange place at last. Remember how they loved my dear father, how attached and faithful they have been to us. They are like our own flesh and blood.'

'I should never willingly part with servants who know my ways, Violet. But as to Bates's dismissal – there are some things I had rather not discuss with you – I am sure that Conrad acted for the best, and from the highest motives.'

'Do you know anything about this place to which I am going, mamma?' asked Vixen, letting her mother's last speech pass without comment; 'or the lady who is to be my duenna?'

'Your future has been fully discussed between Conrad and me, Violet. He tells me that the old Jersey manor house – Les Tourelles it is called – is a delightful place, one of the oldest seats in Jersey, and Miss Skipwith, to whom it belongs, is a well-informed conscientious old lady, very religious, I believe, so you will have to guard against your sad habit of speaking lightly about sacred things, my dear Violet.'

'Do you intend me to live there for ever, mamma?'

'For ever! What a foolish question. In six years you will be of age, and your own mistress.'

'Six years — six years in a Jersey manor house — with a pious old lady. Don't you think that would seem very much like for ever, mamma?' asked Vixen gravely.

'My dear Violet, neither Conrad nor I want to banish you from your natural home. We only want you to learn wisdom. When Mr Vawdrey is married, and when you have learnt to think more kindly of my dear husband——'

'That last change will never happen to me, mamma. I should have to die and be born again first, and, even then, I think my dislike of Captain Winstnaley is so strong that purgatorial fires would hardly burn it out. No, mamma, we had better say good-bye without any forecast of the future. Let us forget all that is sad in our parting, and think we are only going to part for a little while.'

Many a time in after days did Violet Tempest remember those last serious words of hers. The rest of her conversation with her mother was about trifles, the trunks and bonnet-boxes she was to carry with her — the dresses she was to wear in her exile.

'Of course in a retired old house in Jersey, with an elderly maiden lady, you will not see much society,' said Mrs Winstanley; 'but Miss Skipwith must know people — no doubt the best people in the island — and I should not like you to be shabby. Are you really positive that you have dresses enough to carry you over next winter?'

This last question was asked with deepest solemnity.

'More than enough, mamma.'

'And do you think your last winter's jacket will do?'

'Excellently.'

'I'm very glad of that,' said her mother, with a sigh of relief, 'for I have an awful bill of Theodore's hanging over my head. I have been paying her sums on account ever since your poor papa's death; and you know that is never quite satisfactory. All that one has paid hardly seems to make any difference in the amount due at the end.'

'Don't worry yourself about your bill, mamma. Let it stand over till I come of age, and then I can help you to pay it.'

'You are very generous, dear; but Theodore would not wait
so long, even for me. Be sure you take plenty of wraps for the
steamer. Summer nights are often chilly.'

Vixen thought of last night, and the long straight ride
through the pine wood, the soft scented air, the young moon
shining down at her, and Rorie by her side. Ah, when should
she ever know such a summer night as that again?

'Sit down in this low chair by me, and have a cup of tea,
dear,' said Mrs Winstanley, growing more affectionate as the
hour of parting drew nearer. 'Let us have kettledrum together
for the last time, till you come back to us.'

'For the last time, mamma!' echoed Violet sadly.

She could not imagine any possible phase of circumstances
that would favour her return. Could she come back to see
Roderick Vawdrey happy with his wife? Assuredly not. Could
she school herself to endure life under the roof that sheltered
Conrad Winstanley? A thousand times no. Coming home was
something to be dreamt about when she lay asleep in a distant
land; but it was a dream that never could be realised. She must
make herself a new life, somehow, among new people. The old
life died to-day.

She sat and sipped her tea, and listened while her mother
talked cheerfully of the future, and even pretended to agree: but
her heart was heavy as lead.

An hour was dawdled away thus, and then, when Mrs
Winstanley began to think about dressing for dinner, Vixen
went off to finish her packing. She excused herself from going
down to dinner on the plea of having so much to do.

'You could send me up something, please, mamma,' she said.
'I am sure you and Captain Winstanley will dine more
pleasantly without me. I shall see you for a minute in the hall,
before I start.'

'You must do as you please, dear,' replied her mother. 'I
hardly feel equal to going down to dinner myself; but it would
not be fair to let Conrad eat a second meal in solitude,
especially when we are to be parted for two or three days and
he is going across the sea. I shall not have a minute's rest to-
night, thinking of you both.'

'Sleep happily, dear mother, and leave us to Providence. The voyage cannot be perilous in such weather as this,' said Vixen, with assumed cheerfulness.

Two hours later the carriage was at the door, and Violet Tempest was ready to start. Her trunks were on the roof of the brougham, her dressing-bag, and travelling-desk, and wraps were stowed away inside; Argus was by her side, his collar provided with a leather strap, by which she could hold him when necessary. Captain Winstanley was smoking a cigar in the porch.

Mrs Winstanley came weeping out of the drawing-room, and hugged her daughter silently. Violet returned the embrace, but said not a word till just at the last.

'Dear mother,' she whispered earnestly, 'never be unhappy about me. Let me bear the blame of all that has gone amiss between us.'

'You had better be quick, Miss Tempest, if you want to be in time for the boat,' said the Captain from the porch.

'I am quite ready,' answered Vixen calmly.

Phoebe was at the carriage-door, tearful, and in everybody's way, but pretending to help. Argus was sent up to the box, where he sat beside the coachman with much gravity of demeanour, having first assured himself that his mistress was inside the carriage. Mrs Winstanley stood in the porch, kissing her hand; and so the strong big horses bore the carriage away, through the dark shrubberies, between banks of shadowy foliage, out into the forest-road, which was full of ghosts at this late hour, and would have struck terror to the hearts of any horses unaccustomed to its sylvan mysteries.

They drove through Lyndhurst, where the twinkling little lights in the shop-windows were being extinguished by envious shutters, and where the shop-keepers paused in their work of extinction to stare amazedly at the passing carriage; not that a carriage was a strange apparition in Lyndhurst, but because the inhabitants had so little to do except stare.

Anon they came to Bolton's Bench, and then the long straight road to Southampton lay before them in the faint moonshine, with boggy levels, black furze-bushes, and a background of wood on either side. Violet sat looking steadily out of the window, watching every bit of the road. How could she tell when she would see it again – or if ever, save in sad regretful dreams?

They mounted the hill, from whose crest Vixen took one last backward look at the wide wild land that lay behind them – a look of ineffable love and longing. And then she threw herself back in the carriage, and gave herself up to gloomy thought. There was nothing more that she cared to see. They had entered the tame dull world of civilisation.

It was past eleven when they drove under the old bar, and through the high street of Southampton. The town seemed strange to Vixen at this unusual hour. Down by the docks everything had a gray and misty look, sky and water indistinguishable. There lay the Jersey boat, snorting and puffing, amidst the dim grayness. Captain Winstanley conducted his charge to the ladies' cabin, with no more words than were positively necessary. They had not spoken once during the drive from the Abbey House to Southampton.

'I think you had better stay down here till the vessel has started, at any rate,' said the Captain: 'there will be so much bustle and confusion on deck. I'll take care of your dog.'

'Thanks!' answered Vixen meekly. 'Yes, I'll stay here – you need not trouble yourself about me.'

The Captain withdrew to look after the luggage, and to secure his own berth. The stewardess received Violet as if she had known her all her life, showed her the couch allotted to her, and to secure which the Captain had telegraphed that morning from Lyndhurst.

'It was lucky your good gentleman took the precaution to telegraph, mum,' said the cordial stewardess; 'the boats are always crowded at this time of year, and the Fanny is such a favourite.'

It was a dreary voyage for Violet Tempest – a kind of maritime purgatory. The monotonous thud of the engine, the tramping of feet overhead, the creaking and groaning of the vessel, the squalling babies, the fussy mothers, the dreadful people who could not travel from Southampton to Jersey on a

calm summer night without exhibiting all the horrors of
seasickness. Vixen thought of the sufferings of poor black
human creatures in the middle passage, of the ghastly terrors of
a mutiny, of a ship on fire, of the Ancient Mariner on his slimy
sea, when

> 'The very deep did rot; O Christ,
>   That ever this should be;
> Yea, slimy things did crawl with legs
>   Upon the slimy sea!'

She wondered in her weary soul whether these horrors, which
literature had made familiar to her, were much worse than the
smart white and gold cabin of the good ship Fanny, filled to
overflowing with the contents of half-a-dozen nurseries.

Morning came at last, with the skirmishing toilets of the
children, fearful struggles for brushes and combs, towel fights,
perpetual clamour for missing pieces of soap, a great deal of talk
about strings and buttons, and a chorus of crying babies. Then
stole through the stuffy atmosphere savoury odours of breakfast,
the fumes of coffee, fried bacon, grilled fish. Cups of tea were
administered to the sufferers of last night. The yellow sunshine
filled the cabin. Vixen made a hasty toilet, and hurried up to the
deck. Here all was glorious. A vast world of sunlit water. No
sign yet of rock-bound island above the white-crested waves.
The steamer might have been in the midst of the Atlantic.
Captain Winstanley was on the bridge, smoking his morning
cigar. He gave Violet a cool nod, which she returned as coolly.
She found a quiet corner where she could sit and watch the
waves slowly rising and falling, the white foam-crests slowly
gathering, the light spray dashing against the side of the boat,
the cataract of white roaring water leaping from the swift
paddle-wheel and melting into a long track of foam. By-and-by
they came to Guernsey, which looked grim and military, and
not particularly inviting, even in the morning sunlight. That
picturesque island hides her beauties from those who only
behold her from the sea. Here there was an exodus of
passengers, and of luggage, and an invasion of natives with

baskets of fruit. Vixen bought some grapes and peaches of a female native in a cap, whose patois was the funniest perversion of French and English imaginable. And then a bell rang clamorously, and there was a general stampede, and the gangway was pulled up and the vessel was steaming gaily towards Jersey; while Vixen sat eating grapes and looking dreamily skyward, and wondering whether her mother was sleeping peacefully under the dear old Abbey House roof, undisturbed by any pang of remorse for having parted with an only child so lightly.

An hour or so and Jersey was in sight, all rocky peaks and promontories. Anon the steamer swept round a sudden curve, and lo, Vixen beheld a bristling range of fortifications, a rather untidy harbour, and the usual accompaniments of a landing-place, the midsummer sun shining vividly upon the all-pervading whiteness.

'Is this the bay that some people have compared to Naples?' Violet asked her conductor, with a contemptuous curl of her mobile lips, as she and Captain Winstanley took their seats in a roomy old fly, upon which the luggage was being piled in the usual mountainous and insecure-looking style.

'You have not seen it yet from the Neapolitan point of view,' said the Captain. 'This quay is not the prettiest bit of Jersey.'

'I am glad of that, very glad,' answered Vixen acidly; 'for if it were, the Jersey notion of the beautiful would be my idea of ugliness. O what an utterly too horrid street!' she cried, as the fly drove through the squalid approach to the town, past dirty gutter-bred children, and women with babies, who looked to the last degree Irish, and the dead high wall of the fortifications. 'Does your aunt live hereabouts, *par exemple*, Captain Winstanley?'

'My aunt lives six good miles from here, Miss Tempest, in one of the loveliest spots in the island, amidst scenery that is almost as fine as the Pyrenees.'

'I have heard people say that of anything respectable in the shape of a hill,' answered Vixen, with a dubious air.

She was in a humour to take objection to everything, and had a flippant air curiously at variance with the dull aching of her heart. She was determined to take the situation lightly. Not for worlds would she have let Captain Winstanley see her wounds, or guess how deep they were. She set her face steadily towards the hills in which her place of exile was hidden, and bore herself bravely. Conrad Winstanley gave her many a furtive glance as he sat opposite her in the fly, while they drove slowly up the steep green country lanes, leaving the white town in the valley below them.

'The place is not so bad, after all,' said Vixen, looking back at the conglomeration of white walls and slate roofs, of docks and shipping, and barracks, on the edge of a world of blue water, 'not nearly so odious as it looked when we landed. But it is a little disappointing at best, like all places that people praise ridiculously. I had pictured Jersey as a tropical island with cactuses and Cape jasmine growing in the hedges, orchards of peaches and apricots, and melons running wild.'

'To my mind the island is a pocket edition of Devonshire, with a dash of Brittany,' answered the Captain. 'There's a fig-tree for you!' he cried, pointing to a great spreading mass of five-fingered leaves lolloping over a pink-plastered garden-wall – an overgrown old tree that had swallowed up the whole extent of a cottager's garden. 'You don't see anything like that in the Forest.'

'No,' answered Vixen, tightening her lips; 'we have only oaks and beeches that have been growing since the Heptarchy.'

And now they entered a long lane, where the interlaced tree-tops made an arcade of foliage – a lane whose beauty even Vixen could not gainsay. Ah, there were the Hampshire ferns on the steep green banks! She gave a little choking sob at sight of them, as if they had been living things. Hart's-tongue, and lady-fern, and the whole of the asplenium family. Yes; they were all there. It was like home – with a difference.

Here and there they passed a modern villa, in its park-like grounds, and the Captain, who evidently wished to be pleasant, tried to expound to Violet the conditions of Jersey leases, and the difficulties which attend the purchase of land or tenements in that feudal settlement. But Vixen did not even endeavour to

understand him. She listened with an air of polite vacancy
which was not encouraging.

They passed various hunting homesteads, painted a lively
pink, or a refreshing lavender, with gardens where the fuchsias
were trees covered with crimson bloom, and where bright blue
hydrangeas attained a gigantic growth. Here Vixen beheld for
the first time those aspiring cabbages from whose tall stems the
islanders seem to derive a loftier pride than from any other
productions of the island, not excepting its grapes and its
lobsters.

'I don't suppose you ever saw cabbages growing six feet high
before,' said the Captain.

'No,' answered Vixen; 'they are too preposterous to be met
with in a civilised country. Poor Charles the Second! I don't
wonder that he was wild and riotous when he came to be king.'

'Why not?'

'Because he had spent several months of exile among his loyal
subjects in Jersey. A man who had been buried alive in such a
fragmentary bit of the world must have required some
compensation in after life.'

They had mounted a long hill which seemed the pinnacle of
the island, and from whose fertile summit the view was full of
beauty – a green undulating garden-world, ringed with yellow
sands and bright blue sea; and now they began to descend gently
by a winding lane where again the topmost elm-branches were
interwoven, and where the glowing June day was softened to a
tender twilight. A curve in the lane brought them suddenly to
an old gateway, with a crumbling stone bench in a nook beside
it – a bench where the wayfarer used to sit and wait for alms,
when the site of Les Tourelles was occupied by a monastery.

The old manor house rose up behind the dilapidated wall – a
goodly old house as to size and form – overlooking a noble
sweep of hillside and valley; a house with a gallery on the roof
for purposes of observation, but with as dreary and abandoned a
look about its blank curtainless windows as if mansion and
estate had been in Chancery for the last half-century.

'A fine old place, is it not?' asked the Captain, while a
cracked bell was jingling in remote distance, amidst the drowsy

summer stillness, without eliciting so much as the bark of a house-dog.

'It looks very big,' Violet answered dubiously, 'and very empty.'

'My aunt has no relatives residing with her.'

'If she had started in life with a large family of brothers and sisters I should think they would all be dead by this time,' said the girl, with a stifled yawn that was half a sigh.

'How do you mean?'

'They would have died of the stillness and solitude and all-pervading desolation of Les Tourelles.'

'Strange houses are apt to look desolate.'

'Yes. Particularly when the windows have neither blinds nor curtains, and the walls have not been painted for a century.'

After this conversation flagged. The jingling bell was once more set going in the unknown distance; Vixen sat looking sleepily at the arched roof of foliage chequered with blue sky. Argus lolled against the carriage-door with his tongue out.

They waited five minutes or so, languidly expectant. Vixen began to wonder whether the gates would ever open – whether there were really any living human creatures in that blank dead-looking house – whether they would not have to give up all idea of entering, and drive back to the harbour, and return to Hampshire by the way they had come.

While she sat idly wondering thus, with the sleepy buzz of summer insects and melodious twittering of birds soothing her senses like a lullaby, the old gate groaned upon its rusty hinges, and a middle-aged woman in a black gown and a white cap appeared – a female who recognised Captain Winstanley with a curtsy, and came out to receive the smaller packages from the flyman.

'Antony will take the portmanteaux,' she said; 'the boat must have come in earlier than usual. We did not expect you so soon.'

'This is one of Mrs Skipwith's servants,' thought Vixen; 'rather a vinegary personage. I hope the other maids are nicer.'

The person spoke of as Antony now appeared, and began to hale about Violet's portmanteaux. He was a middle-aged man,

with a bald head and a melancholy aspect. His raiment was
shabby; his costume something between that of a lawyer's clerk
and an agricultural labourer. Argus saluted this individual with a
suppressed growl.

'Sh!' cried the female vindictively, flapping her apron at the
dog, 'whose dog is this, sir? He doesn't belong to you, surely?'

'He belongs to Miss Tempest. You must find a corner for
him somewhere in the outbuildings, Hannah,' said the Captain.
'The dog is harmless enough, and friendly enough when he is
used to people.'

'That won't be much good if he bites us before he gets used
to us, and we die of hydrophobia in the mean time,' retorted
Hannah; 'I believe he has taken a dislike to Antony already.'

'Argus won't bite anyone,' said Vixen, laying her hand upon
the dog's collar; 'I'll answer for his good conduct. Please try and
find him a nice snug nest somewhere – if I mustn't have him in
the house.'

'In the house!' cried Hannah. 'Miss Skipwith would faint at
the mention of such a thing. I don't know how she'll ever put
up with a huge beast like that anywhere about the place. He
must be kept as much out of her sight as possible.'

'I'm sorry Argus isn't welcome,' said Vixen proudly.

She was thinking that her own welcome at Les Tourelles
could hardly be more cordial than that accorded to Argus. She
had left home because nobody wanted her there. How could
she expect that anyone wanted her here, where she was a
stranger, preceded, perhaps, by the reputation of her vices? The
woman in the rusty mourning-gown, the man in the shabby
raiment and clodhopper boots, gave her no smile of greeting.
Over this new home of hers there hung an unspeakable
melancholy. Her heart sank as she crossed the threshold.

O, what a neglected, poverty-stricken air the garden had,
after the gardens Violet Tempest had been accustomed to look
upon! Ragged trees, rank grass, empty flower-beds, weeds in
abundance. They went by this paved way to a dingy little door
– not the hall-door, that was never opened – and entered the
house by a lobby, which opened into a small parlour, dark and
shabby, with one window looking into a court-yard. There

were a good many books, and an open desk upon the green-baize table-cover. A spectacle-case on the desk and an arm-chair, before the table indicated that the room had been lately occupied. It was altogether one of the shabbiest rooms Vixen had ever seen – the furniture belonging to the most odious period of cabinet-making, the carpet unutterably dingy, the walls mildewed and mouldy, the sole decorations some pale engravings of naval battles, which might be the victories or defeats of any maritime hero, from Drake to Nelson.

'Come and see the house,' said the Captain, reading the disgust in his stepdaughter's pale face.

He opened a door leading into the hall, a large and lofty apartment, with a fine old staircase ascending to a square gallery. The heavy oak balusters had been painted white, so had the panelling in the wall. Time had converted both to a dusky gray. Some rusty odds and ends of armour and a few dingy family portraits decorated the walls; but of furniture there was not a vestige.

Opening out of the hall there was a large long room with four windows, looking into a small wilderness that had once been garden, and commanding a fine view of land and sea. This the Captain called the drawing-room. It was sparsely furnished with a spindle-legged table, half-a-dozen arm-chairs covered with faded tapestry, an antique walnut-wood cabinet, another of ebony, a small oasis of carpet in the middle of the bare oak floor.

'This and the parlour you have seen are all the sitting-rooms my aunt occupies,' said Captain Winstanley; 'the rest of the rooms on this floor are empty, or only used for storehouses. It is a fine old house; I believe the finest in the island.'

'Is there a history hanging to it?' asked Vixen, looking drearily round the spacious desolate chamber. 'Has it been used as a prison, or a madhouse, or what? I never saw a house that filled me with such nameless horrors.'

'You are fanciful,' said the Captain. 'The house has no story, except the common history of fallen fortunes. It has been in the Skipwith family ever since it was built. They were Leicestershire people, and came to Jersey after the civil war –

came here to be near their prince in his exile – settled here and
built Les Tourelles. I believe they expected Charles would do
something handsome for them when he came into his own, but
he didn't do anything. Sir John Skipwith stayed in the island and
became a large landowner, and died at an advanced age – there
is nothing to kill people here, you see – and the Skipwiths have
been Jersey people ever since. They were once the richest family
in the island; they are now one of the poorest. When I say they,
I mean my aunt. She is the last of her race. The Skipwiths have
crystallised into one maiden lady, my mother's only sister.'

'Then your mother was a Skipwith?' asked Violet.

'Yes.'

'And was she born and brought up here?'

'Yes. She never left Jersey till my father married her. He was
here with his regiment when they met at the governor's ball.
O, here is my aunt,' said the Captain, as a rustling of silk
sounded in the empty hall.

Vixen drew herself up stiffly, as if preparing to meet a foe.
She had made up her mind to detest Miss Skipwith.

The lady of the manor entered. She shook hands with her
nephew, and presented him with a pale and shrivelled cheek,
which he respectfully saluted.

She was an elderly and faded person, very tall and painfully
thin, but aristocratic to the highest degree. There was the
indication of race in her aquiline nose, high narrow brow and
neatly cut chin, her tapering hand and small slender foot. She
was dressed in black silk, rustier and older than any silk Vixen
had ever seen before, not even excepting Mrs Scobel's black silk
dresses, when they had been degraded from their original rank
to the drudgery of early services and daily wear. Her thin gray
hair was shaded by a black lace cap, decorated with bugles and
black weedy grasses. She wore black mittens and jet jewellery,
and was altogether as deeply sable as if she had been in
mourning for the whole of the Skipwith race.

She received Miss Tempest with a formal politeness which
was not encouraging.

'I hope you will be able to make yourself happy here,' she
said; 'and that you have resources within yourself that will

suffice for the employment of your time and thoughts. I receive no company, and I never go out. The class of people who now occupy the island are a class with which I should not care to associate, and which, I daresay, would not appreciate me. I have my own resources, and my life is fully employed. My only complaint is that the days are not long enough. A quiet existence like mine offers vast opportunities for culture and self-improvement. I hope you will take advantage of them, Miss Tempest.'

Poor Violet faltered something vaguely civil, looking sorely bewildered all the time. Miss Skipwith's speech sounded so like the address of a schoolmistress that Vixen began to think she had been trapped unawares in a school, as people are sometimes trapped in a madhouse.

'I don't think Miss Tempest is much given to study,' said the Captain graciously, as if he and Violet were on the friendliest terms; 'but she is very fond of the country, and I am sure the scenery of Jersey will delight her. By the way, we ventured to bring her big dog. He will be a companion and protector for her in her walks. I have asked Doddery to find him a kennel somewhere among your capacious outbuildings.'

'He must not come into the house,' said Miss Skipwith grimly; 'I couldn't have a dog inside my doors. I have a Persian, who has been my attached companion for the last ten years. What would that dear creature's feelings be if he saw himself exposed to the attacks of a savage dog?'

'My dog is not savage, to Persians or anyone else,' cried Vixen, wondering what inauspicious star had led the footsteps of an oriental wanderer to so dreary a refuge as Les Tourelles.

'You would like to see your bedroom, perhaps?' suggested Miss Skipwith, and on Violet's assenting, she was handed over to Hannah Doddery, the woman who had opened the gate.

Hannah led the way up the broad old staircase, all bare and carpetless, and opened one of the doors in the gallery. The room into which she ushered Violet was large and airy, with windows commanding the fair garden-like island, and the wide blue sea. But there was the same bare poverty-stricken look in this room as in every other part of the manor house. The bed

was a tall melancholy four-poster, with scantiest draperies of
faded drab damask. Save for one little islet of threadbare Brussels
beside the bed, the room was carpetless. There was an ancient
wainscot wardrobe with brass handles. There was a modern deal
dressing-table skimpily draped with muslin, and surmounted by
the smallest of looking-glasses. There were a couple of chairs
and a three-cornered washhand-stand. There was neither sofa
nor writing-table. There was not an ornament on the high
wooden mantelshelf, or a picture on the panelled walls. Vixen
shivered as she surveyed the big barren room.

'I think you will find everything comfortable,' said Mrs
Doddery, with a formal air, which seemed to say, 'and whether
you do or do not matters nothing to me.'

'Thank you, yes, I daresay it is all right,' Vixen answered
absently, standing at one of the windows, gazing out over the
green hills and valleys to the fair summer sea, and wondering
whether she would be able to take comfort from the fertile
beauty of the island.

'The bed has been well aired,' continued Mrs Doddery, 'and
I can answer for the cleanliness of everything.'

'Thanks! Will you kindly send one of the maids to help me
unpack my portmanteaux?'

'I can assist you,' Mrs Doddery answered. 'We have no maid-
servant. My husband and I are able to do all that Miss Skipwith
requires. She is a lady who gives so little trouble.'

'Do you mean to say there are no other servants in this great
house – no housemaids, no cook?'

'I have cooked for Miss Skipwith for the last thirty years. The
house is large, but there are very few rooms in occupation.'

'I ought to have brought my maid,' cried Vixen. 'It will be
quite dreadful. I don't want much waiting upon; but still I'm
afraid I shall give some trouble until I learn to do everything for
myself. Just as if I were cast on a desert island,' she said to
herself in conclusion.

'I daresay I shall be able to do all you require, without feeling
it any extra trouble, unless you are very helpless,' said Mrs
Doddery, who was on her knees unstrapping one of the
portmanteaux.

'I am not helpless,' replied Vixen, 'though I daresay I have been waited on much more than was good for me.'

And then she knelt down before the other portmanteau, and undid the buckles of the thick leather straps, in which operation she broke more than one of her nails, and wounded her rosy finger-tips.

'O dear, what a useless creature I am,' she thought; 'and why do people strap portmanteaux so tightly? Never mind, after a month's residence at the Tourelles I shall be a Spartan.'

'Would you like me to unpack your trunks for you?' inquired Mrs Doddery, with an accent which sounded slightly ironical.

'O no, thanks, I can get on very well now,' answered Vixen quickly; whereupon the housekeeper opened the drawers and cupboards in the big wainscot wardrobe, and left Miss Tempest to her own devices.

When she had finished her unpacking she went down to the hall. Not seeing anyone about, and desiring rather to avoid Captain Winstanley and his aunt than to rejoin them, she wandered out of the hall into the many passages of the old manor house, and began a voyage of discovery on her own account.

She found the most curious rooms – or rather rooms that had once been stately and handsome, now applied to the most curious purposes – a dining-hall with carved stone chimney-piece and painted ceiling, used as a storehouse for apples; another fine apartment in which a heap of potatoes reposed snugly in a corner, packed in straw; there was a spacious kitchen with a fireplace as large as a moderate-sized room – a kitchen that had been abandoned altogether to spiders, beetles, rats, and mice. A whole army of four-footed vermin scampered off as Vixen crossed the threshold. She could see them scuttling and scurrying along by the wall, with a whisking of slender tails as they vanished into their holes. The beetles were disporting themselves on the desolate hearth, the spiders had woven draperies for the dim dirty windows. The rustling leaves of a fig-tree, that had grown close to this side of the house, flapped against the window-panes with a noise of exceeding ghostliness.

From the kitchen Vixen wandered to the outhouses, and found Argus howling dismally in a grass-grown court-yard, evidently believing himself abandoned by the world. His rapture at beholding his mistress was boundless.

'You darling, I would give the world to let you loose,' cried Vixen, after she had been nearly knocked down by the dog's affectionate greeting; 'but I mustn't just yet. I'll come by-and-by and take you for a walk. Yes, dear old boy, we'll have a long ramble together, just as we used to do at home.'

Home, now she had left it, seemed so sweet a word that her lips trembled a little as she pronounced it.

Everything without the house was as dreary as it was within. Poverty had set its mark on all things, like a blight. Decay was visible everywhere – in the wood-work, in the stone-work, in hinges and handles, thresholds and lintels, ceilings and plastered walls. It would have cost a thousand pounds to put the manor house in decent habitable order. To have restored it to its original dignity and comeliness would have cost at least five thousand. Miss Skipwith could afford to spend nothing upon the house she lived in: indeed she could barely afford the necessaries of life. So for the last thirty years Les Tourelles had been gradually decaying, until the good old house had arrived at a stage in which decay could hardly go farther without lapsing into destruction.

A door opened out of the court-yard into the weedy garden. This was not without a kind of beauty that had survived long neglect. The spreading fig-trees, the bushes of bright red fuchsia, and the unpruned roses made a fertile wilderness of flowers and foliage. There was a terrace in front of the drawing-room windows, and from this a flight of crumbling moss-grown stone steps led down to the garden, which was on the slope of the hill, and lay considerably below the level of the house.

While Vixen was perambulating the garden, a bell rang in a cupola on the roof; and as this sounded like the summons to a meal, she felt that politeness, if not appetite, demanded her return to the house.

'Three o'clock,' she said, looking at her watch. 'What a late hour for luncheon!'

She made her way back to the small side-door at which she had entered with Captain Winstanley, and went into the parlour, where she found the Captain and his aunt. The table was laid, but they had not seated themselves.

'I hope I have not kept you waiting,' Vixen said apologetically.

'My aunt has been waiting five minutes or so; but I'm sure she will forgive you, as you don't yet know the ways of the house,' replied the Captain amiably.

'We have early habits at Les Tourelles, Miss Tempest,' said the lady of the manor: 'we breakfast at half-past seven and dine at three; that arrangement gives me a long morning for study. At six we drink tea, and, if you care for supper, it can be served for you on a tray at half-past nine. The house is shut, and all lamps put out, at ten.'

'As regularly as on board ship,' said the Captain. 'I know the customs of the manor of old.'

'You have never favoured me with a long visit, Conrad,' remarked Miss Skipwith reproachfully.

'My life has been too busy for making long visits anywhere, my dear aunt.'

They took their places at the small square table, and Miss Skipwith said grace. Antony Doddery was in attendance, clad in rusty black, and looking as like a butler as a man who cleaned windows, scrubbed floors, and hewed wood could be fairly expected to look. He removed the cover of a modest dish of fish with a grand air, and performed all the services of the table with as much dignity as if he had never been anything less than a butler. He poured out a glass of ale for the Captain and a glass of water for his mistress. Miss Skipwith seemed relieved when Violet said she preferred water to ale, and did not particularly care about wine.

'I used to drink wine at home very often, just because it was put in my glass, but I like water quite as well,' said Vixen.

After the fish there came a small joint of lamb, and a couple of dishes of vegetables; then a small custard pudding, and some cheese cut up in very minute pieces in a glass dish, some raw garden-stuff which Doddery called salad, and three of last year's pears in an old Derby dessert-dish. The dinner could hardly have been smaller, but it was eminently genteel.

The conversation was entirely between Captain Winstanley and his aunt. Vixen sat and listened wonderingly, save at odd times, when her thoughts strayed back to the old life which she had done with for ever.

'You still continue your literary labours, I suppose, aunt,' said the Captain.

'They are the chief object of my existence. When I abandon them I shall have done with life,' replied Miss Skipwith gravely.

'But you have not yet published your book.'

'No; I hope when I do that even you will hear of it.'

'I have no doubt it will make a sensation.'

'If it does not I have lived and laboured in vain. But my book may make a sensation, and yet fall far short of the result which I have toiled and hoped for.'

'And that is——'

'The establishment of a universal religion.'

'That is a large idea!'

'Would a small idea be worth the devotion of a life? For thirty years I have devoted myself to this one scheme. I have striven to focus all the creeds of mankind in one brilliant centre – eliminating all that is base and superstitious in each several religion, crystallising all that is good and true. The Buddhist, the Brahmin, the Mahomedan, the Sun-worshipper, the Romanist, the Calvinist, the Lutheran, the Wesleyan, the Swedenborgian – each and all will find the best and noblest characteristics of his faith resolved and concentrated in my universal religion. Here all creeds will meet. Gentler and wiser than the theology of Buddha; more humanitarian than the laws of Brahma; more temperate than the Moslem's code of morality; with a wider grasp of power than the Romanist's authoritative church; severely self-denying as Calvin's ascetic rule; simple and pious as Wesley's scheme of man's redemption; spiritual as Swedenborg's vast idea of heaven; – my faith will open its arms wide enough to embrace all. There need be no more dissent. The mighty circle of my free church will enclose all creeds and all divisions of man, and spread from the northern hemisphere to the southern seas. Heathenism shall perish before it. The limited view of Christianity which missionaries have hitherto offered to the heathen may fail: but my universal church will open its doors to all the world – and, mark my words, Conrad, all the world will enter in. I may not live to see the day. My span of life has not long to run – but that day will come.'

'No doubt,' replied Captain Winstanley gravely. 'There is a slovenliness, so to speak, about the present arrangement of things, and a great deal of useless expense; every small town with its half-a-dozen churches and chapels of different denominations – Episcopalians, Wesleyans, Baptists, Roman Catholics, Primitive Methodists. Now on your plan one large building would do for all, like the town-hall or the general post-office. There would be a wonderful economy.'

'I fear you contemplate the question from an entirely temporal point of view,' said Miss Skipwith, flattered but yet reproachful. 'It is its spiritual aspect that is grandest.'

'Naturally. But a man of the world is apt to consider the practicability of a scheme. And yours seems to me eminently practical. If you can only get the Mahomedans and the Brahmins to come in! The Roman Catholics might of course be easily won, though it would involve doing away with the Pope. There was a prophecy, by the way, that after the ninth Pius there would be only eleven more Popes. No doubt that prophecy pointed at your universal religion. But I fear you may have some difficulty about the Buddhists. I fancy they are rather a bigoted sect.'

'The greatest bigots have but to be convinced,' said Miss Skipwith. 'St Paul was a bigot.'

'True. Is your book nearly finished?'

'No. There are still some years of labour before me. I am now working at the Swedenborgian portion, striving to demonstrate how that great man's scheme of religion, though commonly supposed to be a new and original emanation of one mind, is in reality a reproduction of spiritual views common to older religions. The Buddhists were Swedenborgians without knowing it, just as Swedenborg unconsciously was a Buddhist.'

'I begin to understand. The process which you are engaged in is a kind of spiritual chemistry, in which you resolve each particular faith into its primary elements; with a view to prove

that those elements are actually the same in all creeds; and that
the differences which heretofore have kept mankind apart are
mere divergencies of detail.'

'That, crudely and imperfectly stated, is my aim,' replied Miss
Skipwith graciously.

This kind of conversation continued all through dinner, Miss
Skipwith talked of Buddha, and Confucius, and Mahomet, and
Zuinglius, and Calvin, and Luther, as familiarly as if they had
been her most intimate friends; and the Captain led her on and
played her as he would have played a trout in one of the
winding Hampshire streams. His gravity was imperturbable.
Vixen sat and wondered whether she was to hear this kind of
thing every day of her life, and whether she would be expected
to ask Miss Skipwith leading questions, as the Captain was
doing. It was all very well for him, who was to spend only one
day at Les Tourelles; but Vixen made up her mind that she
would boldly avow her indifference to all creeds and all
theologians, from Confucius to Swedenborg. She might consent
to live for a time amidst the dulness and desolation of Les
Tourelles, but she would not be weighed down and crushed by
Miss Skipwith's appalling hobby. The mere idea of having
every day to discuss a subject that was in its very nature
inexhaustible, filled her with terror.

'I would sooner take my meals in that abandoned kitchen,
among the rats and beetles, than have to listen every day to this
kind of thing,' she thought.

When dinner was over the Captain went off to smoke his
cigar in the garden, and this Vixen thought a good time for
making her escape.

'I should like to take a walk with my dog, if you will excuse
me, Miss Skipwith,' she said politely.

'My dear, you must consider yourself at liberty to employ and
amuse yourself as you please, of course always keeping strictly
within the bounds of propriety,' solemnly replied the lady of
the manor. 'I shall not interfere with your freedom. My own
studies are of so grave a nature that they in a measure isolate me
from my fellow-creatures, but when you require and ask for
sympathy and advice, I shall be ready to give both. My library is

at your service, and I hope ere long you will have found yourself some serious aim for your studies. Life without purpose is a life hardly worth living. If girls of your age could only find that out, and seek their vocation early, how much grander and nobler would be woman's place in the universe. But, alas! my dear, the common aim of girlhood seems to be to look pretty and to get married.'

'I have made up my mind never to marry,' said Violet, with a smile that was half sad half cynical; 'so there at least you may approve of me, Miss Skipwith.'

'My nephew tells me that you refused an excellent offer from an Irish peer.'

'I would not have done the Irish peer so great a wrong as to have married him without loving him.'

'I admire your honourable feeling,' said Miss Skipwith, with solemn approval; 'I, too, might have married, but the man towards whom my heart most inclined was a man of no family. I could not marry a man without family. I am weak enough to be prouder of my pedigree than other women are of beauty and fortune. I am the last of the Skipwiths, and I have done nothing to degrade my race. The family name and the family pride will die with me. There was a time when a Skipwith owned a third of the island. Our estate has dwindled to the garden and meadows that surround this old house; our family has shrunk into one old woman; but if I can make the name of Skipwith famous before I go down to my grave, I shall not have lived and laboured in vain.'

Vixen felt a thrill of pity as she listened to this brief confession of a self-deluded solitary soul, which had built its house upon sand, as hopefully as if the foundations were solidest rock. The line of demarcation between such fanaticism as Miss Skipwith's and the hallucination of an old lady in Bedlam, who fancies herself Queen Victoria, seemed to Vixen but a hair's breadth. But, after all, if the old lady and Miss Skipwith were both happy in their harmless self-deceptions, why should one pity them? The creature to be pitied is the man or woman who keenly sees and feels the hard realities of life, and cannot take pleasure in phantoms.

Vixen ran off to her room to get her hat and gloves, delighted to find herself free. Miss Skipwith was not such a very bad sort of person, after all, perhaps. Liberty to roam about the island with her dog, Vixen esteemed a great boon. She would be able to think about her troubles, unmolested by inquisitive looks or unwelcome sympathy.

She went down to the court-yard, untied the faithful Argus, and they set out together to explore the unknown, the dog in such wild spirits that it was almost impossible for Vixen to be sad. The afternoon sun was shining in all his glory, birds were singing, flickering lights and shadows playing on the grassy banks. Argus scampered up and down the lanes, and burst tumultuously through gaps in the hedges, like a dog possessed of demons.

It was a pretty little island, after all; Vixen was fain to admit as much. There was some justification for the people who sang its praises with such enthusiasm. One might have fancied it a fertile corner of Devonshire that had slipped its moorings and drifted westward on a summer sea.

'If I had Arion here, and – Rorie, I think I could be almost happy,' Vixen said to herself with a dreamy smile.

'And Rorie!'

Alas, poor child! faintly, feebly steadfast in the barren path of honour: where could she not have been happy with the companion of her childhood, the one only love of her youth? Was there ever a spot of land or sea where she could not have been happy with Roderick Vawdrey?

Poor Rorie! She knew how well she loved him, now that the wide sea rolled between them, now that she had said him nay, denied her love, and parted from him for ever.

She thought of that scene in the pine wood, dimly lit by the young moon. She lived again those magical moments – the concentrated bliss and pain of a lifetime. She felt again the strong grasp of his hands, his breath upon her cheek, as he bent over her shoulder. Again she heard him pleading for the life-long union her soul desired as the most exquisite happiness life could give.

> 'I had not loved thee, dear, so well
> Loved I not honour more.'

Those two familiar lines flashed into her mind as she thought of her lover. To have degraded herself, to have dishonoured him; no, it would have been too dreadful! Were he to plead again she must answer again as she had answered before.

'His mother despised me,' she thought. 'If people in a better world are really *au courant* as to the affairs of this, I should like Lady Jane Vawdrey to know that I am not utterly without the instincts of a gentlewoman.'

She wandered on, following the winding of the lanes, careless where she went, and determined to take advantage of her liberty. She met few people, and of those she did not trouble herself to ask the way.

'If I lose myself on my desert island it can't much matter,' she thought. 'There is no one to be anxious about me. Miss Skipwith will be deep in her universal creed, and Captain Winstanley would be very glad for me to be lost. My death would leave him master for life of the Abbey House and all belonging to it.'

She roamed on till she came to the open seashore; a pretty little harbour surrounded with quaint-looking houses; two or three white villas in fertile gardens, on a raised road; and dominating all the scene, a fine old feudal castle, with keep, battlements, drawbridge, portcullis, and all that becomes a fortress.

This was Mount Orgueil, the castle in which Charles Stuart spent a short period of his life, while Cromwell was ruling by land and sea, and kingly hopes were at their lowest ebb. The good old fortress had suffered for its loyalty, for the Parliament sent Admiral Blake, with a fleet, to reduce the rebellious island to submission, and Mount Orgueil had not been strong enough to hold out against its assailants.

Violet went up the sloping pah that led to the grim old gateway under the gloomy arch, and still upward till she came to a sunny battlemented wall above the shining sea. The prospect was more than worth the trouble. Yonder, in the dim distance, were the towers of Coutance Cathedral; far away, mere spots in the blue water, were the smaller fry of the Channel Islands; below her, the yellow sands were smiling in

the sun, the placid wavelets reflecting all the colour and glory of
the changeful sky.

'This would not be a bad place to live in, Argus, if——'

She paused, with her arm round her dog's neck, as he
stood on end, looking over the parapet, with a deep interest
in possible rats or rabbits lurking in some cavity of the craggy
cliff below. If! Ah, what a big 'if' that was! It meant love
and dear familiar companionship. It meant all Vixen's little
world.

She lingered long. The scene was beautiful, and there was
nothing to lure her home. Then, at last, feeling that she was
treating poor Miss Skipwith badly, and that her prolonged
absence might give alarm in that dreary household, she retraced
her steps, and at the foot of the craggy mount asked the nearest
way to Les Tourelles.

The nearest way was altogether different from the track by
which she had come, and brought her back to the old monastic
gate in a little more than an hour. She opened the gate and
went in. There was nothing for the most burglarious invader to
steal at Les Tourelles, and bolts and locks were rarely used. Miss
Skipwith was reading in her parlour, a white Persian cat dozing
on a cushioned arm-chair beside her, some cups and saucers and
a black teapot on a tray before her, and the rest of the table
piled with books. There was no sign of Captain Winstanley.

'I'm afraid I'm rather late,' Vixen said apologetically.

She felt a kind of half-pitying respect for Miss Skipwith, as a
harmless lunatic.

'My dear, I daresay that as an absolute fact you are late,'
answered the lady of the manor, without looking up from her
book, 'but as time is never too long for me, I have been hardly
conscious of the delay. Your stepfather has gone down to the
club at St Helier's to see some of his old acquaintance. Perhaps
you would like a cup of tea?'

Vixen replied that she would very much like some tea,
whereupon Miss Skipwith poured out a weak and tepid
infusion, against which the girl inwardly protested.

'If I am to exist at Les Tourelles, I must at least have decent
tea,' she said to herself. 'I must buy an occasional pound for my

own consumption, make friends with Mrs Doddery, and get her to brew it for me.'

And then Vixen knelt down by the arm-chair and tried to get upon intimate terms with the Persian. He was a serious-minded animal, and seemed inclined to resent her advances, so she left him in peace on his patchwork cushion, a relic of those earlier days when Miss Skipwith had squandered her precious hours on the feminine insanity of needlework.

Vixen went to her room soon after dark, and thus avoided the Captain, who did not return till ten. She was worn out with the fatigue of the voyage, her long ramble, the painful thoughts and manifold agitations of the last two days. She set her candle on the dressing-table, and looked round the bare empty room, feeling as if she were in a dream. It was all strange, and unhomely, and comfortless; like one of those wild dream-pictures which seem so appallingly real in their hideous unreality.

'And I am to live here indefinitely – for the next six years, perhaps, until I come of age and am my own mistress. It is too dreadful!'

She went to bed and slept a deep and comforting sleep, for very weariness: and she dreamt that she was walking on the battlements of Mount Orgueil, in the drowsy afternoon sunlight, with Charles Stuart; and the face of the royal exile was the face of Roderick Vawdrey, and the hand that held hers as they two stood side by side in the sunshine was the broad strong hand of her girlhood's friend.

When she went downstairs between eight and nine next morning, she found Miss Skipwith pacing slowly to and fro the terrace in front of the drawing-room windows, conning over the pencil notes of her yesterday's studies.

'Your stepfather has been gone half-an-hour, my dear,' said the lady of the manor. 'He was very sorry to have to go without wishing you good-bye.'

CHAPTER 35

CHIEFLY FINANCIAL

Violet was gone. Her rooms were empty; her faithful little waiting-maid was dismissed; her dog's deep-toned thunder no longer sounded through the house, baying joyous welcome when his mistress came down for her early morning ramble in the shrubberies. Arion had been sent to grass. Nothing associated with the exiled heiress was left, except the rooms she had inhabited; and even they looked blank and empty and strange without her. It was almost as if a whole family had departed. Vixen's presence seemed to have filled the house with youth, and freshness, and free joyous life. Without her all was silent as the grave.

Mrs Winstanley missed her daughter sorely. She had been wont to complain fretfully of the girl's exuberance; but the blank her absence made struck a chill to the mother's heart. She had fancied that life would be easier without Violet; that her union with her husband would be more complete; and now she found herself looking wistfully towards the door of her morning-room, listening vaguely for a footstep; and the figure she looked for at the door, and the footsteps she listened for in the corridor were not Conrad Winstanley's. It was the buoyant step of her daughter she missed; it was the bright frank face of her daughter she yearned for.

One day the Captain surprised her in tears, and asked the reason of her melancholy.

'I daresay it's very weak of me, Conrad,' she said piteously, 'but I miss Violet more and more every day.'

'It is uncommonly weak of you,' answered the Captain with agreeable candour, 'but I suppose it's natural. People generally get attached to their worries; and as your daughter was an incessant worry, you very naturally lament her absence. I am honest enough to confess that I am very glad she is gone. We had no domestic peace while she was with us.'

'But she is not to stay away for ever, Conrad. I cannot be separated from my only daughter for ever. That would be too dreadful.'

'"For ever" is a long word,' answered the Captain coolly. 'She will come back to us – of course.'

'When, dear?'

'When she is older and wiser.'

This was cold comfort. Mrs Winstanley dried her tears, and resumed her crewel-work. The interesting variety of shades in green which modern art has discovered were a source of comfort to the mother's troubled mind. Moved to emulation by the results that had been achieved in artistic needlework by the school at South Kensington and the Royal Tapestry Manufactory at Windsor. Pamela found in her crewel-work an all-absorbing labour. Matilda of Normandy could hardly have toiled more industriously at the Bayeux tapestry than did Mrs Winstanley, in the effort to immortalise the fleeting glories of woodland blossom or costly orchid upon kitchen towelling.

It was a dull and lonely life which the mistress of the Abbey House led in these latter days of glowing summer weather; and perhaps it was only the distractions of crewels and point-lace which preserved her from melancholy madness. The Captain had been too long a bachelor to renounce the agreeable habits of a bachelor's existence. His amusements were all masculine, and more or less solitary. When there was no hunting, he gave himself up to fishing, and found his chief delight in the persecution of innocent salmon far afield beyond Ringwood. He supplied the Abbey House larder with fish, sent an occasional basket to a friend, and despatched the surplus produce of his rod to a fishmonger in London. He was an enthusiast at billiards, and would play with innocent Mr Scobel rather than not play at all. He read every newspaper and periodical of mark that was published. He rode a good deal, and drove not a little in a high-wheeled dog-cart; quite an impossible vehicle for a lady. He transacted all the business of house, stable, gardens, and home-farm, and that in the most precise and punctual manner. He wrote a good many letters, and he smoked six or seven cigars every day. It must be obvious, therefore, that he had very little time to devote to his middle-aged wife, whose languid airs and vapourish graces were likely to pall upon an ardent temper after a year of married life.

Yet, though she found her days lonely, Mrs Winstanley had no
ground for complaint. What fault could a woman find in a
husband who was always courteous and complimentary in his
speech, whose domestic tastes were obvious, who thought it no
trouble to supervise the smallest details of the household, who
could order a dinner, lay out a garden, stock a conservatory, or
amend the sanitary arrangements of a stable with equal
cleverness; who never neglected a duty towards wife or society?

Mrs Winstanley could see no flaw in the perfection of her
husband's character; but it began about this time slowly to dawn
upon her languid soul that, as Captain Winstanley's wife, she
was not so happy as she had been as Squire Tempest's widow.

Her independence was gone utterly. She awoke slowly to the
comprehension of that fact. Her individuality was blotted out,
or absorbed into her husband's being. She had no more power
or influence in her own house than the lowest scullion in her
kitchen. She had given up her banking account, and the receipt
of her rents, which in the days of her widowhood had been
remitted to her half-yearly by the solicitor who collected them.
Captain Winstanley had taken upon himself the stewardship of
his wife's income. She had been inclined to cling to her
cheque-book and her banking account at Southampton; but the
Captain had persuaded her of the folly of such an arrangement.

'Why two balances and two accounts, when one will do?' he
argued. 'You have only to ask me for a cheque when you want
it, or to give me your bills.'

Whereupon the bride of six weeks had yielded graciously,
and the balance had been transferred from the Southampton
bank to Captain Winstanley's account at the Union.

But now, with Theodore's unsettled account of four years'
standing hanging over her head by the single hair of the penny
post, and likely to descend upon her any morning, Mrs
Winstanley regretted her surrendered banking account, with its
balance of eleven hundred pounds or so. The Captain had
managed everything with wondrous wisdom, no doubt. He had
done away with all long credits. He paid all his bills on the first
Saturday in the month, save such as could be paid weekly. He
had reduced the price of almost everything supplied to the

Abbey House, from the stable provender to the wax candles that lighted the faded sea-green draperies and white panelling of the drawing-room. The only expenditure over which he had no control was his wife's private disbursement; but he had a habit of looking surprised when she asked him for a cheque, and a businesslike way of asking the amount required, which prevented her applying to him often. Still, there was that long-standing account of Madame Theodore's in the background, and Mrs Winstanley felt that it was an account which must be settled sooner or later. Her disinclination to ask her husband for money had tended to swell Theodore's bill. She had bought gloves, ribbons, shoes, everything, from that tasteful purveyor, and had even obtained the somewhat expensive materials for her fancy work through Madame Theodore; a temporary convenience which she could hardly hope to enjoy gratis.

Like all weak women she had her occasional longings for independence, her moments of inward revolt against the smooth tyrant. The income was hers, she argued with herself sometimes, and she had a right to spend her own money as she pleased. But then she recalled her husband's grave warnings about the future and its insecurity. She had but a brief lease of her present wealth, and he was labouring to lay by a provision for the days to come.

'It would be wicked of me to thwart him in such a wise purpose,' she told herself.

The restriction of her charities pained the soft-hearted Pamela not a little. To give to all who asked her had been the one unselfish pleasure of her narrow soul. She had been imposed upon, of course; had fed families whose fathers squandered their weekly wages in the cosy taproom of a village inn; had in some wise encouraged idleness and improvident living; but she had been the comforter of many a weary heart, the benefactor of many a patient care-oppressed mother, the raiser-up of many a sickly child drooping on its bed of pain.

Now, under the Captain's rule, she had the pleasure of seeing her name honourably recorded in the subscription list of every local charity; but her hand was no longer open to the surrounding poor; her good old Saxon name of Lady had lost its

ancient significance. She was no longer the giver of bread to the
hungry. She sighed and submitted, acknowledging her
husband's superior wisdom.

'You would not like to live in a semi-detached villa on the
Southampton Road, would you, my dear Pamela?' asked the
Captain.

'I might die in a semi-detached house, Conrad. I'm sure I
could not live in one,' she exclaimed piteously.

'Then, my love, we must make a tremendous effort, and save
all we can before your daughter comes of age, or else we shall
assuredly have to leave the Abbey House. We might go abroad
certainly, and live at Dinan, or some quiet old French town
where provisions are cheap.'

'My dear Conrad, I could not exist in one of the old French
towns, smelling perpetually of cabbage-soup.'

'Then, my dear love, we must exercise the strictest economy,
or life will be impossible six years hence.'

Pamela sighed and assented, with a sinking of her heart. To
her mind this word economy was absolutely the most odious in
the English language. Her life was made up of trifles, and they
were all expensive trifles. She liked to be better dressed than any
woman of her acquaintance. She liked to surround herself with
pretty things; and the prettiness must take the most fashionable
form, and be frequently renewed. She had dim ideas which she
considered aesthetic, and which involved a good deal of shifting
and improving of furniture.

Against all these expensive follies Captain Winstanley set his
face sternly, using pretty words to his wife at all times, but
proving himself as hard as rock when she tried to bend him to
her will. He had not yet interfered with her toilet, for he had
yet to learn what that cost.

This knowledge came upon him like a thunder-clap one
sultry morning in July – real thunder impending in the metallic-
tinted sky – about a month after Vixen's departure.

Theodore's long-expected bill was among the letters in the
morning's bag – a bulky envelope, which the Captain handed
to his wife with his usual politeness. He never opened her
letters, but he invariably asked to see them, and she always

handed her correspondence over to him with a childlike meekness. To-day she was slow to hand the Captain her letter. She sat looking at the long list of items with a clouded brow, and forgot to pour out her husband's coffee in the abstraction of a troubled mind.

'I'm afraid your letters of this morning are not of a very pleasant character, my love,' said the Captain, watchful of his wife's clouded countenance. 'Is that a bill you are examining? I thought we paid ready money for everything.'

'It is my dressmaker's bill,' faltered Mrs Winstanley.

'A dressmaker's bill! That can't be very alarming. You look as awful, and the document looks as voluminous, as if it were a lawyer's bill, including the costs of two or three unlucky Chancery suits, or half-a-dozen conveyances. Let me have the account, dear, and I'll send your dressmaker a cheque next Saturday.'

He held out his hand for the paper, but Pamela did not give it to him.

'I'm afraid you'll think it awfully high, Conrad,' she said, in a deprecating tone. 'You see it has been running a long time – since the Christmas before dear Edward's death, in fact. I have paid Theodore sums on account in the meanwhile, but those seem to go for very little against the total of her bill. She is expensive, of course. All West-End milliners are; but her style is undeniable, and she is in direct association with Worth.'

'My dear Pamela, I did not ask you for her biography, I asked only for her bill. Pray let me see the total, and tell me if you have any objections to make against the items.'

'No,' sighed Mrs Winstanley, bending over the document with a perplexed brow, 'I believe – indeed, I am sure – I have had all the things. Many of them are dearer than I expected; but there is no rule as to the price of anything thoroughly Parisian, that has not been seen in London. One has to pay for style and originality. I hope you won't be vexed at having to write so large a cheque, Conrad, at a time when you are so anxious to save money. Next year I shall try my best to economise.'

'My dearest Pamela, why beat about the bush? The bill must be paid, whatever its amount. I suppose a hundred pounds will cover it?'

'O Conrad, when many women give a hundred pounds for a single dress!'

'When they do I should say that Bedlam must be their natural and fitting abode,' retorted the Captain, with suppressed ire. 'The bill is more than a hundred then? Pray give it me, Pamela, and make an end of this foolishness.'

This time Captain Winstanley went over to his wife, and took the paper out of her hand. He had not seen the total, but he was white with rage already. He had made up his mind to squeeze a small fortune out of the Abbey House estate during his brief lease of the property: and here was this foolish wife of his squandering hundreds upon finery.

'Be kind enough to pour me out a cup of coffee,' he said, resuming his seat, and deliberately spreading out the bill.

'Great Heaven!' he cried, after a glance at the total. 'This is too preposterous. The woman must be mad.'

The total was seventeen hundred and sixty-four pounds fourteen and sixpence. Mrs Winstanley's payments on account amounted to four hundred pounds; leaving a balance of thirteen hundred and sixty-four pounds for the Captain to liquidate.

'Indeed, dear Conrad, it is not such a very tremendous account,' pleaded Pamela, appalled by the expression of her husband's face. 'Theodore has customers who spend two thousand a year with her.'

'Very laudable extravagance, if they are the wives of millionaires, and have silver-mines or cotton-mills, or oil-wells to maintain them. But that the widow of a Hampshire squire, a lady who six years hence will have to exist upon a pittance, should run up such a bill as this, is to my mind an act of folly that is almost criminal. From this moment I abandon all my ideas of nursing your estate, of providing comfortably for our future. Henceforward we must drift towards insolvency, like other people. It would be worse than useless for me to go on racking my brains in the endeavour to secure a given result, when behind my back your thoughtless extravagance is stultifying all my efforts.'

Here Mrs Winstanley dissolved into tears.

'O, Conrad! How can you say such cruel things?' she sobbed. 'I go behind your back! I stultify you! When I have allowed myself to be ruled and governed in everything! When I have even parted with my only child to please you!'

'Not till your only child tried to set the house on fire.'

'Indeed, Conrad, you are mistaken there. She never meant it.'

'I know nothing about her meaning,' said the Captain moodily. 'She did it.'

'It is too cruel, after all my sacrifices, that I should be called extravagant − and foolish − and criminal. I have only dressed as a lady ought to dress − out of mere self-respect. Dear Edward always liked to see me look nice. He never said an unkind word about my bills. It is a sad − sad change for me.'

'Your future will be a sadder change, if you go on in the way you are going,' retorted the Captain. 'Let me see: your income, after Violet comes of age, is to be fifteen hundred a year. You have been spending six hundred a year upon millinery. If you go on dressing at the same rate we shall have nine hundred for everything else − stable, garden, coals, taxes, servants' wages, wine − to say nothing of such trifling claims as butcher and baker, and the rest of it. You will have to manage with wonderful cleverness to make both ends meet.'

'I am sure I would sacrifice anything rather than live unhappily with you, Conrad,' Mrs Winstanley murmured piteously, drinking much strong tea in her agitation, the cup shaking in her poor little white weak hand. 'Nothing could be so dreadful to me as to live on bad terms with you. I have surrendered so much for your love, Conrad. What would become of me, if I lost that? I will give up dealing with Theodore, if you like − though it will be a hard trial, after she has worked for me so many years, and has studied my style and knows exactly what suits me. I will dress ever so plainly, and even have my gowns made by a Southampton dressmaker, though I know you will hardly recognise me in them. But I will do anything − anything, Conrad, rather than hear you speak so cruelly.'

She went over to him and laid her hand tremulously on his shoulder, and looked down at him with piteous, pleading eyes.

No Circassian slave, afraid of bowstring and sack, could have entreated her master's clemency with deeper self-abasement.

Even Conrad Winstanley's hard nature was touched by the piteousness of her look and tone. He took the hand gently and raised it to his lips.

'I don't mean to be cruel, Pamela,' he said. 'I only want you to face the truth, and to understand your future position. It is your own money you are squandering, and you have a right to waste it, if it pleases you to do so. But it is a little hard for a man who has laboured and schemed for a given result, suddenly to find himself out in his calculations by so much as thirteen hundred and sixty-four pounds. Let us say no more about it, my dear. Here is the bill, and it must be paid. We have only to consider the items, and see if the prices are reasonable.'

And then the Captain, with bent brow and serious aspect, began to read the lengthy record of an English lady's folly. Most of the items he passed over in silence, or with only a sigh, keeping his wife by his side, looking over his shoulder.

'Point out anything that is wrong,' he said; but as yet Mrs Winstanley had found no error in the bill.

Sometimes there came an item which moved the Captain to speech. 'A dinner-dress, *pain brûlé* brocade, mixed *poult de soie*, *manteau de cour*, lined ivory satin, trimmed with hand-worked embroidery of wild flowers on Brussels net, sixty-three pounds.'

'What in the name of all that's reasonable is *pain brûlé*?' asked the Captain impatiently.

'It's the colour, Conrad. One of those delicate tertiaries that have been so much worn lately.'

'Sixty guineas for a dinner-dress! That's rather stiff. Do you know that a suit of dress clothes costs me nine pounds, and lasts almost as many years?'

'My dear Conrad, for a man it is so different. No one looks at your clothes. That dress was for Lady Ellangowan's dinner. You made me very happy that night, for you told me I was the best-dressed woman in the room.'

'I should not have been very happy myself if I had known the cost of your gown,' answered the Captain grimly. 'Fifteen guineas for a Honiton *fichu*!' he cried presently. 'What in mercy's name is a *fichu*? It sounds like a sneeze.'

'It is a little half-handkerchief I wear to brighten a velvet gown when we dine alone, Conrad. You know you have always said that lace harmonises a woman's dress, and gives a softness to the complexion and contour.'

'I shall be very careful what I say in future,' muttered the Captain, as he went on with the bill. 'French cambric *peignoir*, trimmed real Valenciennes, turquoise ribbon, nineteen guineas,' he read presently. 'Surely you would never give twenty pounds for the gown you wear when you are having your hair dressed?'

'That is only the name, dear. It is really a breakfast gown. You know you always like to see me in white of a morning.'

The Captain groaned and said nothing.

'Come,' he said, by-and-by, 'this surely must be a mistake. "Shooting-dress, superfine silk corduroy, trimmed and lined with cardinal *poult de soie*, oxydised silver buttons, engraved hunting subjects, twenty-seven guineas." Thank Heaven you are not one of those masculine women who go out shooting, and jump over five-barred gates.'

'The dress is quite right, dear, though I don't shoot. Theodore sent it me for a walking-dress, and I have worn it often when we have walked in the Forest. You thought it very stylish and becoming, though just a little fast.'

'I see,' said the Captain, with a weary air, 'your not shooting does not hinder your having shooting-dresses. Are there any fishing-costumes, or riding-habits, in the bill?'

'No, dear. It was Theodore's own idea to send me the corduroy dress. She thought it so new and *recherché*, and even the Duchess admired it. Mine was the first she had ever seen.'

'That was a triumph worth twenty-seven guineas, no doubt,' sighed the Captain. 'Well, I suppose there is no more to be said. The bill to me appears iniquitous. If you were a duchess or a millionaire's wife, of course it would be different. Such women have a right to spend all they can upon dress. They encourage trade. I am no Puritan. But when a woman dresses beyond her means – above her social position – I regret the wise old sumptuary laws which regulated these things, in the days when a fur coat was a sign of nobility. If you only knew, Pamela, how useless this expensive finery is, how little it adds to your social status, how little it enhances your beauty! Why, the finest gown this Madame Theodore ever made cannot hide one of your wrinkles.'

'My wrinkles!' cried Pamela, sorely wounded. 'That is the first time I ever heard of them. To think that my husband should be the first to tell me I am getting an old woman! But I forgot, you are younger than I, and I daresay in your eyes I seem quite old.'

'My dear Pamela, be reasonable. Can a woman's forehead at forty be quite as smooth as it was at twenty? However handsome a woman is at that age — and to my mind it is almost the best age for beauty, just as the ripe rich colouring of a peach is lovelier than the poor little pale blossom that preceded it — however attractive a middle-aged woman may be there must be some traces to show that she has lived half her life; and to suppose that *pain brûlé* brocade, and hand-worked embroidery, can obliterate those, is extreme folly. Dress in dark velvet, and old point-lace that has been twenty years in your possession, and you will be as beautiful as a portrait by one of the old Venetian masters. Can Theodore's highest art make you better than that? Remember that excellent advice of old Polonius's,

> "Costly thy habit as thy purse can buy,
>   But not expressed in fancy."

It is the fancy that swells your milliner's bills, the newly-invented trimmings, the complex and laborious combinations.'

'I will be dreadfully economical in future, Conrad. For the last year I have dressed to please you.'

'But what becomes of all these gowns?' asked the Captain, folding up the bill; 'what do you do with them?'

'They go out.'

'Out where? To the colonies?'

'No dear; they go out of fashion; and I give them to Pauline.'

'A sixty-guinea dress flung to your waiting-maid! The Duchess of Dovedale could not do things in better style.'

'I should be very sorry not to dress better than the Duchess.' said Mrs Winstanley, 'she is always hideously dowdy. But a duchess can afford to dress as badly as she likes.'

'I see. Then it is we only who occupy the border-land of society who have to be careful. Well, my dear Pamela, I shall send Madame Theodore her cheque, and with your permission close her account; and, unless you receive some large accession of fortune I should recommend you not to reopen it.'

His wife gave a heart-breaking sigh.

'I would sacrifice anything for your sake, Conrad,' she said, 'but I shall be a perfect horror, and you will hate me.'

'I fell in love with you, my dear, not with your gown.'

'But you fell in love with me in my gown, dear; and you don't know how different your feelings might have been if you had seen me in a gown cut by a country dressmaker.'

CHAPTER 36

'WITH WEARY DAYS THOU SHALT BE CLOTHED AND FED'

Captain Winstanley never again alluded to the dressmaker's bill. He was too wise a man to reopen old wounds or to dwell upon small vexations. He had invested every penny that he could spare, leaving the smallest balance at his banker's compatible with respectability. He had to sell some railway shares in order to pay Madame Theodore. Happily the shares had gone up since his purchase of them, and he lost nothing by the transaction; but it galled him sorely to part with the money. It was as if an edifice that he had been toilfully raising, stone by stone, had begun to crumble under his hands. He knew not when or whence the next call might come. The time in which he had to save money was so short. Only six years, and the heiress would claim her estate, and Mrs Winstanley would be

left with the empty shell of her present position – the privilege
of occupying a fine old Tudor mansion, with enormous stables,
and fifteen acres of garden and shrubberies, and an annuity that
would barely suffice to maintain existence in a third-rate
London square.

Mrs Winstanley was slow to recover from the shock of her
husband's strong language about Theodore's bill. She was
sensitive about all things that touched her own personality, and
she was peculiarly sensitive about the difference between her
husband's age and her own. She had married a man who was
her junior; but she had married him with the conviction that, in
his eyes at least, she had all the bloom and beauty of youth, and
that he admired and loved her above all other women. That
chance allusion to her wrinkles had pierced her heart. She was
deeply afflicted by the idea that her husband had perceived the
signs of advancing years in her face. And now she fell to
perusing her looking-glass more critically than she had ever
done before. She saw herself in the searching north light; and
the north light was more cruel and more candid than Captain
Winstanley. There were lines on her forehead – unmistakable,
ineffaceable lines. She could wear her hair in no way that would
hide them, unless she had hidden her forehead altogether under
a bush of frizzy fluffy curls. There was a faded look about her
complexion, too, which she had never before discovered – a
wanness, a yellowness. Yes, these things meant age. In such a
spirit, perchance, did Elizabeth of England survey the reflection
in her mirror, until all the glories of her reign seemed as
nothing to her when weighed against this dread horror of
fastcoming age. And luckless Mary, cooped up in the narrow
rooms at Fotheringay, may have deemed captivity, and the
shadow of doom, as but trifling ills compared with the loss of
youth and beauty. Once to have been exquisitely beautiful, the
inspiration of poets, the chosen model of painters, and to see
the glory fading – that, for a weak woman, must be sorrow's
crown of sorrow.

Anon dim feelings of jealousy began to gnaw Pamela's heart.
She grew watchful of her husband's attentions to other women,
suspicious of looks and words that meant no more than a man's

desire to please. Society no longer made her happy. Her Tuesday afternoons lost their charm. There was poison in everything. She began to feel wretched in the society of certain women – nay, of all women who were younger, or possibly more attractive, than herself. She felt that the only security for her peace would be to live on a desert island with the husband she had chosen. She was of too weak a mind to hide these growing doubts and ever-augmenting suspicions. The miserable truth oozed out of her in foolish little speeches; those continual droppings that wear the hardest stone, and which wore even the adamantine surface of the Captain's tranquil temper. There was a homoeopathic admixture of this jealous poison in all the food he ate. He could rarely get through a *tête-à-tête* breakfast or dinner undisturbed by some invidious remark.

One day the Captain rose up in his strength, and grappled with the jealous demon. He had let the little speeches, the random shots, pass unheeded until now; but on one particularly dismal morning, a bleak March morning, when the rain beat against the windows, and the deodoras and cypresses were lashed and tormented by the blusterous wind, and the low sky was darkly gray, the Captain's temper suddenly broke out.

'My dear Pamela, is it possible that these whimpering little speeches of yours mean jealousy?' he asked, looking at her severely from under bent brows.

'I'm sure I never said that I was jealous,' faltered Pamela, stirring her tea with a nervous movement of her thin white hand.

'Of course not; no woman cares to describe herself in plain words as an idiot; but of late you have favoured me with a good many imbecile remarks, which all seem to tend one way. You are hurt and wounded when I am decently civil to the women I meet in society. Is that sensible or reasonable in a woman of your age and experience?'

'You used not to taunt me with my age before we were married, Conrad.'

'Do I taunt you with it now? I only say that a woman of forty' – Mrs Winstanley shuddered – 'ought to have more sense than a girl of eighteen; and that a woman who has had twenty years' experience of well-bred society ought not to put on the silly jealousies of a schoolgirl trying to provoke a quarrel with her first lover.'

'It is all very well to pretend to think me weak and foolish, Conrad. Yes, I know I am weak, ridiculously weak, in loving you as intensely as I do. But I cannot help that. It is my nature to cling to others, as the ivy clings to the oak. I would have clung to Violet, if she had been more loving and lovable. But you cannot deny that your conduct to Lady Ellangowan yesterday afternoon was calculated to make any wife unhappy.'

'If a wife is to be unhappy because her husband talks to another woman about her horses and her gardens, I suppose I gave you sufficient cause for misery,' answered the Captain sneeringly. 'I can declare that Lady Ellangowan and I were talking of nothing more sentimental.'

'O Conrad, it is not *what* you talked about, though your voice was so subdued that it was impossible for anyone to know what you were saying——'

'Except Lady Ellangowan.'

'It was your manner. The way you bent over her, your earnest expression.'

'Would you have had me stand three yards off and bawl at the lady? Or am I bound to assume that bored and vacuous countenance which some young men consider good form? Come, my dear Pamela, pray let us be reasonable. Here are you and I settled for life beside the domestic hearth. We have no children. We are not particularly well-off – it will be as much as we shall be able to do, by-and-by, to make both ends meet. We are neither of us getting any younger. These things are serious cares, and we have to bear them. Why should you add to these an imaginary trouble, a torment that has no existence, save in your own perverse mind? If you could but know my low estimate of the women to whom I am civil! I like society: and to get on in society a man must make himself agreeable to influential women. It is the women who have the reins in the social race, and by-and-by, if I should go into Parliament——'

'Parliament!' cried his wife, affrightedly. 'You want to become a Member of Parliament, and to be out at all hours of the night! Our home-life would be altogether destroyed then.'

'My dear Pamela, if you take such pains to make our home-life miserable, it will be hardly worth preserving,' retorted the Captain.

'Conrad, I am going to ask you a question — a very solemn question.'

'You alarm me.'

'Long ago — before we were married — when Violet was arguing with me against our marriage — you know how vehemently she opposed it——'

'Perfectly. Go on.'

'She told me that you had proposed to her before you proposed to me. O Conrad, could that be true?'

The heartrending tone in which the question was asked, the pathetic look that accompanied it, convinced Captain Winstanley that, if he valued his domestic peace, he must perjure himself.

'It had no more foundation than many other assertions of that young lady's,' he said. 'I may have paid her compliments, and praised her beauty; but how could I think of her for a wife, when you were by? Your soft confiding nature conquered me before I knew that I was hit.'

He got up and went over to his wife and kissed her kindly enough, feeling sorry for her as he might have done for a wayward child that weeps it scarce knows wherefore, oppressed by a vague sense of affliction.

'Let us try to be happy together, Pamela,' he pleaded, with a sigh, 'life is weary work at best.'

'That means that you are not happy, Conrad.'

'My love, I am as happy as you will let me be.'

'Have I ever opposed you in anything?'

'No, dear; but lately you have indulged in covert upbraidings that have plagued me sorely. Let us have no more of them. As for your daughter' — his face darkened at the mention of that name — 'understand at once and for ever that she and I can never inhabit the same house. If she comes, I go. If you cannot live without her you must learn to live without me.'

'Conrad, what have I done that you should talk of such a thing? Have I asked you to let Violet come home?'

'No, but you have behaved mopishly of late, as if you were pining for her return.'

'I pine for nothing but your love.'

'That has always been yours.'

With this assurance Mrs Winstanley was fain to content herself, but even this assurance did not make her happy. The glory and brightness had departed from her life somehow; and neither kind words nor friendly smiles from the Captain could lure them back. There are stages in the lives of all of us when life seems hardly worth living: not periods of great calamity, but dull level bits of roads along which the journey seems very weary. The sun has hidden himself behind gray clouds, cold winds are blowing up from the bitter east, the birds have left off singing, the landscape has lost its charm. We plod on drearily, and can see no Pole Star in life's darkening sky.

It had been thus of late with Pamela Winstanley. Slowly and gradually the conviction had come to her that her second marriage had been a foolish and ill-advised transaction, resulting inevitably in sorrow and unavailing remorse. The sweet delusion that it had been a love-match on Captain Winstanley's side, as well as on her own, abandoned her all at once, and she found herself face to face with stern common sense.

That scene about Theodore's bill had exercised a curious effect upon her mind. To an intellect so narrow, trifles were important, and that the husband who had so much admired and praised the elegance of her appearance could grudge the cost of her toilet galled her sorely. It was positively for her the first revelation of her husband's character. His retrenchments in household expenses she had been ready to applaud as praiseworthy economies; but when he assailed her own extravagance, she saw in him a husband who loved far too wisely to love well.

'If he cared for me, if he valued my good looks, he could never object to my spending a few pounds upon a dress,' she told herself.

She could not take the Captain's common-sense view of a subject so important to herself. Love in her mind meant a blind indulgence like the Squire's. Love that could count the cost of its idol's caprices, and calculate the chances of the future, was not love. That feeling of poverty, too, was a new sensation to the mistress of the Abbey House, and a very unpleasant one. Married very young to a man of ample means, who adored her, and never set the slightest restriction upon her expenditure, extravagance had become her second nature. To have to study every outlay, to ask herself whether she could not do without a thing, was a hard trial; but it had become so painful to her to ask the Captain for money that she preferred the novel pain of self-denial to that humiliation. And then there was the cheerless prospect of the future always staring her in the face, that dreary time after Violet's majority, when it would be a question whether she and her husband could afford to go on living at the Abbey House.

'Everybody will know that my income is diminished,' she thought. 'However well we may manage, people will know that we are pinching.'

This was a vexatious reflection. The sting of poverty itself could not be so sharp as the pain of being known to be poor.

Captain Winstanley pursued the even tenor of his way all this time, and troubled himself but little about his wife's petty sorrows. He did his duty to her according to his own lights, and considered that she had no ground for complaint. He even took pains to be less subdued in his manner to Lady Ellangowan, and to give no shadow of reason for the foolish jealousy he so much despised. His mind was busy about his own affairs. He had saved money since his marriage, and he employed himself a good deal in the investment of his savings. So far he had been lucky in all he touched, and had contrived to increase his capital by one or two speculative ventures in foreign railways. If things went on as well for the next six years he and his wife might live at the Abbey House, and maintain their station in the county, till the end of the chapter.

'I daresay Pamela will outlive me,' thought the Captain; 'those fragile-looking invalid women are generally long lived.

And I have all the chances of the hunting-field, and vicious horses, and other men's blundering with loaded guns, against me. What can happen to a woman who sits at home and works antimacassars and reads novels all day, and never drinks anything stronger than tea, and never eats enough to disturb her digestion? She ought to be a female Methuselah.'

Secure in this idea of his wife's longevity, and happy in his speculations, Captain Winstanley looked forward cheerfully to the future: and the evil shadow of the day when the hand of fate should thrust him from the good old house where he was master had never fallen across his dreams.

CHAPTER 37

LOVE AND AESTHETICS

Spring had returned, primroses and violets were being sold at the street-corners, Parliament was assembled, and London had awakened to new life and vigour. The Dovedales were at their Kensington mansion. The Duchess had sent forth her cards for alternate Thursday evenings of a quasi-literary and scientific character. Lady Mabel was polishing her poems with serious thoughts of publication, but with strictest secrecy. No one but her parents and Roderick Vawdrey had been told of these poetic flights. The book would be given to the world under a *nom de plume*. Lady Mabel was not so much a Philistine as to suppose that writing good poetry could be a disgrace to a duke's daughter; but she felt that the house of Ashbourne would be seriously compromised were the critics to find her guilty of writing doggerel; and critics are apt to deal harshly with the titled muse. She remembered Brougham's savage onslaught upon the boy Byron.

Mr Vawdrey was in town. He rode a good deal in the Row, spent an hour or so daily at Tattersall's, haunted three or four clubs of a juvenile and frivolous character, drank numerous bottles of Apollinaris, and found the task of killing time rather hard labour. Of course there were certain hours in which he was on duty at Kensington. He was expected to eat his luncheon there daily, to dine when neither he nor the ducal house had any other engagement, and to attend all his aunt's parties. There was always a place reserved for him at the dinner-table, however middle-aged and politically or socially important the assembly might be.

He was to be married early in August. Everything was arranged. The honeymoon was to be spent in Sweden and Norway – the only accessible part of Europe which Lady Mabel had not explored. They were to see everything remarkable in the two countries, and to do Denmark as well, if they had time. Lady Mabel was learning Swedish and Norwegian, in order to make the most of her opportunities.

'It is so wretched to be dependent upon couriers and interpreters,' she said. 'I shall be a more useful companion for you, Roderick, if I thoroughly know the language of each country.'

'My dear Mabel, you are a most remarkable girl,' exclaimed her betrothed admiringly. 'If you go on at this rate, by the time you are forty you will be as great a linguist as Cardinal Wiseman.'

'Languages are very easy to learn when one has the habit of studying them, and a slight inclination for etymology,' Lady Mabel replied modestly.

Now that the hour of publication was really drawing nigh, the poetess began to feel the need of a confidante. The Duchess was admiring but somewhat obtuse, and rarely admired in the right place. The Duke was out of the question.

Now, in this crucial hour of her poetic career, Mabel Ashbourne wanted something more than a patient listener. She wanted a critic with a fine ear for rhythm and euphony. She wanted a judge who could nicely weigh the music of a certain combination of syllables, and who could decide for her when she hesitated between two epithets of equal force, but varying depths of tone.

To this nice task she invited her betrothed sometimes on a sunny April afternoon, when luncheon was over, and the lovers were free to repair to Lady Mabel's own particular den – an airy room on an upper floor, with quaint old Queen Anne casements opening upon a balcony crammed with flowers, and overlooking the umbrageous avenues of Kensington Garden, with a glimpse of the old red palace in the distance.

Rorie did his best to be useful, and applied himself to his duty with perfect heartiness and good temper; but luncheon and the depressing London atmosphere made him sleepy, and he had sometimes hard work to stifle his yawns, and to keep his eyes open, while Lady Mabel was deep in entanglement of lines which soared to the seventh heaven of metaphysics. Unhappily Rorie knew hardly anything about metaphysics, and a feeling of despair took possession of him when his sweetheart's poetry degenerated into diluted Hegelism, or rose to a feeble imitation of Browning's obscurest verse.

'Either I must be intensely stupid or this must be rather difficult to understand,' he thought helplessly, when Mabel had favoured him with the perusal of the first act of a tragedy or poetic duologue, in which the hero, a kind of milk-and-watery Faustus, held converse, and argued upon the deeper questions of life and faith, with a very mild Mephisto.

'I'm afraid you don't like the opening of my "Tragedy of the Sceptic Soul,"' Lady Mabel said with a somewhat offended air, as she looked up at the close of the act, and saw poor Rorie gazing at her with watery eyes and a despondent countenance.

'I'm afraid I'm rather dense this afternoon,' he said with hasty apology. 'I think your first act is beautifully written – the lines are full of music; nobody with an ear for euphony could doubt that; but I – forgive me, I fancy you are sometimes a shade too metaphysical – and those scientific terms which you occasionally employ, I fear will be a little over the heads of the general public——'

'My dear Roderick, do you suppose that in an age whose highest characteristic is the rapid advance of scientific knowledge, there can be anybody so benighted as not to understand the terminology of science?'

'Perhaps not, dear. I fear I am very much behind the times. I have lived too much in Hampshire. I frankly confess that some expressions in your – er – Tragedy – of – er Soulless Scept – Sceptic Soul – were Greek to me.'

'Poor dear Roderick, I should hardly take you as the highest example of the *Zeitgeist*; but I won't allow you to call yourself stupid. I'm glad you like the swing of the verse. Did it remind you of any contemporary poet?'

'Well, yes, I think it dimly suggested Browning.'

'I am glad of that. I would not for worlds be an imitator; but Browning is my idol among poets.'

'Some of his minor pieces are awfully jolly,' said the incorrigible Rorie. 'That little poem called *Youth and Art*, for instance. And *James Lee's Wife* is rather nice, if one could quite get at what it means. But I suppose that is too much to expect from any great poet?'

'There are deeper meanings beneath the surface – meanings which require study,' replied Mabel condescendingly. 'Those are the religion of poetry——'

'No doubt,' assented Rorie hastily; 'but frankly, my dear Mabel, if you want your book to be popular——'

'I don't want my book to be popular. Browning is not popular. If I had wanted to be popular, I should have worked on a lower level. I would even have stooped to write a novel.'

'Well, then, I will say if you want your poem to be understood by the average intellect, I really would sink the scientific terminology, and throw overboard a good deal of the metaphysics. Byron has not a scientific or technical phrase in all his poems.'

'My dear Roderick, you surely would not compare me to Byron, the poet of the Philistines. You might as well rank me with the author of *Lalla Rookh*, or advise me to write like Rogers or Campbell.'

'I beg your pardon, my dear Mabel. I'm afraid I must be an out and out Philistine, for to my mind Byron is the prince of poets. I would rather have written *The Giaour* than anything that ever has been published since it appeared.'

'My poor Roderick!' exclaimed Mabel, with a pitying sigh.
'You might as well say you would be proud of having written
The Pickwick Papers.'

'And so I should!' cried Rorie heartily. 'I should think no end
of myself if I had invented Winkle. Do you remember his ride
from Rochester to Dingley Dell? – one of the finest things that
was ever written.'

And this incorrigible young man flung himself back in the
low arm-chair, and laughed heartily at the mere recollection of
that episode in the life of the famous Nathaniel. Mabel
Ashbourne closed her manuscript volume with a sigh, and
registered an oath that she would never read any more of her
poetry to Roderick Vawdrey. It was quite useless. The poor
young man meant well, but he was incorrigibly stupid – a man
who admired Byron and Dickens, and believed Macaulay the
first of historians.'

'In the realm of thought we must dwell apart all our lives,'
Mabel told herself despairingly.

'The horses are ordered for five,' she said, as she locked the
precious volume in her desk; 'will you get yours and come back
for me?'

'I shall be delighted,' answered her lover, relieved at being let
off so easily.

It was about this time that Lord Mallow, who was working
with all his might for the regeneration of his country, made a
great hit in the House by his speech on the Irish land question.
He had been doing wonderful things in Dublin during the
winter, holding forth to patriotic assemblies in the Round Room
of the Rotundo, boldly declaring himself a champion of the
Home Rulers' cause, demanding Repeal and nothing but
Repeal. He was one of the few Repealers who had a stake in the
country, and who was likely to lose by the disruption of social
order. If foolish, he was at least disinterested, and had the courage
of his opinions. This was in the days when Mr Gladstone was
Prime Minister, and when Irish Radicals looked to him as the
one man who could and would give them Home Rule.

In the House of Commons Lord Mallow was not ashamed to
repeat the arguments he had used in the Round Room. If his

language was less vehement at Westminster than it had been in Dublin, his opinions were no less thorough. He had his party here, as well as on the other side of the Irish Channel; and his party applauded him. Here was a statesman and a landowner willing to give an ell, where Mr Gladstone's Land Act gave only an inch. Hibernian newspapers sang his praises in glowing words, comparing him to Burke, Curran, and O'Connell. He had for some time been a small lion at evening parties, he now began to be lionised at serious dinners. He was thought much of in Carlton Gardens, and his name figured at official banquets in Downing Street. The Duchess of Dovedale considered it a nice trait in his character that, although he was so much in request, and worked so hard in the House, he never missed one of her Thursday evenings. Even when there was an important debate on he would tear up Birdcage Walk in a hansom, and spend an hour in the Duchess's amber drawing-rooms, enlightening Lady Mabel as to the latest aspect of the Policy of Conciliation, or standing by the piano while she played Chopin.

Lord Mallow had never forgotten his delight at finding a young lady thoroughly acquainted with the history of his native land, thoroughly interested in Erins's struggles and Erin's hopes; a young lady who knew all about the Protestants of Ulster, and what was meant by Fixity of Tenure. He came to Lady Mabel for sympathy in his triumphs, and he came to her in his disappointments. She was pleased and flattered by his faith in her wisdom, and was always ready to lend a gracious ear. She, whose soul was full of ambition, was deeply interested in the career of an ambitious young man – a man who had every excuse for being shallow and idle, and yet was neither.

'If Roderick were only like him there would be nothing wanting in my life,' she thought regretfully. 'I should have felt such pride in a husband's fame, I should have worked so gladly to assist him in his career. The driest blue-books would not have been too weary for me – the dullest drudgery of parliamentary detail would have been pleasant work, if it could have helped him in his progress to political distinctions.'

One evening, when Mabel and Lord Mallow were standing in the embrasure of a window, walled in by the crowd of

aristocratic nobodies and intellectual eccentricities, talking
earnestly of poor Erin and her chances of ultimate happiness,
the lady almost unawares, quoted a couplet of her own which
seemed peculiarly applicable to the argument.

'Whose lines are those?' Lord Mallow asked eagerly; 'I never
heard them before.'

Mabel blushed like a schoolgirl detected in sending a
valentine.

'Upon my soul,' cried the Irishman, 'I believe they are your
own! Yes, I am sure of it. You, whose mind is so high above
the common level, must sometimes express yourself in poetry.
They are yours, are they not?'

'Can you keep a secret?' Lady Mabel asked shyly.

'For you? Yes, on the rack. Wild horses should not tear it out
of my heart; boiling lead, falling on me drop by drop, should
not extort it from me.'

'The lines are mine. I have written a good deal – in verse. I
am going to publish a volume, anonymously, before the season
is over. It is quite a secret. No one – except my mother and
father, and Mr Vawdrey – knows anything about it.'

'How proud they – how especially proud Mr Vawdrey must
be of your genius,' said Lord Mallow. 'What a lucky fellow he is.'

He was thinking just at that moment of Violet Tempest, to
whose secret preference for Roderick Vawdrey he attributed his
own rejection. And now here – where again he might have
found the fair ideal of his youthful dreams – here where he
might have hoped to form an alliance at once socially and
politically advantageous – this young Hampshire squire was
before him.

'I don't think Mr Vawdrey is particularly interested in my
poetical efforts,' Lady Mabel said with assumed carelessness. 'He
doesn't care for poetry. He likes Byron.'

'What an admirable epigram!' cried the Hibernian, to whom
flattery was second nature. 'I shall put that down in my
commonplace book when I go home. How I wish you would
honour me – but it is to ask too much, perhaps – how proud I
should be if you would let me hear, or see, some of your
poems.'

'Would you really like——' faltered Lady Mabel.

'Like! I should deem it the highest privilege your friendship could vouchsafe.'

'If I felt sure it would not bore you. I should like much to have your opinion, your candid opinion' (Lord Mallow tried to look the essence of candour) 'upon some things I have written. But it would be really to impose too much upon your good-nature.'

'It would be to make me the proudest, and – for that one brief hour at least – the happiest of men,' protested Lord Mallow, looking intensely sentimental.

'And you will deal frankly with me? You will not flatter? You will be as severe as an Edinburgh reviewer?'

'I will be positively brutal,' said Lord Mallow. 'I will try to imagine myself an elderly feminine contributor to the "Saturday," looking at you with vinegar gaze through a pair of spectacles, bent upon spotting every fleck and flaw in your work, and predetermined not to see anything good in it.'

'Then I will trust you!' cried Lady Mabel, with a gush. 'I have longed for a listener who could understand and criticise, and who would be too honourable to flatter. I will trust you, as Marguerite of Valois trusted Clement Marot.'

Lord Mallow did not know anything about the French poet and his royal mistress, but he contrived to look as if he did. And, before he ran away to the House presently, he gave Lady Mabel's hand a tender little pressure, which she accepted in all good faith as a sign manual of the compact between them.

They met in the Row next morning, and Lord Mallow asked – as earnestly as if the answer involved vital issues – when he might be permitted to hear those interesting poems.

'Whenever you can spare time to listen,' answered Lady Mabel, more flattered by his earnestness than by all the adulatory sugar-plums which had been showered upon her since her *début*. 'If you have nothing better to do this afternoon——'

'Could I have anything better to do?'

'We won't enter upon so wide a question,' said Lady Mabel, laughing prettily. 'If committee-rooms and public affairs can

spare you for an hour or two, come to tea with mamma at five.
I'll get her to deny herself to all the rest of the world, and we
can have an undisturbed hour in which you can deal severely
with my poor little efforts.'

Thus it happened that, in the sweet spring weather, while
Roderick was on the stand at Epsom, watching the City and
Suburban winner pursue his meteor course along the close-
cropped sward, Lord Mallow was sitting at ease in a flowery
fauteuil in the Queen Anne morning-room at Kensington,
sipping orange-scented tea out of eggshell porcelain, and
listening to Lady Mabel's dulcet accents, as she somewhat
monotonously and inexpressively rehearsed 'The Tragedy of a
Sceptic Soul.'

The poem was long, and sooth to say, passing dreary; and,
much as he admired the Duke's daughter, there were moments
when Lord Mallow felt his eyelids drooping, and heard a
buzzing, as of summer insects, in his ears.

There was no point of interest in all this rhythmical
meandering whereon the hapless young nobleman could fix his
attention. Another minute and his sceptic soul would be
wandering at ease in the flowery fields of sleep. He pulled
himself together with an effort, just as the eggshell cup and
saucer were slipping from his relaxing grasp. He asked the
Duchess for another cup of that delicious tea. He gazed
resolutely at the fair-faced maiden, whose rosy lips moved
graciously, discoursing shallowest platitudes clothed in erudite
polysyllables, and then at the first pause – when Lady Mabel laid
down her velvet-bound volume, and looked timidly upward for
his opinion – Lord Mallow poured forth a torrent of eloquence,
such as he always had in stock, and praised 'The Sceptic Soul' as
no poem and no poet had ever been praised before, save by
Hibernian critic.

The richness, the melody, the depth, colour, brilliance, tone,
variety, far-reaching thought, &c. &c. &c.

He was so grateful to Providence for having escaped falling
asleep that he could have gone on for ever in this strain. But if
anyone had asked Lord Mallow what 'The Tragedy of a Sceptic
Soul' was about, Lord Mallow would have been spun.

When a strong-minded woman is weak upon one particular point she is apt to be very weak. Lady Mabel's weakness was to fancy herself a second Browning. She had never yet enjoyed the bliss of having her own idea of herself confirmed by independent evidence. Her soul thrilled as Lord Mallow poured forth his praises; talking of 'The Book and the Ring,' and 'Paracelsus,' and a great deal more, of which he knew very little, and seeing in the expression of Lady Mabel's eyes and mouth that he was saying exactly the right thing, and could hardly say too much.

They were *tête-à-tête* by this time, for the Duchess was sleeping frankly, her crewel-work drooping from the hands that lay idle in her lap; her second cup of tea on the table beside her, half-finished.

'I don't know how it is,' she was wont to say apologetically, after these placid slumbers. 'There is something in Mabel's voice that always sends me to sleep. Her tones are so musical.'

'And do you really advise me to publish?' asked Lady Mabel, fluttered and happy.

'It would be a sin to keep such verses hidden from the world.'

'They will be published anonymously, of course. I could not endure to be pointed at as the author of "The Sceptic Soul." To feel that every eye was upon me – at the opera – in the Row – everywhere! It would be too dreadful. I should be proud to know that I had influenced my age – given a new bent to thought – but no one must be able to point at *me*.'

'"Thou canst not say I did it,"' quoted Lord Mallow, 'I entirely appreciate your feelings. Publicity of that sort must be revolting to a delicate mind. I should think Byron would have enjoyed life a great deal better if he had never been known as the author of "Childe Harold." He reduced himself to a social play-actor – and always had to pose in his particular *rôle* – the Noble Poet. If Bacon really wrote the plays we call Shakespeare's, and kept the secret all his life, he was indeed the wisest of mankind.'

'You have done nothing but praise me,' said Lady Mabel, after a thoughtful pause, during which she had trifled with the

golden clasp of her volume; 'I want you to do something more
than that. I want you to advise — to tell me where I am
redundant — to point out where I am weak. I want you to help
me in the labour of polishing.'

Lord Mallow pulled his whisker doubtfully. This was
dreadful. He should have to go into particulars presently, to say
what lines pleased him best, which of the various metres into
which the tragedy was broken up — like a new suburb into
squares and crescents and streets — seemed to him happiest and
most original.

'Can you trust me with that precious volume?' he asked. 'If
you can, I will spend the quiet hours of the night in pondering
over its pages, and will give you the result of my meditations
to-morrow.'

Mabel put the book into his hand with a grateful smile.

'Pray be frank with me,' she pleaded. 'Praise like yours is
perilous.'

Lord Mallow kissed her hand this time, instead of merely
pressing it, and went away radiant with the velvet-bound book
under his arm.

'She's a sweet girl,' he said to himself, as he hailed a cab. 'I
wish she wasn't engaged to that Hampshire booby, and I wish
she didn't write poetry. Hard that I should have to do the
Hampshire booby's work! If I were to leave this book in a
hansom now - there'd be an awful situation!'

Happily for the rising statesman, he was blest with a clever
young secretary, who wrote a good many letters for him, read
blue-books, got up statistics, and interviewed obtrusive visitors
from the Green Isle. To this young student Lord Mallow, in
strictest secrecy, confided Lady Mabel's manuscript.

'Read it carefully, Allan, while I'm at the House, and make a
note of everything that's bad on one sheet of paper, and of
everything that's good on another. You may just run your pencil
along the margin wherever you think I might write "divine!"
"grandly original!" "what pathos!" or anything of that sort.'

The Secretary was a conscientious young man, and did his
work nobly. He sat far into the small hours, ploughing through
'The Sceptic Soul.' It was tough work; but Mr Allan was

Scotch and dogged, and prided himself upon his critical faculty. This autopsy of a fine lady's poem was a congenial labour. He scribbled pages of criticism, went into the minutest details of style, found a great deal to blame and not much to praise, and gave his employer a complete digest of the poem before breakfast next morning.

Lord Mallow attended the Duchess's kettledrum again that afternoon, and this time he was in no wise at sea. He handled 'The Sceptic Soul' as if every line of it had been engraven on the tablet of his mind.

'See here now,' he cried, turning to a pencilled margin; 'I call this a remarkable passage, yet I think it might be strengthened by some trifling excisions;' and then he showed Lady Mabel how, by pruning twenty lines off a passage of thirty-one, a much finer effect might be attained.

'And you really think my thought stands out more clearly?' asked Mabel, looking regretfully at the lines through which Lord Mallow had run his pencil – some of her finest lines.

'I am sure of it. That grand idea of yours was like a star in a hazy sky. We have cleared away the fog.'

Lady Mabel sighed. 'To me the meaning of the whole passage seemed so obvious,' she said.

'Because it was your own thought. A mother knows her own children however they are dressed.'

This second tea-drinking was a very serious affair. Lord Mallow went at the poem like a professional reviewer, and criticised without mercy, yet contrived not to wound the author's vanity.

'It is because you have real genius that I venture to be brutally candid,' he said, when, by those slap-dash pencil-marks of his – always with the author's consent – he had reduced the 'Tragedy of the Sceptic Soul' to about one-third of its original length. 'I was carried away yesterday by my first impressions; to-day I am coldly critical. I have set my heart upon your poem making a great success.'

This last sentence, freely translated, might be taken to mean: 'I should not like such an elegant young woman to make an utter fool of herself.'

Mr Vawdrey came in while critic and poet were at work, and was told what they were doing. He evinced no unworthy jealousy, but seemed glad that Lord Mallow should be so useful.

'It's a very fine poem,' he said, 'but there's too much metaphysics in it. I told Mabel so the other day. She must alter a good deal of it if she wants to be understanded of the people.'

'My dear Roderick, my poem is metaphysical or it is nothing,' Mabel answered pettishly.

She could bear criticism from Lord Mallow better than criticism from Roderick. After this it became an established custom for Lord Mallow to drop in every day to inspect the progress of Lady Mabel's poems in the course of their preparation for the press. The business part of the matter had been delegated to him, as much more *au fait* in such things than homely rustic Rorie. He chose the publisher and arranged the size of the volume, type, binding, initials, tail-pieces, every detail.

By the end of May, Lady Mabel's poems were all in type, and there was much discussion about commas and notes of admiration, syllables too much or too little, in the flowery morning-room at Kensington, what time Roderick Vawdrey – sorely at a loss for occupation – wasted the summer hours at races or regattas within easy reach of London, or went to out-of-the-way places, to look at hunters of wonderful repute, which, on inspection, were generally disappointing.

CHAPTER 38

CRUMPLED ROSE-LEAVES

Violet Tempest had been away from home nearly a year, and to the few old servants remaining at the Abbey House, and to the villagers who had known and loved her, it seemed as if a light had gone out.

'It's like it was after the Squire's death, when miss and her ma was away,' said one gossip to another; 'the world seems empty.'

Mrs Winstanley and her husband had been living as became people of some pretension to rank and fashion. They saw very little of each other, but were seen together on all fitting occasions. The morning service in the little church at Beechdale would not have seemed complete without those two figures. The faded beauty in delicate hued silk and floral bonnet; the slim, well-dressed Captain, with his bronzed face and black whiskers. They were in everybody's idea the happiest example of married bliss. If the lady's languid loveliness had faded more within the last year or so than in the ten years that went before it, if her slow step had grown slower, her white hand more transparent, there were no loving eyes to mark the change.

'That affectation of valetudinarianism is growing on Mrs Winstanley,' Mrs Scobel said one day to her husband. 'It is a pity. I believe the Captain encourages it.'

'She has not looked so well since Violet went away,' answered the kindly parson. 'It seems an unnatural thing for mother and daughter to be separated.'

'I don't know that, dear. The Bible says a man should leave mother and father and cleave to his wife. Poor Violet was a discordant element in that household. Mrs Winstanley must feel much happier now she is away.'

'I can't tell how she feels,' answered the Vicar doubtfully; 'but she does not look so happy as she did when Violet was at home.'

'The fact is she gives way too much,' exclaimed active little Mrs Scobel, who had never given way in her life. 'When she has a headache she lies in bed, and has the venetian blinds kept down, just as if she were dying. No wonder she looks pale and——'

'Etiolated,' said the Vicar; 'perishing for want of light. But I believe it's moral sunshine that is wanted there, my dear Fanny, say what you will.'

Mr Scobel was correct in his judgment. Pamela Winstanley was a most unhappy woman – an unhappy woman without one tangible cause of complaint. True that her daughter was banished; but she was banished with the mother's full consent. Her personal extravagances had been curtailed; but she was fain to admit that the curtailment was wise, necessary, and for her own future benefit. Her husband was all kindness; and surely she could not be angry with him if he seemed to grow younger every day – rejuvenated by regular habits and rustic life – while in her wan face the lines of care daily deepened, until it would have needed art far beyond the power of any modern Medea to conceal Time's ravages.

'I am getting an old woman,' sighed Mrs Winstanley. 'It is lucky I am not without resources against solitude and age.'

Her resources were a tepid appreciation of modern idyllic poetry, as exemplified in the weaker poems of Tennyson, and the works of Adelaide Proctor and Jean Ingelow, and a talent for embroidering conventional foliage and flowers on kitchen towelling.

She had taken it into her head of late to withdraw herself altogether from society, save from such friends who liked her well enough, or were sufficiently perplexed as to the disposal of their lives, to waste an occasional hour over gossip and orange pekoe. She had now permanently assumed that *rôle* of invalid which she had always somewhat affected.

'I am really not well enough to go to dinner-parties, Conrad,' she said, when her husband politely argued against her refusal of an invitation, with just that mild entreaty which too plainly means, 'I don't care a jot whether you go with me or stay at home.'

'But, my dear Pamela, a little gaiety would give you a fillip.'

'No, it would not, Conrad. It would worry me to go to Lady Ellangowan's in one of last season's dresses; and I quite agree with you that I must spend no more money with Theodore.'

'Why not wear black velvet?'

'Too obvious a *pis aller*. I have not enough diamonds to carry off black velvet.'

'But your fine old lace – rose-point, I think you call it – surely that would carry off black velvet for once in a way.'

'My dear Conrad, Lady Ellangowan knows my rose-point by heart. No, Conrad; I will not go to the Ellangowans' in a dress made last year; or in any *réchauffé* of velvet and lace. I hope I have a proper pride that would always preserve me from humiliation of that kind. Besides, I am not strong enough to go to parties. You may not believe me, Conrad, but I am really ill.'

The Captain put on an unhappy look, and murmured something sympathetic: but he did not believe in the reality of his wife's ailments. She had played the invalid more or less ever since their marriage; and he had grown accustomed to the assumption as a part of his wife's daily existence – a mere idiosyncrasy, like her love of fine dress and strong tea. If at dinner she ate hardly enough for a bird, he concluded that she had spoiled her appetite at luncheon, or by the consumption of sweet biscuits and pound-cake at five o'clock. Her refusal of all invitations to dinners and garden-parties he attributed to her folly about dress, and to that alone. Those other reasons which she put forward – of weakness, languor, low spirits – were to Captain Winstanley's mind mere disguises for temper. She had not, in her heart of hearts, forgiven him for closing Madame Theodore's account.

Thus, wilfully blind to a truth which was soon to become obvious to all the world, he let the insidious foe steal across his threshold, and guessed not how soon that dark and hidden enemy was to drive him from the hearth by which he sat, secure in self-approval and sagacious schemes for the future.

Once a week, through all the long year, there had come a dutiful letter from Violet to her mother. The letters were often brief – what could the girl find to tell in her desert island? – but they were always kind, and they were a source of comfort to the mother's empty heart. Mrs Winstanley answered unfailingly, and her Jersey letter was one of the chief events of each week. She was fonder of her daughter at a distance than she ever had been when they were together. 'That will be something to tell Violet,' she would say of any inane bit of gossip that was whispered across the afternoon teacups.

CHAPTER 39

A FOOL'S PARADISE

At Ashbourne preparations had already begun for the wedding
in August. It was to be a wedding worthy of a duke's only
daughter, the well-beloved and cherished child of an adoring
father and mother. Kinsfolk and old friends were coming from
far and wide to assist at the ceremony, for whom temporary
rooms were to be arranged in all manner of places. The
Duchess's exquisite dairy was to be transformed into a
bachelor dormitory. Lodges and gamekeepers' cottages were
utilised. Every nook and corner in the ducal mansion would
be full.

'Why not rig up a few hammocks in the nearest plantation?'
Rorie asked, laughing, when he heard of all these doings. 'One
couldn't have a better place to sleep in on a sultry summer
night.'

There was to be a ball for the tenantry in the evening of the
wedding-day, in a marquee on the lawn. The gardens were to
be illuminated in a style worthy of the château of Vaux, when
Fouquet was squandering a nation's revenues on lamps and
fountains and venal friends. Lady Mabel protested against all this
fuss.

'Dear mamma, I would so much rather have been married
quietly,' she said.

'My dearest, it is all your papa's doing. He is so proud of you.
And then we have only one daughter; and she is not likely to
be married more than once, I hope. Why should we not have
all our friends round us at such a time?'

Mabel shrugged her shoulders, with an air of repugnance to
all the friends and all the fuss.

'Marriage is such a solemn act of one's life,' she said. 'It seems
dreadful that it should be performed in the midst of a gaping,
indifferent crowd.'

'My love, there will not be a creature present who can feel
indifferent about your welfare,' protested the devoted mother.
'If our dear Roderick had been a more distinguished person,

your papa would have had you married in Westminster Abbey. There of course there would have been a crowd of idle spectators.'

'Poor Roderick!' sighed Mabel. 'It is a pity he is so utterly aimless. He might have made a career for himself by this time, if he had chosen.'

'He will do something by-and-by, I daresay,' said the Duchess, excusingly. 'You will be able to mould him as you like, pet.'

'I have not found him particularly malleable hitherto,' said Mabel.

The bride elect was out of spirits, and inclined to look despondently upon life. She was suffering the bitter pain of disappointed hopes. 'The Tragedy of a Sceptic Soul,' despite its depth of thought, its exquisite typography and creamy paper, had been a dire and irredeemable failure. The reviewers had ground the poor little aristocratic butterfly to powder upon the wheel of ridicule. They had anatomised Lady Mabel's involved sentences, and laughed at her erudite phrases. Her mild adaptations of Greek thought and fancy had been found out, and held up to contempt. Her petty plagiarisms from French and German poets had been traced to their source. The whole work, so smooth and neatly polished on the outside, had been turned the seamy side without, and the knots and flaws and ravelled threads had been exposed without pity.

Happily the book was anonymous; but Mabel writhed under the criticism. There was the crushing disappointment of expectations that had soared high as the topmost throne on Parnassus. She had a long way to descend. And then there was the sickening certainty that in the eyes of her small circle she had made herself ridiculous. Her mother took those cruel reviews to heart, and wept over them. The Duke, a coarse minded man at best, with a soul hardly above guano and chemical composts, laughed aloud at his poor little girl's failure.

'It's a sad disappointment, I daresay,' he said; 'but never mind, my pet, you'll do better next time, I've no doubt. Or, if you don't, it doesn't much matter. Other people have fancied themselves poets, and have been deceived, before to-day.'

'Those horrid reviewers don't understand her poetry,' protested the Duchess, who would have been hard pushed to comprehend it herself, but who thought it was a critic's business to understand everything.

'I'm afraid I have written above their heads,' Lady Mabel said piteously.

Roderick Vawdrey was worst of all.

'Didn't I tell you "The Sceptic Soul" was too fine for ordinary intellects, Mabel?' he said. 'You lost yourself in an ocean of obscurity. You knew what you meant, but there's no man alive who could follow you. You must take a simpler subject and use plainer English if you want to please the multitude.'

Mabel had told her lover before that she did not aspire to please the multitude, that she would have esteemed such cheap and tawdry success a humiliating failure. It was almost better not to be read at all than to be appreciated only by the average Mudie subscriber. But she would have liked someone to read her poems. She would have liked critics to praise and understand her. She would have liked to have her own small world of admirers, an esoteric few, the salt of the earth, literary Essenes, holding themselves apart from the vulgar herd.

'You are mistaken, Roderick,' Mabel said with chilling dignity; 'I have friends who can understand and admire my poetry, incomprehensible and uninteresting as it may be to you.'

'Dear Mabel, I never said it was uninteresting,' Roderick cried humbly; 'everything you do must be interesting to me. But I frankly own I do not understand your verses as clearly as I think all verse should be understood. Why should I keep all my frankness till after the first of August? Why should the lover be less sincere than the husband? I will be truthful, even at the risk of offending you.'

'Pray do,' cried Mabel, with ill-suppressed irritation. 'Sincerity is such a delightful thing. No doubt my critics are sincere. They give me the honest undisguised truth.'

Rorie saw that his betrothed's literary failure was a subject to be carefully avoided in future.

'My poor Vixen,' he said to himself, with O! what deep regret, 'perhaps it was not one of the least of your charms that you never wrote poetry.'

Lord Mallow was coming to Ashbourne for the fortnight before the wedding. He had made himself wondrously agreeable to the Duke, and the Duke had invited him. The House would be up by that time. It was a delightful season for the Forest. The heather would be in bloom on all the open heights, the glades of Mark Ash would be a solemn world of greenery and shadow, a delicious place for picnics, flirtation, and gipsy tea-drinkings. Lord Mallow had only seen the Forest in the winter. It would be a grand opportunity for him.

He came, and Lady Mabel received him with a sad sweet smile. The reviews had all appeared by this time: and, except in the *West Dulmarsh Gazette* and the *Ratcliff Highway Register*, there had not been one favourable notice.

'There is a dreadful unanimity about my critics, is there not?' said the stricken poetess, when she and Lord Mallow found themselves alone together in one of the orchid-houses, breathing a perfumed atmosphere at eighty degrees, vaporous, balmy, slumberous.

'You have made a tremendous mistake, Lady Mabel,' said Lord Mallow.

'How do you mean?'

'You have given the world your great book without first educating your public to receive and understand it. If Browning had done the same thing – if Browning had burst at once upon the world with *The Ring and the Book* he would have been as great a failure as – as – you at present imagine yourself to be. You should have sent forth something smaller. You should have made the reading world familiar with a style, too original, and of too large a power and scope, to please quickly. A volume of ballads and idylls – a short story in simple verse – would have prepared the way for your dramatic poem. Suppose Goethe had begun his literary career with the second part of *Faust*! He was too wise for that, and wrote himself into popularity with a claptrap novel.'

'I could not write a claptrap novel, or claptrap verse,' sighed Lady Mabel. 'If I cannot soar above the clouds, I will never spread my poor little wings again.'

'Then you must be content to accept your failure as an evidence of the tendencies of an essentially Philistine age – an age in which people admire Brown, and Jones, and Robinson.'

Here Lord Mallow gave a string of names, sacrificing the most famous reputations of the age to Mabel Ashbourne's vanity.

This brief conversation in the orchid-house was the first healing balm that had been applied to the bleeding heart of the poetess. She was deeply grateful to Lord Mallow. This was indeed sympathy. How different from Roderick's clumsy advice and obtrusive affectation of candour. Mabel determined that she would do her best to make Lord Mallow's visit pleasant. She gave him a good deal of her society, in fact all she could spare from Roderick, who was not an exacting lover. They were so soon to be married that really there was no occasion for them to be greedy of *tête-à-tête* companionship. They would have enough of each other's company among the Norwegian fjords.

Lord Mallow did not care about riding under an almost tropical sun, nor did he care to expose his horse to the exasperating attacks of forest-flies; so he went about with the Duchess and her daughter in Lady Mabel's pony-carriage – he saw schools and cottages – and told the two ladies all the grand things he meant to do on his Irish estate when he had leisure to do them.

'You must wait till you are married,' said the Duchess good-naturedly. 'Ladies understand these details so much better than gentlemen. Mabel more than half planned those cottages you admired just now. She took the drawings out of the architect's hands, and altered them according to her own taste.'

'And, as a natural result, the cottages are perfection!' exclaimed Lord Mallow.

That visit to Ashbourne was one of the most memorable periods in Lord Mallow's life. He was an impressible young man, and he had been unconsciously falling deeper in love with Lady Mabel every day during the last three months. Her delicate beauty, her culture, her elegance, her rank, all charmed and fascinated him; but her sympathy with Erin was irresistible. It was not the first time that he had been in love, by a great many times. The list of the idols he had worshipped stretched backward to the dim remoteness of boyhood. But to-day, awakening all at once to a keen perception of his hapless state, he told himself that he had never loved before as he loved now.

He had been hard hit by Miss Tempest. Yes, he acknowledged that past weakness. He had thought her fairest and most delightful among women, and he had left the Abbey House dejected and undone. But he had quickly recovered from the brief fever: and now, reverentially admiring Lady Mabel's prim propriety, he wondered that he could have ever seriously offered himself to a girl of Vixen's undisciplined character.

'I should have been a miserable man by this time if she had accepted me,' he thought. 'She did not care a straw about the people of Ireland.'

He was deeply, hopelessly, irrecoverably in love; and the lady he loved was to be married to another man in less than a week. The situation was too awful. What could such a woman as Mabel Ashbourne see in such a man as Roderick Vawdrey? That is a kind of question which has been asked very often in the history of men and women. Lord Mallow could find no satisfactory answer thereto. Mr Vawdrey was well enough in his way – he was good-looking, sufficiently well-bred; he rode well, was a first-rate shot, and could give an average player odds at billiards. Surely these were small claims to the love of a tenth muse, a rarely accomplished and perfect woman. If Lord Mallow, in his heart of hearts, thought no great things of Lady Mabel's poetic effusions, he not the less respected her for the effort, the high-souled endeavour. A woman who could read Euripides, who knew all that was best in modern literature, was a woman for a husband to be proud of.

In this desperate and for the most part unsuspected condition of mind, Lord Mallow hung upon Lady Mabel's footsteps during the days immediately before the wedding. Roderick was superintending the alterations at Briarwood, which were being

carried on upon rather an extravagant scale, to make the
mansion worthy of the bride. Lord Mallow was always at hand,
in the orchid-houses, carrying scissors and adjusting the hose, in
the library, in the gardens, in the boudoir. He was drinking
greedily of the sweet poison. This fool's paradise of a few days
must end in ruin and despair; but the paradise was so delicious
an abode that although an angel with a flaming sword, in the
shape of conscience, was always standing at the gate, Lord
Mallow would not be thrust out. He remained; in defiance of
conscience, and honour, and all those good sentiments that
should have counselled his speedy departure.

CHAPTER 40

'IT MIGHT HAVE BEEN'

'They are the most curious pair of lovers I ever saw in my life,'
said one of the visitors at Ashbourne, a young lady who had
been engaged to be married more than once, and might fairly
consider herself an authority upon such matters. 'One never
sees them together.'

'They are cousins,' replied her companion. 'What can you
expect from a courtship between cousins? It must be the most
humdrum affair possible.'

'All courtships are humdrum, unless there is opposition from
parents, or something out of the common order to enliven
them,' said somebody else.

The speakers were a party of young ladies, who were getting
through an idle hour after breakfast in the billiard-room.

'Lady Mabel is just the sort of girl no man could be
desperately in love with,' said another. 'She is very pretty, and
elegant, and accomplished, and all that kind of thing – but she is
so overpoweringly well satisfied with herself that it seems
superfluous for anyone to admire her.'

'In spite of that I know of someone in this house who does immensely admire her,' asserted the young lady who had spoken first. 'Much more than I should approve if I were Mr Vawdrey.'

'I think I know——' began somebody, and then abruptly remarked: 'What a too ridiculous stroke! And I really thought I was going to make a cannon.'

This sudden change in the current of the talk was due to the appearance of the subject of this friendly disquisition. Lady Mabel had that moment entered, followed by Lord Mallow, not intent on billiards, like the frivolous damsels assembled round the table. There were bookcases all along one side of the billiard-room, containing the surplus books that had overrun the shelves in the library; and Mabel had come to look for a particular volume among these. It was a treatise upon the antiquities of Ireland. Lord Mallow and Lady Mabel had been disputing about the Round Towers.

'Of course you are right,' said the Irishman, when she had triumphantly exhibited a page which supported her side of the argument. 'What a wonderful memory you have! What a wife you would make for a statesman! You would be worth half-a-dozen secretaries!'

Mabel blushed, and smiled faintly, with lowered eyelids.

'Do you remember that concluding picture in *My Novel*,' she asked, 'where Violante tempts Harley Lestrange from his idle musing over Horace, to toil through blue-books; and, when she is stealing softly from the room, he detains her and bids her copy an extract for him? "Do you think I would go through this labour," he says, "if you were not to halve the success? Halve the labour as well." I have always envied Violante that moment in her life.'

'And who would not envy Harley such a wife as Violante,' returned Lord Mallow, 'if she was like – the woman I picture her?'

Three hours later Lord Mallow and Lady Mabel met by accident in the garden. It was an afternoon of breathless heat and golden sunlight – a day on which the most restless spirit might be content to yield to the drowsiness of the atmosphere, and lie at ease upon the sunburnt grass and bask in the glory of summer. Lord Mallow had never felt so idle, in the whole course of his vigorous young life.

'I don't know what has come to me,' he said to himself; 'I can't settle to any kind of work; and I don't care a straw for going sight-seeing with a pack of nonentities.'

A party had gone off in a drag, soon after breakfast, to see some distant ruins; and Lord Mallow had refused to be of that party, though it included some of the prettiest girls at Ashbourne. He had stayed at home, on pretence of writing important letters, but had not, so far, penned a line. 'It must be the weather,' said Lord Mallow.

An hour or so after luncheon he strolled out into the gardens, having given up all idea of writing those letters. There was a wide lawn, that sloped from the terrace in front of the drawing-room windows, a lawn encircled by a belt of carefully-chosen timber. It was not very old timber, but it was sufficiently umbrageous. There were tulip-trees, and copper-beeches, and Douglas pines, and deodoras. There were shrubs of every kind, and winding paths under the trees, and rustic benches here and there to repose the wearied traveller.

On one of these benches, placed in a delicious spot, shaded by a group of pines, commanding the wide view of valley and distant hill far away towards Ringwood, Lord Mallow found Lady Mabel seated reading. She was looking delightfully cool amidst the sultry heat of the scene, perfectly dressed in soft white muslin, with much adornment of delicate lace and pale-hued ribbon: but she was not looking happy. She was gazing at the open volume on her knee, with fixed and dreamy eyes that saw not the page; and as Lord Mallow came very near, with steps that made no sound on the fallen pine-needles, he saw that there were tears upon her drooping eyelids.

There are moments in every man's life when impulse is stronger than discretion. Lord Mallow gave the reins to impulse now, and seated himself by Lady Mabel's side, and took her hand in his, with an air of sympathy so real that the lady forgot to be offended.

'Forgive me for having surprised your tears,' he murmured gently.

'I am very foolish,' she said, blushing deeply as she became aware of the hand clasping hers, and suddenly withdrawing her own; 'but there are passages of Dante that are too pathetic.'

'O, it was Dante!' exclaimed Lord Mallow, with a disappointed air.

He looked down at the page on her lap.

'Yes, naturally.'

She had been reading about Paolo and Francesca – that one episode, in all the catalogue of sin and sorrow, which melts every heart; a page at which the volume seems to open of its own accord.

Lord Mallow leaned down and read the lines in a low voice, slowly, with considerable feeling; and then he looked softly up at Mabel Ashbourne, and at the landscape below them, in all the glow and glory of the summer light, and looked back to the lady, with his hand still on the book.

The strangeness of the situation: they two alone in the garden, unseen, unheard by human eye or ear; the open book between them – a subtle bond of union – hinting at forbidden passion.

'They were deeply to be pitied,' said Lord Mallow, meaning the guilty lovers.

'It was very sad,' murmured Lady Mabel.

'But they were neither the first nor the last who have found out too late that they were created to be happy in each other's love, and had by an accident missed that supreme chance of happiness,' said Lord Mallow, with veiled intention.

Mabel sighed and took the book from the gentleman's hand, and drew a little farther off on the bench. She was not the kind of young woman to yield tremblingly to the first whisper of an unauthorised love. It was all very well to admire Francesca, upon strictly aesthetic grounds, as the perfection of erring womanhood, beautiful even in her guilt. Francesca had lived so long ago – in days so entirely mediaeval, that one could afford to regard her with indulgent pity. But it was not to be supposed that a modern duke's daughter was going to follow that unfortunate young woman's example, and break plighted vows. Betrothal, in the eyes of so exalted a moralist as Lady Mabel, was a tie but one degree less sacred than marriage.

'Why did you not go to see the ruins?' she asked, resuming her society tone.

'Because I was in a humour in which ruins would have been odious. Indeed, Lady Mabel, I am just now very much of Macbeth's temper, when he began to be a-weary of the sun.'

'Has the result of the session disappointed you?'

'Naturally. When was that ever otherwise? Parliament opens full of promise, like a young king who has just ascended the throne, and everybody is to be made happy; all burdens are to be lightened, the seeds of all good things that have been hidden deep in earth through the slow centuries are to germinate all at once, and, blossom, and bear fruit. And the session comes to an end; and, lo! a great many good things have been talked about, and no good thing has been done. That is in the nature of things. No, Lady Mabel, it is not that which makes me unhappy.'

He waited for her to ask him what his trouble was, but she kept silence.

'No,' he repeated, 'it is not that.'

Again there was no reply; and he went on awkwardly, like an actor who has missed his cue.

'Since I have known you I have been at once too happy and too wretched. Happy – unspeakably happy in your society; miserable in the knowledge that I could never be more to you than an unit in the crowd.'

'You were a great deal more to me than that,' said Mabel softly. She had been on her guard against him just now, but when he thus abased himself before her she took pity upon him, and became dangerously amiable. 'I shall never forget your kindness about those wretched verses.'

'I will not hear you speak ill of them,' cried Lord Mallow indignantly. 'You have but shared the common fate of genius, in having a mind in advance of your age.'

Lady Mabel breathed a gentle sigh of resignation.

'I am not so weak as to think myself a genius,' she murmured; 'but I venture to hope my poor verses will be better understood twenty years hence than they are now.'

'Undoubtedly!' cried Lord Mallow, with conviction. 'Look at Wordsworth; in his lifetime the general reading public considered him a prosy old gentleman, who twaddled pleasantly about lakes and mountains, and pretty little peasant girls. The world only awakened ten years ago to the fact of his being a great poet and a sublime philosopher; and I shouldn't be very much surprised,' added Lord Mallow meditatively, 'if in ten years more the world were to go to sleep again and forget him.'

Lady Mabel looked at her watch.

'I think I will go in and give mamma her afternoon cup of tea,' she said.

'Don't go yet,' pleaded Lord Mallow, 'it is only four, and I know the Duchess does not take tea till five. Give me one of your last hours. A lady who is just going to be married is something like Socrates after his sentence. Her friends surround her; she is in their midst, smiling, serene, diffusing sweetness and light; but they know she is going from them – they are to lose her, yes, to lose her almost as utterly as if she were doomed to die.'

'That is taking a very dismal view of marriage,' said Mabel, pale, and trifling nervously with her watch-chain.

This was the first time Lord Mallow had spoken to her of the approaching event.

'Is it not like death? Does it not bring change and parting to old friends? When you are Lady Mabel Vawdrey, can I ever be with you as I am now? You will have new interests, you will be shut in by a network of new ties. I shall come some morning to see you amidst your new surroundings, and shall find a stranger. My Lady Mabel will be dead and buried.'

There is no knowing how long Lord Mallow might have meandered on in this dismal strain, if he had not been seasonably interrupted by the arrival of Mr Vawdrey, who came sauntering along the winding shrubbery-walk, with his favourite pointer Hecate at his heels. He advanced towards his betrothed at the leisurely pace of a man whose courtship is over, whose fate is sealed, and from whom society exacts nothing further, except a decent compliance with the arrangements other people make for him.

He seemed in no wise disconcerted at finding his sweetheart and Lord Mallow seated side by side, alone, in that romantic and solitary spot. He pressed Mabel's hand kindly, and gave the Irishman a friendly nod.

'What have you been doing with yourself all the morning, Roderick?' asked Lady Mabel, with that half-reproachful air which is almost the normal expression of a betrothed young lady in her converse with her lover.

'O, pottering about at Briarwood. The workmen are such fools. I am making some slight alterations in the stables, on a plan of my own – putting in mangers, and racks, and pillars, and partitions, from the St Pancras Ironworks, making sanitary improvements and so on – and I have to contend with so much idiocy in our local workmen. If I did not stand by and see drain-pipes put in and connections made, I believe the whole thing would go wrong.'

'It must be very dreadful for you,' exclaimed Lady Mabel.

'It must be intolerable!' cried Lord Mallow; 'what, when the moments are golden, when "Love takes up the harp of life, and smites on all the chords with might," you have to devote your morning to watching the laying of drain-pipes and digging of sewers! I cannot imagine a more afflicted man.'

Lady Mabel saw the sneer, but her betrothed calmly ignored it.

'Of course it's a nuisance,' he said carelessly; 'but I had rather be my own clerk of the works than have the whole thing botched. I thought you were going to Wellbrook Abbey with the house party, Mabel?'

'I know every stone of the Abbey by heart. No, I have been dawdling about the grounds all the afternoon. It is much too warm for riding or driving.'

Lady Mabel strangled an incipient yawn. She had not yawned once in all her talk with Lord Mallow. Rorie stifled another, and Lord Mallow walked up and down among the pine-needles, like a caged lion. It would have been polite to leave the lovers to themselves, perhaps. They might have family matters to discuss, settlements, wedding presents, Heaven knows what. But Lord Mallow was not going to leave them alone. He was in a savage humour, in which the petty rules and regulations of a traditionary etiquette were as nothing to him. So he stayed, pacing restlessly, with his hands in his pockets, and inwardly delighted at the stupid spectacle presented by the affianced lovers, who had nothing to say to each other, and were evidently bored to the last degree by their own society.

'This is the deplorable result of trying to ferment the small beer of cousinly affection into the Maronean wine of passionate love,' thought Lord Mallow. 'Idiotic parents have imagined that these two people ought to marry, because they were brought up together, and the little girl took kindly to the little boy. What little girl does not take kindly to anything in the shape of a boy, when they are both in the nursery? Hence these tears.'

'I am going to pour out mamma's tea,' Lady Mabel said presently, keenly sensible of the stupidity of her position. 'Will you come, Roderick? The Duchess will be glad to know you are alive. She was wondering about you all the time we were at luncheon.'

'I ought not to have been off duty so long,' Mr Vawdrey answered meekly; 'but if you could only imagine the stupidity of those bricklayers! The day before yesterday I found half-a-dozen stalwart fellows sitting upon a wall, with their hands in their corduroy pockets, smoking short pipes, and, I believe, talking politics. They pretended to be at a standstill because their satellites – their *âmes damnées*, the men who hold their hods and mix their mortar – had not turned up. "Don't disturb yourselves, gentlemen," I said. "There's nothing like taking things easy. It's a time job. I'll send you the morning papers and a can of beer." And so I did, and since that day, do you know, the fellows have worked twice as hard. They don't mind being bullied; but they can't stand chaff.'

'What an interesting bit of character,' said Lady Mabel, with a faintly perceptible sneer.

'May I come to the Duchess's kettledrum?' asked Lord Mallow humbly.

'By all means,' answered Mabel. 'How fond you gentlemen pretend to be of afternoon tea, nowadays. But I don't believe it is the tea you really care for. It is the gossip you all like. Darwin has found out that the male sex is the vain sex; but I don't think he has gone so far as to discover another great truth. It is the superior sex for whom scandal has the keenest charm.'

'I have never heard the faintest hiss of the serpent slander at the Duchess's tea-table,' said Lord Mallow.

'No; we are dreadfully behind the age,' assented Lady Mabel. 'We contrive to exist without thinking ill of our neighbours.'

They all three sauntered towards the house, choosing the sheltered ways, and skirting the broad sunny lawn. Lady Mabel and her companions were for the most part silent during this leisurely walk home, and, when one of them hazarded an observation, the attempt at conversation had a forced air, and failed to call forth any responsive brilliancy in the others.

The Duchess looked provokingly cool and comfortable in her morning-room, which was an airy apartment on the first-floor, with a wide window opening upon a rustic balcony, verandahed and trellised, garlanded with passion-flowers and Australian clematis, and altogether sheltered from sun and wind. The most reposeful sofas, the roomiest arm-chairs in all the house were to be found here, covered with a cool shining chintz of the good old-fashioned sort, apple-blossoms and spring-flowers on a white ground.

A second window in a corner opened into a small fernery, in which there was a miniature waterfall that trickled with a slumberous sound over moss-grown rockwork. There could hardly have been a better room for afternoon tea on a sultry summer day; and afternoon tea at Ashbourne included iced coffee, and the finest peaches and nectarines that were grown in the county; and when the Duke happened to drop in for a chat with his wife and daughter, sometimes went as far as sherry and Angostura bitters.

The Duchess received her daughter with her usual delighted air, as if the ethereal-looking young lady in India muslin had been a goddess.

'I hope you have not been fatiguing yourself in the orchid-houses on such an afternoon as this, my pet,' she said anxiously.

'No, indeed, mamma; it is much too warm for the orchid-houses. I have been in the shrubbery reading, or trying to read, but it is dreadfully sleepy weather. We shall all be glad to get some tea. O, here it comes.'

A match pair of footmen brought a pair of silver trays: caddy, kettle, and teapot, and cups and saucers on one; and a lavish pile of fruit on the other.

Lady Mabel took up the quaint little silver caddy and made the tea. Roderick began to eat peaches. Lord Mallow, true to his nationality, seated himself by the Duchess, and paid her a compliment.

'There are some more parcels for you, Mabel,' said the fond mother presently, glancing at a side-table, where sundry neatly-papered packets suggested jewellery.

'More presents, I suppose,' the young lady murmured languidly. 'Now I do hope people have not sent me any more jewellery. I wear so little, and I——'

Have so much, she was going to say, but checked herself on the verge of a remark that savoured of arrogance.

She went on with the tea-making, uncurious as to the inside of those dainty-looking parcels. She had been surfeited with presents before she left her nursery. A bracelet or a locket more or less could not make the slightest difference in her feelings. She entertained a condescending pity for the foolish people who squandered their money in buying her such things, when they ought to know that she had a superfluity of much finer jewels than any they could give her.

'Don't you want to see your presents?' asked Rorie, looking at her, in half-stupid wonder at such calm superiority.

'They will keep till after tea. I can guess pretty well what they are like. How many church-services have people sent me, mamma?'

'I think the last made fourteen,' murmured the Duchess, trifling with her tea-spoon.

'And how many "Christian Years"?'

'Nine.'

'And how many copies of Doré's "Idylls of the Kings"?'

'One came this morning from Mrs Scobel. I think it was the fifth.'

'How many lockets inscribed with A.E.I. or "Mizpah"?'

'My darling, I could not possibly count those. There were three more by post this morning.'

'You see there is rather a sameness in these things,' said Lady Mabel; 'and you can understand why I am not rabidly curious about the contents of those parcels. I feel sure there will be another "Mizpah" among them.'

She had received Lord Mallow's tribute, an Irish jaunting-car, built upon the newest lines, and altogether a most perfect vehicle for driving to a meet in, so light and perfectly balanced as to travel safely through the ruttiest glade in Mark Ash.

Rorie's gifts had all been given, so Lady Mabel could afford to make light of the unopened parcels without fear of wounding the feelings of anyone present.

They were opened by-and-by, when the Duke came in from his farm, sorely disturbed in his mind at the serious indisposition of a six-hundred-guinea cart-horse, which hapless prize animal had been fatted to such an inflammatory condition that in his case the commonest ailment might prove deadly. Depressed by this calamity, the Duke required to be propped up with sherry and Angostura bitters, which tonic mixture was presently brought to him by one of the match footmen, who looked very much as if he were suffering from the same plethoric state that was likely to prove fatal to the cart-horse. Happily, the footman's death would be but a temporary inconvenience. The Duke had not given six-hundred guineas for him.

Lady Mabel opened her parcels, in the hope of distracting her father from the contemplation of his trouble.

'From whom can this be,' she asked wonderingly, 'with the Jersey post-mark? Do I know anyone in Jersey?'

Roderick grew suddenly crimson, and became deeply absorbed in the business of peeling a nectarine.

'I surely cannot know anyone in Jersey,' said Lady Mabel, in languid wonderment. 'It is an altogether impossible place. Nobody in society goes there. It sounds almost as disreputable as Boulogne.'

'You'd better open the packet,' said Rorie, with a quiver in his voice.

'Perhaps it is from some of your friends,' speculated Mabel.

She broke the seal, and tore the cover off a small morocco case.

'What a lovely pair of earrings!' she exclaimed.

Each eardrop was a single turquoise, almost as large, and quite as clear in colour, as a hedge-sparrow's egg. The setting was Roman, exquisitely artistic.

'Now I can forgive anyone for sending me such jewellery as that,' said Lady Mabel. 'It is not the sort of thing one sees in every jeweller's shop.'

Rorie looked at the blue stones with rueful eyes. He knew them well. He had seen them contrasted with ruddy chestnut hair, and the whitest skin in Christendom – or at any rate the whitest he had ever seen, and a man's world can be but the world he knows.

'There is a letter,' said Lady Mabel. 'Now I shall find out all about my mysterious Jersey friend.'

She read the letter aloud.

'Les Tourelles, Jersey, July 25th.

'DEAR LADY MABEL, – I cannot bear that your wedding-day should go by without bringing you some small token of regard from your husband's old friend. Will you wear these earrings now and then, and believe that they come from one who has nothing but good wishes for Rorie's wife? –

Yours very truly,
'VIOLET TEMPEST.'

'Why, they are actually from your old playfellow!' cried Mabel, with a laugh that had not quite a genuine ring in its mirth. 'The young lady who used to follow the staghounds, in a green habit with brass buttons, ever so many years ago, and who insisted on calling you Rorie. She does it still, you see. How very sweet of her to send me a wedding present. I ought to have remembered. I heard something about her being sent off to Jersey by her people, because she had grown rather incorrigible at home.'

'She was not incorrigible, and she was not sent off to Jersey,' said Roderick grimly. 'She left home of her own free will, because she could not hit it with her stepfather.'

'That is another way of expressing it, but I think we both mean pretty much the same thing,' retorted Mabel. 'But I don't want to know why she went to Jersey. She has behaved very sweetly in sending me such a pretty letter; and when she is at home again I shall be very happy to see her at my garden-parties.'

Lord Mallow had no share in this conversation, for the Duke had buttonholed him, and was giving him a detailed account of the cart-horse's symptoms.

The little party dispersed soon after this, and did not foregather again until just before dinner, when the people who had been to see the ruins were all assembled, full of their day's enjoyment, and of sundry conversational encounters which they had had with the natives of the district. They gave themselves the usual airs which people who have been laboriously amusing themselves inflict upon those wiser individuals who prefer the passive pleasures of repose, and made a merit of having exposed themselves to the meridian sun, in the pursuit of archaeological knowledge.

Lady Mabel looked pale and weary all that evening. Roderick was so evidently distrait that the good-natured Duke thought that he must be worrying himself about the cart-horse, and begged him to make his mind easy, as it was possible the animal might even yet recover.

Later on in the evening Lady Mabel and Lord Mallow sat in the conservatory and talked Irish politics, while Rorie and the younger members of the house party played Nap. The conservatory was deliciously cool on this summer evening, dimly lighted by lamps that were half hidden among the palms and orange-trees. Lady Mabel and her companion could see the stars shining through the open doorway, and the mystical darkness of remote woods. Their voices were hushed; there were pauses of silence in their talk. Never had the stirring question of Home Rule been more interesting.

Lady Mabel did not go back to the drawing-room that evening. There was a door leading from the conservatory to the hall; and, while Rorie and the young people were still somewhat noisily engaged in the game of Napoleon, Lady Mabel went out to the hall with Lord Mallow in attendance upon her. When he had taken her candle from the table and lighted it, he paused for a moment or so before he handed it to her, looking at her very earnestly all the while, as she stood at the foot of the staircase, with saddened face and downcast eyes, gravely contemplative of the stair-carpet.

'Is it – positively – too late?' he asked.

'You must feel and know that it is so,' she answered.

'But it might have been?'

'Yes,' she murmured, with a faint sigh, 'it might have been.'

He gave her the candlestick, and she went slowly upstairs, without a word of good-night. He stood in the hall, watching the slim figure as it ascended, aërial and elegant in its palely-tinted drapery.

'It might have been,' he repeated to himself; and then he lighted his candle and went upstairs. He was in no humour for billiards, cigars, or noisy masculine talk to-night. Still less was he inclined to be at ease and to make merry with Roderick Vawdrey.

CHAPTER 41

WEDDING BELLS

Vixen had been more than a year in the island of Jersey. She had lived her lonely and monotonous existence, and made no moan. It was a dreary exile; but it seemed to her that there was little else for her to do in life but dawdle through the long slow days, and bear the burden of living; at least until she came of age, and was independent, and could go where she pleased. Then there would be the wide world for her to wander over, instead of this sea-girdled garden of Jersey. She had reasons of

her own for so quietly submitting to this joyless life. Mrs
Winstanley kept her informed of all that was doing in
Hampshire, and even at the Queen Anne house at Kensington.
She knew that Roderick Vawdrey's wedding-day was fixed for
the first of August. Was it not better that she should be far
away, hidden from her small world; while those marriage bells
were ringing across the darkening beech-woods?

Her sacrifice had not been vain. Her lover had speedily
forgotten that brief madness of last midsummer, and had
returned to his allegiance. There had been no cloud upon the
loves of the plighted cousins – no passing gust of dissension. If
there had been, Mrs Winstanley would have known all about it.
Her letters told only of harmonious feeling and perpetual
sunshine.

'Lady Mabel is looking prettier than ever,' she wrote, in the
last week of July, 'that ethereal loveliness which I so much
admire. Her waist cannot be more than eighteen inches. I
cannot find out who makes her dresses, but they are
exquisitely becoming to her; though, for my own part, I do
not think the style equal to Theodore's. But then I always
supplemented Theodore's ideas with my own suggestions.

'I hear that the *trousseau* is something wonderful. The
lingerie is in quite a new style; a special make of linen has
been introduced at Bruges on purpose for the occasion, and I
have heard that the loom is to be broken and no more made.
But this is perhaps exaggeration. The lace has all been made
in Buckinghamshire, from patterns a hundred years old –
very quaint and pretty. There is an elegant simplicity about
everything, Mrs Scobel tells me, which is very charming. The
costumes for the Norwegian tour are heather-coloured
waterproof cloth, with stitched borders, plain to the last
degree, but with a *chic* that redeems their plainness.

'Conrad and I received an early invitation to the wedding.
He will go; but I have refused, on the ground of ill-health.
And, indeed, my dear Violet, this is no idle excuse. My health
has been declining ever since you left us. I was always a fragile
creature, as you know, even in your dear papa's time; but of

late the least exertion has made me tremble like a leaf. I bear up, for Conrad's sake. He is so anxious and unhappy when he sees me suffer, and I am glad to spare him anxiety.

'Your old friend, Mr Vawdrey, looks well and happy, but I do not see much of him. Believe me, dear, you acted well and wisely in leaving home when you did. It would have been a dreadful thing if Lady Mabel's engagement had been broken off on account of an idle flirtation between you and Rorie. It would have left a stain upon your name for life. Girls do not think of these things. I'm afraid I flirted a little myself when I was first out, and admiration was new to me; but I married so young that I escaped some of the dangers you have had to pass through.

'Roderick is making considerable improvements and alterations at Briarwood. He is trying to make the house pretty – I fear an impossible task. There is a commonplace tone about the building that defies improvement. The orchid-houses at Ashbourne are to be taken down and removed to Briarwood. The collection has been increasing ever since Lady Jane Vawdrey's death, and is now one of the finest in England. But to my mind the taste is absurd. Dear Conrad thinks me extravagant for giving sixty guineas for a dress, what might he not think if I gave as much for a single plant? Lord Mallow is staying at Ashbourne for the wedding. His success in the House of Commons has made him quite a lion. He called and took tea with me the other day. He is very nice. Ah, my dearest Violet, what a pity you could not like him. It would have been such a splendid match for you, and would have made Conrad and me so proud and happy.'

Vixen folded the letter with a sigh. She was sitting in her favourite spot in the neglected garden, the figs ripening above her among their broad ragged leaves, and the green slopes and valleys lying beneath her – orchards, and meadows, and pink homesteads, under a sultry summer-haze.

The daughter was not particularly alarmed by her mother's complaint of declining health. It was that old cry of 'wolf,' which Violet had heard ever since she could remember.

'Poor mamma!' she said to herself, with a half-pitying tenderness, 'it has always been her particular vanity to fancy herself an invalid; and yet no doctor has ever been able to find out anything amiss. She ought to be very happy now, poor dear; she has the husband of her choice, and no rebellious daughter to make the atmosphere stormy. I must write to Mrs Scobel, and ask if mamma is really not quite so well as when I left home.'

And then Vixen's thoughts wandered away to Rorie, the alterations that were being made at Briarwood. He was preparing a bright home for his young wife, and they would be very happy together, and it would be as if Violet had never crossed his path.

'But he was fond of me, last midsummer twelvemonth,' thought Vixen, reclining against a grassy bank, with her hands clasped above her head, and her open book flung aside upon the long grass, where the daisies and dandelions grew in such wild abundance. 'Yes, he loved me dearly then, and would have sacrificed interest, honour, all the world, for my sake. Can he forget those days, when they are thus ever present to my mind? He seemed more in love than I: yet, a little year, and he is going to be married. Have men no memories? I do not believe that he loves Lady Mabel any better than he did a year ago, when he asked me to be his wife. But he has learnt wisdom; and he is going to keep his word, and to be owner of Briarwood and Ashbourne, and a great man in the county. I suppose it is a glorious destiny.'

In these last days of July a strange restlessness had taken possession of Violet Tempest. She could not read or occupy herself in any way. Those long rambles about the island, to wild precipices looking down on peaceful bays, to furzy hills where a few scattered sheep were her sole companions, to heathery steeps that were craggy and precipitous and dangerous to climb, and so had a certain fascination for the lonely wanderer – those rambles which had been her chief resource and solace until now, had suddenly lost their charm. She dawdled in the garden, or roamed restlessly from the garden to the orchard, from the orchard to the sloping meadow, where Miss Skipwith's solitary cow, last representative of a once well-stocked farm, browsed in a dignified seclusion. The days were slow, and oh, how lengthy! and yet there was a fever in Vixen's blood which made it seem to her as if time were hurrying on at a breathless break-neck pace.

'The day after to-morrow he will be married,' she said to herself, on the morning of the thirtieth. 'By this time on the day after to-morrow, the bride will be putting on her wreath of orange-blossoms, and the church will be decorated with flowers, and there will be a flutter of expectation in all the little villages, from one end of the Forest to the other. A duke's daughter is not married every day in the year. Ah me! there will not be an earthquake, or anything to prevent the wedding, I daresay. No, I feel sure that all things are going smoothly. If there had been a hitch of any kind, mamma would have written to tell me about it.'

Miss Skipwith was not a bad person to live with in a time of secret trouble such as this. She was so completely wrapped up in her grand scheme of reconciliation for all the creeds, that she was utterly blind to any small individual tragedy that might be enacted under her nose. Those worn cheeks and haggard eyes of Vixen's attracted no attention from her as they sat opposite to each other at the sparely-furnished breakfast-table, in the searching summer light.

She had allowed Violet perfect liberty, and had been too apathetic to be unkind. Having tried her hardest to interest the girl in Swedenborg, or Luther, or Calvin, or Mahomet, or Brahma, or Confucius, and having failed ignominiously in each attempt, she had dismissed all idea of companionship with Violet from her mind, and had given her over to her own devices.

'Poor child,' she said to herself, 'she is not unamiable, but she is utterly mindless. What advantages she might have derived from intercourse with me, if she had possessed a receptive nature! But my highest gifts are thrown away upon her. She will go through life in lamentable ignorance of all that is of deepest import in man's past and future. She has no more intellect than Baba.'

Baba was the Persian cat, the silent companion of Miss
Skipwith's studious hours.

So Violet roamed in and out of the house, in this languid
weather, and took up a book only to throw it down again, and
went out to the court-yard to pat Argus, and strolled into the
orchard, and leaned listlessly against an ancient apple-tree, with
her loose hair glistening in the sunshine — just as if she were
posing herself for a pre-Raphaelite picture — and no one took
any heed of her goings and comings.

She was supremely lonely. Even looking forward to the
future — when she would be of age and well off, and free to do
what she liked with her life — she could see no star of hope.
Nobody wanted her. She stood quite alone, amidst a strange
unfriendly world.

'Except poor old McCroke, I don't think there is a creature
who cares for me; and even her love is tepid,' she said to
herself.

She had kept up a regular correspondence with her old
governess, since she had been in Jersey, and had developed to
Miss McCroke the scheme of her future travels. They were to
see everything strange and rare and beautiful, that was to be
seen in the world.

'I wonder if you would much mind going to Africa?' she
wrote, in one of her frank girlish letters. 'There must be
something new in Africa. One would get away from the
beaten ways of Cockney tourists, and one would escape the
dreary monotony of a *table d'hôte*. There is Egypt for us to
do; and you, who are a walking encyclopaedia, will be able
to tell me all about the Pyramids, and Pompey's Pillar, and
the Nile. If we got tired of Africa we might go to India. We
shall be thoroughly independent. I know you are a good
sailor; you are not like poor mamma, who used to suffer
torture in crossing the Channel.'

There was a relief in writing such letters as these, foolish
though they might be. That idea of distant wanderings with
Miss McCroke was the one faint ray of hope offered by the

future – not a star, assuredly, but at least a farthing candle. The governess answered in her friendly matter-of-fact way. She would like much to travel with her dearest Violet. The life would be like heaven after her present drudgery in finishing the Misses Pontifex, who were stupid and supercilious. But Miss McCroke was doubtful about Africa. Such a journey would be a fearful undertaking for two unprotected females. To have a peep at Algiers and Tunis, and even to see Cairo and Alexandria, might be practicable; but anything beyond that Miss McCroke thought wild and adventurous. Had her dear Violet considered the climate, and the possibility of being taken prisoners by black people, or even devoured by lions? Miss McCroke begged her dear pupil to read Livingstone's travels and the latest reports of the Royal Geographical Society, before she gave any further thought to Africa.

The slowest hours, days most wearisome, long nights that know not sleep, must end at last. The first of August dawned, a long streak of red light in the clear gray east. Vixen saw the first glimmer as she lay wide awake in her big old bed, staring through the curtainless window to the far sea-line, above which the morning sky grew red.

'Hail, Rorie's wedding-day!' she cried, with a little hysterical laugh; and then she buried her face in the pillow and sobbed aloud – sobbed as she had not done till now, through all her weary exile.

There had been no earthquake; this planet we live on had not rolled backward in space; all things in life pursued their accustomed course, and time had ripened into Roderick Vawdrey's wedding-day.

'I did think *something* would happen,' said Vixen piteously. 'It was foolish, weak, mad to think so. But I could not believe he would marry anyone but me. I did my duty, and I tried to be brave and steadfast. But I thought something would happen.'

A weak lament from the weak soul of an undisciplined girl. The red light grew and glowed redder in the east, and then the yellow sun shone through gray drifting clouds, and the new day was born. Slumber and Violet had parted company for the last week. Her mind had been too full of images; the curtain of

sleep would not hide them. Frame and mind were both alike
worn out, as she lay in the broadening light, lonely, forsaken,
unpitied, bearing her great sorrow, just as she must have borne
the toothache, or any other corporal pain.

She rose at seven, feeling unspeakably tired, dressed herself
slowly and dawdlingly, thinking of Lady Mabel. What an event
her rising and dressing would be this morning – the flurried
maids, the indulgent mother; the pure white garments,
glistening in the tempered sunlight; the shower of
congratulatory letters, and the last delivery of wedding gifts.
Vixen could imagine the scene, with its every detail.

And Roderick, what of him? She could not so easily picture
the companion of her childhood on this fateful morning of his
life. She could not imagine him happy: she dared not fancy him
miserable. It was safer to make a great effort, and shut that
familiar figure out of her mind altogether.

O, what a dismal ceremony the eight-o'clock breakfast, tête-à-
tête with Miss Skipwith, seemed on this particular morning!
Even that preoccupied lady was constrained to notice Violet's
exceeding pallor.

'My dear, you are ill!' she exclaimed. 'Your face is as white as
a sheet of paper, and your eyes have dark rings round them.'

'I am not ill, but I have been sleeping badly of late.'

'My dear child, you need occupation; you want an aim. The
purposeless life you are leading must result badly. Why can you
not devise some pursuit to fill your idle hours? Far be it from
me to interfere with your liberty; but I confess that it grieves
me to see youth, and no doubt some measure of ability, so
wasted. Why do you not strive to continue your education?
Self-culture is the highest form of improvement. My books are
at your disposal.'

'Dear Miss Skipwith, your books are all theological,' said
Vixen wearily, 'and I don't care for theology. As for my
education, I am not utterly neglecting it. I read Schiller till my
eyes ache.'

'One shallow German poet is not the beginning and end of
education,' replied Miss Skipwith. 'I should like you to take
larger views of woman's work in the world.'

'My work in the world is to live quietly, and not to trouble anyone,' said Vixen, with a sigh.

She was glad to leave Miss Skipwith to her books, and to wander out into the sunny garden, where the figs were ripening or dropping half-ripened amongst the neglected grass, and the clustering bloom of the hydrangeas was as blue as the summer sky. There had been an unbroken interval of sultry weather – no rain, no wind, no clouds – only endless sunshine.

'If it would hail, or blow, or thunder,' sighed Vixen, with her hands clasped above her head, 'the change might be some small relief to my feelings; but this everlasting brightness is too dreadful. What a lying world it is, and how Nature smiles at us when our hearts are aching. Well, I suppose I ought to wish the sunshine to last till after Rorie's wedding; but I don't, I don't, I don't! If the heavens were to darken, and forked lightnings to cleave the black vault, I should dance for joy. I should hail the storm, and cry "This is sympathy!"'

And then she flung herself face downwards on the grass and sobbed, as she had sobbed on her pillow that morning.

'It rends my heart to know we are parted for ever,' she said. 'Oh why did I not say Yes that night in the fir plantation? The chance of lifelong bliss was in my hand, and I let it go. It would have been less wicked to give way then, and accept my happy fate, than to suffer these evil feelings that are gnawing at my heart to-day.'

The wedding bells must be ringing by this time. She fancied she could hear them. Yes, the summer air seemed alive with bells. North, south, east, west, all round the island, they were ringing madly, with tuneful marriage peal. They beat upon her brain. They would drive her mad. She tried to stop her ears, but then those wedding chimes seemed ringing inside her head. She could not shut them out. She remembered how the joy-bells had haunted her ears on Rorie's twenty-first birthday – that day which had ended so bitterly, in the announcement of the engagement between the cousins. Yes, that had been her first real trouble. How well she remembered her despair and desolation that night, the rage that possessed her young soul.

'And I was little more than a child, then,' she said to herself. 'Surely I must have been born wicked. My dear father was living then; and even the thought of his love did not comfort me. I felt myself abandoned and alone in the world. How idiotically fond I must have been of Rorie. Ever so many years have come and gone, and I have not cured myself of this folly. What is there in him that I should care for him?'

She got up from the grass, plucked herself out of that paroxysm of mental pain which came too near lunacy, and began to walk slowly round the garden-paths, reasoning with herself, calling womanly pride to the rescue.

'I hate myself for this weakness,' she protested dumbly. 'I did not think I was capable of it. When I was a child, and was taken to the dentist, did I ever whine and howl like vulgar-minded children? No; I braced myself for the ordeal, and bore the pain, as my father's child ought.'

She walked quickly to the house, burst into the parlour, where Miss Skipwith was sitting at her desk, the table covered with open volumes, over which flowers of literature the student roved, beelike, collecting honey for her intellectual hive.

'Please, Miss Skipwith, will you give me some books about Buddha?' said Vixen, with an alarming suddenness. 'I am quite of your opinion: I ought to study. I think I shall go in for theology.'

'My dearest child!' cried the ancient damsel, enraptured. 'Thank Heaven! the seed I have sown has germinated at last. If you are once inspired with the desire to enter that vast field of knowledge, the rest will follow. The flowers you will find by the wayside will lure you onward, even when the path is stony and difficult.'

'I suppose I had better begin with Buddha,' said Vixen, with a hard and resolute manner that scarcely seemed like the burning desire for knowledge newly kindled in the breast of a youthful student. 'That is beginning at the beginning, is it not?'

'No, my dear. In comparison with the priesthood of Egypt, Buddha is contemptibly modern. If we want the beginning of things, we must revert to Egypt, that cradle of learning and civilisation.'

'Then let me begin with Egypt!' cried Vixen impatiently. 'I don't care a bit how I begin. I want occupation for my mind.'

'Did I not say so?' exclaimed Miss Skipwith, full of ardent welcome for the neophyte whose steps had been so tardy in approaching the shrine. 'That pallor, those haggard eyes are indications of a troubled mind; and no mind can be free from trouble when it lacks an object. We create our own sorrows.'

'Yes, we are wretched creatures!' cried Vixen passionately, 'the poorest examples of machinery in all this varied universe. Look at that cow in your orchard, her dull placid life, inoffensive, useful, asking nothing but a fertile meadow and a sunny day to fill her cup of happiness. Why did the great Creator make the lower animals exempt from sorrow, and give us such an infinite capacity for grief and pain? It seems hardly fair.'

'My dear, our Creator gave us minds, and the power of working out our own salvation,' replied Miss Skipwith. 'Here are half-a-dozen volumes. In these you will find the history of Egyptian theology, from the golden age of the god Râ to the dark and troubled period of Persian invasion. Some of these works are purely philosophical. I should recommend you to read the historical volumes first. Make copious notes of what you read, and do not hesitate to refer to me when you are puzzled.'

'I am afraid that will be very often,' said Vixen, piling up the books in her arms with a somewhat hopeless air. 'I am not at all clever; but I want to employ my mind.'

She carried the books up to her bedroom, and arranged them on a stout old oak table, which Mrs Doddery had found for her accommodation. She opened her desk, and put a quire of paper ready for any notes she might be tempted to make, and then she began, steadily and laboriously, with a dry-as-dust history of ancient Egypt.

O, how her poor head ached as the summer noontide wore on, and the bee hummed in the garden below, and the distant waves danced gaily in the sunlight; and the knowledge that the bells were really ringing at Ashbourne could not be driven from her mind. How the Shepherd Kings, and the Pharaohs, and the comparatively modern days of Joseph and his brethren, and the ridiculously recent era of Moses, passed, like dim shifting shadows before her mental vision. She retraced her steps in that dreary book, again and again, patiently, forcing her mind to the uncongenial task.

'I will not be such a slave as to think of him all this long summer day,' she said to herself. 'I *will* think of the god Râ, and the lotus flowers, and the Red Nile, and the Green Nile, and all this wonderful land where I am going to take dear old McCroke by-and-by.'

She read on till dinner-time, only pausing to scribble rapid notes of the dates and names and facts which would not stand steadily in her whirling brain: and then she went down to the parlour, no longer pale, but with two hectic spots on her cheeks, and her eyes unnaturally bright.

'Ah,' ejaculated Miss Skipwith delightedly. 'You look better already. There is nothing like severe study for bracing the nerves.'

Violet talked about Egypt all dinner-time, but she ate hardly anything, and that hectic flush upon her cheeks grew more vivid as she talked.

'To think that after the seed lying dormant all this time, it should have germinated at last with such sudden vigour,' mused Miss Skipwith. 'The poor girl is talking a good deal of nonsense; but that is only the exuberance of a newly-awakened intellect.'

Vixen went back to the Egyptians directly after dinner. She toiled along the arid road with an indomitable patience. Her ideas of Egypt had hitherto been of the vaguest. Vast plains of barren sand, a pyramid or two, Memnon's head breathing wild music in the morning sunshine, crocodiles, copper-coloured natives, and Antony and Cleopatra. These things were about as much as Miss McCroke's painstaking tuition had implanted in her pupil's mind. And here, without a shadow of vocation, this poor ignorant girl was poring over the driest details that ever interested the scholar. The mysteries of the triple language, the Rosetta Stone, Champollion – *tout le long de la rivière*. Was it any wonder that her head ached almost to agony, and that the ringing of imaginary wedding bells sounded distractingly in her ears?

She worked on till tea-time, and was too engrossed to hear the bell inviting her to weak tea and bread-and-butter. The ringing of those other bells obscured the sound. She was sitting with her book before her, but her eyes fixed on vacancy, when Miss Skipwith, newly interested in her charge, came to inquire the cause of her delay. The girl looked at her languidly, and seemed slow to understand what she said.

'I don't care for any tea,' she replied at last. 'I would rather go on with the history. It is tremendously interesting, especially the hieroglyphics. I have been trying to make them out. It is so nice to know that a figure like a chopper means a god, and that a goose with a black ball above his back means Pharaoh, son of the sun. And then the table of dynasties: can anything be more interesting than those? It makes one's head go round just a little at first, when one has to grope backwards through so many centuries, but that's nothing.'

'My dear, you are working too hard. It is foolish to begin with such impetuosity. A fire that burns so fiercely will soon exhaust itself. *Festina lente.* We must hasten slowly, if we want to make solid progress. Why, my poor child, your forehead is burning. You will read yourself into a fever.'

'I think I am in a fever already,' said Vixen.

Miss Skipwith was unusually kind. She insisted upon helping her charge to undress, and would not leave her till she was lying quietly in bed. She was going to draw down the blinds, but against this Vixen protested vehemently.

'Pray leave me the sky,' she cried; 'it is something to look at through the long blank night. The stars come and go, and the clouds are always changing. I believe I should go mad if it were not for the sky.'

Poor Miss Skipwith felt seriously uneasy. The first draught from the fountain of knowledge had evidently exercised an intoxicating effect upon Violet Tempest. It was as if she had been taking opium of hashish. The girl's brain was affected.

'You have studied too long,' she said. 'This must not occur again. I feel myself responsible to your parents for your health.'

'To my parents,' echoed Vixen, with a sudden sigh; 'I have only one, and she is happier in my absence than when I was with her. You need not be uneasy about me if I fall ill. No one will care. If I were to die no one would be sorry. I have no place in the world. No one would miss me.'

'My dear; it is absolutely wicked to talk in this strain; just as you are developing new powers, an intellect which may make you a pillar and a landmark in your age.'

'I don't want to be a pillar or a landmark,' said Vixen impatiently. 'I don't want to have my name associated with "movements," or to write letters to the *Times*. I should like to have been happy my own way.'

She turned her back upon Miss Skipwith, and lay so still that the excellent lady supposed she was dropping off to sleep.

'A good night's rest will restore her, and she will awake with renewed appetite for knowledge,' she murmured benevolently, as she went back to her Swedenborgian studies.

CHAPTER 42

THE NEAREST WAY TO NORWAY

No such blessing as a good night's rest was in store for Violet Tempest on that night of the first of August. She lay in a state of half-consciousness that was near akin to delirium. When she closed her eyes for a little while the demon of evil dreams took hold of her. She was in the old familiar home-scenes with her dear dead father. She acted over again that awful tragedy of sudden death. She was upbraiding her mother about Captain Winstanley. Bitter words were on her lips; words more bitter than even she had ever spoken in all her intensity of adverse feelings. She was in the woody hollow by Rufus's stone, blindfold, with arms stretched helplessly out, seeking for Rorie among the smooth beech-boles, with a dreadful sense of loneliness, and a fear that he was far away, and that she would perish, lost and alone, in that dismal wood.

So the slow night wore on to morning. Sometimes she lay staring idly at the stars, shining so serenely in that calm summer sky. She wondered what life was like, yonder, in those remote worlds. Was humanity's portion as sad, fate as adverse, there as here? Then she thought of Egypt, and Shakespeare's Antony and Cleopatra – that story of a wild, undisciplined love, grand in its lawless passion – its awful doom. To have loved thus, and died thus, seemed a higher destiny than to do right, and patiently conquer sorrow, and live on somehow to the dismal end of the dull blameless chapter.

At last, with what laggard steps, with what oppressive tardiness, came the dawn, in long streaks of lurid light above the edge of the distant waters.

"'Red sky at morning is the shepherd's warning!'" cried Vixen, with dry lips. 'Thank God there will be rain to-day! Welcome change after the hot arid skies, and the cruel brazen sun, mocking all the miseries of this troubled earth.'

She felt almost as wildly glad as the Ancient Mariner, at the idea of that blessed relief; and then, by-and-by, with the changeful light shining upon her face, she fell into a deep sleep.

Perhaps that morning sleep saved Vixen from an impending fever. It was the first refreshing slumber she had had for a week – a sweet dreamless sleep. The breakfast-bell rang unheeded. The rain, forecast by that red sky, fell in soft showers upon the verdant isle, and the grateful earth gave back its sweetest perfumes to the cool, moist air.

Miss Skipwith came softly in to look at her charge, saw her sleeping peacefully, and as softly retired.

'Poor child! the initiation has been too much for her unformed mind,' she murmured complacently, pleased with herself for having secured a disciple. 'The path is narrow and rugged at the beginning, but it will broaden out before her as she goes on.'

Violet awoke, and found that it was mid day. O, what a blessed relief that long morning sleep had been. She woke like a creature cured of mortal pain. She fell on her knees beside the

bed, and prayed as she had not often prayed in her brief careless
life.

'What am I that I should question Thy justice!' she cried.
'Lord, teach me to submit, teach me to bear my burden
patiently, and to do some good in the world.'

Her mood and temper were wondrously softened after a long
interval of thought and prayer. She was ashamed of her
waywardness of yesterday – her foolish unreasonable passion.

'Poor Rorie, I told him to keep his promise, and he has
obeyed me,' she said to herself. 'Can I be angry with him for
that? I ought to feel proud and glad that we were both strong
enough to do our duty.'

She dressed slowly, languid after the excitement of yesterday,
and then went slowly down the broad bare staircase to Miss
Skipwith's parlour.

The lady of the manor received her with affectionate
greeting, and had a special pot of tea brewed for her, and
insisted upon her eating some dry toast, a form of nourishment
which this temperate lady deemed a panacea in illness.

'I was positively alarmed about you last night, my dear,' she
said; 'you were so feverish and excited. You read too much, for
the first day.'

'I'm afraid I did,' assented Vixen, with a faint smile: 'and the
worst of it is, I believe I have forgotten every word I read.'

'Surely not!' cried Miss Skipwith, horrified at this admission.
'You seemed so impressed – so interested. You were so full of
your subject.'

'I have a faint recollection of the little men in the
hieroglyphics,' said Vixen; 'but all the rest is gone. The images
of Antony and Cleopatra, in Shakespeare's play, bring Egypt
more vividly before me than all the history I read yesterday.'

Miss Skipwith looked shocked, just as if some improper
character in real life had been brought before her.

'Cleopatra was very disreputable, and she was not Egyptian,'
she remarked severely. 'I am sorry you should waste your
thoughts upon such a person. Had you not better go for a walk
with your dog? Doddery tells me that poor Argus has not had a
good run since last week.'

'How wicked of me!' cried Vixen. 'Poor old fellow! I had almost forgotten his existence. Yes, I should like a long walk, if you will not think me idle.'

'You studied too many hours yesterday, my dear. It will do you good to relax the bow to-day. "*Non semper arcum tendit Apollo.*"'

'I'll go for my favourite walk to Mount Orgueil. I don't think there'll be any more rain. Please excuse me if I am not home in time for dinner. I can have a little cold meat, or an egg, for my tea.'

'You had better take a sandwich with you,' said Miss Skipwith, with unusual thoughtfulness. 'You have been eating hardly anything lately.'

Vixen did not care about the sandwich, but submitted to please her hostess, and a neat little paper parcel, containing about three ounces of nutriment, was made up for her by Mrs Doddery. Never had the island looked fairer in its summer beauty than it looked to-day, after the morning's rain. These showers had been to Jersey what sleep had been to Vixen. The air was soft and cool; sparkling rain-drops fell like diamonds from the leaves of ash and elm. The hedgerow ferns had taken a new green, as if the spirit of spring had revisited the island. The blue bright sea was dimpled with wavelets.

What a bright glad world it was, and how great must be the sin of a rebellious spirit, cavilling at the dealings of its Creator! The happy dog bounced and bounded round his mistress, the birds twittered in the hedges, the passing farm-labourer with his cartload of seaweed smacked his whip cheerily as he urged his patient horse along the narrow lane. A huge van-load of Cockney tourists, singing a boisterous chorus to the last music-hall song, passed Vixen at a turn of the road, and made a blot on the beauty of the scene.

There was a meadow-path which lessened the distance between Les Tourelles and Mount Orgueil. Vixen had just left the road and entered the meadow when Argus set up a joyous bark, and ran back to salute a passing vehicle. It was a St Helier's fly, driving at a tremendous pace in the direction from which she had come. A young man lay back in the carriage, smoking a cigar, with his hat slouched over his eyes. Vixen could just see the strong sunburnt hand flung up above his head. It was a foolish fancy, doubtless, but that broad brown hand reminded her of Rorie's. Argus leaped the stile, rushed after the vehicle, and saluted it clamorously. The poor brute had been mewed up for a week in a dull court-yard, and was rejoiced at having something to bark at.

Vixen walked on to the seashore, and the smiling little harbour, and the brave old castle. There was the usual party of tourists following the guide through narrow passages and echoing chambers, and peering into the rooms where Charles Stuart endured his exile, and making those lively remarks and speculations whereby the average tourist betrays his hazy notions of history. Happily Vixen knew of quiet corners upon the outward walls whither tourists rarely penetrated; nooks in which she had sat through many an hour of sun and shade, reading, musing, or sketching with free untutored pencil, for the mere idle delight of the moment. Here in this loneliness, between land and sea, she had nursed her sorrow and made much of her grief. She liked the place. No obtrusive sympathy had ever made it odious to her. Here she was mistress of herself and of her own thoughts. To-day she went to her favourite corner, a seat in an angle of the battlemented wall, and sat there with her arms folded on the stone parapet, looking dreamily seaward, across the blue channel to the still bluer coast of Normandy, where the towers of Coutance showed dimly in the distance.

Resignation. Yes, that was to be her portion henceforward. She must live out her life, in isolation almost as complete as Miss Skipwith's, without the innocent delusions which gave substance and colour to that lonely lady's existence.

'If I could only have a craze,' she thought hopelessly, 'some harmless monomania which would fill my mind! The maniacs in Bedlam, who fancy themselves popes or queens, are happy in their foolish way. If I could only imagine myself something which I am not — anything except poor useless Violet Tempest, who has no place in the world!'

The sun was gaining power, the air was drowsy, the soft ripple of the tide upon the golden sand was like a lullaby. Even that long sleep of the morning had not cured Vixen's weariness. There were long arrears of slumber yet to be made up. Her eyelids drooped, then closed altogether, the ocean lullaby took a still softer sound, the distant voices of the tourists grew infinitely soothing, and Vixen sank quietly to sleep, her head leaning on her folded arms, the gentle west wind faintly stirring her loose hair.

"'O, happy kiss that woke thy sleep!'" cried a familiar voice close in the slumberer's ear, and then a warm breath, which was not the summer wind, fanned the cheek that lay upmost upon her arm, two warm lips were pressed against that glowing cheek in ardent greeting. The girl started to her feet, every vein tingling with the thrilling recognition of her assailant. There was no one else — none other than he — in this wide world who would do such a thing! She sprang up and faced him, her eyes flashing, her cheeks crimson.

'How dare you?' she cried. 'Then it was you I saw in the fly? Pray, is this the nearest way to Norway?'

Yes, it was Rorie; looking exactly like the familiar Rorie of old; not one whit altered by marriage with a duke's only daughter; a stalwart young fellow in a rough gray suit, a dark face sunburnt to deepest bronze, eyes with a happy smile in them, firmly-cut lips half hidden by the thick brown beard, a face that would have looked well under a lifted helmet — such a face as the sacred Saxons must have seen among the bold followers of William the Norman, when those hardy Norse warriors ran amuck in Dover town.

'Not to my knowledge,' answered this audacious villain, in his lightest tone. 'I am not very geographical. But I should think it was rather out of the way.'

'Then you and Lady Mabel have changed your plans?' said Vixen, trembling very much, but trying desperately to be as calmly commonplace as a young lady talking to an ineligible partner at a ball. 'You are not going to the north of Europe?'

'Lady Mabel and I have changed our plans. We are not going to the north of Europe.'

'O!'

'In point of fact, we are not going anywhere.'

'But you have come to Jersey. That is part of your tour, I suppose?'

'Do not be too hasty in your suppositions, Miss Tempest. *I* have come to Jersey – I am quite willing to admit as much as that.'

'And Lady Mabel? She is with you, of course?'

'Not the least bit in the world. To the best of my knowledge Lady Mabel – I beg her pardon – Lady Mallow – is now on her way to the fishing-grounds of Connemara with her husband.'

'Rorie!'

What a glad happy cry that was! It was like a gush of sudden music from a young blackbird's throat on a sunny spring morning. The crimson dye had faded from Violet's cheeks a minute ago and left her deadly pale. Now the bright colour rushed back again, the happy brown eyes, the sweet blush-rose lips, broke into the gladdest smile that ever Rorie had seen upon her face. He held out his arms, he clasped her to his breast, where she rested unresistingly, infinitely happy. Great Heaven! how the whole world and herself had become transformed in this moment of unspeakable bliss! Rorie, the lost, the surrendered, was her own true lover after all.

'Yes, dear, I obeyed you. You were hard and cruel to me that night in the plantation; but I knew in my heart of hearts that you were wise and honest and true; and I made up my mind that I would keep the engagement entered upon beside my mother's death-bed. Loving or unloving I would marry Mabel Ashbourne, and do my duty to her, and go down to my grave with the character of a good and faithful husband, as many a man has done who never loved his wife. So I held on, Vixen – yes, I will call you by the old pet name now; henceforward you are mine, and I shall call you what I like – I held on, and was altogether an exemplary lover; went wherever I was ordered to go, and always came when they whistled for me; rode at my lady's jog-trot pace in the Row, stood behind her chair at the opera, endured more classical music than ever man heard before and lived, listened to my sweetheart's manuscript verses, and, in a word, did my duty in that state of life to which it had pleased God to call me; and my reward has been to be jilted with every circumstance of ignominy on my wedding-morning.'

'Jilted!' cried Vixen, her big brown eyes shining, in pleasantest mockery. 'Why I thought Lady Mabel adored you?'

'So did I,' answered Roderick naïvely, 'and I pitied the poor dear thing for her infatuation. Had I not thought that I should have broken my bonds long ago. It was not the love of the Duke's acres that held me. I still believe that Mabel was fond of me once, but Lord Mallow bowled me out. His eloquence, his parliamentary success, and above all, his flattery, proved irresistible. The scoundrel brought a marriage certificate in his pocket when he came to stay at Ashbourne, and had the art to engage rooms at Southampton and sleep there a night *en passant*. He left a portmanteau and a hat-box there, and that constituted legal occupancy; so, when he won Lady Mabel's consent to an elopement – which I believe he did not succeed in doing till the night before our intended wedding-day – he had only to ride over to Southampton and give notice to the parson and clerk. The whole thing was done splendidly. Lady Mabel went out at eight o'clock, under the pretence of going to early church. Mallow was waiting for her with a fly, half a mile from Ashbourne. They drove to Southampton together, and were married at ten o'clock, in the old church of St Michael. While the distracted Duchess and her women were hunting everywhere for the bride, and all the visitors at Ashbourne were arraying themselves in their wedding finery, and the village children were filling their baskets with flowers to strew upon the pathway of the happy pair, emblematical of the flowers which do *not* blossom in the highway of life, the lady was over the border with Jock o'Hazel-dean! Wasn't it fun, Vixen?'

And the jilted one flung back his handsome head and laughed long and loud. It was too good a joke, the welcome release coming at the last moment.

'At half-past ten there came a telegram from my runaway bride:

"Ask Roderick to forgive me, dear mamma. I found at the last that my heart was not mine to give, and I am married to Lord Mallow. I do not think my cousin will grieve very much."'

'That last clause was sensible, anyhow, was it not, Vixen?'

'I think the whole business was very sensible,' said Vixen, with a sweet grave smile; 'Lord Mallow wanted a clever wife, and you did not. It was very wise of Lady Mabel to find that out before it was too late.'

'She will be very happy as Lady Mallow,' said Roderick. 'Mallow will legislate for Ireland, and she will rule him. He will have quite enough of Home Rule, poor beggar. Hibernia will be Mabelised. She is a dear good little thing. I quite love her, now she has jilted me.'

'But how did you come here?' asked Vixen, looking up at her lover in simple wonder. 'All this happened only yesterday morning.'

'Is there not a steamer that leaves Southampton nightly? Had there not been one I would have chartered a boat for myself. I would have come in a cockle-shell – I would have come with a swimming-belt – I would have done anything wild and adventurous to hasten to my love. I started for Southampton the minute I had seen that too blessed telegram; went to St Michael's, saw the register with its entry of Lord Mallow's marriage, hardly dry; and then went down to the docks and booked my berth. O, what a long day yesterday was – the longest day of my life!'

'And of mine,' sighed Vixen, between tears and laughter, 'in spite of the Shepherd Kings.'

'Are those Jersey people you have picked up?' Rorie asked innocently.

This turned the scale, and Vixen burst into a joyous peal of laughter.

'How did you find me here?' she asked.

'Very easily. Your custodian – what a grim-looking personage she is, by the way – told me where you were gone, and directed me how to follow you. I told her I had a most important message to deliver to you from your mother. You don't mind that artless device, I hope?'

'Not much. How is dear mamma? She complains in her letters of not feeling very well.'

'I have not seen her lately. When I did, I thought her looking ill and worn. She will get well when you go back to her, Vixen. Your presence will be like sunshine.'

'I shall never go back to the Abbey House.'

'Yes you will – for one fortnight at least. After that your home will be at Briarwood. You must be married from your father's house.'

'Who said I was going to be married, sir?' asked Vixen, with delicious coquetry.

'I said it – I say it. Do you think I am too bold, darling? Ought I to go on my knees, love, and make you a formal offer? Why I have loved you all my life; and I think you have loved me as long.'

'So I have, Rorie,' she answered softly, shyly, sweetly. 'I forswore myself that night in the plantation. I always loved you; there was no stage of my life when you were not dearer to me than anyone on earth, except my father.'

'Dear love, I am ashamed of my happiness,' said Roderick tenderly. 'I have been so weak and unworthy. I gave away my hopes of bliss in one foolishly soft moment, to gratify my mother's dying wish – a wish that had been dinned into my ear for the last years of her life – and I have done nothing but repent my folly ever since. Can you forgive me, Violet? I shall never forgive myself.'

'Let the past be like a dream that we have dreamt. It will make the future seem so much the brighter.'

'Yes.'

And then under the blue August sky, fearless and unabashed, these happy lovers gave each other the kiss of betrothal.

'What am I to do with you?' Vixen asked laughingly. 'I ought to go home to Les Tourelles.'

'Don't you think you might take me with you? I am your young man now, you know. I hope it is not a case of "no followers allowed."'

'I'm afraid Miss Skipwith will feel disappointed in me. She thought I was going to have a mission.'

'A mission!'

'Yes; that I was going in for theology. And for it all to end in my being engaged to be married! It seems such a commonplace ending, does it not?'

'Decidedly. As commonplace as the destiny of Adam and Eve, whom God joined together in Eden. Take me back to Les

Tourelles, Vixen. I think I shall be able to manage Miss Skipwith.'

They left the battlements, and descended the narrow stairs, and went side by side, through sunlit fields and lanes, to the old Carolian manor house, happy with that unutterable, immeasurable joy which belongs to innocent love, and to love only; whether it be the romantic passion of a Juliet leaning from her balcony, the holy bliss of a mother hanging over her child's cradle, or the sober affection of the wife who has seen the dawn and close of a silver wedding and yet loves on with love unchangeable – a monument of constancy in an age of easy divorce.

The distance was long; but to these two the walk was of the shortest. It was as if they trod on flowers or airy cloud, so lightly fell their footsteps on the happy earth.

What would Miss Skipwith say? Vixen laughed merrily at the image of that cheated lady.

'To think that all my Egyptian researches should end in – Antony!' she said, with a joyous look at her lover, who required to be informed which Antony she meant.

'I remember him in Plutarch,' he said. 'He was a jolly fellow.'

'And in Shakespeare.'

'*Connais pas,*' said Rorie. 'I've read some of Shakespeare's plays, of course, but not all. He wrote too much.'

It was five o'clock in the afternoon when they arrived at Les Tourelles. They had loitered a little in those sunny lanes, stopping to look seaward through a gap in the hedge, or to examine a fern which was like the ferns of Hampshire. They had such a world of lover's nonsense to say to each other, such confessions of past unhappiness, such schemes of future bliss.

'I'm afraid you'll never like Briarwood as well as the Abbey House,' said Rorie humbly. 'I tried my best to patch it up for Lady Mabel; for you see, as I felt I fell short in the matter of affection, I wanted to do the right thing in furniture and decorations. But the house is lamentably modern and commonplace. I'm afraid you'll never be happy there.'

'Rorie, I could be happy with you if our home were no better than the charcoal-burner's hut in Mark Ash,' protested Vixen.

'It's very good of you to say that. Do you like sage-green?' Rorie asked with a doubtful air.

'Pretty well. It reminds me of mamma's dressmaker, Madame Theodore.'

'Because Mabel insisted upon having sage-green curtains, and chair-covers, and a sage-green wall with a chocolate dado – did you ever hear of a dado? – in the new morning-room I built for her. I'm rather afraid you won't like it; I should have preferred pink or blue myself, and no dado. It looks so much as if one had run short of wall-paper. But it can all be altered by-and-by, if you don't like it.'

They found Miss Skipwith pacing the weedy gravel walk in front of her parlour window, with a disturbed air, and a yellow envelope in her hand.

'My dear, this has been an eventful day,' she exclaimed. 'I have been very anxious for your return. Here is a telegram for you; and as it is the first you have had since you have been staying here, I conclude it is of some importance.'

Vixen took the envelope eagerly from her hand.

'If you were not standing by my side, a telegram would frighten me,' she whispered to Roderick. 'It might tell me you were dead.'

The telegram was from Captain Winstanley to Miss Tempest:

'Come home by the next boat. Your mother is ill, and anxious to see you. The carriage will meet you at Southampton.'

Poor Vixen looked at her lover with a conscience-stricken countenance.

'O, Rorie, and I have been so wickedly, wildly happy!' she cried, as if it were a crime to have so rejoiced. 'And I made so light of mamma's last letter, in which she complained of being ill. I hardly gave it a thought.'

'I don't suppose there is anything very wrong,' said Rorie, in a comforting tone, after he had studied those few bold words in the telegram, trying to squeeze the utmost meaning out of the brief sentence. 'You see, Captain Winstanley does not say that your mother is dangerously ill, or even very ill; he only says ill.

That might mean somthing quite insignificant – hay-fever, or
neuralgia, or a nervous headache.'

'But he tells me to go home – he who hates me, and was so
glad to get me out of the house.'

'It is your mother who summons you home, no doubt. She is
mistress in her own house, of course.'

'You would not say that if you knew Captain Winstanley.'

They were alone together on the gravel walk, Miss Skipwith
having retired to make the tea in her dingy parlour. It had
dawned upon her that this visitor of Miss Tempest's was no
common friend; and she had judiciously left the lovers together.
'Poor misguided child!' she murmured to herself pityingly; 'just
as she was developing a vocation for serious things! But perhaps
it is all for the best. I doubt if she would ever have had breadth
of mind to grapple with the great problems of natural religion.'

'Isn't it dreadful?' said Vixen, walking up and down with the
telegram in her hand. 'I shall have to endure hours of suspense
before I can know how my poor mother is. There is no boat till
to-morrow morning. It's no use talking, Rorie.' Mr Vawdrey
was following her up and down the walk affectionately, but not
saying a word. 'I feel convinced that mamma must be seriously
ill; I should not be sent for unless it were so. In all her letters
there has not been a word about my going home. I was not
wanted.'

'But, dearest love, you know that your mother is apt to think
seriously of trifles.'

'Rorie you told me an hour ago that she was looking ill
when last you saw her.'

Roderick looked at his watch.

'There is one thing I might do,' he said, musingly. 'Has Miss
Skipwith a horse and trap?'

'Not the least bit in the world.'

'That's a pity; it would have saved time. I'll get down to
St Helier's somehow, telegraph to Captain Winstanley to
inquire the exact state of your mother's health, and not come
back till I bring you his answer.'

'O, Rorie, that would be good of you!' exclaimed Vixen.
'But it seems too cruel to send you away like that; you have

been travelling so long. You have had nothing to eat. You must be dreadfully tired.'

'Tired! Have I not been with you? There are some people whose presence makes one unconscious of humanity's weaknesses. No, darling, I am neither tired nor hungry; I am only ineffably happy. I'll go down and set the wires in motion; and then I'll find out all about the steamer for to-morrow morning, and we will go back to Hampshire together.'

And again the rejoicing lover quoted the Laureate:

> 'And on her lover's arm she leant.
> And round her waist she felt it fold;
> And far across the hills they went,
> In that new world which is the old.'

Rorie had to walk all the way to St Helier's. He despatched an urgent message to Captain Winstanley, and then dined temperately at a French restaurant not far from the quay, where the *bon vivants* of Jersey are wont to assemble nightly. When he had dined he walked about the harbour, looking at the ships, and watching the lights beginning to glimmer from the barrack-windows, and the straggling street along the shore, and the far-off beacons shining out, as the rosy sunset darkened to purple night.

He went to the office two or three times before the return message had come; but at last it was handed to him, and he read it by the office-lamp:

'*Captain Winstanley, Abbey House, Hampshire, to Mr Vawdrey, St Helier's.*

'My wife is seriously ill, but in no immediate danger. The doctors order extreme quiet; all agitation is to be carefully avoided. Let Miss Tempest bear this in mind when she comes home.'

Roderick drove back to Les Tourelles with this message, which was in some respects reassuring, or at any rate afforded a certainty less appalling than Violet's measureless fears.

Vixen was sitting on the pilgrim's bench beside the manor house gateway, watching for her lover's return. O, happy lover, to be thus watched for and thus welcomed; thrice, nay, a thousandfold happy in the certainty that she was his own for ever! He put his arm round her, and they wandered along the shadowy lane together, between dewy banks of tangled verdure, luminous with glow-worms. The stars were shining above the over-arching roof of foliage, the harvest moon was rising over the distant sea.

'What a beautiful place Jersey is!' exclaimed Vixen innocently, as she strolled lower down the lane, circled by her lover's arm. 'I had no idea it was half so lovely. But then of course I was never allowed to roam about in the moonlight. And, indeed, Rorie, I think we had better go in directly. Miss Skipwith will be wondering.'

'Let her wonder, love. I can explain everything when we go in. She was young herself once upon a time, though one would hardly give her credit for it; and you may depend she has walked in this lane by moonlight. Yes, by the light of that very same sober old moon, who has looked down with the same indulgent smile upon endless generations of lovers.'

'From Adam and Eve to Antony and Cleopatra,' suggested Vixen, who couldn't get Egypt out of her head.'

'Antony and Cleopatra were middle-aged lovers,' said Rorie. 'The moon must have despised them. Youth is the only season when love is wisdom, Vixen. In later life it means folly and drivelling, wrinkles badly hidden under paint, pencilled eyebrows, and false hair. Aphrodite should be for ever young.'

'Perhaps that's why the poor thing puts on paint and false hair when she finds youth departed,' said Vixen.

'Then she is no longer Aphrodite, but Venus Pandemos, and a wicked old harridan,' answered Rorie.

And then he began to sing, with a rich full voice that rolled far upon the still air.

> 'Gather ye rose-buds while ye may,
>   Old Time is still a-flying;
> And this same flower that smiles to-day
>   To-morrow will be dying.

Then be not coy, but use your time,
And whilst ye may, go marry;
For having lost but once your prime,
You may for ever tarry.'

'What a fine voice you have, Rorie!' cried Vixen.

'Have I really? I thought it was only Lord Mallow who could sing. Do you know that I was desperately jealous of that nobleman, once – when I fancied he was singing himself into your affections. Little did I think that he was destined to become my greatest benefactor.'

'I shall make you sing duets with me, sir, by-and-by.'

'You shall make me stand on my head, or play clown in an amateur pantomime, or do anything supremely ridiculous, if you like. "Being your slave what can I do—"'

'Yes, you must sing Mendelssohn with me. "I would that my love," and "Greeting."'

'I have only one idea of greeting, after a cruel year of parting and sadness,' said Rorie, drawing the bright young face to his own, and covering it with kisses.

Again Vixen urged that Miss Skipwith would be wondering; and this time with such insistence, that Rorie was obliged to turn back and ascend the hill.

'How cruel it is of you to snatch a soul out of Elysium,' he remonstrated. 'I felt as if I was lost in some happy dream – wandering down this path, which leads I know not where, into a dim wooded vale, such as the fairies love to inhabit?'

'The road leads down to the inn at Le Tac, where Cockney excursionists go to eat lobsters, and play skittles,' said Vixen, laughing at her lover.

They went back to the manor house, where they found Miss Skipwith annotating a tremendous manuscript on blue foolscap, a work whose outward semblance would have been enough to frighten and deter any publisher in his right mind.

'How late you are, Violet,' she said, looking up dreamily from her manuscript; 'I have been re-writing and polishing portions of my essay on Buddha. The time has flown, and I had no idea of the hour till Doddery came in just now to ask if he

could shut up the house. And then I remembered that you had
gone out to the gate to watch for Mr Vawdrey.'

'I'm afraid you must think our goings on rather eccentric,'
Rorie began shyly; 'but, perhaps, Vix—— Miss Tempest has
told you what old friends we are; that, in fact, I am quite the
oldest friend she has. I came to Jersey on purpose to ask her to
marry me, and she has been good enough' – smiling blissfully at
Vixen, who tried to look daggers at him – 'to say Yes.'

'Dear me!' exclaimed Miss Skipwith, looking much alarmed;
'this is very embarrassing. I am so unversed in such matters. My
life has been given up to study, far from the haunts of man. My
nephew informed me that there was a kind of – in point of fact
– a flirtation between Miss Tempest and a gentleman in
Hampshire, of which he highly disapproved, the gentleman
being engaged to marry his cousin.'

'It was I,' cried Rorie, 'but there was no flirtation between
Miss Tempest and me. Whoever asserted such a thing was a
slanderer, and—— I won't offend you by saying what he was,
Miss Skipwith. There was no flirtation. I was Miss Tempest's
oldest friend – her old playfellow, and we liked to see each
other, and were always friendly together. But it was an
understood thing that I was to marry my cousin. It was Miss
Tempest's particular desire that I should keep an engagement
made beside my mother's death-bed. If Miss Tempest had
thought otherwise, I should have been at her feet. I would have
flung that engagement to the winds; for Violet Tempest is the
only woman I ever loved. And now all the world may know it,
for my cousin has jilted me, and I am a free man.'

'Good gracious! Can I really believe this?' asked Miss
Skipwith, appealing to Violet.

'Rorie never told a falsehood in his life,' Vixen answered
proudly.

'I feel myself in a most critical position, my dear child,' said
Miss Skipwith, looking from Roderick's frank eager face to
Vixen's downcast eyelids and mantling blushes. 'I had hoped
such a different fate for you. I thought the thirst for knowledge
had arisen within you, that the aspiration to distinguish yourself
from the ruck of ignorant women would follow the arising of

that thirst, in natural sequence. And here I find you willing to marry a gentleman who happens to have been the companion of your childhood, and to resign — for his sake — all hopes of distinction.'

'My chances of distinction were so small, dear Miss Skipwith,' faltered Vixen. 'If I had possessed your talents!'

'True,' sighed the creator of a universal church. 'We have not all the same gifts. There was a day when I thought it would be my lot to marry and subside into the dead level of domesticity; but I am thankful to think I escaped the snare.'

'And the gentleman who wanted to marry you, how thankful must he be!' thought Rorie dumbly.

'Yet there have been moments of depression when I have been weak enough to regret those early days,' sighed Miss Skipwith. 'At best our strength is tempered with weakness. It is the fate of genius to be lonely. And now I suppose I am to lose you, Violet?'

'I am summoned home to poor mamma,' said Vixen.

'And after poor mamma has recovered, as I hope she speedily may, Violet will be wanted by her poor husband,' said Rorie. 'You must come across the sea and dance at our wedding, Miss Skipwith.'

'Ah,' sighed Miss Skipwith, 'if you could but have waited for the establishment of my universal church, what a grand ceremonial your marriage might have been!'

Miss Skipwith, though regretful, and inclined to take a dismal view of the marriage state and its responsibilities under the existing dispensation, was altogether friendly. She had a frugal supper served in honour of Mr Vawdrey, and they three sat till midnight talking happily — Miss Skipwith of theology, the other two of themselves and the smiling future, and such an innocent forest life as Rosalind and Orlando may have promised themselves, when they were deep in love, and the banished duke's daughter sighed for no wider kingdom than a shepherd's hut in the woodland, with the lover of her choice.

There were plenty of spare bedrooms at the manor house; but so bare and empty, so long abandoned of human occupants, as to be fit only for the habitation of stray bat or wandering

owl. So Roderick had to walk down the hill again to
St Helier's, where he found hospitality at an hotel. He was up
betimes, too happy to need much sleep, and at seven o'clock he
and Vixen were walking in the dewy garden, planning the
wonderful life they were to lead at Briarwood, and all the good
they were to do. Happiness was to radiate from their home, as
heat from the sun. The sick, and the halt, and the lame were to
come to Briarwood; as they had come to the Abbey House
before Captain Winstanley's barren rule of economy.

'God has been so good to us, Rorie,' said Vixen nestling at
her lover's side. 'Can we ever be good enough to others?'

'We'll do our best, anyhow, little one,' he answered gently. 'I
am not like Mallow. I've no grand ideas about setting my native
country in order and doing away with the poor laws; but I've
always tried to make the people around me happy, and to keep
them out of the workhouse and the county jail.'

They went to the court-yard where poor Argus lived his life
of isolation, and they told him they were going to be married,
and that his pathway henceforward would be strewn with roses.
He was particularly noisy and demonstrative, and appeared to
receive this news with a wild rapture that was eminently
encouraging, doing his best to knock Roderick down, in the
tumult of his delight. The lovers and the dog were alike childish
in their infinite happiness, unthinking beings of the present
hour, too happy to look backward or forward, this little space
of time called 'now' holding all things needful for delight.

Violet's portmanteaux were packed. All was ready. There
would be just time for a hurried breakfast with Miss Skipwith,
and then the fly from St Helier's would be at the gate to carry
the exile on the first stage of the journey home.

'Poor mamma!' sighed Vixen. 'How wicked of me to feel so
happy when she is ill.'

And then Rorie comforted her with kindly-meant sophistries.
Mrs Winstanley's indisposition was doubtless more an affair of
the nerves than a real illness. She would be cheered and revived
immediately by her daughter's return.

'How could she suppose she would be able to live without
you!' cried Rorie. 'I know I found life hard to bear.'

'Yet you bore it for more than a year with admirable patience,' retorted Vixen, laughing at him; 'and I do not find you particularly altered or emaciated.'

'O, I used to eat and drink,' said Rorie, with a look of self-contempt. 'I'm afraid I'm a horribly low-minded brute. I used even to enjoy my dinner, sometimes, after a long country ride; but I could never make you understand what a bore life was to me all last year, how the glory and enjoyment seemed to have gone out of existence. The dismal monotony of my days weighed upon me like a nightmare. Life had become a formula. I felt like a sick man who has to take so many doses of medicine, so many pills, so many basins of broth, in the twenty-four hours. There was no possible resistance. The sick nurse was there, in the shape of Fate, ready to use brute force if I rebelled. I never did rebel. I assure you, Vixen, I was a model lover. Mabel and I had not a single quarrel. I think that is a proof that we did not care a straw for each other.'

'You and I will have plenty of quarrels,' said Vixen. 'It will be so nice to make friends again.'

Now came the hurried breakfast, agitated adieux to Miss Skipwith, who wept very womanly tears over her departing charge, and uttered good wishes in a choking voice. Even the Dodderys seemed to Vixen more human than usual, now that she was going to leave them, in all likelihood for ever. Miss Skipwith came to the gate to see the travellers off, and ascended the pilgrim's bench in order to have the latest view of the fly. From this eminence she waved her handkerchief as a farewell salutation.

'Poor soul!' sighed Vixen; 'she has never been unkind to me; but O, what a dreary life I have led in that dismal old house!'

They had Argus in the fly with them, sitting up, with his mouth open, and his tail flapping against the bottom of the vehicle in perpetual motion. He kept giving his paw first to Vixen and then to Rorie, and exacted a great deal of attention, insomuch that Mr Vawdrey exclaimed:

'Vixen, if you don't keep that dog within bounds, I shall think him as great a nuisance as a stepson. I offered to marry you, you know, not you and your dog.'

'You are very rude!' cried Vixen.

'You don't expect me to be polite, I hope. What is the use of marrying one's old playfellow if one cannot be uncivil to her now and then? To me you will always be the tawny-haired little girl I used to tease.'

'Who used to tease you, you mean. You were very meek in those days.'

O, what a happy voyage that was, over the summer sea! They sat side by side upon the bridge, sheltered from wind and sun, and talked the happy nonsense lovers talk: but which can hardly be so sweet between lovers whose youth and childhood have been spent far apart, as between these two who had been reared amidst the same sylvan world, and had every desire and every thought in unison. How brief the voyage seemed. It was but an hour or so since Roderick had been buying peaches and grapes, as they lay at the end of Guernsey pier, and here were the Needles and the chalky cliffs and undulating downs of the Wight. The Wight! That meant Hampshire and home!

'How often those downs have been our weather-glass, Rorie, when we have been riding across the hills between Lyndhurst and Beaulieu,' said Vixen.

She had a world of questions to ask him about all that had happened during her exile. She almost expected to hear that Lyndhurst steeple had fallen; that the hounds had died of old age; that the Knightwood Oak had been struck by lightning; or that some among those calamities which time naturally brings had befallen the surroundings of her home. It was the strangest thing in the world to hear that nothing had happened, that everything was exactly the same as it had been when she went away. That dreary year of exile had seemed long enough for earthquakes and destructions, or even for slow decay.

'Do you know what became of Arion?' asked Vixen, almost afraid to shape the question.

'O, I believe he was sold, soon after you left home,' Rorie answered carelessly.

'Sold,' echoed Vixen drearily. 'Poor dear thing! Yes, I felt sure Captain Winstanley would sell him. But I hoped——'

'What?'

'That someone I knew might buy him. Lord Mallow perhaps.'

'Lord Mallow! Ah, you thought he would buy your horse, for love of the rider. But you see constancy isn't one of that noble Irishman's virtues. He loves and he rides away – when the lady won't have him, *bien entendu*. No, Arion was sent up to Tattersall's, and disposed of in the usual way. Some fellow bought him for a covert hack.'

'I hope the man wasn't a heavy weight,' exclaimed Vixen, almost in tears.

She thought Rorie was horribly unfeeling.

'What does it matter? A horse must earn his salt.'

'I had rather my poor pet had been shot, and buried in one of the meadows at home,' said Vixen plaintively.

'Captain Winstanley was too wise to allow that. Your poor pet fetched a hundred and forty-five guineas under the hammer.'

'I don't think it is very kind of you to talk of him so lightly,' said Vixen.

This was the only little cloud that came between them in all the voyage. Long before sunset they were steaming into Southampton Water, and the yellow light was still shining on dwarf gorse and purple heather, when the brougham that contained Vixen and her fortunes drove along the road to Lyndhurst.

She had asked the coachman for news of his mistress, and had been told that Mrs Winstanley was pretty much the same. The answer was in some measure reassuring; yet Violet's spirits began to sink as she drew nearer home, and must so soon find herself face to face with the truth. There was a sadness too in that quiet evening hour; and the shadowy distances seemed full of gloom, after the dancing waves, and the gay morning light.

The dusk was creeping slowly on as the carriage passed the lodge, and drove between green walls of rhododendron to the house. Captain Winstanley was smoking his cigar in the porch, leaning against the Gothic masonry, in the attitude Vixen knew so well of old.

'If my mother were lying in her coffin I daresay he would be just the same,' she thought bitterly.

The Captain came down to open the carriage-door. Vixen's first glance at his face showed her that he looked worn and anxious.

'Is mamma very ill?' she asked tremulously.

'Very ill,' he answered, in a low voice. 'Mind, you are to do or say nothing that can agitate her. You must be quiet and cheerful. If you see a change you must take care to say nothing about it.'

'Why did you leave me so long in ignorance of her illness? Why did you not send for me sooner?'

'Your mother has only been seriously ill within the last few days. I sent for you directly I saw any occasion for your presence,' the Captain answered coldly.

He now for the first time became aware of Mr Vawdrey, who had got out of the brougham on the other side and came round to assist in the unshipment of Violet's belongings.

'Good evening Mr Vawdrey. Where in Heaven's name did you spring from?' he inquired with a vexed air.

'I have had the honour of escorting Miss Tempest from Jersey, where I happened to be when she received your telegram.'

'Wasn't that rather an odd proceeding, and likely to cause scandal?'

'I think not; for before people can hear that Miss Tempest and I crossed in the same boat I hope they will have heard that Miss Tempest and I are going to be married.'

'I see,' cried the Captain, with a short laugh of exceeding bitterness; 'being off with the old love you have made haste to be on with the new.'

'I beg your pardon. It is no new love but a love as old as my boyhood,' answered Rorie. 'In one weak moment of my life I was foolish enough to let my mother choose a wife for me, though I had made my own choice, unconsciously, years before.'

'May I go to mamma at once?' asked Vixen.

The Captain said Yes, and she went up the staircase and along the corridor to Mrs Winstanley's room. O, how dear and familiar the old house looked, how full of richness and colour after the bareness and decay of Les Tourelles; brocaded curtains hanging in heavy folds against the carved oaken framework of a deep-set window; gleams of evening light stealing through old stained glass; everywhere a rich variety of form and hue that filled and satisfied the eye; a house worth living in assuredly, with but a little love to sanctify and hallow all these things. But how worthless these things if discord and hatred found a habitation among them.

The door of Mrs Winstanley's room stood half open, and the lamplight shone faintly from within. Violet went softly in. Her mother was lying on a sofa by the hearth, where a wood-fire had been newly lighted. Pauline was sitting opposite her, reading aloud in a very sleepy voice out of the *Court Journal*: 'The bride was exquisitely attired in ivory satin, with flounces of old *Duchesse* lace, the skirt covered with *tulle, bouillonè*, and looped with garlands of orange-blossom——'

'Pauline,' murmured the invalid feebly, 'will you never learn to read with expression? You are giving me the vaguest idea of Lady Evelyn Fitzdamer's appearance.'

Violet went over to the sofa and knelt by her mother's side and embraced her tenderly, looking at her earnestly all the while, in the clear soft lamplight. Yes, there was indeed a change. The always delicate face was pinched and shrunken. The ivory of the complexion had altered to a dull gray. Premature age had hollowed the cheeks, and lined the forehead. It was a change that meant decline and death. Violet's heart sank as she beheld it: but she remembered the Captain's warning, and bravely strove to put on an appearance of cheerfulness.

'Dear mother, I am so happy to come home to you,' she said gaily; 'and I am going to nurse and pet you, for the next week or so; till you get tremendously well and strong, and are able to take me to innumerable parties.'

'My dear Violet, I have quite given up parties; and I shall never be strong again.'

'Dearest, it has always been your habit to fancy yourself an invalid.'

'Yes, Violet, once I may have been full of fancies: but now I know that I am ill. You will not be unkind or unjust to

Conrad, will you, dear? He sent for you directly I asked him. He has been all goodness to me. Try and get on with him nicely, dear, for my sake.'

This was urged with such piteous supplication, that it would have needed a harder heart than Violet's to deny the prayer.

'Dear mother, forget that the Captain and I ever quarrelled,' said Vixen. 'I mean to be excellent friends with him henceforward. And, darling, I have a secret to tell you if you would like to hear it.'

'What secret, dear.'

'Lady Mabel has jilted Roderick!'

'My love, that is no secret. I heard all about it the day before yesterday. People have talked of nothing else since it happened. Lady Mabel has behaved shamefully.'

'Lady Mabel has behaved admirably. If other women were wise enough to draw back at the last moment there would be fewer unhappy marriages. But Lady Mabel's elopement is only the prologue to my story.'

'What can you mean, child?'

'Roderick came to Jersey to make me an offer.'

'So soon! O, Violet, what bad taste!'

'Ought he to have gone into mourning? He did not even sing willow, but came straight off to me, and told me he had loved me all his life; so now you will have my *trousseau* to think about, dearest, and I shall want all your good taste. You know how little I have of my own.'

'Ah, Violet, if you had only married Lord Mallow! I could have given my whole mind to your *trousseau* then: but it is too late now, dear. I have not strength enough to interest myself in anything.'

The truth of this complaint was painfully obvious. Pamela's day was done. She lay, half effaced among her down pillows, as weak and helpless-looking as a snowdrop whose stem is broken. The life that was left in her was the merest remnant of life. It was as if one could see the last sands running down in the glass of time.'

'Dear mother, there will be no pleasure for me in being married if you do not take any interest in my *trousseau*,' pleaded

Vixen, trying to cheer the invalid by dwelling on the things her soul had most loved in health.

'Do not talk about it, my dear,' her mother exclaimed peevishly. 'I don't know where the money is to come from. Theodore's bill was positively dreadful. Poor Conrad had quite a struggle to pay it. You will be rich when you are of age, but we are awfully poor. If we do not save money during the next few years we shall be destitute. Conrad says so. Fifteen hundred a year, and a big house like this to maintain. It would be starvation. Conrad has closed Theodore's account. I am sure I don't know where your *trousseau* is to come from.'

Here the afflicted Pamela began to sob hysterically, and Vixen found it hard work to comfort her.

'My dearest mother, how can you be poor and I rich?' she said, when the invalid had been tranquillised, and was lying helpless and exhausted. 'Do you suppose I would not share my income with you? Rorie has plenty of money. He would not want any of mine. You can have it all, if you like.'

'You talk like a child, Violet. You know nothing of the world. Do you think I would take your money, and let people say I robbed my own daughter? I have a little too much self-respect for that. Conrad is doing all he can to make our future comfortable. I have been foolish and extravagant. But I shall never be so any more. I do not care about dress or society now. I have outlived those follies.'

'Dear mother, I cannot bear to hear you talk like that,' said Vixen, feeling that when her mother left off caring about fine dresses she must be getting ready for that last garment which we must all wear some day, the fashion whereof changes but little. 'Why should you relinquish society, or leave off dressing stylishly? You are in the prime of life.'

'No, Violet, I am a poor faded creature,' whimpered Mrs Winstanley, 'stout women are handsome at forty, or even——' with a shudder – 'at five-and-forty. The age suits their style. But I was always slim and fragile, and of late I have grown painfully thin. No one but a Parisian dressmaker could make me presentable; and I have done with Paris dresses. The utmost I can hope for is to sit alone by the fireside, and do art needle-work.'

'But, dear mother, you did not marry Captain Winstanley in
order to lead such a life as that? You might as well be in a
béguinage.'

Vain were Vixen's efforts to console and cheer. A blight
had fallen upon her mother's mind and spirits – a blight that
had crept slowly on, unheeded by the husband, till one
morning the local practitioner – a gentleman who had lived
all his life among his patients, and knew them so well
externally that he might fairly be supposed to have a minute
acquaintance with their internal organism – informed Captain
Winstanley that he feared there was something wrong with
his wife's heart, and that he thought it would be well to get
the highest opinion.

The Captain, startled out of his habitual self-command,
looked up from his desk with ashy countenance.

'Do you mean that Mrs Winstanley has heart disease –
something organically wrong?'

'Unhappily I fear it is so. I have been for some time aware
that she had a weak heart. Her complexion, her feeble
circulation, several indications have pointed to that conclusion.
This morning I have made a thorough examination, and I find
mischief, decided mischief.'

'That means she may die at any moment, suddenly, without
an instant's warning.'

'There would always be that fear. Or she might sink gradually
from want of vital power. There is a sad deficiency of power. I
hardly ever knew anyone remain so long in so low a state.'

'You have been attending her, off and on, ever since our
marriage. You must have seen her sinking. Why have you not
warned me before?'

'It seemed hardly necessary. You must have perceived the
change yourself. You must have noticed her want of appetite,
her distaste for exertion of any kind, her increasing feebleness.'

'I am not a doctor.'

'No; but these are things that speak plainly to every eye – to
the eye of affection most of all.'

'We are slow to perceive the alteration in anyone we see
daily and hourly. You should have drawn my attention to my

wife's health. It is unfair, it is horrible to let this blow come upon me unawares.'

If the Captain had appeared indifferent hitherto, there was no doubt of the intensity of his feeling now. He had started up from his chair, and walked backwards and forwards, strongly agitated.

'Shall we have another opinion?' asked Dr Martin.

'Certainly. The highest in the land.'

'Dr Lorrimer, of Harley Street, is the most famous man for heart disease.'

'I'll telegraph to him immediately,' said the Captain.

He ordered his horse, rode into Lyndhurst, and despatched his telegram without the loss of a minute. Never had Dr Martin seen anyone more in earnest, or more deeply stricken by an announcement of evil.

'Poor fellow, he must be very fond of her,' mused the surgeon, as he rode off to his next call. 'And yet I should have thought she must be rather a tiresome kind of woman to live with. Her income dies with her I suppose. That makes a difference.'

The specialist from Harley Street arrived at the Abbey House on the following afternoon. He made his examination and gave his opinion, which was very much the same as Dr Martin's, but clothed in more scientific language.

'This poor lady's heart has been wearing out for the last twenty years,' he told the local surgeon: 'but she seems, from your account, to have been using it rather worse for the last year or so. Do you know if she has had any particular occasion for worry?'

'Her only daughter has not got on very well with the second husband, I believe,' said Dr Martin. 'That may have worried her.'

'Naturally. Small domestic anxieties of that kind are among the most potent causes of heart disease.' And then Dr Lorrimer gave his instructions about treatment. He had not the faintest hope of saving the patient, but he gave her the full benefit of his science. A man could scarely come so far and do less. When he went out into the hall and met the Captain, who was waiting anxiously for his verdict, he began in the usual oracular strain; but Captain Winstanley cut him short without ceremony.

'I don't want to hear details,' he said. 'Martin will do everything you tell him. I want the best or the worst you can tell me in straightest language. Can you save my wife, or am I to lose her?'

'My dear sir, while there is life there is hope,' answered the physician, with the compassionate air that had grown habitual, like his black frock-coat and general sobriety of attire. 'I have seen wonderful recoveries – or rather a wonderful prolongation of life, for cure is, of course, impossible – in cases as bad as this. But——'

'Ah!' cried the Captain bitterly, 'there is a "but."'

'In this case there is a sad want of rallying power. Frankly, I have very little hope. Do all you can to cheer and comfort your wife's mind, and to make her last days happy. All medicine apart, that is about the best advice I can give you.'

After this the doctor took his fee, gave the Captain's hand a cordial grip, expressive of sympathy and kindness, and went his way, feeling assured that a good deal hung upon that little life which he had left slowly ebbing away, like a narrow rivulet dwindling under a July sun.

'What does the London doctor say of me, Conrad?' asked Mrs Winstanley, when her husband went to her presently, with his countenance composed and cheerful. 'He tried me dreadfully with his stethoscope. Does he think me very ill? Is there anything wrong with my lungs?'

'No, love. It is a case of weakness and languor. You must make up your mind to get strong; and you will do more for yourself than all the physicians in London can do.'

'But what does he say of my heart? How does he explain that dreadful fluttering – the suffocating sensation – the——?'

'He explains nothing. It is a nervous affection, which you must combat by getting strong. Dear love!' exclaimed the Captain, with a very real burst of feeling, 'what can I do to make your life happy? what can I do to assure you of my love?'

'Send for Violet,' faltered his wife, raising herself upon her elbow, and looking at him with timorous eagerness. 'I have never been happy since she left us. It seems as if I had turned her out of doors – out of her own house – my kind husband's only daughter. It has preyed upon my mind continually, that – and other things.'

'Dearest, I will telegraph to her in an hour. She shall be with you as soon as the steamer can bring her.'

'A thousand thanks, Conrad. You are always good. I know I have been weak and foolish to think——'

Here she hesitated, and tears began to roll down her hollow cheeks.

'To think what, love?' asked her husband, tenderly.

If love, if tenderness, if flattery, if all sweetest things that ever man said to woman could lure this feeble spirit back to life, she should be so won, vowed the Captain. He had never been unkind to her, or thought unkindly of her. If he had never loved her, he had, at least, been tolerant. But now, clinging to her as the representative of fortune, comfort, social status, he felt that she was assuredly his best and dearest upon earth.

'To think that you never really cared for me!' she whimpered; 'that you married me for the sake of this house, and my income!'

'Pamela, do you remember what Tom Jones said to his mistress when she pretended to doubt his love?'

'My dear Conrad, I never read "Tom Jones." I have heard dear Edward talk of it as if it was something too dreadful.'

'Ah, I forgot. Of course, it is not a lady's book. Tom told his Sophia to look in the glass, if she were inclined to question his love for her, and one look at her own sweet face would convince her of his truth. Let it be so with yourself, dear. Ask yourself why I should not love the sweetest and most lovable of women.'

If sugarplums of speech, if loverlike attentions, could have cured Pamela Winstanley's mortal sickness, she might yet have recovered. But the hour had gone by when such medicaments might have prevailed. While the Captain had shot, and hunted, and caught mighty salmon, and invested his odd hundreds, and taken his own pleasure in various ways, with all the freedom of bachelor life, his wife had, unawares, been slowly dying. The light had burned low in the socket; and who shall reillumine that brief candle when its day is over? It needed now but a breath to quench the feeble flame.

'Great Heaven!' cried Captain Winstanley, pacing up and down his study, distraught with the pangs of wounded self-interest; 'I have been taking care of her money, when I ought to have taken care of her. It is her life that all hangs upon: and I have let that slip through my fingers while I have planned and contrived to save a few beggarly hundreds. Short-sighted idiot that I have been! Poor Pamela! And she has been so yielding, so compliant to my every wish! A month – a week, perhaps – and she will be gone; and that handsome spitfire will have the right to thrust me from this house. No, my lady, I will not afford you that triumph. My wife's coffin and I will go out together.'

CHAPTER 43

'ALL THE RIVERS RUN INTO THE SEA'

For some days Violet's return seemed to have a happy effect upon the invalid. Never had daughter been more devoted, more loving, fuller of sweet cares and consolations for a dying mother, than this daughter. Seeing the mother and child together in this supreme hour, no onlooker could have divined that these two had ever been less fondly united than mother and child should be. The feeble and fading woman seemed to lean on the strong bright girl, to gain a reflected strength from her fullness of life and vigour. It was as if Vixen, with her shining hair and fair young face, brought healthful breezes into the sickly perfumed atmosphere of the invalid's rooms.

Roderick Vawdrey had a hard time of it during these days of sadness and suspense. He could not deny the right of his betrothed to devote all her time and thought to a dying mother; and yet, having but newly won her for his very own, after dreary years of constraint and severance, he longed for her society as lover never longed before; or at least he thought so. He hung about the Abbey House all day, heedless of the gloomy looks he got from Captain Winstanley, and of the heavy air of sadness that pervaded the house, and was infinitely content and happy when he was admitted to Mrs Winstanley's boudoir to take an afternoon cup of tea, and talk for half an hour or so, in subdued tones, with mother and daughter.

'I am very glad that things have happened as they have, Roderick,' Mrs Winstanley said languidly; 'though I'm afraid it would make your poor mamma very unhappy if she could know about it. She had so set her heart on your marrying Lady Mabel.'

'Forgetting that it was really my heart which was concerned in the business,' said Rorie. 'Dear Mabel was wise enough to show us all the easiest way out of our difficulties. I sent her my mother's emerald cross and earrings, the day before yesterday, with as pretty a letter as I could write. I think it was almost poetical.'

'And those emeralds of Lady Jane Vawdrey's are very fine,' remarked Mrs Winstanley. 'I don't think there is a feather in one of the stones.'

'It was almost like giving away your property, wasn't it, Vixen?' said Rorie, looking admiringly at his beloved. 'But I have a lot of my mother's jewels for you, and I wanted to send Mabel something, to show her that I was not ungrateful.'

'You acted very properly, Rorie; and as to jewellery, you know very well I don't care a straw for it.'

'It is a comfort to me to know you will have Lady Jane's pearl necklace,' murmured Mrs Winstanley. 'It will go so well with my diamond locket. Ah, Rorie, I wish I had been strong enough to see Violet's *trousseau*. It is dreadful to think that it may have to be made by a provincial dressmaker, and with no one to supervise and direct.'

'Dearest mother, you are going to supervise everything,' exclaimed Vixen. 'I shall not think of being married till you are well and strong again.'

'That will be never,' sighed the invalid.

Upon this point she was very firm. They all tried – husband, daughter, and friends – to delude her with false hopes, thinking thus to fan the flame of life and keep the brief candle burning a little longer. She was not deceived. She felt herself gradually, painlessly sinking. She complained but little; much less than in the days when her ailments had been in some part fanciful; but she knew very surely that her day was done.

'It is very sweet to have you with me, Violet,' she said. 'Your goodness, and Conrad's loving attention, make me very happy. I feel almost as if I should like to live a few years longer.'

'Only almost, mother darling?' exclaimed Violet reproachfully.

'I don't know, dear. I have such a weary feeling; as if life at the very best were not worth the trouble it costs us. I shouldn't mind going on living if I could always lie here, and take no trouble about anything, and be nursed and waited upon, and have you or Conrad always by my side – but to get well again, and to have to get up, and go about among other people, and take up all the cares of life – no dear, I am much too weary for that. And then if I could get well to-morrow, old age and death would still be staring me in the face. I could not escape them. No, love, it is much better to die now, before I am very old, or quite hideous; even before my hair is gray.'

She took up one of the soft auburn tresses from her pillow, and looked at it half sadly.

'Your dear papa used to admire my hair, Violet,' she said. 'There are a few gray hairs, but you would hardly notice them.'

Mrs Winstanley was always at her best during those afternoon tea-drinkings. The strong tea revived her; Roderick's friendly face and voice cheered her. They took her back to the remote past, to the kind Squire's day of glory, which she remembered as the happiest time of her life; even now, when her second husband was doing all things possible to prove his sincerity and devotion. She had never been completely happy in this second marriage. There had always been a flavour of remorse mingled with her cup of joy; the vague consciousness that she had done a foolish thing, and that the world – her little world within a radius of twenty miles – was secretly laughing at her.

'Do you remember the day we came home from our honeymoon, Conrad,' she said to her husband, as he sat by her in the dusk one evening, sad and silent, 'when there was no carriage to meet us, and we had to come home in a fly? It was an omen, was it not?'

'An omen of what, dearest?'

'That all things were not to go well with us in our married life; that we were not to be quite happy.'

'Have you not been happy, Pamela? I have tried honestly to do my duty to you.'

'I know you have, Conrad. You have been all goodness; I always have said so to Violet – and to everyone. But I have had my cares. I felt that I was too old for you. That has preyed upon my mind.'

'Was that reasonable, Pamela, when I have never felt it?'

'Perhaps not at first; and even if you had felt the disparity in our ages you would have been too generous to let me perceive the change in your feelings. But I should have grown an old woman while you were still a young man. It would have been too dreadful. Indeed, dear, it is better as it is. Providence is very good to me.'

'Providence is not very good to me, in taking you from me,' said the Captain, with a touch of bitterness.

It seemed to him passing selfish in his wife to be so resigned to leaving life, and so oblivious of the fact that her income died with her, and that he was to be left out in the cold. One evening, however, when they were sitting alone together, this fact presented itself suddenly to her mind.

'You will lose the Abbey House, when I am gone, Conrad.'

'My love, do you think I could live in this house without you?'

'And my income, Conrad; that dies with me, does it not?'

'Yes, love.'

'That is hard for you.'

'I can bear that, Pamela, if I am to bear the loss of you.'

'Dearest love, you have always been disinterested. How could I ever doubt you? Perhaps – indeed I am sure – if I were to ask Violet, she would give you the fifteen hundred a year that I was to have had after she came of age.'

'Pamela, I could not accept any favour from your daughter. You would deeply offend me if you were to suggest such a thing.'

This was true. Much as he valued money, he would have rather starved than taken sixpence from the girl who had scorned him; the girl whose very presence gave rise to a terrible conflict in his breast – passionate admiration, bitterest antagonism.

'There are the few things that I possess myself – jewels, books, furniture – special gifts of dear Edward's. Those are my own, to dispose of as I like. I might make a will leaving them to you, Conrad. They are trifles, but——'

'They will be precious *souvenirs* of our wedded life,' murmured the Captain, who was very much of Mr Wemmick's opinion, that portable property of any kind was worth having.

A will was drawn up and executed next day, in which Mrs Winstanley left her diamonds to her daughter, her wardrobe to the faithful and long-suffering Pauline – otherwise Mary Smith – and all the rest of her belongings to her dearly-beloved husband, Conrad Winstanley. The Captain was a sufficient man of business to take care that this will was properly executed.

In all this time his daily intercourse with Violet was a source of exceeding bitterness. She was civil, and even friendly in her manner to him – for her mother's sake. And then, in the completeness of her union with Rorie, she could afford to be generous and forgiving. The old spirit of antagonism died out: her foe was so utterly fallen. A few weeks and the old home would be her own – the old servants could come back, the old pensioners might gather again around the kitchen door. All could be once more as it had been in her father's lifetime; and no trace of Conrad Winstanley's existence would be left; for, alas! it was now an acknowledged fact that Violet's mother was dying. The most sanguine among her friends had ceased to hope. She herself was utterly resigned. She spent some part of each day in gentle religious exercises with kindly Mr Scobel. Her last hours were as calm and reasonable as those of Socrates.

So Captain Winstanley had to sit quietly by, and see Violet and her lover grouped by his fading wife's sofa, and school himself, as he best might, to endure the spectacle of their perfect happiness in each other's love, and to know that he –

who had planned his future days so wisely, providing, like the industrious ant, for the winter of his life – had broken down in his scheme of existence, after all, and had no more part in this house which he had deemed his own than a traveller at an inn.

It was hard, and he sat beside his dying wife, with anger and envy gnawing his heart – anger against fate, envy of Roderick Vawdrey, who had won the prize. If evil wishes could have killed, neither Violet nor her lover would have outlived that summer. Happily the Captain was too cautious a man to be guilty of any overt act of rage or hatred. His rancorous feelings were decently hidden under a gentlemanly iciness of manner, to which no one could take objection.

The fatal hour came unawares, one calm September afternoon, about six weeks after Violet's return from Jersey. Captain Winstanley had been reading one of Tennyson's idylls to his wife, till she sank into a gentle slumber. He left her, with Pauline seated at work by one of the windows, and went to his study to write some letters. Five o'clock was the established hour for kettledrum, but of late the invalid had been unable to bear even the mild excitement of two or three visitors at this time. Violet now attended alone to her mother's afternoon tea, kneeling by her side as she sipped the refreshing infusion, and coaxing her to eat a waferlike slice of bread-and-butter, or a few morsels of sponge-cake.

This afternoon, when Violet went softly into the room, carrying the little Japanese tray and tiny teapot, she found her mother lying just as the Captain had left her an hour before.

'She's been sleeping so sweetly miss,' whispered Pauline. 'I never knew her sleep so quiet since she's been ill.'

That stillness which seemed so good a thing to the handmaid frightened the daughter. Violet set her tray down hastily on the nearest table, and ran to her mother's sofa. She looked at the pale and sunken cheek, just visible in the downy hollow of the pillows; she touched the hand lying on the silken coverlet. That marble coldness, that waxen hue of the cheek, told her the awful truth. She fell on her knees beside the sofa, with a cry of sharp and sudden sorrow.

'O mother, mother! I ought to have loved you better all my life!'

CHAPTER 44

THE BLUEBEARD CHAMBER

The day before the funeral Captain Winstanley received a letter from his stepdaughter, offering to execute any deed he might choose to have prepared, settling upon him the income which his wife was to have had after Violet's majority.

'I know that you are a heavy loser by my mother's death,' she wrote, 'and I shall be glad to do anything in my power to lessen that loss. I know well that it was her earnest wish that your future should be provided for. I told her a few days before she died that I should make you this offer. I do it with all my heart; and I shall consider myself obliged by your acceptance of it.'

The Captain's reply was brief and firm.

'I thank you for your generous offer,' he said, 'which I feel assured is made in good faith; but I think you ought to know that there are reasons why it is impossible I should accept any benefit from your hand. I shall not re-enter the Abbey House after my wife's funeral. You will be sole and sovereign mistress of all things from that hour.'

He kept his word. He was chief mourner at the quiet but stately burial under the old yew-tree in Beechdale churchyard. When all was over he got into a fly, and drove to the station at Lyndhurst Road, whence he departed by the first train for London. He told no one anything about his plans for the future; he left no address but his club. He was next heard of six months later, in South America.

Violet had telegraphed for her old governess directly after Mrs Winstanley's death; and that good and homely person arrived on the day after the funeral, to take up her abode with her old pupil, as companion and chaperon, until Miss Tempest should have become Mrs Vawdrey, and would have but one companion henceforward in all the journey of life. Rorie and Vixen were to be married in six months. Mrs Winstanley had made them promise that her death should delay their marriage as little as possible.

'You can have a very quiet wedding, you know, dear,' she said. 'You can be married in your travelling-dress — something pretty in gray silk and terry velvet, or with chinchilla trimming, if it should be winter. Chinchilla is so distinguished-looking. You will go abroad, I suppose, for your honeymoon. Pau, or Monaco, or any of those places on the Mediterranean.'

It had pleased her to settle everything for the lovers. Violet remembered all these speeches with a tender sorrow. There was comfort in the thought that her mother had loved her, according to her lights.

It had been finally settled between the lovers that they were to live at the Abbey House. Briarwood was to be let to any wealthy individual who might desire a handsome house, surrounded by exquisitely arranged gardens, and burdened with glass that would cost a small fortune annually to maintain. Before Mr Vawdrey could put his property into the hands of the auctioneers, he received a private offer which was in every respect satisfactory.

Lady Mallow wished to spend some part of every year near her father and mother, who lived a good deal at Ashbourne, the Duke becoming yearly more devoted to his Chillingham oxen and monster turnips. Lord Mallow, who loved his native isle with the ardour of a patriot, but who always found six weeks in a year a sufficient period of residence there, was delighted to please his bride, and agreed to take Briarwood, furnished, on a seven-years' lease. The orchid-houses were an irresistible attraction; and by this friendly arrangement Lady Mallow would profit by the alterations and improvements her cousin had made for her gratification, when he believed she was to be his wife.

Briarwood thus disposed of, Rorie was free to consider the Abbey House his future home; and Violet had the happiness of knowing that the good old house in which her childhood had been spent would be her habitation always, till she too was carried to the family vault under the old yew-tree. There are people who languish for change, for whom the newest is ever the best; but it was not thus with Violet Tempest. The people she had known all her life, the scenes amidst which she had played when a child, were to her the dearest people and the loveliest scenes upon earth. It would be pleasant to her to travel with her husband: but pleasanter still would be the home-coming to the familiar hearth beside which her father had sat, the old faces that had looked upon him, the hands that had served him, the gardens he had planted and improved.

'I should like to show you Briarwood before it is let, Vixen,' Mr Vawdrey said to his sweetheart, one November morning. 'You may at least pay my poor patrimony the compliment of looking at it before it becomes the property of Lord and Lady Mallow. Suppose you and Miss McCroke drive over and drink tea with me this afternoon?'

'Very well, Rorie, we'll come to tea. I should rather like to see the improvements you made for Lady Mabel, before your misfortune. I think Lord Mallow must consider it very good of you to let him have the benefit of all the money you spent, instead of bringing an action for breach of promise against his wife, as you might very well have done.'

'I daresay. But you see I am of a forgiving temper. Well, I shall tell my housekeeper to have tea, and buns, and jam, and all the things children — and young ladies — like, at four o'clock. We had better make it four instead of five, as the afternoons are so short.'

'If you are impertinent we won't come.'

'O yes you will. Curiosity will bring you. Remember this will be your last chance of seeing the Bluebeard chamber at Briarwood.'

'Is there a Bluebeard chamber?'

'Of course. Did you ever know of a family mansion without one?'

Vixen was delighted at the idea of exploring her lover's domain, now that he and it were her own property. How well she remembered going with her father to the meet on Briarwood lawn. Yet it seemed a century ago — the very beginning of her life — before she had known sorrow.

Miss McCroke, who was ready to do anything her pupil desired, was really pleased at the idea of seeing the interior of Briarwood.

'I have never been inside the doors, you know, dear,' she said, 'often as I have driven past the gates with your dear mamma. Lady Jane Vawdrey was not the kind of person to invite a governess to go and see her. She was a strict observer of the laws of caste. The Duchess has much less pride.'

'I don't think Lady Jane ever quite forgave herself for marrying a commoner,' said Vixen. 'She revenged her own weakness upon other people.'

Violet had a new pair of ponies, which her lover had chosen for her, after vain endeavours to trace and recover the long-lost Titmouse. These she drove to Briarwood, Miss McCroke resigning herself to the will of Providence with a blind submission worthy of a Moslem; feeling that if it were written that she was to be flung head foremost out of a pony-carriage, the thing would happen sooner or later. Staying at home to-day would not ward off to-morrow's doom. So she took her place in the cushioned valley by Violet's side, and sat calm and still, while the ponies, warranted quiet to drive in single or double harness, stood up on end and made as if they had a fixed intention of scaling the rhododendron bank.

'They'll settle down directly I've taken the freshness out of them,' said Vixen blandly, as she administered a reproachful touch of the whip.

'I hope they will,' replied Miss McCroke; 'but don't you think Bates ought to have seen the freshness taken out of them before we started?'

They were soon tearing along the smooth Roman road at a splendid pace, 'going like clockwork,' as Vixen remarked approvingly; but poor Miss McCroke thought that any clock which went as fast as those ponies would be deemed the maddest of timekeepers.

They found Roderick standing at his gates, waiting for them. There was a glorious fire in the amber and white drawing-room, a dainty tea-table drawn in front of the hearth, the easiest of chairs arranged on each side of the table, an urn hissing,

Rorie's favourite pointer stretched upon the hearth, everything cosy and homelike. Briarwood was not such a bad place after all, Vixen thought. She could have contrived to be happy with Roderick even here; but of course the Abbey House was, in her mind, a hundred times better, being just the one perfect home in the world.

They all three sat round the fire, drinking tea, poured out by Vixen, who played the mistress of the house sweetly. They talked of old times, sometimes sadly, sometimes sportively, glancing swiftly from one old memory to another. All Rorie's tiresome ways, all Vixen's mischievous tricks, were remembered.

'I think I led you a life in those days, didn't I, Rorie?' asked Vixen, leaving the tea-tray, and stealing softly behind her lover's chair to lean over his shoulder caressingly, and pull his thick brown beard. 'There is nothing so delightful as to torment the person one loves best in the world. O, Rorie, I mean to lead you a life by-and-by!'

'Dearest, the life you lead me must needs be sweet, for it will be spent with you.'

After tea they set out upon a round of inspection, and admired the new morning-room that had been devised for Lady Mabel, in the very latest style of Dutch Renaissance – walls the colour of muddy water, glorified ginger-jars, ebonised chairs and tables, and willow-pattern plates all round the cornice; curtains mud-colour, with a mediaeval design in dirty yellow, or, in upholsterer's language, 'old gold.'

'I should like to show you the stables before it is quite dark,' said Rorie presently. 'I made a few slight improvements there while the builders were about.'

'You know I have a weakness for stables,' answered Vixen. 'How many a lecture I used to get from poor mamma about my unfortunate tastes. But can there be anything in the world nicer than a good old-fashioned stable, smelling of clover and newly-cut hay?'

'Stables are very nice indeed, and very useful, in their proper place,' remarked Miss McCroke sententiously.

'But one ought not to bring the stables into the drawing-room,' said Vixen gravely. 'Come, Rorie, let us see your latest improvements in stable-gear.'

They all went out to the stone-paved quadrangle, which was as neatly kept as a West-End livery-yard. Miss McCroke had an ever-present dread of the hind-legs of strange horses: but she followed her charge into the stable, with the same heroic fidelity with which she would have followed her to the scaffold or the stake.

There were all Rorie's old favourites – Sultan, the big chestnut; Blue Peter, broad-chested, well-ribbed, strong of limb; Pixie, the gray Arab mare, which Lady Jane used to drive in a park-phaeton – quite an ancient lady; Donald, the iron-sinewed hunter.

Vixen knew them all, and went up to them and patted their noses, and made herself at home with them.

'You are all coming to the Abbey House to live, you dear things,' she said delightedly.

There was a loose-box, shut off by a five-foot wainscot partition, surmounted by a waved iron rail, at one end of the stable, and on approaching this enclosure Vixen was saluted with sundry grunts and snorting noises, which seemed curiously familiar.

At the sound of these she stopped short, turned red, and then pale, and looked intently at Rorie, who was standing close by, smiling at her.

'That is my Bluebeard chamber,' he said gaily. 'There's something too awful inside.'

'What horse have you got there?' cried Vixen eagerly.

'A horse that I think will carry you nicely, when we hunt together.'

'What horse? Have I ever seen him? Do I know him?'

The grunts and snortings were continued with a crescendo movement; an eager nose was rattling the latch of the door that shut off the loose-box.

'If you have a good memory for old friends, I think you will know this one,' said Rorie, withdrawing a bolt.

A head pushed open the door, and in another moment Vixen's arms were round her old favourite's sleek neck, and the velvet nostrils were sniffing her hair and cheek, in most loving recognition.

'You dear, dear old fellow!' cried Vixen; and then turning to Rorie: 'You told me he was sold at Tattersall's!' she exclaimed.

'So he was, and I bought him.'

'Why did not you tell me that?'

'Because you did not ask me.'

'I thought you so unkind, so indifferent about him.'

'You were unkind when you could think it possible I should let your favourite horse fall into strange hands. But perhaps you would rather Lord Mallow had bought him?'

'To think that you should have kept the secret all this time!' said Vixen.

'You see I am not a woman, and can keep a secret. I wanted to have one little surprise for you, as a reward when you had been especially good.'

'You are good,' she said, standing on tiptoe to kiss him. 'And though I have loved you all my life, I don't think I have loved you the least little bit too much.'

EPILOGUE

Vixen and Rorie were married in the spring, when the forest glades were yellow with primroses, the mossy banks blue with violets, and the cuckoo was heard with monotonous iteration from sunrise to sundown. They were married in the little village church at Beechdale, and Mrs Scobel declared that Miss Tempest's wedding was the prettiest that ever had been solemnised in that small Gothic temple. Never, perhaps, even at Eastertide, had been seen such a wealth of spring blossoms, the wildlings of the woods and hills. The Duchess had offered the contents of her hot-houses, Lady Ellangowan had offered waggon-loads of azaleas and camelias, but Vixen had refused them all. She would allow no decorations but the wild flowers which the school-children could gather. Primroses, violets, the firstlings of the fern tribe, cowslips, and all the tribe of innocent forest blossoms, with their quaint rustic names, most of them as old as Shakespeare.

It was a very quiet wedding. Vixen would have no one present except the Scobels, Miss McCroke, her two bridesmaids, and Sir Henry Tolmash, an old friend of her father, who was to give her away. He was a white-haired old man, who had given his latter days up to farming, and had not a thought above turnips and top-dressings; but Violet honoured him, because he had been her father's oldest friend. For bridesmaids she had Colonel Carteret's daughters, a brace of harmless young ladies, who dressed well and looked pretty.

There was no display of wedding gifts, no ceremonious wedding breakfast. Vixen remembered the wedding feast at her mother's second marriage, and what a dreary ceremonial it had been.

The bride wore her gray silk travelling-dress, with gray hat and feather, and she and her husband went straight from the church to the railway-station, on their way to the Engadine, whence they were to return at no appointed time.

'We are coming back when we are tired of mountain scenery and of each other,' Violet told Mrs Scobel in the church porch.

'That will be never!' exclaimed Rorie, looking ineffably happy, but not very much like a bridegroom, in his comfortable gray suit. 'You might just as well say that we are going to live among the mountains as long as Rip Van Winkle. No, Mrs Scobel, we are not going to remain away from you fifty years. We are coming back in time for the hunting.'

Then came kissing and handshaking, a shower of violets and primroses upon the narrow churchyard path, a hearty huzza from the assembled village, all clustered about the oaken gate-posts. The envious carriage-door shut in bride and bridegroom, the coachman touched his horses, and they were gone up the hill, out of the peaceful valley, to Lyndhurst and the railway.

'How dreadfully I shall miss them,' said Mrs Scobel, who had spent much of her leisure with the lovers. 'They are both so full of life and brightness!'

'They are young and happy!' said her husband quietly. 'Who would not miss youth and happiness?'

When the first frosts had seared the beeches to a fiery red, and
the berries were bright on the hawthorns, and the latest bloom
of heather had faded on hill and plain, and the happy pigs had
devoured all the beech-nuts, Mr Vawdrey and his wife came
back from their exploration of Alpine snows and peaceful Swiss
villages, to the good old Abbey House. Their six months'
honeymoon had been all gladness. They were the veriest boy
and girl husband and wife who had ever trodden those beaten
tracks. They teased each other, and quarrelled, and made friends
again like children, and were altogether happy. And now they
came back to the Forest, bronzed by many a long day's
sunshine, and glowing with health and high spirits. The glass of
Time seemed to be turned backward at the Abbey House; for
all the old servants came back, and white-haired old Bates ruled
in the well-filled stables, and all things were as in the dead and
gone Squire's time.

Among Roderick's wedding gifts was one from Lord
Mallow: Bullfinch, the best horse in that nobleman's stable.

'I know your wife would like you to have her father's
favourite hunter,' wrote Lord Mallow. 'Tell her that he has
never been sick or sorry since he has been in my stable, and
that I have always taken particular care of him, for her sake.'

Among Violet's presents was a diamond bracelet from Lady
Mallow, accompanied by a very cordial letter; and almost the
first visit that the Vawdreys received after they came home was
from Lord and Lady Mallow. The first great dinner to which
they were bidden was at Briarwood, where it seemed a curious
thing for Rorie to go as a guest.

Matrimony with the man of her choice had wondrously
improved Mabel Ashbourne. She was less self-sufficient and
more conciliating. Her ambition, hitherto confined to the desire
to excel all other women in her own person, had assumed a less
selfish form. She was now only ambitious for her husband;
greedy of parliamentary fame for him; full of large hopes about
the future of Ireland. She looked forward complacently to the
day when she and Lord Mallow would be reigning at Dublin

Castle, and when Hibernian arts and industries would revive and flourish under her fostering care. Pending that happy state of things she wore Irish poplin, and Irish lace, Irish stockings, and Irish linen. She attended her Majesty's Drawing-room on St Patrick's Day, with a sprig of real shamrock – sent her by one of her husband's tenantry – among the diamonds that sparkled on her bosom. She was more intensely Irish than the children of the soil; just as converts to Romanism are ever more severely Roman than those born and nurtured in the faith.

Her husband was intensely proud of his wife, and of his alliance with the house of Ashbourne. The Duke, at first inclined to resent the scandal of an elopement and the slight offered to his favourite, Rorie, speedily reconciled himself to a marriage which was more materially advantageous than the cousinly alliance.

'I should like Rorie to have had Ashbourne,' he said mournfully. 'I think he would have kept up my breed of Chillingham cattle. Mallow's a good fellow, but he knows nothing about farming. He'll never spend enough money on manure to maintain the soil at its present producing power. The grasp of his mind isn't large enough to allow him to sink his money in manuring his land. He would be wanting to see an immediate result.'

As time went on the Duke became more and more devoted to his farm. His Scottish castle delighted him not, nor the grand old place in the Midlands. Ashbourne, which was the pleasure-dome he had built for himself, contained all he cared about. Too heavy and too lazy to hunt, he was able to jog about his farm, and supervise the work that was going on, to the smallest detail. There was not a foot of drain-pipe or a bit of thatch renewed on the whole estate, without the Duke having a finger in the pie. He bred fat oxen and prize cart-horses, and made a great figure at all the cattle-shows, and was happy.

The Duchess who had never believed her paragon capable of wrong-doing, had been infinitely shocked by Lady Mabel's desperate course; but it was not in her nature to be angry with that idolised daughter. She very soon came back to her original idea, that whatever Mabel Ashbourne did was right. And then the marriage was so thoroughly happy; and the world gladly forgives a scandal that ends so pleasantly.

So Lord and Lady Mallow go their way – honoured, beloved, very active in good works – and the pleasant valleys around Mallow are dotted with red brick school-houses, and the old stone hovels are giving place to model cottages, and native industries receive all possible encouragement from the owner of the soil; and, afar off, in the coming years, the glories of Dublin Castle shine like the Pole Star that guides the wanderer on his way.

In one thing only has Lady Mallow been false to the promise of her girlhood. She has not achieved success as a poet. The Duchess wonders vaguely at this, for though she had often found it difficult to keep awake during the rehearsal of her daughter's verses, she had a fixed belief in the excellence of those efforts of genius. The secret of Lady Mallow's silence rests between her husband and herself; and it is just possible that some too candid avowal of Lord Mallow's may be the reason of her poetic sterility. It is one thing to call the lady of one's choice a tenth muse before marriage, and another thing to foster a self-delusion in one's wife which can hardly fail to become a discordant element in domestic life. 'If your genius had developed, and you had won popularity as a poet, I should have lost a perfect wife,' Lord Mallow told Mabel, when he wanted to put things pleasantly. 'Literature has lost a star, but I have gained the noblest and sweetest companion Providence ever bestowed upon man.' Lady Mallow has not degenerated into feminine humdrum. She assists in the composition of her husband's political pamphlets, which bristle with lines from Euripides, and noble thoughts from the German poets. She writes a good many of his letters, and is altogether his second self.

While the Irishman and his wife pursue their distinguished career, Rorie and Vixen live the life they love, in the Forest where they were born, dispensing happiness within a narrow circle, but dearly loved wheresoever they are known; and the old men and women in the scattered villages round about the Abbey House rejoice in the good old times that have come again; just as hearty pleasure-loving England was glad when the stern rule of the Protector and his crop-headed saints gave place to the reign of the Merry King.

From afar there comes news of Captain Winstanley, who has married a Jewish lady at Frankfort, only daughter and heiress of a well-known money-lender. The bride is reported ugly and illiterate; but there is no doubt as to her fortune. The Captain has bought a villa at Monaco – a villa in the midst of orange-groves, the abandoned plaything of an Austrian princess; and he has hired an apartment in one of the new avenues, just outside the Arc de Triomphe, where, as his friends anticipate, he will live in grand style, and receive the pleasantest people in Paris. He, too, is happy after his kind, and has won the twenty-thousand-pound prize in the lottery of life; but it is altogether a different kind of happiness from the simple and unalloyed delight of Rorie and Vixen, in their home among the beechen woods whose foliage sheltered them when they were children.

THE BERTRAMS

ANTHONY TROLLOPE

In an attempt to escape from the seeming chaos around him George Bertram journeys to Jerusalem and the Holy Land full of transcendental enthusiasm and religious zeal, searching for the higher things of life.

Instead he loses his faith completely, falls for the rebellious Caroline Waddington and enters into an agonising power-struggle with this liberated lady. In order to avoid the drudgery of 'love in a cottage' Caroline refuses to marry George immediately and by a series of silly misunderstandings they are taken down a road which leads to guilt and a desire for revenge.

Their struggles are at the centre of this dark comedy from Trollope's early period with its many sub-plots, its descriptions of exotic cities and whirling dervishes, and its further exploration of the themes raised in the Barsetshire Chronicle.

THE BISHOP AND OTHER STORIES

ANTON CHEKHOV

The last week in the life of Bishop Pyotr in 'The Bishop' introduces the themes of clerical abuse, social class, religiosity and poverty which are taken up and explored in these six brilliantly conceived and characterized tales.

The bishop is consumed with loneliness in his high position as he is rarely spoken to 'genuinely, simply, as to a human being', and he experiences a powerful sense of having missed that which is most important. Bishop Pyotr is witness to the drunkenness and discontent of the clergy, such as Father Demyan, nicknamed 'Demyan Snakeseer', and Father Sisory, as well as the poverty of his own family as Katya, his niece, begs for money.

Chekhov paints a world where the undignified and pitiful priests fail 'to satisfy the ideals which the Russian people have in the course of centuries formed of what a pastor should be'; the 'aged-looking faces' make the young look old; and the 'well-intentioned but unreflecting and over-comfortable' point to greed where there is grinding poverty.

DOCTOR PASCAL

ÉMILE ZOLA

Doctor Pascal is the final novel in the twenty-volume *Rougon-Macquart* series which follows the fortunes of this family of disparate characters through the Second Empire in France. It is, in Zola's own words, 'a scientific work, the logical deduction and conclusion of all my preceding novels', in which he presents a final formulation of his theories on atavism, and the role of heredity in shaping men's lives.

In *Doctor Pascal*, Zola creates a vivid and moving picture of passionate love between an old man and a young girl, and of the persecution of an ageing savant by his own family. Most of all, however, *Doctor Pascal* offers a fascinating and thought-provoking discourse on the social and religious issues surrounding the lives of the characters, many of which are as relevant to today's readers as those when Zola was writing towards the end of the last century.

THE BITER BIT & OTHER STORIES

WILKIE COLLINS

This collection contains five skilful tales of detection, mystery and suspense, from the author of *The Moonstone* and *The Woman in White*.

The title story is an investigation into the curious circumstances of an unusual robbery, revealing Wilkie Collins's lesser-known comic talents. 'The Lady of Glenwith Grange' is an intriguing mystery, while 'Gabriel's Marriage', set during the French Revolution, looks into the lives of a Breton fishing family after a storm at sea . . . In 'Mad Monkton' we have a fine thriller, and 'A Terribly Strange Bed', set in a Parisian gambling den, presents the dilemmas and delusions of a young Englishman who encounters a 'fiendish murder machine' after breaking a bank.

THE BLACK MONK
AND OTHER
STORIES

ANTON CHEKHOV

Chekhov's pages are peopled with psychopaths, degenerates of genius and virtue and satirically comic characters who succumb in feeble revolt against the baseness and banality of life. They are quite unfit to combat the healthy, rude, but unintelligent forces around them.

Kovrin, Likharyóff and Dr Andréi Yéfimitch, three heroes in this collection, are characteristic of Chekhov's outlook. Andréi Vasilyevitch Kovrin, the chief character in the title story, had worn himself out and unsettled his nerves. His doctor advised him to spend the spring and summer in the country and in the nick of time came a long letter from Tánya Pesótsky asking him to come and stay with her father at Borisovka. It was a journey which was to lead to marriage, madness and death. With the other stories and characters in this collection we have the best of Chekhov.

THE DEAD SECRET

WILKIE COLLINS

Rosamond Treverton lay dying at Porthgenna Tower, the family mansion in Cornwall. But what was the terrible secret from her past which was about to go with her to the grave? Calling her lady's maid to her side she confesses but dies before she can extract a promise from Sarah to reveal all to her husband.

Hiding the written confession in a remote part of the mansion, Sarah carries the burden alone for fifteen years. Worn out by the strain, it is at this point that she is pitched headlong into a chain of events which could lead to discovery by the innocent she is trying to protect.

Will the secret be revealed? What lies in store for the young Rosamond, her blind husband and their infant son, heir to Porthgenna?

A CHANGED MAN

THOMAS HARDY

This collection contains, as well as the title story, 'The Waiting Supper'; 'Alicia's Diary'; 'The Grave by the Handpost'; 'Enter a Dragoon'; 'A Tryst at an Ancient Earthwork'; 'What the Shepherd Saw'; 'A Committee-Man of "The Terror"'; 'Master John Horseleigh, Knight'; 'The Duke's Reappearance' and 'The Romantic Adventures of a Milkmaid'.

Hardy's love of the eerie and the supernatural are brought out in full measure here. His skill at depicting topographical detail is also apparent, particularly in 'A Changed Man' — set in Casterbridge and instantly recognizable to readers familiar with that town. The story is that of a young hussar captain who resigns his commission to preach in a poor parish and, by so doing, causes his wife to leave him for another soldier. It is a fine portrait in a vivid set of stories guaranteed to delight all Hardy devotees.

THE YELLOW MASK & OTHER STORIES

WILKIE COLLINS

The letter was anonymous but its message unmistakable: 'Neglect my advice and you will repent it to the end of your life. I have reasons for what I say – serious, fatal reasons, which I cannot divulge. If you would let your wife lie easy in her grave, if you would avoid a terrible warning, go not to the masked ball!'

The ball at the Melani Palace promised to be sensational, the old Marquis had a reputation as the most hospitable, as well as the most eccentric man in Pisa. Arcadian bowers, fantastic dances, the extravagant disguises were but a few of the attractions, until the Yellow Mask appeared – silent, inscrutable, relentless, gliding from room to room . . .

Told as the curious anecdotes of a poor painter, 'The Yellow Mask', together with 'Sister Rose' and 'A Stolen Letter', make up another superb collection from this master storyteller.

WITHIN THE TIDES

JOSEPH CONRAD

Four tales from this modern master. *The Planter of Malata* is a man who does not count the cost to himself or others and his heart is set on Miss Moorsom. Cloete is *The Partner* of George Dunbar and an unscrupulous on eat that. George needs money – lots of it.

The Inn of Two Witches is in Spain, but the story begins in a box of books bought in London, in a street which no longer exists. *Because of the Dollars* rounds off this quartet with a tale of the East, an exotic world peopled with characters like Captain Davidson. He used to smile a lot, but not any more . . . for there was very little to smile about on the night he ran his little steamer full of dollars into a jungle creek.